SECRETS OF THE CITYSPIRE

A Familiar Love Song

SECRETS OF THE CITYSPIRE
A Familiar Love Song

Published by NRM Books.

ISBN: 978-1-965179-31-4

CREDITS
Written & Cover Art by: Nathan Reese Maher
Edited by: Judy K. Kingyon

COPYRIGHT

Dedicated to my mother Judy,
for always believing in me.

Prelude

Flakes of ash trickle above in soft whirlwinds of soot. All is tranquil, like waking to a fantastical dream; the world braved anew. I smell lilacs…*the scent must have been hiding in the walls.*

My ears ring against the stress of the prior explosion, a dull hum that comes from the striking of a tuning fork. I'm on my back, disoriented and my vision blurred. My back aches from having struck my lower vertebrae on the curb. In moving, tiny shards of broken glass shift in my skin. I try to get up—I can't get up—as the shavings of burnt wood tack me to the pavement and a swirl of dizziness overcomes my sense of balance.

I hear muffled cries around me, people crawling about—one touching my boot—as their fuzzy silhouettes strive to pick themselves up and scurry away to some distant hospice. People are shouting, but I can't quite make it out. My head wavers from the impact; a heaviness that brings back memories of those previous nights when I drank myself to sleep – to muddle things, to forget.

A man lies next to me. His skull is caved in from the left eye socket to the temple. A smoldering piece of lumber rests next to him splotched with a familiar red lacquer, black with heat and covered with the shreds of his missing hair. I shake him, hoping that the damage only pertains to the outside. He doesn't move. I don't expect he ever will again. His remaining eye stares vacantly in front of him, a look that makes me believe he accepted the inevitable before impact. Despite his wounds, he looks serene. His blood is everywhere, mixing with remnant puddles along with the variety of dead and injured. I'm sure it won't be long before the rains will come to wipe it away.

Someone secures my arm and I struggle to yank it free. A panic induced reaction, but I'm held fast. It's Marty. His baby face is marred by a gash across his left temple which is bleeding, but his short brown hair is still intact; much unlike that of my gutter mate. I check to see if my own is in place. There's blood on my hand.

He smacks me across the face. I'm unsure if it's due to the impact, but every sound rushes me at once. The tone in his voice reflects that he's had to repeat himself.

"Snap out of it boss, we have to get out of here!" He struggles lifting me to my feet. He never was one for sympathy.

His strength surprises me for how short he is, a 5'7" nothing; must be the adrenaline at work. Unfortunately for him, I'm not ready to stand and we are both back on the curb before finding a stable equilibrium.

As we get to our feet, I point to where the red-haired man had fallen. "What about him?" I ask coldly, for I'm having problems committing to any one emotion while staring at his ill-begotten form. I think this disturbs me more than the carnage around us: a leg here, a woman? or a man caught by shrapnel, layers of baked clothing and calloused skin. It may just be too much – something to haunt me in future years.

Marty grabs the back of my head and pulls himself to my ear. "There's nothing we can do about him boss. We've got to go, or the Count will have us for sure."

"Marty," I tug at his arm to keep balance, "don't call me boss."

He takes my arm and supports it over his shoulder, chuckling. "At least you've kept your sense of humor."

From his dust covered jacket, I'm able to steal a glance towards the old convenience store. The roof is still intact. The walls are a different story. The once radiant glass walls are replaced by empty frames, loose bricks and rubble. The insides are scarred black and all the desperately needed food is gone. It was our only supply. And they thought it was hard before. The shortage just got worse.

The bomb was set up to explode out into the street, to catch as many people as possible. It is obvious the way the roof didn't fly off. How did I know that? The gigantic neon Open sign that once dominated the street is missing the 'O'. I imagine that if it wasn't destroyed in the fireball, it may have rolled farther down the street. The bulbs of the other three letters have only shattered. With my vision returning, I look at all the faces of the dead; thirty-two in all.

"The fools…" I mutter. Instead of the usual pity, all I can muster is anger. "I warned them…" A large knot in my throat descends and attaches itself to the inner lining of my stomach; a call for the previous comment. I struggle to defend myself. "I tried to stop them, but they wouldn't listen." But that's the way of this, mobs never do.

My strong-arm walking beside me doesn't say a word, too intent on getting us to safety. It seems to be the common consensus with those remaining. Those who are capable of standing stoop to save one of the survivors. Finally, I muse, an act of humility. It's ironic in a way. Just a few seconds ago they planned on tearing each other apart.

A figure catches my attention, perched five stories up on a window ledge. His crimson hood is drawn over his face to hide his monstrous visage and the permanent smile that rends across his cheeks descends upon us all. His presence dictates his responsibility in the massacre and acts as evidence to the severity of his laws. He looks at me. His eyes bulge with thick veins, as they issue a past silent warning, *Heed that the Rue du Bourreau is my domain, and I its malicious sovereign.*

Part I
Sleepers' Wake

1

It's 10:43 a.m. but I'm unsure of which day. I've been sitting here thinking to myself for the first time, or at least   it feels like the first time. I run my fingers over the ivory keys of the white piano that sits in front of me. A light drizzle touches the glass of the apartment windows and something strikes familiar. I press a few of the keys, allowing my hands to sort out the feelings that I've been searching for. Gone. Just like that.

A glass of water perspires off my left atop the nearby end table. The ice cubes shift and I wonder how long they have been sitting there. I'm not even thirsty. A white card with elegant gold embossment, no larger than a business card, takes the place of the sheet music. "You are Samuel Bell". That's it. That's all I know.

The first thing I remember is watching the front door shut out the light of the hallway. The sound of the door knob latching still echoes in my mind. I remember dancing. I remember drifting in and out of consciousness, and a sense of falling. The room shifts by a touch of dizziness.

Above the music stand and behind the piano, a wall ledge displays an assortment of bare antique picture frames. I watch as reflections of water lick their plates, as the rain resounds chillingly over my right shoulder. My hands are freezing so I rub them together for warmth. I'm not dressed in much, just a simple silk button down loose sleeve shirt and matching white pants. The thermostat, a steel plated touch panel, reads a startling seventy-two degrees. Why am I so cold? I look at my palms and then test my forehead. Is there something wrong with me? Am I ill? Why can't I remember? My only answer is the returning ticks of the wall clock.

Beside me is a line of windows set between the occasional bit of plaster that divides one from its neighbor. The glass is decorated with black steel muntins and accented above by a circle top. Beyond the windowpanes is a massive cityscape, marked by sullen grey skyscrapers. The buildings are constructed of plain concrete blocks and steel framed windows that run the entire length of the structure.

look to the empty streets. No pedestrians, cars or action in the windows. The rooms are vacant, devoid of all objects and of habitation. They all appear that way. At least the ones I can anyway. Emptiness. Silence. Something feels wrong with the d. I try to force the thought but my head throbs in protest.

Something moves – a fleeting shadow across the glass and my jumps at the sudden motion. My forehead begins to sweat as the windows across the street I perceive a ghostly couple dancing. is draped in a chic red dress and him in black tux and coattails. ther the duo sweep across the glass, twirling and spinning to the of the pain pounding in my head; a headache, I fear, that spawns toms. They drift hauntingly, the fabric twirling like tattered ories, escape soundlessly and invisible into the rain. I am struck with a rending of my chest, one bleeding from a hidden sadness.

Then there's a song, one that sits at the border of my ears and plays against my mind. Just four notes, four titillating sounds that flaunt of some greater melody. I play them on the piano and realize that they have something to do with everything, like a drop of living history or perhaps the secret to existence. I sense something distant, like something that I am supposed to know – something important. Yet, every time I reach my hand out into the waters of acuity, I startle the memory and it buries itself. My nose twitches. The scent of lilacs is fresh in the room.

The smell is all around me, hanging in the air like some curtain waiting to be pulled back. Seeking it out, I find that the apartment is well furnished: lilies in the corner—though they appear fake—a pearl suede loveseat with a grey fleece throw, the morning paper lain neatly on the glass coffee table, the kitchenette not far off separated by a white painted bar, and a short hallway leading to a bedroom with adjoining bath. It's the purveyed version of the flat across from mine, a surreal enigma in comparison to the rest of the block. Yet the smell persists.

I waver when I stand, the dizziness still swims about the room like a pair of fish in unfamiliar waters. I try and steady myself on the piano and sniff the air. The odor is high in the room, like a haze that's longing to dissipate but has been trapped by some maleficent cage. I follow my nose, careful not to trip over the coffee table, as I reach out to the couch to prevent my stumbling. My inhalations lead me to a small vent nearest the bar. When I place my hand over it I am greeted by a touch of heat. The lilacs are strongest here. The smell is billowing up from the vents, possibly the very bowels of the building. It is strange – as not long after the discovery, the scent diminishes.

When I turn back to the piano, I notice an explosion of broken glass alongside the tattered remains of a red painted music box. It must have fallen off the piano and rolled underneath. Did I knock it while stirring in my slumber? I exhaustively make my way to its current resting place. Atop the center turntable stands a single ballerina in arabesque. Something strikes me familiar about her, but the feeling lends me no recognition. The lack of memory forces me to ask the plastic belle, *Who are you?*

Jagged pieces of glass cling to its edges, all rounded as if it had once encapsulated it in a globe. My fingers activate the turnkey to squeeze some remnant tune out into the air, but the mechanism is loose. I return the item to its rightful place on the piano.

I try the familiar chords again, hoping that I can recognize another key to that song's measure. Yet all I get is the silence of the streets and the tinsel of rain continuing to fall. When nothing comes to mind, I collapse back onto the piano bench and I slide my head into my hand. My stomach churns with an unsettling nausea that comes from a constant waver in vision and concentration. I think the notes have something to do with it. I play them again, wishing that perhaps something will come of it. But like many times before when my fingers gracefully press the last key, I am greeted by a void.

I allow nihility to pay me visit, to invite a moment of clarity to free itself from the clutches of silence. I mull over, whilst my hands nurture the keys, if whether or not my musc is embedded deep within the granules of the ivory. I focus on my breath, to add a bit of noise into the background—something else to concentrate on. I believe it is the stillness of this world that makes me somber. I need something, so I play a piece by Chopin, Nocturne No. 20 in C Sharp minor. My hands glide across the piano and I close my eyes to let the music enthrall me.

PART I - SLEEPERS' WAKE

In my mind I can see the desolate streets of the city: empty, dusk, and chilling. The rain adds tears to the performance that collect in tiny pools on the sidewalks. Above, the street lamps go unheeded and unnoticed. Somewhere there are birds flying, pigeons that caress the sky in hopes of finding the people they once knew. A cat knocks over an empty garbage can, but no one is able to hear, and before long the clamor is enveloped by the ever present quiet. A dog stares at the sky, forlorn in its lack of master. It wishes to give off a cry, but is choked by the stillness. All is as if the world did cease to exist. The city's monuments go unseen, its past unheard, and its culture slowly fading in the dismal sea.

For a moment, I briefly hear the passing of voices, the sound of laughter and bemusing conversation belonging to hidden phantoms. I imagine figments walking toward the distant horizon and slowly sinking in the west. Soon all is taken by the setting sun, forever sworn to cast its shadow upon the earth no more.

My hands halt when all is done. I slam the fall of the baby grand piano, hoping to trap my encroaching disparities beneath it. I cringe at the thought of having harmed the instrument, yet the melancholy persists. At least the sound is still fresh and I managed to dispel the feeling of being swallowed by oblivion, but my head… I ease it down upon the fall to stop the room from spinning.

I dream of a face lying next to me. Her skin is smooth and pale, reflecting the white light that occupies the obscured background that is bleached by an overhead light. Her hair is long, platinum, no… blonde? It's hard to tell with the strength of illumination. We both lay on opposite tables, necks resting to the side. She smiles at me with the type of affection that comes from familiarity.

"Is this a dream?" I ask harmoniously. My voice ripples around us like water.

She blinks slowly, as if the action itself conveys some hidden meaning. "No…" her cheeks hide dimples. "Not a dream."

Then, "How did I get here?"

She laughs, like the sound of tiny bells kissing my soul. I awake mouthing the words, *"You've always been here."*

CHAPTER 1

The shadows have changed on the exterior o[f the] buildings, but the sky is still drenched in an ashen overcast and [ra]ins continue to fall. I look to the wall clock, 1:31 p.m. I must hav[e slep]t for almost three hours. The woman from my dreams, did I simp[ly ma]ke her up? Have I dreamt of her before?

A creak in the building's foundation, a floor board [com]ing from a loose nail, I hear it as it moans from outside my apar[tmen]t door. My ears now on alert, I watch with startled eyes as a shad[ow] passes from beneath the crack of the door.

I spring from the bench. "Wait!" I scream.

My knee slams into the piano leg during the flight and I b[a]rely catch myself from falling. A few additional steps and I man[a]ge to reach the closet door knob to steady myself. I quickly grab fo[r the] adjoining front door, turn the knob and pull it open. I see – nothing.

Empty like the rest of the world, the hallway is simple: white walls, grey carpet, dim lighting and white closed doors. I am number 147. The letters are gold like the card.   I walk out across the plush carpet, my feet sinking into the hidden cushion beneath. I look down both directions, hoping that the angle from my door had obstructed some individual, but nothing. Something isn't right. The carpet smells new, the walls untarnished from passing finger prints, and the numbers of each apartment shine clear and bright. I find the creak in the floor, just about mid-hallway between my apartment door and my neighbors.

Someone has to be here. I sense that there is still something lingering in the stillness of this place. My body is on guard, stiffening every hair to help listen for anything that may belong to the shadow I saw passing beneath my door. Frigid from earlier, I hastily return and open the closet. It is there I find a long black trench and matching jackboots. They fit me perfectly. I find the apartment keys instinctively in my right pocket. After everything else, I'm not surprised. I step back out into the abandoned hallway and lock the door behind me.

I test the apartment door across from mine and find it unlocked, clean and left for bare. A deserted building of fourteen floors or more and I am the only tenant? It is a grim reality that I don't wish

to give in instance with the light beneath the door is enough
to keep sing that there is someone here or if not, then there
might b as to where they went. But an entire empty building?
It is eno send my spine into tingles.

A about to step within, a metallic door slams and echoes
from er down the hallway. My stomach leaps into my throat,
and kly dart out into the hallway to see what caused it. Again,
everg is still. I know that my mind isn't playing tricks on me,
too y things have happened to simply attribute it to imaginings.

ush down the hallway as quickly as possible. Down to where
and brass-plated elevator stands vigilant with a half-circle and
nedle to point the current floor – 14 out of 28. To the right, is a
metalic door with a single rectangular window that beyond leads
onto a staircase that allows access to the other floors. I place my
hand on the push bar and look out the tiny window in hopes of
catching something hiding within the stairwell. My heart beats
heavily in my chest, warning me of something both terrifying and
unknown. I swallow a hard lump in my throat and ease onto the
push-bar to open the door. The chime of the elevator startles the
lump back to its previous place, as the doors reveal a red tufted
interior.

With a hand to my chest to calm the sudden surge of adrenaline,
I give the staircase one last chance to reveal me some obscured
character. When nothing's produced, I cautiously step inside the
brass construct and push the button for the first-floor lobby. I make
note of the twenty-five floors the panel has listed, that alongside a
button for the basement.

After many floors wait, the elevator doors unveil an elegant lobby
with a marble floor, white Roman Greco pillars and brass child-size
vases cradling extravagant plastic ferns. There is a wall set with brass
mailboxes with a small window to allow one to see in. Only one is
graced with a tag set on the inside reading, "Samuel Bell". Sadly, like
everything else, it is just as empty.

The front doors are wooden and double pane. I notice that one
of them is slightly ajar. I see the rain touching against the windows,
rolling down the flawless glass, and it is then that I am reminded
about the weather. However, it seems to me that something is

spurring me to follow it out into the city. [...] are toying with me, as if playing some w[hat]ever it is, it is as if they with the madness that has come from [l]ittle game to coincide however, will leave me no better off than [w]aking. Ignoring it know what has happened here, and what ha[s] ently am. I must following whatever it is will bring me closer to t[he] pened to me. If be it. The thought of it rallies me forward and o[ut] answers then so [...] door.

The wind brushes against me in silent serenade, d albeit my earlier mood, simply being outside of the empty apart[ment] t building gifts me a much needed escape. Here I can breathe easi[er] Outside the streets are desolate. I had half-expected that there [wo]uld be some sort of noise, some wrestle of ambiance that would gr[ee]t me, but there is nothing—no dog waiting on the street corner or bird sheltered beneath a building overhang to keep its feathers dry. Not a soul.

"Hello?" I call out into city. "Is anyone there?" All I can hear is the delicate kiss of the rain falling around me, and beyond that— apathy.

My breath takes to a fog. It must be October, feasibly even early November, though I really can't be sure. I bury my hands deep inside my coat, desperate that it'll keep what warmth I have. I look down the street, desolate for which way I should go. A street sign hangs above a metal pole at the corner, reading Gnosh and Rhine— Rhine being the street that I now currently inhabit.

I take a step toward what I believe to be east, when I hear someone's whisper press against my neck. I spin around and swing with my fists, believing that I'd connect with some manner of denizen. I'd hope to knock them to the ground, or at least connect with something physical so as to acknowledge my senses. But my fists simply pass through thin air, and all I hear are the fleeting sounds of footsteps heading off to the west.

"Wait!" I shout after. "Come back!"

With no sign of them stalling, I give pursuit.

I chase them as far as my legs can carry me, faster and faster I speed down the flawless streets and adjoining structures. I try to listen for them, hoping to catch the sound if they were to turn down

PART I – SLEEPERS' WA

...some alley way or a quiet street. Though despite all my efforts, the footfalls distance themselves. The harder I run, the farther they seem to hurry away and it isn't before too long that I slow completely and begin to cough from a choke in my chest. I stop and listen to determine where they are bounding off to. But with my ear to the air, I no longer hear them – it is as if the footsteps never existed at all. I regain my breath and continue westward, this time at a slower pace, wide-eyed and cautious.

The buildings are massive, like ancient monoliths that were built to withstand the pendulum of time. Some of the lower windows reflect like mirrors that run parallel along the sidewalk to create an ever-expansive road. In viewing them, I feel part of some estranged carnival, as my reflection creates the illusion of multiple silhouettes walking the streets; sometimes behind me and others in front. The images are like cruel specters, there to remind me of what once possibly was, a city filled with people and history. It pains me to think that some day I too will be nothing more than a fleeting reflection hidden deeply in the past, forgotten and never staring.

The sky is swollen with drudgery, both smoky and lifeless. Everything is clean, the streets are smooth and unsoiled, the gutters are unused save for the drainage of water, and the sidewalks are finely chiseled with no identifiable cracks or nicks. I wonder if the world's maker had built the city in a single thought and decided at the last minute not to fill it. It all seems unnatural, a likewise abomination to all things known and here I am walking through the middle of it.

I catch something moving from the corner street—just another me. The reflection bends at a window's edge as I wave my hand, severing the images at the frame. I step up onto the curb and then, cupping my hand to close off the light, I peer within a window to discover an empty lobby. There is no furniture, chairs or other pieces belonging to human inhabitants, just tiled marble flooring, light fixtures, white painted walls, speckled ceilings and well-polished brass door handles. The absence of it all invokes a terrifying despondency that sticks with me as I continue down the street.

With luck, I come across a quaint convenience store. It is peculiar, as it doesn't fit with the other buildings that are at least seven times its size. There is a gigantic pink neon sign, at least my size in height, lurking above the door that reads, 'Open'. I do not know what it is about the letter, but the gigantic 'O' bares into me like the opened eye of some dark god. I shiver off a chill to escape the sensation.

The store is a rogue property, nestled snug between high-rise skyscrapers as if it were a stepping stone for giants. How it has managed to stay untouched beneath the shadow of the city is a mystery filed amidst all the others. There is enough light for me to see within from the street side. However, there isn't anyone inside. All is a brilliant white. Oddly, there isn't a payment counter, just transparent plastic shelves storing food, and with stocked refrigerators garrisoning the back walls. Here is my chance to get out from beneath the rain and a break to investigate, as it's the first building that I have seen that isn't empty. Besides, whoever I was chasing before has long disappeared. I reach for the handle of the door and push to enter. It swings easily to one side.

I am struck with a creeping terror, a missing delicacy that I expected on entering the store: the sound of an angelic bell to alert the proprietor of my presence. Instead, I am greeted with a cold silent frame. Beyond the occasional buzz bounding from the overhead fluorescent lighting and the vigilant humming of the refrigerator units, the place caters to its own unique tune of quiescence quite similar to the rest of the city.

I take off my coat to get dry and perchance wait out the remainder of the downpour, although I am almost convinced that it won't ever let up. Staring at the food suddenly makes me hungry. I try not to think any longer on things, as not to disrupt my appetite. It is time I should savor my good fortune instead of squandering it on what ifs and the insanity that's born from them. I bite into a pastry and then select a heatable entree from the freezer now bound for a nearby microwave.

The rain is now a light sprinkle, something temporary before the rains inevitably pick up again. Somewhere, hidden in the darker places of this city, is a being who feels commissioned to drown the city in perpetual rains—an arbitrator for the final days. With him at my back, I now take the road in strides—a steady pace—reinforced with a collection of weary determination. I still see no birds, nor any other animal that might have come before that initial moment when I first opened my eyes, when I originally saw the fading glimmer of light disappear within the cracks of my apartment door.

I wish that I had been more aware of my environment; able to get up and pursue whoever it was that shut me in. I couldn't. It was a fleeting moment that was witnessed in the single fluttering of an eye. It was the light that caused me to rouse to begin with, the sharp entry of luminescence that squeezed across my face, and then the sound of the door knob latching in place that lulled me back to slumber. I wonder if it had been the same individual who drew the creak out of the floor. Though oddly, I feel as if the first was less invasive than the second and though both equally as startling, the last felt far more malicious. It was as if I had been poisoned towards unconsciousness, and by some sheer luck had witnessed that original something that I was not meant to see. Perhaps it was by force of will alone that I was able to glimpse as much as I had.

I press on, towards the west I trudge, racing a concealed sun to the end of the horizon. The skyscrapers loom above me, touching a near endless expanse. There are no residents to claim the towers as home. Each window is excruciatingly visible, every room just as bare as those I saw from the uneasiness of my apartment. There is no one here, the entire city sighs from a lack of activity and the streets are now covered in a shroud of wistfulness that only I get to witness. What ever happened to those who would walk the sidewalks toward a preset destination? Where have they gone and why was I left to my own defenses against the ever-creeping silence that threatens to break my nerves?

Finally, in a few hours after the clouds have shifted toward a darker cast and the light of the invisible sun slowly filters through the haze of the bleak horizon, I reach the city docks—breathtaking! The pier extends far over the sea, wide enough to compensate for an influx of cargo, passengers and whatever else would choose its use. I had long since left the presence of the skyscrapers, they being replaced by industrial warehouses and smaller brown brick buildings. There is a thick concrete promenade with a metal railing, and then a lower wooden dock set with moorings. A hemp rope closes off the sea from the clumsy traveler. Below that lies a rocky beach, scored by shells and white sand. A concrete ramp leads down to the shoreline. The sea is placid, with little waves brushing against the foundation of the docks. The constant lapping of water makes my heart surrender a palpitation.

As I stand in awe amongst the salt-filled air, I witness a slight parting in clouds and through it, the radiant beams of the setting sun poke beyond the fissures and cracks of this mirthless world. I can not help but think of her, the woman in my dreams who looked upon me with such indescribable reverence. I can not look away. I can not resist the passions in which the sight evokes. Somehow I hear the knob of my apartment door turning, and as the sun falls back beneath the choking brume, the sound of it latching follows gently afterwards.

I feel the unsettling sensation that someone or something is watching me, hidden away somewhere in the city's shadows – laughing. I am cold, tired and far too unsettled to remain. I no longer wish to be a participant in this game of hide and go seek. It is well enough past the time I should return to my apartment, and leave this mischief-maker to the abandon of this city; whoever or whatever it may be.

I nod to the omnipresent waters of the sea, turn and take my leave of it.

I stand at my apartment windows looking from my well-lit perch out across the dark cityscape with a glass of chardonnay I had poured from the bottle I found beneath my kitchen sink. Whoever it was that stocked my home with necessities had exquisite taste. I for one am grateful. Though even with the intoxicating nectar seeping into my blood stream, my stomach sits in knots.

Upon my return to my apartment I take stock of everything the apartment has and may possibly need if I am to survive for a long period of time. When I check the cupboards I find that they are all full of food items: pasta, can goods, fruits, seasonings and baking supplies. They are all here. The refrigerator holds the same—stock full. It's all out of place. There is enough food to last me a few months, perhaps even longer depending on my appetite. It is as if I, or someone else, had ensured that food wouldn't be a worry, but for what purpose? Was I to stay alive while everyone else was simply meant to disappear? It unnerves me. This whole city unnerves me.

I sit on the loveseat while keeping the throw tightly around my shoulders. Here, I take up the newspaper. The date is missing: "Sunday, The CitySpire Gazette," without any notation of month or year. The articles are blank, just boxes without text and random pictures of places around the city: buildings, monuments, graveyards; yet no detail on what the structures are for, or even their names.

The Gazette reminds me of the business card on the piano. So ambiguous, undefined and lacking in all the essentials, it is as if everything had been purposefully erased so as not to spark any bit of remembrance. It is simple, lonely and cruel. Like the glass that was resting next to the piano, like the room, like the streets, everything appears tied together somehow like clues leading to some hidden truth about the state of things. I feel like I've unveiled some deep philosophy, then a note!

I rush to the piano, casting off the blanket as if it were chaining me to the cushions, and play the previous four notes while quickly adding the fifth. I play it a few additional times, always believing the next to be destined for more. However, when nothing immediately comes of it, I grow weary. I try not to force it in order to avoid bringing frustration to bear. What I have isn't much, but it's a start.

After closing the fall, I recapture the paper sitting on the coffee table. Perhaps I had missed a clue, I think as I shuffle through the empty news. Nothing — just photographs. I stop about page four. The picture there shows the city docks that I had visited earlier. Strangely, it shows a pigeon perched atop a mooring. Just like when I visited, it shows no ships in the harbor. It seems that even when this picture was taken there wasn't any traffic. .

I take a pair of scissors from the kitchen drawer and cut out the image. Photo in hand, I grab one of the antique frames off the wall ledge and remove the back. I place the clipping behind the glass. It fits awkwardly, especially since the frame was designed for something larger, but I have nothing else to fill it with. Partially satisfied, I replace the frame on the shelf and continue to browse the remaining pages of the newspaper.

There are many such places depicted throughout the paper, and some I believed would be harder to find than others. One in particular frightens me—the city graveyard. My fear does not stem from the supernatural or that of human fragility that would usually prevail in most others, but a fear of finding nothing but empty tombs and blank gravestones. If there are no bodies in the graveyard then I worry for the past. Without monuments for the dead, what would be left after my passing? Who will bury me when my turn arrives? And would a stone bear my name, or shall I be left nameless and forever unknown? These are the thoughts I wish to leave unanswered.

Disjointed, I take this opportunity to distract myself with the music box. I imagine that if I'm somehow able to correct the loose key that I'll be able to discover part of the melody that's kept me vexed. To my astonishment, after lifting the top off the base, I realize that the insides aren't actually broken, but are just missing the pronged cylinder entirely. Someone or something had removed it. Without the teeth to touch against the musical pins, there is no way of finding out the tune. It is just another frustration to add to my existence. I grow tired of all this.

I take one last look out of my apartment window and see little but the glow of the street lamps and the titanic shadows cast by the neighboring structures. I leave the light on, finishing off the last remnants of the wine, and head towards my only respite—long, though preferably everlasting sleep.

2

Two weeks, twenty nine notes, dreams and silence, the city has given me far less than what I could ultimately desire. Nothing. This city offers nothing in regards to companionship and yet I firmly believed that there would be someone, possibly a handful of individuals left who either know more about this place, or share the same affliction as I. Two weeks! How it unnerves me. Beforehand, I had fallen into a grievous depression and for a few days I refused to leave my apartment. Sure I had found a few local stores, but material things offer me little comfort. There are times that I sit at my piano, playing one requiem to the next, something to help lighten my spirits as the moments flicker by. And although I strive to make an attempt at accomplishing something: such as going to see a new site, locate a few more businesses, and familiarize myself with the layout of the streets *all in the name of discovery*, I am oftentimes thwarted by the question of "To what purpose?" and whether or not my actions hold sway over this uncaring place.

I even made a game of seeking out the locations depicted in the newspaper. Each time I found one of the areas, I cut the photograph out and placed it in its own frame. In my journeys, I saw the city square's statue of Hermes, surrounded on all sides by department stores that are filled with clothes of varying styles. Another day I managed to locate a dilapidated cathedral whose Gothic spires and buttresses chilled me with a fear that accompanies mortality; and across its street I discovered a well-trimmed forested park, despite its lack in caretakers. Then just yesterday, I located a hidden trove of Victorian mansions nestled atop the northern hill-face, passed the concrete towers and apartment complexes. Everything was beautiful, clean and empty. In each place I left a note describing my whereabouts and a desire for any who find it to seek me here in my apartment at the corner of Gnosh and Rhine. Not a word. Each night since my waking I have stood here at my window, tending what is to be the only lit building in the city.

Every time I step outside my apartment door, I cannot shake the dreadful feeling that something lurks somewhere in the CitySpire. Every so often, I'll hear something shift in an alley, a scuff of a shoe and occasionally something of a whisper off in the distance. I will not lie, for it truly terrifies me, as whatever being hides just shy of my view is my sole tormentor. Who is it? And what does it want? Am I the victim of some denizen's tricks or is this city haunted by the missing inhabitants? I cannot truly say, for no matter what I do or say in hopes of coaxing it, ends in the city's ever persistent silence.

I've also dreamt of her nightly. The dreams are much the same and still there is an air of familiarity about her. I woke on Sunday, but it is hard to say whether or not I had a past. Can I be suffering from a mental condition, possibly amnesia or other memory deficiency? But if such were the case, why is it that I remember some things and not others? And if so, that still does not explain the reason as to where the rest of the world disappeared to. Many things are not clear. I've been going over the details since my waking and I have yet to find any answers concerning my condition. Something had happened to the inhabitants of the CitySpire, but something to the extent where old buildings are camouflaged to appear as new. History has been completely erased, covered over by a thick layer of paint. My mind cannot help but wonder towards darker things, and believe that whatever creature is out there may have had something to do with the previous tenants. Why else would it constantly hide from me? Such is the reason I try and remain inside, else I fall victim to the same fate as they had.

It does not take long before the depression tries to nest inside me, and the only means for its cure is to escape the confines of my apartment. I find it better to brave the passing of some unknown specters than to dwell upon what horrors befell those before me. Finding its way to me once again, I take this opportunity to egress from my building and return to the west-side pier. In my outings, I've discovered that the city is surrounded on all sides by water, which is endless in all directions. The extra thought of isolation surely hasn't helped my state of mind, and although trapped on this island, I still feel an overwhelming calm while I look out across the water's expanse.

"So this is where you find me, Rachel," the name for her, the woman of my dreams, "here at the water's edge."

PART I - SLEEPERS' WAKE

As the sun makes its descent toward the horizon, I cannot help but hear gulls crying out in my mind. I close my eyes and I take in a breath of sea breeze. Things are much easier to imagine when my vision is dampened. I harbor thoughts of them flying above, their wings flapping gracefully in the saltine winds, each striving to maintain an aerobatic maneuver that permeates seagull legend. Here is my day's end, my little cup of coffee to ease me into an idealistic mood before facing the lonesome nights of piano play, and acting as an inland lighthouse for a city that receives no visitors.

I open my eyes, sighing from a slow gathering of motivation, and look slightly off toward my left and there! lying leafless on the beach no more than a foot from the rolling tide is a battered silhouette—a woman! I rush across the wooden boards, tripping, and catching myself in mid-stride. My heart pounds in emergency. She is lifeless, pale and face down in the rock ridden sand. I lower myself from the dock, careful not to do myself injury in case she needs to be carried. I reach her side, my lungs, not used to such activity, heave with desperate gasps. Her hair is littered with debris, short and auburn in color, her body covered in bruises and scrapes. She looks as if coughed from the sea floor.

I take her pulse—faint, but there. I check her eyes to look into her pupils regardless that I have no idea what I'm looking for. She is freezing, shivering from her body's natural response to frigidity. She breathes. I might be able to make it to the convenience store. Perhaps there I could try and get her warm—break until I feel able enough to brave the rest of the way. My mind is racing with everything that can go wrong, and I swallow to keep my doubts inside—I have to act!

Quickly, I take off my coat and wrap her inside it. I sit her up, throw her arms over my shoulders and heft her onto my back with extreme difficulties. The extra body is awkward, my center of balance shifting between multiple locations. I make a grab for her legs and hoist her higher, with my head crashing into her hip. It hurts, but I fear whether or not I had inflicted some horrendous wound on her more. As my muscles tense and my body quivers from her weight, I command myself, "Hold together!" I take a couple steps toward a distant ramp.

As my legs strive to find their lost dexterity, I stagger slightly forward. The city's stillness now carries the feeling of judgment, watching as if all things depend on me. I tell myself that she will live, to press on and to ignore the pain from the albatross. My heart is racing, my muscles straining and all I can think about is getting her to safety. I look to the horizon one last time, noting the sun poised to set on another evening of emptiness. I think to myself, "Not today."

I ease my head back to rest against the glass door of one of the refrigerator units, my body twitching from both exhaustion and strain. I made it, difficult, but I made it. The woman rests not far from me, lying on the cold tile since there are no counters to sit her on. I found some hand towels, wetted, and heated them in the microwave. They now serve to keep her warm, as I stuffed them in the crucial locations throughout my coat so that they would bring her a little life. I am thankful that she doesn't weigh more than she does, one hundred pounds, if that. I try to rationalize that this is all that I can do for her and yet it grieves me to think that it may not be enough. Happenstance tends to be a cruel master and me the ever-so-ready pawn.

My limbs hang helplessly to my sides. My nose itches, yet I refuse to muster the energy to fight it off. I sit in silence, listening to the sound of her breathing, watching as her lungs lift and fall. I can't help but stare, her presence gives me a sense of purpose, something that I had been lacking during the previous weeks. Above all, I yearn for conversation, though I am sure that it will not come for some time. She will take days before her vigor returns, and who knows how many more it will take for her to wake, if at all. Alive or dead, she has relieved my greatest sorrows—dismissing the belief that I was the only one left in this world. With her here, that would mean that there are others elsewhere.

Yet where did she come from? A ship? Did she decide to swim in the nude, swam too far and was later overtaken by fatigue? Or perhaps, and an even darker possibility, did she attempt to drown herself and was pushed ashore before the suicide was completed? I can't be certain, and I would hate to think that such a beautiful girl plotted to end her own life. I wouldn't blame her if she had. The city had me contemplate the same notion on a few unmentionable occasions. She looks like a regular Emily Dickinson. I trust that she wouldn't share the same fate.

I lull my head in a half-circle in an attempt to expel the kinks from my spine. I hurt, but it is a sweet pain. For once my body feels the harm from an outside source instead of toiling beneath ill-gotten woes. I swear that the human brain holds the cork to a draught of poison that if left unattended could reap a man of his soul. And here it is when an outside influence—though as small and delicate as the woman before me—interrupts my string of thought, I am given remedy. It is as if there had been no suffering, and the loneliness is now nothing more than a dream violently snatched after waking— quick, faint and gone. I'm forever in her debt, "Thank you, oh sweet dearest woman."

Not a stir or welcome, though she continues to breath. That is enough for me. Now all I have to do is to wait, recoup, and continue the rest of the way. That is the plan as I proceed to watch her lungs fill with air. I tell myself that it won't be long now. I envision myself standing and taking her upon my back, but my muscles sit, refusing to comply.

As soon as I lay her on my bed, I collapse by her side. My arms are weak, my calves taken to the flame, and all other sort of aliments consort with one another in plans of my torpidity—I am spent. I bring the covers from the foot of the bed overtop us, and I embrace Emily with hopes of bringing her warmth. As my eyelids falter and my vision blurs, I swear I can see faces staring at us; all huddled around the bed. I have little time to identify the specters, for what comes after is a silent lightless lethargy where not even dreams can penetrate.

I awake in the same position. Emily has not moved and I worry that she may have passed while I slept. Then I notice her breathing and all is well again. My body still aches from before. Though as painful as movement brings me, I know that it is the best counter agent for the cause. I pull back the covers and remove the constraint of my coat from her body. She's gorgeous—slim physique, perfect breasts. I try not to look for too long, especially under these circumstances. I cannot help but steal a glimpse as I examine her wounds… so vulnerable. Some are mere scratches, while others such as the three-inch gash across her right thigh and the cut above her lip, gives me cause for worry. I grab the first aid kit from before and I make use of it as best as I know how.

Cutting bandages and gauze seem to be second nature to me. I find some comfortable clothes, sweats and white cotton polo to dress her in. I decide to shift her to her back, and tend to her forehead with a warm cloth. She is still cold to the touch, but not as frigid as she had been on the beach. I am sure that the weather didn't help much, nor the hyperborean waters. I fear the coming of a fever and if such is the case, I worry whether she will have the strength to overcome it.

The hours pass as I sit by her side. I feed her water, though most of it ends up being coughed up as she struggles momentarily. It takes a couple of tries to get her to accept it—a long grueling process. At times I think that I am doing her more harm than good. Exactly, how much of a struggle did she have to persevere before wearing herself out, succumbing to the darkness of unconsciousness with the fear of the inevitable depths stinging her mind. I have so many questions, and I catch myself speaking them aloud in anticipating a coherent response. But the most I ever receive is a sharp twitch of her head. She dreams. Her eyes move beneath her lids in rapid succession. Perhaps there is something left of her after all. I assure myself that it's only a matter of time before she wakes. Though as dawn lifts from beneath the veil of night, I cannot help but shed a tear for her, still asleep—fighting against the toils of ebb.

For days I tend to her every need: I spoon feed her soft foods, and blend up others to make them easier to swallow; I change her clothes along with the sheets; above all else I strive to keep her warm. During the moments that I have for myself I spend them at the piano, resurrecting old dirges and the accustomed piece from Beethoven. At times I dream of the notes rousing Emily from her slumber, and enticing her from her bed. I watch as the gloomy days pass, from cloud cover to misty haze, and from one drizzle to fleeting rain. At nights I leave the lights on to attract any others that may be lurking around the dark crevasses of the CitySpire. I often catch myself believing that others had washed heartlessly ashore by the forgiving tide and that they too need my help. My biggest fear lies in leaving her alone, that after searching the myriad beaches, that I'd return to find my home empty and Emily nothing more than a fleeting memory. So despite my gnawing concerns for others, I am chained here in responsibility. Besides, it is far too much for a single man. As far as I know, Emily is all that washed ashore that day. Trusting so, I am the better for it; else I'd drive my conscience to madness.

Four times have I woken beside her and each time she continues to sleep beneath the shroud of injury. Sometimes I consider that Emily dreams of death, and how her spirit haunts the bottom of the seabed. I, for one, can't imagine the horror of it all, but remind myself that I am simply being over-dramatic. Ever since Emily's arrival, I have noticed that I have been more predisposed toward the romantic, though dark as the circumstances suggest.

As I sit at my piano, I tap out the few measures of the song that constantly flows through my head. I've managed to remember a few other notes since my last count, and since then I desire another breakthrough. What I have is enough to allow a continuous loop in which to provoke my memory into summoning the remainder of it. Each time I try to recall the melody it's a constant barrage that leaves me exhausted, and above all else frustrated.

And it is at this time, where my head has finally met my hand in tireless effort, that I am stirred by an angelic thing—"I heard music."

I turn over my shoulder and see her standing in the doorway of my bedroom, her body leaning against the framework in order to support her weight. It looks as if she is having difficulties moving—still in pain I imagine—but refuses to give notice. Her hair is in a disheveled tangle, her eyes are shadowed and her skin pale with sickness. She wears one of my white shirts which hangs down to her thighs.

For awhile we exchange glances, each searching for something to say. "I'm glad to see you finally awake," I expel in an awkward fashion. She pays it no mind.

"How long have I been out?" She asks.

"Five days."

"Five days?" She bites her lip and shifts her eyes to identify her surroundings, takes a breath and snaps her eyes back to me. "Did I snore?"

Her question strikes me funny, but by the sound in her voice the question was posed in a serious manner. "No – you dreamed a lot, but rarely moved. You were very quiet."

"What did I dream about?"

I worry she is touched. "You tell me."

She shrugs her shoulders and rubs her arms. "I'm cold."

I rub my hands across my lap hoping to stimulate a sympathetic response. "There are extra shirts in the bedroom closet and you may take any of the blankets from the bed. Help yourself."

She doesn't move, but continues to rub her arms and looks around. She staggers toward the window, and my heart skips thinking that she is about to leap. I hastily get up from the piano, but deaden my speed as she stops short and looks out across the city. I stand at the other side, relieved, and follow her gaze in order to discern what she is thinking. She doesn't say a word, but her face keeps to a neutral expression.

I can't help but ask, "Do you know where you are?"

She turns to me with a foreboding glare. "Do you?"

Her eyes are as grey as the weather and she holds me in place with them. I don't know how to answer that question, and I wouldn't be able to even if I did. The ironic thing is that she probably doesn't know either. She looks back out the window without saying a word.

"I found you by the shore. You almost drowned."

"Did I?" She doesn't flicker, doesn't move, as if her body can't react due to the coldness in her limbs.

"My name is Samuel Bell. What's yours and where did you come from?"

"The sea."

I'm perplexed and my stance must be giving me away, as she quickly looks back to me with blank expression. "You said you found me on the shore, so I must have come from the sea."

"Yes, but where exactly?"

She sighs.

I decide not to press it any further. "Do you know your name?"

"My name?" Her face becomes hard, as if trying to squeeze out a memory that is lodged somewhere in her mind—"Rachel."

I am taken aback. "Rachel?"

"I heard you say Rachel," she pauses, "at the docks. So I must be named Rachel."

Instinctively I retort, "I was talking about someone else."

"Someone else?" She looks about the apartment, partially afraid that she'd missed someone's introduction.

I shake my head. "Not here, someone in my dreams."

She taunts me with a queer expression, "You talk to your dreams?"

"There was no one else to talk to. I was more talking to myself, really."

"But I was there."

"Yes! but you were—" It is a lost cause. I can't argue with her. She had caught me talking to myself. Though I wasn't aware it was a social taboo. Other questions bug me, "So your name is Rachel?"

"No."

"But you just said..." I stop myself. "What's wrong with Rachel?"

She turns away from me and stares banefully out the window once more. "It's not me."

I do not know how, but I think I have insulted her, though I can't follow the reason for it. She leaves me in silence, the very thing I believed I had been rid of. The frigidness between us consumes the room.

"You pick." She quickly stammers, the stillness obviously getting to her as well.

"What about Emily Dickinson?"

"Who's she?"

"A poet."

She looks at me with the most malicious eyes and there is a touch of resentment in her voice. "Did you dream her up too?"

"No – she's real. She lived a long time ago."

"Was she beautiful?"

"I believe so." Her body shivers, manifesting a chill down her spine.

In a blink her features soften and a smile creeps up the side of her cheek. "Then my name is Emily."

"Dickinson?"

"Waters." She tilts her head back and laughs. I can't help but feel that I missed the joke. Perhaps her shift in mood comes from some hidden moment in her psyche, or from the excitement of hearing her name for the first time. Somewhere deep inside, I cannot help but feel partially cheated of this same occasion. My moment came on an embroidered card with no one to share it with. The change in her character is most welcome.

I cannot help but smile. "Emily Waters it is then."

Her giddiness ends abruptly. "I'm cold Samuel Bell."

I become locked in those grey eyes of hers. In them I cannot help but remember the first moments of my initial waking and how cold I felt. Amidst the strangeness of it all, I feel a connection to Emily: her bite, her mood, and her appreciation for the mundane. I wonder if she had experienced her waking on the beach, as I had at the piano in this apartment. Suddenly, I didn't just sympathize with her and her suffering, I pitied her. I startle her accidentally as I hastily glide toward the bedroom in hopes of curing both our aliments. And when I return with a thick bedspread and drape it across her shoulders, she casts me a smile that I know I shall never forget.

"Now – how about something hot to drink?"

She nods and watches me with the cat's eyes – glittering with appreciation, curiosity, and a hint of self-canonization.

Emily lays across the sofa as if she were the jewel of the Nile, listening as Cleopatra, to the music I play. She keeps the blanket nearby just in case the chill returns to her once more. The hot tea and occasional cocoa adds color to her face. Each song I play she contemplates some deep hidden meaning and later taunts me by claiming she hadn't thought a thing. Every so often she interrupts me and asks me which composer wrote the song and then very trivial questions about their lives such as, if Bach ever owned any horses or if Chopin had ever used a curling iron. I find the majority of them silly, but never do I dismiss them as agitating or in the least bit out-of-place.

No – Emily caters to an enormous, if not overactive, curiosity that reminds me of a child. And yet, despite whatever answer I give, I notice her retreat back into herself to calculate her latest finding, and begin the formulation of new questions. I rather enjoy hearing them, as her companionship offers my soul a break from my previous mentalities. It occurs to me that I have fallen into a mentor's position.

We go on like this for hours, with her laying there occasionally chiming in with yet another question, while I shift between our short conversations and the latest serenade. Then without any explicit reasoning, Emily dismisses herself from the warming thralls of the couch and announces that she is bored. I am forced to end Bach's Cantatas 140 prematurely. She walks up to the picture frames, the ones filled with the clippings from the newspaper, and leans in eye-level with the glass. When I reach her side she asks, "What are these?"

"Pictures of places around the city."

She picks up the clipping of the harbor and stares at it in blank expression. "Is this where you found me?"

"Yes, you were lying on the shore. It was a far distance to carry you. I had to stop at the convenience store and rest." I laugh. "I was sore for days."

She puts the picture frame down and starts looking around for some particular photo. "I don't see a picture of this convenience store. Are you sure it exists?"

"Of course it exists, just because I don't have a picture of it doesn't mean that it isn't there."

"Take me." Her face is filled with vehement conviction.

I ponder whether she had cause not to believe me, and thought that perhaps I was being untruthful. Then I remember her health.

"Are you sure you want to go out right now? You haven't had enough time to recoup. Technically, you should still be in bed."

She takes inventory, halting in thought to dedicate all her senses to the condition of her body. She closes her eyes and takes in a deep breath. Her face tightens up, as what I can only postulate, due to some grievous pain she had just become aware of. She brings her hand up to her head and wobbles a bit—I hasten to catch her. She drops her hands onto my arms and grips me with desperation in order to regain her lost balance. I consider that she might have done that on purpose, but when her eyes slowly flutter open and the sweat on her brow collects in beads, I aver she had been faking her wellness the entire time. Emily is a masterful deceiver, although I do not know from what she intended to gain from the facade. Was it her means of finding out whether she could trust me? Was it all in part to satisfy her sense of pride? Or did she do so to save me from worrying? As I stare at her while holding a portion of her weight, and when her eyes finally reach mine in a deadlock, I come to realize how incredibly fragile she is. She swallows, and it is then that I know that she realizes it too.

"Don't worry, I got you."

Her eyes sparkle with a rising dampness. "I've seemed to overstep myself, Samuel."

"Indeed you have."

"Can you tell me something?" I nod to reassure her. "Did Bach ever eat pancakes at midnight?"

I can't help but laugh and while I help her back to her feet and slowly over towards the couch once more, I tell her that I highly doubt that he had.

"Do you think *we* can have pancakes at midnight?"

I smile to the point that my cheeks hurt, like I've acquired some level of connection—some trust. She is soft, docile, staring at me with misty eyes. She needs me more than ever, to save her from whatever dangers try to overcome her. For now I am her savior, her protector, her friend. Together we are safe from the plights of the world.

"Pancakes it is."

Emily's fainting spells increase as the next two days spiral on. I am consigned to her side, ever-ready to offer her balance and a steady arm for an inconsistent affliction. Her dizziness is always accompanied by an unsettling cold that begins at her fingertips and slowly moves toward her chest. I sometimes wonder whether her body still believes it to be at the mercy of the frigid sea.

Every time that I ask Emily if she recalls what she was doing in the waters she replies with a shortness that only follows agitations. So far her answers have been absurd, such as when she claimed that someone had probably just roughed her up, stole her clothes, and threw a bucket of water on her. Her latest thought has been that she was born of the sea, like some water nymph chosen to live amidst the mortals of the world. I've come to the conclusion that Emily's faith resides in which telling favors her most, and to convince her otherwise would be a needless trifle. She is happy, albeit her condition, and until such improves I am content in her conviction.

Discovering her origins might piece more of the puzzle together, but if left to her, she would have none of it. She finds me irritating, as she later claimed one day after a delightful dinner, informing me that my delving into the mystery about the city's inhabitants is superficial. When I inquired why she thought such, she said that for all I knew they could be hiding. But her annoyance doesn't lend itself solely to my questions about the city's lack in occupation, but to all questions dealing with a plausible past. In her eyes the world began when she washed ashore, and all concepts of a before is a headache best left unfelt. With Emily, things don't exist until she sees them, all experiences mute until she experiences them. And the more I speak about composers and other artists, the more she is convinced that I made them all up.

Emily does not share the knowledge that I woke to, or the expectations of a thriving city. She enjoys things as they are, and feels that I can't accept—which she believes—never was. The stronger she grows in her assuredness, the more I question my own. I can't be sure, for I may be the one who is misinformed. The more I give into self-doubt, the more I wish to do away with the entire affair. I am relieved by Emily's inability to hold a philosophical conversation for long, as I have noticed that she is easily distracted. I can never be angry with her, and no matter how foreign her opinions, I appreciate the opposition and am glad neither of us have the stomach for lengthy disagreements.

After those few days of rest, Emily and I decide that some fresh air will do her good. Our consensus arrives on a day when the rains are drawn back into their beds and a few slivers of light beam down to warm the moist streets. We walk arm in arm, more as a means of an innocent flirtation than one would expect from the affectionate gesture. It also enables me to monitor Emily for signs of yet another episode. We both are dressed in long coats, a spare I had found from an earlier adventure. Our first order of business is to visit the convenience store as a means of proving its existence, and then continue to the shore—as she has been dying to see it. The streets, as previous ventures before, are bleak.

I am amazed at Emily's calm during the long westerly walk toward the pier. I keep a sharp observance of her, watching her gaze move from building to building as if for her first time – wide-eyed with wonder. At times we pass mirrored windows, and at each she stops to gaze at our reflection. She tips her head back to giggle at our image and comments on how becoming we look. I am careful to avoid mentioning how abandoned I find the buildings to be and how lonely they make me feel. Preferring to keep her ignorant of my mood, it is best that I refrain from any sign of melancholy or despondence. I must be a convincing actor for she remains oblivious to it all.

Something tugs at my mind, something hidden about the city and its condition. Nearly the whole trip we bask in each other's company, allowing the silence that the CitySpire imposes on a body settle in our throats. Then it comes to me like a splash of cold water—debris! When I found Emily she was covered in mud and soil from the shore. It is obvious, merely common sense, that with all the winds and the rains that some debris should eventually find its way into the city. Yet the windows are all perfectly clean, without smudge or streak! One could say that city exists in a state of perpetual perfection, clean and without flaw.

I recall being careful during all my previous outings, to prevent myself from harming—at least what I perceived to be—a delicate thing. There is only so much a single man can do in order to fight off the challenges of inevitable decay, but it is as if all things have been spared. Everything is left to its own accord, free from the eventual fate that all things share. It's all unnatural. I want to scream out my discovery. I want to confirm my suspicion and gain Emily's insight on the matter, but then I rationalize that she would become angry with me for thinking about "trivial" things and should focus on our journey instead. So I save myself the extra step, keeping my revelation secret in order to keep our procession enjoyable, both for her sake and for mine. It will be something to discuss when conversation finally runs dry.

The farther the distance from the apartment, the more the city's stillness creeps up on me in the form of a manifesting anxiety. I feel that familiar feeling, that uncomfortable horripilation that skitters across my body when I sense that once again we are being watched. But now, I feel a strong oppressive force within my chest, as if the buildings—though the same stone monuments as before—now hold some kind of spell over me, towering like concrete giants glaring down at me with mal-intent. I can not identify our stalker's location and no matter how hard I try to subdue it, the anxiety only inches a little deeper, stinging the interior of my chest. Then she hums.

She hums the exact measures that took me weeks to construct from the fragments in my mind. I grow angry, and if it weren't for my blasé nature, I might have clenched my fist in her face.

"Where did you learn that?!" I demand as flames lick the confines of my ribs, scarring the flesh and leaving an acrid taste in my mouth. My teeth clench as my throat stiffens, with the putrid sensation crawling out to greater affect my tongue; doing everything in my power to restrain a most certain outburst.

"Hmm?" Emily cocks her head toward me, her eyes drifting out of a far-off stare acting as if she had been distant. "Oh – I don't know." She shakes her head and gives me a questioning look. "You did." Her features grow angular, sensing the disruption in my character.

I station myself to prevent a miss word. "I never played that for you. It's an unfinished work. You must have—" I stop mid-sentence while happening upon a realization, like a door opening to reveal the next room's secrets. I did play it! In fact I believe it was the song that brought her out of her coma. I do not know why I hadn't thought of that earlier.

Her face is stern, and she tightens her grip on my arm to drive her point. "Well you did play it for me! I didn't even know who Moat-zart was before you told me about him!"

"It's Mozart. And you're right, I apologize. I did play it." I don't understand why I am so angry. I've worked very hard on putting that composition together. Perhaps hearing her throw it around like an everyday tune may have upset me in some fashion. Maybe it is because I thought she may have had the secrets all along and that all my work was for naught. The anxiety hadn't helped in the matter and somehow I cannot shake that my state of apprehension was born of that exterior source. The feeling of being watched has fled and I am left horribly guilty.

"Mozart! That's what I said. He's the one that wrote Moonlight Sonata right?"

I don't feel up for conversation, especially after how easily angered I became. But to deny her now would only make matters worse.

"That was Beethoven." At least I restrained myself.

"Well it doesn't matter. It's a pretty song and I like it." If her hands were free, she would have crossed them to emphasize her point.

"I like Moonlight Sonata as well. It has a dark romance about it."

"No! that song makes me depressed. A lot of the songs you play are depressing. I mean the one I was humming, what's its name again?" She starts snapping her fingers as if the noise would help conjure it to her tongue.

"It's unfinished, I don't know if it has a title."

"Well it's gorgeous. I don't know what it is about it, but you play it in my head all the time. You should play it for me again Samuel." She stops and pulls my arm so that we are standing perpendicular to the curb. "Now aren't we the pair?"

We continue the rest of the way in conversation about particular pieces of architecture that catch our attention. Most of the buildings are plain, with lines of windows and uncountable stories. Emily mentions how she finds the modernity of the combination of concrete and glass to be unexciting and for the most part dull. She adheres in her opinion that the buildings should be more like music, both pleasing and inspiring. I happen to agree with her, as there is something about the towers that add a feeling of dejection. I tell her that I am particular to Baroque and Victorian styles myself. I promise to take her to see the terraced manors at the north end of the CitySpire, as I am sure that she will enjoy them better.

Her eyes brighten and then she shakes my arm vigorously. "Why aren't we living there?!"

"I would if we could. But there's a problem, we don't have any means of transporting our things. Besides, I don't know what we'd do with all that space. I don't even know if there is any power."

She sighs heavily and bites her lip in disappointment. I'm sure that she is trying to think of a means of residency, but the problem holds firm. By the time we reach our destination, she has since long abandoned it.

She stands next to me, absorbing the sight while biting on her fingers. For a time we are bathed beneath the neon glow of the open sign. Emily staggers partially, and as I tighten my grip to ensure her safety she pulls hastily away, takes a few steps forward, and points to the store's sign and asks, "Why didn't you just tell me it was called 'Open'?"

I scrunched my eyebrows in an attempt to see past her riddles. "It's just a sign letting people know that the store is open for business. It has no name."

"No it's not." She races up to the store window nearest the door and peers inside.

From my location the store looks exactly as I had left it. I shake my head at her prior announcement, refusing to accept her naming. I approach the storefront, and once reaching her side, I brush lightly against her hand to gain her attention to convince her otherwise.

"Emily I —"

"You sure are a messy person, Mr. Bell." She says as she lifts her finger up and points past the glass.

There are a few chip bags on the ground, a couple of wrappers strewn about the shelves, and the microwave door left open.

"That wasn't me."

"Wasn't you? Who else could it have been? I don't see anyone else." She looks around as she had in my apartment, seeking out the missing link.

"Emily, please…" She now stares apprehensively at me with those beautiful eyes, searching for some manner of fib. Her gaze abates and she places her hand on my cheek while smiling.

"You're so polite to me."

I interrupt her compliment. "Someone else has been here!"

She looks around, shifting her eyes toward the darker corners between the looming buildings and deep into their shadowy alcoves. She turns back to me with a frightened visage.

"Maybe they are still here!" Her teeth chatter and I worry that her hypothermia is returning. I feel her forehead, but all is well. Emily clenches my arm tightly and presses her face hard into my coat. "I dwn lyk eht ere!"

I pull her from me in order to better hear past her muffles. She latches tightly onto a section of my coat, pulling me closer to her for safety.

"Take me home Samuel! Please take me home!"

I hold her as best as I can and look around the area for additional disturbances. The streets are lorn, the windows of the neighboring buildings are clear and the interiors are bare. Curiosity scratches at my temples and regardless of Emily's protests, I want to investigate, to find all that had occurred inside the store and follow it out into the city.

As I make toward the doors, I am halted by my companion's steadfastness. "Don't go in there!"

"It's alright. I just want to get a better look. Maybe there is another like you who recently washed ashore." I take another step toward the entryway, but once again I am restrained as Emily tugs at my arm with her entire weight, as her body slowly sinks toward the ground.

"Another like me? Don't leave me out here with myself! I'd go mad. Please don't leave me alone, Samuel! Just take me home!" Tears stream down her face. "Please take me home!"

I try to reassure her. "I'll only be a minute. You can come with me inside if you want. I'll make sure you're safe."

She drops to her knees and wraps her arms about her, sobbing uncontrollably.

"Don't leave me alone! I'll die out here. Please don't leave me alone!"

Overwhelmed by her disparity, I feel compelled to restore every ounce of security she has lost, to dry her tears and see her happy again. I do not know what has come over her. Ever since that brush with anxiety, it feels as if there is something malicious in the air, stemming from an unperceivable source.

Grabbing her by the shoulders, I hoist her up to her feet. Emily continues to cry, sniffling between breaths, each one heavy in order to compensate her heart's demand; it is racing. I take little time securing her around the waist. I retreat from my earlier inclinations and support her toward the direction we had originally come; sorry I hadn't the opportunity to discover the one responsible for the mess, and ever the more penitent for her sufferings.

I steal one glance over my shoulder as soon as we are far from the foreboding luminescence of the neon glow, and it is there that my stomach leaps into my throat. Squatting just shy of the light and partially concealed by the shade of an alley is a sinister silhouette beneath a crimson cowl, beaming a demonic smile which spans from cheek to swollen cheek.

I quicken our pace, she later to claim for her sake, and I in flight from the creature of the convenience store. Its image now burnt deathly into my mind. Be it man or beast, it had been watching us the entire time from the darkest places few have dared. And as we egress farther away, whilst keeping an eye behind us, I watch in relief as the fiend silently slinks from my vision, forever hidden from the muddled rays of the sun.

Emily's mood improves much faster than my own as the streets shape toward the familiar. Laughter accompanies nearly every step and her trek has morphed from the sullen trudge, to a jovial skip. Sunlight manages to peek from the cloud cover enough to cause the water beads to shimmer each with their own miniature sun. The air is fresh, carried by the northern winds, accompanied by a sweet aroma that smells of melting ice. Winter must be near, and the endless grey will end its persistent rains and crystallize into tiny flakes in its stead. I fear whether the electricity and food will carry the both of us through the harshness of the coming snows.

At times I envy Emily's ability to ignore such concerns. Whether it originates from an inability to manage complex troubles, or due to a mental unwillingness, is far beyond my current understandings. Either or, the self-proclaimed nymph is joyous more times than not, preferring her state of bliss to the exertion that my thinking tolls. Already, she acts as nothing transpired at the store. I wish forgetting was that easy.

I am glad we left when we did. The thing that stood dismally in the shadows may have had foul intentions. It makes me think about what Emily had said, about how there could be others but hiding from us. I thought the prospect to be ridiculous at first. Now, it is because they are devious or horrid things, left to the darker portions of this city—as per that creature—to unleash their evil. Why else would it be hiding there and not introduce itself, knowing full well the city's condition? Yet there it sat, fringed between the worlds of light and dark and at any moment could have descended upon us, yet didn't. Maybe it was content squatting there, watching us with deleterious desires, but failed to act on them. Or more probable, it didn't know whether or not it could handle the both of us at once and was waiting for the right moment for me to separate. If such were the case, poor Emily would have suffered an attack had I not taken pity in seeing to her care. I am fearful. I can't endure the chance of her loss—it reminds me of how dear she is to me and that our minor disagreements shouldn't be seen as anything more than a blessing else I'd have nothing at all.

My companion tosses her short auburn hair, brushing it from her eyes and beams me a youthful expression that one would have troubles saying 'no' to.

"Take me somewhere I can find new clothes, Samuel."

Held by the hands, I raise them to about chest level and am beset by her greyish orbs. "But didn't you want to go home earlier?"

"Did I?" She pauses slightly with a frowned face directed at the curb, but quickly returns to a pleasing smile, "It's no matter. I don't feel like going there now. I want new clothes. Please!" She weaves her fingers around mine. "It'll make me feel better."

I don't have it in me to object. She is right. She does need new clothes and the trip would have seemed a waste had we not come back with something—besides nightmares. It is the best I can offer her, what better to shed my horror of the previous encounter. I'm still unsure of whether it would be wise to tell Emily. Perchance there will be an appropriate moment to relay it all, but better to be in the safety of our home than here, vulnerable to the figments of imagination.

We reach Hermes Square around the dawning of twilight. The quaint shops are lit by distinguishable four-arm streetlamps that greet us at every twelve feet or so. The Square is more of a circle really, with the bronze statue on a center pedestal surrounded in bushes and half wilted flowers. The stores' entrances all face toward the street, eagerly displaying garment adorned manikins, cloth, and enough dress accessories to accommodate a royal retinue and here we have a run at it! Emily doesn't even allow for the beating of an eyelash before she chooses a startling boutique and drags me in tow.

In a few hours we emerge with formal garb: Emily in a red-lace number, fit snuggly in an under bodice that accentuates her breasts and I fit with cap and cane. We were both inspired by an imaginary invitation to some high societal event and therefore dressed appropriately. My escort also found a few darling outfits that she couldn't do without, though luckily we were able to find a box to carry them in.

"I am a princess!" She shouts while dancing excitedly in the street. "And you sir are my coveted cavalier."

"And where would you be off to this evening, Milady?" I dash after her in an enthusiastic bout of play.

Taking up her role, she races behind the statue keeping the pedestal between us. "To the grand ball, a charity auction, a devious masquerade, the opera!"

"All of that in one night? How have you the time?" We corner each other off, keeping sharp eye in which direction the other dodges to. She laughs, I laugh—a childish game that before now would have seemed impossible.

Emily is far overtaken by laughter, her mouth frozen open to better suit the continuous chain of mirth. She gasps and bares her teeth in an erotic fashion, "I'm magic!"

I leap further into the hilarity, chasing her around the statue until the grass slips from beneath my feet and I tumble into her, the both of us falling in a mixed mosaic of limbs. Still caught up in our gaiety, we manage to pull ourselves free. I am the first to emerge, enough to return to my feet and offer my hand to Emily. She sticks her tongue out at me—the little flirt—and flings herself on her back stretching into the ground. She must have found some perfume, as she smells like jasmine. I give it the good laugh and start brushing off the slivers of grass, yet stop in a dead face. Standing together, like two lodestones, at the mouth of the eastbound street, is a pair of human-like figures dressed in high attire; watching us from beneath a streetlight.

"Look Samuel!" She points to the couple – I noticing a twig sticking out of her hair. "Mannequins."

She extends her hands and I quickly hoist her up, too quick as she scrambles with her heels to get her proper footing. The end result comes in her latching onto my waist and climbing me as a ladder until situated. The entire foolery almost ends with us on our backs again. I am sure that our audience would have found it to be the most entertaining introduction yet.

As we finally step foot in their direction they mime us. Each of our boots click across the pavement like a rehearsed marched. Upon closing, we stop a few paces from one another, none daring to speak, but staring at the other like a pride of lions. Others have awakened from the recesses of the CitySpire, standing in front of me like a pair of specters, both dream-like yet substantial. Their eyes matched ours, each seeking, each searching, trying to discern the other as either physical or fiction. I want to speak, but am stuck in the dither of the moment. Here they are, present before me, and I am unable to form the most simplest of words.

3

"Splendid to see others out and about, especially at this time of night – don't you agree, Natalie?" He is dressed in a grey suit, matching tie, with a cleft chin, short dark hair and eyes. His appearance is flawless and he walks as a gentleman should, with a hat and cane much like my own.

"Of course, we haven't seen anyone for days and thought something awful had happened." Her lips are painted with a dark copper tone to match her brown eyes. Her hair is dark, much like her suitor, and wears a long black dress and fur lined coat. Her eyes flirt with mine and her lips crack a tiny smile. They are in arms, as lovers tend to do.

Emily is afraid to speak, as she turns her face from the couple in a shyness that I am not accustomed to. Her grip tightens on my hand that until now, I wasn't aware it had been there. They captivate my every intrigue and I barely notice the slip in silence when I'm brought to retort by a clearing in the woman's throat. Twice now, I must be terrible at introductions.

"Forgive me." I extend my hand to the man in front of me. "My name is Samuel Bell. I live in the apartment complex on the corner of Gnosh and Rhine."

He grips my hand in a ravishing handshake. "Michael Rawlings Locke, and this is my sparrow, Natalie." He smiles with debonair flair.

"Natalie Silver Locke." Her eyes dart to her companion in a mild displeasure. Her beauty swells with a tenacious glow. When her escort retracts his hand, she places hers in mine. "It's wonderful to meet you. And who is your charming lady?"

"This is –" I am elbowed in the side by Emily, causing to invoke a wicked glance.

"I can do it." In a short step, she comes between us and extends her arm full and stiff. It is enough to cause Natalie to jolt backwards from the invasion, bringing her hand to her chest to smother her quickened heart. "Emily Golden Waters."

Golden? This is the first time I had ever heard Emily use the name. Either she had given it to herself in secret or this was something she made up. I am leaning on the former. I worry that Emily's display may be in violation of some societal taboo, breaking boundaries and doing away with tradition, whatever tradition that may be. If so, I couldn't imagine the consequences that her actions may cause to our future relationship with the Lockes. Yet, despite Emily's rude display, I think that both of them are more startled than insulted.

Mrs. Locke is a good sport as she takes Emily's hand in earnest and returns her face from that of a disheveled bird. "I'm gracious to meet you Emily – both of you." She slips me a smile as Emily's hand is given to Michael.

"So… days you said?" I can not yield my wonderment to their earlier statement. "How long have you been looking?" I must sound dreadful, but the company doesn't pay it any mind.

Mrs. Locke, on the other hand, begs her husband with a silent plea and when he doesn't respond—save for a mild flirtation of his own—she replies with, "To be honest, we woke up yesterday morning. We left our apartment in hopes of finding someone. Is the city as deserted as it seems?"

"This morning? Have you met with anyone else?"

"We're afraid not, Mr. Bell." Michael says while in the process of removing his hand from Emily's. "You two are all we have seen. However, it has been a short stroll, no more than a couple of hours, and we might have missed someone."

"Unless there are others who happened to wake the same time as you did, I believe that the CitySpire is just as deserted as it seems."

"Dreadful." Mrs. Locke takes a step backwards with a frightened look about her surroundings. "This place is lonely and so—"

"Quiet?" Emily interjects regardless of the amount of fingers that now hang from her lip. I had never seen her with such a grave expression on her face before, and wonder whether she is being genuine. Her actions remind me of the first interactions we had when she arose from her coma.

"One can feel friendless in a short while. I braved it for two weeks before I met Emily."

Mrs. Locke is overtaken by emotion as her eyes light up in sparkle. "It must have been utterly romantic for you."

Yet before I can answer, Emily is quick to pipe in, "I was coughing up sea water."

The Lockes are taken aback. "Figuratively speaking–" I interject. "She wasn't actually coughing up seawater." I laughed nervously. "I found her by the shore."

Emily quakes as if she just hiccuped and then adopts a smug mien. I sense that she is plotting something jumbled with flamboyant performances and questionable manipulations – things for which I want no part of, but know I will come beneath her scrutiny in some shape or form. One could think her evil. Perchance her actions are based on personality insufficiencies, petty jealousies, and the desire to be well-liked. I am sure that all people are guilty of such actions from time to time, and I couldn't blame her in the least.

"It sounds like a lovely tale, but I'm afraid we'll have to hear it another time." Mr. Locke motions with his hand as if crumpling up a piece of paper. "It's going to storm soon."

"Don't mind him – he has an acute talent for predictions. I would think him a prophet, were he not my husband."

It always rains here. On the other hand, I am sure that Mr. and Mrs. Locke didn't know that themselves. It isn't as profound of a prediction as the two might think, yet I decide to let their delusion continue without challenge.

"I'm not sure if we'll be able to make it back to our apartment in time before the first bout falls. How far away is your apartment from here, Mr. Bell?"

"It's only an hour or so, maybe less."

"Would you mind if Natalie and I were to stay in your building until the storm lets up?"

I am enraptured by the request as I hadn't expected to keep their company as long as they are suggesting. I am glad for it. If there is a storm coming, as Mr. Locke has suggested, then I would wish it to persist through the night so that we may have additional conversation. Emily doesn't say a word.

"My apartment? That sounds like a wonderful idea."

"Then best we off?" Mr. Locke takes Natalie's hand and warms it under his arm.

Emily grabs mine and insists that I do the same. As he best put it, we are off – though for the majority of the trip, in silence.

I am in disbelief, startled as I am now, glaring out my apartment window at the rolling thunderhead's booming with life, drowning the city in a harsh torrent of rain – like dastardly little knives stabbing at the city-isle for some past vengeance. Michael had been right. He has the soothsayer's eye.

The winds snake between the buildings and lash out against any testament to their maneuverings. This storm grants me a disheartening reassurance about the antiquity of the building in which I reside, as the foundation's creak now wails beneath the might of the tempest. It is times like these that I find myself unfortunately living on the fourteenth floor. It could be worse, I could be living on the twenty-fifth.

Behind me Mr. and Mrs. Locke sit together on the couch, while Emily crouches far from the windows, preferring as much distance between her and the like-nebula as possible. Fingers of lightning grip the sky only a few buildings down and within seconds, a resounding boom steals the breath from the room and all are hiding beneath their hands and arms as if their appendages would protect them.

I cannot help but feel awed by the strength and formidable display of power harnessed by the brume and, at the same time, frightened to think that the same entity that perpetuates the teeming rains has an even darker side. I am glad that I hadn't first awoken to this and pity those who do.

As the rumbling subsides, Michael is first to speak from a half-hour's worth of silence, shouting above the deafness that all of us have acquired. "You said you met Ms. Waters by the shore, did you not?"

I have to mimic his tone as my ears are still ringing from the previous thunder crack. "Yes – she was bruised from the trauma, unconscious and on the verge of hypothermia." I decide to leave the part out about her being naked, as I don't want to embarrass her in front of our new friends.

"Really?" He rests his arm on the back of the couch and addresses Emily. "Ms. Waters, do you remember anything before that?"

Emily, her hands still cupped over her ears, shakes her head and then tucks it between her legs. I feel sorry for her, and think that I could lessen her fears by giving her some comfort to hide under. It is the least I can do. Excusing myself momentarily, I retreat to the bedroom and take up a blanket. I return in nearly no time at all, dressing her shoulders with the majority of it, and I manage to convince her without saying a word to join the rest of the party on the piano bench.

"It must have been terrible for you, Emily." Natalie, apparently tiresome of addressing everyone formally, leans in toward the piano bench where now sits the huddle of conversation. "I am hopeful you share very little memory of it. I swear I would have nightmares if it had been me in your place."

Emily casts a feral smile that looks to hold secret Natalie's fate, a sinister side that is somewhat in resemblance to when we first spoke. I imagine that Emily doesn't appreciate the exuberant amount of attention she is receiving and though always a woman of attention, she doesn't take lightly to discussing her moments of vulnerability. She may as well be feeling as if she is being ganged up on, and rather than seeing a cat pushed into a corner, I decide to change the subject.

"Where do you two live?"

Mrs. Locke is first to take the bait and sighs. "We have this gorgeous apartment suite on the north side of Flint Street. It has a beautiful view of the park and there is a cathedral not far from us. Unfortunately, we weren't as lucky to have a piano like you do. Do you play?"

As I am about to part my lips, Emily interrupts which would have been a prompt response. "He plays all the time! At times I lay and listen to music from Chopin, Bach and Mozart. He also has been working on his own work, but he tries to keep that one a secret. Isn't that right Sam?"

She gives me a look that is supposed to inspire me to follow along with whatever game she is playing but for the most part, her answer was true—that is—all for the part about my own work. It isn't like that at all. I know it's not mine, but I am at a loss for its origins. I figure it is just as well, it would be difficult to explain how I know of it while having no recollection of hearing it. I still can't explain it to myself.

I nod my head in agreement.

"Can you play us something—something to take our minds off of the horrid storm?" Mrs. Locke pleads in a very coquettish manner, though the rest of the room seems not to take note of it.

I do as I am asked. It would be rude not to. Squeezing in next to Emily on the bench, I manage to fall into a soft medley, all the while Emily watches from over her shoulder. And I notice from time to time that her eyes dart back and forth as they attempt to register the notes with the right key—infatuated. The notes disrupt the chaotic turbulence that lies just outside the window, and as the lightning flashes and the approaching booms sound, each are drowned in a less threatening harmony. Once I finish, the usual silence is met with a short burst of applause from my couch audience, grateful that I had given them a deserving respite from the previous onslaught.

"You know what this calls for?" Mr. Locke asks. "This is the perfect time for a ghost story."

The room agreed, save for Emily who hides herself deeper in the blanket, enough that only her faced shows beneath a quilted cowl. Though as the turn for telling circles round my guests, they concede that they know none. As it returns to me, I decide to wow them with Emily's and my visit to the convenience store. I told them about how we were seized by an unnatural bout of anxiety, me nearer the street-side and Emily at the store. Then I told them about the shredded wrappers and pieces of litter that were strewn about quite savagely. And then I told them about the being who lurked in the alley, watching us from the dark.

"His face was mangled, scarred with strips of linen covering portions of his charcoal colored skin. The rest of his body was bandaged from the neckline down. I couldn't make out the majority of the details as he kept mostly to the umbra. But as our eyes met, he flashed me a demonic smile that sent chills down my spine."

"Oh how awful!" Shrieks Mrs. Locke.

"My word." Gasps Mr. Locke.

"You made that up!" Emily cries. "You didn't see anything like that at all!"

"I didn't tell you because I was afraid you may have fainted, and then I would have to contend with the monster myself."

"Ghoulish! Now I'll never get to see the pier! All because of that terrible Open."

"Open?" Mr. Locke is bewildered.

"Emily believes that 'Open' is the name of the store due to the large neon open sign hung above the doorway."

"Is there no other title?"

"None."

"Seems logical to me. I'll be sure to stay away from this 'Open' place, I'd hate to have a run in with that fiendish creature. It'd probably spell the end of my life."

The rest of the conversation slowly dwindles into minute and occasionally mundane topics such as the city layout, favorite shopping locations, and the like. It isn't until nearly an hour passes that Mr. Locke decides that it is time for bed and asks if it would be bothersome for a few pillows and an extra blanket if I could spare it. After rummaging up the items, I realize that instead of sleeping here that the Lockes intended on adopting the apartment across the hall for the night. After bidding them adieu and then closing the door behind them, Emily creeps toward me in a sorrowful manner while fidgeting.

"Samuel… can you promise me something?"

I look at her sincerely, realizing that this is the first time she has ever asked me for a favor.

"Never play that song of yours for anyone, except me. I know it's bizarre, but it makes me feel special. At least—not until it's done… please?" She pauses. "You will finish it won't you?"

I smile at her and tell her I had no intentions otherwise and follow it by making the promise anyway. She leaps toward me, drapes her arms around my neck and presses her cheek close to mine. I am stunned by the sudden alteration in mood and am somewhat with odds of how to receive her. But it's only a few moments before she drops her arms and moseys into the kitchen, pulling out a spatula, milk, and pancake mix.

Asleep, I dream of Rachel staring at me from across the room, the bright lights from before now dimmed to near nothingness, yet she still retains that loving countenance. I find myself sitting back at my piano in full view of the embossed card resting on my piano, reminding me who I am. The door to the apartment is open, releasing a blinding display of light, but slowly closes. As the brilliance disappears beneath the cracks, I hear the knob turning and latching into place. I awake instantly in the dark of our bedroom.

Emily is sound asleep, curled on her side with nearly all the covers at her disposal. The storm has settled into a light drizzle, as I hear that familiar tapping against the windows. As I am about to reclaim the comforter that was usurped from me, I hear a door opening from across the hall and its latching. I swear I'm attuned to it. I can't imagine the Lockes leaving at this time of night, especially without saying goodbye. My dreams have spirited me awake and now I am filled with an unbearable curiosity pulling me in the direction of the disruption. Escaping from bed, I silently gather some heavier clothes and by the time I reach the living room in search of my coat and shoes, I hear the elevator sounding its chime.

I follow in pursuit, noting the lit first-floor indicator above the elevator doors. After summoning the carriage, I soon find myself released into the lobby. Everything is dark, though slightly aglow by the artificial moonlight provided by the streetlamps. Standing in the doorway of the apartment building entrance, is Mrs. Locke leaning against the wooden frame, dressed in her nightly fur and taking a short drag off a cigarette. The smoke trails up and outward into the night sky, as the sprinkling rain attempts to douse its source. She looks off into the distance, gazing out across the street with a forlorn look.

"I needed to get out." Her obviously aware of my presence from the elevators announcement. She speaks with her eyes turned from me, unknowing whether I am her husband or someone else. Her voice is somber, unlike the Natalie I knew back in my apartment. "Did I wake you?"

"I was already awake," I reply, "—bad dreams."

I walk up, and lean against the opposite frame, getting a better glimpse of her face, but not what she was looking at. She just stands there, letting the smoke from her cigarette drift out into the CitySpire.

"Something has been bothering me since I first woke. This may sound silly, but I can't remember things like where I have been, what I had been doing, or why I am with Michael. I don't even remember moving into my apartment or why the city is so cold and empty. It frightens me, Samuel. It's like everything has been taken away." She shivers from a course wind that rustles the fur on her coat, and in its determination manages to steal a tear from her eye.

"I wondered whether you and Mr. Locke had any recollection about the past. I see now that we all suffer the same."

"Michael pretends that nothing is wrong, that everything is the way it should be. I wish I could adopt his beliefs, but no matter how hard I try, I cannot deny this feeling. Call me crazy, but there is something terribly wrong with this city."

Her words remind me of the first time I woke, it was all wrong to me as well. I also remember how cold, lonely and broken-hearted I felt. It seems that Natalie is experiencing the same. I feel sorry for her, and wish there could be something that I can do to ease her anguish but I, more than anyone, know that there isn't much that can be done. The city, the stillness, the rains, the emptiness are all things that I can do little about—perhaps Michael is right, things are the way they are or should be. I wonder if it is *we* who are out of place.

"I don't think you're crazy."

"You've been here longer than any of us," she finally loses the object of her attentions and focuses on me for the first time in our conversation. "Was it like this for you?"

"It was and for the most part, still is. I find the company of others to help reduce the sway of the stillness. Music helps, soothes the soul. But I do not know if the feeling will ever go away, or whether the city's secrets will be unveiled. I just don't know."

"For the two days that I have been here, I have yet to catch a glimpse of the sun. Does it ever come out?"

I recall standing at the pier, the first time I saw it when the clouds momentarily parted and allowed a few stray beams to brush the grey streets and concrete buildings. "Rarely—but when it does it is quite the sight to see."

"At least," she pauses as she returns her watchful eye back to the street, "there's something to look forward to."

We stand there for a time in silence, enough time to allow her cigarette to diminish to ash. She stares for the longest time out the window, looking for something, searching for answers to the questions that are traipsing through her mind. I don't think she finds any. As near the hour's end, her and I retreat from the lobby and back toward our respective suites, but not before she kisses the side of my cheek, wraps herself in the security of her arms and then vanishes behind the shadows of her apartment door; her lips massage every question in the world.

4

The storm settles and Emily and I find our friends parting, as both Natalie and Michael insist that they freshen up and deal with a few items at home which need their attention – whatever that may be. When I offer them an opportunity for breakfast, they refuse, claiming they're unsuited for a proper meal and would rather to take us up on the offer once they were presentable. I don't mind their mussy appearance, but I don't wish to force them into anything uncomfortable. Besides, the Lockes have graced us with their presence longer than what I had anticipated.

Honestly, I thought they would have left us in the street, had not it been for Michael's prediction. Mr. Locke comes across as a man of higher standards, respectable and pristine in comparison to Emily and me. I could not help but feel that Natalie has already grown bored with his gentry appeal, but then again I just met them and first impressions are never what they seem. Who knows what lies behind closed doors? I do hope to see them again, as I enjoy their company immensely.

Emily, on the other hand, sighs heavily after she watches the couple exit the lobby from our apartment window.

"I don't like that Natalie person. And her husband is horrid, simply horrid! They wouldn't stop with the questions. Always questions!" She puts one hand on her hip and traces 'YAWA OG' on the glass.

"They aren't that bad, Emily. Just a little different, that's all. They were interested in you, you should be happy. They'll grow on you eventually, you'll see."

"I would certainly hope not! Having one of them attached to me is a terrible thought." She rotates toward me and sighs once again, but this time with a heavy-heart. "You're not going to leave me for them are you?"

"Leave you?! What on earth do you mean?"

Her eyes glisten with newly formed dew. "I saw how they looked at you, acted like you were the sun. They couldn't keep their eyes off you." She sniffles and wipes her nose with her sleeve. "You're going to leave me for them aren't you?"

Her body shakes while she sporadically opens and closes her left fist. She must have been keeping all this in. It is all ludicrous but I dare not laugh, as her face is on the verge of swelling. I study her, first and foremost trying to bide by time before giving an answer that won't break her, while a portion of me looks for any sign of a farce. Still in doubt, I answer from the heart.

"Emily, I'm not going to leave you just because we met some new people. I enjoy your company, and you've been an inspiration to me and still are. I don't know how these ideas came about, but I'd dismiss them. They do neither of us any good and you need not fear of such a thing coming from me. Besides, how many women can I claim have been plucked from the sea? You're one of a kind, and you needn't worry about being replaced."

She laughs, claps her hands together in front of her face and screams, "Bravo! My dearest Samuel, bravo! What would I do without you?"

Her jubilance gets me thinking, and at long last since the moment I first knew her, I place my finger on it—that special something that is a constant with her no matter the circumstance. Life for Emily comes across as a play, each little moment a simple scene in the epic script. I find myself caught up in her fancies, brought into the world of theatrics and illusion. I do not know why she does it. Perhaps she is like Natalie, hiding her loneliness and doubt beneath a clever deception – grasping at tradition and a higher society to tiptoe around her fears. Emily is a different breed, as her cries for attention manifest in harmless manipulations rather than hiding behind the showmanship of class; though still closely related nonetheless. I'm never quite sure whether her feelings are genuine or an act for attention.

She jumps on the cushion next to me and raises herself up on her four limbs to resemble a perched cat.

"Play me a song Samuel! I want to hear that love song – the one you're working on." She stifles a bit. "Please, it would make me very happy. Then maybe we can be like the Lockes someday, and you wouldn't need them. It'll just be me and you again."

I humor her, unsure of how to retort without harsh feelings between us, I would hate to miss out on the Lockes' friendship. The thing about what Emily said, 'like the Lockes'—marriage? Is Emily thinking about marriage? I am sure people have married for lesser things, but the whole idea makes me ill. It isn't the thought of marrying Emily that repulses me. It's that I can't escape this feeling of devotion to Rachel.

Everything about it makes me sick, weak in heart, and reminds me of all the feelings I associate from the first instance I saw the light disappear behind the crack of my apartment door—loneliness. That's what it is, plain simple loneliness. And here I have come to adopt the emotion again. For some reason or another, I cannot dismiss my feelings for Rachel, despite the fact that currently she's just a phantasm of my waking world. I take to the piano and play Emily's song, the one that makes her happy, and in doing so I try to draw some color back into my world. Oddly enough, I remember a few additional keys to add to the piece and it brings a smile to both our faces. That is how we spend the rest of our morning, her on the couch, whilst I massage the ivory keys into something divine that only her and I share.

A few days pass and there is no word from the Lockes. Emily on the other hand, has enjoyed every minute of it. I hear her occasionally humming to herself, humming the same song that she continually begs to hear. I swear the music has had some profound effect on her, as recently she has been cleaning the apartment from top to bottom. I cannot describe her unnatural vim; I do wish I knew the exact motivation behind it. I try to keep in step with her, but too often have my breaths been smothered by her energy. I am thankful that the apartment isn't as large as some of the other flats scattered about the city. Although, I am sure if I gave them mention that Emily would insist we locate a couple and start to clean them as well.

When my muscles are spent, and Emily starts to pull out the food items in the cupboards in order to dust, she demands that I make myself useful and play her the song once more. I am flattered that it is in such high demand, but I wonder whether she is taken with it more than a drunk would a bottle. Her productivity should not be considered a bad thing, as I recall the first few weeks Emily barely lent a hand. At first I thought it was due to depression, perhaps she was contemplating her sordid state on the beach, while still beneath the effects of her fever. Later, I found it was partially due to her watching me, learning things as a child would, gaining a feel of the world. This had led me to conclude that Emily may have suffered a greater loss of memory than I, having to relearn certain aspects whilst others remained intact. This explains her shyness, her mood shifts—due heavily in part because of frustrations—and of course the unlimited questions and irrational jumps in thought.

Each time I try to bring up her state of memory, the conversation tends to end in dismissal, so I can only theorize. Each day I have with Emily is another for which I can learn to understand her better. She is a fragile thing. With her affliction, I can't help but feel a closer kinship to her. Unlike the Lockes, I do not feel like I have to impress her in order to keep her company, which is a good thing since it becomes tiring as the hours drag on.

Just today Emily has taken interest in learning to play the piano. I am eager to teach her as much as possible, despite the lack of sheet music and a metronome. I improvise as much as possible, writing down a string of notes for her to follow, teaching hand placement, and tapping out an easy beat to ensure that her notes are on cue. Emily is vexed easily and some of her lessons have ended in her slamming the fall—with one such instance landing on my hand. It doesn't take much coaxing, usually after a brisk walk to regain a sliver of courage, to attempt the piece again. Her favorites are minuets, as it gives her a sense of accomplishment whenever emulating songs she recognizes. She absolutely hates reading notes—down right despises them—due in part to her hand-eye coordination, but prefers to play easier by ear. I'm amazed on how quickly she converts things to memory.

There are times between Emily's lessons when I wish I could pay the Lockes a visit. After three hours of straight piano lessons, I long for a change in surroundings and a chance to relax before Emily calls me to her side to fix some error in her playing. I could always scour the CityScape in search of their residence, but it may take hours, even days and there is no guarantee of finding them. No – I figure that the Lockes are well aware of our residence. If they are as desperate for company as I, then they wouldn't hesitate to drop by.

Their knock comes Thursday morning during another of Emily's lessons, whilst the rains have since dissipated. Mr. Locke is dressed in his usual garments and Natalie has adopted some fresh albino fur with a white underlay. I'm greeted with a candid smile from both the darling couple.

"I'm glad to see you again Mr. Bell, and Emily as well. How are the two of you getting along?"

"Well—and you? It's been nearly a week." I reply.

Emily cranes her neck from her seat at the piano. I notice that she has stopped entirely and sits with her hands folded on the keys, now having found a mute face.

Natalie keeps her hands inside a muff that blends with the rest of her outfit. Then I notice a scarf that hangs around Michael's neck, as well as a pair of leather gloves covering his hands.

Mrs. Locke angles her head to see into our dwelling in hopes of something, and when her curiosity is disappointed, she answers with a half-frown, "We've been well. Michael predicts some cold weather heading our way. We thought it would be neighborly to take you shopping for winter coats, that is, if you haven't already?"

"Also," Michael chimes in. "I was wondering whether the two of you would join us in a tour of the cathedral. I have yet to see it and I would be honored to have *you,* Mr. Bell, escorting us around your city."

"*My* city?" I ask confused.

"A turn of phrase – You've been here longer than any of us and I am sure that you have a couple of things to say about it. If there is anything out of place, you would be the one to inform us. There may be another one of those creatures you met guarding the buttresses. I'd hate to have one get the jump on us; strength in numbers."

"Very well then, I hope that we are not going to run into another one of those storms." I joke.

Michael's face changes rapidly, staring quite serious with his brown eyes, his brows aligned for a curse. "Worry not my dear friend. The rains will soon be gone."

I worry that I have insulted him somehow.

Natalie touches her husband's shoulder and gives him a push. "Dear, don't be so sober. Forgive him, he's a thespian at heart. You'd think with that kind of a face, he was predicting our deaths."

His malediction vanishes to that place where actions never were, "You'll both have to excuse me. I've picked up a copy of Shakespeare's 'The Tempest'. I can't get the character Caliban out of my head. He's quite the villain, you know."

I stammer that I haven't read it, but already Mr. Lockes' attentions are drawn elsewhere.

"Emily, we would be delighted if you joined us. Your company has always intrigued me. Besides, with your loving Samuel showing us the city it would make each of us an odd party—nothing good ever comes of that."

Emily gives a comforting smile. "I would love to come! Sam has been keeping me locked up in this place for an eternity, with nothing but the charm of the piano to keep me entertained."

"Wonderful!" Natalie cries. "We'll make a day of it! Just the four of us."

A quick run to Hermes Square and Emily and I are fit with the latest in winter fashion, a thicker lining for my coat, a new one for Emily, and of course scarves, gloves and heavier socks. Each time we come to the stores there is a crisp smell in the air; unique in every way—it is difficult to describe, though warming nonetheless.

Now that Emily and I are dressed, with the Lockes' approval, I am more confident in showing them around the cathedral as best as

I am able. I recall that the upstanding couple lives closer to the Gothic structure and had plenty of opportunities to explore it in the past. Curious as to why they desire to search it now? I'd hate to think they kept themselves distant from it simply because of a ghost story. To be honest, I do not know whether the creature I saw was dangerous.

We reach the shadow of the gloomy cathedral, its stone oddly blackened by years of neglect and rain. Out of the entire city, this is the only place that I have noticed affected by entropy; whether it is due in part because of the structure's nature or because of some hidden mystery is unclear. If I wasn't in mixed company, or rather any company at all, I would try and find out the reason for its neglect. Black gargoyles crouch on the higher bulwarks, smiling down at us, their mouths agape in howl as the winds whistle through them. The spires, which reach near fifty-stories in height, are decorated with tiny iron spikes. The single most notable item is the enormous stained glass circle window, set in the pattern of a rose. In its center is a crimson crystal the size of a moon that glistens despite the cloud cover.

I am the first to make the initial moves toward exploring the rest of it, as all the others are paralyzed by the design. Emily clings to my coat as much as she can, claiming that her legs have fallen asleep and needs only to use me as a crutch until they are awake. The massive oak doors open without effort and allow us to proceed into the inner sanctum without further delay.

The place is empty, with only a few wooden pews and dusty candelabrums. An aged organ rests at the foot of three arched windows that stretch the full length of the wall. Flanked alongside the instrument are brass pipes fitted with marble statues of men and women dressed in the dishabille. There are no electric lights or other means for which to lift the gloom of the place. Our only source of illumination manifests in twilight that pours in from the stained glass windows from the higher floors, and a single beam of daylight dominates the center chamber, originating from a missing shard out of the right most arched window.

Michael is exceptionally enthusiastic, as once beyond the threshold he immediately chases down the center floor and bathes in the afterglow, looking at various designs and shadows as if he had been dreaming of this place all his life. Natalie keeps back with Emily and me, preferring our company to the relentlessness of her husband.

"Can you believe this?" Mr. Locke's baritone echoes, reverberating off the ceiling vaults. "How long do you think it took them to build this?"

Emily tightens her grip. "What do you mean *them*?"

Natalie shuffles closer, perhaps wondering the same as I, about a possible prediction that her husband has decided to keep to himself—mayhap he intends for some frightening encounter that we are not aware of?

"*Them* – the ones that built this city, you don't think that it just came into existence, do you?"

My side companion lessens her hold and shifts her auburn hair from her face, as if to brush away her previous fears. I capture her hand as a means of reassurance.

"Who do you think built this?" Natalie reluctantly asks, apparently her method of keeping a steady conversation.

"I don't know, love." He thumbs his chin. "I'm sure it's possible that they could have erected themselves."

"Like a divine being?" I inquired, due in part to our surroundings and eager to hear my voice rebound back to me.

"Yes – exactly like that! This city is desolate. Where did all the inhabitants go? I highly doubt they just got up and left. Maybe there never were any to begin with?"

Emily rolls her eyes and pulls away her hand. She seizes Natalie's arm and drags her toward the far end of the hall, eager to catch a glimpse of the antique organ. The sudden shift in speed causes Natalie to catch herself, as her boots nearly kick from beneath her. She tosses me a look of utter desperation but before I can say anything she is already half-way there, leaving me alone with Michael's musings.

He acts as if unaware of the sudden loss in company. "What do you think Samuel? I cherish your opinion. Was it man or a higher being?"

"The city is older than what it looks. When I first woke, I had a feeling that everything had just been recently replaced: the carpet, fresh paint on the walls, everything finely polished. I'd hate to attribute all of it to a single unseen hand."

"So you're saying that men built the city and just left it here?" Cross at the whole concept, his features droop in dissatisfaction. I can't help but feel baited, like he goaded me previously to inspire a theological debate.

"I'm saying I don't know who or what constructed this place. It could be that there were people here once, that some tragedy overtook them and they were killed or even fled. It may also be, though it sounds ridiculous but perhaps the city was constructed for our purpose. Who knows? I cannot remember anything beyond the weeks before when I first woke up in my apartment."

"Are you denying the possibility that this was created by a divine being? Since you mentioned it before, I am sure that you have at least considered it."

"I won't lie. I occasionally feel like there is something hidden in the shadows, watching me at every turn. I've never felt threatened by it but at the same time, I wondered if it was my arbiter—but those were thoughts that came during a desperate time."

"Ah-hah!" His demeanor channels a higher spirit. "Ever since I woke, I have felt a *presence* of sorts as well. Wouldn't that be the thing! If all of this had been created by a single being—an unseen hand—for us to live in? Wouldn't that be grand?—the arbiter of all things, how nicely put Mr. Bell."

"It's very romantic, but it would be a hard thing to prove – beyond that it's simply conjecture. I'd rather find something more solid before I start attributing what I don't know, to—"

A middle-C erupts in a billowing of dust and smoke from one of the organ's pipes. Both the women jump back from the ancient device, soon laughing at their silly reactions.

Michael takes a step closer to me, one that I notice after the fact; distracted by the women's play.

"I was wondering if you would be so kind," he whispers, "to indulge me in a little experiment of mine."

He waits for some change in me before continuing, "I noticed that the city has a graveyard. What better place than to test your theory?"

I think I know where this is going and it leaves a lump in my throat. I motion for a means out of it. "I don't think that Emily would—"

"Forget Emily on this one, I do not intend to expose a lady to the particulars. I would prefer if we kept this secret to ourselves as I am sure that it would bring them nightmares."

I know now that there is no way for me to escape. He doesn't even have to say it, as I know what is on the foremost of his mind— grave digging.

"Just what do you intend to prove by this?" I ask in a perturbed fashion.

"If the city had prior inhabitants, then obviously they would have buried them, correct? That *is* the purpose of a graveyard after all. Tonight we shall go and see whether those old tombs have anything buried beneath them. Then we will know for certain and we can put this matter to rest. I'll come for you two hours after midnight, down in your lobby. I'll meet you with the necessary provisions."

Michael hadn't asked me to go, he demanded. I feared this would happen. I had come up with the same idea during the first week of my waking. I swore that I wouldn't dare set foot in that graveyard and now here I am, soon to trespass against my own promise. I didn't want to know what is buried beneath hollowed ground. There is something about Michael's eyes, a zeal that I hadn't seen before, as if possessed by some infernal drive. Nothing I can say will dissuade him from this purpose, and I feel that I am caught in a frightening surf. I am startled by a shout from Emily.

"Sam! Come quick!"

I catch her standing at the base of the organ, a few steps from Natalie, staring upwards toward the three arched windows at some object of interest. Michael and I hasten to their side and, once halted, Emily points at the broken window. Snow - tiny flakes of winter float gently through the cracks, allowing the frost to collect on the inside of the cathedral.

"It's snowing." I mutter aloud.

"No." Emily continues to point, "Look!"

I stare for what seems to be the longest time, listening to the sound of my ears giving off a slight harmonic. Yet then I hear something! I hear the near-silent of fluttering and the flashing of sunlight and in a short instance catch glimpse of a white something passing by the window. As I strain my eyes to perceive past the muddled glass, a small head pokes into the chamber. I am astonished, as from out of the ebb strolls a paunchy pigeon, white in feather, cooing from the experience of shelter.

"It's beautiful Samuel." She grips my hand and draws herself close to me. Pausing before asking, "What is it?"

I wait until Emily falls asleep. I watch her chest rise and fall. I listen to her breathe. For once I no longer hear the pattering of the rain against the window and in over a month's time, I sense the emptiness of the world again. Despite my bedmate, the world still feels desolate, as if all things have been plucked from the universe in one gigantic sweep. Perhaps Michael is right. Maybe there is a being out there, but whether it is of good conscience is another question entirely.

My mind is filled with pigeons and their symbolic nature in respect to their role in the CitySpire. On a funny note, if there are others who are yet to wake in this city, I would hate to inform them of their respective hierarchy: first the pigeons, then them. I am curious if it will sit well with those of high ego, or whether or not it will be believed. Here I am thinking of pigeons while Emily sleeps soundly in our bed. It's the only thing, I imagine, keeping me sane while I wait for my two o'clock rendezvous. I cannot shake this overwhelming sensation of impending doom that waits for me beyond the iron gates of the city's graveyard. Regardless of my concerns, it won't be long before Michael will stalk his way into the lower lobby, waiting for me to aid him in his deed.

I can always pretend like I slept through it, ignoring the appointed time and wake the next day having escaped from the event, though I am sure it would not reflect well on my future relationship with Michael. I also fear leaving Emily here alone. What if she wakes by some sound or lingering nightmare and realizes that I am gone? I'd never hear the end of it—no matter which route I pursue.

I cover Emily as best as I can, ensuring that she will be in comfort during the hours I'm gone. She sleeps soundly, muttering a few things under her breath faintly enough that I am unable to understand. I grab the set of clothes that I had hidden away for tonight's activities and change in the living room to keep her from stirring. It is not long before I am well into my winter clothes, thankful that we had purchased them when we had, and out the door, locking it behind me.

The elevator's tune puts Michael on alert, he leans closest to the door in the exact spot his wife had those many nights before. He's dressed in black, rough clothing, attire that I am unused to seeing. Along side him is a brown tote bag, assumedly carrying the tools meant for our little adventure.

"For awhile I wasn't sure whether you were coming." His voice dispels the quiet with conspiracy. "I'd hate to think that I dragged these all the way here for nothing." He takes an instance to look me over. "You didn't tell Emily did you?"

I shake my head. "No, she wouldn't approve – nor would she allow me to go." I pause. "Did you tell Natalie?"

"She doesn't even suspect." He smiles a devious grin. "She's a deep sleeper. Won't even notice I'm gone. I tend to go on walks by myself. She'd be none the wiser." He takes a moment to look me over. "Are you ready?"

A lump rises in my throat, choking me slowly, causing a quiver in my voice. "Lead the way."

He hefts the sack across his shoulder and I can hear the clanking of instruments banging against one another. Together, though as hesitant as I am, we walk out across the snow cover.

There's a heaviness in the air, like the gathering of clouds. I'm tense, flexing in anticipation for what lies hidden in obscurity. The snow falls in a gradual descent, cuddling against whichever object it touches. Were it not for the packing of snow beneath our feet, I would believe myself deaf—as all sound is coveted beneath the cold.

At about a half mile Michael hands me the bag. When I swing it atop my shoulder I am surprised at its weight, though nothing in comparison when I carried Emily. Oh Emily, she is the foremost on my mind. I wish I wasn't in this position but Michael is right, this sort of business would make her uneasy, and impossible at the most. The entire trip, neither of us passes a note.

After a half-hour of walking, we are greeted by a pair of huge black iron gates, which marks the boundaries of the land of the living and the place of interment for the dead. Michael doesn't miss a step. The gates are wide like a beast's maw, which—as Emily once put it—forces my legs to fall asleep. I convince them to press on, to follow Michael down a brick path that weaves its way like a spider's web amongst the hundreds of graves and standing crypts. Each stone is unmarked, wiped clean like the rest of the world, in attempts at hiding its history. I am thankful that there are lamps, those dangling from grooved cords that are strung from wooden poles and through the trees, each shedding enough light to grant us passage through the blinding darkness, swinging like pendulums from the momentum of the snow.

We pass several monuments such as tall obsidian obelisks, granite orbs, and concrete angels. My anxiety is so thick that my body takes to trepidation; one would think due to the chilliness, but I know better. I am sure that by now poor Emily may have noticed my absence and is worrying herself in a corner. I could always go back, explain my urgent need to return home, forget the idea entirely. And in one last hesitant step…

"We dig here!"

PART I - SLEEPERS' WAKE

Before us lies a gravestone, no different or extraordinary than the others. I've come all this way and it is far too late to stop now—the point of no return. Michael takes the bag from off my shoulder and throws it to the ground, pulls out the two shovels—among other tools of the trade—and hands one to me.

"Where did you get these?" I ask in hopes of relieving my nerves.

His eyebrow arches and a sly smile skitters up his face. "I'm very resourceful. I found a hardware store on one of my walks. This city is filled with tiny wonders. It just takes a little time in finding them." He plunges his shovel in the earth, eager to begin his investigation. I do so as well, in order to avoid chastisement.

The dirt pries up easily, the ground not yet hardened by the change in temperature. We dig endlessly for an hour and as we near about two feet I turn and ask, "Wouldn't it be easier if we just opened one of the crypts instead?"

He leans on his shovel and replies in deep breath, "I don't want to disrupt anything that we can't put back in place. It's bad karma as is." And so ends our conversation.

We continue to dig, constant digging, shovel after shovel full of upturned soil and snow. Each time I stab at the earth, my heart skips in beat, a pain already beginning to grow with each motion of my spade. I feel like every inch I toss to the side is another inch closer to my own grave—the metaphor made physical.

A many more hours and Michael's shovel hits wood. We both clear away the top portion of dirt, pushing away the excess in order to reveal what we both know to be the coffin of the nameless grave. In mere minutes the coffin's edges have been traced; the topsoil removed to expose its bare surface. I move away from the lid as Michael starts to pry at its edges to open the casket—in desperation to solve what appears to be the ultimate question of existence. I clamor out of the pit and bring my glove to my mouth to keep in the nausea that has just stirred in my stomach. Above, I watch in growing terror. There is little light for him to see by and most of the work is done blindly. But this doesn't stop the sound of wood snapping as it echoes out across the barren landscape. Michael throws back the lid with a hollowed fever. For me, there is nothing to see but darkness, but somehow I manage to make out Michael's kneeling form reach with his hand into the void.

There is a stillness between us, a period of restlessness that ties my stomach in a hangman's noose. It is this same lack in noise that lives, there! in the darkness of the grave, how it frightens me beyond all things. It is like reaching into the unknown, staring in the face of eternity; like being touched by the cold palm of death. And then, a sound! Quiet at first but rising by the moments, the sound of weeping—no, giggling! Michael's shoulders quivering from this uncanny laughter, a dark terrible thing that I wish he'd cease. He is possessed! It is a ghoulish thing, a sound that I would attribute to that creature that hides in the alleyways near the convenience store. He is delirious from the toil, broken from what he stares or at least expected to see, laughing on and on, maniacal in his conscription, giving into the thing in which man was never meant to see. And when my nerves are near their break, after his cachinnations have played far out of hand I scream, "What is it?! What do you see?!"

He stands up and addresses me, his face veered upwards in a sinister smirk, he jets out his hands as if he had just strangled someone to death and then turns them upward in reverence. "The coffin is empty!"

The coffin had indeed been empty. There wasn't even a pile of dust or a remnant of anything remotely human. But what does it mean?—for Michael it meant that the CitySpire had never been in the thralls of men and that it had been constructed by some unknown force. For me it only raises more questions. It is as I feared during those days when I was alone, a fear that said that there never was a past and would be no future—things are different now. Emily had arrived, the Lockes and now pigeons. The past has proven that the CitySpire will be inhabited again and that it was just a matter of when. Creation did not begin the moment prior to me opening my eyes. What about my apartment door? What of Chopin and Mozart—of Rachel? What about the song that consumes my every thought and whim?

PART I - SLEEPERS' WAKE

I am lost in a jumble of thoughts while I lay next to the still slumbering Emily who, despite her complex nature, still finds it easy to evade such questions and exist peacefully. I'm tired. No matter how long my night has been, the horrors that I have witnessed are now multiplying in my head.

I close my eyes and focus on the one thing that has ever brought me peace: the face of an angel, the light passing over her body, my beautiful Rachel as she stares at me with the passion belonging only to an ardent lover. I will see her again and put all this madness behind me…

5

My dreams come in a gentle breeze, like leaves drifting down a stream, silently passing me by—touching upon an occasional memory—and continuing into a empty morrow. I can hear the song that I have been searching for playing harmoniously in the background. Somehow, I am safe.

The building creeks, a low whine, yet silent in its composure and for some reason I wake by it. Emily lays next to me with her arm wrapped around me snuggly as if she had some horrid nightmare and needed the comfort to expel the consternation from her mind. Her face is soft, completely pacified from any disturbance that she may have experienced. A barren wind pushes against the outside windows and I can hear its whistling coming from the hallway.

Maneuvering beneath Emily's arm, I take care not to wake her. I am unsure of how many hours I have slept. I think it may be nearing afternoon, usually Emily is up by now. She may not have slept well last night, especially when she was deprived of her respective bedmate. I lay her arm across her chest, in belief that it'll be safer there, without lending her cause to rouse. Instead, she accepts her limb, crinkles up her lips in pout and drags my share of the covers over herself in transfer to her left side.

The living room is exactly as I had left it the previous night. Nothing has changed, despite what Michael insists had occurred. The snow hasn't let up from the night before as it is still drifting down in concentrated torrents around my building. Now I am able to see its full effects on the streets and neighboring buildings, as everything is covered in a thick layer of snow. In fact, I am unable to tell where the sidewalk ends and the street begins.

I walk over toward the window and lean against the right supporting wall, looking out across the cityscape. I catch a thought trekking across that initial memory of waking for the first time in this city. It seemed then that there was no one around and that this city was completely empty. There was something about antiquity and polish? That history had been wiped away and that all traces of the world had been obscured and hidden. The footprints, something about the footprints—like memories being erased.

The snow had covered both Michael and my tracks in the snow, it was a sure sign that the both of us had been out on some nightly errand. Due to the weather, everything we did is now covered by thick powder, making it impossible to imagine that we had embarked on anything at all. Even though the memory is there and I can relive exactly what had transpired in that cemetery, there is no worldly proof that either of us had left our respective apartments. The unseen hand has once again taken out its handkerchief and wiped away all traces of history and events. Remembering what I have done and where I have been appears the only real way of determining a concrete past.

It inflicts a thought about what Michael said, about how there is something that lies beyond the shadows of the CitySpire watching and listening to everything that occurs, and quite possibly acting out as an arbiter. He prefers to hand it all to a single being, a deity or some divine entity. I think it's more complicated than that—a perpetual state of being, perhaps like entropy or other governing force such as time. But all these are mortal concepts. The closest thing I can compare it to is this sinking feeling in my chest I get when I think about how everything has been spirited away—just a general spiral into oblivion. I do know that if I think about it too much, that I begin to feel unavailing and should better leave the point of investigation for another time. Besides, the piano is something more deserving and the song that I keep hearing in my mind, I believe, held a few additional notes that played in my dreams.

The snows continue to fall, like a never ending fount that pours from some hidden crevasse deep within the rimy brume. My world has been turned upside down and then right side up again with all the snows spinning about in a glass sphere. Emily on the other hand, pays it absolutely no mind at all. In fact, she appears quite content at the fact that she can stay inside with me by her side and the ivory keys of the piano at her fingertips. She giggles occasionally whenever she hits the wrong note and then after a bout or two, decides to try the measure again. She hasn't said a word about my disappearance last night, and probably suspects nothing.

I sometimes wish that she would have seen something, at least enough to cause me to give her some explanation as to why it was imperative that I journey with Michael to the graveyard. No matter how I could explain it, I am sure that she wouldn't fully understand—and in fact, may take it personally, as if the reason I left her alone was because of something that she had done, or otherwise hadn't done. I still want the conversation to take place in order to get it off my chest and reassure myself that no harm had come by it. But not everything goes according to plan and I would hate to enter into an argument that couldn't be resolved or at least result in worse feelings than one would have going in. So I shall keep the event to myself. Besides, the feeling that is currently in the room is a pleasant one.

At times Emily's attitude while playing is trying, especially since I had been gifted with the talent to play the piano without the memory of lessons. Yet, I take a greater share of solace from her playing than perhaps she does. I imagine myself in her place, learning the piano from trial and error, experiencing how much she struggles and how quickly she learns in an attempt to ignite the same memory in myself. It's an appreciation that I can respect—something to take pride in.

I am glad that Emily keeps me busy and rarely allows my mind to wander. I am sure that without her presence I would be enveloped much like the streets, caught up in the utter depression that winter tends to bring. There is nothing more disheartening than seeing the trees without their leaves, the flowers without their bloom, and nothing but a white canopy hanging over the sky and ground. It makes even the lost seem hopeless. But I am comforted now by the fact that I have someone here to speak with, to at least enjoy the shallow benefits that winter brings, and enjoy the homey atmosphere that our relationship affords us. Perhaps the coming months will not be so bad.

A few days and the snows have stopped. There is perhaps a foot, maybe a little more, guarding the ground with an overlay of white. Today Emily has insisted that we go outside, enjoy the chance at fresh air, and "see what fruits winter has given us"—her words. I can see my breath expel in puffs of smoke. One would think it wouldn't be long before both of our breaths would join the clouds above to forever keep out the sun. Yet despite the continually grey, my eyes squint against the onslaught of the blinding whiteness of ice and snow.

Regardless of the handicap, Emily rushes out onto the street and immediately lies down to create her first nightingale in the middle of the street. The way in which she moves her arms and legs reminds me of the pigeons in the cathedral and I wonder whether or not they will have enough food to cater them throughout the coming months—paunchy or not. Then again, perhaps I should be worried more about our own food supply. We should really schedule a time to take inventory before worse weather approaches and take advantage of the lift in wintry siege to restock. All this can be left for another day for I highly doubt that we are in for harsher weather at this moment—of course I am not Michael Rawlings Locke.

"Come on Sam! Stop daydreaming and live them! The snow is grand and my bird is so lonely by itself."

Emily's cheeks are rosy and covered in partials of snow. She laughs a laugh that is common to children on first winter's morn and I cannot help but be overwhelmed by sensibility to join her. It has been long since we have had an exchange of play and since that night where we danced childishly in Hermes Square, I have been secretly yearning to do so again. I join her and for the rest of the day as we build other wonders of merriment, objects of which I desire most, a city filled with people, constructed from ice and snow.

It isn't until when dusk arrives, after hours of play, a couple of silhouettes appear trudging through the cotton covered streets carrying each a box of things only imaginable at this range. As I squint my eyes, hoping that I can dismiss a portion of the white blindness that has been afflicting my vision, I make out the familiar frames of the Lockes. I rouse Emily to our guests, as she finishes off our fifteenth snowman by setting the head atop its torso. She stands limp at my direction, pointing out the coming shadows and I cannot help but hear a muffled sigh as she decapitates her latest creation with a single push of her hand. I wait for her as always before heading toward them in jovial greetings.

"Michael! Natalie! How wonderful it is to see you two again." They still approach with boxes in hand, looking as perfect together as usual.

"Samuel…Emily." My greeting being returned only by Michael's casual nodding.

"What brings you two out this direction and with such a heavy load?"

The Lockes exchange glances between them, their faces forcing back whatever strain the boxes are putting on them. Natalie is the first to answer.

"Michael has predicted a long and troublesome winter and is worried that something horrible could happen while our parties are split up."

"Yes, Mr. Bell – we are hoping that you will grant us permission to take residency in one of your apartments for the winter. This way, if the winter does prove to be monstrous, we can watch out for each other and tend to one another's needs. Besides, I have been dying to have you two pleasant people as neighbors."

"What a splendid idea!" I exclaim. "Here, allow me to help you with your things."

As I am about to lend a hand to lessen Mrs. Locke's burden, Mr. Locke quickly and rather preemptively interjects, "That won't be necessary, Samuel. You have done more for us than you know. We can manage our own things but appreciate the gesture just the same."

I wonder if it has something to do with the Lockes' sense of pride, preferring not to become anyone's onus. I'd rather wish that as friends we were over that little inclination and realize that each other's help comes without price. Though if I were to push the issue and insist on aiding them the rest of the way, I could plant some seed of guilt or otherwise damage an ego, something difficult to repair, for our coming neighborly future. At the least, I could get the door – and in doing so, as I rush with Emily in toe to relieve their buckling arms, I hear Emily whisper, "A troublesome winter indeed."

"I just don't see how we would be able to get the furniture from your apartment, carry it all the way over here—during the dead of winter no less—and into the respective residency." I muse while the four of us sit together for what I have come to realize as our first meal ever.

The one thing that my apartment lacks is a proper dining table so that we could at least have a near-formal dinner. As it is, Emily has taken the piano bench with plate in hand, the Lockes enjoying the love seat, and myself on the floor. I have found candles and instead of using artificial, I bath the room in firelight.

Despite my spoken grievances, Michael appears relatively unconcerned with the matter and Natalie completely oblivious to my asking. I observe a slight change in Emily's demeanor, as hidden beneath her smiles and elegant manner is a boisterous nature. I do not understand her moods as previous outings with the Lockes have never been, in any shape or form, disastrous in effect to warrant such a reaction. But as I have said many times, she keeps to herself well and knows how best to manipulate the situation to better her needs. My greatest fear lies in her silence, when conversation has worn thin and all that's left is her ceaseless plotting. Somehow I feel responsible for her foul mood and no matter what I do to lessen the situation it all comes out the same. I am sure that when the Lockes depart to their new apartment on the twenty-fifth floor, I will receive a sliver of her inner monologue that she has been preparing the entire night through.

"We had found during one day of searching, that when our own apartment was a bit lacking, a cache of furniture covered in sheets in the building's basement. Tomorrow, Natalie and I will delve into the realms of discovery…" he takes his wife's hand, "and see what treasures lay waiting in your basement Samuel – that is, of course, if you have no objection. With a bit of luck, since this is a larger building than our own, we may be able to find the right pieces for both necessity and décor."

"I have none what so ever. In fact, although I cannot speak for Emily, I would be delighted to join you two in your search and help as best as I can. Besides, I hadn't even thought of going down there.

I confess that I was more interested in looking outward than ever exploring the secrets of this building in particular. For some reason, I overlooked it."

"That is quite alright, Samuel," Natalie counsels. "We wouldn't wish to ask you and Emily to help us any further. We don't want to inconvenience you."

"Nonsense!" Emily blares with a new found excitement. "It isn't an inconvenience in the least—as we have nothing planned. Samuel and I would be absolutely tickled to help you and in fact, the both of us insist. You two are, after all, our neighbors! It is our responsibility and Samuel's duty as host, to ensure that his guests are well taken care of. Isn't that right, Sammy?"

She has a predator's look, her eyes glistening by the flame of a nearby candle. Her continence is rehearsed, her manner absolute and with it I notice the Lockes sinking into themselves in defeat. A silence deadens the room and I see, for what the candles try to conceal, a paleness stricken on both the Lockes' faces. I question what it is that Emily called them out on—relinquish of pride? Was it not them who wanted to become our neighbors out of worry for Emily and my safety? I can see what Emily is doing, making them see that we are capable of being as helpful to them as they intend on being to us. But what is it that causes the shrewd awkwardness that now afflicts us? I look upon each face, trying to see what it is that each is feeling, what each is hiding, but no matter how hard I strive, I feel as if I am at an even greater loss of what has just occurred. I must dispel the silence and keep it at bay for as long as I can.

"Aren't you worried about leaving some of your possessions behind? We could always help carry a few of your more sentimental items back here for you. I know there is one object in particular that I could not do without." I look toward Emily, beneath were rests the piano, and she gives me a broad smile of concurrence.

"Don't worry about it, as there is very little that we hold as dear to us that we couldn't do without for the remainder of the cold. We'll be just fine with what items you have afforded us. We are simple people, dear Samuel, living simple lives. We'll take what's available and be happy, no need for mawkish behavior during a time like this. Wouldn't you agree dear?"

Natalie looks up from a glass of wine that she has been nurturing, takes a quick sip again before answering and brushes a lone strand of hair that falls in front of her face. "Agreed."

Dinner comes to a close shortly after and I am still in low spirits as if I had stolen something from the Lockes that could never be returned. I must be overdramatic, perhaps not seeing everything as clearly but as I say my goodbyes I cannot help but feel somber at their leaving. Yes it is clear on them as well, a sullen dilapidation in their usual characters, like a portion of their soul ripped from their bodies and hung dangerously high above a cliff in blackmail. If this is the result in offering aid to those who wished nothing from us save the same, I would have dismissed the notion if, by chance, it would lead to their happiness. Sadly it is too late already, as tomorrow Emily and I will assist them in their apartment. With hope—as a night's sleep tends to do— they will retire into a more pleasant mood and acquire some newly found appreciation for our involvement. If they are indeed simple people, they will soon be able to accept a simple gesture of hospitality.

Emily startles me when she reaches her hand around my waist and follows the Lockes with her gaze as they enter into the elevator, then disappearing behind its steel doors.

"Such a fuss over furniture—you'd think they didn't appreciate us." Emily cuddles her head into my ribs. "The snow where they lived must not pack as well as ours, or otherwise they'd be making snowmen about now."

"I'm sure that's not the reason. It's like they said before, Michael saw harsher weather ahead and thought we'd all survive it better if we lived closer to one other. Michael conveys to me as someone with a lot of pride and it must have been difficult for him to ask for an apartment from me, on the other hand I've never really considered owning them. I'm happy that they are our neighbors, now we're not alone anymore. I think it may have been the food that put everyone in a sour mood."

"I had the food and I'm great!" She leaves my side and heads deeper into the apartment singing, "—if the spirit tries to hide, its temple far away… a copper for those they ask, a diamond for those who stay."

The stairs groan beneath our feet as we descend the wooden beams into darkness. Candles are our only instrument of illumination and even then, the soft light fairs little against the porous veil of blackness. An iron railing snakes down along the side of the stairs, leading us into dissolution. I take up the front with the rushlight extended far before me as a warning to whatever denizens lurk in the dim, trusting to ward them away.

Emily clings to my backside, following the glow with her eyes as best as she is able to manage, while Michael takes the rear, keeping his beau in front. The farther we descend, the stronger raises the scent of dust and a hint of mold. It is apparent that the entire city is not protected against the dissidence of entropy's breath. I wonder whether all dark places cater to the same environment and if so, create a foul nesting place for creatures of evil such as the one guarding the convenience store 'Open'.

With luck, we reach the bottom of the well and as I extend the taper far over my head, tossing wax across the concrete floor, the brilliance reveals the very thing that Michael believed nestled beneath the building. There are little oddities of furniture covered in dust-laden sheets, pieces of this city's past, all arranged in tight little rows. There are many of them, easily judged by how many shadows are cast across the basement walls; many items entombed in this place by someone or something of antiquity.

"There they are! Just like I said Samuel, I'm glad I hadn't been wrong. It would have been a very uncomfortable stay if there was nothing here. But just look at all of them—"

And look I do, as many as hundreds, all positioned side by side, differing furniture with no system of file, all scattered about in rows and rows. There are a couple candelabrums standing beneath the unscathed sheeting, which makes me nervous for some reason, like how they've kept prevalent against the holes of moths. Michael is first to withdraw a sheet to reveal the stand in its full majesty. All its candles are there partially melted with rolls of wax dripped solid along their sides to signifying previous use. I'd make mention of it, but I'm partly afraid of entering into yet another segment of debate concerning the divine and even so the conversation could lead to revealing our graveyard deed. Plus, this place simply does not contend well as a fine atmosphere for such a discussion. I am on edge as it is.

I hand him the candle so that he may light them himself and so that in earnest, he may come to the same thread of thought as I. If he does so, he is ever more talented at concealing it, for as the candles take to the flame, there is no hesitation in his step and returns the one back to me.

In one gallant stride, Michael strips the linen off another piece of furniture and then another, each throwing a cloud of dust high into the air, churning in some foreboding brume above our heads before slowly settling atop us. Beneath are constructs of fine oak and blackened iron – dressers, mattresses, chairs, all pieces of mediocrity and oftentimes plain design. The expression on Michael's face, though it could be the shadows deceiving me, drops in disappointment. Mayhap he was expecting some ancient treasure for which to call his own or, at best, didn't meet with his patrician side and appeal.

"What's the matter?" I ask. "Not what you were expecting?"

"They look fine to me." Emily scoffs, "Simple right?"

Natalie breaks in smile with a near laugh, "They are lovely. Don't you agree love? These would look beautiful in our apartment – such a step in class."

"They do look a little drab. Your right dearest, they'll liven up the place. Nothing in comparison to the elegance of our other apartment, but a step up from the now, most assuredly."

The Lockes exchange a secret message to each other, a look that Michael initiates with a stern glare that douses Natalie's mood.

"Yes, of course dear." She glances over at me, begging me with her eyes for some manner of relief.

There is obviously something going on between them, a strangeness that haunts the room. Come to think about it, they wore the same skin the previous day, like some unresolved conflict brewing in the background. "None of my business," I'd like to say, and have said to myself plenty of times before. But now as my neighbors and constantly reminded "guests", would it not be in my best interest to resolve whatever qualm that has risen between them? However, in the long run, perhaps my greatest ally in this is patience. In time the matter will most likely resolve itself. Besides, I wonder how long this charade will last before someone will leak a little more of that which troubles them.

"Everyone, keep an eye out for a piano similar in style to Mr. Bell's. I have the perfect place in mind where to put it, perhaps close to the window? I've been admiring that conversation piece of yours since you first showed me your apartment."

"Our own piano?" Natalie's spirit ignites at its mentioning, as her eyes are now as large to take in the entire floor. "Samuel – you would be kind enough to allow us one? Such a friend."

"What's the excitement?" Emily poses, while clutched to my side for comfort.

"Oh dearest Emily," Mr. Locke remits. "You are far to used to having a piano than knowing the familiarity of not. It is a fine luxury that neither of us has experienced. You are both blessed in its ownership."

"Yes – and had we one, you'd probably never see us at all." Mrs. Locke adds jokingly.

Emily pulls ecstatically against my clothing, a new found joy in her eyes. "Samuel! We must find a piano for the Lockes! It is the very least we can do!"

I cast a dispelling glare to my side companion, knowing full well her vying intentions. We each spread out just the same, looking beneath all the sheets at anything that remotely resembles a piano. Emily even locates a chest of drawers that she wants for our bedroom. Besides that, we find little trace of another piano or any musical instrument, for that matter. The search comes to a halting close once every cloth has been either pulled off or peeked under. The Lockes are desolate.

"It would have been difficult to get it up the stairs anyway, had we found one, that is." I claim while looking on the brighter side of things.

Michael tarries from his somberness. "You're right, it would have been a horror. Perhaps we are all better off."

"Well – shall we get started moving some of these into your apartment?"

Michael shrewdly turns away with Natalie giving me an apologetic look. She shrugs her shoulders and says, "It would have been lovely. Perhaps we'll find one elsewhere." Then returns to her husband's side to help pick out exactly which ones will be sent upstairs. We cover the rest.

While I watch, something stirs inside me: an ominous feeling that refuses to release me from its grasp. So much furniture, the used candles, everything pointing to a plausible past in this very building and then a stone of thought – *it's all used furniture*! There is a ding here, or a miniscule scratch there. There is even enough for every apartment, maybe more. People must have lived here, but something had to have happened to take that factor away. What would inspire so many individuals to deposit their belongings in one place, and in the basement no less? The elevator only runs to the ground floor since the key is missing and the basement is now accessible only via an old staircase. On top of that, each item is covered in order to shield them until their owners' safe return? It doesn't make sense.

When the Lockes left their apartment to come here, they didn't take their furniture to the basement and cover it for convenience. No, why would they? They intend to return as soon as the winter months let up with the desire to rest in their already pre-furnished loft. If people had been living here like I suspect, they would have left their apartments in much the same condition. Someone or something had gathered all the furniture from the separate apartments and then covered them for future use—but why? Then again, everything has been repainted, the carpet replaced, and the whole feeling of newness has been implicated throughout the building all in preparation for newer tenants. There is something out there, watching from the alleys, waiting for some unknown purpose – the true landowner.

I'm overtaken with it all. Fearful, I now desire a sturdier bolt on my door. I can't tell the Lockes, can't tell Emily, as I wouldn't want to cause panic and distrust amongst us. I'll have to be the one that keeps a lookout. After all, I may be jumping to conclusions. There is no way of being certain. It is not like we had any problems in the past, but it doesn't hurt to be cautious.

"I think we'll go with these items here Mr. Bell, if that is alright with you? Some of these may prove a bit difficult to get up the stairs, but once we can get them into the elevator its smooth sailing from there."

I peak a glance at all the lit faces in the room, seeing what we are—just people—and wondering how long it would be until our furniture will be dragged from our apartments and back down into the recesses of the building's vault.

At night, I wake by the sound of the elevator passing through the floors above me and settling at mine, its chime alerting me to someone's presence. I slide out of bed, careful not to rouse Emily—especially if this be a situation of alert. I creep slowly into the kitchen, feeling the frigidness of the linoleum floor against my feet. A light rapping passes across my door as soon as I locate a knife from one of the utensil drawers. I catch the person's apparition shifting beneath the crack in the door as I stalk up to withdraw the bolt. I open the door a hair's length, just enough to allow the light to filter gently into the room. Only Natalie is there, wrapped in her night robe with that same look of distress she bore when I found her that night down in the lobby.

"Can I speak with you a moment?"

I toss the knife aside on the carpet to dampen its sound and where the door will hide its presence. I allow the door to ease open. Natalie's eyes are moist in newly formed dew and from the looks of things she is worried about something drastic as her eyes constantly shift down either side of the hallway with explicit attentions on the elevator.

"Are you all right, Natalie? Is something wrong?" I'm surprised I don't see a cigarette in her hand, something to calm her down. She takes a deep breath, only then do I notice the envelope in her hand.

"All is well, Mr. Bell. Call it a voice of a guilty conscience. I have something I want to tell you."

"Do you want to come in?"

"That won't be necessary. I've only a moment. If Michael knew I was down here he—it isn't important. I need you to do something for me. It would make my nights here more pleasant."

"What is it?" Something about a woman on the verge of crying makes my heart yearn to set things right.

"—at least sleep a little better. You've been an honorable host and a twice proven friend. I've left something over in our apartment that is very sentimental to me, it's a picture, the only one we have… there's something you need to see for yourself. I can't go, as Michael wanted me to destroy it. He made me promise never to speak about it." Her face pales with its mentioning. "Please go tonight, as I don't think you'll get a better chance."

She hands over the envelope and I feel something heavy sliding around on the inside of it. She twists to leave with her arms wrapped around her chest, yet halts mid-stride. "Please leave Emily out of this, I don't trust her discretion in these types of things—but I trust yours. I'll listen for the elevator on your return and meet you back here."

I watch her go as she retreats down the hall and into the elevator. The envelope is heavier than what it looks, and the majority of its weight comes from the simple ownership of it. After shutting the door, I pick up the knife and open the seal on the letter in order to examine its contents: just a key and address. This whole situation is preposterous. The dead of night, just to retrieve a picture?

There was substance in her voice, a commodity that went beyond the simple errand of having to retrieve a photo, an article—like she said—I had to see for myself. Whatever it is, Natalie has lent me the fulcrum in solving the feud behind her and her husband, to relieve some sliver of tension and expel her guilt in conscience. I grab what clothes won't cause a ruckus and slip as silently into my winter wear as I can. As sure as the constant grey above, I lock the door behind me and expel myself into the nightly frosts.

For the first few blocks, I disguise my steps by tracing the Lockes previous tracks. Since they had been carrying heavy boxes, their steps were short and dragged. I'm able to track through them without difficulty. Like that night before, where I was kidnapped by Michael's morbid fascination, everything is still and burdensome. A tight breeze pushes its way from building to building, canvassing the street for some unfortunate to sting with its winter tail. It reminds me of a sea creature, weaving its way through the icy depths, looking for a bite amidst the darkness of oblivion. For the most part, the city is just as silent, with the buildings' heights vanishing slowly in the night sky, far too distant for the ambience of the street lights.

It is here, as I trudge diligently through the snows, when my mind returns to thoughts of the true landowner—to his purpose and ultimately his intended design. Are we to live the rest of the days unbeknownst of those who came before us, only to disappear as they did? Is the city stuck in a perpetual cycling of vacancies and non? These questions frighten me, to think that I am at the mercy of some grand scheme, unable to fend off the same inevitable fate that touched those before us. I know fairly little of this city and the more I find out, the little clues here and there, have turned it into something monstrous.

I traverse beyond Hermes Square, past a few streets next to the park where the Lockes claimed they had once lived. The address is quite clear, 1712 Herbertson, apartment 7, past Richmund and Lowel, a location which places their loft far from the cathedral's view. The farther I continue toward its acclaimed destination, the more rundown the buildings become; a section of the CitySpire that I had not known about and swear had not been here before.

Herbertson Street begins at the base of a hill, with three-story habitations looming over the narrow street-side. A few streetlamps dot a corner here and there, but for the majority of the place, it is dark, seething and cold. Wrought iron fences stick up around the property lines and metal bars guard every window. Portions of dried vine cling to the buildings grey sidings. I have never seen a more twisted place, even in my dreams or dreaded nightmares, to better compare to the wickedness of the street called Herbertson. And as my better reasoning encourages me to turn away, to forget this place and return home, do I happen upon the dilapidated address of 1712.

I push beyond the iron gate, across the continuing march of footprints and up to the front door. It opens easily enough, with little resistance and the lights that had been smothered now flicker wildly to my movement that sets the entire house alight. A hallway leads to the other apartments on the floor, a set of brass mailboxes to my left, each of them empty in title. The numbers on the doors tells me that their apartment is located on the second floor. My feet instinctively ascend the worn staircase. The Lockes couldn't possibly have lived here. Michael would not have been able to stand it as he is a gentleman in all considerations. I reach the apartment door and find it locked. I almost forget that Natalie gave me the key and it creeps into the hole with little difficulty. I turn the knob.

I let the door swing on its own, preparing myself in case something catches me off guard. The lights, with motion again, flicker in their fluorescent tubes and tick a few times before stabilizing in constant illumination. The walls are coated with peeling plaid wallpaper, a dark rustic purple color, with a wooden chair rail that runs to the floor. The ceiling is cracked and there are exposed wires that hang from particular outlets along the base of the floor. The ground is a kind of grey wood that has absorbed its fair share of moisture and dirt. As suspected, their furniture was left behind in a relatively cozy arrangement and it seems that they only packed personals before heading to me.

The apartment is arranged, much in the same style as my own with a large living room, a full-kitchen and a single master bedroom and bath. In all respects the place is larger than mine, but not even close to habitable. In the center of the room is a small picture frame lying face down in a shamble of broken glass. I lean down, careful not to step in it, and flip over the frame with the length of the key.

The picture is of a little girl around twelve years old, playing in a field of leaves. Her hair is black, with strikingly resemblance to Natalie, especially in the face. The portrait is in black and white, the leaves are a detailed brown and green, and the sky is a picturesque shade of blue.

There must have been a struggle, an argument about taking it with them. It all reminds me of Michael's belief in the divine, a single being creating the city around us without past or reason why. He may have thought the picture a fake—and as Natalie claimed, held a personal significance—that lay cause for a disagreement with the end result here on the floor. But who is the little girl? A memory perhaps? Natalie once said that she can't remember anything about her past. I puzzle over how much of that is true. Maybe she does remember something or at least has a familiarity with this photo that makes her believe in a yesterday. I'll have to ask her, she at least owes me that much.

Everything is coming together now, especially why Michael and Natalie have come to live with Emily and I in our building. I don't blame them. I don't understand why they hadn't moved before, maybe it's that same familiarity that made it so difficult in the first place. Moving was most likely Michael's idea. Emily wanted to know why we couldn't live in the manors on the edge of town. I made excuses but mostly I didn't want to leave my apartment in case Rachel would seek me out. Maybe Natalie wanted to wait for the little girl in the picture.

I take the picture out of its frame and steal it into a coat pocket. I'm glad that the Lockes decided to move. I can't imagine living here, what it was like, or how terribly it may have affected their psyches. Here I thought that my situation was grim. I give one last look about before exiting the apartment, locking the door behind me and waiting quietly outside for the lights to shut themselves off.

The elevator brings her arrival, still wearing that same number she came down in. She refuses to look at me, keeps her head to the ground, knowing full well what I saw—with inclinations of what I think. I've been waiting for her at my doorway as I still haven't changed out of my winter coat, still cold from the night's chill. I give her the photo and she stares at it for the longest time. Eventually she musters up the courage to say, "Thank you."

"Don't worry about anything. I don't care where you came from."

"It's not that, Mr. Bell. It's—" she pauses to swallow. "It's that we lied to you about it. It was mostly Michael's idea, he went on and on about wanting to live the good life. He wanted us to live it as close as possible, even wanted to live in one of the manors on the hill. I just didn't want to go."

"Because of her?" I motion toward the picture.

"Silly isn't it? She's was just a dream until I found her photo hidden beneath a loose floorboard. Then I thought she would return. I don't know who she is, or how I know her."

I pitied her, much as I pity myself. Natalie has her Rachel, but instead of a woman—a child. Memories. She and I are holding onto dreams and memories, a struggle against familiarity and forgetfulness.

"It's okay, I dream too."

Natalie chokes back a tear and starts to leave. I watch her go. At least she'll be able to sleep better at night, even if she is far from home. For now, winter will lead their trail here in case the child does happen to show up.

"Natalie?" I halt her as she nears the elevator. "Who do you *think* she is?"

She stands there, asking herself that very question over and over again in her head. She looks up from the floor before finally meeting me at eye level.

"She's my daughter."

The proclaimed mother hits the call button. I repeat the exact words she said in my head. *She's my daughter*, words spoken in absolute. It forces thoughts on my own dreams, of Rachel and if she is real or not. With the chime of the elevator, Natalie steps back into the carriage. With a distant look, somewhere between here and distant memories, the doors close her off to me—back to the 25th floor, to dream once more across the threshold of Nod.

6

I wake to barren sheets. I can hear music playing from the other room, the sound of the piano drifting harmoniously through the cracks of the bedroom door. I blink a few times to let the dust fall from my eyes, a means of distinguishing reality from dreams. I think on last night and how desperate Natalie was to acquire her picture. A floorboard—she claimed that she found it beneath a floorboard. How she came upon it is beyond my comprehension. I'll have to ask her about it the first chance I get. That is of course, once Michael and Emily are out of earshot. She is right about not putting her trust into Emily, especially since she has expressed distrust towards the Lockes. I do not know whether to attribute it to paranoia, a reluctance to share attention or due to a keen intuition. But I can't blame Michael or Natalie and I can't bring myself to condemn them for trying to cover up their environment—I still can't imagine, even now, how horrible it must have been. It's ironic. Here I was looking up to the Lockes, when it was they who were looking up to me. At least now I know why they keep insisting that it's *my City and everything within belongs to me*. Despite recent events, I still wish they wouldn't.

I take my time today: shower, primp, and change clothes. Like many other days, there really isn't any reason to hurry. The entire time I listen to the chords that Emily plays; a few missed notes, her timing is off, but overall a greater improvement over the previous days. When I enter the living room I bid her a good morning… my only response is the sound of hammers striking taught strings. She wears a white dress, something one would wear during the summer months. It's somber in appearance.

There is something hanging in the air, something decaying right before me, yet without the smell. Just a feeling. I check the cabinets, an after thought of the previous, to discern how far the food will take us into the next few weeks. I count boxes, inventorying what it is we have when I hear Emily move into Beethoven's *Moonlight Sonata*. I thought she hated that song.

I watch her from my angle at the kitchen and see enough of her side, focused on her eyes and her fixation with the keys. Her body sways, leaning into the keys as she keeps tempo. I'm amazed at her perfect timing. The notes are on. It is like she has entered an inescapable trance, hitting each key as if it were a part of her, as if there was nothing left to her existence but to play. Hearing little drops of her soul pouring out, washing against the piano, inspires that impossible fantasy that she has always been able to play. But when a tear streams down her face, my world comes crashing down.

As she nears the end of the sonata, the notes take on a life of their own, picking up a new complexity—the likes I haven't heard before. Her hands weave above and beneath each other, planting themselves in concise location and caressing each key as if it were a newborn child. Something is dreadfully familiar about what she plays, something that I've heard before and then—the same that I've been hearing in my head! but her part is somewhere between where I left off, and the end – a tiny glimpse of what is to come. I never knew she heard it too. The pain from before rises in my chest, the one I felt the day I woke, as my heart palpitates to the sway of the music.

The playing only lasts a minute, enough to leave me dazzled and questioning why or how she was able to play so beautifully. And then, without warning or breath of air, she stops. Her hands curl up inside her palms and a few tears seep from her eyes like water running down the glass during the rain. Her fist reaches her heart, her hand clenching even further, struggling to keep everything in. She coughs a breath of air and blinks for what seems to be the first time in years.

"That was beau—" my words cut off by her flight from the bench and out the door!

I give pursuit, following the sound of her footfalls as they race past the elevator. I catch a glimpse of her fleeting white as she squeezes past the door guarding the stairwell.

I scream her name, desperate that she'll stop, praying that she will hear me. My heart beats against the wall of my sternum, screaming for her as well. I take up the chase, my mind spinning with the events, flashing through every second of this morning's waking. I am disoriented by the entire episode and as I pass out of the hallway, I accidentally slam my shoulder into the framework—hard—before meeting the stairwell, the pain branching across every nerve ending and stopping at my teeth.

Over the white railing I can see the flowing trails of Emily's dress fluttering behind her as if she were a phantom. I call out once more, in case she hadn't heard me, before hastily descending with a maddening flurry. The wind whistles through the well, a perpetual squall in a land of silence. I know not where it originates from, and the base greyness of the concrete walls only adds to the sensation of being drawn into oblivion. Emily is pulling me, drawing me down into some recess of despair for reasons that I know not. As I reach the fourth-floor I hear the door to the lobby torn aside and bangs off the wall in harsh echoes striking a ringing in my ears.

When I reach the final step, I leap to the base floor and into the lobby where there! crawling on the ground is the fallen spectre. She slowly pulls herself toward the door, sobbing uncontrollably in a fit *far* surpassing the anxiety of 'Open'.

I rush over to her, "Emily!" and attempt to take her up in my arms but she fights me, throwing her arms against an otherwise unknown assailant. She screams, sobbing all the while—until she sees me, stares momentarily in my eyes, with hers darting between my left and right orbs, debating whether she recognizes me or not. And then, in an outpour of tears and emotion, she falls into my arms, throwing her own around my neck in an attempt at saving herself from her misery. She is cold to the touch—like ice.

"The waves! I can hear the waves—I can see them! Don't let me drown!" She inhales dramatically, gasping for air as if previously suffocating. "Please Sam, *don't let me drown!*"

Emily sprained her ankle, having slipped on the tiled floor. I do not know what caused her mania, I don't even question it. I carry her back up to our room and take care of her as best as I can. I ice her wound and later wrap it in gauze. It's snug and beyond the occasional whimpers from my patient, I believe that everything is going to be fine. It isn't until after I wrap her in a blanket, in order to bring some color back into her cheeks, that she points to something on my face with a grimace—"Sorry."

PART I - SLEEPERS' WAKE

I touch the spot and a sharp pain jolts me in surprise. My fingers reveal blood; a souvenir from the struggle, no doubt. I excuse myself from Emily's care and look to the mirror in the bathroom, to see exactly what it is that bleeds so. And there it is… a scrape across my left temple, a deep wound, precisely cut. Emily must have scratched me. I didn't even feel it before and hardly feel it now. Such a minor trifle in this encounter of ours that it really doesn't deserve much attention; it is just a scrape, after all. I clean it as best as I can and leave to attend other things.

Emily rests peacefully on the couch, as if the whole experience has siphoned every ounce from her body. She shivers from the unnatural chill that has been gifted upon her by the hyperborean waters; the icy hand of the deep refusing to release its treasures so willfully. I thought we had seen the last of her condition, but something had triggered it again. It would be foolish of me to dismiss the happening with the piano that her skills happened to flourish, and she began composing a segment of a very complex, if not unknown song that even I can't fully remember. It's the biggest mystery of them all, and no matter how much I pry Emily for information, I am most positive that the outcome will turn up without a single explanation. She would know as little as I.

I make her a cup of hot tea and wait by her side as she finishes it. Pulling her hair out of her face, I pet her head in reassurance that everything shall be alright, her eyes droop in a struggle between wakefulness and slumber, a losing war that buries her in a paralyzing sleep.

A week goes by with the occasional visitation from the Lockes. There is a new found awkwardness between Natalie and I, though I can tell with the every-so-often glance that she has a new found respect for me, not to mention admiration for keeping her secrets. The last thing I want is to damage the Lockes' loving relationship, not to mention my own. Regardless of Michael's fabrication, they are still my friends and welcomed neighbors. Since the move, the couple has been a bit more relaxed and no longer declines my invitations to dine, and in fact, has offered a few invites themselves. Their apartment has been arranged with perfection and the new units, which we dragged from the basement floor, look splendid in their new home. On the other hand, the Lockes do concede that when it comes to dining, nothing can dismiss the ambience of candles and piano play. I try to meet their wishes as often as possible, but I have noticed a sharp decline in our stored supplies and worry whether it will last us through the rest of the season.

It isn't until the Tuesday of the second week of Emily's recuperation, a date which will never leave my mind, after the last of the pancake mix has finally dwindled to nothing, that by sheer principle of the matter, Emily forms an exploration party to, in her words—"Seize all pancake mix in the name of the queen!" We all are to brave the cold with nothing but shrewd containers and pillow cases to help carry a portion of food from the only place that caters, the convenience store 'Open', all in dread of its malicious guardian.

At times it caught me funny to watch Emily hobble around our apartment in an attempt to keep the pressure off her foot, now her ankle has finally healed to an extent that the walk to 'Open' may do her some good. As the ladies slowly get ready to venture into the crisp air, Michael takes me aside with concern chiseled on his lips.

"What are we to do about that horrible creature of yours, Samuel? It terrorizes us by the mere telling of it, and I would not wish to be caught unawares."

"It didn't attack Emily and I while we were together, perhaps it's best that we just keep close and not stray from one another. I think this—above all—is the greater policy."

Michael opens his coat to reveal the handle of a knife. Something about the way he carries it or possibly even the concept of him branding such a thing is enough to send my heart on the quiver. "Even if that be so, it isn't enough insurance. He may have set an ambush for us and I'll not be some degenerate's lunch simply because I wasn't prepared."

"Michael – bringing that into the creature's lair may set it on the prowl. It didn't attack us then, I see no reason to why it would attack us now, especially since we have twice the number. If you bring it along, then you will be more apt to using it, maybe even rely on it, in circumstances with other alternatives. You may be putting us all at risk just by bringing it."

"And I may be putting us all at risk by *not* bringing it. If you don't plan on equipping yourself properly, and Emily suffers for it, I'd hate to be the one to console you for the mistake." His face is stern and filled with a zealous determination that I'm unable to break.

I look at Emily and recognize her smiling face, her delicate features and then imagine her at the hands of some diabolical abomination. Michael is right, though as reluctant as I may be. I have to protect Emily above all other things, as without her, I'd be lost. Returning to my opponent, I concede with a painful sigh. I am regretting ever telling the story about the creature at the convenience store, the fear that it inspires has ensnared them all. Michael nods his head in approval and hands me the knife from his pocket.

"If your theory holds and the monster decides not to bring us any harm, then there will be no need for it and we can forget we ever brought it, alright? Don't worry, Samuel. You're doing what is necessary for our survival. No one can fault us for that."

I hope that everything is as Michael said and that the creature will keep at bay, allowing us his charity to the stock. But, I'm afraid so many things can go wrong given Michael's fanaticism, especially when attempting to prove a point, he leaves our journey in a shroud of doubt. His words are convincing enough, but it's not words that I fear, it's the result of them. Against my better judgment, I take the knife and slide it dolefully in my inner coat pocket.

With Emily finishes, she seeks me out to walk arm in arm with a box under her other. I maneuver myself so that I keep her on the opposite side of the instrument of paranoia. I'd not wish to taint her innocence with the musings of men, the darker recesses of the mind, nor give her reason to hate the Lockes even more.

There is something about the trek toward the west end, an unnatural touch to the air that quiets even the most outspoken. After loosing sight of the apartment building, our journey is a wordless one steeped only in footfalls, the crunching of snow, and the sound of the wind brushing against the forest of skyscrapers. It isn't as cold as previous days and certainly not as chilling as the trips that I had made before. It is strange. No matter how many times I see the empty streets, the collection of quiescence building in the stratus, and the grey in which it brings upon the world, I can't accept that this is how the world has always been—that there is something hidden, far beyond the reaches of man. I see it on everyone's face, they being bothered by the perpetual state of things. We are misplaced beings in a land far different than our dreams and tormented by the lack in memory of it.

Past a couple hours' time we catch sight of the enormous sign that hangs diligently above the convenience store, still illuminating the shadowed section of the city in its brilliance under the word of 'Open'. As I stop, everyone else does as well, peering across the street ahead, worried that I had spotted some nefarious devil lying in wait. I look across the snow hoping to catch some manner of tracks, a sign that someone had recently traversed the area. Yet there is nothing except a virgin line of white powder stretching presumably as far as the rocky shore. I push myself forward, under the strict motivation of our common necessity and the others follow in turn. By this time Emily is shivering, teeth chattering from the immutable dread that has slowly developed about the place - the results of a simple telling of a story. I can only imagine that the Lockes are experiencing the same, but Michael and Natalie are better poised for such things. There is still a hint of reluctance in their motions, keeping a stride behind as Emily and I proceed closer in step.

"Keep an eye out and be careful." I call back to them.

Their response is naught but a series of nods and grave countenances. The store is as it was many months ago, the glass as spotless as the day I had discovered it. I still cannot imagine how or by what graces the city happens to avoid the clutches of entropy. The church tends to be the only monumental proof of what the passage of time can inflict upon the world. I chuckle silently to myself, quickly remembering on how Emily rushed to press her face against the window the first time she had seen the store. It is ironic how now, in comparison to then, she trembles in its presence. How rapid things change, one emotion to the other, the same in a state of being; it's a truth that I have experienced many times, where at one point I felt stagnant in life and suddenly, out of the folds of existence, comes a new element. All things considered, change happens to be the one thing I hope not to experience here today.

Now nearly ten feet from the store, we are caught beneath its radiance. The Lockes act as if they attribute the light to a subscribing curse, for they keep just shy of the reflecting snow. I cast my eyes squarely where I last saw the creature, the alley's mouth now minus occupation. I am relieved for it and at the same time, afraid of where it might be now. Past the glass of the store windows, I confirm the familiar settings within: back refrigerator units, plastic shelving, white walls, florescent lighting, everything as it was before. I creep closer towards the store's doors, yet am impended by the unyielding weight that Emily has now become. She captures me an arms length between us, shaking her head to and fro to prevent entry into the place, as if it spelled our permanent end.

"Emily we have to go inside."

She continues to shake her head in disapproval, keeping her eyes directed toward the ground where I'm sure she's convinced herself that in that direction, no harm could come to her. I sigh deeply, noticing a quiver to the exhalation that I attribute to my own succession of inner fear. A fear, I believe, spawned from the musings of others. I was the one who saw the thing first hand, and yet I am the one who is at the front of the venture.

I carry my agitation to the Lockes who are still standing beyond the lights incandescence. "Michael? Natalie? Would you mind?"

They look between another expecting the other to take up the flag, their stance shifting like a lottery to designate who is to lead. After a short instance of their contentions, I decide to intercede once again. "Michael!"

He snaps his attentions back to me. "Yes of course," he manages to stifle between clearings in his throat. It is not long before the two manage to make their way to our side, enough to convince Emily that we are all in this together and to loosen her steadfastness.

I am surprised, after a closer examination of the inside of the store, that the wrappers and pieces of trash that Emily brought to my attention the time before are gone, with no evidence that they had been there in the first place. Carefully, I peer around the rest of the store, to make sure that there are no shadows or dark corridors for one to hide behind. Satisfied, I try the door, pushing it inward to give way beyond the wall of glass. A ring! the sound of a tiny bell chiming above the door as the top passes over it. It wasn't there before! The toll sends chills down my spine, throwing my neck into horripilation and my eyes into a desperate dance about the room. My pause is not recognized by my fellows and I am pushed into the store by their crowding. I try to brace against them, lock my knees and dig into the floor with my feet but despite my strongest efforts, I am uprooted and the door shuts behind us.

"This isn't as extravagant as I had imagined, more formidable from the outside, but very quaint on the inside. Smoke and mirrors, Samuel! Smoke and mirrors…"

Natalie expels her breath like she'd been holding it for sometime. "We should feel lucky that there was nothing here to greet us."

"Luck may have little to play in this my dear. But let us not worry about that now, I'd prefer to get what we came for and be gone as soon as possible."

I listen to everyone's movements, the gathering of items from the shelves and into the boxes – but no matter how hard I try, I cannot take my eyes off the tiny bell. It is like some morbid atrocity, a sign of welcoming by the only being whom I saw inhabiting this place. Michael is right, there is no luck about it, and he's here – somewhere, watching us as we make way with his possessions. My mind flashes to when Emily pointed out the wrappers, all strewn about the floor in some feral fashion and then the time I first discovered the store, took my fill, and left it accordingly in the same state it was prior to my arrival. Was it he who created the mess? I previously assumed, but what if it had been left by someone else? What if—my thoughts are interrupted by a frigid touch, Emily's hand lifting me out of my concentration; still fixated on the bell above the door I greet her worrisome face.

"Everything okay?" Her voice is a mixture of concern and sobriety.

I'm about to speak, about to tell them all but I'm hushed by how it might affect them. Emily tries to read me, tries to see what it is that has captivated my haunted parlor and when she notices the bell she sees nothing beyond herself looking back in a distorted image.

I lie. "Things are fine."

With Emily close by, I do what it is that we originally set off for – collect food that'll get us through the remainder of the winter. And as soon as we are done, I look back over the store and notice a few items that had been dropped and accidentally kicked about the floor.

"Are you coming, Mr. Bell?" Michael stands with Natalie just outside the door, holding their boxes close to their chests.

"One moment…" I mutter, as I set down my load and seize the fallen items and place them back upon their fragile shelves. I arrange them to ensure that everything is in its proper order, give the place another look about, and follow Emily back out into the cold.

The four of us proceed in a line, trudging homeward, bound for a pleasant meal and each other's company until near the end of the night. I stop slightly, just shy of the place I halted before, and look over my shoulder to the desolate alleys and niches expecting to see some fleeting glimpse of the horror of 'Open'. To my relief, as a hand-like gale sweeps across the snow banks, I find nothing but the emptiness of streets staring back.

Like many nights before, Emily and I enjoy the company of the Lockes for dinner under candlelight and piano play. The conversation revolves around the "utter disappointment" of not being able to encounter the creature I had so willfully described that stormy night. But at the evening's close, and when all is said and goodbyes are exchanged, Emily and I are left to our own devices.

After cleaning up the dishes, I fall upon the couch while Emily takes her turn at the piano, giving into a few minuets that she has memorized to perfection. The candles are still alight and all I can see beyond the blackness of the window are our reflections. Many things are still running through my mind, thoughts about our visitation to 'Open', the creature who guards it yet remains concealed, about our first encounter with the Lockes, finding Emily, being alone and then Rachel. Some nights she comes to me in the same way she usually does, lying on our sides staring lovingly at one another in a bright room – dreaming the impossible dream.

"Do you think Emily," I ask her during a soft period of one of her songs. "Whether we will find others, like ourselves? Perhaps see a time when all one would have to do is look outside their window in order to find another person?"

The music stops and for a instance there is nothing but the silence of the walls to keep me company.

"Why do you care so much?" Her melody picks back up.

"I'm not sure. I just can't shake this feeling of depravity, loneliness and abandonment. It all tends to run hand in hand. Perhaps I feel that if there were more people who lived here, things would be different."

Her timing slows to mere absence and now finger plays one note at a time. "I'm sure it would be. Wouldn't that be the thing… to see people just by looking out the window." There is a hint of hesitation to her answer.

"Think of it, the whole city filled with people to talk to."

The music ends once again and she walks to my side. "Oh Samuel…" She climbs into my lap and nuzzles her head against my chest. "Aren't you happy? Is the world so empty that you can't be still? Can't you bask in what is instead of what could be? Is change all that important?"

Her voice is coupled with a longing of sorts. All I can do is stare at the reflection of us in the window, surrounded by the candlelight and the night of the city. My mood slowly wanes, dropping into a despair reminiscent of the moment of my waking. The room grows cold and our image dancing by the candlelight grows distant and blurry. For awhile, we just lie here listening to the silence, the disturbing absence of all things.

As I shift, Emily raises her head about a few inches from my own. There's tension in the room as our eyes look between each others, wondering what could come and the fears which employ it. I can feel my heart beating, increasing as the silence between us grows in a rich heaviness that threatens to consume us. She leans into me, bringing her lips closer to mine and at the moment when I am about to take a breath from the building anxiety, our lips meet. I'm lost in the emotion, caught between thoughts and feelings. And then, with a sharp pain in my heart, my mind flashes to Rachel…

Emily pulls away, looking at me as if the world had crumbled away, that her heart had been crushed under the weight of the action. She turns her face and regretfully says, "I'm not her…" A tear streams down her cheek and she lets it fall.

I cannot explain what it is that betrayed me to her – my thoughts, my composure, the kiss? I want to deny it, to take it back, but there is nothing to excuse and nothing to forgive. The tear has been shed, the memory of it ingrained forever in my mind.

"I'm sorry." I whisper, but I don't think she hears me.

She leans back into me, she too looking at our reflection in the window. I am sure that as the minutes pass, she too perceives the image getting blurry and distant. Her fingers find her mouth and she chews on her nails nervously. We sit together in the awkward stillness of the room, contemplating the meaning of our existence and the concept of loneliness.

My dreams are filled with horrors and phantoms, strange things that not even I can understand. I hear whispers in the void and as I turn toward the source of sound I am gripped by the throat by some monstrous being. I face the guardian of 'Open', dangling me over the side of a building as I struggle to wrestle free from his grasp. His body is covered in bandages, wrapped snuggly by a master's hand, and what flesh that does show is as black as coal. I can smell the scent of burnt flesh flaring in my nostrils and his eyes bare down into me like blazing embers.

His voice as deep and dark as any torturers pit. *"We are all subject to a tyrant, a sorcerer, that by his cunning hath cheated you of this island."*

From his grip I pull out into the waking world, sitting upright in my bed with sweat glistening from my brow. I gather myself in the darkness next to Emily's sleeping form. The vividness of the dream still clutches at my brain, refusing to release the horrid vision of the guardian. My throat stands parched – tight as if hands from the dream had physically wrenched it shut. I escape from the bedroom, hoping to leave the taint behind, desperate for it not to follow me.

In the dark I manage to find my way over to the sink and draw a glass of water. After quenching my thirst on half the glass, I find a place of solace on the couch, looking out into the night. I rub my face to grant me a greater sense of lucidness, to push back the thoughts of the dream. I try and relax, falling back into the cushions – but it is then that a light turns on in the opposite apartment across the street.

Standing at the other apartment's window is a figure dressed in a long red coat and hood, obscured in the face with the shadows of the place. He stands in a peculiar way, staring as if able to see me from his perch. I am overwhelmed by fear, a sudden blast of terror as the remnants of my dream play over in my head. The figure throws his palm against the window and then writes an invisible message across the glass with his finger. I cannot see what he is writing, nor can I recognize the motions as letters or symbols. I find myself in trepidation, shaking as the words from the guardian repeat themselves in my head. *"By his cunning…"*

I close my eyes direly wishing him to disappear, vanish from both this world and my mind! I shove my hands over my eyes, to plead to whatever being controls the constant brume to make him disappear. And when I open them again, I find that the apartment is empty once more and the light across the way slowly dimming until it returns to the state of nothingness it knew before.

"Are you *sure* he was here?" Emily huddles close to me, hiding beneath the hood of her throw-on, keeping her perceptions narrow in case danger crept up on her – a means not to see it.

"This apartment is empty – clean to say the least for someone as filthy as that creature to have stalked through here. So you say he spoke to you from this apartment?" Michael looks out the window, a flat of the same proportions as my own, to my window across the way.

"No – I dreamt that he spoke to me. He had me by the throat hanging over the side of a building. He spoke to me then. When I woke up and went to get a glass of water, it is then that I saw him."

"Writing on the window?" Michael queries with an arched eyebrow. "Sure you weren't dreaming at the time?"

"Michael!" Natalie scorns in an attempt to silence her husband. "We trust your telling of it Samuel. It's just that it's sounds—"

"Scary!" Emily bleats, her eyes now completely within her cowl.

The air is crisp, frigid to the lungs and numbing to the limbs. I wonder how long it's been like this, as empty as it has, governed by the whims of the city's temperatures without the freedom of stability? This room might have once belonged to someone, but all traces have been lost to the handkerchief of some unseen hand. Yet… someone was here the night before, writing its message with a single finger – like that day Emily had written hers "YAWA OG", on mine. She used her breath to write it, and some days when the temperature drops and the heat rises I could still read it. That is, of course, until after *I* wiped *it* away, afraid that the Lockes would see.

I walk up to the window, shifting my head side to side, looking for a blemish of sorts to capture my attention. I breathe heavily against the glass, watching as the window takes to the condensation – spreading around the lines of oil left by the figure.

"There!" I point at the cursive strokes.

Michael blinks in disbelief, raising his lips to mark the discovery with an impish smile. "Forgive me. I had modest doubt of your telling, Mr. Bell. I thought surely we were on another ghost hunt."

"Are we to blow until we are out of breath?" Natalie sweats.

Just then the familiar click of the thermostat and the rattling of the registers stifle our conversation. We all examine the perpetrator—Emily—as her hand drifts back to her side from touch panel.

"What?" She stammers. "I'm cold!" She hides her face even further by pulling the drawstrings to her hood, now completely shut off from the world.

The room struggles in an onslaught against the cold as the ventilators expel heat that shifts around the room to cater to every corner to ensure the designated setting. The window fogs from the meeting, revealing the secret message from the night before, with small beads of condensation threatening to erase the entire thing.

"Emily you're a genius!" I excitedly profess, as I step back from the window's proximity in order to take in its full perception. It is not long, after reading the first few lines of the message, before my enthusiasm drops to a state of grave vexation – I quote as follows:

Burgess of the CitySpire,

Heed that the Rue du Bourreau is my domain and I its malicious sovereign. The city gives to those in equal share. Take nothing less than fairness and nothing beyond deserving. Least thou suffer beneath Count Champ de Croix.

Our monster has a name. Beneath a raised hand to her lips Natalie mutters in whisper, "There really are devils."

"It sounds like this city no longer belongs to you, Mr. Bell. I can't say that I envy the usurpation."

I can't believe it, yet here it is. Staring at me in the face, a proclamation of the deadliest sorts, here in the CitySpire we are to be ruled by monsters.

7

The days each set aside their own manner of nervousness and dread. It is when the sun sets that the unscrupulous feelings draw to their heights as we all huddle about our dinners, casting glares at the apartment across the way, worried that some new proclamation would be written there. I think that this time, as the paranoia seeps in me, how I am now the true bearer of the emotional flag. The Lockes have built up this Count de Croix character and made him into some cannibal, despite how he is the most real to me. And why wouldn't he be? It is this same Count who persists in allowing none but me to see him, to alert others of his existence, enough so that fear can build on fear. Maybe that is his plan all along, to get others to fear him so that none would be foolish enough to challenge him or his proclamations.

Aside from the drama of it all, his request isn't all that imposing, to take nothing but what is needed and no more, is rather common sense really. Yet it was the way in which everything was presented— all so theatrical—and now Michael, how he looks at me strangely, ever since he declared it usurpation. I catch him staring at times, his eyes betraying a tenebrous thought – a thought that I was dead already or could be at any moment. I wouldn't cosign myself to the graveyard just yet, especially because there is no reason as to why the creature-Count would do me harm. Perhaps it is due to a Machiavellian mind, a state to which confers his ultimate belief that I was overthrown. It seems my wish has come true for no longer will I have to suffer in hearing that this is *my city*. Count de Croix claimed that his domain is the Rue de Bourreau, a name for which he has established for the general area surrounding 'Open'. I wish I had a better idea of boundaries so that I know if and when I am beneath his scrutiny.

Emily seems to be taking this instance with her usual flightiness and detachment, as she handles most other things. Times previous, I had found this trait of hers a bit off-shore, but now I am seeing it in a new light as I am glad to have someone who isn't looking so grim and is open to conversation outside of the malevolent Count. Natalie keeps her head down as if dodging the attention of some callous oppressor, but smiles at me from time to time to say how appreciative she is of being granted our company. I am all the more glad for it as without their friendship, I'm afraid that this existence would be a hollow one.

Four weeks transpire and the majority of the snows have dwindled away, leaving little save a moist street and tiny pockets of white dunes that have collected against portions of buildings and other large obstacles unmoved by the winds. I've noticed a sharp decline in the Lockes visitation, no longer are Emily and I invited over for dinner or tea. It isn't until the third week that Michael stops showing up entirely and only Natalie allows us her time. Every instance, I inquire about Michael's well being and what has kept him from our presence. Natalie gives some excuse that he isn't feeling well or that he has stumbled upon a collection of books and that it is nearly impossible to have him break from. But I know just the way that Natalie presents his reasons that something has been severed between us.

Our visitations used to be a nightly affair, but in the past weeks it has been four nights, then three and now nothing at all. Emily is first to point it out saying, "First you lose a section of the city, and now a friend? How interesting…" but I think she is quick to dismiss.

It does seem coincidental that Michael has suddenly lost interest in our get-togethers but I wouldn't ascribe his withdrawal completely to that reason. Perhaps he is in need of some time to himself, or mayhap he actually had been sick or is too engrossed in some study as Natalie claims. Her disappointment—Emily claims it is guilt—stems from her lack of influence over her husband. I can't blame her really. I've been caught up in one of his evangelisms before and hadn't been able to think of a way to slink beneath its fervor. It's the way he is. Once he gets an idea in his head, it's difficult to dissuade him from it. I'm taking it as a matter of faith that he will rejoin our company, but until then, we'll have to make do without him.

That afternoon Emily and I are once again without their company, sharing a tune together by the piano side. She is playing a melody from a time I cannot remember; a waltz of an almost dreary composure yet touched by a hint of longing. She plays continuously, hour after hour, one song after the next, but always returning to the same song as before.

I finally build up enough nerve to ask, "What is it that you keep playing?"

She looks up partially from the keys and blankly at the wall in front of her, "Hmm – oh… I don't know. Something that I've been working on, just playing really…"

"It's nice." But my compliments may not have been what she was expecting, as she bows her head once again and switches to another piece.

Ever since that night that she kissed me things have been different between us. She rarely looks me in the eye, keeps to herself, and isn't as responsive as I would like. I'm sure it has a lot to do with a bit of embarrassment, confusion and maybe mixed with bits of rejection. I didn't consciously push her away, but how she retreats from me is enough to bolster that idea. I don't know what it is with me, chasing after some dream, continually being reminded of that instant when the door shut me in my apartment with nothing save a heartache and anxieties.

It could be out of my love for a woman who may or may not exist. Subconsciously, perhaps I feel no one else can compare to Rachel, and yet… I do have feelings for Emily. But what good are feelings when I am conflicted with another? How is it that I can even conceive of a life with Emily when there are so many questions unanswered about myself: Rachel, this city? Everything is veiled. Everything is a huge mystery. As long as things continue as they are, I won't be settled. I could try and explain things, tell Emily how I feel, and what goes on inside my head, but I don't think she would understand. Where I am weighted down by this city, Emily is oblivious of it and its condition. She is in the now, where as I am in the past, still searching for answers.

She is mid-way into one of Tchaikovsky's numbers when a flutter catches my eye and lands gracefully at the window's ledge.

"Emily!" I stifle from my seat in surprise. She looks at the window, both of us in a moment of silence as we watch the grey pigeon strut beyond the glass and bounce its head from one side to the next.

"Isn't this wonderful?" I ask in a fit of enthusiasm. "It looks like we have a new friend."

Yet Emily just sits there in somber continence, looking at the bird but seeing something far beyond it – something that I cannot perceive. Not a word, just staring at the creature, a silent miserable stare. And when the pigeon takes flight out into the cityscape, I find Emily at the door of the apartment already in her winter shoes and putting on her coat.

"Where are you going?"

Her statements are bold and without her usual character. "Out," she opens the door and squeezes half way across the threshold before finishing her sentence, "for a walk."

"Hold on," I stammer as I rise from the couch, "I'll come with—."

The door slams behind her. I remain in the same position for nearly five minutes, caught in making for my coat, but halted by a closed door. It's as if everything inside me shut down, believing that perchance the door may open and Emily emerge demanding that I hurry up. Nothing.

I manage to sit on the couch, waiting silently, listening to the emptiness of the room and imagining the stillness of the city. I suffer through it painfully. I worry. Was it something that I said? Something I had done? And though unbeknownst to it, there is nothing that I can do to shake this feeling of guilt that slithers about my chest. I'm wounded. Abandoned. My thoughts are filled with Emily and that kiss and how badly she must have wanted it. Maybe she's jealous, jealous of a dream... jealous of Rachel. She could be frustrated with me for some unspoken offense, she could not have heard me, or simply preferred to be alone. I'm making a bigger deal of this than is necessary. What if I'm not? What if Emily never comes back? And what if Michael never seeks my company? What if? What if—Stop!

I rush over to the piano—something is wrong with me—and open the fall. I play as if I never have played before, like I have been deprived of music my entire life and that somehow knew exactly how to play, how to describe and portray the hidden recesses of my soul. I play loudly, to keep the thoughts from returning in my head, to keep out the sound of the door latching shut, and to keep the silence that comes after from throwing me into a darkness from which I may never dawn. I play as Emily once had, drifting into the chords like some pleasurable caress. Yet with me there wasn't any epiphany into that mysterious melody that runs through my head – just a strong passion for absorbing every musical note I can wreck across the taught strings of the piano.

I play until I sweat. I play until my fingers pain me from the marrow and still I press myself to play. On and on, as the clock's hand makes a full swing, several rotations, as the world proceeds to turn on its spindle I play. My music forsakes the sun as it sets far beyond the scope that my window allots me, with the glove of night soon crawling after. And then, as my absolute disparity takes its last leap, my fingers proven numb, I lie helplessly on the closed fall and wish that Emily would return.

My heart cracks as I'm struck by how long she's been gone and blame myself for her disappearance – that it was my hand that drove her away. I curse my dreams; curse myself for allowing Rachel to possess me so, for turning away my only bedfellow and dearest friend of whom I love! I find myself a wretched thing, something tortured, to be alone simply to suffer beneath the thralls of the stillness. I start to cry, convinced that Emily will never return or worse, has come under some terrible danger. I think of how I found her near lifeless on the shore, how fragile she appeared. I think of all the times she kept me from the depressions I met without her company and how at the very least I could return her love and spare her the indignities of my dreams about a girl who I don't even know.

I retire to the bedroom while revolving through all the times Emily and I shared, all the times we spoke together and the moments she brought a smile. Each memory, each passing thought, manifests as yet another stab at my heart until exhaustion overtakes me.

In my dreams Rachel looks on with the same somber look that Emily had when she stared at the pigeon. She turns her face from me and the lights of the room, normally brilliant with ecstasy, now dim to darkness as her figure slowly slips into the void. But then I feel a cold hand pressed against my cheek and I stir into a half-dream where the bedroom wavers like the ripples of a stream. I can make out Emily's silhouette amidst the shade. She still carries the aura of winter.

I fade in and out of reality, but I manage to expel, "Emily – I'm so sorry… the stillness…"

And she curls up next to me, still in her coat, snuggling from behind, she sings, "Oh dearest Samuel, they've gotten the best of you…"

She says more, but I cannot hear her as my eyes are fixed in between the now and dormancy. She soothes me with a gentle shush. Emily is home, and the added relief grants me all that I need to fall back to sleep once more – an empty fruitless sleep where dreams no longer tread.

I wake as if from a tenebrous nightmare, as if the events from the day before had all danced about my mind as dreams tend to do. My muscles are sore as perchance the covers had constrained my body from shifting about in my sleep. I remember seeing Emily the night before and quickly turn to her side of the bed – empty. The sheets haven't moved, nor does her pillow have the imprint that she usually leaves behind. In her place is a silver embroidered box – a jewel case of sorts. I brush my fingers over the engravings, feeling the grooves and appreciating the masterwork of the piece. I wonder where she got it. It is large enough that I am able to take it in both my hands, nearly three pounds. I open it.

At once my heart is seized in the same fit of despair as it had the night before, the song—the one that Emily had been playing and I couldn't identify—that waltz, chiming on some hidden music box, as a plastic dancer spins in tiny pirouettes, plays throughout my being. There's a note:

PART I - SLEEPERS' WAKE

Someday my love, when winters breath is song,

with many nights alone, and all the dreams have gone.

I shall wait for you, by the frigid tide,

when the boat sails in, as it rounds seaside.

I'll be looking on, as lovers often tend,

knowing you loved me, discovered in the end.

My face flushes with fear as the wrongness of the silence reminds me of the emptiness of the city. I throw the covers and rush out into the living room shouting Emily's name. But the room is abandoned – still, like the times before. I grab my boots and coat and rush out of apartment without locking the door. I take the stairs all the way to the twenty-fifth floor and find the Lockes' apartment, rapping heavily until Natalie answers with nothing but a bathrobe. She gives me a quizzical look, her hair wet from the shower.

"Emily's gone." I stagger from amongst the heaves in my breath.

Surprise flashes across Natalie's face so quickly that one would contest if she wore her expressions any other way. "Why – what happened?" She stammers but already she rallies to the urgency in my voice. "Come in and Michael and I will get dressed."

I grow impatient, shaking my body to encourage haste. I have no idea when she left, but I think I know where she went. But Natalie sees the light to reason.

"We'll go together. Don't worry Samuel. We'll find her."

We take the elevators and once the carriage touches the lobby I spring out to the streets. The Lockes keep up as I flood across the snow-laden pavement, headed toward the western shoreline – the place where Emily had mentioned in her poem, the place where I originally found her. The buildings pass quickly. My figure's reflection leaps from window to window. The entire time I am overtaken by the fears of what I may find. I cannot believe what is happening – Emily gone! My heart pounds uncontrollably and the sharp pains that anxiety brings, the mania that has overcome me, causes me to stumble from time to time. The Lockes don't say a word, but they are with me the entire way, following just a few feet behind, struggling to keep up. Every alley we pass I throw a look in that direction, hoping for any sign of Emily or where she had gone and each time I find one empty it is yet another stab at my being.

Before long we pass by the dreaded convenience store and I am reminded of how I insisted on the store's name and wish that if only I had conceded to the name 'Open' instead of being emphatic that it was there only to encourage visits. The skyscrapers slowly disappear with small warehouses and rundown office buildings taking their place. I'm bothered by the entropic grime that has collected in sparse patches on the north sides of the buildings. It makes me think how everything is falling apart; a sinking feeling that I can't shake, that only gets stronger the closer I get to the shore. Then the streets bend into a decline, a barely noticeable ramp of concrete that ends at the far reaches of the promenade. I take the stairs down and race out onto the docks. I search all about me, scanning the rock bed, beneath the planks and when I reach the end of the pier, across the sea, nothing. There is nothing here, not a sign of Emily, not even a disruption of sand, earth or wood that could foretell that she was here at some time. I scream her name out into the wind yet despair when it is swallowed by the surf. I call out again and again and still no answer.

The Lockes are silent. Michael leans against the promenade's railing, bearing down at me the entire time as he tries to catch his breath. Natalie sticks to her husband but keeps her eyes about her, looking as well. The weather is chilling and I just now feel its cold brushing against the insides of my lungs. I call out a few additional times, staring out across the waters, fearing where she had gone. I stand here for what seems to be hours when I hear footsteps across the wood and Natalie's voice behind me.

"She's not here, Samuel." She pauses as a wave crawls across the beach. "She's probably elsewhere, Hermes Square, the church, terrace manors, maybe even the park. We can check there if you like."

She's cold and I feel horrible for having dragged them into this. I can see Michael still staring at me from the promenade, thinking that I've lost it. "She's not there." I finally reply.

"What makes you so sure? We can at least try." She is sincere, concerned, and weighted by the toll Emily's disappearance is having on me. I must look terrible. I didn't even shower this morning, my hair in shambles. Sweet Natalie.

I claim defeat even before we check all the stores of Hermes square, the insides of the church, the area surrounding the park, as well as briefly canvass the terrace manors. The entire time, Michael tries to convince his wife that the CitySpire is too large for the three of us to locate a single person, especially someone who doesn't want to be found. He even backs up his arguments by citing the elusive Count Champ de Croix. Yet every time Michael brings up the subject of ending the search, she burrows into him with a glare, glances at me and then shakes her head. Oftentimes she grabs my hand and pulls me down the street when all I want is to sit and rest. Natalie refuses to let my disparity get the better of me. I realized long ago that Emily is important to me, but I never imagined how awful it would be without her. I never imagined feeling like this. *If I had only kissed her...*

It isn't until night returns when we all give up the search and together return to the apartments. All the way home Natalie suggests that Emily may have returned in our absence and may be waiting for us. But I know, even before I find the lonely emptiness of my apartment, that Emily wouldn't have come back. I sit on my couch staring out the window at the apartment across the street. I don't see anything, just the dark and the reflections of the Lockes as they stir about my threshold. Michael concedes after a short whispered debate and returns back to their room. Natalie decides to stay.

She makes us both something to drink, some hot cocoa from the cupboards, as I used to do for Emily. How it pains me to sip it. She joins me on the couch and together we sit in silence. She doesn't say a word, but cares for me without question. I'm sure she's curious about the events surrounding the disappearance, though it's not hard to conclude that it was voluntary on her part. The whole thing has left me empty and I feeling numb. I rot here accepting my defeat. Finally, the stillness creeps in – the long fight against the city has ended in my desolation.

In time it all gets to her, poor Natalie. She shifts in her seat and takes up my hand in hers, though strangely avoiding eye contact.

"You know," she swallows, "sometimes I find myself asking whether I am with Michael out of love or out of convenience."

I take my gaze from the window, feeling as if dust had settled on my line of sight, laying cause for my difficulties in severing my eyes from the glass to my couch mate.

"He's headstrong, domineering, and at times neglectful. He takes a fancy to you though. You should have seen him before we met you…" she trails off reflecting on those times past before continuing. "Our 'union', as Michael likes to call it, hasn't been an easy one. I get scared… I'll admit it that I've been jealous of you and Emily. Other times, I questioned if you were intimate... or together at all."

I just look at her. I can tell that she's uncomfortable, but what she is saying keeps my mind away from my current troubles. She's loaning me a short reprieve by relating her inner thoughts, her secrets – she's giving me the chance to get away from myself.

"Want to know something funny?" She swallows hard, with her anxiety showing clearly as her fingers fondle her mug. She pulls up her left hand and displays it in front of her. "I don't even have a ring. For all I know… *Michael could be my brother.*"

There it is. She expels her breath as if it had been nestled up inside her for years. She smiles at me as tears well in her eyes. "That is…" she persists, "If you believe what the card tells us." Natalie laughs lightly in hopes of dismissing the awkwardness of the situation.

I cannot take my eyes off of her. I cannot comprehend how she has managed to function beneath these weighted thoughts. Her love, a love of convenience; Michael her brother; her relationship with Michael constantly in question, and still she is able to drag me across the city to help find Emily. She didn't do it for Emily, she did it for me, to try and give me back that happiness that she herself is missing. She's a strong woman, capable of doing what is necessary, despite personal sacrifices. My gaze must inspire discomfort, for she sets her cup down and motions to get up.

"I-I-should be going."

But before she fully stands, I grab hold of her hand and pull her effortlessly back on the couch. After absorbing the months of denial and burden from her face, I pull her into me, kissing her as Emily had kissed me many nights before. At first she is hesitant, squirming from the suddenness of it all, but eventually she leans into it, accepting my sorrows and feeling my heartbreak as if it were her own. I run my fingers up the side of her leg—she shivers—up her torso and ending with my hands cupping her breast.

In a burst of unbridled passion she undresses me and I her, shedding each other's clothing and tossing them across the floor. Our skin touches skin, our limbs embracing until we are one person. I bed her here on the couch and then when cushions and creases become too restrictive, I carry her into the bedroom. The windows fog as we sweat, she moans quietly beneath me – both of us giving into the others pain, releasing pent-up desires, along with months of frustrations and giving into the desire to be loved. And when it is all over, as we collapse from the exhaustion of our climax, the room starts to spin. As I lie here, with her warm body next to mine, the both of us slipping between the veils of dreams, I am touched by a brief guilt that spawns from such things. Why Natalie and not Emily? I question love and meaning as the room slips to blackness, before drifting into sweet unconsciousness.

I dream of water, with lights sparkling in incandescent ribbons in the deep. I can see ocean blues and how all color eventually dissipates into the inky depths. I can hear the stillness more clearly, as here there are no walls. It is an acute deafness that lingers beneath the waves. Before me is the grim cast of Emily's face, sinking beneath me, her dress—the same white summer garment she wore the day she sprained her ankle—flutters in wisps about her kelp-like hair. I cry out for her but my lungs fill with water and I too begin to feel that tenacious pull that is slowly bringing Emily into the darkness. I'm being choked! My lungs burning with the absence of air and I reach for Emily, trying to catch her arms as they trail above her, far from reach. Her eyes reflect the swaying lights from the surface, but as I try to read her features, all I see is a giving in – a lack for the luster of life and all its meaning as she accepts the inevitability of the depths. I struggle against the undercurrents, trying to acquire a quicker descent so that I may be able to reach her in time and try to bring her to the surface. Still wanting to gasp for air, I force myself to keep what little air I have left.

I reach the tips of her fingers. We touch momentarily. She doesn't move; still descending farther into the dismal ebb. Something stirs. Beyond Emily, I can see pairs of pin-sized orbs, all lighting up from the reflecting surface. The heart that beats heavily in my chest now cries out against this unknown terror. The orbs swarm in spiral, growing bigger as they draw nearer from their watery graves. Bubbles engulf Emily as it pushes past her hair and then tickles against my skin. I make another desperate grab for Emily's hand, I am able to hold just long enough for it to be pulled violently from my grasp. The eyes draw themselves up her feet, and slide up her legs.

I can now see—by the Maker—all the people clawing their way up Emily's body! Every handful toward me is yet another Emily is taken away, all being weighted down by the tens—no! hundreds of people—many thousands of pairs of orbs glittering in the dark! I try and pull away, try to retreat towards the surface but I am grappled, my feet now wrestled by the people of the deep. Their hands are like ice, so cold that it feels that their touch is liquid fire. I kick at them, thrash and swim as hard as my limbs can take, but I am pulled thrashing into their world, while they invade my own. It isn't until they reach my neck, as their fingers dig into my flesh, probe into my mouth, nose and eyes, that I am forced from the terrible visions to sit upright in my bed. The dream passes as softly as a whisper.

I wake to the warmth of sunshine filtering through the windows. I am alone. It has been months since I've been able to spy a break in the gloom. The smell of lilacs is fresh once again, I can barely recall the last time I had smelled it. I am sore from yesterday's search.

One look at my nakedness and all of last night washes back against me – Natalie. I've made a horrible mistake! I've betrayed Michael, despite Natalie's doubts on the legitimacy of their union.

They are still by all definition of the word, married. Then let's not forget how hurt Emily would be if she were to find out. But do I regret what happened? No – not in the least. Natalie is a dear friend and confidant. It was a wonderful thing we shared. We were both vulnerable. How can we be blamed? But if Natalie were to tell – who would she tell? She has as much to lose as I and any burden on her conscience tends to be redirected to me. I shouldn't worry, but the sun – how glorious.

I take my time showering, something I hadn't done the day before, and dress myself so that I can show some physical signs that things were improving. No sooner do I finish, when there is a knock at my door. I answer it as promptly as possible hoping that Emily has returned. I find the Lockes instead, both of whom have smiles across their faces.

"Good morning Mr. Bell, I hope you are feeling better from the previous day, especially if you are to accompany us to the very rooftop of this building."

Seeing both the Lockes this early and unprepared draws rocks in my throat to which I am forced to swallow, but there is something in Natalie's features that place my tensions on hold. She beams me that flirtatious eye of hers.

"We're taking the stairs to access the roof. The sun, Samuel! The clouds have parted. We can see the sun!"

With my coat and boots we take the elevator to the twenty-fifth floor. The stairwell leads us onto a twenty-sixth, all run with wires, ventilation and other hidden necessities that modern structures require. Surprisingly there is no dust and the place smells of fresh rain, then a flight of stairs that lead to a covered skylight that, once flung open like the doors to dusty cellar, envelopes us in the light of morning sun. There is no wind and with the sun now caressing the city in its glow, the temperature is comfortably cool. The skies aren't clear of the clouds, but there's a large enough gap where the sun is able to be seen, with smaller holes that filter its beautiful rays across the cityscape. Michael races across the flat of the roof and to the edge of the building, stopping premature of the edge by a torso high wall.

He lifts his hands as if addressing a phantom audience. "This is beautiful! You two should come see this!"

Natalie takes up my arm and escorts me toward her joyous husband. I look at her, nervous that her gesture of affection could be construed as a hint to last night. She doesn't flinch or take a misstep in acknowledgment to the same thought. She is acting as she normally would in this situation, as the Natalie before our affair. The way that the light dances across her skin casts her as a harmonious spirit.

"Natalie… about last night—"

"Don't mention it, Samuel. It was my pleasure to take care of you in your time of need. I would hope that had I been in your situation, that you would have afforded me the same. That's what friends are for, are they not? To…" she pauses, "be there for each other?" She smiles with her eyes, and her lips accentuate her thoughts as the corner turns upward.

We join Michael at the edge of the building, taking in the city for what seems to be the first time—as the sunlight glistens off the remaining snow. It occurs to me, as the beams of sunlight filter across the cityscape, that it has been quite some time since the last moment I saw it. I'm reminded of my first encounter, when I saw the sun creeping from behind the solemn clouds at the docks the day I woke. It was just as touching then as it is now. There is something about when the light caresses you, while warming your skin, that for a short instance one feels cleansed of all past pains and guilt. But beneath all the jovial sensations, I cannot help but wish that Emily were here with us to share in the moment – how I miss her.

"This does place one in a rather unique perspective on how much beauty the CitySpire is capable of. Wouldn't you agree, Mr. Bell?"

"It does…" as I continue to look out across the shimmering city-isle, a dark cloud must have began to form above my head, as I start to question how much longer the weather would last. I don't voice it, as I am sure that Michael already knows the answer. I don't want to spoil the moment besides, seeing how wonderful the skies are grants me a sliver of hope that it will continue. Sometimes life is easier when you don't expect the worst to come.

For the moment I just sit in awe with the rest of the company, enjoying what precious moments the roof has to offer.

The unfortunate truth of it is that the weather doesn't last. By the late afternoon, the sky is once again blanketed by a thick haze that chokes the remaining sunlight, pushing the light back toward the horizon. Already tiny drops of precipitation are touching the outside windows and the smell of moisture is thick in the air. I spend my time tuning the piano in an attempt at keeping my mind off of Emily's whereabouts. Once over my manic episode, I later realize that there aren't very many places she can go. She is not the type to strike out on her own as the lack of social contact would drive her mad. And she did say something to me while I was half-asleep that I couldn't make out, perhaps something important. Between each manipulation of one of the piano's strings, I concentrate as hard as I can to remember what exactly she had said; try as I might, I simply can not recall.

In the distance I can hear the approach of thunder echoing somewhere off to the southwest. I hope it won't be another one of the fluke storms that Michael predicted the first night I met the Lockes. Emily is not fond of thunderstorms. Her disappearance, on the other hand, has given me quite a lot to think about. For all I know, Rachel could be nothing more than a dream, something my mind manifested to keep me company while I was alone. And still, the strength Rachel has in my waking life is near being unbearable. What can I do when dreams are as strong as memories? If I knew that Rachel was alive or if I had something that could confirm that I was in love once, then things would be different. But all I have are these feelings, these dreams, and a song that plays continuously through my head, even during times of troubles such as these. I don't feel like I have any control over the events that are transpiring, nor the events that are soon to come. It's almost as if everything that has occurred, the motivations behind my actions, the muscle beneath my convictions, are all based around those first few moments I found myself in existence. Back then, I had nothing more than my thoughts and whatever clues that were scattered about the apartment to keep me preoccupied.   Alternatively, I can't set aside the responsibility for my actions and blame them on a longing desire to be with Rachel.

After tuning the last chord, I set the tools aside—the ones I had found in a hidden compartment beneath the bench—and strike up a short melody to ensure I had tweaked everything accordingly. What was Natalie in all this?   Have I been desirous of her since the moment I met her, and was her conviction in Emily's search and her admission afterwards, enough to have waken them? Can I say that I love her? I think that is the true indicator.   I do care for Natalie but not in the way I wish to love Emily. Is that the thing? Do I turn Emily away out of fear of betrayal to Rachel, as a betrayal in sharing love?

Natalie is a creature of desire, but one that comes in a sexual attraction and not for the sake of devotion. I do not find my heart yearning for her during her absence as I do with Emily – as I do for Rachel. I love Emily as I love Rachel, and that's that hardest part, for where does my loyalty lie the most? Rachel is more than a dream to me, she is someone who existed in a particular place, at a particular time, and shared it all the while with me. I simply cannot abandon the memory of her, or the hope that I'll one day see her again. But then again, can I afford to gamble Emily and my future happiness on a dream?

I begin once again in the composure of the familiar love song, reminiscing of those hollow moments of being alone and that feeling of being lost. I think of Emily and of how I miss her, how if things were any different I could be with her in the way that she wishes us to be. All the while I add additional notes, a full measure this time, while thinking that at the same time *I wish it too.*

8

The next morning, I rouse by the sound of knocking at my door. It is early, and the night has just sunk beneath the horizon. I had been dreaming again and as the knocks first rapped across my door I had thought, originally, that it had been Rachel returning from some excursion. It was a foolish notion that I later realize once passing beyond my bedroom and into the living room. The knocks were soft, like those coming from a tiny wrist. Making my way across the grey carpet, I assume that it is Natalie on the other side, though when I open the door I am sure that my face turns a stark white.

"Hello stranger." Emily stands just an inch shy from the threshold; dressed in clothes I've never seen her in – a pinstripe suit, skirt and fedora hat. She looks well. Not a scratch or hint of illness.

I am overwhelmed by both confusion and an uncontrollable happiness that forces my hands to reach out, quickly grabbing her round the waist, lifting her high into the air and spinning her into the apartment. The room is filled with laughter, both hers and mine, as I'm overjoyed in her return. My heart beats excitedly as I bring her back to the ground. There is a touch of serenity in her face, an enthralling peace that had been missing the day she disappeared from the apartment.

Overwrought with the moment, I beg her to, "Never, ever, leave again."

She laughs as if I had asked the absurd and that her absence couldn't possibly have been missed as desperate as my plea made it sound.

"I was only gone for a short while. I told you I would return, you sound as if I planned to abandon you completely." Emily taunts me.

"When did you tell me that?" I ask between smiles and laughs.

"When I woke you up a couple nights ago, you were mumbling. I told you it was something I needed to do." Her eyes narrow as if her squinting could jostle my memory.

"I don't recall—," my face growing somber with the strain of remembrance, as I think back to the night in question. There was something she said but I couldn't make out amidst the sands of slumber. My attentions are better directed to the joyous occasion. "It doesn't matter. The important thing is that you are here now."

Emily exposes the full whites of her teeth as she flashes a powerful grin. "Did you see my present?"

"Yes, it's wonderful! Where ever did you get it?"

"I found it at a silver shop. You wouldn't believe all the beautiful things you can find there."

"Well, you'll have to take me one of these—"

"Ahem." A low clearing of the throat robs me of any further enjoyment, as huddled in a half-bow is a man I've never seen before. His hair is short, blonde and fairly thin enough for his roots to show semi-transparently. His frame is wiry in most places and the suit that he wears is enough to make one wonder if it was explicitly tailored. He knocks lightly on the frame to add his bid for acknowledgment and now that my eyes are set directly upon him, he straightens his back to match my exact height.

"I almost forgot!" Emily breaks from my embrace—I realizing that my hands had been on her hips the entire time—walks over and takes this man's arm in her own. "This is Henry Boenger. I found him wandering aimlessly about the city. He was rather perplexed and delusional at the time, but I was able to bring him to his senses and here we are!"

I hate him. Without even a chance to meet him, to get to know his mannerisms, or even learn of his wants or dreams – I despise him. One could blame this on the waves of jealousy that now pulse through my veins, how she puts her arm so willfully in his as she used to do to mine. My eyes burn with utter loathing and yet as he extends his hand to me I cannot—by sheer principle in character— deny him proper etiquette. As I grip his hand, without misstep, Boenger speaks with a fine craftiness that hides his devilish intentions toward *my Emily*:

"A pleasure to meet you Mr. Bell, I've heard so much about you."

And as much control as I can muster, I refrain from crushing his hand as I am secretly doing with my teeth. I can't remember a time when I've felt such ire. Though the couple—if they noticed my affliction—are covering it all too well, as there is not even the slightest indication in their steps that I had fallen to foul moods.

"I see that my reputation precedes me for the first time, I hope Emily hasn't been speaking ill of me." I meant it as a half-joke, predisposed toward rooting out previous conversations the two may have had in the past. But Emily and Boenger—as I will not even grace his name with a mister—laugh as jokes were intended.

"No – Mr. Bell, nothing of personal insult. Emily has been very flattering in the description of your hospitality. I can see why it is that she was so skilled in returning the same to me. Had she not found me when she did, I don't know what I would have done."

"And the best thing about him is that he likes pancakes, Samuel! We can have him over for breakfast, lunch and dinner! He'd be a much better sit-in than our usual guests. I've already talked him into adopting one of the empty apartments in the building."

"That is of course with your permission. I would hate to intrude." He looks at me as if I would be the one to relinquish a blessing.

"Nonsense!" Emily chimes in. "There is plenty enough room for everyone. Don't you agree, Samuel?"

I smile the false smile and bear the rage as best as I can. "Plenty of room for everyone... like you said."

"You see! Come – the two of us can go find the right one!" She leads him by the hand and all I can do is stand there struck down from the higher points of grace that this morning first opened with. I am hardened by his flawless skin, his bright blue eyes and bastardy charms, and I have emerged as something far worse than the dreaded tyrant of the Rue du Bourreau.

They practically skip out into the hallway, the door latching shut behind them to further open my wound. I can hear them as they reach the elevator, the sounding of its ring, and the drawing of the carriage's doors. It isn't until I am sure that the two have left the floor that I walk into the kitchenette to pour a glass of water. Bringing it over to the center of the floor, I take a few sips, while staring out into the grey city and swollen sky. And it is then, while contemplating the recent events in a continuous circle, that I lose all sense of higher rationality—I throw the glass against the apartment window and it shatters, sending tiny shards of glass and water spewing against the impenetrable window.

I find myself fuming with the darker side of passion. Yet if one were to look at my recent endeavors, in particular at my spontaneous affair with Natalie, that I should be judged harsher. But at least I have the decency not to flaunt a newly acquired lover in the face of one that is still under courtship. It is as if Emily has forgotten me completely, or the moments for which we shared together in times of hardship and other. Is it possible that Emily and Boenger's flirtations with one another are nothing more than harmless banter? No – something tells me otherwise. Why is it that I am left here, still alone in this apartment, as the one I suffered for is out for a stroll with another man, and why wasn't I given invitation? All the while, I clean up the shards of glass. If I'm not careful, my jealousy could turn to self-pity. What I need is a second opinion, someone to help reassure, or deny what it is that I see in them. Once all the glass is carefully swept away and disposed of, I put on my boots and take a carriage to the twenty-fifth floor.

Natalie is the one to answer the door, with Michael just a room beyond her shoulder reading deeply from a leather-covered tome at a desk where my piano would sit. Her face brightens to see me, a quaint tranquility left from the previous day when the sunlight sparkled off her face. She's dressed this time, wearing a slim chiffon dress that's looks elegant on her like the many ones prior.

"What's the news, Sam?" She takes a large breath of air, that's purposefully sensual in nature.

"Emily's come back."

The playfulness falls from her features faster than water pouring from a glass. She strikes up a sober note and says, "Judging by the fact that you're here, things aren't going well."

"She's not alone."

Michael lifts his head as if the words themselves pull him out of his book. "What is it about you bringing bad news to our doorstep?"

"I think it has something to do with thresholds. They have never been the best place for pleasant conversation."

She sighs sympathetically, "Do you want us to come down?"

"Of course he does!" Michael carries himself majestically from his hiding place. "Who is this new addition to our little society – hmm? A gentleman I hope."

I cannot help but sneer, "I have other words for him."

"Come, come – he can't be all that bad. I'm sure there's some good in him somewhere."

Natalie puts a hand up against the frame to intercept Michael from, quite literally, pushing his way past the door and all those who stand in it. "Perhaps now is not the time to focus on his positive features. We don't know anything about him yet."

"Oh dearest, you're such a pessimist at times."

Natalie closes the door partially and smiles reluctant to her husband's urgings to be let through. "Perhaps *now* isn't the time for introductions. Shall we meet you for dinner?"

"Why not make it lunch? It is, after all, nearer to the hour." Michael says matter-of-factly.

I'm not in the mood to deal with Michael's enthusiasm. I need to return to my apartment to ensure that things are put to order. "Fine – make it lunch. I'll expect you in an hour, as Michael says." I give Natalie a fleeing look as I start my way back to the elevator, seeing that her beautiful face has been replaced by one of apology. "You needn't be so," I call back to her, "everything is fine." I don't think she believed me. I don't believe it myself.

As I reach my apartment, I hear them talking, though it is impossible for me to make out. Something tells me they are talking about me. I enter into the room quickly in an attempt to catch a sliver of their conversation. They are sitting together on the couch, facing each other in the vilest of ways, both enamored with their topic of dialogue, as their cheeks are rosy from smiles. But it's their speech, the things that they are speaking that halts my progression into the room. I am confounded—lost—so far as to be absolutely perplexed at the meaning of their words.

"Up ewohsd oyua ehwn cafei ihs on oolk htei veilebei nact io. Oulaejs sou ihm eesn evenr viei." Emily expels ecstatically.

"Mei drawots lil dlohs hei nihtk oyua dou? Oisserpmin abd ae kamei tou tahei id."

"Nifei sujt oyua dnifs hei nihtk io nou. Rabei nact hei ahtt us tis." She laughs a terrible laugh.

"Mei at mocei vahei luowd hei aewsr io oyua nissikg sniagat edicedd io algd im. Cneloivei estedt sou io. Nividei sio niyalpg raei wei magei ihts ubt!" Boenger notices me still standing at the door and switches to something more intelligible. "Welcome home, Captain!"

"We came back and you were gone. Is everything okay?" Emily smiles her usual smile, the one she always gave whenever the Lockes were around. "I was hoping that you'd play a few songs for Henry. He says he's never heard a piano before."

"Perhaps another time when the mood is right – I've invited the Lockes down for lunch." I take a deep breathe of air. "They are very eager to meet you, Mr. Boenger."

"The Lockes?" Emily fidgets with her hands, her smile moving towards a half-frown. "They always put me in a mood as well. Are you sure you won't play something then? Chopin, perhaps?"

"I think Mr. Boenger would appreciate hearing it from you." I suggest while meandering towards the kitchen. There's hope that the sectioning of rooms will quiet her insistence. Today, I don't feel like indulging the fancies of an adversary.

"Emily, you didn't tell me that you could play."

Emily hides her face beneath her hands. "No! I'd make a mess of everything."

"Oh, come now. I'm sure you play marvelously." He leans over the loveseat and outstretches his hand to me. "I do not wish to be a bother, but could I ask you for a drink. I'm terribly parched."

By the end of the night, my teeth will have taken a new set of grooves, as even now they clench together in irritation at his manners. Ask for a drink? I pour a glass of water and bring it to him. I refuse to lose face in this matter, and instead respond accordingly as any decent host would.

He takes it lightly and nods to me in thanks while brushing me a kind smile. "What do you think, Mr. Bell? Is Emily being too modest?"

"She does what she does." The kitchen being no longer a safe haven, I retreat to the wall nearest the window and lean there with my arms crossed.

Emily peeks from beneath her closed palms at her couch companion. "I never know the right thing to play."

"Play whatever's easiest. You'll find no critics here."

It is a rare thing to see Emily blush. And here I thought it to be impossible to entice her towards doing something outside of her own wishes, but never the less she gets up from the pillows, while smiling wickedly, and deposits herself at the bench. It's not long before the fall is opened that the familiar melody of chopstix assaults the room.

"This city of yours," he manages between the turmoil of the piano, "is a marvelous place."

"I assure you Mr. Boenger, it's not mine."

"Yes, I hear it's in contest. And you say you saw this Count character just across the way, writing his edicts on the glass?"

"Something in that regard."

"Amazing!"

The man tries my patience. It's as if Emily has spent the past few days filling him in on every little detail that has occurred and he's now making use of it in light conversation; a means, by chance, for him to fall into my good graces or make suitable friends. It isn't working. Each time he opens his mouth or any act of camaraderie only reminds me of how he first arrived, bowing, smiling, and taking arm with Emily as if they're the best of friends. The whole instance burns inside me and as my mind wraps around circles of hate, additionally fueled by the song Emily is engaged in, it only makes me feel more isolated and above all, bitter.

"And what is it that you find so 'amazing' about it, pray tell? I'm always interested in an outsider's point of view." Perhaps, if circumstances were different, I'd have a greater sensibility towards him but he continues untouched as if my previous statement wasn't full of venom.

"That such a figure as menacing and primitive as he's been described to me can have such impeccable timing to catch you in the dark and your attention at the same time. Simply amazing."

I wonder if he's implying that I conjured up the whole thing! that I went next door and wrote the words myself. "What are you getting at, Mr. Boenger?"

"That our Count is either a meticulous observer of human behavior or has powers beyond our understanding. Maybe, just maybe, he can delve into our minds and read every thought."

Emily slams the keys down in interruption. "Don't say that! He's bad enough as is without you adding to it."

His blue eyes sparkle with curiosity and invention and he sweeps them off of me and settles them on the accompanist of conversation. "My apologies dear Emily, I shall not speak of it further."

The Lockes arrive on the hour. I answer the door as both Emily and Boenger have taken to games in counting the number of skyscrapers and guessing how many more stand behind us. Natalie wears a dark shawl around her shoulders, still wearing the same chiffon dress from earlier, whereas her husband has dressed himself in a fine suit. He peers over the both of our shoulders, hoping to be the first to catch a glimpse of the new arrival and to draw his own conclusions of whether Mr. Boenger is a man of standing or not.

"A pleasure to see you as always, Samuel." Natalie kisses me on the cheek, her rosey painted lips add a slight comfort for the past hour I've had to endure.

Michael, not wanting to appear ungentlemanly, shakes my hand and pats me on the side of the arm before I lead them into the apartment.

"Mr. Boenger, may I introduce you to—"

Michael steps beyond me and extends his hand. "Michael Rawlings Locke. I can't tell you how excited I am to meet you. Conversation runs dry when all one can speak about is the weather."

As Henry had done for me, he bows slightly and takes up his hand in a firm handshake. "It's wonderful to meet you. As our esteemed host was going to permit, my name is Henry Boenger. I've heard a lot about you and your predictions. I'll be sure to come to you directly whenever I plan an outing."

"Please do! Please do." His excitement almost outdoes his vim in the cathedral and I can tell from Natalie's expression that I'll be hearing another apology for her husband's actions.

Once there is a break in their acquaintanceship I say, "And this, Mr. Boenger, is Natalie Silver Locke."

Natalie holds out her gloved hand, which is then delicately taken up and cupped in a sincerity that makes me wonder if the man has any shame. "It's absolutely fabulous to meet you." He nods back to Michael. "To the both of you, what an honor."

Emily creeps up to me between the exchange and nuzzles into my shoulder. She bounces up on her tiptoes to whisper into my ear, "This has to be the worst introduction ever. No one is falling down."

In this instance, I'd have to agree.

The tension, if it were a physical thing, I could serve it both for lunch and for dinner. Since the addition of the Lockes, Emily has instructed me that pancakes is completely out of the question and so we dine on other things. The seating arrangements are a bit more difficult than those times before. Both Michael and Boenger sit well upon the couch, whilst Natalie and Emily manage next to each other on the piano bench, and I? I stand an inch away from the events, feeling the riled conversation that touts between the two gentries like scratching one's fingernails against the bark of a tree, splinters and all. The women keep to themselves, occasionally a whisper from Emily into Natalie's ear, but as much as Natalie struggles she cannot help but be lured by curiosity into the questions her husband feeds his couch mate.

"And she found you where?" Michael inquires from the rim of his cup.

"I was sitting on a bench in the middle of the park surrounded by pigeons, completely dazed at how I arrived here and wearing nothing but rags. I had no memory of who I am, or what had happened to get me here; all I had was this embossed card with my name scrolled across it to let me in on my identity. I swear that if Emily hadn't come along to rouse me out of my stupor, I would have conceded to being a bum and thought nothing more of it."

The room laughs, a thing completely foreign to this building until now. I want nothing more than to forgive Henry for his earlier slight and to join them in jovial times but the feeling keeps gnawing at me – the thought that Emily had abandoned me for him.

"I remember I was looking up at the sky and all of a sudden the clouds broke. By this time, I had been feeling a bit down on myself, when out of the light came Emily's face and she said, 'You're a strange one for being a pigeon! Care for some seed?'"

The Lockes erupt again, Michael with a boisterous laugh and Natalie clutching at her chest while trying to keep hers down.

"I was so flabbergasted, here with this beautiful light display and a gorgeous creature such as Emily looming above me, that I had birdseed all over me by the time I managed a response."

"That must have been when the sun came out yesterday morning. We went up to the rooftop to see it. It's a rare thing with the cloud cover and all. You are most fortunate to have woken to it." Natalie explains.

"After that awkward introduction, Emily took me for some better clothes and together we toured the entire city talking about the two of you along with Samuel and his knack for music. It's been a grand adventure so far. Everything is so new and exquisite that it made me forget about not remembering anything before my waking in the park. Emily tells me it's a condition we all share."

Michael shifts in his seat, a momentary pause in what I know is about to come. I hope that it will taint the mood, that his next few words will bring the scene to a terrifying close.

"One could consider it a condition of all things. This city and all its inhabitants share a common key element that we're all new and have been created by an unseen arbiter or who I'd like to call the grand architect. I've been doing some reading and have come to the conclusion that this city and all within share some purpose here. And that in serving according to his designs there will be a great reward awaiting us in the end."

He said it, the very thing that turns Natalie's eye's skyward in hopelessness and even Emily releases a sigh of irritation. Boenger, on the other hand, doesn't flinch.

"That's a very interesting perspective, but I ask you what is it that this arbiter wants from us? If this grand architect is building towards something, what is it that he's building and how are we a part of it?"

Michael leans back into the cushions. "I wish I had the answer to that. I just don't know. But I believe it has something to do with the natural state of things. The clues are there, I just have to look harder."

"It sounds difficult, especially with what you have to work with. I've been working on a little something of my own here and there. I don't really know what it is, just lines and schematics, but I'm sure with enough time I'll be able to flesh it out. Until then, I'm sure we'll all have time to bounce ideas off one another. I'd be very interested in what you find, Mr. Locke." And there it is: Michael won over by Boenger's interest alone, Emily enamored and Natalie bound to her husband. I am the odd man out.

Conversation continues through lunch, afternoon, dinner, and night. During such time, Emily is asked to play a few of her Sonata's, whilst I refuse any and all requests by making the excuse that my hands ache from the days prior. Natalie every so often gives me a comforting look and tries to express to me how very sorry she is, but it does not stop her from joining in the great times they each afford one another. As Michael once put it, I have been usurped, my role no longer needed in the birth of a new generation. Least that is how I feel. Out with the old and in with the new, as the saying goes.

When all is said and done and the conversationalists are fleeting in the eyes, I escort them willfully to the door and bid the Lockes a good night. Meanwhile, Emily and Boenger both help in the collection of dishes, the happy couple. I tell them to leave them and that I will take care of it in the morning. No one argues.

And when Henry readies himself to leave, Emily gives him a generous hug and kisses him on the side of the cheek. "It was a real pleasure to have you, Mr. Boenger." Emily says in a playful scrunch of her face.

He picks up her hand, bends low and kisses it just above the knuckles. "Until later. I'm sure we'll be seeing each other quite regularly. And in such time, there will be many pancakes."

She giggles. "How gallant you are. So many pancakes for us all." She pokes him in the nose.

Such ire. Boenger looks me in the face, his features smoothing to a warm continence, of which he hopes to pacify me or, in the least, convince me of his innocence. I can see his ruse and know full well that Mr. Boenger is intelligent enough to know exactly what he is imprinting, a masterful deceiver of the callous sort. He extends his hand to me.

"Thank you for your hospitality, Samuel. You have been very generous. I hope to see you again."

I am stuck to principle and he knows it. He holds the upper hand, and I am expected to meet it. My skin boils as I take his hand in a shake, harnessing every ounce of my self-control not to twist his arm and send him stumbling across my threshold and into the hallway. As he nods goodbye, I take satisfaction in the fact the he now trudges off to some empty apartment where he'll sleep, like a ragged man, on the floor without sheets and without pillow. Emily sees him out, and whispers something in their language that I cannot comprehend before shutting the door.

I glare at her from across the way, thinking ugly thoughts, and revealing in tainted fantasies that involve taking a stroll with Mr. Boenger through the Rue de Bourreau and abandoning him to the whims of the creature. They're interrupted prematurely when Emily turns to me and says, "That was fun. I think the Lockes had fun as well."

I cough up, "So it seemed." A distasteful event that for some reason she wishes to bring up again. Wasn't my suffering enough?

"I'm surprised at you, Samuel. You didn't say a word the whole time. Being as polite as ever?"

"I didn't want to intrude in the conversation since it was going so well." Lies.

"Always playing host, what ever am I going to do with you?" She runs a hand through her hair, stopping occasionally due to a knot. It appears like she hasn't brushed it for days.

Something jumps in me with association to time which I prescribe to the condition of her hair. "Boenger claims you found him yesterday when the sun was out, yet you've been gone for two days. What were you doing during that time?"

Her face drops from her earlier mood and she walks slowly towards the window and stares at her own reflection. "I went for a walk."

"A fairly long time for a walk, don't you think?" I ease towards her but stop at the back of the couch, a fair enough distance where I can see her looking at both our reflections. I am reminded of the time we used to walk arm and arm and she'd call us 'quite the couple'. I'm angry at her, angry at her for leaving me as she did, for putting me in such a vulnerable state and for returning with a man who's proving twice the better all around. What angers me more, is how she's trying to replace me and doing so publicly.

"I needed time to myself, that's all. Staying around you, day after day can be unbearable at times."

"Unbearable! And I suppose that good ol' Henry Boenger is that breath of fresh air that you've been searching for. Well Brava, I'm glad things worked out for you."

She turns me an evil eye, her face hardened like marble. "Stop it." I can see the vehement in her eyes, the conviction of pain. This isn't a topic she wants to endure.

Stop it? How I wanted to. But this isn't something that can just end abruptly, this is something that started the minute Boenger walked into the room and she put her arm in his. Stop? No – I want it to end.

"Oh, of course! I wouldn't want to inconvenience you in any way. Especially not after everything I've done for you."

Her body is steady, her eyes narrow, "That's not fair."

"No, it's not fair is it?" My hands grip the tops of the couch pillows in angst. "What do you want me to do? Keep quiet, play the dutiful role of host as you and your bedfellow count buildings and speak gibberish to one another? Hell, I'm surprised you're still here. Plan on sneaking out again while I'm asleep? There's no need for such secrecy here. Enjoy yourself. Please, be my guest!"

She storms off to the bedroom and emerges moments later with a pillow and blanket. She doesn't say a word to me as she passes; straight face and fire. I hold my countenance. It's like everything is playing out and there isn't a thing I can do about it.

Emily opens the door, steps out into the hallway and shouts, "You should have left me at the beach!" The door slams behind her.

I listen as she walks at first, then runs to the elevator. I hear the heart-piercing chime of the carriage as it settles at the floor, and then the all too familiar sound of the doors closing and it whirring up to the higher floors.

My chest burns like sulfur and before long all I hear is the dreaded sound of silence closing around me. I stare off at my own reflection… this is the beginning of the end. This is the start of the fall. I can feel it in the apartment drifting along the walls, that sense of entropy clutching at the core of the building – that little creak that moans when the winds blow. It's that sound of the door latching shut, it's the sound of darkness, and it's the sight of memories fading beneath the ebb.

Stop it? Emily… I wish I could.

9

The day is empty, my apartment is quiet and all I do is sit on the love seat and face out towards the apartment across the way. I didn't sleep last night. How could I? The whole event plays out in my mind like something that had happened before, something that I was powerless to stop – like a line of dominoes falling in a continuous spiral. I don't feel bad for what I said, it needed to be said. I feel bad because I had to say it and because I had to say it to her. I was hoping for a sense of reprieve and that one of us would give and apologize. Yet here I am, alone in this place.

Earlier this morning I went up to the Lockes' apartment, hoping to speak to Natalie about last night, but when I arrived at the floor all I could hear was laughter and the detestable sound of Boenger's voice spouting another story of his. It amazes me how many he can tell with having just woke a few days past. Even still, it amazes me how easily he slips into his role and comes out as popular as he is.

Is it an act? Perhaps, I've been too hard on him. He is who he is. And really… how can I be angry at him for attracting people's interest, for doing what it is he does and for attracting Emily's affections. She wanted me. I wasn't ready. She found someone else. It's that simple. Who am I to fault her for that? Especially for my involvement with Natalie not but a day after Emily was gone. I thought Boenger the monster, and now? I wonder how they view me in all this. I didn't stay on their floor, I returned to my apartment. If they had wanted me they knew where to find me.

I stray from the couch and stretch my fingers that have been yearning to release the emotions that I've been experiencing since yesterday. I sit at the bench in front of the piano, open the fall, and start playing a piece of Chopin: Prelude in E Minor, Op.28, No.4. In all instances of disparity, I always resort to him; it tends to help. While I play, I wonder if I am better or worse than the first time I played him.

I'm reminded of Rachel, how I haven't been able to dream of her, and that how all of a sudden I'm faced with darkness—that haunting touch of oblivion that waits for us all after we close our eyes. I feel cut off from everything like I'm being pushed out and segregated from the rest of our so-called society. And for some reason, though it bothered me many times before, it would be a great comfort to hear someone say that it is my city again.

Now? It seems like it's slipping through my fingers and the younger generation is picking up where I left off. Granted, he is just one man, but what about the possibilities of others? What more will they steal from me? It's funny, in a way. How can I claim a sentiment of ownership over something of this magnitude? I laugh and then my face grows stagnant. Why does it bother me? Emily warned me of having aspirations towards meeting new people, but I wouldn't listen, I figured it would bring happiness. So far, it's brought me nothing but misery. Maybe she is the wiser. The tragedy is that it took all this to occur before I managed to understand. The city seems apt to spawning more inhabitants and as more arrive I'm sure I'll experience an even smaller role in this world.

I close the fall after the song is finished and lean on the piano. I hang my head and bury it into my arms just thinking of the whole affair like some grand carnival ride that I'm not invited to.

I'm buried for hours, listening to the silence that seeps through the boards, and the light drizzle that has just started to hug the outside window. My eyes are closed and I focus on the one thing that I once dreamed daily about, my beloved Rachel. I remember the dream with profound clarity. She, leafless though indistinct and her hair alit by the glow of the lights behind her. We lie parallel to one another, gazing into each other's eyes.

I'm standing in a dark office. Books lavishly decorate the back shelves, all leather volumes, take an air of maliciousness. The scent of gun oil is strong, mixed with the warm miasma of sweat and dread. I stand clutching the weapon aimed steadily at the man's head, his face shadowed by the closed blinds that guard against the city lights. He stands not far from me, a person's length or so, in a well-tailored suit. His hand is on the desk, the bridge of his palm arched like a spider.

He looks at me in a queer fashion, as if I should know him. "So what's it going to be, Mr. Bell? What's it going to be?"

PART I - SLEEPERS' WAKE

There's resolve in his voice, one that issues from those who ask questions but already know the most rational answer, as if there were no other course of action – like he is talking to a child. But I'm not here out of rationality. I'm the one holding the gun. There's a shot, a loud thunderous bang that pierces my insides like a javelin. Then the dream fades.

I tip over the bench as I grab at my chest to keep whatever exploded inside. I'm back in my apartment. The rain heavier than before taps at the pane, the droplets run down the glass like splatters of blood. In the distance a drum line of thunderclaps grumble about the cityscape. I poke at my sternum to ensure that all was a dream. It must have startled me; the thunder that is. My hands are quivering as I remember the weight of the dark implement that I had held in my dream.

"Guns." I say aloud so the rest of the silence can hear me, so that it too can feel the tinge of fear that creeps up the length of my neck. "I know guns. There are guns here."

To think that I was afraid of carrying a knife when we returned to the convenience store 'Open', now there are guns, had been guns or I've known of guns at sometime? And in this dream of mine I had one in my hands, ready to use it, not just to fire it, but to murder a human being. I'm about to dismiss it—a dream, nothing more— yet, something inside me won't let it go. If it's not real, then what is real? Is Rachel real? These dreams of mine, are they memories? I bring my hands up to my head and dangle my nose over the keys of the piano, a means of which to stop myself from thinking too hard and to stop the shivers in my fingers.

It bothers me, it all bothers me. I try and put it all out of mind while reassuring myself, "I make my own fate."

The way in which the rain titters against the glass, the sound of the approaching storm and the state of the rest of the apartment, all I can think about is that smell: the smell of desperation, oil and sweat wafting off my own hands. I withdraw them from the piano, careful not to taint the ivory with my touch.

Grabbing a glass of water from the kitchen I sit myself on the couch and look out across the city. Pulling my legs close, I rock in contemplation, thinking about the details of the nightmare. But like all dreams, I find it harder to recognize the finer details of the scene the longer I contemplate it. There were a few titles on the shelves, the color of the carpet, the wood of the desk he so rapturously guarded, all of which were clear and now they have faded into the depths like a sinking ship. Depositing the glass on the table in front of me, I watch in one of those bleak stares that accompanies struggles of remembrance. A tear of condensation drips down its side.

Whatever it is, I lose my concentration, whether due to having noticed a dark splotch reflecting where one should not or the encroaching feeling of something malicious in the air, I cannot say for certain. But everything points toward the apartment across the way, the one veiled in darkness and with the veins of water seeping down the opposing windows. I feel as if tiny insects are crawling beneath my skin and a disparaging weight pounds at the inside of my rib cage as my heart struggles to flee and hide. And then, I see him — there! in the silence of the other apartment, skulking in the shadows of vacancy, and eyeing me with feverish interest is Count Champ de Croix!

Everything tells me to run, to find some other place to escape to in order to hide from his terrifying gaze, but his eyes! It's too late, he has hold of me. He's come and for the life of me, I'm reminded of the previous trip we made into his liar, the trespass we embarked upon. He claimed the Rue de Bourreau and, by all accounts, we took from his charge and he allowed us to pass without harm. He wants something, and as his self-assumed title imposes, his presence bids me summons. I fear him. And though my body, riddled with anxieties, wants to retreat from him, I fear what may come from ignoring him more.

So it is that I don my coat and boots like piece-mail, and ride the carriage to the first floor lobby and race across the water swelled streets and into the building across the way. Silence follows me though not of sound but of spirit, as if my very soul has abandoned me to a horrifying end.

Somewhere in the distance I can hear a haunting chord, a ghostly sonata, or is it the sound of a dirge? I can't quite place my finger on it. I follow it as it echoes down the freshly painted walls, across the marble tiled floor and up a Romanesque pillar towards the cake pan ceiling. The sound dances, mockingly, jeering at some memory that I should recognize but don't. The song retreats towards the elevator that lies beyond the abandoned front desk and past the wall of bronze mailboxes like a fleeting spectre. In a few inescapable moments, the phantom melody calls to me from the higher floors, where horror shall have it, some callous oppressor lay in wait.

There's a detestable scent in the air, one of dust and matches that causes the hairs on my back to perk. I no longer think about Mr. Boenger, save the half-wish that he was in my stead. It is here, as I enter the foreboding carriage, that all manner of social depravities I've had to endure the past day vanish from my mind; replaced by the violent terrors that race through my brain and trip into my throat. I hesitantly press the button to the fourteenth-floor and quash my breathing entirely until the sinking sensation of the ascent transforms into goose bumps. The elevator settles. The doors draw back.

A few tablespoons of light manage their way beneath the cracks of the closed apartment doors and spill their contents into the hallway. Would it not be for the frightening nimbus that hovers from the opened portal to apartment number 148, the hallway would be drenched in darkness. I cannot imagine what the Count would want of me, would ask of me, to bring me to this place where he first instituted his original proclamation, staking his claim to the Rue de Borreu. As I take the tiniest of steps down the carpeted path, my heart beats heavily and I am reminded of the time Michael insisted that I take the knife to protect ourselves, to protect Emily above all else, from the evil mechanizations of the Count's intentions. I wish I had brought it here now in the off chance we are to do battle.

At last I reach the inside threshold of the apartment and I peak inside, using the outside drywall as a partial shield from anything that could assault me from within. But the place lies empty save a small card, about four times the size of the one that holds my namesake, facedown and blank side up, near the window. My first inclination is a trap and that the Count lay in wait in the adjoining bedroom and could, at a moment's investigation, spring upon me in surprise.

These are the fancies of our nightly sessions of ghost talk which are followed by the exaggerated tales of usurpation. And as frightened as I am, I find it difficult to imagine that he'd lure me here with such abysmal tactics only to prey upon me when it is just as easy—if not more so—to murder me in my bed. Therefore, with the courage of a pigeon, I make my way inside carefully and, after cautiously peering into the adjoining room and seeing no danger, I kneel down and turn the piece over. There are few words. It's Rachel – by keepers of this city, it's a portrait of Rachel!

It's another of those artistic shots, black and white but with touches of color on her jacket and in the background of Hermes Square. Her hair is long, blonde in color, with the sky a greyish-blue. She stands next to the stone statue, wearing a long black coat that fits her perfectly. Her eyes—yes, I remember now—her eyes are the color of a cloudless sky; how I had forgotten. This confirms it all! Rachel exists. It's like the photo Natalie holds dear, the one she claims to be her daughter, it proves that people at one time or another existed here in this city, but how many? What happened to them? Where did they go? My questions are stalled by a returning presence that darkens the serenity that the picture has woven. I have to get out of here, back to my apartment where I feel safest. I pocket the photo and walk hurriedly out into the hallway.

I hear nothing, save the disturbing quiet that places me on edge. I slow my steps to the elevator so that I may hear any shift or change. As I reach mid-way to my salvation, the scent of ash permeates the hall and a hellish groan skitters across the walls like a handful of centipedes.

His voice is deep and disturbing – like the echoes of the grave. "Never put your trust in wizards, Mr. Bell."

I turn, expecting to see his wicked smile gleaming from out of the darkness of the furthest end of the hallway, but worse! He stands but an inch from reach of light, loitering in the twilight, not far from where I stand. He wears a thick coat of red and black, which is tattered by age, frayed edges, and many loose threads. His face, though shadowed beneath a hood, is bandaged and what peaks between the cracks is a blackness of skin that only results from fire. His lips are cracked and grey. His hand grips the wall, while his fingers dare beneath their bandages to trespass into the light. His nails are yellow, sharpened to a point and partly jagged. I whisper a curse, if one could call it a whisper, as the words escape me in the form of short incomprehensible shriek. He looks at me with a cold glare, one that makes me believe he's seeing more than any single being should. My muscles tense as if waiting for an inevitable collision.

The nefarious Count passes a few breaths from his nostrils before speaking again.

"Go home, Mr. Bell. As they say, there are devils here." He diverts his eyes to the door of apartment number 148, though keeping me in his peripheral.

I back away slowly, ensuring not to stray my eyes else risk missing a shift in his body that'll betray aggression. I hold one hand on the wall, feeling the surface as a means for direction. I count the thresholds, naming each door in my head as I near the boundaries of the carriage, 147…145. I watch each of the Count's heavy breaths, like some rabid creature racing between sanity and the insane. He keeps his gaze poised in the same location, stalking me from the corner of his eyes.

As I reach the carriage, my heel dips into the crevasse between the floor and the elevator. I stumble backwards and I panic. I grab one of the copper railings before slamming into the back wall. The elevator creaks from the impact and the above florescent light flickers momentarily above me. I look up, having lost sight of the Count in my blunder, and realize that he is gone. I hear the door latching shut at the other end of the hallway, and see a shrewd reflection of light catching off the glass pane in the stairwell's door. He had gone, just like that, and without a single word or sound.

I wait in the safety of the enclosure, listening for anything that could be construed as dire or perilous. And while the Count, who stood not but a few feet from me, didn't give much cause for alarm, his presence simply suffocated all means of rationality from my person and chucked it down the elevator shaft. It may be awhile before I gather my courage enough to reclaim it. As I swallow a bit of bile, I think back when Emily and I walked down to the convenience store and were both overcome by fits of anxiety.

Perhaps he had followed us the entire way, watching us as we paraded down Rhine Street. It's the feeling of being stalked, of feeling the frigid touch of death creeping across our backs, a feeling of some horror lurking in the darkness of every shadow but being completely unaware of it all. It's how the rabbit knows when the fox is upon them, a precognitive sensation before the chase, an untailored paranoia that something is amiss. But what then, what would he have to gain by giving me a picture of Rachel? Why here? Why now? And how did he know?

I shouldn't think about it, I shouldn't give answers that I know I would only question later and possibly fear. No, I should get out of here and leave as quickly as I had come. I reach out from the far back portion of the carriage, my finger trembling as it presses the button for the lobby. I grip the rails tightly as the mechanical locks release above and the carriage slowly descends toward the lower floors. The sinking feeling of the descent only adds to my apprehension.

I store the photo behind the newspaper clipping of the west side pier, hiding it as best as I can from anyone who'd take the time to examine the picture frame. I reason to myself that it's temporary until I can find better hiding place. I'm still trembling. Regardless of the terrifying experience I had in meeting the Count, his words play over again in my mind and I've come to accept them as a viable source for concern, *"Never put your trust in wizards, Mr. Bell."* I cannot be sure of exactly who he means, as he himself could be considered something of a wizard on account of his unnatural ability to know where I am and what I am thinking. But it wouldn't make sense for him to lure me up to the other apartment just to warn me about himself, when it is obvious that everyone is already frightened of him. No – though easy to pit him against his own words, it's not what he was referring to; Michael, perhaps? Since I've first known him, Michael has always concealed some aspect of his livelihood and can predict when bad weather approaches. But that's no more wizardry than having a keen knowledge of weather patterns and not wanting to be looked down upon, although Michael did have Natalie forsake the picture of her supposed daughter when he made the ultimate decision to move here.

Maybe that's it? Maybe the Count is warning me about those people who aren't very accepting of a plausible past. Maybe, in his own peculiar way, he's warning me to protect certain secrets such as Rachel, such as… that song? Emily expressed her own concern about me playing it in front of others. What is its importance? I figured it had something to do with her wanting to feel a part of something that no one else was, but maybe unconscious or otherwise, she feared what would happen if others knew of its existence. I can't jump to any conclusions, but it may be in my best interest to be cautious in these things. When it all comes down to it, I don't even know how much credence I can give to the Count's warnings.

My thoughts are interrupted by the sound of the doorknob turning. Looking over the top of the loveseat, I am able to identify the familiar face of Emily as she enters through the door wearing the same clothes from the day before. I stand up in acknowledgment but her face is turned down and combative. She doesn't look at me, and it hurts to see her like this.

She pauses momentarily and mentions, "I'm just here to pick up some clothes," before taking a path through the kitchen and toward the bedroom.

I get up and intercept her, blocking her way as she rounds the bar that separates the kitchenette from the living room. She must not have noticed, as she startles when we meet. Her hand rises instantly to her heart.

"Samuel, please. Just let me…"

I wrap my arms around her, pulling her into a loving embrace. Her arms hang limp at her sides and her muscles clench.

"What? I—" her hands come up to my elbows. "You're shaking." Her flat intonation is lost to a comfortable concern.

I hold her closer, tightening my grip around her waist and I lean my head on her shoulder. I can feel her relaxing into me and eventually her arms slip beneath mine and her hands end cupping my back. I am shaking. Trembling more than I originally thought. With everything, I don't want to be angry anymore. Standing here, I realize how much I need her, how much her voice keeps me together and from falling victim to those past feelings of isolation and abandonment. She feels it to, I think. As we stand there holding one another, the past few days slowly melt away to a time when the two of us existed in a state of perpetual bliss, a time when things weren't so complicated. I bring my hand up to the back of her head and brush my fingertips through her hair.

"I've seemed to overstep myself, Emily."

She nuzzles her head into my chest and repeats a bit of the past, "Indeed you have."

"Can you tell me something?" I ask as she remains in silence, stealing a hand up to my heart. "Did Bach ever eat pancakes at midnight?"

She hiccups and my shirt feels wet from rain. She sniffs, perhaps from some allergy before saying, "Pancakes it is."

At the day's celebration, I invite the Lockes and even sent Emily to rouse Mr. Boenger from his apartment for dinner. Since early afternoon, after things between Emily and I have rekindled into our usual friendship again, I've turned to lighter moods. I realize that it does not matter who Emily chooses to be with, either Boenger or myself, as her company is all I truly desire. And there's no real alarm as of yet, since the two haven't made any official declaration that they are a couple—as much as my heart would be pained—I'd have to accept her decision.

The Lockes arrive first, Natalie—as always—taking the lead with her husband filing in behind her. We say our usual greetings and I take whatever garments they find too heavy or decorative to carry any longer. Despite their short walk from the twenty-fifth floor, I always find it of high character to bring down coats or scarves, as if coming out from beneath the rain. Michael tips his ribbon traced fedora at me before handing it off to go with the rest of their things.

"Lovely weather. Once again I am complete shocked at the recent shift in dynamics. Don't you agree, love?" Michael smiles with a tinge of sarcasm as he helps his wife out of a frill coat.

"Oh, stop." Natalie passes me a hint of agitation, the type that comes after having to endure hours of his lecturing on one topic or another. But she smiles, as if the joke had been funny.

"It is ghastly isn't it? Especially for Mr. Boenger to up and leave as he did without indication of where he was going. And though I love the good chap, I've never been one for secrets."

"I'm sure he had his reasons." Natalie interjects. "He had that same look in his eye that you get whenever something strikes your fancy. I'm sure he'll be back once he gathers what he's looking for."

I take their belongings and set them atop the bar as delicately and well arranged as possible before speaking my mind. "Boenger is not here?"

"Of course he's not here. He got up quite unexpectedly and said he's 'found it' or something or other. Don't you rem—" he stops in realization of a misstep. His face tightens and his eyebrow twitches. "I'm sorry, Mr. Bell. I've seemed to have forgotten your invitation. I could have sworn that you were there."

I lie to save any unwanted awkwardness. "It's alright. I wasn't feeling well this morning. I would have had to decline regardless."

"Well, no harm then." An invisible hand wipes away his troubled face. He slowly strips off a pair of white gloves from his hands and pockets them. "Yes – Mr. Boenger, after many wonderful hours of entertainment was in mid-sentence and then grew incredibly pale. He sat in silence for a few seconds, his eyes wavering back and forth. I thought he was going to faint. But then this glow came to his features and stood with declaration that he had found it and excused himself from our company. When I asked him in what he was referring to, he simply said it would win the day. It was very theatrical and all rather sudden. I haven't seen him since."

"Do you know when he'll return?" I start to worry. If Boenger had indeed left in the middle of this morning's get together, I wonder if Emily knew where he was going. And if so, where was Emily now?

"No, Samuel." Natalie puts a hand on my arm. "We haven't the foggiest."

"If you don't mind me asking," Michael pardons as he walks over towards the window, "Where is Emily? Not on the stroll again, I wager?" He eyes me from over his shoulder like a snake to an unprotected egg.

"I sent her in search of Mr. Boenger to invite him for dinner. I wanted to make him feel that he was welcome despite my earlier mood."

"Inviting him into the den, my word Samuel – I *have* misjudged you. This shall be a marvelous sport."

"I beg your pardon?"

"How does the old phrase go? Gentlemen at war?"

"You must be joking."

"Am I wrong to assume that you and Mr. Boenger are both after the same thing? Love is not a resource that can be shared, Samuel. I presume you are taking the necessary precautions not to lose what you hold dearest. It is Emily we speak of is it not?"

Michael has changed over the course of his isolation. He's always managed to be a little outspoken, but never to the severity of bluntness. He smiles and I wonder if he benefits from some manner of entertainment in all this.

"Intentions are still being determined." I say. His grin puts me to anger, "Have I missed some joke?"

"No, no joke. I see no hilarity in this. What propels my face sir, is my profound interest in the due process. Two worthy gentlemen vying for the love of a single woman, it's reminiscent of the classic romances. I envy you." He takes his usual seat on the couch and directs me to join him. "I wonder if you could grant me a favor, Mr. Bell. I haven't heard you play in such a long time. Can we expect something from your piano tonight?"

I'm unsure of whether to take him as friend or foe, but for everyone's sake I force myself to accept the former. I bow to him, as a musician would his audience and eventually take my hands to the ivory keys of the baby grand.

Emily returns within an hour, just in time for dinner but without Henry Boenger. She doesn't say a word and keeps to herself.

Somber. And though as quick to the tongue as Michael had been earlier, he simply offers a smile and unrelated conversation. I imagine that he is just as curious as I am about Mr. Boenger's whereabouts, but sits back in observation, reveling as if seated in a grand theater.

Natalie takes it upon herself to dismiss as much of the contention as possible. She tells a few jokes that she had read the other day and even goes as far as suggesting the possibility of coming to me for proper voice lessons. And though I remind her that I am a pianist and not much of a vocalist, she shrugs her shoulders and claims that she still believes that I could offer her some manner of instruction, if not a steady accompanist. She says she's been studying music in her free time and, as impressed as we all are at ambitions, we manage to expel the strange heaviness that has acquired in my apartment for the past few days.

After dinner we continue with a switch between Emily and I at the piano, each playing our favorite tunes and for the first time a four hand duet to musicians such as Czerny and Brahms. During one of the waltzes, Michael gathers enough gall to stand up and ask Natalie to dance. They then slide back the loveseat and adjacent coffee table, and take to the center floor. I can not remember a time when things were as light-hearted. And since a long time coming, I could not recall that last I have seen Emily smile as widely as she did now.

When it is all finally over and the night comes far too soon, when the Lockes are nearly out the door, Michael grabs me by the shoulder and presses close to my ear and whispers, "Longing makes the heart grow fonder." Before I am able to ask what he means, he then shakes my hand, wishes me a goodnight and walks arm in arm with Natalie toward the elevator door.

A week passes and still no sign of Boenger. During those days, Emily and I entertain each other in conversations; walks through Hermes Square and along the park; piano play and for once a slow dance to the sound of rain. She doesn't speak much of him and whenever I bring up the topic she grows increasingly quiet and refuses to go on with a tight-lipped silence. I'm afraid that he's become a mute point and I wonder if she misses him, worries about him or feels guilty? I've come to find that no one knows where he's gone, not even Emily. Whatever it is, it allots for a schism between us. Though she looks at me with those wondrous eyes and uncanny spirit, she still acts hesitant. I keep thinking of what Michael said, about the longing of the heart. Maybe she longs for him. Maybe not.

There's one thing that I've found bothers me more than the rest, it is that Emily has shifted from a fragile creature to one who is capable of managing without me. She proved that she's capable of going out into the city on her own and capable of disappearing for a couple of days. She met Boenger, can play her own games, and needs very little instruction from me when it comes to the piano. In fact, I'm depressed that I am no longer needed in her development as a person and that my role as a mentor has finally come to its end. Now my pupil is ready to mature into whatever it is she wishes to be. Perhaps, what stops her from being completely with Boenger is that she feels obligated or, at the worst of it, indebted. Is it possible that I am stifling her with my needs as an individual? Is it possible that all I was and will ever be is the old mentor? There may come a time when Emily decides that she no longer wishes my company and that she'd rather pursue a life elsewhere. It saddens me to say, but will I be able to handle it?

By the ninth day, when the rains have ceased and a few small droplets of light drip from the clouds, a hard and frantic knock is forced against our door. Emily is first to answer and without invite or word otherwise, Michael forces his way inside up until he is able to see the both of us.

"Quickly! You two! To the roof – there's something marvelous to see!" He's out of breath and though winded he spends no time waiting on us before he's back out into the hallway and racing for the elevator.

We chase him, though an entire elevator ride apart, we chase him; all the way to the twenty-fifth-floor and then up the stairwell and into the attic, that is easier described as a floor between floors, before we reach the ladder of stairs that lead out onto the roof.

The rain is barely noticeable, but I can taste the moisture. Tiny droplets find their way to me here and there, while I cast my eyes about the vacancy of the roof. Natalie is there. Her eyes are cast skyward, squinting beneath the indirect rays of sunlight that trickle through the vapors above. Her coat flutters slightly to match the inconsistent winds, but she keeps it wrapped snuggly around her to guard against the remnant winter chills. Michael waits for us at the top stair, ready to offer his hand in the case of a stumble due to the slick roof.

"What is this about?" I ask as I emerge fully into the light. "Are we due for some sun?"

"We are here to witness a marvel, Samuel! Simply a marvel!" Michael touts as he pulls Emily out of the darkness.

I take a glance about, hoping to catch some mysterious prize that was hiding behind one of generators or the elevator's mechanisms, but nothing. The three of us make our way towards Natalie in the center.

"Can you see it?" Natalie breaks in with her hand shielding her eyes from the glare of the stratus.

"More pigeons?" Emily asks while attempting to mimic her stare. "I've already seen a flock today."

I struggle to look beyond the clouds, searching desperately to find some manner of portent written in the odd shapes. Still nothing. I'm about to give up, call it a practical joke and demand the meaning of rousing us all the way up here, but Michael points to a once empty bed of sky fog.

"There she is! Oh – Samuel, you're in for a treat."

I hear something, quiet at first, but growing in intensity; a light hum and whirring above. I stare down Michael's finger, leaning my head in order to better follow it. At times I spot a small speck that teams with the light, but it isn't but a millisecond before it disappears in the brume, and I question whether I had truly seen anything at all. Then, a while longer in search I see it! – an object, small but growing on approach. It is teardrop in shape, bubbled near the center, with four arms that extend from its underbelly. Lights flash beneath it, a strange rotation of blue, reds and whites that coincide with whatever direction the machine floats. It is indeed a wonder, as never in my life would I imagine seeing such a construct. It nears, and I am able to judge the exact size, a vehicle no more than eight feet across, perhaps four foot wide maybe more. I can see the disruption of air as it circulates fumes from the wind-swept turbines attached to the end of each extended arm. The windows are tinted, each reflecting its surroundings, like mirrors.

The flying car reaches about twenty feet and then rotates around us so that we may view it up close and in-flight, before it levitates away not ten feet from our location before landing; a pair of wheels flip from out of their hidden compartments and settle on the tar-coated roof. None of us move. We are all enraptured with its sleek design, curves, and its well-polished gleam. Beads of condensation slip off its silver surface and as a hiss of air breaks the suffocated sounds of the engines, a door stretches open like a bird stretching its wing. A figure steps out and leans on the front portion, baring the grin from the Cheshire cat, one that only comes from a high ego.

Emily rushes to him and hugs him around the waist like a child would their parent's leg. "Where have you been?"

Michael only reaffirms the source of the bad taste in my mouth.

"Splendid work Boenger! Just absolutely magnificent! So this is what you've been up to the past week. However did you manage it?" Michael says gleefully with adoring eyes. "May I?" His hand hovers over the hood, his fingers just itching to pit its realism to the test.

Henry pats the body. "Be my guest." He chuckles as he attempts to pry Emily from his belt. "The design has been in my head since I woke. I just couldn't figure out how to stabilize the aerodynes. It just didn't make sense to me. Then all of a sudden I had it!"

Natalie walks up to her husband to catch a better glimpse, "How were you able to manufacture it? Where did you get the metal?"

"There are a few factories scattered about the warehouse district. Luckily, some of them had old car parts lying about. I just took what I needed and handcrafted the rest from pieces of scrap metal and plastic I found tucked away in the northern quarter."

"What's it run on?" I ask amidst the sea of questions. Despite my dislike for Boenger, I can not withhold my wonderment.

"Kerosene at the moment until, that is, I can find something else to run off of. My goal is electricity, but that would require a whole new blueprint."

Emily runs to the other side of the flyer, opens the door and jumps inside. "Take me for a ride! I want to see the world!"

Beonger waves his hand in a coquettish manner. "I think we have fuel enough for a couple trips around the city, but only four people at a time. We'll have to make multiple trips."

I am about to issue Natalie to join her, but Michael steps back and hastily interjects, "Natalie and I will wait for your return." A sly grin snakes its way across his cheek and I cannot help but question whether his patience is inspired by friendship or to allow others to test the car's safety.

The thought of plummeting to death in the steel contraption doesn't make it easy for me when I slip into the backseat. But the thought of letting Emily go out alone, not to mention with *him*, is too unbearable. I can see it now, the turning of the gears in Michael's skull, as he thinks—no doubt—of the sheer competitiveness that I'll have to top in order to prove myself the better to Emily. His whole manner is beginning to unnerve me, especially in his belief that Emily could be won by simple creations or youthful charm. Boenger plops into the driver's seat and instructs the two of us on the location and proper procedure—in case of an emergency—to fit ourselves with parachutes that are velcroed beneath our seats.

With the pressing of buttons and a flip of a switch, the vehicle's turbines begin to oscillate with a low-pitch hum. Michael nods to me from the front window and steps back to where Natalie lights a cigarette. I've only seen her smoke when she's nervous.

"Here we go." Henry warns as his right hand pushes a metal lever towards the dashboard.

A sinking feeling, one like I previously experienced when meeting with the Count, bathes in my stomach acids as the car lifts slowly off the ground. Emily scoots to the edge of her seat in order to peer out the front passenger side window, as the Lockes – I imagine – disappear in the height. I find myself pressed against the seat, in fear of a sudden drop, my hands already ensuring that

Boenger hadn't been lying about the parachutes. I try and think of something to keep my mind busy once the car accelerates and dips down closer towards the cityscape.

"What do you call it?" I swallow a lump. "Your car?"

"It's a whirly-gig!" Emily interrupts as she ganders at the grey sky.

"Actually—" Boenger jets in, "I was thinking about calling it the Model-A1 Boenger or an Aircar."

"That's a stupid name! Whirly-gig is much better, I think. Who in their right mind would point at this thing and say, 'I'm going to fly in my Model-A1'. People would much rather say, 'Get in my whirly-gig'. And that's what you should name it."

"I have to hand it to you, Emily – you have the knack for the unusual." He offers with a hesitant chuckle.

This is my cue. "I think I like whirly-gig myself." I mention, knowing full well that it is an attack on Boenger's pride.

I can see Henry's face in the upper portion of the front windshield which acts as a rear view mirror. His face shifts from a self-righteous grin to sobriety. "I built it, I get to name it."

"Well, you can call it what you want." Emily mentions uncaringly. "But I'm going to call it a whirly-gig."

Silence pursues as we fly between buildings. It's just as well, as the three of us are caught up in the grand sight of witnessing the city from a bird's eye. The skyscrapers are focused in the center of the island, all magnificent in their splendor. The island itself is shaped like a gourd: fat in the south, but skinny and round near the top. We pass over Hermes square, over the top of the Gothic cathedral, and around the terraced manors in the northern section. What would have taken hours, possibly a half-day to reach by foot, we reach in the matter of minutes by air.

We pass by a flock a pigeons, ones that Emily is quick to point out; smudging her fingerprint against the glass. Everything whooshes by in a calm whirring of the fans, and for the first time we are able to see the far stretches of the ocean and its empty expanse. We round the western shoreline, making view of a small patch of forestry before cutting through a thick area of warehouses and factories as we make our way above and beyond the Westside pier, the one I point out to Emily as the place I had found her. She smiles at me from a failed reminiscence, but the look in her eyes is enough to let me know she appreciates it. Boenger cuts easterly up Rhine Street and the three of us eagerly wait to pass the convenience store.

All is going well, until Emily jabs her finger once more against the glass and cries, "Samuel, look! Mannequins."

"Where!?" Both Boenger and I say in unison. I lean out of my seat and hang partially in the forward compartment in an attempt to see what Emily had been referring to.

"Just back there! I saw one."

"Was it the Count?"

"No! It was a person. I saw it standing on the right-hand side."

"Henry! Go back!" I yell as I grab his shoulders.

He halts the vehicle in mid-air and spins us back around. It isn't long before I see what Emily is talking about. But there isn't just one, there are two figures standing there, looking up at us from the sidewalk. Their faces and clothes are a little difficult to make out from our height, but they are people none the less.

Emily raises my excitement when she points out her window a few seconds later. "There's another one! In the apartment building over there! That's three for me." She giggles.

Boenger flies us closer as we swing up a neighboring street.

"There's one." He points, "On the balcony."

"Another there! Five…six…"

"Seven!" Emily yells, "No – Ten! There were three by the streetlamp."

The excitement drains from all our faces as we start counting more and more littered amidst the streets and peering at us from the apartment windows.

"They weren't here yesterday." Henry mutters. "I did a test flight. There was no one."

"Samuel…" Emily casts me a visage caught between confusion and fear. "The apartments… they're furnished."

Dread. Absolute dread. Emily is right. They are *all* furnished! We pass by windows, apartments, skyscraper condos and flats, every one of them have furniture of some kind. A bed, a dresser, a couch and the people who sit on them; some active, some limp. Those who are awake peer at us with their beady little eyes; all staring their vacant stares, like a human apocalypse in reverse. We aren't witnessing the spread of a miracle, we are witnessing something that we don't understand, something so harrowing that it causes my bones to shudder. They all look ridged in their motion, like automatons learning to walk. I am overwhelmed with a disturbing notion that the silence of the city has been swept away by the confused cries of its inhabitants. The barren streets are now a wasteland of activity. It is a different city than we had woken up to. My mind calls out, *flee, flee, run away* but my lips are unable to mouth them.

Emily grabs Boenger by the arm, her eyes never leaving the window as she strangles out the words, "Take me home!"

We return to the top of the apartment, both Michael and Natalie still wait for us diligently so they may have their trip. They rush to us with smiling faces, but their features melt at the sight of us.

Natalie brings a gloved hand to her mouth and cries, "You're all so pale."

Emily crawls out of the car and onto the roof like some deranged dog. She sits and stares blankly at the blacktop hoping for sanity to return.

Boenger stays in the car, and it is I who must speak the unexplained. "We found people, but not just one, tens, twenty, maybe hundreds of them." I look at Michael's perplexed face. "The apartments Michael, they're all full."

He rallies a cloak of courage behind him, a strength I never knew he was capable of showing. He grabs me by the shoulders. "Then we must hurry! We've spent enough time dallying in this apartment, we need to go."

"Go?" The blink the question, "Go where?"

"If there are people, then that means we need to stake our claims as quickly as we are able. We should have moved to the northern manors in the first place, we need to grab them before anyone else does. Mr. Boenger, how much weight can your vehicle carry?"

I swat his hands from off my shoulders. "You're just going to leave?!"

"It's simply economics, Mr. Bell: the greater the demand, the higher rate of consumption. We need to consolidate. We need to let people know that we were here first and deserve a better style of living."

"But we are just fine right here. What does moving have anything to do with economics?"

"Because Samuel – if we do not take what's rightfully ours, then someone will take it from us. There comes a time when we must pursue something greater than ourselves. It is our duty to assume the mantle of the higher class. And without the distinction of class, there will be no order. If we are to survive this we need to go now! It is safer there."

I shoot a glance among the rest of our society, looking from face to face in order to acquire some form of support. Emily lifts her head and now nods rapidly; Natalie looks away, while Boenger silently agrees. I am outnumbered in the vote, and all I can do is feel this inescapable feeling I first felt when the door to my apartment door latched shut – a sense of looming oblivion and the loss of all hope.

Michael is making the decisions now. No matter how I plead, Michael would have some retort that'd ring true with the rest of them. He thought this out. He knew this day would come, or at least he planned for it. We are allowed a small box worth of items, essentials mainly: food, health kits, blankets and so on. The aircar can only carry so much. The entire time I help Emily pack her pancake mix and other favorite dinner items, I cannot help but look at the picture frame that held the photo of Rachel behind it and ask myself, *"Will I ever find her now?"*

I look at the piano and remember all those nights of piano play and conversations. I glance in the bedroom, to the time when I managed to carry Emily all the way from the shore, where I had collapsed and dreamed. Lost, everything is lost. Soon everything we did, everything we experienced would be nothing more than a memory. I knew, nestled deep within me, that someone else would take habitation in this place and I would be forever barred from it.

Once everything is packed, we join everyone on the roof. I watch as Michael counsels with Natalie, as Boenger helps Emily into the car as they beam half smiles between one another. At that point, I realize something Michael had said about pursuing things greater than ourselves. I grasp the importance of memories and the importance of dreams. I envision sitting at the piano alone, seeking out those notes to that familiar song that still chimes in my head. I daydream of Rachel and mouth the words *maybe*. Then my lips mouth another set of words, but this time with voice.

"I'm not going." They all look at me like I've stabbed them in the heart.

"Samuel…" Emily begs.

"What do you mean that you're not going?!" Michael protests. "Of course you're going!"

"I'm not leaving." It's hard for me. It feels like a huge rock is weighing upon my chest. But who was I to change my lot. "This is where I belong." This is where I'll find Rachel, this is where I woke, and this is where life had originally sprung.

"Do you realize what might happen? People are going to be crawling over themselves like a horde of frenzied rats. Do you realize the anarchy that might erupt over territory disputes, food, and shelter?" He is angry. I can see it in his wrinkled face, the arch in his eyebrows, and tiny flames in his eyes.

I refuse to relent. "And the northern manors will be different?"

"At least it'll be away from the mess of it! There's less housing up there, and the hill will act as a deterrent for most."

"Just the same, I'm not going."

Michael stares at me, rending a vicious glare deep into my soul. "Then so be it." He grabs his wife's hand. "Come on Natalie. Our *host* is not coming." He drags her towards the car and hoists up the driver-side door for her to enter.

Emily pushes past Boenger in a fit of hysterics and crumbles in my arms. "You have to come with us, Samuel. I can't eat pancakes alone. Who will play me Mozart? Who will play me Beethovan?" Her eyes fill with dew.

"I can't. My place is here. This is where I belong. I can't just leave everything behind. There's purpose here, since the day it all began. You have friends now. They'll take care of you. You don't want to be here if things get out of hand."

"But—you saw all those dreadful people. They're all monsters, every one of them." Her eyes swell and she lightly hits her palms against my chest. "This isn't the way it's supposed to be. Who will take care of me?"

"Boenger will. He'll keep you safe." I steal a look for compliance and he nods. "He's a good friend. Everything will be fine. I can't keep you bound to me. There should be no debt between us. I realize that now."

"No debt…" Her eyes lapse into a stare. "No debt… someday when all the dreams are gone…discovered… for when will that be, Samuel? Three times and then declines forever." She sobs uncontrollably and I motion with my head for Boenger's help. With all the stress, she's lost her rationality.

He takes her by the waist and leads her back toward the car, the entire time she mutters incomprehensible things. It all must be too much for her.

Emily claws Boenger's chest before she sinks into the passenger seat. "He doesn't understand, Henry. He just doesn't understand."

He looks at her with a face scarred by guilt. "I know."

I walk up to him after he closes the door.

"Take care of her, Henry. I'm sure you'd prove the better man. She needs constant attention. Do not take your eyes off her else she'd be spirited away by one of her fantasies. Keep her warm. Above all else, keep her warm."

"I will." He shakes my hand the way competitors do, as they wish for a few seconds to be in the other's place.

I escort him to his place as the driver and Natalie's face emerges from the descending backseat window. "I'll be sure to write." She says in goodbye. "When all this is over."

I nod. "I look forward to it."

The aerodynes hum with life as the car rises from off the roof and is drawn into the sky above like a set of invisible pulleys. The car roars as it speeds off, leaving a trail of vapor behind that is visible for a few minor seconds before dissipating. The old pain has returned to my chest, that seeping venom that manages to make its nest in the lower portions of my veins that creep along the narrow passages and branch throughout the rest of me like tainted blood intent on spoiling the rest.

There on the roof, I am plagued with a discomforting tingle as my limbs grow weak from seeing them go. I am on the verge of collapse as emotion hits me all at once: Emily's crying face, her debilitating state – how I hope she will be well without me. The true test is whether I will be without her. I must keep in mind that this is not forever. In remembering her tears, I cannot help but shed a few of my own. And as the clouds churn above they release their day's work across the entirety of the CitySpire. I am caught in the downpour. The water from me is lost in the torrent as the aircar disappears from sight.

Part II
The Sea Waifs

10

The crunching sound stirs a nervous shiver to coil itself round my spine. As well, an apprehensive bubbling manages its way up and out of my throat as my jackboots grind against the pieces of glass that are scattered across the street. My teeth chatter as I take a deep breath of damp air once reaching but a foot from his body. The man I knew from the past week, he who lived across the street and in the apartment where the Count had once left his messages, now lay motionless on the cold concrete. He jumped – just like that – from out of his apartment window, through the glass and then… I was fortunate to not have seen him land. The sight of it would have been unbearable.

He's wearing a white silk shirt matched with shinny metal buttons with black tops, bleached trousers and barefoot. It's something one would lounge in, nothing comparable to social elite, or in the least presentable for greeting company. It reflects some semblance of a makeshift funeral shroud. Perhaps he wanted to be comfortable, or perhaps he didn't feel that his final demise would draw a crowd. Surprisingly there isn't much blood, just a few traces on his shirt where the glass had cut and a slow trickle that slides out of his mouth and onto the pavement. Seven floors. I thought he would be worse off. Not a single protruding bone.

His eyes are closed. His mind must have come to grips with his decision the moment he broke through the glass. It was something that I had once contemplated my first week in the CitySpire. The fear of never being buried or ever being remembered was enough to scare me from the deed. Now, with so many people arriving every day, it is no longer a deterrent. I crouch down for a closer look and I notice the white edge of a card jetting out from his pocket, "You are Richard Farley" I wonder if he believed it. It is identical to my own: gold embossed, hard matte. Seven floors… I can't imagine what went through his mind the last few seconds he had left.

His black hair is groomed, a bit rustled from the fall. His skin is pale, paler than mine, as the city's temperatures have already sucked the warmth out of him; well shaven. I look up to the very height of his fall. A large gaping hole now takes the place of the smooth window pane. The glass is tough, but not indestructible. He had a running start. I saw something in him those many days before…

The apartment sighs from the downpour. I sit just hours after their egress: Boenger, Michael, Natalie and dearest Emily. I see a part of them – a representation of our past interactions – shown clearly in furniture, picture frames and music. My mind caves and while the decay caused by the painful parting grips at my organs, I am whisked away to walk with passing haunts, to glide through memories.

I brush the smooth stained wood of the baby grand with my finger tips and stop short of the apartment window to watch the rain begin to fall. I return my attention towards the silent room and see myself sitting on the couch in conversation with Natalie; Michael replaces me not long after, ranting on about the Count and the ever-present feeling of the divine; and then Emily, fiddling with some ditty on the piano, laughing at her mistakes and I smile at her progress.

I retreat my gaze not wanting to put myself through the pains of memories. I breathe against the glass. My breath fogs the window and I mimic Emily's tiny prints, "YAWA OG". It seems so long ago. I chuckle a pitiful laugh that squeezes a couple drops from my eyes, as in realization of the irony of those words. She never wanted to be a part of any society. She wanted nothing more but the simple pleasures of my company and my company alone. What gets me is how she was fearful that I would inevitably leave her for the Lockes, and yet here I am being the one completely alone. I feel as if they have abandoned me. Instead of staying and fighting for what was ours, they have all fled to hide in a life they only dreamed of having.

I long to escape from fantasies by retreating to my room. The bedspread and sheets have all been kicked off the bed – a tendency Emily would adopt during the middle of the night and always when I was cold. Sitting on the nightstand, nearest the bed, is the small music box that she gave to me. I only wish that she had asked to stay with me, albeit the consequence of danger. Maybe it is better this way. Emily shall no longer feel that she is indebted to me, that she can make her own decisions without touching any semblance of guilt. But above all else, she is far from the waking city, far from the influence of the Count, and in the hands of Boenger who swore to protect her from harm.

"Remember me dearest Emily, remember me."

I wrap myself in covers and with regret and sorrow in my heart, I curl up and fall quietly to sleep.

I wake in the dismal hand of darkness. The apartment keeps to the silence I must now reacquaint myself with. I dreamed something about the waves, high rolling surfs and the thunderous crash of water turning over on itself. There is more to it. It is one of those many dreams that held some significance, but prefers to remain a mystery as the lift in consciousness buries the thoughts in some remote portion of my mind. It is cold. So is the loneliness that has settled against the window pane in light, though frequent, sprinkle.

I do not wish to spend my time basking in memories of the past. Nor do I desire to keep company with the figments of old friends. I need to get out, a chance to escape the inner workings of my soul. And so, without stopping for a change of clothes or a coveted snack, I decide to leave my abode with my coat and boots, ensuring to lock the illusions of yesterday within.

Not wishing to go outside, at least not to have to deal with whatever devil happens to be walking the street, I breathe in the isolation of the building. I just don't have the courage to contend with anyone's lapse in memory or questions on what has become of the world – especially since I have nothing to give them except sympathy and the truth of our predicament. I just don't have the spirit for it. The hallway is empty and still no sound of habitation raps against my ears. I exhale from a breath I forgot to expel; a rise of nervousness that is now manifesting in my chest. Perhaps a trip to the roof will give me room to breathe and not fall into any troublesome memory. But then a thought, or more like a brush of curiosity, plays rhythm against my brain. What is the state of the Lockes' old apartment?

One could call it snooping, as I make my way towards the elevator and press the button that sends me to the 25th-floor, but the place is as good as abandoned. The Lockes took with them what they considered to be the most important pieces of their lives. What interests me is what they decided to leave behind. I think its Michael's prior isolation that interests me the most. What was he doing during that time? Natalie had mentioned that he found an obsession and that it was nigh impossible to draw him away from it, but what could have harvested his utter devotion? Emily thought he had simply grown weary of us and especially lost interest in me since our discovery of the Count's request on the glass. She never really said it outright, but it was very apparent that she felt his friendship was based solely off my ownership of the CitySpire.

The elevator reaches their floor in a matter of seconds and only a few more before I am able to reach their door at the farthest end of the hallway. The door is shut. An apple bounces into my throat as I touch the brass doorknob and check to see if it's locked. In me there is the fear that the Lockes did not actually vacate their apartment and that I was going to walk in on them. As I rotate the knob and push in on the door, I am assaulted by the odd sensation that I'm breaking into some long forgotten tomb.

The lights catch the motion of the door and brighten enough to make out objects strewn about the room. I'm reminded of my encounter with their previous habitation back on Herbertson Street; apartment number 7, a lucky number for such a dark and decrepit place. It is different here. Much different. The layout is the same as my previous venture, the time when Emily had gone missing and I was able to catch a glimpse of the inside. However, it had been awhile since I was able to stay long enough to take it all in. Of course the design is much the same as mine, a separated kitchenette via a white bar from the living room, as well as a side bedroom and attached bath. Michael's desk rests against the wall where my piano would be, a leather sofa and veneer coffee table in the same position as my own.

I'm not all too interested in what their cupboards hold, although I'll have to grab whatever food items they left behind and add it to my personal stock. Since packing, I didn't have much left. In place of the picture frames I have scattered about the wall-shelf just left of the door, are a line of books with varying titles: "The Origin of Species", "The Prince", "Paradise Lost", "Faust", and "The Tempest" among others. I draw the previous one off the shelf and flip through the pages, a few dog-eared and quotes circled: "In few, they hurried us aboard a bark, / Bore us some leagues to sea…", and then a few pages in, "The island's mine by Sycorax my mother," followed by, "His art is of such power, / It would control my dam's god, Setebos,". I flip to the end, where written beneath the last line of Caliban is "You disappoint me" in pencil, both underlined and circled.

A folded piece of paper drops from within the notes and definitions sections. I replace the book back on the shelf and recover the article. When unfolded, it reveals the picture of some ungodly beast devouring the moon. Written next to it in the same handwriting are the words, "Make that good mischief".

It is all cryptic to me. I'm led to believe that Michael had been working on something that pertained to his idealisms on the divine, or at least his thoughts on the nature of the island. It would take me weeks to go through all the books, to read and speculate what's been flowing through his head. Those past feelings of drowning, being trapped and being on an unstable course causes a touch of anxiety to swell in my chest. It's like he's dragging me through the graveyard again, digging in the tainted earth to answer whether anyone is buried beneath. I decide that it's best left for another time. I reopen the book and slide the picture back in and sort it alongside its brothers.

Michael's desk is laid out neatly: a stack of paper on the top with a sharpened pencil waiting nearby, a bottle of glue and rubber cement. The drawers are empty. Nothing too important. He must have done some writing here and possibly took notes. I shut the drawers and move towards the bedroom.

The bed is unkempt, much like mine, the comforter tossed and the sheets practically falling off on their own. There's a dark armoire on the left-hand side and a few cardboard boxes in the right-hand corner. I find my way to the wrought iron handles of the wooden closet and draw back the doors. Inside are remnant suits, left over lingerie and dresses. At the bottom is a black leather purse, and inside are an assortment of makeup, a hand mirror and tissues. The cardboard boxes on the other hand, carry a few more books, a couple knick-knacks from local stores, a porcelain doll with black locks, and a newspaper that reads: Saturday, "The CitySpire Gazette" of course there are no articles, just photos. The front page is dedicated to a single picture, that of the statue in Hermes Square. It's identical to the picture of Rachel, save this one is in black and white and she's missing from the photo. I'm unsure of what it means.

I shuffle through the rest of the paper looking for more clues. I see photos of the cathedral, the graveyard, and even a lovely up-front photo of one of the Victorian mansions that rests in the northern portion of the city. I wish I knew where the newspaper had come from, if it had been printed ahead of time, or if it—along with how everything else—appeared when the Lockes first awoke. Perhaps then, after realizing its point of origin, I can find some answers into the reason of its publication. I snatch it up with intent of taking it with me. Besides, I still have a few picture frames that I haven't been able to fill quite yet. Before I leave, I also decide to take a few of the aforementioned books for comfortable study in my apartment, the doll as well.

When I return to my apartment I am startled enough that I nearly drop everything, as across the street, nestled where there was once nothing before, is a man. He stands there staring in a white shirt and trousers, his hand in place where the Count had once rested his. His hair is black, short, but slicked back from some manner of hair gel or grease. He blinks at me from across the way, non-hostile or in any particular threatening way, but more absent than what I am comfortable with. His apartment is furnished with a sofa, loveseat, desk and chair. It is troubling, especially for how quickly his apartment filled in the meager time that I was away.

As I continue into my apartment and set my things atop the coffee table, he continues to watch me as intently as I had upon entering the room. His shoulders are slumped and his body unmoving. I'd think him dead if there wasn't an occasional fog of breath against the glass. It's the same feeling that Emily came out of her coma with. Perhaps he is an empty slate just waiting for his surroundings to imprint him with a personality. How on earth did the furniture arrive so quickly?

I unload as casually as possible atop the glass coffee table, setting the books to one side and placing the doll in the farthest seat on the sofa. The doll is comprised of a porcelain face, painted pale white, with glass eyes that shine with a sky blue. The doll's hair is long and black that highlights the white batiste dress it wears. I'm vaguely reminded of the girl in Natalie's photo. Perhaps this was her way of comforting herself during those dreams of longing. I wonder if Michael ever made the same connection.

Finding the couch, I bury my head in my hands—my elbows press deep into my knee caps—as I search for a gasp of air that had cleared my lungs of that lurking depression that stings their inner edges. One hand manages to meet my chin and as I pull myself up with intent of drawing open a neighboring book and researching further into Michael's obsession, I realize that the man from across the street is mimicking me, sitting and all. When I reach for a book and place it into my lap, he grabs at nothing, but just the same he places the airy item in his lap for mime's sake.

I humph at his childishness. Irritatingly, it reminds me of those same types of games Emily and Boenger had the tendencies of playing together. Despite my agitation he persists in turning the front cover and sits in stares at a set of illusionary words that only he can read.

The book I picked up happens to be Milton's "Paradise Lost". Underlined in many places are quotes from the 2nd book, "Armed with hell flames and fury all at once / O'er heaven's high towers to force resistless way, / Turning our tortures into horrid arms / Against the torturer;" and "what can be worse / Than to dwell here, driven out from bliss, condemned / In this abhorrèd deep to utter woe;". Michael writes along the side of the page, "Where does this guilt stem from? Where will it take me now? – Sympathetic, but what one must do to find his place in heaven?"

It all gives me a headache. If there were any clues as to what he was up to, or at least what he was thinking, they are obscured in riddles throughout the pages of every book he has on his shelves. It would take me perhaps a lifetime, or the better half of the year, to get at least a general idea of his beliefs. Michael had claimed that he was working on something, a secret of sorts that pertained to the divine and quite possibly the overall state of the CitySpire. But then again, by the look of his choice in reading material and side commentary, he might just be out of his mind. I close the book and so does my mime.

I set the book aside and bring up the newspaper belonging to the Lockes. The paper is a tinge yellower than the photos I had in my picture frames. I wonder if it had been printed on a different sort of paper – although it feels the same. Some of the photos I already had, but the major ones that interest me are the photos of the statue in Hermes Square, the convenience store, and another of a mansion that sits somewhere in the northern section of the city. My mime follows me in gesture to the kitchen where the two of us brandish a pair of scissors from one of the counter height drawers. Returning, I start cutting carefully so as to get an exact size so they'll fit snuggly inside some of the remaining frames that I have left.

In my peripheral, I notice the man from across the way fidgeting with his pair of scissors. He has his own newspaper, but something in him prevents the motions. I look up as he looks up and with a sober face he opens the scissors fully and rakes it across his left temple, drawing a line of blood. My head pains me like rubbing alcohol to an open wound and when I cup it to ease the pain, I withdraw in shock as a trickle of blood stains my palm. I rush to the bathroom, the man following in step, and examine the wound. The cut that Emily had made with her fingernails had returned and reopened. It doesn't make any sense. It had healed perfectly and now? What is this madness?

I rush back to the living room and stare across the synapse between us. My doppelganger follows through in kind, keeping a straight head and face, completely emotionless and separate from the wound he inflicted upon himself. I watch him, keeping tabs on his motions and waiting for any form of hesitation in his movements as I lead our pas de deux. He doesn't waver and if there is a delay in his reactions, it is unnoticeable. It is as if I watch a reflection of myself, cast across the street in perfect order.

He breaks the illusion by his eyes shifting towards the street side. I follow them, part due to having been caught up in the fantasy and the other due to curiosity. Beneath a street lamp stands a couple, dressed in wool coats and hard sole shoes. They're embracing one another, her with long blonde hair and him in a dark colors with his ponytail that reaches past his shoulders. They kiss. The pain hits my chest, like a cold iron poker and I hiss with a startling intake of breath. It sickens me and I feel the bile gathering in the back of my throat.

I'm reminded of Emily, I'm reminded of everything I've been trying to hold back and trying to forget. He led me into it. The man across the street knows something more than what he's revealed, and with some manner of hypnosis he's manipulated me to follow along with his tricks. That's it, he's tricked me! That's all there is to it. I place my hand up to my sternum trying to swallow both the poison and added pains that come with the territory of memories.

I'm hunched over; the blow hit me lower than what I initially realized. I ease myself back to the window, to reveal my deceiver for what he truly is – hoping to catch some demonic smile hidden at the crease of his lips or perhaps a glitter in his eye exposing his enjoyment of the entire affair. But when I cast my gaze across the rain filled street I catch, beneath the transparency of a fog message, his broken form laying with his back turned now huddled upon the loveseat. The message written on the window is the simple word, *Live*.

I don't know what it is, something perhaps that Michael underlined, "what can be worse / Than to dwell here, driven out from bliss, condemned / In this abhorrèd deep to utter woe;" I feel sorry for him having to be here. I feel sorry for myself.

Two days pass and I continue my research. I have been pleased that my counterpart across the way hasn't resorted into any of his tricks and kept his movements independent of my own. He's been keeping busy cutting out newspaper clippings, reading what books were left for him in his apartment and writing, always writing. I've been curious as to what sort he's committed to. I've seen him, from time to time, standing up from his work and pace about his apartment – back and forth, back and forth – pondering something that I can only guess at. His facial expressions range from frustration to wonder and from absolute epiphany to discouraging abandon.

While I rest on my sofa and take up one of Michael's books, my friend—as I've been secretly enjoying his silent company—lays across his loveseat with a hand placed up to his temples and he massages them for hours on end. Whoever he is, I can see a bit in myself there, that consistent search for answers. I'm curious as to what it is he dreams of. Perhaps he dreams of a long lost love, a parent, or maybe a child. Perhaps he even dreams of a time long ago, a time when the city was new and memories came easily. On the other hand, maybe it is just the romantic in me. Perhaps he doesn't dream at all.

In my studies, I've found that Michael paid especially close attention to "The Prince" written by Niccolò Machiavelli. Many of the phrases and wording are underlined in regard to the governing of state and even in the manner in which one can ascend beyond poverty into the state of princedom. I wonder if his obsession in this title's reading lead towards anything of the imaginary dispute of ownership over the CitySpire between the Count and I. After reading the whole thing, I find that it may have been the reason for Michael's observance—more like encouragement of competition— between Boenger and I. There are times when the questions turn difficult, when everything becomes befuddlement and confusion. So I turn to other things.

Watching the pedestrians, as they are no longer the sorry looking sort that I first encountered a few days prior, are soothing to my troubled mind. Some have managed to stumble toward the clothing stores huddled around Hermes Square as I recognize a few pieces that I myself had once considered adding to my wardrobe. I observe a man stopped by another on the opposite street side. One is dressed in an excellent coat and tie, and the other in a rather ragtag style. The one with the coat is asked to open it, to show off his newly acquired threads. He then points in direction of the street where he had gained it. They nod to one another and proceed on with the rest of their way. Traffic is still a bit too infrequent for my tastes as I only get to see a newcomer every few hours at the most and other times I miss them entirely.

When my attention dries up, I take to the piano as I have many times before. When I play mournful pieces, they instill in me visions of the end of the song, some distant memory that continually drifts through my head. I catch my window mate looking up from his exhausting work to gaze on me, or rather through me, as if he too can hear what it is that I'm trying to reach.

As for my "masterpiece", as Emily would have me call it, I've been unable to reach any new notes for quite some time. I'm unsure whether the muse has died or if I didn't really know the whole thing to begin with. It's a funny thing, this remembering business. It's liable to drive me to utter frustration before anything useful comes of it. But I keep reminding myself of the broken carousel music box, of the dancers that once danced within, and I ask myself whatever was it for? Yet, all I know of is its importance and the feelings it invokes in me – my ever longing for Rachel.

The man across the street nods his head at me, a tip if you will of the proverbial hat as if he acknowledged what it is that I'm thinking. He is a strange sort, an interesting enigma, and at the same time frightening.

A week! A full week has gone by. I lay in my bed staring at the ceiling. It is sprinkling now as it usually does. It's near noon, perhaps a bit later. I can't really tell. Time is slowly consuming me. I haven't left my apartment. I've read all Michael's books, and I've done all I can to keep myself from going outside. I have all that I need here. I've been staring at the ceiling for some time, trying to swallow the ticks of the wall clock that resounds from the living room over the patter of little droplets on my window pane. My head has been spinning since I woke up, a slight fever; my forehead a bit warm to the touch. I think only of Emily.

Shivers – that's how I first found her. I had to carry her quite a distance and all she would do was shiver. I'm afraid I've caught her sickness, the one that had overtaken her during those several days while she slept. While I lay buried beneath the covers, I ponder how she managed to wash up on shore. Did she simply appear like all the rest of the CitySpire inhabitants? Not there one moment, then there the next? And if she had, would not she and the Lockes disappear in the same manner again? Is that what happened? What *is* happening? Will my Rachel return much the same as all the rest? Or will they all disappear again and leave me here alone? Have they done so already? Have I imagined them all? Have I gone mad in a city where there are no inhabitants and I've invented them as part of some deranged method of dealing with loneliness?

Chimes. Notes. A song is playing. It is soft, like the churning teeth of a music box – each note an individual pick. They float above me as sporadic moths fluttering about the room looking for purpose. The melody is familiar, like a various blend of songs that rattle through my head, both past and present. For a moment I share a glimpse of what is to come and in an instant of fever-induced delusion, I'm at peace with the world. Yet as quickly as it came, I forget it all having lost it in the heap where all other memories have vanished to. And then—

"You're doing it again." Her voice, if it could be seen, would twinkle like a cloudless night.

It's all so nonchalant, as if she's always been here. "Doing what?" I hear myself respond.

"Thinking." Her curls drop over my face and I see her, my dearest Rachel, her cheeks swollen in smile. "You know it gets you into trouble."

"I wouldn't dream of it." I can feel the warmth from her body, the pressure as she hikes her leg over mine and the touch of her hand as it eases onto my chest.

"As if life here isn't filled enough with those." She lays her head down on my chest. "Do you remember what you promised?"

"Remind me."

"You said you'd finish it."

Gone - her weight, her hair, her smile, everything is gone. In an instance she was swept from me by the great invisible hand of the

CitySpire. I still hear the notes dancing in the air, twirling like a pair of ballerinas. It pains me. I was hallucinating.

The sound doesn't dwindle it just hangs there, beckoning me to get up and to move outwards and into the living room where the piano lays. I need to catch them. I shimmy through the covers and out onto the floor where I stumble towards the instrument of my delusions. I pass beneath the doorway where I stop. A woman sits at the piano, her hair is auburn in color, her skin a white cream, she looks up at me. It's Emily.

"I heard music." I rub my face with familiarity and hear the rest of it in my head. *"How long was I out?"*

"Five days."

"Five days—" the words I speak startle whatever illusion has entwined my mind as the phantom-Emily dissipates like a light rain.

I grip the wall and follow the trim along the kitchen before passing myself to the sofa. I don't believe it, everything my mind is showing me is a product of stress and fever. It's Emily's sickness that's lain dormant inside me all this time. I wonder what it was that *she* had seen. The rolling surfs? Or perhaps being underwater, struggling to catch her breath – as she's acted in her more manic bouts. I crash on the piano bench and open the fall. I still hear the notes playing, now drifting through the walls, and hovering there and then wafting to the ceiling above me. I place my hands on the keys and begin that familiar song once more.

My mind wraps around a distant meaning, a hidden phantom of sorts that lives amidst the melody. I breeze through the opening and then into the rest. It's like a complex puzzle of pieces that come together through the rotation of the notes. And as I move into each unknown measure, I find the pieces coming to me more clearly than ever before. I simply pluck the notes from the room and place them in their corresponding locations and the song continues to build. Then after exhausting what the room has to offer me, when there are no longer any notes fluttering to and fro, I find myself invigorated.

I decide to play the song a few more times through, eager to memorize the newer portions so I may continue with the love song's construction. And after the fourth time, realizing that it had completely sunk in, I bound off to the kitchen to fetch a glass of water. Returning to the living room, I take a seat on couch and watch as the glass fogs from my finger tips. I take a drink.

I'm surrounded by a feeling of uneasiness. I see my neighbor dressed in a ghostly white, his loveseat turned to the side and him at the farthest end of his living room. My hands shake uncontrollably, an unusual reaction but something triggers inside me and I brace for what's coming – something in his eyes, an event attached at the tip of my tongue. He runs.

The window shatters into a kaleidoscope of fragments—each flashing like a stringent of Morse code—as a white spectre spreads his arms before him and in a rustling fabric that levitates momentarily above the street, he plummets; eyes shut to the ground below. His descent throws a sinking feeling in my throat that travels down my arms and to my hand where, upon the wet thump that comes from the street, cracks the glass in my hand.

11

"That's the third one this week," says the man leaning against a column of concrete that serves as both support and décor of the nearby building. "You'd think these folks would realize the cruelties of gravity." He blows a cloud of smoke into the air. It dissipates silently into the chilly day as he curtseys his hand in greeting.

He wears a brown suit, nothing from Hermes Square, a bit too dingy for that. There are holes in his sleeves, making it appear as if moths got to it – that is, if there were any moths. His hair is brown but well kept, and his eyes are a startling baby blue. Height happens to be his less prominent feature, a tad shorter than Natalie, perhaps a good five foot five, maybe more.

Ignoring him, I turn over the card and examine it again: *You are Richard Farley.* It appears unaffected by the long fall once taken by its previous owner. I compare it side by side with my own.

"Contemplating changing names? I've been doing a little of that myself, but no one will switch with me." I find his humor a bit ill placed.

"I prefer the one I have." I reply coldly.

"A pity. What about the stiff? Anything exotic?"

"A Mr. Richard Farley."

"I'm afraid I'll stick to the one I have. The name's Marty Kessler." He continues to lean and observe.

I run my fingertip over the corpse's lips like the rim of a wine glass and bring them to my nose to smell. I was expecting alcohol, but there's nothing except the lingering smell of lilacs. I wonder if it's from a cologne.

Returning the favor, I dust off my knees and come to standing. "Samuel Bell."

"Has a nice ring to it, don't you think? Let me know when you're done with it."

I look at him beneath the light sprinkles of the day and try and figure out his angle. I'm really not in the mood to deal with the street raff.

"You look a bit out of place. Did you just tumble down the rabbit hole?"

I'll assume he means waking into the CitySpire. "I've been here."

"No shit? And here I was thinking of being the welcoming party. How long?"

"Since before the snowfall."

"Snowfall? You have been here awhile then. The oldest I've managed to gather in conversation is the old harbor master: claims he's been here a few weeks. You're talking months now. I'll be damned."

I take my coat off and cover Mr. Farley's body.

He throws his hand out as if to stop a falling vase. "I wouldn't do that if I were you boss, unless you have an extra one. I don't know if you noticed or not, but a coat like that is hard to find."

"I'm sure others will uphold to decency when contemplating stealing from the dead."

He snickers. "You have a lot more faith in people than I do, sir. But you interest me, so I'll go along with it. I'd just hate to see a nice coat go to waste."

We continue to keep our distance. "You are an odd sort Mr. Kessler. Have things come to the point where individuals have lost all morality?"

"Call me Marty. When I grow a beard and my hair is grey, then you can call me mister. As for morality? I'm unsure of your comparison."

I sigh. "Never mind."

I look up to the window from where Richard had taken his plunge. I remember seeing him jotting down a few things in journals and loose pieces of paper. Perhaps they may give me a little introspection into what he was thinking, or even an explanation as to how he had arrived in the CitySpire.

A bit rude on my part—partially absent minded—I bypass Marty and make my way towards the door to the apartment complex across from my own.

"Don't tell me you're planning on heading up there?"

I slip my hand through one of the handles of the doors. "No one said you had to come along."

"You're the most interesting chap I've met thus far. I'm not letting you go and disappear on me. There's enough of that as is."

I shake my head – another person to lead around. I don't want him tagging along, but I just don't have the energy to convince him otherwise. I'm sure he thinks that I have all the answers and that by some trick of patience I'd divulge all the information at once and everything would finally make some sense in the world. I'd hate to disappoint him. He figures he has all the time in the CitySpire to wait me out. Something tells me that I'll have to break it to him slowly. This is the exact thing I hoped to avoid by staying in my apartment.

Beyond the swing of the doors I'm met with an unusual sensation. Those many times before, I was welcomed with apprehension and dread, however the only thing lurking around is Marty in the threshold.

The smell of lilacs is strong. Too strong.

With a little hesitation I cross the lobby and enter the elevator that waits at the other end of the room. I hit the button to send us to the seventh floor, but this time the carriage has decided to take its sweet time, leaving me to contend with the curious pedestrian.

"You seem to know where you're going." Marty suggests while leaning on the back wall and planting his hands squarely on the waist high copper railing. His eyes scan the ceiling as if hoping to catch our destination before the carriage does.

"I've been here before." I reply in monotone.

"Long history of folks jumping, eh?"

"Let's just say this isn't the first time I've been to this specific apartment."

"Wait—" Marty stands full upright, "this wasn't an acquaintance of yours was it?"

A smile grapples the side of my cheek. "Never met him."

He lets out a breath of relief. "And here I was thinking I owed you an apology. Based upon your reaction I just figured you a bit rattled from the whole thing. It's the same expression everyone else has when they witness a body slamming into pavement. It's just getting a little too common around here."

"Does this happen a lot?"

"More than I'd like to admit." Behind his roguish face there's a hint of remorse to him. "But what can you do? A lot of people have contemplated it from time to time. Seems everyone has a hole inside them that they can rarely place. It's rare to find someone willing to talk about it." For a moment he looks bothered by something, but his features soften back to the interests at hand. "So what's *your* interest in all this?"

The elevator slows and then comes to a silent stop as it levels with the designated floor.

"I've seen him around. Just curious is all."

We start down the hallway. A light haze drifts about the place, like a smoky plume of incense traveling towards the staircase at the other end of the hall. The door is shut, but I cannot help but wonder if the Count lays in wait at the other end. Marty's voice interrupts my daydream.

"You know what they say about curiosity?"

We stop and I look to him as if to question who "they" actually refer to in this instance. "No—what do *they* say?"

Marty smiles a devious grin. "'Tis the stuff of true adventurers. Brigit Box, you'll meet her. Nice gal."

In this particular regard, I believe he is right, especially how the CitySpire tends to have so many twists and turns, side streets and hidden buildings tucked away in some remote pocket. The city is enchanted. There is always something new. No doubt about it. Here I was irritated he was going to say, "It killed the cat."

We continue down the hallway.

The scent is heavier here, like a garden of flowers hidden beneath the carpet. Each step we take is like shuffling through a pile of pedals, tossing their fragrance into the air with every step.

"Do you smell that?" I ask as I count the gold numbers that decorate each door.

"What's that boss?"

"Flowers."

"Oh, that? It's everywhere. Mostly it's around those who just wake up, and strongest around those who die. Can't really place the source of it though. It may be someone's perfume or maybe an air freshener. It must have spilled or something because I've never smelled it this strong before. Although I've never gone to a jumper's apartment before, so there's a first time for everything."

We stop at the door. The paint still looks new and the hardware is polished down to the letter. I'm beginning to believe that Mr. Farley never left his apartment. From beneath the cracks of the door, I can hear a low whistling blowing in from the broken window. The door lifts momentarily and knocks softly in its hinges. There's a slight premonition, a touch of a future familiarity that glances across my brain, a feeling that this door will always stir by a draft even after the window is repaired.

Marty's eyebrow questions me if I'm serious about going any further. His countenance reminds me of the time we all stole into the Gothic cathedral. Looking at him I question myself, what *is* the better part of valor? before turning the knob and entering the room.

The door wrestles from my grip and slams into the wall, bouncing before settling. The room is turned into a whirlwind of loose papers and then they scatter. Utter catastrophe. The loveseat is pushed off to one side and piles of books lay in small nests around the legs of his desk and other random pieces of furniture. The pages flutter in communication to one another with each gust of wind.

Marty kills the ambience. "Not much of an organizer. I guess that's a lot to expect from someone who committed suicide."

"Marty…" This isn't the time to kid around. "Check out the kitchen for me will you?"

His head turns to his right and with sly intent says, "Yes…the kitchen." And he follows through to the refrigerator as if it harpooned him in the heart. I hear the familiar relinquish of the door's suction and then glasses clinking together before I feel I'm safe to go about my investigation.

Where to begin? There are papers everywhere. If there had been an order to which these were all supposed to be read then it has long since been lost to the whims of the wind.

As I dig my toe into the ground in mid-step, I hear a slight crinkle under foot. One of the pages has managed to find its way beneath my boot. I stoop to pick it up and find the images befuddling. It's a hand drawn picture of a spiral starting from the edges of the paper and then disappearing into the infinity of the center. There are a few others like it as well, differing in some particular shape or form. There's one that spirals from two points in the center of the design and then flows outwards and another that curls around like a coil, all perfectly drawn. It's all very mathematical.

A book by his desk is pushed open by the force of its pages and I catch some writing in my peripheral. With a wide collection of drawings in my hand I pick up the journal and read:

I am not dead and neither are you. It is imperative that you understand this in all things. The CitySpire may have you believe it is some secluded prison or hell. Others may have you believe it is a construct of the divine. But remember no matter what you believe, you must believe that you are indeed alive.

We all must yield to whatever purpose has brought us here, the purpose of our existence—be it to seek revenge on those who wronged us or watch for signs of sails on the horizon—purpose is our reason in all things; it is life.

Do we not each dream of dreams? Do we not dance on the notes of lost memories? Then are we not each dreamers of tomorrow and yesterday, since dreams play when time is askew? Are we not all adrift in the constant sea of trial and when all is done, do we not all yearn for ships to carry us home?

Remember, that no matter what you see here, no matter where your purpose takes you, we all walk in different directions but there is only one destination. Inevitable end is simply the door to the beginning. We are alive my friend, never for once doubt that. We are all alive.

Peculiar to read this in knowing he had only written them a few days ago. Stranger that he'd write something as uplifting and positive as this and then throw himself from the window. A touch of irony perhaps? I don't sense any identifying patterns of depression or madness wafting from his latest entry that would cue me into the reason for his demise. It doesn't make any sense. There's nothing to pinpoint the reason for his plummet. He jumped, but why? He was a mystery in life and in his writings, funny how he'd remain a mystery after his death.

I just don't think I'd be able to let it all rot. It'd keep me up at night. I'm going to have to recover as many pages as I can from around the apartment and maybe it'll later afford me a hint of insight into the entire affair.

Marty's voice catches me off guard, as I had forgotten he was even here.

"Hey ya, boss? The man is loaded. We got an entire refrigerator piled to the ceiling with fresh meats—little sausages, ham—what's this, a turnip? Everything I've been eating lately has been out of a can and in fact…" he closes the refrigerator door and throws back a pair of high cabinet doors. "He's got those too! It's like he's been hoarding food. He's all settled in nice and cozy."

It's all too familiar. "He didn't go anywhere. He didn't have to." Something about purpose. Marty isn't listening.

"What I don't understand about these jumpers is that here they wake in a well furnished apartment, food galore, and they just let it all waste by leaping out the windows. I woke up in an alley, how comfortable is that?"

The hardware of his door was still polished, hadn't seen much use. Even mine looked a bit smudged after I touched it. Now he could have been a clean freak, but something like an exterior door knob is a bit obsessive. Judging by the chaos of his apartment, something tells me he wouldn't have left it in such a mess if he was overly concerned about cleanliness. Since he leaped through his window in essentially pajamas he obviously didn't care about appearance, therefore he must not have been the obsessive type.

Now what about the food? Like mine had been, his pantry is stocked full – in anticipation of a prolonged stay, was it? There was the light from my apartment door, the sensation and belief that there had been someone in my apartment prior to my waking which then led me out into the CitySpire in search of them. What about Mr. Farley? If he hadn't experienced anything similar, he may be content to stay inside his apartment, to do what? To write?

I walk to the edge of the window and peer down the cracked glass and onto the street where below I'm able to make out the outline of my coat. And to jump? Is this the purpose in which Farley wrote about? Cause and effect, or is he referring to something greater than that such as fate?

"I am not dead." I'm sorry Mr. Farley, but I don't think I believe you.

"What was that, chief? Oh, look at this—Pancake mix. I haven't had pancakes in forever… literally." He pulls the box from the shelf and shakes it towards me.

"It's time for us to go." I muse on a painful memory. "We'll come back for the rest."

I secure the lot of papers so more are not lost in the winds of the city, before excusing the both of us from the room.

"You've got to be kidding me." Marty complains while staring over the pallid corpse of Richard Farley. "It's not our job, boss."

"Then whose job is it, then? Certainly not the rest of the population. He'll start to rot and then he'll smell. Besides, it's the right thing to do."

"And who dictates these rules, Mr. Bell? Certainly not him." He stares at the body for a period. "Did I mention that I have a soft stomach? I'm really not feeling this right now." He taps his heart.

"Trust me, you'll feel it afterwards. We don't have to bury him. There're plenty of tombs to go around. We'll just break the lock and set him inside."

"Didn't you have a thing about disturbing the dead? Some morality question you poised earlier?"

"There aren't any bodies in those tombs. I checked."

"You must have been bored during those many months ago. I don't think I would have ever gone in there. It's a tad creepy."

"Creepy or not, you need to grab his legs. I'm saving you some grief and taking the heavy end."

"Looks like you're causing *me* grief. This is what I get for trying to be on the welcoming committee."

"By the way," I chuckle. "Welcome to the CitySpire."

"Gee thanks. Is that what this place is called? Nice." He looks back down at the corpse. "I'm still not feeling it."

He is impossible. "I'll give you my coat if you help me."

"You mean the one that's been covering a cadaver for the past half-hour?" He cocks his head to the side. "Tempting."

"It would mean a lot to me."

"Now how can I say 'no' to that? His legs you say?" He hoists up his end like a pair of pants. "How far away is this graveyard of yours?"

"About twenty to thirty minutes or so?" I point to the north. "That way."

He drops his end. "You have to be kidding me? We get to lug him all the way down Rhine Street, parade him through the square, and then stuff him in a tomb?"

I look at him disappointed. "That's the plan."

He picks up his end once again. "Just wanted to make sure is all."

I'm struck by an epiphany. "Now we could make a stretcher. It'd probably make the job a lot easier."

Marty once again drops his end. "Now you're talking! I knew you were a smart one the first time I laid my eyes on you."

"But then again…" My thinking rounds the inside of my brain in search of tiny tidbits I may have locked away. "I don't know anywhere we could find the necessary materials to make one."

Marty's hopeful expression flattens. "Let's just get this over with."

He waits for me to pick up my end before taking up his own. "You'd think that with all the time you had been here that you would have had this entire place mapped."

"You're serious?" I ask as I walk backwards, my muscles starting to hate the dead weight. "This city is like a labyrinth. You turn down the same corner every day and you're bound to run into something you missed. I'd probably know more but I was a little preoccupied."

"And what would that be, boss? Got a woman up there in that tower of yours?"

I keep it simple. "I had a few friends, yes."

"Friends, huh? Maybe we should round up a few of them and get *them* to move the body."

"They've had a change of address. I haven't heard from them in awhile."

"Did you scare them away with your bedside charm?"

I sigh while trying to put this nicely. "Something about not wanting to be on the welcoming committee."

"A lot of work that is. I don't blame them." Seems he buys it.

I keep quiet for the next few blocks in an attempt to bypass any additional questions he may have about them or just to change the topic entirely. Marty is the eager sort, there's no doubt about it. But I'm unsure if his interest lies solely in me or if he is more eager to learn about the city. Oddly enough, he keeps quiet. Since there are no pedestrians walking the street side, nor is their any noise to keep the sound of our boots company, it is I who asks the next question, due to the stillness frightening the sound from my throat.

"You mentioned something earlier that there is enough disappearing of late. What did you mean?"

Marty is quick to respond, he too perhaps disturbed by the silence. "The city, boss. Cities are supposed to be crowded, overpopulated at times. What we have here is a poor population to city ratio. Not enough folks to go around, if you catch what I mean. Something had to happen to them, I feel it in my gut. And it isn't a nice feeling either."

"What do you think happened to them?"

"Don't rightly know. It's difficult to say when apartments are empty one minute then filled the next. People are waking up around every corner and no one has the faintest clue who they are, why they are here, or where they come from. No one knows anything about the CitySpire, but when questioned if there's somewhere they'd rather be *other* than the city, it's like asking a mole if he'd rather live in a tree. Is there some place other than the CitySpire that we all came from? Did the rest of the population just vanish? It gives me a headache just thinking about it. I woke a week ago, and I don't remember anything before that."

"Someone once told me their theory about what may have happened."

"Really?" His features entertain a new query. "And what was that?"

"Loose translation? Rapture."

"What?!" He yells. "That's the most ridiculous thing I've ever heard! Freaking Rapture. So some divine being whisked the majority of us away and left some behind? Doesn't make any sense to me, especially when you look at the chronology of it all."

He intrigues me. "How is that?"

"Because those left behind would have been here en masse, not scrambling about trying to find out who's been here the longest. Hell, as far as we know day one may have started with you. But then there's history to explain, and I've got a little of it churning around in my head. History doesn't start with a tall building and a card with your name written on it, but jokes do. I think someone is taking us for suckers and is playing a mean game. Freaking Rapture. Nothing brings hope to you more than feeling like you weren't good enough. What sorry sod made that one up?"

It churns in my brain, and though he doesn't carry the best in social graces, it's his last statement that makes me decide I truly like him.

"Nobody important."

We reach the cemetery after multiple breathers, an hour or two since we started walking. The black iron gates are open wide like the maw of a gigantic beast which whines to the pitch of last winter's fleeting winds. I can see the graves now, a lot easier to make out from their snow-laden blankets when Michael and I had laid siege to the ground in hopes of finding a body. Returned, I bring one to rest. It's funnier the more I think about it.

"So just toss him into a tomb, right? No need to break out a shovel. Not like we have one."

"If I remember correctly, the majority of them are locked. Unless we can find one unlocked, we may need a rock or its equivalent."

"Maybe we'll get lucky. In the meantime, should we let ol' Richard here be a temporary gate guard? My arms could use a bit of a rest."

"Just leave him here at the gate? Doesn't that seem a bit risky?"

Marty's right eyebrow raises as he scrunches his forehead to something queer. "What? Do you think someone's going to run off with him or something? Last I heard, there isn't much of a demand for dead bodies. The fact that we took one is odd enough."

He has a point. I shrug my shoulders as I have nothing to counter my previous concern.

The two of us wander past the gates and take a cobblestone path deeper inside the cemetery. The grass still remains sickly brown, having grown little during the encroaching spring. Yew trees stretch over the roof tops of most tombs that are scattered periodically throughout the grounds. A few roots poke out from beneath them like a sea serpent, fervent to devour the thoughtless. There are more headstones than I remember. Perhaps it is due to the darkness that we stole beneath to shield our actions from both Natalie and Emily. All are unnamed.

"Can't say I've ever had the courage to wander through a graveyard." Marty says as his eyes dart from stone to stone. "It's weird that none of them are marked."

"It's because there's no one beneath them. This graveyard is a huge façade, it gives the illusion that there were others before us."

"Well, it's very convincing; convincing enough that I'd rather stay out of them as much as possible."

"I'm not one to enjoy them myself. It does have a certain serenity about it. Just the same, it's not a place I enjoy visiting. It reminds me of wrongness of the city. It's like some terrible dream."

Just around the cobblestone path, it winds between a set of three separate tombs, one of black granite, another built of limestone, and the other built of glass. Each has a unique design to them, blending a differing allotment of architectural styles ranging from Gothic to modern. They aren't but an eyeshot from the location where Michael previously dug, but I swear they weren't here before. I figure it's either the city or possibly my mind playing tricks on me.

"Well boss, whad'ya think? Should we choose door number one, door number two, or door number three?"

"I guess any of them are as good as any. I don't really have a preference, to be honest."

Marty walks up to them and sizes each of them from head to toe, contemplating with his hand upon his chin as if it were a riddle of importance.

"Let's stick him in the granite one."

"Any particular reason?" I muse in his bit of hilarity.

"I like the other two better. It'll make me feel better knowing they're not occupied. Besides, I'd rather not stick him in the glass one because I'd hate to find myself a stroll and have to look at his decaying mug through the transparency. You know what I mean?"

"I see." I say with an inch of bemusement.

Apparently sensing my understanding Marty then adds, "Plus, it's the only one without a lock on it."

"Ah, I see. Shall we be off to acquire Mr. Farley from his post?"

A few stretches and Marty is good to go.

We lay his body atop a stone sarcophagus that's been cemented shut. There really is no point to breaking open the mortar, especially if someone was interested in getting at the corpse. We have no way of resealing it. At least not at the moment. Marty helps me slide the stone door back in place to seal it from the city's weather. I make a vow to return here with a lock.

Now, with the grinding of granite against a cement foundation finally drifting out of our ears and from our memories, the day grows silent.

Marty stares at the tomb during a short moment of reflection. "You know, you were right, boss. I'm feeling it now. Gives ya that long lost sense of accomplishment. Now *that's* something you don't get here every day. Feels good."

He turns out all right after all, though still a bit rough around the edges. I pick up the coat that I retrieved off Mr. Farley's body, fold it and hand it to him; a bit sorry to see it go.

"I believe you've earned this."

Marty looks down at it a bit confused and then his face ignites in remembrance. "Naw, that's alright boss. It's too big. Looks better on you anyway. Besides, you're going to need it for tomorrow."

"And why is that?"

He turns, spins, and puts his hands on my shoulders. "Cause we got a whole city filled with corpses. I think it's 'bout time they were given a home."

More than all right, he turned out well.

I invite him to join me in my apartment for a little after-hour celebration – that is, of course, after we raid Mr. Farley's apartment for food, his first aid kit, books and other necessities. After all the work is done, I catch a mild return of my sickness. I had almost forgotten.

I find my way to the sofa and rest for awhile, my hand keeping to my head to stabilize an emerging pain that throbs at the temples. Marty pays it no mind. Neither does he seem insulted that I haven't given him a tour or isn't playing the proper role of host. I guess he figures that all the apartments look the same. You see one, you see them all.

But instead of joining me at the couch, I hear a rattling in the kitchen. It's enough to rear my head to see what he is up to and am surprised at what I see. Marty is gathering bowls, a few utensils, and even flips up a frying pan in a manner that's near acrobatics. He spreads them across the counter, apparently not concerned about the order in which they're in, nor the diminishing space he now has to work with. He whistles an impromptu song without any real structure to be worth writing down. It's unusual to watch anyone cook, especially in my kitchen. It's always been the other way around. It's nice just the same.

He makes the two of us chicken cacciatore with a bed of pasta. I swear he used twice the needed amount of garlic in it, but it doesn't disturb the flavor. I have him break out a bottle of wine, a nice chardonnay that I've been saving since the first night I stood vigilant as an inland lighthouse. The taste of it reminds me of the overwhelming silence of loneliness, dreams and love.

Marty doesn't ask me any questions, but I feel obligated to let him in on everything. I can't help but say, "This is how it all began…" at least from my perspective. I tell him about Emily, how I found her and how she acted. I tell him about Michael and Natalie, how we met them at Hermes Square and Michael's fascination with the cathedral and the divine. I tell him about Count Champ de Croix, of Henry Boenger and the marvelous aircar. He knows of Rachel, but the song I keep to myself; following through on the promise I once made to Emily.

After all the telling, it seems so short – the time we had spent together that lead up to the now. Marty doesn't speak, he just absorbs like a splash of sun. He doesn't question, instead he simply revels in knowing it. And in his knowing, he realizes that I'm just as touched by the state of the CitySpire as everyone else. He knows that I'm no better than any of the pedestrians in the streets. Yet for some reason those few months act like a currency, and to him I am the wealthiest man in the CitySpire.

When the night reminds us of our weariness, I offer him the comfort of the Lockes' old apartment or if he preferred, he could have my bed and I the latter. He takes the couch, offering himself as a loyal guardian against the night's terrors.

After I see to his comfort, I ease into my room, shut the door, and drift into a sea of sheets and blankets.

12

I dream of Farley standing at the edge of his window looking at me from across the way. He's dressed as he had the day of his death. His white clothes are still, hanging like drapes. He mouths something from across the way. I cannot hear him. Richard's features are soft but sorrowful, his face torn down to the street below. I believe his disappointment—I know—it's because of the way I'm dressed. His feet are bare, whilst mine are in jackboots; his shirt is of silk, mine is of cotton and heavy wool; he is naked against the winds, I wear a coat. He turns his head from me, ashamed. He leaps.

I see him emerging from the shattered glass of his window, staring straight through me as the day he heard me play, staring deep into the great beyond. I see the lack of fear in his eyes, the conviction painted across his soul. I see him descend. I watch as he falls.

From the street the rain tumbles like a trapeze performer who lost his grip, soon to burst atop the pavement. Above me, I see the swollen sky stir like a sky-born maelstrom. All is mute, even when all the windows—thousands of glittering shards—break out across the synapse between buildings, followed gracefully by hundreds. People! Their clothes flutter like silk, their garments whip against the wind, as they dive willingly—collectively—like a symphony into the bowels of the street below. I'm shrew struck as others follow suit, apartments exploding with flying glass, a torrent of white throwing themselves like a waterfall to the city below, one after another. All around me, I see the city's population mixing with the rain. I hear as they strike the ground, chiming like an overpowering gong, each ringing—each a distinctive note—as they collapse in down scale.

I awake sore. The dream haunts me, leaving a lingering feeling of dread that slips down my esophagus the more the morning is absorbed into my skin. Nightmares – how they've become more frequent. I shower and dress quickly, eager to have the day's activities drown out the visions beheld in the land of Nod.

My living room is how I left it the night before save one important piece: Marty is gone. I wash my eyes over the coffee table, across the piano and amidst the kitchen, yet there is no sign of a note or evidence to where he had run off to. Then I understand that he has no more need of me. I divulged all that there is to know about the past months. He offered me his temporary services and I paid him handsomely.

Unknowingly, perhaps due in part to past habits, I find myself leaning against the frame of the window gazing out across the cityscape. The shattered window from Mr. Farley's apartment still greets me with its jagged teeth, a cruel reminder of yesterday's events. I'm about to muse on the whole affair when something below catches my eye. I blame my sluggishness on early morning rousing as below, gathering in a large group, near in twenty, are a ragtag collection of men and women running in and out of local buildings. Some, farther down the street, race to join the encroaching mob, whilst others off in the opposite direction on errand.

I mutter quite bewildered, "What in the world?"

I gather my effects and rush out and into the elevator so I may meet this posse of individuals. It is but a few breaths before the familiar ring of the elevator's chime announces the ground floor. There, leaning up against one of the columns, is Marty conversing with a short youngling – perhaps a little over twenty, bowl-cut brunette, wearing men's pants, suit and tie.

It's she who notices me first. "Well, ain't that a flower." She says with a tough guy voice that would serenade a rock. It is obvious she is referring to me.

Marty makes a play on her prior sentence. "Morning, sunshine. It's about time you got up. I guess you older folks need your beauty sleep, eh?" He snickers silently, the only give away is his rapid intake of breaths.

"What's all this?" I ask with as much gentility as I can muster. I can tell instantly that I'm in the presence of a new breed.

"The Welcoming Committee, boss." Marty boasts. "I gathered them all early this morning. Thought we could use the extra hands in carving out a few graves for the recently departed. Can't have them smelling up the streets now can we?"

The lean woman opens her grey coat and places her hand on her hip. "This the one you've been gabbing about, Mart?" She humphs. "Doesn't look like much to me."

"Mr. Bell, may I introduce you to Miss Brigit Box." He crosses his arms and smiles.

I extend my hand to her, somewhat taken aback by her choice in dress. "A pleasure, Miss Box."

She raises her penciled-in eyebrow, fakes a half-smile, and then takes my hand in kind. "Yea, sure." She then withdraws to brush the ghost of a hair out of her eyes. "So are we going to lollygag or are we going to get started? We don't have all day."

Marty laughs the good laugh. "My goodness, that's all we have."

"Can it Marty." Brigit walks impatiently out the door. "I don't have time for this shit."

Marty calms himself by wiping the tears from his eyes, all the while watching as she muscles her way out the door. "Oh, that tommy always gets me." He walks over to me and places his arm around my shoulder. "I told you you'd like her."

"What's with the suit?" I ask while watching the enigma through the glass.

"Oh, that? Pay her no mind. She's a charming little tootsie once you get to know her. I'm so glad you're awake."

We start towards the doors.

I eye him with skepticism. "And why is that, Marty?"

"Well, I've managed to round them all up, but no one's really willing to do anything without some convincing. And you're just the thing to get everyone motivated."

"And why would that be?"

"Because you're the boss! You're the only one who knows what's going on around here and people are just looking for a bit of direction, know what I mean? They just need a little push to get the ball rolling. People have been all zombie-like the past few weeks, naught but moaning and groaning, and nothing is getting accomplished."

Something about Marty's presentation is making me uncomfortable. "Listen, Marty." We stop. "I don't know these people."

"You didn't know me a few days ago, but that didn't stop you from enlisting me into your service." He looks me square in the eye. "Look - all you gotta do is be you. Yesterday you showed me that you knew what you were doing, and that's saying a lot. These folks out here are lost and just need someone to look to in order to find their way. You don't have to do anything fancy, just tell them to pick up their shovels and get to work. Now how hard is that?"

"If it's not so hard why can't you do it?"

He sighs. "I've already done that bit. They wouldn't even listen to me until I told them about you."

"What exactly did you tell them, Marty?"

"Just that you're the oldest chap on the block and that you may have some answers for us, that's all."

"But I don't have any answers."

"Answers aren't always found in a sentence, boss. You have to look at the big picture."

It didn't sound like his sort of insight. "Where'd you hear that at?"

"Actually, it was written in magnets on Mr. Farley's refrigerator. Thought it was catchy at the time."

I take a deep breath and give. "Alright, let's just get this over with. At least we can get those bodies off the street."

"Now you're talking, chief." He slaps me on the back and aims me for the door.

With my hand on the knob, I turn and look on him squarely. "Just what is your motivation in all this, Marty? Yesterday it took a bribe to get you to even go near Mr. Farley's body and now, all of a sudden, you want to take on those that are a few stages in decay."

He halts, not just in movement but in face. I've caught him in some sort of mental quandary, one that's free from his usual jibes. He loosens his features, raises his eyebrows and says, "To distract the mind, boss. Give them something better to think about. That's all. Give 'em a day where they feel good to be alive. I promise you, you won't regret it."

I never took Marty to be a humanitarian, caring about other peoples' state of mind. I suspect there is far more to him that he lets on.

Hesitantly I give into his request. "Very well, I'll see what I can do."

Past the glass doors that separate us from the growing crowd, I get a whiff of the day. It is calm, a light breeze, but nothing that would cause rise to any foul weather. It's clouded over like most days and if you take a deep enough breath you can taste the accumulated water in the stratus above.

The people have gathered in the thirties, a rough-in-tumble sort, their clothes are an assortment of varying garments that range from the luxury jackets that used to belong to the hangers in the shops of Hermes Square to others like bits of rags eaten away by hungry rats. They're all so pitiful: their faces pale with the morning chill and their breaths all mixing together in steam. Someone points Marty and I out. It isn't long for the rest of them to see what the hush is all about.

I can see Miss Box hanging off the side speaking to a few large gentlemen towards the back row, and a few other familiar faces that I recognize from passing by when I used to observe them from my apartment window. None of them know me, but that doesn't stop their begging stares from ambushing me at once. It's very nerve wracking. I try and think of something dramatic, hoping Michael's books have left some impression on me. I open my mouth to speak.

"I don't know how long you've all been here. Nor do I know what you've all experienced since then." I swallow to keep myself from shaking. "I've seen the passing of two seasons. I've seen the emptiness of this city and the horrors it that can create. I've even come face to face with a devil and managed to tell the tale." With the previous sentences I gain a bout of courage to continue unabated. "But I am no different than any of you. I'm just a man who came before the rest and had to suffer the CitySpire with less than what you have now." I cast a glance at Marty. "Some would have me be their savior, but I would rather you be my comrades. I am willing to share with you everything I know in hopes of giving you history and a place to start. Though right now there are things that need to be done. Some of us chose the unfortunate path by ending their life. I know many of you may have even contemplated it yourself at some point. I know, because I have done the same. This city has a way of tricking your emotions and doing away with rationality. There is no shame in it, but the albatross now lies on our shoulders. Instead of wasting away searching for memories we can't reach, it is fine time we all do something to better our situation. First and foremost, our kinsmen need to be put to rest, to be buried in the northern cemetery. With them at peace, perhaps we can find some of our own. We can use their sacrifice as the foundation for a new start, to make the CitySpire our own."

I stand there in silence for a few moments, hoping that what I said would be enough to spur some sort of action. Yet the crowd remains still, chewing over my words as if it were an old stick of gum. Brigit Box is the first to speak up.

"So if we bury these chumps, you'll let us in on all your secrets eh?" She doesn't look all that convinced.

"I'm not asking for much." I drop in before anyone else has the chance to pick up on her doubt. "It's one day of work for two seasons of history. It'll level the playing field and give everyone the same opportunities as the next guy. It's an opportunity for us all to do some good."

The crowd remains silent.

"Oh – come on people!" Marty bellows. "It's not like you have anything else better to do. We'll even celebrate afterwards. Who's with us?"

No one moves until a voice issues through the crowd.

"I'll do it." A call from Miss Box herself followed by, "You're right about one thing. We haven't anything better to do."

A couple others join her as well, a few men and women who flag themselves by raising their hands into the air and walk forward to join Marty and I near the front of my apartment building. Slow at first but gathering in number, the amount of hands and "I"s spirit through the gathering until each and every member of the aporetic mass lays down their dissent and joins us in turn.

Marty whispers over to me, "Not the best speech in the world chief, but you got their attention. What now?"

"Alright listen everyone, I don't know the entire layout of the city. As we all know, there's something always new around the corner. What we need is a hardware store, or a place that has shovels, picks, wheel barrels, you name it. I know one exists, because I've seen tools around. It's got to come from somewhere. Who knows where one is?"

A red-headed man, a little under 5'10", thin and young, perhaps best representing late teens, calls from amongst the crowd. The locals pull him up towards the circle that has formed so as everyone can get a better view. He stumbles as he trips over another's foot but manages to retain his balance.

"Who are you?" Marty manages from the spectacle.

"Frankie Jacobson, sir. Woke just a few days ago by the side of the old cathedral. Saw an old shop round there off a side street. Place is named the Brick, lot of tools and such."

Marty laughs. "Good lad. Glad someone's paying attention 'round here. Alright everyone, looks like Mr. Jacobson will lead the way. Take us to this Brick of yours."

The crowd moves away from him, egging him on to take the lead. I move with him, knowing that he will serve as the catalyst to the crowd's fuel, and also because of Marty's tender shoves. I don't feel up to this — leading a group of people I don't know and automatically assuming a role best left for scapegoats if something should go wrong. Everything is quiet, not a word is uttered in our march. The city itself has fallen into yet another one of it's moments of quiescence, perhaps holding unto the wind to see what shall transpire in the next several hours. I know I'm not looking forward to it.

We pass the old sites. I note the difference from when the new comers hadn't existed. Now the fine shops around Hermes Square lay empty, the clothes gone and the manikins now in the nude and staring on as we walk on. Shoes, menswear, accessories, those tiny little delicacies that Emily and I had fawned over so many times before are forever lost. Seeing the place in dishevel causes a small bit of pain to reach around and squeeze my heart. Nobody else pays it any mind and why would they? It was they who had stripped the place bare. Something in me is painted in anger, accusing, despite how they took simply what they needed to survive. I glare at each of them. Is nothing sacred anymore?

Mr. Jacobson jogs once he catches eye of the top turrets of the dark cathedral looming above. "We're getting close now, it's just a few blocks away." He waves for us to follow him in a refreshing boyish way. His excitement is boyish like drawing a club of friends to a pool.

His eagerness only helps to dismiss the silence that's been chaining the majority to closed mouths and steady pace. I quicken my stride and with little effort it is Marty, who after falling a bit behind, looks like he's the one needing the tender shove. Together, in one large mass of joggers, we round the corner where the cathedral sits, eyeing the park no more than a stone's throw away. We turn off down an opposite direction and delve into a series of cobblestone alleys where aluminum downpipes and steam expelling vents reside. The usual sort of buildings change from the concrete exterior to more of an exposed red and black brick the deeper we go. This is a piece of the city that I neither had, nor would have ever, found on my own. I prefer to keep to the main streets as it is easier to find my way home but this—this is certainly an aspect of the city that I never could have imagined.

We turn down a few additional passages before the alley widens to the size of a small pedestrians' circle where street-hugging shops are set and left to entropy's breath. Mr. Jacobson points to an orange brick building that looks to have taken the brunt of the years. The outside is flaking, and a few bricks have fallen from their nesting place and gathered around the base of the building. The glass windows are dirtied and difficult to peer through, but large enough to have once displayed its goods proudly to the passersby.

"This is it." He says in marvel at his accomplishment.

"Good job, Frankie." Marty exclaims.

I'm astonished – so much in fact, that I don't register at first the amount of stares I receive in anticipation of the next order. I try and pay them no mind, focusing more on the building and its state of disrepair. The only other structure that's come close is the cathedral, but I always associated some form of magic to the place. It seems magic is everywhere these days.

My legs take me to the front stoop, just a few paces away from the wooden door, where etched in the side of a large datestone is the engraving "B. Rick". Perhaps it belongs to the builder or the architect, perhaps even the original owner. I thought that the name Brick for a hardware store was a tad questionable, but remembering my encounter with Emily I'm not at all poised to have another such debate over the name. B. Rick is it? I wonder what all Mr. Rick had to do with the city.

Marty catches me touching the engraving. "Hey Boss. It's cold out here so let's get the show on the road, eh?"

Right. I look to our red-head guide. "Mr. Jacobson will be responsible for inventorying everything we take. I want to be sure that when we're done everything is returned in kind." I'd hate to see these tools scattered across the CitySpire. More the less likely, if I didn't keep track of them, we'd never see them again. "Miss Box, you and I are responsible for making stretchers so we can get the bodies to the graveyard without killing ourselves. I need you to take lead of a handful of people, ten will do, and get started." She scoffs quietly to herself, but I believe she is pleased with playing a major role. "Marty?"

"Yes sir?" He smiles happily to himself.

"You and the rest are responsible for digging graves."

"All due respect, I think it'd be better if I came along with you on your body hunt. Besides how else are you going to be entertained?"

I walk back to him and whisper beside his ear so as not to offend those around us. "I need you to take charge. I can't trust anyone else to ensure those holes are dug by the time we return. This is important. Can I count on you?"

He sighs without losing his smile. "Alright chief, if it's that important to ya."

Returning to the awaiting crowd I request, "Mr. Jacobson, fetch some paper and something to write with. Keep ahead of the masses and jot down everything that is taken. What we'll do now is form a chain, since not all of us can fit in there, and just hand out the tools appropriately."

I dare not to go in. I just don't want to. The crowd takes care of that for me. They are all frenzied in a strange, yet organized way. I yell out to be careful. I don't want the CitySpire to suffer any damages. It strikes me odd in regard to my sentimentality. I want to preserve it. Best to keep everything the way it is. I'm unsure of whether it has to do with a special form of attachment, an investigative nature, or fear of the Count himself. If they ruin anything, it'll be difficult to piece it all back together. B. Rick. Why do I feel that the name is significant?

The rest of the buildings are not as disheveled as the hardware store. There's a quaint music shop, with no discernable label, that displays a crimson violin nestled up against a purple lace, staring at me from a dusty window. Off to another side there is a silversmith shop, denoted mostly by the silver bowls, pitchers, and snuff boxes. There in the lower portion of the window is a tiny music box, fit with a ballerina in relevé. The door to the shop has a glass window, shattered in one pane that's closest to the knob. The thought of Emily's gift draws me to the threshold. Marty, noticing my sudden detachment, is quick to follow curiously after.

"What are you doing, boss?"

"Just give me a moment." I retort as I check the door handle. Locked. Perhaps it locked itself on her way out.

"We don't have much time for this you know, they'll be asking for some direction in the next few minutes. Be a bit odd if they found you window shopping."

I choose to ignore him. I'm not about to follow any picture that Marty has painted for me, be it as some fearless leader or some dedicated taskmaster. I reach my hand through the exposed hole and turn the knob from the inside. The door gives and I easily push it aside.

The shop is covered in a thick layer of dust with tiny cobwebs hanging from shelves like tiny wedding veils. The things that hide within are uncountable, so many, in fact, that I find myself stalling just to marvel at them and muse on how they'd appear if the dust is wiped away. I could spend hours here. Hanging from wall pegs are several silver pocket watches whose lids are glass allowing one to see both its musical and non-musical mechanics within. There are wooden boxes, no larger than a briefcase, which carry elaborate dinnerware in varying sizes. And there are also small gifts of all sorts: rings, necklaces, cufflinks, earrings, tiaras, combs, broaches, hairpins and hand mirrors. All this and more are strewn about in some manner to attract the attention of a customer or two.

Like the store Open, there isn't a single counter or place for one to make a purchase; more like storage really. It's the same with the shops in Hermes Square and I'm sure it's the same in the hardware store. The CitySpire isn't built to accommodate a seller—odd that it's built to accommodate a buyer.

Marty whistles through his teeth. "My my, isn't this a beaut. Don't think I've ever laid my eyes on anything like this before."

"One person has." I say in a half-whisper.

The dust bothers me. What makes one building antiquated from those around it? What significance do they carry? It's as if the main portions of the city are built and cared for to create some sort of illusion, an illusion to hide something. My apartment building is older than it looks, I could feel it. Often I can hear the wind inspiring the floors to creak. Then there is the furniture that is hidden in the basement of the building. The city didn't just appear out of nowhere. It's been here for a long period of time. What is it hiding? What secrets are buried in the CitySpire?

My concentration is halted by the overhead sound of a flutter. I look above to the wooden rafters. There, on the cherry stained beams, stand rows upon rows of white feathers. An entire flock of pigeons are roosting above, fluttering to and fro neighboring boards in order to gain a better position in watching their bipedal intruders. One in particular coos at us from his lofty perch and a few others answer it as if it were a question directed to them.

There are many, an entire family or possibly an army, all huddled together to survive the long winter temperatures that have yet to dwindle with the snow. I count them as if in race with Emily, but her voice echoes in my head, *"I've already seen a flock today."* And I stop. I do not know why I think of it. Funny that the memory of her disappearing into the clouds inside Boenger's flying machine comes to the forefront.

Marty glances once at the birds above and chuckles. "Don't stand too long under those pigeon tails, boss. This *is* a gift shop after all." He waits for his reaction like he always does and this time he strangles a laugh out of me.

Shuffling toward the window, he watches the progress of the workers outside. His humor always amazes me, even as trying of a time as it is. He places his finger on the dirtied glass and slashes an opaque stripe across the pane.

"So what exactly are you sniffing around for? It's like you're in Farley's apartment all over again, silence and all. It gets to me, you know? The quiet."

I pick up a silver music box with tiny embroidery and turn it over in my hand, looking for the cylinder. Unable to find the panel to the inner workings, I turn the key and get a couple of notes out of it. I remember to answer him.

"I don't know what I'm looking for. Just something…" I finish in mutter after replacing the item on the shelf.

"You're thinking about her, aren't you?"

I swing around to interpret who exactly he's referring to and am surprised to find him not many feet away.

"Her *who*, exactly?"

"That Waters tart you spoke so fondly of last night. Emily was it? You think you found one of her little getaways?"

I sigh from a pain as delicate as the pins in the box. "Could be."

"You know, if you still have something for her boss, you should do something about it. Life's too short to sit around moping about love that shoulda' been."

I puff a breath of regret from my nostrils. "She's better off where she's at. What matters is that she is safe."

"Safe from what exactly? You?"

I look at him with disdain, eager for him to pick up the hint that I don't want to discuss this any further.

Marty relaxes his shoulders in defeat. "Well, if you say so, Mr. Bell. They say love only comes twice in your life."

"Another one of Miss Box's sayings?"

"No, don't really know where I heard that one." He returns to the window and squints through the stripe he made. "It looks like they're almost done. I can see Brigit's foot tapping."

He doesn't wait for an answer from me. Instead he walks towards and then out the door as if he was a customer who was just browsing.

Marty's an okay guy and I think he's trying to do what's best for those around him. What really impresses me is that he didn't take anything from the shop. Knowing how these ruffians have treated all the others around the city, I'm confounded he didn't take up the fad and line his pockets. Then again, he didn't take anything from Hermes Square either.

Once I had him figured out, I thought he was out to satisfy some notion of grandeur, but that would paint him vain and ambitious. He doesn't seem the type. Helping others, without taking anything for himself – an honorable philosophy. In his own little way he's dedicated to seeking out what best benefits the majority, despite where it places him on the ladder. I can see him helping old ladies across the street regardless that he's bound for the opposite direction. Perhaps it's too early to judge him, to figure out his inner character, but so far I'm liking what I see – a man of action.

The cylinder will have to wait. It's not like I'd recognize it if I had found it. In the end, that is all one can hope for in this place: just a little familiarity. I wave to the pigeons above in pardon for the intrusion. I leave the flock as they look on in indifference.

The streets are engulfed by the dress of the city. The fog is thick, leaving only a few stories visible before rendering the rest of its towers in bleak vapors. Brigit takes the front like a grey she-wolf ahead of the pack of unskilled laborers. It's terrible business walking the streets for corpses and the troupe's silence only reaffirms it. With a little ingenuity we managed to create a makeshift stretcher out of rake handles and canvas, as well as a cart with a piece of plywood, rope and wheel barrel frame. But now fully equipped to deal the simple task of carting the dead to their final resting place, we've been interred in a severe disadvantage. Every street is looking the same.

I've been to this section of the city before, but the fog is making things a little disorienting. I reaffirm what street we are on, remembering back to when I used to take walks in search of Rachel not long after I first woke up. But I can not shake the feeling that streets are moving behind us like a dismal labyrinth. It is doubt that serves as the major muddle.

Sometimes I can make out Briget as she eagerly strolls forward as if she can pierce through the smoky veil as if it were thin air. *"It's those grey eyes of hers,"* I heard from one of the other men. And with the way she traverses the street without need to reach out in fear of running into something, I'm starting to believe it.

My traveling companions, a sorry lot consisting of seven men and two women, flank me on all sides. Their faces have taken to a pallid coloration, in part due to the thickness of the fog and the frigidity of the season. Occasionally, I can see tiny wisps wafting around their bodies like ghostly hands caressing them for a moment's remembrance of what it was like to once to have physical limbs.

Every face is grave and dirtied from the many days of living on the streets. A question comes to the forward portions of my mind and I wonder why any of them haven't taken residence in any of the empty buildings. One would think that they would seem inviting to those who are forced to suffer the frigid temperatures and incessant ice-water rains. It's like what Marty had said earlier, *"It's the silence that gets me.*" Could the constant sound of nothing keep them from seeking residence? I regret not taking Marty up on his offer to come with me, at least then I'd have someone to talk to.

Without wind or rustle from the cityscape, I adopt the same expression as those around me as desolation finally sets in. But then a roguish man, black hair and brown eyed, catches the return swing of my shirt cuff. He looks to be in his late thirties. He's rather round, his shoulders are sloped downward and a round pair of glasses hugs his face. I notice a few strands of premature grey collecting around the roots of his bangs. Appallingly, he wears a brown smock coat that I distinctly remember from Hermes Square window display.

He speaks cautiously and quiet as if the entire city were to collapse upon him should he speak too loudly.

"You-you were here when it began, right?" He stutters, but I'm unsure if it's part in due to the cold or some mental aliment.

"Not sure. I was here when there wasn't anyone else." I rethink my answer adding, "At least no one that wanted to be found."

He whispers and I have to lean in to hear. "The-then, can you tell me something?" His teeth chatter in fear that he may have said it too loudly. What do you know about *them?*"

I'm confused. "Who, exactly?"

Brigit returns to us, pushing back the fog like a well-seasoned fisherman. Her face however is flat with a level of seriousness that I've not seen before on a lady. Her once pink skin is the color of apparitions and her grey eyes have now taken on the same wisp-like qualities of the mist.

She replies to the unspoken question in our minds, "Something's following us."

"Like what?" I beg as she rushes by.

She nabs a shovel handle and tears it from one of the stretcher's loops. She then turns around glaring at my question as if it's absurd.

"Something lookin' for trouble, that's what."

The crew cast weary eyes around them, each squinting to pierce the thick miasmas that seem to encroach upon us as the seconds roll on. Those around me stiffen in the neck as they strain to see beyond their neighbor – albeit their curiosity. I reflect the fear in their faces as their last remaining color melts to reveal veins turning varicose. Everyone has stopped and I am stuck in the middle of the outfit as folks subconsciously circle in case an attack could come from any direction. No one utters a word. No one moves. I'm thrown further to edge, as I watch as all breathing ceases at once so everyone can put their ears ahead. Occasionally, there is a scuff of someone's shoe against the pavement and the sound sends a ripple of cringes through my spine.

The mist has perhaps played a trick upon our noble scout and my continence lightens until my spirit hides in my chest as distant footsteps break the silence of the ground fog. I hear them off the side street, walking like a pair of jackboots, and then stopping when the sound bounces off to the left. The footsteps draw nearer, slow at first and then quicken their pace. So quick, in fact, that the footsteps cross the entire length of the street, pass through us, and then zip behind. People jump as they grab at their arms or sides as if something had just brushed against them. The circle pulls inward and people bump into one another to take comfort in a warm body.

My heart trembles. The ground clouds act only to amplify my imagination of some nefarious demon gambling against us from the sidewalk to see how many he can fell.

Brigit pushes her way to the forefront, waving the handle above her head as if it were a club. "Show yourself!" She screams while baring her teeth at the invisible phantoms.

The footsteps fall quiet. The feeling of being watched is unshakable and perhaps more this time than not, stronger. The footsteps begin again, swooping by like some feral animal looking for a morsel to sink its teeth into. Patting against the ground in a full sprint, they approach and pass through the middle of us. A skid of boots against concrete and Brigit is knocked to the ground.

A pair of men rush to her side, taking up the call of the fallen comrade to bring her back to the safety of the tightly pressed circle. Brigit resists.

"Let me go! I'll fucking kill them." But the men ignore her pleas, figuring her anger a mild punishment to witnessing her being gobbled up by the vaporous creature.

The dark-haired vagrant besides me starts muttering a prayer; his teeth barely allow him the words as they chatter uncontrollably.

There's a shift in the vapors, a movement of some humanoid shape twisting like an apparition in the natural rolling of the mist. The being is faceless and its arms stretch out long before it grasping at whatever is near it. Then it disappears with a draft of air.

I see others in the distance, the fog revealing at first their heads, then later their shoulders and torsos. Each marches its way towards the west. Their faces: all jeering – as they proceed in their grisly procession. I can hear their steps, their long trudge up Panset Boulevard. Headed where, I know not.

The army of spirits passes through us, bumping here and there into a man or two, knocking one to the side, or touching the wrist of another bewildered. A woman lashes out at her hair as it rises as if by static.

Brigit breaks fast from her guardians and out into the street. She takes up the shovel handle and once again renews her swinging at the haunts. Perhaps more due to the disruption of air than the object itself the fog rolls on, taking the image of the figures with it.

I am awed in its wake, as I can do nothing. Paralyzed in the whole scene of it all, the mist lessens as it continues further along the street, soon far from sight, leaving us mystified with a lingering sense of dread that can only come with a brush from the supernatural. A drizzle of fog is all that remains.

13

We walk together, still dazzled from the eerie experience. Those forms, those mist-walkers, were far from the normal expectations. None of us were prepared when they descended upon us, and neither are we prepared to understand even partially what just occurred.

The man who had first mentioned them, I found, is named Thomas Cagney. This plump man's nerves have yet to relieve themselves of the entire affair. I can't say that I blame him. However, where as the rest of our company have returned to a straight back, Mr. Cagney is still hunched in figidity. I'm unsure as why Brigit chose Cagney over any of the other strong backs. Then again, I can't picture him down in a ditch digging graves either. Though as spooked as he is, it doesn't prevent him from talking to me. I now, his only voice of salvation.

"Ca-can't say th-that I'm s-surprised we ran into them. Th-they tend to be curious sorts." He says as a form of rationalization.

"You've ran into them before?" I ask.

Cagney blinks more than a man should. "Yes. Pl-plenty of times. By the s-sound of your voice, you must n-not have known about them. I f-find that odd, f-for someone who's been here so long."

If I didn't know any better, the little man is insinuating something.

"I find it odd that people suddenly appear out of thin air, that there is furniture where there used to be none. And it's a little odd, personally, that the shops are now bare where they once were filled with clothes." I cast his coat a horrid glare.

Mr. Cagney halts momentarily, fearing I'd strike him, before he then takes up walking again.

"Many apologizes, mis-mister Bell. I did not mean to off-offend you. I som-sometimes say th-th-things and they-they come out wrong. I-I just find it odd, is all, na-nothing meant by it."

If Brigit had reason for choosing Mr. Cagney as part of our group, it would be more to keep an eye on him so he wouldn't get himself into any trouble. Then again, the man looks harmless enough.

"No offense taken. It appears that there are a lot of things about this city that many of us are still getting used to." It's strange and I feel myself compelled to indulge as to the amount of information that this small fellow may have acquired in his short life here in the CitySpire. "Tell me about them."

"I d-don't know m-much about them as you think. B-but, I have seen them before—yes. You see, they aren't ones to sti-tick around for long. They usually ka-come when someone is about to-to die. But, not everyone ca-can see them, Mr. Bell. Th-this is the first—I think. I jus-just fig-thought that you being here for so-so long that you would have seen them by now."

In fact, now that he mentioned it, I have seen them. When I brought Emily home the first time I saw their faces staring at me from the foot of the bed. I thought that they were a hallucination caused by physical exhaustion, but no. They were there, as Mr. Cagney has pointed out, for her death. But Emily didn't die, so perhaps Cagney has misinterpreted the omen.

"Are you sure? Then does that mean someone is going to die?"

"Na-na-not necess-ss-arily, Mr. Bell. As I said, they ar-are the curious type. They are-are harmless, really, just there to-to watch. De-de-death tends to linger on, and it-it-it's sometimes the-the people around you who-who bring them. App-a-rently, there were enough ba-bad thoughts for everyone.

"Harmless you say? Brigit got knocked down by them. I don't see that as being harmless."

"Na-not knocked d-d-down, I was watching her, she-she won't admit to this, and pl-please don't-t-tell what I said bu-bu-but she slipped."

Slipped? It is a possibility, just one that I hadn't considered until now. The ground is moist and she could have easily thrown herself off balance when she was swinging that pole around. Then I remember something else, "But if they are so harmless, why were you afraid? I heard you praying."

"Pr-pra-ing? I'm s-s-sorry Mr. Bell, if I may have again offended y-you. It wa-wa-was not my intention. I wa-was saying a prayer for a-all of us. You see, I wa-was af-afraid that they wa-wa-were coming to wa-atch someone die. I don-on't like seeing my fr-fr-friends dying, Mr. Bell. Br-br-breaks my heart."

There I have it. The very reason that Brigit brought him along: innocent honesty. It's been awhile since someone's managed to reach me inwardly and it's a very comforting feeling — a feeling that I'm not used to.

I place my hand upon his shoulder. "You're a good man, Thomas Cagney."

"Th-thank you." He says while adjusting the glasses on his nose. "I w-w-would surely ha-hate to disappoint you, Mr. Bell." He lets out a cold breath. "Now, I think Miss Brigit would l-ike to ta-alk to you."

"Why's that?" I ask dumbfounded.

He unravels his finger slowly towards the nearby buildings. "Bec-cause, the ghosts are in the windows. We-we must be getting close."

And close we are. Brigit waits at a break in the fog, watching the mists swell around a lump in the road, the clouds drawn to death itself. We are all hesitant, even myself. The workers stand aback, waiting for their cue to begin the process of carting this one back to the graveyard. Brigit and I stand not far from one another, a foot or so, and stare in wait for disruption of any kind. The mound at the center of obscurement sends a shiver through my fingers and up my arms, as where Farley had been fresh as the moment he jumped, this one has a few days head start towards ol'man Rigor.

Brigit doesn't show any initiative to press forward: her legs are locked, her shoulders are tense and from the expression of anxiety poking at her dimples, she won't be moving in that lonely direction any time soon. I can hear Marty's voice in the back of my head, *"Tis time to shine, boss. Show them a thing or two."* And so I take a breath and drag my feet across the pavement.

The walk there is a desolate one. My heart beats to the melody of Chopin's Marche Funèbre, its intro playing across my mind like a dark procession of instruments and banners. It is no surprise, as I draw nearer, of the dress the fallen victim chose for his final display. He has no shoes and barefoot, with white silk pants and a loose-cut pearl shirt, and nearer—his pale blue skin, shoulder length blonde hair, and white glossy eyes, a sight that I could have done without. His mouth is opened, a slight brown rust caked to his lips.

At his side I squat, where I draw his card from his shirt pocket. Same card alright. I speak his name in whisper, "Raymond Keel."

His chest heaves a breath and in its spasmodic exhalation he sings in a sawdust voice, *"Here lies one whose name was writ in water."*

I sprawl backward, carting myself like a crab a few feet before halting. My soul screams out as if it were once more a part of the phantom army. My lungs absorb the fleeting words like the inhalation of soil. Caught within my throat is a long gasp that should have been shrieked and now forever trapped within me to remind me of this terror. Yet his corpse, a sound and yet unmoved thing, rests once more in its original position as if nothing had occurred.

I hoist myself cautiously back into a squat, pick up the card that I dropped—now soaked by a puddle—and return it with a trembling hand to his pocket. Not a motion from the corpse. It is as if the whole thing were part of some dismal day terror.

A cold hand presses itself against my shoulder and I spin with thoughts of some ghoul, but I am met with the boyish Brigit.

"What happened? Did he bite ya?" Under the ashen ambience generated by the ether, her concern is no more warming than the corpse below me.

Remembering what Cagney said. I reply with, "No, I just slipped." It does me no good to demoralize them into a fitful retreat from the direful whisperings of a corpse. At the moment, I'd rather be seen as clumsy than inspire horror-fed tales that'll forebear future adventure. Better for all that I bear it alone.

"I see." She says without judgment in her voice. "Are ya done poking it then? I'd like to get him in the ground before sunset."

"Well said." I return as I ease back into standing, me eager to agree in order to end her questioning.

Brigit thumbs to a few laborers. "Let's get a move on, gents. This day ain't over until the ground swells with bodies. Mr. Bell likes his streets clean."

I stand there and ponder, while the men roll the corpse onto one of the stretchers. Mr. Keels spoke. Were they his last words before he struck the ground? Did I disturb the final breath to release? No—that's impossible. *Here lies one whose name was writ in water.* Another ditty to frighten me in the late hours of the night.

We carry his body from the scene, turning at Wood and proceeding towards Cherry Street—a place where Brigit claims she saw a few others lying about. All the time, I eye the corpse with a tremble in my heart worried if he, in some manner of disruption from the workers that carry him, will mouth the words once more. But he lays there, his head now forever star gazing and his eyes closed by Brigit's hand.

With many steps behind us, our troupe stumbles upon the next fell pair. They look to have jumped at the same time, perhaps, in fact, from the same window. Of course it is fairly difficult to determine since the moisture blocks our upward view. I'd like to take a look at what their habitation was like, how they lead their existence until that fateful moment when they leapt from the towers—if or if not, hand in hand. A Warren and Lucille Barnett. Everything lays the same: pearl white clothing, silk, no shoes, the card in the left hand pocket. They are all like my dream, all part of the same phenomena surrounding Farley's death.

I aid with the woman by hoisting her up and onto the wheel barrel frame alongside a few of the men. The stench is with this one; a foul decaying mixture of worms and refuse playing tricks on the inner portion of my throat. As soon as her body raps against the rickety boards, her hand drops and catches my wrist with tight black fingernails.

"Cry no tears for us, my friend." I pry at her fingers, panicking to be released in fear that she may drag me into death with her. She croaks again, *"Lend no aches to the dreams of yesterday."*

From the corpse of Warren, his greyish gums smack from whatever goo has settled in his mouth, *"Allow the tide sweep free the bay."*

Then together they sing in zombie choir, *"And home the ships sailing send."*

Her hand releases, dropping as lifeless as the moment we found them. Lucille Barnett's eyes stare at me through their translucency, begging me to forever remember their portentous dirge.

"Mr. Bell – can we get a move on?" Brigit requests without indication of witness. "Are you going to stare longingly at every dead girl you meet or is this a one-time thing?"

"Forgive me, she—" *Think.* "—reminds me of someone I once knew."

"Better than her being so." She pats my shoulder as it were a good joke and tarries lightly forward as if in wait for me to join her side.

In the corner of my eye I can see the timorous face of Thomas fixated on me as if I were a practiced doomsayer. He swallows something far too ill-conceived and hardy to be a usual swallow, his throat all the tighter in his walk. I nod my head to him, then repeating to let him know that yes—I heard them and that they were speaking to me. He bares a wry grin, then turns his head with his eyes in unison ahead. I know that he understands the message.

Again we trudge, through the dark synapses of the CitySpire, making passage through alleys deemed shortcuts to the other streets teeming with bodies. There we find others, sprawled out on the streets like lost children in the night, waiting in place for the rescue parties to find them. These are by far not the hugging sort. And as we gather the others, I—in anticipation of unearthly tune—do not jump when the next three corpses expel a few additional lines:

"Bury us low beneath the cold,"

"Deep in swollen womb, at silent end."

"Perched there, the old cypress tree bends"

"With wing, to carry us westward told."

I judge Thomas' reaction to be much the same as my own. Some would subscribe the dampness and the boreal winds to Mr. Cagney's and my bloodless cheeks, however the two of us share—never to relay—the gross nightmare of our citywide search upon our face.

We end in the gathering of six, though many of the laborers make mention that they may have seen one off Shore Street, or perhaps one not far from the last over off Daltier. But six would make the company of seven, and seven is a lucky number to stop on. Any more this day and I'm afraid the workers would collapse.

Brigit and I manage the sixth, a raven-haired man with deep emerald-set eyes—the freshest of the day. He keeps voiceless the entire way, never moving or even a whisper to make this trip any more unbearable. We take the current street back to Rhine and march in procession up to the lurching black gates of the CitySpire Cemetery.

Marty greets us immediately.

"'Bout time you joined us, we were all getting a bit distressed sitting out here all by our lonesome. Did you bring us any goodies?"

A bit out of breath, I stammer out, "How many?"

"Well, there are about twenty of us; twenty-one if you count me. So if you brought any for yourselves I imagine we would need at least—"

"Graves, Marty. How many graves?"

"Oh, that! We managed about eight graves. I think they are just finishing up the last one. These men and women are hard workers. You've certainly inspired something in them."

"Good. We're ahead of schedule."

Marty looks around me in count. "Only six? Couldn't you and Brigit have carried one each yourselves?"

I tear him a spiteful glare.

"Okay, okay—no need to be giving me that look. There's something I'd like to make mention to you, nothing big. But did you know that these graves come equipped with their own caskets?"

"Yes, I already knew that." I reply.

"Don't you find that a bit deranged? Why would you go through the trouble of digging a grave—which isn't very fun, mind you—and bury an empty casket? It doesn't make sense."

He's right – it doesn't make any sense, but what part of the CitySpire ever did? Tired, frigid, and still quivering from the corpse's ballad, the query just isn't very high on my priority list.

"You doing okay, chief? You don't look like yourself."

Brigit irradiates her impatience by bypassing any future order and waves the laborers to bring the bodies.

"The city hasn't been kind—"

A Miss Marylyn Crootch is carried by us. Her lids flutter half open, enough that I can see her milky orbs oozing from beneath her eyelashes. Her flaky rust colored lips breathe open, struggling like a fish, to expel the remaining words that are lodged in her throat.

"Slumber we now, beyond the sunlit shown. Ne'er to wake in favored listless breeze."

She passes like the rest, without additional word or visible proof she had spoken. I look for Cagney, desperate in search to see if he too had heard, but he is nowhere to be found. Alone. I am to hear their morose callings in disturbing isolation, here in the company of the deaf.

Marty grabs at my shoulder. "What's wrong, boss? You look a bit spooked. Recognize any of these chumps?"

"No… I—" My words are snuffed. It is as if my lungs have finally shriveled up, as if the deceased have leeched out the moisture to lend aid to their final words. I'm exhausted and, without fair warning, my legs buckle from beneath me.

Marty catches my arm and hoists me to partial standing. "Whoa there chief." He eyes those who are nearby. "The ground's a bit wet now. A little slippery. You got to be a bit more careful."

"Marty." I plea. "Walk with me. I've seemed to overstep myself."

"Aye, I can see that." He helps to gather my balance and in so he brushes against my neck. He then mentions in whisper, "You're feverous, boss. Best if you rest awhile."

"There'll be plenty of time for that." I push off of him into steadiness.

Brigit is already at work, directing the men to deposit the bodies in their respective coffins. I make it a point to plunder each of their cards and write the respective number on the back according to how they lay. Somehow, their gravestones will need to be marked.

When I come across the last gentleman, the black-haired fellow with emerald eyes, he stirs in his box. His lips quiver, as if having difficulty in relaying his final words. I kneel closely to him. Marty watches intently the strangeness in my actions.

The cadaverous lips continue to struggle, as if the world were no longer filled with air. I place my ear close to his mouth and release a pent-up breath within me. His voice is faint.

In one dark exhale he releases a dying breath, *"Farley."*

A chill creeps down and settles within the pores of my back. I can feel the rearing of hairs and for the life of me, I cannot shield the chaos that burns through my mind. I step away and order his coffin to be nailed shut.

Then as the last board is in place, all the rest of the coffins are lowered deep into the ground below. I look up and above as if hearing a distant sound. And there, on an ill desired hill, lies a gnarled cypress tree. Upon it, there roost six pallid pigeons in white stares.

I hear the fallens' ballad in my ears, ringing over again:

"...no tears for us... no aches for yesterday...allow the tide sweep free the bay... and home the ships sailing send."

The birds raise their shouldered wings and take to the dark brume that lies to the west, I hear again the song shifting in the wind.

"Full those sails in silk raised sheaves."

"Fare us well, spirit bound for the unknown."

I shelter my eyes from the experience and listen as Brigit gives a sorrowful eulogy for those we'll never know.

It is madness after the final shovel of soil is patted against the last mound. The laborers all burst in merrymaking and conversation— all jubilant voices—that for once drowns out the persistent quiet. It has been known to grapple the inhabitants of the CitySpire, it attempts to quaff them like a fleeting candle flame. Yet now, it is a solemn victory that all are willing to celebrate. Marty looks on as Brigit is picked up by a handsome beau. She shrieks with as much boyish aptitude as she can muster without sounding like a blushing maid.

"If you know what's good for you, you'll put me down!" She wails.

Yet it seems that with the sudden energy none are willing to come to her rescue, at least not this time.

"Well now," Marty says. "Didn't expect this much out of them. Who would have thunk there could be this much happiness swimming out of a graveyard." He ponders a bit to himself. "Perhaps we should move this party elsewhere before the environment *soils* the mood."

I shake my head at him before uttering, "I humbly agree." I extend my hand out to him after having spent the past few moments resting on a gravestone. He draws me up to standing and, in near echo of one another, we both spout out, "To Open?"

"Yes," I respond to our query. "To Open it is."

And like the conductor of a marching band, I muster a call that gathers everyone's attention, "Wine for everyone! Follow me to wine!"

Together we march down Rhine Street. We pass Hermes Square and salute my apartment building as we all continue westward. In the glass windows of buildings we appear as an army, all dirtied from a hard day's labor – enlarged to such effect that our thirty easily replicates to the three-hundreds. Judging by rapturous cheers, the screams, and the boisterous nature of us all, our company could easily be mistaken for foreign invaders, hell-bent on seizing this section of the city for ourselves.

Yet, as we approach the neon glow of the Open sign, a bitter sight hangs from one of the cross-shaped street lamps. It's the feet we see first. Then the red. Two men sway silently from each arm of the crossbeam, a rope taut against their neck suspends them a good eight feet off the ground. Their clothes are neatly folded and set to the side, their boots are displayed at the bottom base of the lamp.

Torn. Their bodies are bled and scratched as by claws or a jagged knife. Their faces are mangled so badly that it would be impossible to identify them. Their heads are limp, with their jaws extruding far more fiercely from its hinge, allowing air to whistle through it. A deep sanguine trail leads from the door of Open and out onto the street, as well as a few scattered entrées and a couple of burlap bags filled by—what I can only imagine—as food from the convenience store. It's easy to determine what they were up to.

A note, in familiar script, is carved into the flesh of their exposed chests. It reads:

"Licentious and sans worth – CCdC"

The sound of jubilance has been choked by the ropes as each imagines their necks squeezed beneath the hemp. What frightens me, perhaps more so than the rest, is the full knowledge that such violence was done by a single man – hoisted and displayed for all those to see. The Rue du Bourreau has finally lived up to its name, beneath the ever terrifying eyes of Count Champ du Croix.

Marty is the first to break the barrier of ill-quiet. "Ladies and Gentlemen, looks like we have two more."

We bury them much the same as the rest. These men, however, have no identity. The Count made sure of that. Even if their faces were not disfigured, no one here would know them. In the pockets of the men's clothes I find nothing but a burnt edge of a card and ashes. They were intentionally marred to be forgotten – to rejoin the legion of the nameless who now trudge through the streets as a mist walker. The Count is merciless.

Once the pit is covered, I'm despaired to witness a few of our lot exhaling a fit of worry, some fear, while others a poorer countenance than before we started.

Swarms of pins and needles kamikaze themselves against my brow and I shiver from encounters past. The Count truly is a murderer. It appears that the fearful water everyone had bathed him in has finally soaked in. Ghastly.

It's only when we all converge outside the gate of the now haunted place that Brigit breaks through the destitution and speaks her mind.

"This is bullshit! Who the hell does he think he is? What gives him the right?"

"Calm yourself, love. They were taking all the food and last time I checked there wasn't all the much to go around."

"That doesn't justify it, Mart! Sure – they shouldn't have been doing that, but they shouldn't have been hanged for it! He's a damn murderer!"

Marty attempts to shush her violently, pointing at her with dire warning. "Careful there, sweet cheeks. You don't want to bring his attention to yourself. Judging from that rope work, he'd have to be fairly strong to string them up on his own. Wouldn't take him much on your account."

"I'd rip his eyes out." She argues, but her voice lessens in volume. And I can tell simply by a spasm in her cheek and a twitch of her left eye that she knows what Marty is saying to be true and all the more chilling.

It isn't right – not just the murders but how quickly everyone is robbed of their celebration. It was a short instance where the concerns of the city no longer burdened anyone else's shoulders. For a short fleeting time I had forgotten my earlier depressions. I felt invigorated, vivacious and deep within fools' paradise. It's all come crashing back upon us. It isn't fair, especially for them who've worked so very hard to have it all rinsed in the gutter.

"Listen everyone," I hold up my hand so that people are able to see who it is that is speaking. "I'm not about to let the Count take away what it is that we worked for all day. We should be proud of our accomplishment and are entitled to everything that comes with it. Forget Open. I invite you all to my apartment, where there should be enough perishable succor to orchestrate the event. All in favor follow me."

There are no arguments, only an overwhelming desire to forget—at least for a short while—what we all witnessed hanging from the posts in the Rue de Bourreau. So, people agree and people follow. And I know in our walk back that my stocks aren't plentiful enough to feed such a population, but I'm sure that with the aid of Farley's pantry that it will make it a memorable occasion.

Marty is still pale with the apparition of feet dangling in his mind, so I slap him on the back—a quick jolt to boost him into his usual self—before he or anyone else pollutes the tenor.

We return from whence we started, between my building and Farley's – smack dab on the corner of Gnosh and Rhine. Everyone waits for their just due, each stretching their neck—but not too far— to see beyond his neighbor, as if being first to hear will be imparted some supernatural powers that'll give them an edge over his lesser kin. It's time I told them.

I study them and drink in their exhausted eyes, all desperate for the information that I promised at the day's start. I wet my lips and there is a gasp from somewhere in the crowd. I bleed sweat beneath my clothes and somewhere within there is a screaming voice crying beneath the pressure of anxiety, muffled through a blanket of the day's work and the flayed skin of the dead. I feel stronger than I have ever before and for once I feel in control of the next few seconds. It's as if the world has turned over in lull.

Carefully, and without giving too much of myself to the vanity of the stage, I give them exactly what I told Marty the night before.

And as the words ink out of my mouth, the people form a circle, each eager to lap them up.

I begin with the light disappearing beneath the door and the songs that swam through my head, my familiarity with Mozart, Brahms and Chopin; about the way things once were, where the silence was ruled by the ambience of the city and the people who lived within. I tell them of the emptiness and the loneliness it provided in turn. I speak of Emily, and as my heart wraps around the idea of her, so too do the faces of my audience. I move on after noting the yearning glimmer in their eyes, feeling I have portrayed her correctly and without any malice.

I continue in tale regarding our discovery of 'Open' and then frighten them with the introduction of the Count. I speak highly of the Lockes, of Michael's ability to predict the weather and Natalie's unconditional kindness. I describe to them our trip to the Cathedral, of pigeons and the graveyard. I mention our astonishment in finding the furniture beneath the apartment; of Boenger and his amazing flying car. When they ask what he called it, I tell them "a Whirly-Gig". I reveal their mysterious appearance and in that, I conclude the tale with watching as Farley leaps from the top of the seventh story.

They stand lost in their own imaginations of what once was and some stand as if clutching the edge of the abyss — held there by both disparity and curiosity. Yet for some, they look love struck, or perhaps I have mistaken it for heartbreak. I really cannot tell. Whatever their emotions may be, it all has some profound effect on them. It is as if watching one surface with relief from the ebb of the sea, after having been under for far too long. I see a woman's face, one who helped in the digging of the graves, wipe her eyes. Those who don't release tears, I feel as if they're on the verge. It is not from sympathy for my past or because they were moved by the telling, but from something deeper. It stems from finding commonality with all those around them. Without a past there can be no future. Here I've given them a stepping stone. I've given them history. It no longer stems from what they did the day before, but now it illuminates into something far greater. It's a common nostalgia for something that once was or had ever been. And no matter how indirect my "answers" to any unspoken question had been, it serves them as a better understanding for the condition of things. A release, I'd wager, from a chain of uncertainty and misdirection.

"And now my friends, my comrades, I would like to invite each and every one of you off the streets and into the apartment of your choice. My building is empty and so is the one across the street. I almost guarantee that there are still pieces of furniture hidden deep below the ground floor. I am more than willing to help everyone move into their respective dwelling. You don't have to decide now as now is the time to celebrate a new beginning. We've all earned it. So stay, drink with me, and let's starve off the coming silence that waits on the morrow."

The streets are filled in applause.

14

The bottles uncork to hurrahs and cheering. The room wavers as if watching everything beneath water. A toast. *Here's to me, here's to them.* There is a succulent feast spread throughout the room: dishes in hand, some on the counter and others on the floor. There are people in the hallway. I can hear them laughing. But the window! The Count is there in the window! How his eyes blaze with fire!

I wake. The night's festivities dance's a jig inside my head. It is a party I can't quite remember. How much did I drink? I can't recall. It was obviously more than my share, as I've slept in the same clothes from yesterday. It's time for a shower. I make it a long one. As the warm water massages my dehydrated muscles, I think on the prior night.

Marty and I, Brigit and a few other strong hands gathered a few boxes full of food from Farley's pantry. The three of us cooked until, of course, we were overthrown from our kitchen duties by a few others. I can't remember their names. It turned out well, it was very delicious. I played piano and was usurped from classical into a free-spirited jazz. Apparently, I'm not the only one who knows how to play. Drinks were served and people shared experiences. Something about nude beaches? There were many waking stories: alleys, warehouses, back streets, dark suburban housing with frayed wallpaper… a generation born on the streets. My head – how it pains me…

I don't remember how much I drank. I don't remember if there had been enough bottles to get anyone snockered. Somehow I managed it. Perhaps with all the work we had done, since I hadn't had all that much to eat that day – it could have been the cause. It doesn't matter, I guess. It doesn't change the fact that I'm suffering for it now. I contemplate taking some medicine, but decide that it's better to take it when I absolutely need it and not due to something I did to myself out of carelessness. Who knows if there will be any more? The throbbing of my head can serve as a good reminder of that.

After dressing I check the damage in the next room. Nothing too serious. The guests weren't without heart, as everything waits patiently for me in the kitchen next to the sink. I'll get to it later. As an ode to habit, I check the window for news.

The streets are quiet like the many months before, although I am surprised by a little activity. A couple walks out of my building. I've seen them before. It's the lady with the long blonde hair, hanging towards the crease of her back, being escorted by a brown haired cavalier. I don't see their faces. They walk arm in arm, she pointing off to the east and they then make their way up Gnosh. They were at the party I think, inseparable, as I recall. They fell in love with my Sibelius. That is until the rest had me change the tune.

A knock and Marty lets himself in. His clothes are wrinkled, but his shirt is half buttoned, his hair disheveled and wet, and his tie is unknotted and hangs loose. A few eye-sweeps about the room and Marty jests, "Haven't you got this place picked up yet?"

I glare at his reflection in the window, slightly irritated from his sudden intrusion. "Why don't you come in." I chew over the next few moments before swallowing the offense. "And where did you bound off to last night?"

Marty scratches his head. "You don't remember? I took Miss Box up to that sky apartment belonging to those old neighbors of yours. You said we could have it for the night."

"Did I?"

I try and think back through the fog of forgetfulness. I see them cuddling on the couch. I'm playing the piano. I see them kiss, and she looks at me; her eyes are alight like a wicker flame. At some point, Marty's arm is snug around her waist. He presents me with a question and I wave them merrily to standing. Together they walk out the door and into the hallway. He clicks his teeth with the motion of a finger pistol.

"I guess I did." I can't recall all the details, but I'm not about to let on about it.

"Some party, huh? I don't think I've seen so many happy faces at one time. They'll never forget this event, I can assure you of that. My compliments to the host."

Marty pokes at one of the saucer stacks and examines a burgundy lipstick stain along the rim of one of the wine glasses. "Do you want help with these?" He asks while rubbing his fingers together to kill off any skin cells that may have been infected.

I shake my head and I can easily feel the grey matter swishing in my skull. "Leave it. I'm not feeling up to dishes today."

"Well, I hope you're up to keeping promises. A couple of lovely finches from yesterday want to move into one of your apartments down below. And from what I heard spreading amidst your guests, is that they may not be the only ones. A lot of people want to take you up on that offer."

That painkiller is tempting. I need some water, but there aren't any clean glasses left. A part in my brain nudges at my skull and I question, "So where is Miss Box?"

Marty shrugs his shoulders. "Don't know. She was gone before I woke. She's certainly a sneaky devil – I'll give her that."

"Did you two…?" I trail as the asking is too uncouth.

"A gentleman never tells, Mr. Bell, you know that. So yes, to answer your question – we did. You could have yourself you know, if you would've taken the proper initiative."

I part from the window and look at him over my left shoulder, the rest of my body unwilling to rile the aches.

"You're joking?"

He walks closer to me, stopping at the back of the sofa as if it were a wall. "She may put up a stiff face but she's all heart. She likes you. I can tell. You can see it too if you look hard enough" He grins one of those wry smiles of his that sheds doubt on whether he's being serious or playing me a fool.

"What about the two of you?" I study him carefully for any change of face. "It seems the two of you have something special."

"If it was anything more than what it was, she wouldn't have disappeared come morning."

"Don't you find that to be a little unusual for a quality in a lady?"

He laughs. "Brigit is no lady, boss. She makes ill at playing the part and proud of it. Even so, there's nothing wrong with a little unusual from time to time, especially when all you're looking for is a little break in the world."

I don't want to argue, especially not about this. But perhaps he's right, maybe I'm struggling to see her as a lady when it is something that she's not. It's obviously apparent in all aspects of her life. Perhaps it's a bit unfair of me to attach the label. I concede.

"I'll give you that. Your words. Quoting anyone in particular this time?"

"That's all me, boss. Now come on. Those skirts won't be waiting for us forever, and it isn't everyday that they get help from the owner of the Cityspire."

Despite my head's condition, his insistence will have to wait. I find a glass that may have once been mine, give it a quick rinse and down a cool glass of water.

"I'd say 'that's disgusting', but you don't even want to know where I had to get mine a couple weeks back. Not necessarily the most accessible commodity while living in the alleys."

I grab my coat and boots, and march out into the hallway, all the while prodding Marty to take the lead.

The so-called finches happen to be men or promised couples. I suspect that Mr. Kessler's label of "skirts" was his way of creating a sense of urgency. Effective — as if he had mentioned the truth, I would have taken a few more gulps of water and take a pill or two.

The good news is that Marty manages to find the basement key to the elevator hidden in a secret compartment in the elevator console. Fancy that. His usefulness continues to astound me. Things would have been a lot easier had Marty been around. I'm sure events with prior relations would have turned out differently. Then again, he may have started some public works project and exhausted every one of us. Yet, I have no one to blame but myself for this one. I was the one who promised to help others move into their respective apartments in order to get them off the streets. I don't know what I was thinking. A couple days of this and I may be in the clear.

Marty introduces me to Sonia and Jacob Richardson, Christopher Bark, and Terry Insley. Each has his own unique story, and for folks that were to share the same building as mine, I strive to make a point in learning them.

From what I gather about the Richardsons, they are self-proclaimed biologists who are interested in the local plant life – or in this case, the lack thereof. Jacob is the first to ask my permission—as if he needed it before—to categorize and possibly help cultivate the park for future growth. The two of them together exchange a rather wide vocabulary of terms, ranging mostly from their Latin origins, from which I can only guess at their meaning due in part to connotation alone. Mrs. Richardson is quick to catch on to my occasional stupor and promptly changes the subject to something less complex. Our meeting with them is short, as they are more eager to break out into the day than worry much about matching pieces.

Christopher Bark is a small statured man, whose lanky limbs prefer to dangle lazily at his sides whilst Marty and I struggle with each furniture piece—from table stools to armoire—which takes him forever to decide upon. As the two of us sweat from the basement to the elevator, and from the elevator on, he entertains us with his theories on weather phenomenon and celestial mappings. He mentions his disparity in the lack of a clear view almost as if he blames me or some other corporeal entity for the consistent cloud cover.   Under the right circumstances, were it not for the large amount of physical labor that I am forced to undergo, I would love to sit and talk with him about any topic in general. But, Mr. Bark's incessant questions as to *when I woke, how many days have since expired*, that sort of rubbish is causing me to think dark things that are best left unmentioned. For both our sakes, Marty is quick to excuse us from Mr. Bark's presence as soon as the last piece is dropped in place. We leave him to his questions without any shed of guilt.

Terry Insley is a different sort. He is stout, broad-shouldered and built as solid as they come. To me, and I may be a bit biased at this point in the move, Mr. Insley appears more than capable of lifting the pieces on his own and even still, over his head. He greets both of us with a handshake that instills a new meaning to the word torture. His head's shaved and his eyebrows are arched. Yet despite his intimidating stature, I cannot find a shed of aggression. Besides sharp efficiency, I can't see the reason for helping Mr. Insley since he is so capable himself. Then a rationale explanation occurs as we're moving a few non-descript pieces into his new apartment on the fourth floor, he starts up with something interesting.

"I'd like to thank you gents for allowin' me to move into your building. I've been looking fer a kip, but I wasn't sure which one or to whom they belonged."

Marty leaps in to garden a space in the conversation. "No problem. You are more than welcome here in Mr. Bell's Tower."

Bypassing Marty's entrance, he redirects himself to me. "Is that true, Mr. Bell? You're honestly glad ta have us?"

"I'm all for the company, Mr. Insley. The sound of others helps to keep the quiet at bay. Silence has the tendencies of teaching you terrible things about yourself."

"Completely understandable, sir. This place has the tenacity to harbor such nasty things. I'll be glad of it, if it's what grants me the company of you and yer friends. I have a request for you, something that I've been sittin' on since the moment I've laid eyes on her. I'm not sure what siren calls me here, perhaps it's the things you did, Mr. Bell. You see, I'm somewhat of a sculptor. I've been looking for a place to lay my hands, some studio space to do my art. I'm willing to earn my keep."

"I'm very touched, Mr. Insley—"

"Terry, sir."

"Terry, then. I'm touched and we are both gracious to have you. But I don't believe there is much space beyond the apartments for a studio."

"Not in the apartments, sir. I wasn't expecting ta dirty the place with chips and dust. But I was hoping, once a few more pieces of furniture are settled above, that you'd allow me to make use of the space down below."

Marty coughs in. "You mean the basement?"

"Yes, Mr. Kinsley, the basement. I'm not expecting you to lend it to me exclusively—as I'm sure you may have other uses for it—just for the time being and all. I would appreciate the lending and for doing so, I'd be more than welcome to offer you any assistance with building maintenance and even help future tenants move in. I'm sure you'll have yer hands full with other things."

Marty nods his head extensively as if a bobbing bird. "I don't think we'd be needing the space for a good long while, what do you think Mr. Bell?" He continues to bob.

There's a lift in my cheek. "I would be honored to have your help, Mr. Insley. I do have one request, if I may."

"Certainly, what can I help you with?"

"How good are you at engravings?"

Though sore from the previous day and acquiring an even greater load today, I manage to commission Mr. Insley to etch the names of the recently departed on the gravestones. I stress to him the importance of the correct order of the names—else we'd have to swap stones around—dated, Spring, xx00. Who knows the year? Richard Farley is the first to have his name carved in the tomb; Raymond Keel, and then the others.

During one such inscription, we are approached by Briget and her two hulking companions. Her face is taught, stretched to its contour by the crunch of her brow and narrowed eyes.

"Mart, I need to talk to you and yer pal." She stands a few yards away.

I appreciate the approach on her part, but I feel she needs to work a little more on the delivery. Properness and manners do not seem to be in her repertoire, and while some of the newer generation offers a bit more in politeness, she voluntarily does away with the whole tradition. I question whether or not she was at the tail of this new breed's waking, as if etiquette could determine date of birth.

Marty shuffles from his pensive stance over the gravestone; lost in captivation over Mr. Insley's handiwork. I can't say that I blame him. I too listen quite mesmerized at the crack of his hammer against the chisel, listlessly engulfed in the sway of his brush—flinging of the dust—and his smooth rubbing of the stone. It's all very captivating. I think the mason enjoys the audience.

"Well, there's my missing heart." Marty taunts as he closes within a foot from her.

She crosses her arms. "Cut the crap, Mart. I've got something important to talk to ya about."

I scuffle down the low swept incline of the graves to meet them. "What seems to be the trouble, Miss Box?" I ask as stately as I can muster, without letting on to my disdain for her company of other men.

"Have the two of you been down to Open today?"

I drop my limbs and suspire. "Don't tell me the Count has—"

"No – nothing like that, but I promise that bastard will get his due. I'm talking about the kettle of vultures clogging up the joint. Ol' Cagney got a fist full of threats when he wanted a snack. Now I hear they aren't letting anyone in. Says they own the place."

I square with her in the eyes and raise my voice infuriated. "Who's not letting anyone in?" I grit my teeth in the audacity. "Who dares?" I bark louder.

She takes a step backward. "I don't know." She tosses her hands to the side, as if trying to cast blame from herself, before they settle on her hips. "Some mutts that think they have a right to the place." She reclaims her previous step with a witch's glare. "You gonna to do something about it?"

I desperately search the coloration of her grey irises for a precognitive vision. All I see is a reflection of outrage and anger. I cock my head to my side companion.

"Marty, see who you can rally up. We'll show these braggarts who owns what."

He smiles in glee and runs down the path toward the front gates of the cemetery.

"One hour at the apartment." I call after him.

He directs his hand to the center of his chest, raises his eyebrows and purses his lips in one of those, *"Hey, it's me,"* sort of looks before continuing on his way.

"Mr. Insley?" I project over my shoulder loud enough to compensate for the distances between us.

His chipping ceases and answers back, "Aye, sir?"

"Care to accompany us to the store?"

He blows on his tools to rid himself of some lingering dust before replacing them in his leather belt.

"You know, now that you mention it… I do need to pick up some groceries."

Brigit thumbs to the gorillas behind her. "This is Harvey and Brent. The Parson boys."

The six-foot plus duo are dressed in white-cuffed shirts with the sleeves rolled up over their massive arms. Black untarnished suspenders keep their moth-eaten brown slacks from falling off their hips. Their brown hair is cut short, their eyes dark and brown. They don't wear a coat, despite the constant chill. They don't look like they need one.

At the mention of their names, they both cross their arms to bulge out their muscles. It's not until now that I notice their uncanny resemblance. Twins, I suspect.

"They don't say much, but they got it where it counts."

I surely hope she was referring to their overall strength or even the weight of their heart, and not to some other *hidden* characteristic. Considering her one night stands, I wouldn't put it past her.

My hand twitches in anticipation of a coming introduction, but in remembrance of Terry's friendly shake, I decide to weight towards caution and nod to them instead.

"A pleasure, gents." I do not wish to waste any more time on pleasantries. "We should make our way to my apartment. We'll try and snag anyone that happens by."

Brigit smiles in eagerness. "I knew I could count on you, Sam." Be it a sigh of relief or maybe the urgency of the matter, her voice echoes a softness when she says my name. Her features are struck in shock as she too recognizes it. The woman scans me rigorously in order to discern a reaction. I must not be good at faking my observations, as she turns from me quickly to usher forward her larger companions. I swear that her cheeks flushed a slight pink.

"Let's go, boys. Don't wanna keep Mart waiting."

The walk could be shorter had we wished it, but the five of us are in no hurry. We know it will take Marty a good part of the hour to gather as many men as possible to help handle the current situation. Though appreciative of Miss Box informing us of the blighters hold on Open, I'm not up for sharing the coming encounter with her, though I believe she wouldn't have it any other way. As useful as she's proven in the past, we may be walking into a violent situation. I'd hate to see her get hurt.

I want to say something to her, perhaps get my disapproval out in the open so that things between us would lessen in ungainliness. Be it Mr. Insley's nature, or some unknown ability of his to pick up on the ire of others, he too casts a few unusual glances at our company. He talks, so I don't have to.

"So what's yer story, sweetheart? Got a thing for wool?"

She angles her head to peer around at my left sided compatriot. "I ain't your squeeze, Johnny boy. And wool happens to fit me just dandy."

"Johnny boy, eh?" He nudges me. "This tart thinks she's a regular hoot. Look doll, I'm not lookin' to wrinkle your tie, I'm just interested and all."

"Yea?" She grits her teeth. "What's there to be interested in? Do *you* got a thing for cotton?"

"I was refer'n to yer jacket."

"And I was *refer'n* to your shirt."

"I'm not try'n to talk shop wid ya. I'm ask'n why yer dress'n like a blade."

"I can't cut anyone with knitties, now can I?"

"You can cut the blather and tell me why yer dressin like a fella."

"Because I ain't a tootsie, that's why! I act how I want, when I want. And I don't give into cat calling schmucks that are look'n for long legs, sweet cheeks, and a fine teat to suckle on – you got that?"

"I got it. Gesh – it's like try'n to bathe a kitty, talk'n to you."

She leans back in her walk. "Then keep that in your skull and ya won't get scratched."

We all walk in silence for a block, my eyes wide with shock.

"Alright –" Brigit says to the street in front of us. "You want somethin' done? I'll do it. You need someone to get their hands dirty? I'm your gal. But if you're lookin' for a gussied-up floozy with perfect skin and an upturned nose, ya best be lookin' elsewhere. If that's eatin' you up inside, then the problem's not with me. It's the fact you've been fed too much crap and now everything doesn't taste the same anymore."

Dire silence. She's right. Call me old fashioned, I just prefer her in a dress. It's against everything that had been or ever was, those past few months ago. But that's the thing: she's not Emily, Natalie, or a Rachel. She's not even close to high society. She's something else. Why couldn't I accept that, and why am I having problems with it still?

Thoughts quake as a sudden burst of laughter explodes out of Terry. He's red in the face and his eyes water from a joke the rest of us missed.

"She's a spitfire, this one!" He heaves a short breath. "I like it! A regular gutter rat!"

She bites back. "Quiet, brick face – or I'll shove a poker in that gab of yours."

He stops walking to try and catch his breath between laughs. "Fish rag!"

"Shaved gorilla!"

"Alter boy!"

Be as it is, Terry's laughter turns contagious and she catches the giggles. The Parson Brothers start, still the every silent observers, now victims to the plague of hilarity.

I don't laugh. I don't find any of it funny at all. Maybe the problem doesn't lie with Brigit. Perhaps it's me. Maybe, I'm the one who doesn't belong. These are different people, with different expressions. It's I who is the outside society, not them. And the more they laugh, the worse I feel.

There are nine of us walking in close formation with nothing but the seriousness of anger across our faces. The clacks of our boots once were a jumbled mess but somehow on the way down Rhine Street, they managed to conjoin into a single beat. Marty riled up four others along the way, four faces I recognize from the party and from what I heard in his explanation, they weren't all too happy about being barred from the store Open, especially since it is the only source of food.

I take the lead and with the band following close behind, I am sure that we'll be able to extinguish the firebrands ahead. Even with the occasional jibe between Terry and Brigit, we keep our minds focused on what is at hand. My blood builds its pressure behind my eyes so strongly that it feels like my insides are about to implode. Then when I catch the first eyeful of the would-be-tyrants, my heart gorges itself on a hidden reserve of blood and adrenaline.

I hear one of them shout over to a man closest to the convenience store, "General" and then a mismatch of words that I cannot understand.

They gather into a swarm of blackened ants, as the thin veil of vapor still scurrying about the cityscape favors shadows this day. There are many of them, more than what I would have thought. I figured Marty had gathered the majority of these sea waifs yesterday. Apparently, there were some he had missed. There are seven of them in total, with their trusted 'General' coming to the front.

We march but a few feet between us and them, forming a line like the crusaders of the past to better show our numbers. I glare at them with as much malignity as I can muster, with the words—*How dare they!*—splattered on the walls of my skull in red.

His hair is black, his face as pallid as the rest of us, and his eyes gleam of emeralds. He isn't stocky, but lean and athletic. His black satin jacket and flawless slacks leads me to believe that he had taken his share of Hermes Square long before anyone else had gotten to it. His vest flap lies open like an army officer, though his epaulets and silver painted buttons add more to his general-like appearance; these I'm sure were added to the outfit. I stare him down at the level for we are the same height.

"The store is closed." He directs me with his head over his shoulder towards the quaint little building with the large neon sign staged above it. "So you might as well go home."

His band of loyal followers consist of a rag-tag group of men and a single woman dressed in the familiar moth eaten attire that has become a recent trend in CitySpire fashion. All nervously glare at us from the opposing side, each trying their best to be imposing.

I point to the sign that casts his fellow hate-mongers slightly pink. "Looks to me that the sign says, 'Open'."

"Looks can be deceiving, sir. I assure you that the store is quite closed." He issues without a flinch. His face doesn't give way to any inner thought or emotion. He's steadfast, but I don't believe that he's prepared to deal with any physical altercation. The Parson brothers alone would mop the floor with half of these scoundrels. Such confidence allows me to speak with certainty.

"As much as I'd like to give credence to your claim, I'll have to insist upon my previous statement – the store *is* open and will remain that way unless of course you plan to stop us from taking our share. I reassure you that it won't bode well for you or your friends."

He assesses our line as if for the first time. He feigns being unimpressed.

"You want something to eat? Be our guest—"

"Genero!" Growls a gaunt-faced man with a misshapen lip. "What the hell are you—"

Their straight-faced leader holds up his hand to quiet his subordinate. With him hushed, he's able to continue with his original sentence.

"Yes, they can be our guests." His last sentence more for his own thugs than directed at us. "And when the red devil comes to enact his revenge for the theft, I can reassure you that it won't be me cutting you down for a burial."

"Oh, he is frightful." I reply with venom. "But perhaps you don't know who I am. I've had my run-ins with the Count, and I'm well aware of his laws: 'Take nothing less than fairness and nothing beyond deserving', least you suffer beneath his hand. And may I be the first, sir—since we are now getting so well acquainted—that you are encroaching upon the Rue de Bourreau. I pity the man who thinks he can usurp Champ de Croix's claim, especially for this place, as he holds such a fondness for it."

"You know this demon?" His lips turn up into a sneer. "Those were friends of mine!"

"He stalks even me." I spit back in order to dismiss notions of an unholy alliance. "But if I were you, I'd consider picking your friends more carefully. From what we gathered, they were taking way more than what they needed. Some may even consider it stealing. There are other people in the CitySpire that are in need of food. Careful for what you take boys or it'll be your necks swinging from that lamp post."

A few from his side swallow hard. I can see that I'm demoralizing them. Perhaps a just a little more might take the bite out of them.

"And what, might I ask, makes you think you are so deserving?"

"Because – I am the first that woke in the CitySpire. I braved these streets long before you were even a thought. I've been in and out of this store on several occasions, and I'll be damned if I'll let some eye-rubbing sea waif think he can bar me from *my* city."

"You can't own something that you can't personally protect. We've staked this place out for weeks now and all of a sudden you come in here saying you own the place. That's hypocritical, don't you think?" He crosses his arms as if he won something.

"Not particularly, for the difference between you and I is that you make a claim and obstruct, whereas I include. These people behind me have earned their right to be here. This is *their* city too. And while you and your malcontents have been focused on keeping others from eating, they've been busy clearing the streets of the dead, not to mention those friends of yours. What have you done? What right do you have to impede others? for surely, it isn't in your numbers."

His eyes slip silently to the side as if listening to a voice of guilt. He returns with a larger breath in his lungs.

"There's not enough to go around." My heart sinks. "If I let every desperate soul take as they will, there eventually won't be anything left to eat. We'll all starve." He says it so matter-of-factly he catches me off guard.

Thankfully, Brigit reminds me while we are here. "So yer plan was to hoard the food and let everyone else starve to death?" She flashes her teeth. "Let's beat their heads into the curb. It'll be fewer stomachs to fill that way."

"Better you than us." He jabs back at her.

She leaps forward only to be caught beneath the arm by one of the Parson boys.

"Best keep a leash on that one." Says the man with the deformed lip. "Hate for a pretty face to get marred."

"She makes a good point." I add to dismiss this threat. "Hoarding the food isn't going to solve the situation. Eventually you'll run out of options and you'll be forced to turn on each other."

"At least keeping others out and our numbers small, it'll give us enough time to figure something out. Maybe enough time for a ship to come by and get us off this rock."

I feel as if the air has turned heavier and is pressing down upon me. He sounds absurd. "Listen." I try and say calmly. "There are no ships. This is it. This is all that there is."

My words—I did not think well on them—for I can see from everyone's reaction, even Marty beside me, that many believe that we are in need of rescue and that sooner or later a ship will make berth.

Genero unintentionally saves me from the debate.

"Then what do you suggest, huh? Shall we just let people waltz inside and take their fill? Because if so, you will doom us all and I'm not going to let a fool bring us to ruin."

All turn their eyes on me, even my own compatriots, and I don't waste the opportunity to read the desperation growing on peoples' faces. I can see the mistrust and the suspicion turning like gears in their minds. I foresee this turning into something ugly. I think fast.

"Then we'll have to ration it."

"Ration it." His nostrils bat away my words with a puff of cynical air. "And who's going to do that? You?" He shuffles his feet for a well planted stance. "I know we just met, but I don't trust you enough to not skim a little off the side."

"Likewise." I think aloud, but care little enough to allow it to pass beyond my lips. "Fine then, I think I have someone in mind. We'll each chose someone that we can trust to do a good job, that way we can keep a close eye on one another."

Genero stands and stares for a moment in contemplation. He fingers his chin before coming to a decision. "It still doesn't solve the food problem."

"Those who woke in apartments may have their pantries stocked. If we all work together and bring the food back here, we'd be able to last a little longer. That is, until we are able to find a solution to the problem –" I pause. "Or in the off chance a ship were to dock."

"Sounds like a reasonable plan." He contends.

"In the meantime, if I hear that you or any of your lot are hoarding food or preventing others from their share, you won't have to worry about the Count for I'll hang you from the lamp posts myself."

We scowl at each other in a moment of cooling and in his stance and the way that he locks his pupils dead set against mine, he communicates that he's a man of his word. He'll keep his end of the bargain, at least for now.

"Don't worry about us. The same goes for you, sir, so as to avoid any double standards." He points to the dreadful spot of where the last two swayed.

A direful accord.

Genero commands his people behind him. "Let's go ladies and gentlemen. We've got some apartments to search."

He bows his head slightly to me before slowly, though seemingly undefeated, turns in retreat down Rhine and deeper into the Rue de Bourreau. The gauntly faced man, with his deformed lip that's swollen on one side, points two fingers at his eyes and then turns a single one against me. The wrinkling of his brow and the sharpness of his pupils carry with it more than just a warning. It's as if he has just marked me down somewhere in his mind so that he'd never forget.

Marty stands next to me and asks, "So who exactly do you have in mind for this? All I got to say is that it better not be me."

I wait until they disappear completely from sight before breathing easier.

"Two people, actually."

15

"Y-y-you want me t-to-do what?" Asks the ill-at-ease Thomas Cagney. He tries to busy his fidgety hands inside his suit pockets despite that they are stitched shut.

"Thomas, consider this an opportunity to do good for all those around you." I say while trying to convince him. "It's a very important job."

"But, but-tt I'd have to-to work with those people from the s-store?"

Marty decides to put his charisma to the test. "Think of all the perks. You get to meet new people and ensure that we all live a little longer. What more can you want?"

Even when he's trying to be serious, it's very difficult for me to take him that way. I wonder if that's the reason he needed my help inspiring people. From how Cagney starts rubbing his hands against his chest, I can tell he isn't keen on the idea.

"Mis-mm-ister Bell, all d-due respects, but is-isn't there anyone else more qu-qual equipped for the job?"

"No one that I can trust. I've already enlisted Mr. Jacobson into keeping track of the inventory. All you have to do is ensure that everyone is getting their fair share. He did a wonderful job back at the Brick, but he doesn't have the right qualities that I'm looking for."

He puts his fingers to his mouth. "A-and what is-is that, Mr. Bell?"

"Heart." I let the word soak into him. There's a shift in his position and for a short moment there's a pause in his hands. "Thomas, you're the only person I've met without an agenda. So far I see nothing but selflessness in what you do. I need someone who won't line their pockets if things turn desperate. I need someone who would rather die than take from his neighbor. Mr. Cagney, I need you."

His eyes well with the brume overhead and I can tell from past experiences that rain may come. His shoulders, normally raised into his neck, droop and square into proper posture. He releases a pent up breath of anxiety, perhaps the one that's been making him squirm all this time, and watches it as it diminishes like fog.

He looks me straight in the nose, just a few inches shy from eye contact and declares, "Alright, Mr. Bell. I'll do it" His voice is as torpid as the picture of the west-side docks. "Jus-jus tell me wha-at to do." For that last moment anyways.

I pat him on the shoulders and thank him. "You won't regret it, Thomas. I promise you, you won't regret it."

On the way back to the apartment, Marty speaks after a long while of silence between us.

"Did you really mean it?" His eyes are forward, staring blankly at the road ahead, watching as the panels of glass and slabs of concrete that make up the surrounding structures stare blankly back.

"About Cagney?" I'm struck by the possibility of having misspoke yet again. I hope that Marty didn't take too much offense. "Most of it—about not having an agenda—but, to be honest when push comes to shove I'd rather have you at my side. You're a good friend."

"No, no – not that." He waves his hand to a figment of a passerby. "You say what you have to say to get things done. Only a fool would have taken offense to that. I'm referring to our earlier conversation with Genero. Did you mean what you said about ships not coming?"

It's really bothering him. His face is shallow with concern and his eyes are looking far beyond what's in front of him. He has been for some time.

"I don't know everything, Marty. To be honest, I never thought about it. For me it seems that this is all there is and ever will be. I do not know why, perhaps it's because everything feels so permanent, fixed."

He stares a little longer. "Everyone talks about it, you know – of the ships sailing into port. Why else would we have one? This may sound strange, but I dream of them coming; big tall things made of wood and vast sails – like the frigates of old. It makes it difficult to *not* believe in them. A lot of people dream about them."

"I'm not going to tell you what to believe in, Marty. Earlier, I spoke quicker than I could think and truth be told, I got a little carried away. Here – I guess anything is possible. But we all shouldn't live expecting one around the corner. If a ship does come, it won't be at our convenience and if we live as if it were, then a lot of people will die on that premise alone. We need to live as if there will never be a ship, it's the only way people will survive."

He continues in his stare, possibly watching those sails catch wind somewhere in his mind or a reflection in a nearby puddle. "Perhaps you're right, Sam. Perhaps you're right. But they are real and I know they'll come some day. Maybe not today or tomorrow, or even after the food shortage passes, but they'll come. I know they will."

"Let's hope you're right, Marty."

He may believe I referred to the ships, I meant the food shortage. Maybe it's the suddenness of it or perhaps it's the way everyone looked at me back during my conversation with Genero. The city is dark, the city is loneliness and silence, but it's beginning to fill with things that I care about – people, places. By and large, it's the only place where I could one day find my Rachel.

As the two of us continue our walk through the desolate streets, the clouds churn above, threatening rain. From the slight scent of the sea sweeping by the buildings like a powder brush, I don't believe we are in for anything more than a light sprinkle. Marty digs his hands deep inside his worn pockets, keeping his thoughts tucked inside and his emotions absent. I drift into my own reclusive day dreams, thinking about things that I haven't had time to in the past few days since.

I remember those nights I spent awake playing that song, the one that once occupied my thoughts day in and day out. It's been wanting, and from it a missing part of myself. I can still hear the words drifting through the tops of the buildings, lost in a bank of fog at some time, and now waiting to be found again. If memories were such things to be lost, amidst the labyrinth of the CitySpire, it certainly would be a task to find them all without losing oneself.

I think of Rachel and of that moment when the light did cease from beneath my apartment door and the resounding sound of the doorknob returning in its place. It's a strange feeling that comes with every resurfacing. I can recall her face, the detail of her lips and the tiniest lines that define her sky-blue eyes. I imagine her painted on the glass, the like-mirrors that edge the sidewalks, simply bending with the light. There's a slight tingling in my shoulders and chest like the light touching of her hands caressing my skin. And it is then that my feet halt in stride, whilst Marty—caught in the daze of dreams— trudges by, that my imagination is made physical in the glass.

Rachel! She's there, adorned in a white dress that flutters from some ethereal breeze, pressing up against the pane, looking out from the other side. I hear music, a dark harmonious melody, a phantom tune that drips down the walls of the mirror. Her cheeks swell with a smile whilst her teeth radiate an uncanny whiteness. Her hair is blonde, though lighter than most, like tiny strands of silver. She places her hand on the glass and begs me with her eyes to follow it, to reach out and touch the pane separating our worlds.

I raise my hand and let my fingertips settle upon hers before easing my palm to do the same. I'm reminded of something: a fall. I remember the old music box in my apartment, the two dancers, twirling together in the center – one chasing the other round and round. Then I see it drop, the music giving off its final note before the box hits and the glass shatters into tiny pieces on the floor.

"—boss? Is everything alright?"

I shake my head to clear the vision inside, not realizing that my sight had gone black. The color returns, much as if I had rubbed my eyes for too long. My hand is still on the glass, but there is nothing on the other side. All I see is a lobby, the insides to another apartment complex that's seen no visitors.

"Are you alright, boss? What do you see in there?" Marty worries from over my shoulder.

"Nothing." It is an awkward nothing that has me retract my hand slowly from the window, leaving a deep print on the glass. I investigate in the building once more, hoping that I hadn't hallucinated or worse, but there isn't anyone there. There never was. "Nothing at all."

I step back from the building and Marty staggers backward as to not bump into me. "You had me worried there, chief. I was half-way down the street before I noticed that you were missing. You were standing there for some time just staring. It's just a bit eerie. Please don't make a habit of it."

I pretend to pay attention by nodding, but this building has something. I strain my neck to count the floors.

"I understand." I say aloud, while struggling to perceive beyond the reflections. "There." I point with my hand to a broken window cast in illusion to make it look like the rest of the structure. "The seventeenth-floor."

He shrugs his shoulders. "I don't see anything."

He doesn't have too. He follows me, like those many times before, he follows me. I shove my way past the doors and into the elevator just like Farley's building a couple days before. With little time wasted between his bewildered expressions cast from across the elevator, we soon are standing inside the apartment of one of Farley's disciples, a white clad jumper that had shattered the window on his way down. We must have picked up the body the other day.

"Well, I'll be." Marty exclaims with his hands on his hips. "How did you manage to see that?" He nods to the broken window.

I give the apartment the once over. Not much different, a bit larger, but overall the floor plan is the same. A half-empty glass of water rests on the kitchen counter.

"Marty, did you see any pieces of glass on the street?"

He blinks at the broken pane trying to interpret my path of thinking. "No not really. Wasn't really looking for any – why?"

"I didn't see any either." There should have been plenty. It would not have been hard for us to notice it, but there was nothing. "Where did they go?"

Marty scratches his head. "Beats me, maybe there's a neat freak out there who can't stand a little disorder." He ponders on it. "Or maybe the city took it." He smiles as if fresh from a thieves den.

I move to the hall closet nearest the door while displacing Marty into the kitchen. He seems not to mind while his hands make noise at the pantry. The closet is empty, save the fresh smell of paint and carpet.

"There aren't any shoes." I pause. "There isn't a coat, either."

"But there's food," he shows me an aluminum can of mixed vegetables before continuing with, "Jackpot! Now, what more can you ask for than a good medley?"

I nod my head. "This will likely help us out in the long run."

He breaks into the cupboards between pulling, not long after, a bottle of Merlot. "Not bad sir, not bad."

"The real question is." I contemplate aloud. "How are we going to carry this?"

Pillow cases and dresser drawers. We set them all on the counter of my apartment, shifting amongst them for refrigerated items to place in my freezer for the night. Marty pulls out the Merlot he had found and uncorks it.

"What are you doing? That was supposed to go to the convenience store along with the rest of this." I exclaim in mild irritation.

He shrugs his shoulders with a smile before wiping out a couple glasses. "Wine is not an essential item for survival. I don't think anyone will miss it." He then nods to the stack of bottles that were finished off the night before. "Don't think anyone counted, so we're in the clear. Besides," he pours a glass and then hands it to me. "I think we've both earned it."

I take it without additional complaint.

"I never got the chance to congratulate you on how you handled Genero and his goons. I was very impressed." He takes a drink.

"Although, I would have preferred seeing them get their teeth kicked in. That would have taught them a lesson." He laughs.

I swirl my glass, letting the wine take in some air before drinking it. "It would have been the sight to see, wouldn't it?" I picture Genero's face. Beneath the hard emotionless façade, I think he was more concerned about it his friends; just trying to do what it takes to survive. "I don't think he felt good about what he was doing. There was something in his face."

"Felt good about it? His plan was to starve the rest of the CitySpire so that his cohorts could live high on the hog. I don't see how anyone could feel good about it. If he had any remorse for what he was doing, it obviously was a small price to pay. I don't trust that man and I don't think we can trust his minions either."

"Better to hold up our end of the bargain and to catch them in the act, than to accuse them of the same crimes we commit ourselves."

Marty finishes off his glass. "I can't agree with you more. I just don't think that when it comes down to the final go anyone will be willing to adhere to the bargain. Call it human nature. It may very well turn into a free for all."

I down the rest of my wine as if it were stiff hard liquor. I rest the glass on my lip. "That's what I'm afraid of."

One bottle of wine turns into another while Marty and I lounge about my apartment. The city darkens as the sun disappears beyond the scope of cloud cover. We talk about those we know, share a little more of our history, and laugh to the stories that seem most hilarious – such stories became more frequent as the more bottles we empty. I play the piano during times of silence, fingering out a tune or two; nothing jovial. I don't think any of us are really in the merrymaking mood.

As soon as the sun drops out of the horizon and the night is fully upon us, the windows take to a light tapping as the first signs of a drizzle starts to fall. I play simple songs. Songs that remind of me the past that's long forgotten and I fall into a nostalgic daze. Marty sits slumped next to the piano, his head resting against the wall with his emptied glass in hand. He stares those longing stares for, as I can only imagine, a misplaced dream or those things that lie beyond our world that only philosophers see.

After the hours pass, and the lights from the city dim, he hefts himself up to standing all the while weighing his balance. He sets the glass next to the pictures of the Westside pier.

"You'll have to excuse me, Mr. Bell. It seems that I have had my fill of wine and piano playing. But I do wish to extend you my sincerest thanks for this marvelous opportunity to bask in your company." He clumsily bows to me in such a foppish way that it steals a smile.

I raise my half-emptied glass to him in respects. "Until tomorrow, then."

He waves a gentleman's wave, which he does so in mock of me, before turning towards the door and then stumbles into the hallway. The intoxicated Mr. Kessler manages to shut the door behind him.

I law awake listening to the patter of the rain licking the glass, and to the sounds of the building vibrating through the walls. I can feel the floors breathing, slowly climbing its way out of the cold grave of silence. The city finally has a pulse. Every so often I can hear someone walking around, the nudge of a piece of furniture or a few voices coming up through the vents. I can imagine Mr. Insley clearing room in the basement in anticipation of finding some stone to hammer his imagination into the physical.

The alcohol has run its course and I breathe that dehydrated breath, as my head is now amiss from the wine. I can't sleep, no matter how long I close my eyes. Usually wine puts me out, but not this time. This time the air is too thick with worry, like a cruel humidity that refuses to dissipate with proper fanning. It bothers me. Everything is starting to close like an inward spiral.

Michael was right. His words still burn in my mind, right next to the feelings of resentment for his abandon, *"People are going to be crawling over themselves like a horde of frenzied rats. Do you realize the anarchy that might erupt over territory disputes, food, and shelter?"* The food, I could not have predicted—could not have contemplated—as being the first to go. It hadn't even been a fleeting thought until the now.

The warning signs were right in front of me, but really what more could I have done? Preserved the food? Not eaten as much? It all hasn't burrowed fully into me yet, but as the stocks slowly dwindle, I'm sure it'll leave a gaping hole right in my soul. Was Michael right all along? Is he right about everything? Should I have gone with them to the terrace manors? Held out until the worst was over? But then—

The swish of the elevator rumbles down its shaft, dropping from the higher floors before settling at mine. The chime follows not long after, a resounding haunt of a thing. The doors open and then... silence. I lay with my hands behind my head and try and convince myself that Marty has comeback for a nightcap. I listen but hear nothing. It seems that the entire building is listening as well, bringing nothing more than the dreaded quiet that once dominated the CitySpire. It still chills my blood, this emptiness, this loathsome absence of noise.

There is a rustle, followed by a pressed crinkling that emanates from my apartment door. My imagination churns with the ichors of all things horrid and I hold my breath in case of a night intruder. A long minute passes and after letting my breath slowly out, as not to make a sound, I'm able to identify nothing except the fear in my veins. Marty would have tried the knob and upon realizing that the door was locked, he would have knocked or given up entirely and headed back to his habitation in the Lockes' old apartment. I know it isn't Marty. I can tell. It's not until the elevator's doors shut and the carriage starts to pick up speed that I decide to creep from the safety of my bed to investigate the previous ruckus.

I touch the wall plate to slowly bring up the lights without damaging my eyes. Upon rounding the kitchen, I'm able to spy it. Pushed from beneath the crack of my door is a small white envelope sealed in a red wax. I pick it up and feel its contents shift from one end to the other, something loose. I break the seal carefully with a butter knife from a kitchen drawer. Inside is a small silver key attached to a red rabbit's foot. A note:

Dearest Sam,

I know that you may hold some resentment towards us, perhaps feel like our leave was unjustified and that we left more out of the horrifying picture Michael illustrated for us instead of thinking beyond our fears. I've been feeling guilty myself, wondering if leaving was such a great idea when there are so many things we could be doing to help those who are misfortunate. I've sat alone at night questioning if what we did was the right thing, by moving up here to escape the coming troubles. What's more is that I cannot help this overwhelming feeling of abandonment for leaving our home on Herbertson Street. I fear that in my absence, I may have lost my chance in finding my daughter. I haven't let Michael know about her, the woman you see in your dreams. But I want you to know that I understand why you decided to stay and wish you the best of luck in finding her.

The manors up here on Terrace Hill are quite lovely. There's a gorgeous front porch surrounded by a white picket fence. The porch wraps around the entire home and leads into the back where there's a garden and a pond. I generally spend most my days resurrecting flowers from the winter. There are large bushes of roses on the western side, and I think they're getting ready to bloom. It's the only thing that makes me happy now a'days. I really miss our old get togethers.

Michael has been out on walks more frequently of late. He doesn't talk to me very much anymore. He doesn't talk to anyone. When he's not out walking, he usually sleeps in. When he's awake I can find him in the study, pondering over volumes and volumes of books we found previously nesting here. I can tell however, that he doesn't enjoy them as much as he used to. He sighs more. I think he generally misses you. But bringing you up in any conversation usually ends badly where he shuts himself up in one of the many rooms, demanding to be left alone.

Henry has been keeping out of sight. Not due to any spat between Michael and I, but because he's been busy with those flying cars of his. Just yesterday he managed to finish his third one. I don't understand how quickly he is able to produce these. And frankly, he doesn't let anyone follow him or watch in the process. He's so secretive. However, he has confided in me of how terrible he feels about what happened between you and Emily. He wants to apologize to you in person, but I told him that it would be best that he kept his distance… at least for awhile.

I'm sure you've found the key in the envelope. It goes to the present that has been left for you on the roof. Mr. Boenger insisted that you have it. I've even taken the liberty to give you a little luck in your future struggles. It seems that everyone needs a little luck these days.

I miss you, Samuel. Things haven't been the same since we left. I'd give anything to go back and relive the times we spent together, when it was just the four of us. I still look fondly on the first time we met.

Feel free to visit us when you have the chance. We live at 322 Rose Quartz Blvd. You will always be welcome here.

Sincerely,

Natalie Silver Locke

Such a good friend. With all the turmoil of the recent weeks, I had forgotten what her words do to me. I feel a renewed vigor in my limbs, a strong conviction in my heart in which to aid me in future days to come. I rub the lucky rabbit's foot, feeling the smooth fur between my fingers. Clutching the keys tightly in my hand, I don my boots and coat before heading towards the elevator and whisking up to the top floor.

I take the roof access. The door is cracked slightly open as if someone had left it that way intentionally. Beyond the building's inner ducts and cabling, and up the stairs, I break out into the cool night air.

Like I had imagined, there it sits, the very vehicle from before, the tear drop Whirly-Gig that Boenger had taken Emily and I in, just once around the CitySpire. I run my finger along it's curvature on the front hood before unlocking the driver's side door. There atop the seat is a small little note that reads: *Kerosene Only ~ You'll figure out the rest. – HB.*

I recall watching Henry pilot the vehicle and am confident that with a little go I'd be able to fly without crashing into a building. And though I am excited to place the key in the ignition and fly about the city, I realize that perhaps now wouldn't be the best time. I gaze out the driver's door, looking up at the city's reflection in the mirthless clouds. Now is the time to conserve. This should only be used in an emergency. I want to visit them up on Terrace Hill. But I'm afraid that if I do, with events as they are, I'd want to stay. Things are going to be tough around here for awhile. People need me. They rely on me. I'll get some practice in here and there, but for now my place is here more than ever.

I sit, I stare and I wonder what the future will hold for us.

A few days or a week? I'm not sure exactly at this point. Things have been very hectic. Each morning we wake at the first signs of dawn and we canvass the city for any apartments that are furnished. "Where there is furniture, there is food" – or so the saying has evolved. Our general team has been Marty, Brigit, the Parson Brothers, Mr. Insley, and a few others that we happen to come across with nothing else better to do with their time.

At first we would try and spot the apartments from the ground, but Brigit brings up the point of, "What happens if we miss one?" to think that people will starve in the future simply because we happened to miss a furnished apartment sent spiders down my spine. So we choose streets and go building to building in search of consumables. More likely than not, we come up empty handed. I figure if we find at least one cache then we've had a good day. Unfortunately, the days aren't always good to us.

Today, of all days, something dark creeps out of the CitySpire that adds even more worry and fear. At the base of a thirty-six story building, covered in fragments of glass and blood, is a man lying face first on the pavement. His eyes are wide open and his jaw has been dislocated. Whenever the wind stalks its way through the streets and wails whenever it bends, I cannot dismiss the throb in my chest – believing the scream to issue from the corpse's throat. Brigit sends the Parson Brothers to get a stretcher from the Brick whilst Marty and I examine the body.

Of course Marty's examination, if he had one, would involve poking it with a stick. He covers his nose and takes a few moments to stop to fight back the nausea. I think he's getting used to it.

"Another one, huh? You'd think that jumping out of windows would eventually go out of style." He comments.

I shake my head at the corpse. He wears black slacks and a white collar shirt. The shirt is missing some buttons. This guy is fresh. I don't imagine he's been here for too long.

I look up to the window from whence he fell. "I don't think this one jumped."

Brigit crosses her arm. "Whad'ya mean he didn't jump. Yer starin' at the very window he flew out of." She spreads her hand apart as if sowing seeds. "See? Lots of glass. Don't think it needs to be spelled out any more than that."

"As I said Ms. Box, I don't believe he jumped." I try and swallow the word blockage in my throat. It feels like my esophagus is closing up. I check his pocket and my heart skips in beat. There isn't anything there. "No… he didn't jump at all."

Marty squints his eyes and leans closer towards me. "Just what are you getting at, boss?"

"His clothes are wrong, and all the other jumpers were face up. This one is face down."

"Can't always land on your feet, I imagine." He chuckles.

"He doesn't even have a card in his pocket." I hoist myself to standing, giving Marty a hand as soon as I reach the extent of my knees. "Something is very wrong here, Marty." There's a tug at my sternum, a rope of anxiety that grows taut inside me. The peaceful serenity of Farley's followers doesn't accompany this one. I can feel the sensation in the air, the last few emotions of his life, it all clings to the outside of the building like a vine. Terror. I head for the building's doors.

"Now where is he going?" Brigit demands before shouting after, "We've got to wait for Harvey and Brent."

"No stopping him now, sweetheart. I know that look on his face, and it ain't pretty."

Inside the lobby, I'm caught from the return swing of my arm. "Just where do you think you're going pal? The food can wait." Worry bleeds from her pores while she struggles to maintain her aggravation.

"It's not the food, Ms. Box. Like I said, something is wrong here. I don't think this man committed suicide." My heart pounds with the next sentence I'm about to reveal. "I think he was murdered."

16

His apartment is unique. He doesn't have a counter or walls separating his kitchen from his living room. Nor does he have anything that separates his bedroom from the rest of the apartment. He lived in a studio. White walls and all. He was a photographer, a very good one at that.

Scattered throughout the place, born upon walls and easels, are aspects of the CitySpire done in black in white. I don't recognize the angles, but the places are known to me. There's one of Hermes Square after it had been ransacked, one of a close up of the cathedral's buttresses and some wide shots of the park. There are other photos that catch my eye, one particularly of the store Open, done up so that the background is black and white and the neon lights are bright pink. It reminds me of the photos Natalie gave me, but I doubt they were by the same person. Just not the same style.

His camera is on the floor, dropped between the sofa and coffee table, with its lens broken.

"Don't touch anything." I say with pause between the words. Marty and Brigit huddle up next to me in the doorframe wanting a peak inside.

There's mud on the carpet from someone's shoes. The carpet's neutral color makes it easy to spot. The partial tracks lead up towards the camera, yet are less profound the farther in. I think the photographer may have been a nostalgic, as his camera is an old folding job with the words "Pinkfyne" stenciled on the side of it.

The broken chips of the lens lay mostly beneath the glass coffee table, with a few having dug themselves beneath the brown nappy sofa. There's a nick at the corner of the table, like something had ran into it, or someone. With some of the glass falling into the studio from the window, it's hard to tell which pieces, if any of them, belong to the coffee table.

There are shards everywhere. I wouldn't have suspected so many to have been thrown so far inward. It looks like the bottom half was broken in and the top later collapsed. The wind may have jostled it loose. It would only take a push, as some of the remnant pieces appear fairly loose. Strange – the apartments from before, those previously belonging to Farley's disciples, broke the window in the center. This guy may have struck it head first.

As I reach down for the camera, trying not get disrupt any of the broken shards beneath it, something small catches my eye in the shadowed fibers under the sofa. I scrunch down to my knees, steady myself on the table, and then peer beneath before taking it up into my hand. It's a small white pressed shirt button with a pattern that reminds me of the inner shell of a clam.

"What you got there, chief? A present for the Misses?"

"A button." I hold it up between my fingers to get a better look at it, away from the shadows of the furniture.

"Oh, that'll charm the ladies." Brigit adds. Her arms are crossed as she waits by the door. I can tell she's not used to being told what to do, not to mention against her nature to follow patiently. A gal of action, so I'm told.

I place the button in my pocket, planning to match it with the corpse's shirt on the street later on. After nabbing the camera, and returning to standing, I thumb back to Brigit.

"Check the food, will you?"

The back panel is easily removed and inside is a roll of film still loaded in the camera. Brigit mentions something to Marty, but I can't hear her. I rewind the camera and pry out the spool of film. The side of the cartridge reads, "Daylight safe", which strikes a cord of irony in this sort of a place.

"No chance of that." I say aloud.

I hear a cabinet door slam then followed by another. "How did you know that?" Brigit exuberates out of disbelief. She must be referring to me.

I turn over my shoulder sluggishly, still caught in a wonder. "What's that?"

The suit adorned femme quickly opens a cabinet door, showing nothing inside. "How did you know it was empty?" She hangs on one of the doors while waiting for a response and when nothing comes back save my confusion she slams it in recant. "I said to Marty that, 'I bet there's enough here to last us a month', and then you said 'Not a chance'.

This is one of those rare instances when you can make yourself look like a genius. "Lucky guess."

"Stop playing games with me, Sam. I don't like games. First you drag me up here on some murder hunch and then you have me check the pantry when it's already empty. This does not bode well for our continued *healthy* relationship." She clenches her fists just to reiterate her point. Seeing her angry makes Marty smile.

The food's gone. Of course it is. Why else would someone kill another person unless there was something to gain?

"So now we're screwed?" She asks while taking another glance at the cabinetry. "Some asshole beat us to it. I can't believe this!" She throws her hands in the air. "I'm going back down to meet with my boys. You two enjoy each other." Brigit storms off towards the door.

"Looks to me," I say while coming out of a thought, "that there was a struggle and our photographer friend got pushed out the window. Whoever did it, then took the food."

Marty breaks into my scenario after watching Brigit exit. "How do you figure that, boss?"

"He wouldn't have broken his only camera. It most likely was damaged during the struggle. His door was unlocked so they must have caught him while he was fiddling with it."

Marty guns at the camera with his hand and asks with a raised eyebrow, "Maybe the camera has something on it. Photographers are always itchy on the trigger finger."

I inspect the film closer. "It's possible." I turn it over a couple of times in my hand hoping to release some of its secrets, though nothing comes of it. "In the meantime, we better let everyone know that there's a murderer out there."

"You mean besides the Count?" Marty mentions matter-of-factly.

"Yes, besides him."

"Any idea who you think would have done this?"

There are only a few people who I'd suspect of doing this, Genero or a member of his gang. They were the ones willing to let others starve just so that they could live. What's stopping them from killing others? To quote Brigit from our previous confrontation, "…less stomachs to fill," the only problem is… I can't prove it.

"I have my suspicions." Is the best that I'm able to reply. "We need to set up a meeting with Genero."

There's an old brick warehouse out there on Cadence Street, a beautiful three-story beast with arched windows and sliding metal doors. The place is flawless on the outside, not a single mark of wind-carrying soot. I wish the same could be said about the inside.

The walls are cracked, with chips of mortar lying at the base. There are rusted metal girders stretched across the top for support, that then run down as corroded beams that help keep everything aloft. There are numerous crates tucked off to the north end, each stacked on top of one another with nothing but a series of numbers burned into the side of them. The numbers hold little significance.

Genero's men occupy the openings of the place, leaning up against the framework of the doors while others sit nearest the loading dock as if expecting a truck shortly to unload.

Marty and I are far more west that what we would have liked, but as the messenger said, it was I who wanted to speak to him, so we would have to speak to him on *his* terms. We brought a few of our people as well, but they were to remain outside and wait for us. It's our insurance that our encounter won't turn to fighting or worse. With what happened to the photographer, I'm not about to place trust in others as easily as I may have in the past. For all I know, it could have been any of my people. I just hope it's the other way around.

Genero walks up to the both of us. Just him against Marty and I. He doesn't appear to be bothered by the confrontation, nor does he seem riled when surely he's outnumbered in the conversation. He's confident and unconcerned. He catches me eyeing the crates.

"Ball bearings – the warehouses are just filled with them. If we had as much food as there were ball bearings, perhaps we might have been friends. Instead, the situation places us as adversaries. Fate is cruel is it not?" He asks with a calm demeanor.

His back is straight, his shoulders are pressed firmly down, and his arms are held behind his back like an admiral inspecting his ship. He looks at Marty. "I remember your right hand man from our encounter at the Open store. What's his name?"

Marty coughs. "I'm right here, you know. You could ask *me* that."

"This is Marty Kessler. He's a very good friend of mine." I cast an apologetic look to him, knowing that Genero is purposefully ignoring him.

"Well then, what can I do for you, Mr. Bell? My man tells me that you wanted to speak with me. At first I was going to say 'no' but after thinking on it awhile, I realized that it's not everyday that you get to have a conversation with the *owner* of the CitySpire."

I could tell he is still sore from our initial encounter. I really don't want to be here.

"I'm going to make this quick. We stumbled upon a dead body during one of our excursions while looking for furnished apartments."

"A body you say? How was the burial? You just absolutely have to let me know about these events. I've been considering attending." A couple laughs echo through the warehouse, all stemming from his gang of muskrats. "You surprise me, Mr. Bell. Were I in your place, I'd gather the bodies up and simply burn them."

"Call me sentimental, now about the body…"

"Mr. Bell, perhaps I've been unclear. I don't care much in hearing about the remains of some poor waif who jumped out a window."

"He didn't jump."

"Skipped, maybe?" There's laughter again. "Perhaps he was a jovial screwjob, eh?"

"He was pushed." And all the laughter ends abruptly.

Some of the hot air releases from Genero's face though his voice still fringes on the disbelief. "Pushed? Really? Now, how does someone push themselves through a window?"

"Someone else pushed him. He was murdered."

He momentarily absorbs the ideal as if it were a poisonous black cloud. He yells at the ceiling, "Everybody out!"

I watch them all get up from their locations, hustling to exit the very doors they were charged to protect. None say a word or grumble at having to leave so hastily. I will say that I'm very impressed to see this man carry such a strong hold over his followers.

And once everyone has exited the warehouse, he glares angrily at Marty. "You too."

Marty takes a step forward. I know exactly his reaction, a, "*Not on your life pal*" sort of comment, but I stop him—

"Marty, could you wait outside, please? This shouldn't take long."

He grits his teeth and from his locked eyes I can tell he's consciously forcing his lips from snarling. I've never seen him so enraged, but Genero is treating him like a dog. If it were me, I probably would be fuming too. Marty solidifies his contempt before joining the rest of our men waiting on the street. I half expect Genero to say something degrading but he just watches him go without saying anything further. It's a good thing, because Marty may have killed him.

Genero slumps in his composure, then he looks off to some invisible sanctuary before returning his attentions back on me.

"How do you know that he was murdered?" In less than a few seconds notice, the commander has reverted into a man.

"Those who committed suicide did so in a ritualistic fashion. They all fell face up, they all wore white garments, and they were all barefooted. This man was face down and dressed casually. Inside his apartment there were muddy footprints that led to where he may have been sitting at the time. His door was unlocked, so whoever did it didn't have any trouble getting in. He was a photographer and his camera lens was shattered during a struggle. I found some buttons that matched the shirt he was wearing. They must have ripped off during the confrontation. Then there's the missing food. His cabinets and refrigerator are empty, despite how lived-in the place looked. Every apartment I've encountered, especially one well furnished, was always stocked full."

"Murdered?" He covers his nose and then lets his hand slide down the rest of his face. "Who did it? The Count—?" I note a quiver in his voice.

"I think it was someone else; someone who has a stake in the dwindling food supply. I am curious if you may know anyone."

His shoulders press down once more and his back regains its natural arch. His eyebrows flash with insult. "Are you suggesting it was one of my men?"

"Everyone is a suspect here, even you."

"You think I did it?" He flashes his arms out to their fullest length like a pair of damaged wings. "Look around you, Mr. Bell. I'm never alone. If I murdered anyone then everyone would know. With all these men following a murderer, then you'd have bigger problems then you originally thought."

"So then, it's probably someone acting alone."

He rolls his eyes from one side of he warehouse to the other before stating, "Maybe it's one of your people, Mr. Bell. Ever think of that? How well do you know those around you? Enough to stake your life on it?"

"A grand majority of them – yes, but what about you, Genero? Who of your people can you trust?"

"Unlike you, Mr. Bell, I don't trust anyone." Genero walks over to one of the crates and removes the lid. "So we have nothing to go on then except trust?"

"There is one thing. I believe that the photographer may have captured the murderer on film. All I have to do is develop it before anyone else dies."

Genero reaches inside the crate and then returns back to me carrying a couple of solid steel balls about the size of a finger. He rattles them together in his hand while musing. "Fate is a cruel arbiter, don't you agree, Mr. Bell?"

He tosses me one and without much thought or warning, I manage to catch it.

"Ball bearings – enough to fill the entire CitySpire. If only we could eat them. Pray you're fast enough with those photos, I'd hate to make a trek out to that horrid graveyard of yours. Call me superstitious."

That's my cue to leave. I nod my head to him and walk Marty's familiar path out towards the door.

He calls after me, "We should make it a habit of hunting down murderers, Mr. Bell. There's more than one, you know."

I leave him to muse over the ball bearings that he still holds drearily in his hand. Genero may be a strong leader and very charismatic—as he seemed to have fallen in his leadership role a lot better than I had—but in all, he is ruled by the common fear of a single foe, Count Champ de Croix. Is it due to the death of his fellow comrades? Or is it because the Count is so inhuman? He's almost a symbol really, the right hand of the CitySpire. No one knows where he lives, just where he frequents – that little place he calls home, the Rue du Bourreau. With the food shortage, I believe Genero's truly frightened. I'm scared too. This murder doesn't help matters much.

I walk past the front doors and out towards the concrete stairwell that leads down onto the street. I catch someone out of my peripheral, figuring it to be Marty, but when I look again it's the man with the cleft lip, puffing on a cigarette. He leans with his foot up against the wall, while he stares uncaringly across the way.

He holds his cigarette between his pointer and middle finger and waves it in front of him as if he is cursing me by tracing smoky symbols in the air.

"Tough luck about that photographer. Landed face down on the asphalt, did he?" He takes another hit off his cigarette and blows a tiny cloud of smoke at me. "What a pity." His eyes gleam with a cold detachment. I can almost see the sadistic replay of the photographer's death playing across his features. All I want to do is wring his throat, especially with the way he looks at me, with a smug smile that zigzags across his cheeks.

He throws the leftover filter of the now exhausted cigarette onto the concrete and stamps it out, smearing it against the stone for good measure, before lighting up a second one with an old kerosene lighter. I manage to catch a peek at his cuff that pokes out from the moth eaten jacket, a clean pearl shirt with clam shell buttons.

"Nice shirt." I say with contempt. "Now where would I go and get myself something like that?"

Marty must recognize the tone for what it is from off the street as he has already made it to the bottom step, grabbing hold of the railing as if it were the thing that is halting my progression out onto the pavement.

He points the filtered end of his new cigarette at his eye. "Gotta keep your eyes open. You'll never know what you'll find."

"I'll take that advice to heart." I take a step down. "Oh, speaking of which, you wouldn't know anyone who is good at developing film would you?"

His fist clenches around the butt while his misshapen lip curls slightly into his mouth. "Wouldn't know anything about that." He looks behind me somewhere in an attempt to ignore me.

"Just thought I'd ask." I pull the roll of film out of my pocket and twirl it about with my fingers. "I came across some today. Who knows what I'll find on it?" I place it back in my pocket, ensuring he sees where I put it. "You have a good day." I say with detailed pronunciation.

I walk down the steps with a feeling of his imagination knifing me in my back. My apprehension has now amplified as my chest drags on me and my lungs now fight to adjust to the anxiety. I signal to Marty which direction I want to go. I cannot speak. And if I could, I do not know how well I'd be able to say it and to what degree of volume. I know it was him! The man with the cleft lip, he is the murderer, and I've called him out on it! He'll be coming after me now. It's the only way to cover his tracks. Genero may have been the one to sentence the CitySpire to starve if it hadn't been for me, but he wouldn't tolerate a murderer in his midst – especially considering how much he hates the Count.

My side companion picks up on the miasma of dread and horror that now have overridden the colors of my mind. He stares at me, not sure what to say or how to say it, but he knows my perilous thoughts. And as we are further up the road, as our bodyguards veer off from our street and towards their own haunts, he gathers the gall to speak the nagging things that have reared the hairs on his cheeks.

"What are you doing, boss?" His voice is short and emotionless.

"You know what I'm doing." It's all I can say in the muddle of my thoughts. Where will he try and strike at me? When I'm alone? Yes, that would be the most opportunistic time.

"That scum has it out for you, Mr. Bell, and I don't know if you noticed, but there's a murderer on the loose and he'd jump at the opportunity to see you dead. I can see it in his face. He hates you."

"I saw a lot more than that, Marty." I respond while staring dismally ahead. "He's the one. I'm sure of it."

"And *how* do you know that?" He's angry, and I'm not sure why.

"He's got the same shirt and buttons as the photographer had. I'm certain he took it when he was in the apartment. That's why I showed him the film. He reacted to it, which only verified my suspicion."

He grabs me by the arm. "Just what kind of game are you trying to play here, Sam?" His face is stern, but his hand quivers. I can feel it through my coat. "This guy has already killed one person. Are you trying to be number two?"

I pierce through his eyes and am able to see his anger for what it truly is. He's frightened for me.

"Listen Marty, I have to draw him out. If I don't try and stop him then he'll just go out and kill someone else. This way I'm forcing his hand." I pry off a couple of his fingers and the rest follow. "I'll be able to end this."

"Yes – or he'll kill you! Then where will I be? I can't do this Sam." He turns his back on me, while bringing a hand to his forehead as if to quall a headache.

"You can't do what?"

He lets his hand drop with a slap against his thigh. "This!" his hands extend outward as if to bring in the entire city block. "I can't do *this!*" He spins around. "Don't you understand, Sam? I can't do all this without you." He grabs the back of my neck and bumps his brow against mine. "I need you here, doing what we're doing. It's the only real thing that matters."

I don't fully understand what he means. "And what exactly are we doing?"

He lets go and tries to regain his composure. "I don't know, boss. But we're doing something meaningful, and I can't let someone else take that away from me. I won't allow it."

"Then help me, Marty. It'll be tough on my own."

He lets go and races in that little skull of his. "What is it that you want me to do?"

I shush him. "Speak softly now." I wrap my arm around his shoulder and bring him closer to hear the things I've been contemplating. And between those times I speak to him my inner web, I swear against a third pair of footsteps shadowing us from behind – keeping to dark and terrible places.

The wind sweeps against our brows, the air itself is fresh and moist, seasoned with the flavor of the sea. I can see that there are dark clouds on approach from the north and it instills in me a feeling so immutable that I wear it as a funeral shroud across my features. We stand in watch over the building's expanse and gaze across the city and all its concrete towers that look more like gravestones. Marty waits in ready as my fingers nervously stroke the rabbit's foot on my key chain, wishing—no, praying—to whatever denizen rules the CitySpire from beyond the dismal brume.

I haven't been able to swallow for the last few minutes now and already my heart has quickened its pace in anticipation of the trial ahead. I carefully pass over the letter, concentrating heavily in order not to give my hand over to the shakes – a response to Natalie's previous correspondence. The note explains the current state of affairs that have been plaguing us for the past few weeks, including the most recent incident involving the photographer. I warn her of murderers in our midst, to stay home and lock her doors. I wrote it after our trek up the stairs, stopping momentarily—and announcing my intent quite loudly—to pen it and then follow its departure up to the roof. He waited, I'm sure of that.

I fiddle with a handled instrument I procured from the butcher's block of my kitchen. It gleams, even from the obscurity of my inner coat pocket.

"Are you sure of this, boss?" His voice wavers like an ill struck tuning fork. He peers at the envelope with a feigned interest, more disjointed from the possible terror that it may bring. He keeps his eyebrows down as if trying to hide his reservations beneath the brown follicles.

"It's too late to back out of this. Remember, ring two times then leave the note, you got it?"

He hesitantly takes it, then letting my fingers brush over the crimson fur one last time, I toss him the keys. He catches them with the vertical closing of his palm.

"You can count on me, Mr. Bell." His eyes are attracted to the tar of the roof, before he lifts up again. "Samuel I—" he pauses as if frozen in time and then relaxes. "I'm still not sure how to drive this thing. You said there are parachutes beneath the seat?"

I chuckle beneath the weight of the city. "You'll do fine. But if not, I don't think you would have enough time to open the chute. Try to bring it back without running into anything."

"Thanks for the vote of confidence." He looks at the whirly-gig and then catches me in the corner of his eye. "Are you sure you don't want to take a chute with you?"

It feels as if a furnace is lit in my chest; glowing embers trickle up neck, as the fear of the void holds me in its grasp.

"You'd better hurry. The weather isn't getting any better."

He gives the wayward salute before lifting the driver's side door like a vet inspecting a bird's wing for injury. He gives me one last forlorn stare, soundlessly communicating his lack of confidence and with a shake of his head he slips silently within.

PART II - THE SEA WAIFS

The aerodynes spring to life as they expel a familiar hum as they spur into rotation. I imagine him pulling on the throttle, much like Boenger had the first day I saw it. And with that, it lifts slowly in the air, spewing exhaust that appears as a liquid vapor beneath it. It hovers for awhile as the driver gets acquainted with the feel of the car. Then, with a single press of a button and without protest from the engines, the vehicle ascends into the clouds where it's swallowed noiselessly into the heavens.

I watch them — those laggard mists that stir in obedience of the incessant winds. I attempt to lap up the coming rain, to soak in the moisture through my pours, hoping that with enough water I'd be swept away, caught up in the tide and sent beyond the isle. Anywhere but here. Any feeling than what lies behind me.

I glare back at the stairwell that leads into the dysphoria of the floor between floors. I know he is there, waiting amidst the darkness, ready to dine on whatever death he has affixed in his mind. Down there he's a hiding blackguard consorting with devils and their whispered-like cachinnations. I could always leave, yes!—the thought has crossed my mind. I could take Boenger's skycar and retreat to the terraced manors where I could hide from possible extinction. In waiting, I'd go mad, born from the constant threat of an assassin dwelling in my mind and at the edge of dreams, unsure whether it be my time today or tomorrow. What type of life could I live in such horror? If indeed I would face him and fall against his blade—that horrid man, that slayer of dreams—I'd die with good intention and none could say anything poor against me. I'd die protecting the CitySpire and the lives of those he'd otherwise bring to an end.

I swallow a hard painful swallow before stepping closer to the abyss. I touch the railing, focusing on the texture of the wood. My mind swirls with emotion, warnings and memories. There are visions that play against my brain like a tricky spirit that traces shapes beneath the sanctuary of my eyelids. It is here that I contemplate the void beneath me; a few steps and then the descent. I hold my breath to become lightless and be taken into the overcast above. Vertigo deceives me and I take a step forward.

Below, I drift into a fantastical realm of ventilation ducts, wires, wooden beams and insulation all exposed, all vulnerable to whatever creatures call it their home. My skin gives into horripilation, stretching to its fullest reaches to sense the environment around me. My ears open wide, allowing sound to flood into my head without dampeners or filter. I hear the shifting of wood, a light creaking that gives at the slightest brush of the wind. My feet take me down.

I can see the light pushing beneath the door to the twenty-fifth floor. It gives this place little in illumination, and though the sky lends some of its rays to aid this shadowed world, I notice them dwindling by the second. I count each step as if it were crucial for my escape; one misstep and I'd fall into oblivion. From the base stair, it's only an additional fifteen feet before I'd reach the safety of the lighted hallway. I hear a scuff coming over my left shoulder and I veer quickly to catch a glimpse of some unwonted attacker, but there is nothing. Just echoes. I step out slowly on the ground floor, and when the stillness brings me nothing but an acute sensation of the environment around me, I feel a shift of air and I dodge.

A metal something slams into my right shoulder, my muscles tighten against the impact and I yelp. The blow sends me staggering to the left and in order to keep my balance, I must twist to face my attacker, my back slamming into an aluminum panel to some unknown device. Blackness and dust, the charcoal silhouette recovers from the last swing and with a long pipe he bears it down again.

Roll!—is the strong command that issues from my subconscious and I spin to my right, sending waves of pain through my shoulder and down my side. My previous location screams with the collapsing of aluminum. I keep him in sight – I watch in a paralyzing terror as he kicks the panel that now bars his path to me and once again takes a swipe at the distance between us.

I jump backward, glad that I've yet to run into a wall. The pipe echoes painfully with the displacement of air, ringing in my ears like being too close to a gong. His swing carries through, and with his one full section of his body exposed, I charge him! connecting at the waist we both tumble over one another and to the ground.

I lash out with my fist, slamming my knuckles into his face before I get a boot to the abdomen. I spin away and over his right side, where upon smacking the ground, I elbow him in the kidney.

I hear a gasp, reminding me of his mortality, until the pipe strikes against my right arm and I feel something crack. I grab at it instinctively and kick with my legs to be free of him. The pain rushes through my body, every nerve firing in warning of the wound; my brain struggles with the next few seconds. Shimmying on my back, my head hits the first stair and I lift my body to slide up the step.

He picks himself up, clutching the horrid instrument of death with both his hands, he laughs and spits off the side.

"Where's the film, Mr. Bell?" Lurching forward, he makes a swing against the stair, misjudging and misses. The stairs reverberate into my teeth.

I try and grab hold of the railing but my arm only pulses with pain.

The dastardly form leaps atop the first step and descends over top me. He pins the pipe against my neck and he forces me against the next stair. I can't breath. I choke!—I emit a gurgle that sounds like the bubbling of water.

"Give me the film, and I'll make this quick."

My eyes are going to burst, my head swims with a whirlpool of grey matter, making it difficult for me to discern which way is which. The void slowly slithers at my peripherals, threatening to consume the entire world. My left hand pushes hopelessly against the pipe to squeeze me out a few additional seconds of breath.

The room explodes from a single beam of light pouring in from behind my attacker, like a goodly spirit dispelling all is horrid. He eases up briefly, diverting his attention to the sudden intrusion.

I force my right hand into my coat pocket, the pain no longer registering as my brain gasps for oxygen. My fingers fumble around the handle of the butcher knife and with all my remaining strength, I pull it from its secret confines and bury it into his chest.

The pipe releases, clamoring down and off the stairs. He howls. Blood pours down over top me, his insides releasing like a leaky facet. I can hear someone say in the distance, "What the hell?" as my assailant grasps frantically at the wooden handle and pries it form his chest, where the rest of his precious ichors vomit out of him.

Heavy footfalls rush across the roof and toward the stairwell. It's Marty! I'm able to make out his fuzzy shape appearing at the top step while I make a desperate plea for air. I kick my attempted murderer square in the stomach, eager to send another spurt of sanguine fluid out and down his front, watching in glee as he tumbles backward and onto the floor.

Where once stood my attacker, now reveals a diminished shape of a man looking out into the dismal blight of the floor between floors, caught in the terror of his plight as he flails on the ground.

"Samuel!" Marty screams as he skids down the steps, gaining momentum as his heels bounce off each of their edges.

The man with the split lip—yes, I can see him now—covets his newly acquired wound. Yet in seeing Marty, knowing full well that his efforts are at their end, he scrambles to half standing and rushes the door—knocking the petrified Christopher Bark aside—and him into the hallway. A red palm drips off the door's frame.

Marty checks with me for a second and after receiving a nod, I point at the fleeing psycho and release a guttural voice, "Get em." I try and force my collapsed vocal chords to say more but they refuse, all I get is the passing of air.

He snatches up the pipe like a hungry bird-of-prey, the gritty metallic scrapping that comes from an end of it brushing against the ground sends shivers through my wounds. Marty gives chase out into the hallway where the still stunned Christopher Bark stares in complete confusion. He steadies his glasses, as if they were the cause of the entire affair, and looks over at me for answers.

My response translates to movement as I try—staggered—to standing, but the dizziness which has settled within my skull makes it difficult to determine which direction to head. I lean on the railing of the staircase, my arm and shoulder returning with the strength of the injury. His blood is all over me, a few spots of my own as well.

It's everywhere. I must have hit an artery of sorts. The floor is slick so I wait for my balance to return.

"What's the meaning of all this, Mr. Bell?" Christopher hesitantly cries with a weary eye against me. "I don't think I properly know what's going on."

I inhale like a fish, the air catching against some stubborn trapdoor in my throat, and I cough. "That man is a murderer, Mr. Bark. Your timing was impeccable." I wave him over. "A hand here?"

He startles as if I just caught him daydreaming, as if my present condition was unbeknownst to him. Hustling, he makes it to my side to give me a shoulder to lean on.

"Are you alright, sir? You're neck is all bruised."

"Fine, thanks." Is all I'm willing to offer at this point, especially since it hurts to talk; like sand rubbing against glass.

"You certainly picked a fine place to be ambushed in, Mr. Bell." He helps me towards the door.

I nod in acknowledgement of his statement. A question in regards to why he happened upon us when he did passes my lips, "Why are you here?"

"Me? Well – if you must know, I've been stealing looks at that vehicle that's been parked up on the roof the past few days. I saw it the last time I was stargazing and haven't been able to take my eyes of it since."

"Stargazing?" A pain strikes my elbow after moving it the wrong direction. It may be fractured.

"Oh, yes! Mr. Bell. At night I'm able to get a little glance here and there from pockets in the stratus. I'm hoping that by slowly charting the stars' location that I'll be able to make a guess as to what months we are in, maybe even get it to the week. Seeing that you've been here the longest, I'd like to ask you a few questions in regard to the day you woke up and the weeks that progressed. You didn't happen to count the days did you? And that storm you spoke about, could you tell me anything unusual about the clouds in their formations or—"

I see Marty running back up the hall, the pipe still strong in his hand. I wish it had been bloodied more. Mr. Bark prattles on, but I no longer register it. I'm more concerned about what Mr. Kessler has to say.

He reaches me nearly out of breath; his huffing quiets my side companion. "The bastard took the elevator. As fast as it is, he'd be halfway down the street before I'd get to him. Sorry, Sam, I really tried. I managed to get a few flights of stairs out of it, before realizing his gain."

"We need to see Genero. We'll catch him yet." I grab onto his shoulder. "Help me there."

Marty nods, and helps me back towards the stairs.

"But Mr. Bell, what about my questions?" The extremely thin man asks, now a few patches of blood stain his dress, his hands reaching out like a beggar.

"All in good time, Mr. Bark. I promise you that."

His arms drop, as if realizing the full severity of the situation. He nods and smiles a sorrowful smile as he watches Marty and I quickly, though somewhat painfully, ascend the flight of stairs up towards the roof.

17

The door to the warehouse opens as the bloodied form of my attacker stumbles his way out of the accusing streets. One of Genero's men informed us that he was making his way here. They are efficient, I'll give them that. But I'm unsure of whether he returns in order to sway his leader that it was *I* who attacked him, or whether he believes that, despite his crimes, he would still be harbored as a friend and kept from any harm.

"Genero!" He calls out, allowing his voice to carry up into the iron girders of the place. "Help me, Genero!"

I watch him from behind a crate, where both Marty and I lie in wait, so not to frighten him off. It amazes me now to see what the knife had done to him, a large cut that has penetrated through a space in his ribs. He still clutches it, stooped over, like some hunchback creature, pale, with dried blood now caked at his lips. He's ruined, from the proud egotistical maniac to the now miserable being that skulks like a whimpering dog back to his master.

When he's far enough from the door where a quick burst of adrenaline couldn't take him back onto the streets, Genero's men, his own compatriots, descend upon him. They grab his arms and contort them around and up his spine to lock him from performing any additional harm.

"What's the meaning of this?" He wails. "I'm one of you! Let me go! Where's Genero? Where's my Genero?!"

They push him forward and in front of their waiting god. He stands in his usual affair, keeping tall as if he were suspended by his epaulets. Genero stares at him with emotionless eyes, a distancing of that part which makes us human, the forgiving part, to better issue the sentence we ourselves had discussed.

Genero grabs the murderers face, pinching his cheeks together to better make prominent the man's split lip. He looks him in the eyes to try to peel what remnants of a soul he may have hiding in the darkness of his deeds.

"I want to hear it from your lips, Edgar." So the monster has a name. "Tell me that you killed the photographer."

He looks to his captors, once friends, but no longer. Edgar looks into himself and off to the side to keep his teeth from showing. He looks up with a newly forged confidence.

"Yea, I did it. The screw-job wasn't about to share his food, he was hording it, keeping it for himself. So I took the initiative and sent him sailing. Justice served."

Genero releases Edgar's face in disgust and walks a few feet away.

"Don't turn your back on me!" He cries with a mouth filled with hate. "No one was complaining when they shoved morsels into their mouths. And wasn't it you who struck the bargain with that bastard Samuel Bell, that those who hoard food were to be hanged? So don't get all self-righteous on me simply because I did what everyone else just talks about doing."

Genero spins around, his face arched into a fiendish rage and screams far more powerful than a man should be allowed, "That was his food!" Even I cringe from the sheer strength of his wrath. "You do not take what is not yours! You ask for it. He was born into it, he didn't steal it. But you stole from him far more than what was yours to take." He takes in a deep breath. "And for that, you'll hang for it."

He motions for both Marty and I to enter, and as fitful as I dare to see him I refuse to tempt our alliance by ignoring him. And as soon as we are revealed, the murderer wails in such pain as if our image burns him.

"No – that's impossible! You sold me out, Genero! He'll sell us all out!" He kicks with his legs and the men restraining him knock them out from under him. He slams onto the ground, his face connecting with the pavement.

Genero waves his hand. "By their testimony and your own, I sentence you to death."

They slip a noose around his neck, a brown furry piece of hemp, one similar to that belonging to the two men who were hanged in front of the convenience store. He tries to scream, tries to say something that would otherwise save him from his current fate, but they tighten it, and it quashes anything that may have been uttered – only a gurgle of unfamiliar words.

"Goodbye, Edgar." Is all that Genero says as they drag the defiant creature across the warehouse floor and out onto the street. He bids us to follow, as a few additional members of his gang sally after.

They fling the rope over a two-headed lamp post, catching between the rung so the rope won't slip. Kicked to his knees, Edgar scrambles to get the noose off his neck, but to no avail. They draw. The rope tightens and so does the noose, pulling him into the post where his spine connects against the metal, sending a foul ringing against our ears. Edgar digs his nails into the rope, still desperate to remove the piece from squeezing against his skin. He tries to speak, but nothing pours from his mouth. He lifts off the ground as four men take up the end, he kicks, trying to disrupt their grip so he'll be let back down, but they hold fast.

They draw him a good seven feet up the fifteen-foot lamp. His hands grip the rope from the back knot, perhaps to pull himself up the rope. He isn't strong enough, doesn't even move an inch, before his hands drop back to the noose itself. He continues to wrestle the air, beating frantically at an invisible street – to escape his inevitable fate. His face is reddened by the minute, his eyes bulging to their ends, and I swear I can see them fill with blood.

It takes a total of eight minutes before his legs slow and then finally cease to flail; his hands at his side. Genero's men tie him off at the base of the pole and then silently, and without as much as a look back, they disappear into the dark of alleyways. Strange to it all, I receive no proper satisfaction watching him sway there, nor did witnessing the execution make it any sweeter.

Genero walks up to him and touches his boots, coupled with a sign of remorse for the man who was once known as murderer.

I try and sooth a troubled spirit. "I want to thank you for all the help you've given us to—"

"—Do not thank me, Mr. Bell, for doing what needed to be done. To you, you've brought a man to justice and should feel right doing so. To me, I've lost a man. I do not know if it is right to call him friend, but he was always at my side. He was good comfort when called upon."

"But Genero, that man was a monster."

"A man is not a monster for doing what he believes is necessary to survive. It's called desperation, Mr. Bell. He was just preemptive, is all. Desperation was his true downfall and the need to survive his demon. Take heed I found no comfort in doing what I did. Simply acknowledge 'what is done, is done' and go."

Friends? Whatever color I have left in my face has now run into the gutters and down into a sewer grate. I cannot imagine what he is going through. Thoughts construct around the relationship for which Genero shared with the man now suspended by a rope. He did what was required of him, sacrificing for the safety of city and those dearest around him, giving up a friend so he may execute a murderer. I can only nod to him and nudge for Marty to follow me to the car hidden away at the back of the warehouse.

I stop a good distance away and turn to the still staring, still emotionless, Genero and say, "For what it is worth, I'm sorry."

"Sorry? Let us hope, Mr. Bell, that you will one day face a similar decision as I have. You'll likely discover something new about yourself. Let us pray it doesn't take you to a darker place. My light is responsibility. Don't forget we've done a good thing here. We must always remind ourselves of that." He inhales in remembrance before taking his eyes off his former comrade and looking directly at me. "Good night, Mr. Bell."

I leave him to the corpse, to escape the madness that still clings to the wind. Together, Marty and I return homeward, to breathe that breath of clarity that comes in knowing that this night. We'll sleep peacefully or, in the very least, without fear of being thrown out a window. As for Genero, only time will tell.

A few weeks and my arm is as good as new. Surprising what a little bed rest and relaxation will do. I give Christopher Bark that interview, it is the very least I can do considering the circumstances. He asks me all sorts of questions, occasionally prodding me to elaborate on certain things, especially those pertaining to the weather, the count of days, the printings in the newspaper and, of course, in regard to those rare moments when the sun slips through the clouds and gives us a glimpse of blue. He never interrupts, just sits there and ponders and then writes something down.

I ask him what it's for and he tells me that it's for establishing a timetable, to get an idea of what day it is, what time of year. Above all he says it's for genealogy.

"People will one day be interested in who came before whom. It's very important, you know. I think someday you'll appreciate it as well, Mr. Bell."

After the interview, he thanks me for my time and starts to leave with his findings in hand. He reaches near the door before stopping.

He snaps his fingers. "I almost forgot." He looks up to the ceiling as if searching through a web of thoughts while at the same time shuffling about in his coat pocket. He pulls out an envelope, walks back, and hands it to me. "I recall you dropped a roll of film a while back during your confrontation on the twenty-fifth floor. I took the liberty of developing it for you."

I turn the envelope over in my hands somewhat frightened to look inside, having hoped to put the entire thing behind me. I wanted no real reminder of the happening.

He smiles briefly before returning his cheeks to a relaxed position. "Unfortunately, it seems that the chemicals on the film were botched somehow. All I could get out of them was fog. I certainly hope that you didn't have anything important on there."

He then nods at me then retreats out my door, closing it behind him.

Shocked, I open the envelope and take out the negatives. I hold them up to the glass with an unsteady arm to allow the light to bleed through to better see the portraits within. Yet he was right. There is nothing but a wispy fog with the tiniest splotch of background behind them. I drop them on my coffee table.

"He could have gone free." I mutter, placing my hand over my mouth to quash any sounds that could escape my lips.

I search the apartment hastily, keeping note of places to seal the negatives away forever and out of my mind completely. I burn them in the sink, watching as the black smoky swirls dissipate into the air of my apartment. It leaves a terrible stench that lingers for the next several days.

Genero has closed Open! The words echo through my ears like an unforgiving voice, everything screeching at once. My heart tears against my chest, trying to force itself out, to get ahead of the sprinting Marty.

Our boots click against the pavement in desperation. *A mob has formed and Brigit's at the front of it!* By the maker, what is she doing? What can she be thinking? These are the questions that repeat themselves in my mind. The very same questions I asked Marty when he roused me early in the morning with the dire news.

He heard it from a sprinter who was heading towards the store himself. Said the whole affair has spread by word of mouth that a woman wearing a man's suit was gathering folks to force Genero to reopen. That was the word anyway, and he kept running farther down Rhine to meet up with the rest. Knowing Brigit, she's out for blood.

A small man makes his way slowly up the street, his left foot exposes a limp, his clothes are dusty and his hair is matted. His glasses are bent. His rounded lenses continually reflect the city around him. Marty passes and halts, skidding his boots against the pavement before turning suddenly and latching onto Mr. Cagney as if he were a life preserver.

"Thomas! Thomas—" Marty pants to gather more breath and swallows. "What's going on? Tell me what's happening."

I catch up and lean over my knees as if I were going to faint. Oxygen doesn't come as easily as it used to.

"M-m-m-mister Genero, he-he closed the store. The food is g-g-gone, all-all of it. I c-c-an't understand it, Mister K-k-essler. We had enough to last us a-a-a few more months."

"Gone!" Marty grabs him by the neck of his shirt. "What do you mean gone? Who took it? Where did it go?"

"I-I-I—"

"Spit it out!" Marty yells.

"Marty! Let him go! Let him talk." I relieve him by the shoulder and he releases the tiny man. Marty grabs his head, closing his ears off to the world and tilts it back to the sky.

"No, no, no – this can't be happening." He curses under his breath.

I place my hands on Thomas' shoulders and he flinches. I haven't the time to calm him. I'm as sincere as possible.

"Thomas, how did this happen?"

"I don't know! It happened on Mis-mister Jacobson's shift. He says he may have fallen asleep. One blink he says, one b-b-blink and it was all gone." Thomas grabs my hands and looks me square in the face. "You've got to-to stop them, Mr. B-B-Bell. I don't want anyone to get hurt."

I pull away, not giving Mr. Cagney the chance to reclaim his balance. He staggers a bit but holds himself aloft. I run and it doesn't take much notice to have Marty follow alongside.

The shouting can be heard over four blocks away. Our legs burn with the ills of haste and the pain in my lungs has me coughing up much needed fluids. The run turns my insides raw. I see them, a large brown mass of people all circled around the convenience store, all awash in the brilliant pink glow of the Open sign. Some of them have lead pipes, others knives, boards, broken bottles or whatever else they could get their hands on. I see Genero and his gang all stretched out, each blocking the glass doors from the insanities of the mob.

"I'll kill the first man who tries to make it past us." He screams out over the crowd. "Open is now closed."

"Give us our food back," shouts one, "You're not the law," and, "Thieves, all of you thieves!" Cries the mob. It's difficult to tell who is saying what but it seems that the main instigator is Miss Brigit Box, who—flanked by her men at arms, the Parson Brothers—rallies beneath the banner of war.

"Open is not yours to close, it belongs to everyone! We know you're hoarding it somewhere and we're going to have at it even if we have to tear this place apart!"

"Yeah!" Returns the crowd.

She lobs a brick out towards Genero, but it misses – sailing into the paned glass and shattering it. A few of his guards duck to avoid the bombardment.

Genero stands firm. "If it's a fight you want young miss, then it's a fight you'll have! I certainly hope you're brave enough to step from behind your muscle –"

"Enough!" I scream at the edge of the mob. "This ends now!" I tear a protester from his stance so that I may push my way in.

"You've had your chance, Mr. Bell!" Brigit keens. "We are going to do this the way things should have been done the last time this happened!"

"Funny that you should mention that, lass," Genero taunts. "Mister Bell has done more good then you'll ever be worth."

A man grabs me by my cuff and punches me in the stomach. For a moment I can't breathe, but I do get to witness Marty punching him in the kidneys and then throwing him out onto the street hacking.

"I'll show you exactly what sort of good I can accomplish, you piece of gutter trash!" She grabs a pipe from one of the masses and raises it high into the air. "Let's teach these assholes what we're made of!"

One in the crowd launches yet another brick at Genero and his men, catching one of his members horribly in the chest. It's the very thing that sparks the fight and I'm too late to stop it!

The mob rushes the convenience store, pipes swinging, knives slashing, and tongues crying out for a taste of blood. I charge in after, hoping to pull back anyone who gets in my way. I don't really know what my goal is – to reach Brigit, to somehow get between the clashes of bodies in order to say something, do anything that may prevent someone from getting hurt?

I can hear Marty screaming my name. But it's difficult to know exactly what he's after. I snatch a table leg from someone, and before they are able to react, I bring it down across their back, grab them on the fall and shove them back out into the street.

"This is not going to happen!" I hear myself shout. "Not in *my city*!"

A woman is knocked back and bumps in to me in a fit to regain her dexterity. She falls to the ground. Her shoulder is cut from a knife and bleeding profusely. I take her by the hand and bring her to standing in order for her not to be trampled upon by the tens of twenty pairs of legs. I speedily shove her towards safety.

There's a full conscious push made by the mob against Genero and his men, all are within distance of the store. The screams, the cracking of instruments against bone, and bodies stiffen then drop into silence. My head pressurizes like an invisible palm pushing from the storefront. My attention is captured in the remnant windows of the convenience store. By the Maker! The ghosts are in the glass! Their wispy forms are there, staring, looking beyond the veil of the afterlife into our own! And in doing so, I take a step back and I let loose a noiseless scream. The convenience store explodes!

It is as if time itself has decided to slow, the remaining panes shatter, sending shards spiraling into the crowd like a spray of needle-like snow. Then the fireball: a large rolling cloud of red, orange, and yellows creeping out of the vacancy of the store, engulfing people like the maw of a giant devil. People are lifted off the ground, tossed like sullied dolls and thrown in every which way, their destination careless and cruel. Then there comes a swat of the mighty divine, as I'm lifted off my feet, my body both lightless and lethargic.

Flakes of ash trickle above in soft whirlwinds of soot. All is tranquil, like waking to a fantastical dream; the world braved anew. I smell lilacs…*the scent must have been hiding in the walls.*

My ears ring against the stress of the prior explosion, a dull hum that comes from the striking of a tuning fork. I'm on my back, disoriented and my vision blurred. My back aches from having struck my lower vertebrae on the curb. In moving, tiny shards of broken glass shift in my skin. I try to get up—I can't get up—as the shavings of burnt wood tack me to the pavement and a swirl of dizziness overcomes my sense of balance.

I hear muffled cries around me, people crawling about—one touching my boot—as their fuzzy silhouettes strive to pick themselves up and scurry away to some distant hospice. People are shouting, but I can't quite make it out. My head wavers from the impact; a heaviness that brings back memories of those previous nights when I drank myself to sleep – to muddle things, to forget.

A man lies next to me. His skull is caved in from the left eye socket to the temple. A smoldering piece of lumber rests next to him splotched with a familiar red lacquer, black with heat and covered with the shreds of his missing hair. I shake him, hoping that the damage only pertains to the outside. He doesn't move. I don't expect he ever will again. His remaining eye stares vacantly in front of him, a look that makes me believe he accepted the inevitable before impact. Despite his wounds, he looks serene. His blood is everywhere, mixing with remnant puddles along with the variety of dead and injured. I'm sure it won't be long before the rains will come to wipe it away.

Someone secures my arm and I struggle to yank it free. A panic induced reaction, but I'm held fast. It's Marty. His baby face is marred by a gash across his left temple which is bleeding, but his short brown hair is still intact; much unlike that of my gutter mate. I check to see if my own is in place. There's blood on my hand.

He smacks me across the face. I'm unsure if it's due to the impact, but every sound rushes me at once. The tone in his voice reflects that he's had to repeat himself.

"Snap out of it boss, we have to get out of here!" He struggles in hefting me to my feet. He never was one for sympathy.

His strength surprises me for how short he is, a 5'7" nothing; must be the adrenaline at work. Unfortunately for him, I'm not ready to stand and we are both back on the curb before finding a stable equilibrium.

As we get to our feet, I point to where the red-haired man had fallen. "What about him?" I ask coldly, for I'm having problems committing to any one emotion while staring at his ill-begotten form. I think this disturbs me more than the carnage around us: a leg here, a woman? or a man caught by shrapnel, layers of baked clothing and calloused skin. It may just be too much — something to haunt me in future years.

Marty grabs the back of my head and pulls himself to my ear. "There's nothing we can do about him boss. We've got to go, or the Count will have us for sure."

"Marty," I tug at his arm to keep balance, "don't call me boss."

He takes my arm and supports it over his shoulder, chuckling. "At least you've kept your sense of humor."

From his dust covered jacket, I'm able to steal a glance towards the old convenience store. The roof is still intact. The walls are a different story. The once radiant glass walls are replaced by empty frames, loose bricks and rubble. The insides are scarred black and all the desperately needed food is gone. It was our only supply. And they thought it was hard before. The shortage just got worse.

The bomb was set up to explode out into the street, to catch as many people as possible. It is obvious the way the roof didn't fly off. How did I know that? The gigantic neon Open sign that once dominated the street is missing the 'O'. I imagine that if it wasn't destroyed in the fireball, it may have rolled farther down the street. The bulbs of the other three letters have only shattered. With my vision returning, I look at all the faces of the dead; thirty-two in all.

"The fools…" I mutter. Instead of the usual pity, all I can muster is anger. "I warned them…" A large knot in my throat descends and attaches itself to the inner lining of my stomach; a cancer for the previous comment. I struggle to defend myself. "I tried to stop them, but they wouldn't listen." But that's the way of things, mobs never do.

My strong-arm walking beside me doesn't say a word, too intent on getting us to safety. It seems to be the common consensus with those remaining. Those who are capable of standing stoop to save one of the survivors. Finally, I muse, an act of humility. It's ironic in a way. Just a few seconds ago they planned on tearing each other apart.

A figure catches my attention, perched five stories up on a window ledge. His crimson hood is drawn over his face to hide his monstrous visage and the permanent smile that rends across his cheeks descends upon us all. His presence dictates his responsibility in the massacre and acts as evidence to the severity of his laws. He looks at me. His eyes bulge with thick veins, as they issue a past silent warning, *Heed that the Rue du Bourreau is my domain, and I its malicious sovereign.*

Marty forces us both to standing and tugs to get me moving. "We've got to go, Sam. We've got to get out of here *now*! No telling what that demon will do."

We support each other under the waist and over the shoulder. Dizziness still swims in my head as a touch of nausea boils in my stomach. I can feel the inner acids working their way up my esophagus and I throw up. Luckily for Marty, I turn my head. I wipe my mouth with my sleeve and with the loss of weight, try to move faster.

But then it hits me. "What about Brigit? What about the Parson Brothers? What about Genero?"

"They brought this upon themselves, let them sort things out. We need to worry about us and I hate to tell you this boss, but you don't look all that well."

The day is beginning to look much darker as my eyelids continuously falter. Maybe it's the blow to the head or maybe it's something else, but I don't remember getting home. I wish I didn't remember the rest.

My head is covered with an ice pack that Marty recently made me from the freezer. Everything hurts. I can't get them out of my mind. I keep hearing the shouting, the flying bodies, the flames... When I close my eyes I can see them crawling on the ground, shifting through the limbs and lifeless husks that were alive a few moments before. I think back and wonder, *if I only had been quicker.* Would things have matter much? Would I have been able to prevent all this from happening?

The Count – that horrid monster! The disappearance of the food, the rigging of the bomb, I'm sure he was behind it all! But why? To teach us a lesson? To teach us about death? His smile… he enjoyed what had happened. Murderer. Beast. Demon. I would kill him if I had the chance, the opportunity to seek revenge.

I sit up when Marty rests from pacing. He still hasn't taken time to clean his wounds. We then spend the better part of a good hour pulling out the glass from each other's skin.

"We have to do something! We have to go after him." The pain hits me, and I hiss.

Marty helps to ease me back down. "They brought this all upon themselves." He repeats from earlier. "They should have waited and thought things through. Face these people with a smidge of desperation and they forget whose side you're on. As for the Count, he'll get what is coming to him." He shakes his head and rears back as if by breath alone. "But don't be getting any ideas of trying to hunt this one down, boss. No disrespect, but he'd kill you if need be. He'd kill any of us."

I look out the window and hint at the cloud cover. "Should we just forget this one then? Just let it all go?" I don't want to let it go. I want vengeance. I want the Count to suffer as much as everyone else who was there.

"If you want to live, then yea – you let it go. The Count only kills when people break his laws. As you recall, Brigit was well warned about that. And you saw what happened to her."

I swallow my rage to allow the passage of remorse. "Did you see her amidst the bodies? Did you recognize anyone?"

He gets up from his chair at the piano bench and returns to pacing. "No – no, I didn't. Everyone looked the same. I was too busy worrying about you and getting the hell out of there than to bother with the rest."

He moves behind the kitchen counter and removes one of the few remaining bottles of alcohol, a bourbon of sorts that I've always seemed to avoid. I never like the taste of the hard liquors. He pours both of us a drink and brings the bottle.

"Here this'll help get your mind off things or, in the very least, help the pains go away."

He puts one in my hand and clicks his and my glass together. "Cheers." We both swallow. The sheer touch of it stabs the back of my throat and cauterizes the rest the way down, perhaps the very reason I avoided it for so long. My mouth tingles its way to being numb.

"You're a good friend, Marty. I don't think I've ever said this to you aloud, but you've always been there for me. Well, except for the time when that Edgar fellow tried to kill me. You were a bit late on that one."

"Hey —" he points out with his drink. "I couldn't figure out how to park the blasted thing. But better late than never, huh?"

"If it wasn't for Mr. Bark, I probably wouldn't be able to talk."

"Yes — that would be horrible." He sponsors a roguish smile and kicks me gently in the leg.

I slap at him, only to strike empty air and he laughs.

"I would have given anything to see ol' Chrissie's face when he walked into the room while the two of you were trying to kill one another."

I nearly spit out my drink as I burst out laughing. "Absolutely petrified!" I remember something. "Marty." I point with my glass hand a couple fingers in the direction of the front door. "There's something in the closet that I've been meaning to give to you. Can you go get it?"

He sets his drink down and makes his way to the closet door, opening it and stooping slightly to peer inside.

"It's the grey one."

He grabs it and draws the coat out into the room. "This one here? Where'd you find this hunk of junk?"

"Now that, sir, used to belong to a fine young lady who I was once graced with the chance to share quarters with." I say after downing the rest of my drink and cautiously pouring myself another.

He gets serious for a moment's passing. "Sam. I can't take this. What happens if your lady friend comes back and is shy a coat?"

"Emily?" I sit and absorb the coat into memory. I take another drink. "She isn't coming back, Marty." There's a moment of awkwardness. "Besides you'll look good in it. I do happen to owe you a coat, remember?"

He smiles. "So you do."

He puts it on, the very same trench I loaned to Emily the first day we walked down to Open. She didn't wear it much after that. We found her other things.

"Well, I'm honored. Thank you."

I fill up his glass. "You're welcome."

And then we drink the rest of the night to forget.

Marty's on the bench and I am on the couch when we're woken by a crude rapping against my door. It's still night and the lights catch our motion and slowly brighten to give our non-acclimated eyes a chance to adjust.

I get up, still dizzy and in pain from the earlier explosion. The bourbon didn't help matters much either. Neither of us has showered. And by our smudged faces and exposed wounds, it's apparent we're not prepared to entertain guests. Then I realize the company I keep and do away with it all. Propriety has long ago taken his own life. I open the door.

Her hair, though shortly cut is matted and tarnished by ash, and her face is cut. Her once beautiful white shirt is marred with blood, her suit coat open due to lack of buttons and her tie forgotten somewhere. Her greyish eyes yield a constant stream of tears and have long since reddened from the irritant.

She wrings her hands and tries to speak but a short breath catches and she loses the words in a fit of emotion. Her knees buckle and she falls forward, catching herself on my waist.

Brigit weeps as I try and hold her up, blubbering out, "I'm s-s-sorry, Mr. B-b-bell." She breaths in hysterically between words making them choppy and difficult to understand. "I'm s-s-s-orry. I'm so…so… sorry."

She slides down my legs and she grabs onto the left one as if it were a life preserver, clawing at the fabric to draw me into herself. "So, sorry, so… please, for what it's worth… sorry. Please!… sorry. Please…" She wails, breathes three breaths and looks back up at me. "It was me… I killed them all. No one else. All me. I was only trying to help. I wanted to make things better. But I killed them. All of them." Her eyes clench and she starts coughing uncontrollably.

I squat down to help her, a being struggling to find redemption. She brings her fist against my shoulder lightly to throw away her fit. It sticks with her.

"Never forgiven. Never. Poor… weak… Brigit. I didn't know. I didn't know! Please, forgive me, Mr. Bell. I can't forgive myself. Someone has to forgive poor Brigit for what she's done. I never wanted any of this to happen. I'll never eat again. I'll get food and I'll give it away, give it to someone else. I don't deserve this. I'll just starve, that's all. That's all I'm good for. That's all I'm ever good for!"

She claws at my torso and I bring her closer to me. I hug her to help her hold onto whatever sanity she has left.

I can't stand to see her like this, or anyone for that matter. And for a short fleeting moment, she reminds me of Emily. "I'll forgive you, Brigit. It's alright. We'll take care of you. You won't have to starve. I'll forgive you."

She sits there and cries. For two hours she cries and I hold her there between the hallway and my apartment – in the threshold of insanity and security. She repeats herself for a fine hour, apologizing and blaming herself for everyone's death. Refusing food, refusing life, just wanting to sit there and waste away into nothing. I hold her and I look to Marty, he's off facing the window, his head against the pane.

After those long many hours, she cries herself to sleep, and I'm able to employ the red eyed Mr. Kessler to help me lift her into my bed. Together we strip her down to the fundamentals and cover her up for the night.

Marty looks to me after rubbing the remaining moisture from his eyes, "She's still human, boss."

"Are you all right?" I ask after shutting the door to my room, leaving but a hair open in case she were to wake in the middle of the night.

"I just can't stand seeing a lady cry. Especially her. I guess it does a lot to a person, feeling responsible like that. There's nothing that we or anyone else can do that she hasn't already done to herself."

"It may not seem it sometimes, but we are all in this together. We all have to do our part."

We spend the rest of the night watching the stillness of the city, breathing in life, and the pains that come from it.

18

The next morning we attend the mass burial. Those who remained, and weren't injured beyond reproach, were more than willing to offer their aid in the matter. It affected all sides. What was surprising about it all is that Genero and a few of his cohorts made their way to the cemetery to offer what bit of help they could muster.

The list of those who died is longer than I expected. Some of the names I don't recognize, but there were others that only made the sorrow more unbearable. Among those who died were Frankie Jacobson and one of the Parson Brothers, Brent, who had thrown himself on Brigit to shield her from the debris. That is the saddest part of the day. Nothing is more tragic than to learn the death of a twin.

Twelve deaths in all, nine men and three women, and not everyone died due to the explosion. A good majority of people died because they bled to death, or suffered some form of head or spine injury that took them later in the night. For those who were left behind at the remains of the convenience store, the nefarious Count Champ de Croix watched from his perch atop one of the buildings until the very last standing retreated from the place of horror. The most infuriating thing of it all is that there isn't anything anyone can do to make him pay for his crimes.

After digging the graves and placing the remnants of bodies—guessing which arm or foot belonged to whom—in their own respective caskets, Brigit offers to say a few words.

She wrings her hands, having stayed silent up until this point, perhaps pondering the entire day on what to say to those that she lead into disaster. Her eyes are transfixed on the coffins that lay sprawled out in front of her and I can see a battle in the muscles of her neck trying to force her head up and meet the gaze of all those judgmental faces. The audience numbers in the forties.

"Sometimes people do da things they do because they believe themselves in the right. And sometimes, these same people are blinded by the very things that drive them: anger, hate…" She looks up and swallows hard. "And fear. I'm not trying to justify what I did by leading you against Genero and his people. I don't think that anything I can ever do or say will justify what I did. I mean… I was so outraged by the fact that he closed us off to Open." She looks at him, crushing her brow harshly against her own eyes, a means to pen up a squall. "I mean, how dare you!" She looks up to the sky and lets her hands release to her sides, her fists clenching and knocking into her thighs. "He had cut us off to food, the only things that me and many other good people have worked hard to ensure we had a future. And now it's gone." She crosses her arms. "You know it wasn't that he closed it. It wasn't about that at all. What did it matter that the store was closed? There wasn't anything inside. What did it matter?" She trails while looking off into the distance. After a short pause she continues. "The fact of the matter is I thought you took it." She nods at Genero. "Whatever you were doing… I don't know what you were doing. But I knew somehow that you were responsible. But I was wrong. It wasn't you, was it? It was the Count. That awful Croix that just sat there and smiled – he watched us die, and all he did was smile. I'll never forgive him. He took one of my dear friends from me. His name was…is… Brent Parson. He always tried to keep me out of trouble, always pulling me from the good fight. He saved me. Just threw himself on top of me, and…" She brings her fingers to her mouth and starts to chew on her nails. "I'm forever in debt to you, Harvey. I'm so sorry."

Brigit doesn't stick around for anyone's reaction. She wipes her eyes as if expecting tears and starts down the hill. People move out of her way.

Genero, a man who just stood through her speech without as much as giving a hint of emotion, takes the opportunity to walk over towards the casket and take his stance against the somber stares of his lessers.

"This is not the time for forgiveness. We act in accordance to what we believe is right, and it is history that proves to be our ultimate arbiter. These people here died not because of a mob, not because of a fight, but by the cowardly and heinous acts of a one dastardly Count Champ de Croix. He murdered two that could have easily been reprimanded, and then murdered twelve out of spite. There was no cause for their death. There were no laws that they broke. Champ de Croix murdered these people simply out of the fact that he could." He lifts up his right hand in front of the crowd to greater emphasize his next statements. "People of the CitySpire, when monsters threaten the security of our wellbeing, there is no further negotiation. You cannot reason with a tiger, nor sway an animal that feeds upon the blood of others. And when you turn a blind eye, hoping the creature's hunger has abated, do not feign surprise when there is yet another clasped in his teeth. Champ de Croix has proven himself outside human law, so who are we to judge him against the same set of rules that he himself ignores. Allow these dead to bear witness that the one who goes by the name of Count Champ de Croix forever be considered an enemy to humanity. By his own words, let him be found 'Licentious and sans worth'!"

The crowd cheers as by some unknown power transforms their sorrow into a unified call for vengeance. "Praise to Genero! Death to the Count! Praise be to Genero!"

Marty looks about him as if now finding himself in a foreign land, he looks onto the people recognizing their calling for what it truly is, a demand for vengeance. He pulls me to the side hoping that by some order I'd be able to stop it.

"The answer to our problems isn't more bloodshed. Going after the Count is just suicide. People are only going to get hurt. We have to do something, boss. This is getting far too out of hand."

I listen to the chant. I hear their souls crying out for justice, I can see the conviction embedded in their features. I shake my head at him and at Genero, as he lifts his hands like a conductor for the ghoulish choir. "It's too late, Marty. It's already out of hand. Blood is blood in the maw of the beast."

I can do nothing but stand hopelessly and listen to the cries of the mob.

It was the very last thing I wanted to be a part of in this world. Where I wanted life, everyone else simply wished for death. So with little urging from Marty, I take his advice and we sequester ourselves from the rest of them. From my present stock of food items, I estimate that we are able to hold out for a few months if rationed sparingly.

Of course, my decision isn't made alone as a few additional members of my building take to the isolation as well: the Richardsons, Mr. Bark and Mr. Insley. Though as large of a building as it is, it would be at times difficult to locate the majority of them.

In Christopher Bark's travels, he has managed to find a bronze telescope which he mounts on an oak tripod at the very top of the building. His goals, we have found, consist mainly of recognizing cloud formations. When night falls, he spends hours seeking out holes in the brume, hoping to catch a glimpse of the stars. I ask him to keep an eye out about the city to see what the general population is up to.

He tells me from time to time, as the days and nights pass on, that a mob will form and gallivant about the city. Most of the time a few windows are broken and a few fights break out, but nothing catastrophic. Though a couple nights the skies hint of fires burning inside the warehouse district and all watch from the rooftop as it is consumed entirely.

Marty and I invite our select few inhabitants, Mr. Bark and Mr. Insley mostly, as the Richardson's are impossible to reach, over for a minor dinner and piano playing. After awhile, I feel a smidge of how things used to be – minus the occasional hunger pains I have in my stomach. I'm reminded of the song that used to possess my every waking breath, but has somehow dwindled due to the previous excitements. Unfortunately, with Marty constantly around, I haven't much time to add to it.

Christopher Bark informs us of his recent findings, claims that he has located Cassiopeia and Ursa Minor. I'm unsure of what to make of it, but he says that we must be located somewhere close to the northern hemisphere which would explain the constant cloud cover and fog. However, he still says that we experience far more than our share and that he still needs to perform additional research. I wish him luck as any clue as to the city's condition is always a welcomed one.

Mr. Insley spends most of his time hidden away in the basement. When he comes to dinner he is always late and covered in a thin layer of dust – byproducts from his recent sculptures. He doesn't let us in on what he is up to nor do I believe he enjoys anyone prompting him about it. I leave it be, for the most part, especially since he's always willing to come up and fix whatever needs to be fixed. The pipes seem to have found a niche in dripping more than they should.

It isn't until well into the second week that Brigit joins us at night from her tiny seclusion somewhere in the city. She empties out a backpack full of canned food and other such foodstuffs.

"Found them stashed away in one of the apartments at the west side of the city. Bon appetite boys, there's plenty more where that came from."

I pick up one of the cans and then look back up at her. Her coat has been cleaned and she uses safety pins to keep it closed. Her shirt isn't as marred as before and somehow she managed to locate a new tie – though it has seen better days, as it appears the invisible moths have had their way with it. Her grey eyes are no longer red as if her pain had evaporated with the tears.

"Always appreciated, Miss Box. I sincerely hope that you didn't have to toss anyone out a window to get to it." I jest.

Her eyes narrow and lips purse. "Only yer sorry ass for insinuating such a thing."

Terry laughs from his gullet. "She's still a saucy little thing isn't she? One would think you'd be a bit more polite, considering recent events." He smiles with a wink.

"Screw off, Sandy." She throws a can at him and he catches it right in the stomach with a loud 'umph'. "I'd trade *you* for any morsel."

"See now, that's the girlie I've grown to love. We were afraid you forgot."

Brigit bares him a stark glare of disdain. She's about to throw out an insult or two, but restrains herself; mouth half agape.

"Any word from the street?" I interrupt them, so as not to bring up painful memories.

She clears her nostrils and blows out a silent humph, before honoring me with an answer. "People are out chasing shadows, is what they're doing. Someone swears they hear or see or smell the Count and they're off on another crusade."

"What about you, love?" Marty beams from his seat in the far corner of the room. "What crusades have you embarked upon?"

"Don't make the mistake of linking me to those Neanderthals, Marty. I don't run around tapping trashcans with a stick, hoping that he'll come slithering out. I hate the Count, don't get me wrong. But I need something more than a board with a nail in it to get the drop on him. One thing I give that tyrant credit for is that he's playing it smart. He's seen only when he wants to be seen and if that means leading folks on a wild goose chase then so be it. Did you see? They burned an entire warehouse down because they believed he was inside it. After it all, they didn't find nothing. Not a single trace."

"*Anything*, darling." Mr. Insley corrects her. "They didn't find *anything*."

She shakes her fist at him. "You got enough cans over there, Warhol? Or do you need another?"

He just laughs at her, producing perhaps the most beautiful sound I've heard in a long time.

I try for her attention. "I heard there was some fighting. Is anyone seriously hurt?"

She shrugs her shoulders. "Not that I have heard. Just a couple broken noses and bruised egos is all. People are frustrated. I got to hand it to Genero though."

Marty breaks in. "And why is that?"

"Because no one's mentioned the food shortage. He's got everyone so riled up about the Count that nobody's put a second thought that they're on the brink of starvation. They are more afraid of being murdered in their sleep than dying a few months down the road."

"Seems Genero has everyone distracted from the real problem." Marty muses.

"A problem Genero realized cannot be fixed. The less people are out there looking for food, the more there'll be for those who are." I suggest.

"Son of a bitch." Brigit half whispers. "Do you think that mooncalf's been keeping people busy so that he and his army of ants can store away for the winter?"

"I wouldn't put it past him." I dig deep inside myself to see if it's all a giant façade. "I believe he honestly hates the Count. Ever since two of his men were hanged for stealing food, he's had something against him."

Marty chimes in. "But I don't believe he's complaining when everyone else is looking for the Count, he's out stocking up."

The door bursts open and the scrawny Mr. Bark is outstretched at the knob of it. "Mr. Bell —" he takes a desperate gulp for air and looks around the room. "Everyone — one of the northern mansions is in flames!"

All of us race to the roof. The fiendish glow of the inferno can be seen blazing against the night sky. The black smoke is washed against the horizon as if it had given birth to the gloom above. *Emily! Natalie!* There's a feeling in my gut, the one that presses my heart into the shape of a bowl.

"This can't be happening." I mutter in shock.

"Another one bites the dust eh, Mister Bell?" Terry pats me on the shoulder, his hands leave a print on my shirt.

I run to the whirly-gig and jostle the door to open. Marty tries to intercede on my egress.

"What are you doing, boss? Where are you going?"

"My friends are in trouble. I got to go." I squeeze into the seat and make a grab for the door.

He halts it before I'm able to slam it shut. "I'm coming with you."

"Not without me you're not!" Brigit shouts and then rushes to the other side.

I don't have time to argue, as by the time that I stick the keys in the ignition and rev up the aerodynes, they're both inside the car closing the door behind them – Marty in the passenger side and Brigit in the back. The turbines squeal as I force the vehicle into a quick climb in elevation and then I shove the accelerator clear to the floor, smashing my passengers into their seats and us clear across the cityscape.

The vehicle climbs in speed to 240 miles per hour and steadily increases: 260…270…280. A dull hum issues from the beneath us as the gig shakes. My mind isn't centered on the condition of the car, but more poised towards time and getting there without wasting a second more.

It takes us little under two minutes to get there and I land on a small patch of open grass, a good distance away from the mob of angry people holding their torches, pipes and broken bottles in the air.

Once out of the car, a person rushes from the crackling home, a dark silhouette against the blinding white of the flames. The mob descends upon her. I hear her scream. I know who she is.

"Natalie!" I yell as I bulrush the posse.

As before, I steal a pipe from some unsuspecting hand and clear myself a path, swinging where ever the pipe will take me. Many see me coming and dodge, backing away from what could be described as an enraged berserker. Those who try and take a step close I catch in a return swing which is enough to dissuade others from getting in my way.

Marty and Brigit are a few steps behind me, pushing and exchanging the occasional fist to those would be martyrs.

I draw out Natalie's name once more as the crowd circles in on the manor's defector. She screams again, a long ghastly screech that weights strongly against a death knell. And as I near, I drive the pipe from over my head and against someone's shoulder blades. Terry's words ring in my ears, "…*another one bites the dust.*" The man drops to the lawn unmoving.

Seven, maybe eight more surround her, scratching at her dress and tearing pieces of cloth as if they were flesh.

I recover my swing and yell, "Get away from her you sons of bitches!" before slamming it into another. A loud crack issues as the pipe connects with yet another soul, forcing the brigand backwards.

My weapon's return isn't as lucky, whiffing overhead with a slight whistle that comes from the air pushing through the hollow shaft. I'm kicked hard in the stomach and fall backwards into the crowd where I'm caught and held. Somewhere drops the pipe. Whoever is behind me tightens their grip on my arms. I pull all my weight forward and then launch my head backwards, striking them in then nose. The impact rattles through my brain and I stagger free.

Natalie's screams again, this time she recognizes her attempted hero. "Samuel! Save me!" I can see her hand reach out for me from the confines of the crowd.

I rush forward once more and pull off one of her attackers. Marty and Brigit reach my flanks and pry a member of their own, kicking from the entangled mass of people.

Someone plants their hand on my shoulder and I real about with a left hook, which is caught by a familiar hand – Harvey Parson. He nods at my recognition, before letting me return to the human pile. Once he steps in on our behalf the rest of the mob retreats, only to crawl back to the side lines of onlookers where it's safe from two half-crazed men, a woman and her giant.

"Samuel." Natalie reaches out for me, half in and out of clothes. Her face is cut and spots of red bleed from under her dress. I'm sure it was beautiful at one time.

I snatch her up in my arms, allowing the fight's adrenaline to pick her up and carry her back to the car. We are escorted by both Marty and Brigit, and she by the remaining Parson Brother. Natalie fades in and out of consciousness, the whole ordeal too much to bear.

Easing her into the passenger seat of the gig, I shake her enough for her eyelids to open. "Natalie! Wake up, Natalie. Where is Emily?" She barely responds and I shake her again, this time yelling. "Where is Emily?!"

She points back towards the engulfed manor, muttering incomprehensibly under the breath. It is all I need.

I toss the keys to Mr. Kessler. "Marty! Get her out of here." Without waiting for a response I sprint towards the house.

I hear him calling after me, but I cannot make it out. I run past the crowd, they quick not to inspire my wrath and part like water. Past the white fence I feel the billowing air baking against my face. It grows hotter as I kick in the otherwise half-open door and leap through a ring of flames.

It's difficult to breathe as the fire swallows the oxygen, stifling my only means of life. I find myself in the foyer, the stairs an upside-down waterfall of liquid holocaust. I certainly hope she's not on a higher floor. The blaze devours ancient treasures, old furniture sets, beautiful paintings perhaps oils on canvas, and the arches – the conflagration wanders up them like a spirit of chaos.

"Emily!" The first yell is swallowed by the smoke. I strike again. "Emily!" I remember another and shout, "Michael?" I cover my mouth with my sleeve.

I duck into the next room where the howl of the fires, the snapping of wood and the consumption of the tinder-like house is more sufferable; best here, where my skin doesn't feel as if it were melting. I pray that my clothes don't conspire with the hellish scene and erupt in accordance with some demonic pact. It's really all I can do.

"Emily!"

A sitting room of sorts, I can see the scorched skeleton of a sofa, a few shelves and the black bindings of a score of precious books now lain to ash. The candelabrums run red with candle wax, the wicks already fed to the fire.

"Emily, please! Where are you?" I bellow in the heat of the abyss.

Then I hear something, an eerie stringed melody floating in from behind a pair of double white sliding doors. It triggers in me the fear of the void as if I were standing at the precipice of oblivion staring into the bleak nothingness. Beneath the cracks, firelight dances in a frightening pas de deux as a plume of black smoke claws at the scarred finish of the door. I place my palm against the wood—still cool—and force it open, more troublesome now that it's warped from the heat. I squeeze in. My heart stops.

There in the center of the dining room, with the table cast aside and the chairs set aflame, fiddling on a blackened violin is a crimson hooded figure, his back to me – the infamous Count Champ de Croix.

Had it not been for the flames, had it not been for my desperation, had it been somewhere else at a different time, I would have run from him. But my fists clench and my heart pounds from the heat rolling off my brain.

"Where's Emily you fiend?!"

He continues his ghoulish melody while gazing into the inferno that spans around him. He watches me from the reflection in the glass, one cast off a set of scorched French doors that lead outside onto a stone promenade – still untouched by the hands of hell.

His voice is a deep base that echoes with the creaking of the house that sets my nerves to jitters. "All are gone, Mr. Bell. There's just I, he who dwells in mystery and the dark."

"Where is she?" I demand.

He taunts me. "Gone – to who knows where? She's been gone for some time now. You do have the knack of losing her."

"What did you do with her?"

"I did nothing. From what I can remember, I believe you released her to Mr. Boenger's charge the day the sea waifs encroached upon our city."

"*Our* city?" As if the two of us signed a mutual agreement.

"Yes, Mr. Bell, *our* city – yours and mine. I cannot tell you how often I long for the days when it was just the four of us; a pity that we must tolerate that pathetic rabble." He points with his bow the way I came without missing a beat. His music sweeps against my mind; like a drug, like a dream.

I shake my head to clear the notes. They crawl away like spiders. "They want to kill you, you know?"

The nightmarish beast turns quicker than I can register and now burns me with his coal-like eyes set aglow by the blaze. And when he speaks, it is as if he were feeding the inferno as the room grows hotter. "Do you?"

My voice escapes my throat before I even will it. The heat tears at my face. "You must be brought to justice."

He laughs - a dark laughter that is found dwelling in vacuity. And as he laughs the house laughs with him, a sharp intense billowing of heat, a rise in the fires crackle, and a snapping of the abyssal flicker. I draw my hands to shield my eyes causing my palms to scream from the strength of it.

He tosses the violin into the blaze and cackles horrendously as he watches it ignite in a wide array of colors. He spins around to address me fully. His face is an unfriendly reminder of my own burning flesh.

"Justice?" He spits like the stabbing of a pen. "Have they enchanted you, Mr. Bell? For when did the blind hag turn in her scale for a torch and her sword for a club?"

"You murdered fourteen people in cold blood."

He spews nothing but the equivocal. "Did I? If their blood was cold, then it would seem that I'm more guilty of mutilating corpses than of murder. What then do they matter to you? They've brought nothing but ruin. They contribute nothing, they believe in nothing, therefore they are nothing. They are not like us, Mr. Bell. They don't appreciate. They don't respect."

"A life is still a life." I manage over the roar of the consumption.

"Shall we relinquish blood for blood then? Pour our precious ichors into vials and assess their properties? Have you the proper weights for measure? And when all is done, will all be found wonting? Whose blood will be next, Mr. Bell? Yours?"

I step backward, pressing myself against the door in case he rouses to attack. His scarred lips turn upwards revealing a haunting pleasure he gains in seeing my reaction.

"You can't stare up the rope and not expect recourse, Mr. Bell. Blood begets blood, where all will be washed away with the next tide."

"And who are you to escape the criminal of your deeds?" I accuse, frightfully. The doors to the previous room refuse to budge. I am trapped here and at his mercy.

"You forget, Mr. Bell. I am the state. You and I claim sovereignty over our lessers. You are the face. I am the hand. And it is they who must be punished for their transgressions."

"Punished for what?" I yell.

His lips reveal a set of sharpened fangs. "Treason."

The floor above me snaps and splinters. I hear the support beams collapsing from the weight. The wood is failing and I draw my attention to the smoky haze that's collected amidst the blaze. Knowing it'll fall at any moment, I look back to the Count.

He speaks. "Do not concern yourself with those who transgress against us. They will soon know the error of their ways." He chuckles. "On a lighter note, do offer my regards to Miss Waters when you see her next. You never know when it'll be your last."

A board drops from the ceiling and I duck to avoid it, my exit now utterly blocked as it has wedged itself against the doors. When I return my attention to the Count, I find nothing save a preserved pair of footprints left in the scarring of the floor.

Knowing that my time is soon spent, I rush toward the French doors, avoiding the mounds of scorching oak and the approaching cinder storm. It is there that I bull rush the portal, sending the pair of them shattering outwards and into the garden. I manage to leap through, as the room behind is crushed by the floors above, a mass of hellish planks and crumbling furniture.

The flames take the house. I watch from the sanctuary of the grass, huddling close to fresh dew, as the once magnificence of the architecture is brought to ruin. The mystifying arches, the stained glass windows, vaulted ceilings and marble all now a pile of rubble destroyed by the hands of the desperate and destitute. The heat of the home still lingers inside me, a burning anger planted by the Count himself at those who came into the CitySpire and raped it of its treasures. They stole from Hermes Square, they plundered Open, and now turn against the elegant manors. How dare they destroy my buildings? How dare they threaten my friends? All these things bubble inside me and I must concentrate to not grind my teeth.

Though hesitant to admit it, the Count may be right. They could have killed Natalie. They could have even killed Emily. Marty has it all wrong, the Count isn't the true threat. It's *them*. But as much as the Count may be right, it doesn't justify murder.

I storm out of the gate that opens beyond the enclosing stone wall, around the side, and then toward the front where the mob watches in hopes that the pyre scores the demon that is Count Champ de Croix. They chatter amidst themselves, startled that I've emerged alive. Though familiar as they may have once seemed, the shadows drawn by flames render their bodies faceless. They are like harlequins set before a stage.

My coat is covered in a thick layer of soot and I still shed the layers of smoke that managed to hitchhike from their devilish home. I glare at them all, those dark savants of the night, allowing them to feel the fires that I have endured in search of my beloved Emily. I shout from my invidious core and release upon them the wrath I bore witness to.

"Listen to me – all of you! I will tolerate your impertinence no longer! You and your sticks, your torches and your mobs, for two weeks now you've been chasing shadows, poking around in the dark daring to frighten the Count from his hiding place. But the Count was right there," I point to the tragedy behind me, "inside that house! And none of you had the gall to follow him in. So you lit it ablaze despite the innocents who resided within." I pause as the scene plays out angrily in my mind once more. "I spoke with him—the tyrant of the CitySpire—and I can tell you that he cannot be killed. He simply basked in the flames and laughed at your failure whilst I cringed beneath the heat. He warned me that he has marked you all for your crimes! He claims you've committed treason against the state of the city, which is punishable by death."

The lawn erupts in outcry, many voices panicking in the night in knowing their end has come. They sputter out a mixture of questions like some wretched receipe, some pleading at me, others for the arbiter of the city.

"What will we do? If we can't kill him, we're all doomed. He'll come for us in our sleep. Where shall we go, where shall we hide. Tell us, what shall we do?"

"As far as I'm concerned, you all can go home and wait for death. But perhaps by sheer touch of compassion he'll let you live if you undo what you've sown. By making yourselves useful and seeking his forgiveness, maybe then he'll spare you. Either way it doesn't matter to me. I'm through with the lot of you. From now on, you are on your own."

Somewhere deep inside I'm taken aback by my own words. Condemned by my own mouth. Yet my anger refuses to subside, the very audacity—everything I've done for them—and this is how it goes.

How they've earned it.

"But whatever you do decide, this here ends tonight! I will not suffer another mob. And I swear to you, if any of you bear torches against my city again it's not the Count you'll have to worry about, for I'll kill you myself. Unlike him, I won't give into the pleasure of toying with you first, before putting you to the rope. Now go home! Go home or be damned!"

I leave them in silence. Their long shadows cast an unsettling feeling of the bleak across the hill, down the road which winds to the poorly lit cityscape, and across my back. I can feel their eyes watching me as I abandon them, reaching out like frightened children in the night. Was I ever the guiding parent or perhaps the leader for which Marty wished me to be? I cannot truly say. My quandary's retort come in the form of wordless clicks as my boots scuff against the archaic cobblestones that are paved to the bottom of the hill. There a set of wrought iron gates stand tall and overbearing, designating this portion of the city as Terrace Hill.

As much as it pains me, as much as a part of me yearns to aid them in their dismal hour, I cannot forgive them. What they did to Natalie was a product of their desperation, the very price of betrayal I hadn't expected from those who had once worked side-by-side burying the corpses of strangers. Instead of coming together to work towards a common goal, people instead turned to vicious savagery. Is this the society in which I wish to preserve?

A life is a life. My words ring in my head like an unfriendly reminder of naivety. Yes, a life is a life, but what of the value of a life? Natalie and Emily hold value to me, and apparently to the Count. Michael – how I had forgotten about him... What value does he hold? What of Boenger? What of Marty? What of myself? And those faceless beings that contend to do harm against the CitySpire, what value do they hold in the grand scheme of things? Can death pay for death? Or does death only pay for peace of mind? In such case, is peace of mind worth more than a life? It bothers me. It all bothers me.

And when I reach the welcoming gates of Terrace Hill, leaving beneath the lingering taste of contempt, I'm reminded of the true meaning of value: Emily – how I've wronged you. I ran into hell looking for you with no question as to my safety. And I'd do it again, not knowing if you were within or not. There may have once been a Rachel, but it is now that I'm in love with Emily Waters. Oh dearest creature, where are you?

19

The walk is long and arduous. The city has never seemed so empty. I could still see the dwindling fires of the terrace manor glisten like a dying sun, poking out between the obstructions of skyscrapers. Yet I see no souls, I hear no voices. It is as if the entire city holds its breath. Not even the wind blows. Quiet. Never was a walk so exhausting.

It takes me several hours. And as I reach the silence of my building's door, cross the dismal lobby, and ascend up the despondent elevator, I realize the full emptiness of the world. Had the unseen hand whisked away the inhabitants yet again? Am I, once more, sole? Tired. All I want to do is to lie down and sleep, and dream of those things I truly miss.

The apartment is dark and vacant. I close the door behind me and shed the stink of the night's labors on the floor in the kitchen. I'll deal with them in the morning. I shower, paying close attention to remove the black and grey residue off my skin. I spend more time than usual, allowing the water to wash away more than just the soot. *Letting it go with the tide.*

When I'm done, I collapse in bed and fight hard not to dwell on the moment in which I made the decision to stay behind, when Michael had decided to leave and avoid those people and the troubles they bring. I try not to focus on her face, the very moment I had decided to send Emily with Boenger. She was trying to tell me something, *"Three times and then declines forever."* What did she mean? I had believed it was just nonsense, but now it may have held some unknown significance. It's ironic how things turned out. In the end, it was Samuel Bell, who proved the fool.

I drift off, thinking back on the days when the four of us were together; wishing that someday, I'd be able to live them again.

I wake to the music of Bach's Cantata no. 140, my eyes flutter open just in time to watch the tail end of a forgotten dream drift back behind my eyelids. The music yields from my piano, a very slow yet perfectly orchestrated composition that soothes my tormented conflictions that there is an intruder in my home.

I dress, knowing well that Marty had let Natalie into my apartment. I was not aware that she had taken up the piano, nor had the opportunity or time to perfect her craft so quickly. In my exhaustion from the previous day, I may have forgotten to lock the door. During the completion of choosing my attire, I am able to note the end of the piece and then continuance of it once more.

Then, after stretching the soreness from my limbs, I twist and push back the knob to my door. But what I see strikes me hard in the chest and I grab onto the frame of the door to stop my legs from buckling. I'm not to witness the recital of a black haired beauty, but one of auburn, crimped and curled – now shoulder length. She wears a lavender off-the-shoulder dress with delicate lace and beautifully tied ribbons. I stand there, listening to the uplifting melodies that her fingers call from the ivory keys, paralyzed by the sheer joyfulness of her presence. My Emily, my dearest Emily has returned!

When she finishes, I try to catch her before she begins anew.

"I heard music."

The pianist turns on the bench fully so as not to strain her shoulders. She smiles a radiant row of whites that flush her cheeks with a soft pink, bathing the room in warmth.

She fidgets with her hands in her lap before remembering, "I'm glad to see you're finally awake."

"How long was I out?"

Emily chuckles, squinting her eyes straining her cheeks ever more with her grin. "For days and days."

I walk to the couch, placing my hand on the back to ensure that this encounter is real. My face reflects hers and my cheeks do strain beneath my next question. "Did I snore?"

She shakes her head viciously. "Terribly so, I could hear you for miles." The bench is pushed back as she quickly spirits from the piano and tackles me round the waist. I fall backwards and take the eager nymph with me, laughing even after we impact the carpet.

I laugh from both the giddiness that has overtaken me and in part to being knocked off balance. I manage between bouts, "Liar. I do not snore."

"I'm afraid you do, Mr. Bell." She scrunches her face in foolery. "I'm afraid you've scared all your tenants away."

"I thought the building seemed quieter." I follow in fancy.

She giggles and then rolls off to the side. Emily looks at me with strong affection. Her skin is smooth and the light from the day brightens the color of her hair.

She whispers, "I have a confession to make."

"What is that?" I return in whisper.

"I've been working on a present for you."

"Oh? What kind of a present?"

"The secret kind."

"Am I not supposed to tell anyone about it?"

"Nope." She takes up a strand of my hair and plays with it, before returning her gaze. "You'll have to promise to keep it a secret, okay? It's just between you and me."

"Alright then, I promise."

She scoots closer to me. I can smell her perfume, a combination of lilacs and jasmine. Her eyes have changed from their sea-grey to a dreamy blue and with but a stare she captures mine with an ocean of hypnotic color. Her forehead creeps closer and without hesitation I allow myself to dive. She presses her lips up against mine and I'm dazzled by the sweet serenity that comes from the connection. My head swirls with the sensation, a mixture of an irregular heart beat, longing and love. All of it comes crashing together and overwhelms my sense of gravity. In but a few second's tick from the wall clock, the kiss ends and I'm set adrift in the memory of it.

With a quick push she shifts to standing and is able to pass the piano before I'm able to say a word about it.

"Where are you going?" I ask in fear of abandon.

"It'll take me some time to get everything put together. Don't worry. You're going to love it."

"Wait —" I struggle to get up, hefting myself from the back of the couch to my own two feet. I move toward her. "Please stay. We can have breakfast. I've saved some mix so we can have pancakes together."

Emily returns to me and wraps her arms around my neck. Her body is pressed close to mine as she looks up in an assuredness. "There'll be plenty of time for that after. Trust me, you don't want to miss this."

My hands run over hers and I close my eyes in the pain of remembrance. "Emily, I want to apologize for—"

My lips are sealed by a finger and a shush. "Don't apologize. Everything is alright now. You'll see." She kisses me again, this time on the cheek. "Here." She retracts her hands and pulls a pen out of a dress pocket. She takes my hand and writes down an address: 251 Nereid Street, #29. "Meet me there in an hour. We'll talk then."

She pulls back and hesitantly I let her. Blowing me a kiss, she opens up the door to my apartment and then disappears into the hallway with the door shutting behind her.

I watch it for a few minutes, half expecting her to bound back inside for having forgotten something or perhaps to change her mind, or for me to go with her. But she's Emily, I muse after breaking my stance. When she has something on her mind, she's determined to have her way. Going after her would only prove to my frustration. From prior experience, it would seem that Emily knows the city better than I do, especially how difficult it was last time when I sought her out on the streets. Hours, days, and I turned up with nothing. But now I have an address, I have a place where I can meet up with her, and all will be well. I shall see her in the hour.

The apartment is filled with the sound of playing a wide variety of songs, mostly anything that really comes to mind. I sit there calculating to myself how many melodies I will have to play before I can leave. Occasionally, I find myself looking up at the wall clock and count how many times the second hand must round before I'm through. The waiting, it kills me. Nereid Street, as I recall, is a tiny street towards the eastern portion of the city. The buildings there are generally well kept, though small, from what I recall during my treks out in search of food.

When the clock's hands are nearer to twenty minutes from our designated time, and as anxiety threatens to swallow my sanity, I lift myself out of the middle of a sonata, adorn my soot infested coat and boots and head out onto the street.

My pace is quick, a series of long strides that spur my egress. I navigate solely by memory, turning down one street and then heading up another. I pass the concrete monolithic buildings that beg for an artist's touch, and then along alleyways and loose brick buildings of no name. Constantly, I think of Emily. It is as if I've awoken from a nightmare and all has rendered itself anew. The streets are empty and the city is once again devoid of sound and whisper. There's a harmony to the air, a tinge of hope that sails on the light breezes that catch my coat from time to time. It's like how everything used to be.

When I'm about to turn down Nereid Street, I catch a huddled something gazing out at me from one of the street-side windows. There's a faceless form, a greyish silhouette that has propped its hands on the glass, climbing it to stand, and then seeking out what lies beyond its world. A ball of cancer grows in the pit of my stomach and it branches out like the showering of hundreds of needles in my chest; a feeling of apprehension grows from the silence of all things.

I try and ignore it, walking quicker now down the street that holds my destination. My peripheral is again bombarded by the misty beings that press themselves against the glass. I start to think the unthinkable and cringe against evil portents. My legs turn to a full-out sprint, and my mind screams something hidden in my subconscious where true horrors dwell. *No.* I repeat in my head. *Stay away! Go away!* The creatures manifest in armies, all lining the walls of glass that face the entirety of the street.

I close my eyes and I run, as far as I can go, as fast as I am able — anything to outrun the possibility of them and the horrors they bring. I'm drowned in urgency, speeding past the ghastly mirrors as if they would explode in a frenzy of glass. And as the addresses spur closer, and the buildings change from concrete slabs to detailed masonry, I stumble upon a distant white mound lying face up to the sky.

"No!" I scream. Dreading far more in my soul than what I'm willing to believe. "Please, for the love of –"

I speed towards it, my legs dropping from under me, and I having to catch myself before collapsing as well. And when I reach it, my heart caves and expels its sorrowful poison throughout body. Her beautiful auburn hair, her smooth pallid skin, her lips—by the Maker, her lips—and the sweet sound of her voice. "Emily!"

I drop to my knees and as I reach for her, my fingers recoil, and I must concentrate to push them forward to test if my eyes aren't deceiving me. I touch her face. Cold. Frigid like the moment I first found her, a life hanging by the balance. I shake. My eyes well with the dew of the past seasons, the memories all flooding into my mind like a gate that's forever been torn open. I feel her pulse—the pain—there is no rhythm.

My hands slide beneath her and I cradle her, bringing her closer to my chest that an hour ago was still warm and vibrant. Her cheeks are no longer pink with smiles. The glass beneath her tells her story, the top most window of the eighth-floor. The shards beneath us crack as I shift her, chime as I breathe.

"No. Emily, please don't be d—please." I kiss her lips and then smell the death the creeps out of them. I howl. Tears drop from my eyes like those storms we used to watch from the safety of inside. I can no longer feel the breath coming from her, and in reaction, I can no longer feel the breath coming out of me. I blubber, I cry, I cough. I gasp whilst I paw at her with my fingers, trying to pull her inside of me, to make the two of us whole again.

"Please not like this. Please come back to me, Emily. I'm sorry. I'm sorry for everything jus—" Not a word, not a response. There is no telling that things will be okay, there is no witty response or shush to be quiet. There are no more pancake breakfasts. There are no more midnights. No more dancing in the streets, nightingales, or snowmen. There are no pigeons to count. There is simply this, the cold lifelessness that comes from a vacant body of Emily.

She's gone. My beautiful sea nymph is gone! And thus I tumble after as I hold her, refusing to let her go. Sanity, a thing lost to time. There is only this in this world — *the ever uncaring silence of the streets.*

I refuse. Her body is limp in my arms and I am no stranger to her weight. She is adorned in a pearl white dress, the same off-the-shoulder fixation that she wore in her flight those several months before. At the time she complained of the sea, the rushing of the waves, and the frigid waters that had claimed her so long ago. She scratched my temple then. How it pains me now.

Her dress is made of white satin, a trim of lace around her shoulders and cuffs. Her sleeves are long and wispy that trail behind me with a portion of her flowing dress. The corset is tight and I wonder how she was able to tie it herself. That accents her breasts far beyond what I've ever imagined them to be. She is perfect in her form, beautiful in skin and in cheek. A motionless being, how it solidifies her like a statue, a perfect image that would accent poor lonely Hermes in the square. Beautiful. Dead.

I tear my vision from her towards the sky, and I call out in my mind and soul and ask those questions that will forever pain me, "Why her? Why now?" and I cry when there are no answers.

I remember nursing her from death's bed. She was pale, if not paler now, and as still as currently — unresponsive. Yet then her heart did beat, and her breath was shallow, and I could feel a slight warmth in her trying to escape the bonds of the waters. There was a chance, the possibility of ending my loneliness that stemmed from that empty muscle. And now it all comes racing back again, a draught of water to douse the flame that once kept the darkness away.

I take Emily from her bed of glass, whisking her away from this place, and to the world I had her leave behind. I struggle down the street, my boots scuffing off the occasional dip in step. I feel is if I'm carrying my bride towards the distant lighthouse that I set up for us to spend the rest of our days. Her head hangs limp over my arm and she looks as if she is simply sleeping.

Fog grows and then settles as though manifesting from the surrounding windows and walls of glass. The ground is swallowed by a thick cumulous-like vapor and, while coupled with the ever-so-greying of the strata, the higher floors of neighboring buildings seem not nearly as affected, like giant tombstones.

The air turns chilly, transforming Emily into a creature of ice. At times, I can see hands reaching out for her in the mist: creatures of untold shape attempting to lift her from me, to spirit her away into the unknown. I pass through them without a sound, all the while keeping my hands clenched tightly so not to lose what remnants I have left.

I keep her aloft. In my arms I continue with her forward. I trudge through the wasteland of my depression, a sorrowful being, lost forever without cure for future ills. There isn't a sound, not a single presence of person or motion. All I can hear is the clicking of my boots and the pounding of her heart. Her heart! I—no… just the empty rhythm of my own echoing through her. If only it is enough to start hers running again. How I'd carve mine out if I knew it would bring her back.

I'd give anything: my hair, my eyes, the left side of my brain – just anything to bring back her voice, to let me know she lives and is happy. The silence, how it confirms all that I've feared in my life, the absolute inevitability of all things. Nothing looks familiar. The world is now frozen in a perpetual mist, which will soon erase all from the pages of existence and worry.

Squeezing her, I continue my trek through the dismal thickness of the city, seeking out the familiar, walking the streets from memory, and hoping – just wishing for salvation.

She's so picturesque, lying here with me, watching out the window of my apartment together – waiting for the world to pass us by. She lies between my legs, her head lulled on my shoulder, staring with those closed eyes into oblivion. I pet her hair, feeling the softness of her auburn curls, remembering those nights she snuggled against me for warmth.

I talk, believing she can hear me in some way – some how. "We should have done this long ago, you and I. I can't recall when the two of us took a break from life and just admired the city." I hiccup in breath, the tears from my eyes continuing to fall like the drizzle from rain spouts. "You know, you were right. It should have just been the two of us. No one else to tell us what to do or hand us expectations. I should have ignored all of it, and just listened to you. And now… see what we have for it?"

I breathe out and hold my lungs still, wanting to feel what she feels to not breathe. I imagine the darkness of oblivion, all the while feeling the swirl of dizziness from the lack of oxygen. My lungs struggle and my head grows light and throbs. I inhale – weak.

"Do you remember, back in the cathedral, when the snows first fell? Do you remember the pigeon climbing in from the weather?" I pause to swallow. "Wasn't that a sight? My eyes burn me and I close them. "I wonder where it came from?"

I hear the door opening behind me, followed by the shuffling of feet and the swishing of clothes. I cannot budge, I refuse to move. Emily and I are here, and together we'll stay. I have no need of material things, no more food, no more wind, and no more air. Here I am content to stare out the window with my beloved in my arms, forever more. I write along the walls of my mind, *"YAWA OG"* and stare into the silence that is forever to be my place in life.

Part III

The Sorcerer

20

They call it the Creep.

I watch it from my apartment window in the late hours of the night, absorbing the black mold that scales the concrete like a choking vine, a defilement of the building's coloration that returns no matter how hard you scrub it. Some say it comes with the winds, a combination of ash and salty air. I say it has always been here waiting in the cracks. I call it desolation, the stain that's left behind when all that is beautiful has been torn from the world.

Three years I have struggled to forget her, but when you dwell in the same place where she once breathed, it is difficult. I catch myself plucking memories from the air, left there to be discovered again and with it a growing devil that pains my chest, the longing listless poison that inwardly condemns a man to death. Memories – the silent killer.

Times like these I cannot stop thinking of her. A half-empty bottle of bourbon stands on my coffee table, a label of a lighthouse overlooking the sea, made by a couple of gents down by the wharf. They know me by name. Across from it a black leather chair replaces the pearly loveseat I once had. I no longer in need of it, not since I stopped entertaining that is. Guests have grown rarer by the day.

Marty took the loveseat hesitantly. I think it was because he felt as if he were contributing to my self-imposed isolation. I swapped it on condition of receiving Michael's desk, which I lied and claimed it held some personal significance to me. In reality, it was my way of focusing on work, a means by which to distract myself from the things that once mattered. A drink rests in my hand whilst the other hand cradles my head by the window frame allowing my continual stare across the nightscape. I look despairingly out across the city, seeking things that lie hidden from my unlit corner of hell.

A couple had moved in across from me not but a few months ago, now in occupation of Farley's old apartment. From afar, the two remind me of Sonia and Jacob Richardson, the true saviors of the CitySpire in their discovery of rapid pollination, words they used to describe the ability to grow food overnight, thus ending the shortage. R&R Labs and Conservatory sprung up as quickly as their food entrees. It wasn't that long after Emily had died. I remember because pancakes were part of the initial menu.

As far as the belated Mr. Farley, I'm sure the landlord left that little tidbit out and overcharges his tenants for the space — just like everyone else. It's not as if space were a hard thing to come by. It's not that there isn't plenty of room, but it's the quality of those you're sharing it with. I don't know how they get away with it, overcharging to live, but it keeps people segregated.

If people want something free, there are always places like Herbertson Street, though you'll be lucky if anyone responds to a plea for help. No one patrols there. We simply don't have the manpower. Move in at your own risk, they say. However, there are enough stories of disappearances to keep people from complaining about the rent. Then again, maybe such a high rate isn't so bad. It's a fee to keep you from lying face down in an alley somewhere. Life can be cruel in the CitySpire. I let Mr. Kinsley deal with the renters. I still have the final say on who stays and who goes. I like things quiet and Terry does a great job at it. I let him keep the majority of the money.

Unable to find any respite from the blackening buildings, I swallow the remaining half of my drink and revel in the short instance when the burning sensation quashes the gnawing that's tearing my heart apart. It certainly is taking its sweet time of it.

I brought some of Emily's things from her apartment, a spill of unknown clues and memories, each a piece that somehow adds together in meaning even a passing thought or whim—above all else, her whims—to gift me insight into what she had been doing prior to *the incident.*

Michael's desk rests opposite my piano, where stuffed in a corner is a cardboard box filled with an assortment of things: a jack-in-the-box, a bag of marbles, a carousel horse figurine, a spatula, twine, a corkscrew, and piano rolls of music by varying classical artists. A tuning fork lies on my desk, perhaps the most interesting item of them all. Her place has a player piano, a worn contraption that is missing one of its black keys. She kept it tuned and with my continuous visits to her apartment on Nereid Street, she had to maintain it often.

I've listened to the rolls more times than I can count. I've sat there and listened to them all in the dark, late at night when I cannot sleep. I sit there and dream of those things that she may have dreamed and wish for the things she may have wished. I imagine her repertoire of playing styles increase and fantasize about how it would have been to hear her play. I remember how she played Bach's Cantata no. 140. It's forever inscribed in my head and listening to it time and time again fills me with both a sliver of happiness and always remorse. I don't play anymore. I don't know if I ever will.

The piano stares at me from across the way, out of tune and dusty. I've let it sit. The song that once dwelled in my head is forever gone. The notes I recall, but there is nothing else beyond what has been composed. It's unfinished and shall hereby forever remain. It was my song. It was hers. And now I have no one else to play for.

I drop into my chair, at least a comfortable seat that I had dragged up from the building's basement. I pour myself another drink. I listen to the quiet of the room and the hush of the city. I let the silence waft over my skin and into my mind and with it I take a long sip; focusing on letting the nothing bleed into my head. Forget, forget. Please, please forget. The pain does not let up, does not release, and with it comes the continued thoughts of her. Thinking of that time when…

I press myself flat against the black concrete as I struggle with footing along a six-inch ledge on the ninth floor of the Samson building. One misstep and it'll all be over. The serpentine wind slithers up against me, rustling the loose fabric of my coat, and shifting my balance for what seems to be the entire skyscraper shaking.

At night it is here, overlooking the precipice towards the street down below, that I'm able to spot my quarry: not beneath, but above. He's reached a drainpipe a few panes of glass to my right and is currently climbing, his knees squeezed tightly against its dark rounded surface, his arms quickly shimmy his way up towards the next level.

He's wanted for questioning. I was going to put the red-eye on him, hopefully to make the night easier on the both of us, but he didn't give me a chance. What makes this dangerous, while resting my head against the window behind me, is not necessarily the height. The scariest part is that *he has my gun.*

A quick struggle, a few holes burnt into the walls of a nearby restaurant, and now nine floors later, jumping is looking mighty good right now.

"If you give up, I could be looking past this whole affair. A couple questions and we could both go home, what do you say?" I shout above the whipping of air.

He ignores me. It was worth a try but I don't expect him to bite. They never do.

I start across the next window, grateful that the building is nearly abandoned. That's just the thing I need, to be blinded by someone turning on the lights staring half-naked in their bathrobe. Once I'm able to reach the pipe myself, the sound of hallowed metal echoes with the sound of shattered glass. Tightly, I close my eyes, as a few fragment pieces rain on my head and shoulders. Shaking them loose, I steal a glimpse, noting where my adversary had gone—into the room above—and quickly, though cautiously, ease out onto the drain pipe.

Miming my charge, I hoist myself upward through a series of movements involving the tightening of my knees and then a pull upwards. The pipe is as thick as my thigh, securely bolted into the concrete and bound by steel which serves well as handholds. I do not understand how he was able to make it up so quickly, and I worry that if I'm not fast enough, I could lose this one.

Truth be told, this isn't how I pictured spending my night. My hands are sore and covered by the same residue that has collected against the building's exterior, the black mold that has been growing over the past years. I've been reassured that it isn't toxic, not this type anyway. With determination, I'm able to clear the edge of the tenth-floor and then squeeze through the broken window.

I'm greeted by the roar of a pistol, the scent of scorched ozone and the shattering of the next pane over. The blast was close, shot by an untrained if not shaky hand. I dive into the room and behind an empire sofa. Another excruciating cough of gunfire stings my ears. The wall now takes to the offensive odors like burnt metal, a scent that comes from an electric-fed projectile. Everything has changed since rail weaponry. How I'm nostalgic for the simple crowbar or broken bottles.

I flip the sofa for cover. The old girl may not be able to stop a sabot, but it'll certainly help obscure my location. I hug the floor in anticipation of the next few shots. I start my count. One at the window, two and three when I rolled, and then another two scream into the sofa, followed by a showering of stuffing and the twang of coils. That's five! And the familiar sound of the pistol's meter chirps to indicate a recharge.

I spy him in the threshold of another room. Scrambling to my feet, I leap over the sofa and charge, catching him unexpected in the chest and slam to the ground. The gun spins from his hand across the hardwood floor, sliding beneath a fixed radiator next to a wide bay window.

The fray has dropped into someone's personal office. I quickly discern the shadowed details of a polished oak desk, bookshelves opposite the door, cabinets and an embroidered rug. I throw a couple of well-aimed punches, both in his face before missing and then taking one square across the jaw. The impact stuns my brain for a short second before I elbow him in the sternum. Unfazed, he grabs me by the collar and attempts to roll, where I break his grasp and palm him in the chin.

The gun chirps once more as the room is lit by a flash of green from the chirper's handle, indicating a complete recharge and an additional dreaded five shots. My nemesis forces his legs between us and kicks outward, landing them hard in my stomach and I stagger. He hastily stands and rushes toward the window, hoping to snatch up the gun and be done with it all. But I leap at his legs, and draw him back down onto the floor. The wind is knocked out of me and he jostles one of his legs free just in time to kick me in the head. I lose his other one and for a moment, my orientation.

As I ready myself for the next attack, my foe draws the chirper from beneath the radiator, stands and aims it in my direction. I grind my teeth in anticipation of the shot, thinking those inevitable thoughts, but am instead blinded by a strobe that beams directly into the room from a floodlight.

The hum of aerodynes breaks the dread and a loud speaker wails, "Drop your weapon!" My eyes adjust as my assailant's body casts a pillar of shadow shielding me from the abrupt change in illumination. There, beyond the window, hovers an aircar with the flashing of red and blue lights designating its allegiance.

The man turns his weapon on the whirly-gig, a mistake that costs him. I duck into a ball, full knowing that the driver has an itchy trigger finger and cringe as a spray of rails decorate the room in searing heat, static electricity and splatters of blood. I watch struck by both awe and horror, as the perpetrators body convulses like a marionette whose strings are tied too tightly, twists and falls lifelessly in a heap on the floor.

Lights score the room in a variety of blues and reds, enough for one to see every detail – like a pair of 3-D glasses. Flashlights, spotlights, and a variety of other sources are used to better light the area. A stray sabot damaged the wall panel and must have short-circuited the wiring.

Marty stands with me, having his gig idle outside the broken window. He turns a white card over and hands it to me. "Mathew Collins, a fake – must have picked it up off some unfortunate near the docks on his way in." This one is easy to tell, it's the third Mr. Collins this week.

I look at it briefly knowing that once you've seen one, you've seen them all. I watch as a pair of officials, Rockword and Slovene—members of Govennet Cleanup—starts picking up the pieces of Mr. Collins and stuffs them into bags.

"Were they able to put the red-eye on him?" I ask out of morbid curiosity.

Marty shakes his head. "Didn't need to. I put enough holes in him for them to verify that he was a mannequin. Synthetic. Nothing but tubes and wires. Good riddance, if you ask me."

"Am I to assume that we need to step up our efforts on the beaches?" I ask with a measure of detachment that comes in dealing with their kind, a real pit in the stomach.

"Too much ground to cover and they have sympathizers. They're becoming more frequent as the months progress."

It was a year ago that a doctor named Victor Dreval discovered that there were monsters living among us. They bear our skin, they wear our clothes and model human behavior, but they aren't human. They are synthetics, genetic machines that imitate society. They'd kill without an acrid taste in their mouth, even their own kind if it was advantageous to them. He said their psychology was equivalent to a serial killer—sociopaths, megalomaniacs, and pathological narcissists. I didn't quite understand all the other fancy Latin terms he used, but from what I did grasp, it's all scary stuff.

They're said to bubble up from beneath the ocean. Most of it was simple rumor, a couple of eye testimonies claim naked men or women wash ashore and then slip stealthily into the city. All such witnesses are questioned rigorously and then given the eye exam themselves—a tiny hand held device that detects abnormalities in a person's physical makeup. Green results always indicate a pass, but rare red results mean you were one of them. It isn't unusual for a body to be found, having been deposited in an alley murdered, usually strangled or beaten to death. They always take the clothes. All is said to be the product of mannequins. Some call them puppets, plasties or plastic-heads. Some have even resorted to calling them screw-jobs. No matter what you call them, it all translates out to being a cold-blooded killer.

A fellow officer, Reginald Blake—rough skin, black hair, pencil mustache—hands my missing pistol to Marty. His voice delves into the rough draw of the wharf. "Mitei xent ihts tou on dlohs hei rusei kamei. Tio of suacebei ruht egt us of noei esei tou tahei louwd I."

Marty snatches it quickly and spouts, "Cepsert mosey ohsw. Etsixed even oyua rofebei redrums nisahcg aws hei. Us of nay tou eneppahd vahei luocd it."

Whatever it is they are talking about, Officer Blake seems to disagree. He shakes his head and spits back. "Siwh taedh ai ahs or seleracs ehtier is eihcf htei mei sak oyua if. Egnadr in noyreveei tups it, or ehtier."

"Calsk mosey ihm uct. Capsei mosey ihm vigei tou ogt oyua, ltnecery eidd ahs ihm tou solcei noemosei. Hguorht aws hgint htei rofebei etomedd lkciuqy oyua vahei louwd hei oitanidrobusnie uoyr uobat enkw hei if, edisebs."

"Marty." I try to interrupt.

But the other officer adds his retort, "Gaou raeys erhtei evor aws ahtt. Bei evenr liwl hei ehtn, onw by it evor ont is hei if."

"That's enough, Sergeant. I believe you have some work to do." Marty glares at him with animosity. The sound in his voice is enough to let the Sergeant know that he better let things lie.

Marty returns with his usual roguishness. "Yes, chief?"

"Do you mind cutting that out while I'm around?"

"Cut what out?" He asks.

"You know what I mean."

"It's just street talk. There's no harm in it."

"I don't like it. It makes you sound like you just crawled out of the gutter."

"Duly noted." He passes me my gun. "I think you lost this." He caters a sly smile that comes from a joke he's told in his head.

"Thanks." I say without recognizing his making light of the matter. "I figure it was best to leave the chirper where it was in case there were organs inside. Hate for you to get pinned as plugging an innocent whose only crime was admiring the view."

Marty's face sobers up, dropping in both smile and joyful rise in cheek. "He had a gun?" The smile returns quickly.

"Nice." Is really all I can muster from beneath the morbid fantasy of his sarcasm.

"So do you plan to stick around for the police, file some paperwork, or did you want to go get a drink somewhere?" Marty asks. "I know this great place that'll just knock your socks off."

I shake my head, not wanting to embark on any of Marty's adventures. I'd hate to have to spoil it all by pretending to have a good time. Besides, nobody loves a depressing drunk.

"Will you take a rain check? I have some work left unfinished."

"You know, chief," he tilts his head to the side, starring at me with those bright blues of his to reinforce the actual rarity of his seriousness. "It rains in the CitySpire almost everyday. I could buy myself a building for as many rain checks as you've given me."

He's concerned for me. Has been for years. Whatever keeps him close to me is a mystery. It's always been a subject that we've never explored. As may times as I've kept him at arms length, one would think that he would have stepped away for good. But he's still here, following me at arm's length. It lends me comfort knowing that he's there if ever I need him. One of these days I'll make it up to him. Tonight, on the other hand, I won't be much company. Tonight is different.

"Some other time perhaps, I promise you."

He nods his head just as he has nearly a hundred times before. He bows suddenly, opening his arms wide, leading with his right, and directs me properly as an usher.

"Then allow me, good sir, to offer you a ride home. The car is already parked out front and is ready for your every whim."

I crack a grin up one side of my cheek. "I don't want to inconvenience you."

He keeps in character, overdoing his arm movements by planting his leading hand on his chest. "Not at all, good sir. It would be my pleasure."

The charlatan. We live in the same building. However, the night is through. Once blood is spilt in the CitySpire, be it organic or synthetic, a disturbing hush carries its way through every niche and cranny. The streets quiet as the population turns sparse with everything crawling back into their holes to wait out the night. Let the Sergeant handle it. I have no desire to explain the situation to the watch.

"Sure, Marty. Lead the way."

It's the same vehicle, the same company, but the tension thickens as the Creep. The ride in the gig is an awkward one. I contend to distance myself from whatever thoughts are weighing the compartment, and instead watch both police and Govennet radio channels converting to digital green text on the tinted windshield.

Halfway to our destination, Marty decides to break the natural order of silence with another breath of concern.

"So what's so special about tonight, boss? You got a sizzling date or something?"

"It's her anniversary."

"No kidding?" He focuses forward, his eyes darting back and forth every so often. There's something he's calculating, something that he's searching for in the past. "Has it been that long? I didn't realize." He chuckles nervously from the mistake. "Sorry, chief."

We sit in quiet for the passing of a minute. "I guess that's understandable." He mentions from the halls of his mind.

"Why, what's understandable?"

"Why you're off."

I turn from him and look out the passenger side window. "There's a first time for everything." I mutter with disdain.

He's right though, he shouldn't have been able to get the drop on me. I'm smarter than that. For some reason, I hesitated and he got the upper hand. I saw him on the street but he wouldn't make eye contact, as if he was trying to avoid me. I tried asking him some questions but before I could, he overpowered me. I would have died if Marty hadn't been there to back me up. I was sloppy. I was careless. I was distracted.

I think on the past half hour. "Is that what you and the sergeant were talking about?"

"More or less. I wouldn't worry too much about the sergeant, chief. He's just an asshole. He's been walking around the past few weeks with a chip on his shoulder. He's gone and bagged himself six screw-jobs and thinks everyone should worship the ground he walks on. Forget him. The rest of the team looks up to you. You've been devoted to your job since day one and quite frankly, I can't remember the last time you took a couple days off."

I continue to stare out the window watching as the camouflaged buildings fly by, the passing of windows, and the forming of rainclouds.

I sigh. "I don't want to take a couple of days off. I don't want to take *a* day off. I just made one mistake. I'll be fine. Let this day pass and I'll be good as new."

I can tell Marty isn't into having this conversation, but from the conflict in his cheeks reflected in the window, he's pushing himself out of worry.

"You know as well as I do that we can't afford to make mistakes. Remember who we have to deal with on a day-to-day basis. If we let them have an inch, they'll take you for all you got. They'll kill you, Sam, and they won't think twice about it."

I stare off into the silence of the city. Occasionally, I catch Marty taking a breath for words, but he halts and decides to leave well enough alone. It's eating him up inside, him seeing me like this. I wish it were only possible to flip a switch and everything would be back the way they were three years ago. But there is no switch, only the knowledge of how things were, and how they are now. The sad thing is that there is nothing either of us can do about it.

He returns me to the rooftop of our building, the aerodynes slow in hum and vibration drowns itself into a soft whirl. I place my hand on the door handle, but am held by the shoulder by a quick hand.

"Sam, as a favor to me, take a couple days off to get your head straight. You owe it to yourself. You owe it to me."

I sigh once more. "Fine. I'll take tomorrow off."

"That's all I ask." And he returns his hand back on the wheel.

"Not coming?" I ask.

"Naw, I think I'll go toss a few back before calling it quits." He gives me a salute. "You have a wonderful evening, Mr. Chief Inspector."

"You too." I open the gig's wing and step out onto the blacktop of the roof. But before I close it completely, I poke my head back in. "Make sure our friend the sergeant gets a royal share of tonight's paperwork."

"Oh, I'm sure he'll get his due." Marty laughs the good laugh before resurrecting the aerodynes into a full spin.

Once away from the vehicle, I catch the driver giving me the thumbs up before he's levitated into the air, turns, and then hovers back out into the city.

The strangeness of it all is that home is the last place I want to be. I take the stairs down to the twenty-fifth floor and then, after stopping shortly at my apartment for a few piano rolls—plus a map case to protect them from the rains, I take the elevator to the lobby and then step out onto the streets.

It is a nightly affair and I a miserable creature of habit. If the lights of the city reached the darkness that huddles above us, I'd be able to see the rolling thunderheads on approach. I can feel the change of air currents and pressure as well as smell the encroaching moisture from the east, a touch of salt and a hint of rot from the Creep that follows like the tail of a kite.

The streets are vacant, still glistening with the dampness from the previous rain, reflecting the cast iron street lamps that hug the edge of the sidewalks. Even with Boenger's Model what-is-what being made every day, there are still very few of them using the streets, and fewer still that frequent the air, especially this late at night. I hear he's cut back in production, preferring the custom job over a mass assembly line. Not much demand for a city stagnant in population with more apartments than inhabitants. But I don't like to think about *his* fortune. This all could have been prevented had he been out of the picture. I still blame him partially for Emily's "accidental suicide". At least, that's what is in her file.

I remember an altercation between us a year ago. I walked into his office and accosted him in front of his coworkers, in front of everybody. I was drunk at the time. Marty managed to get me out of that one, claimed it had something to do with parking violations, code restrictions, and permit indiscretions. No charges were ever filed. As if it would have done him any good. The complaint would have disappeared somewhere and any inquiries would have been met by the frustrations of Govennct bureaucracy. I never felt sorry about it, just wish I could have landed a few good hits on him instead of tripping over myself.

A raindrop. One of many, I'm sure. I'm still in uniform, a garb consisting of a black double-breasted trench coat, knee high patrol boots and a silver badge in the shape of a nautilus shell—Brigit's idea. They all are waterproof. Seems everything needs to be these days if you want it to last.

I follow the absence of life as if it were a pathway leading to my obsession. Occasionally, I can discern a set of voices farther along an adjoining street, but sound never travels here in a direct line. It always ricochets off a few items before ever reaching your ears. I'm sure Christopher Bark could explain it better. I continue forward, up Rhine Street and into Hermes Square.

The shops are now restored businesses, the fashion boutique of the CitySpire, along with a quaint little chocolate and coffee cafe designed in the old style, decorated in neon lights that read "Midnight Rendezvous". They sometimes call it lovers' corner. I've never frequented it, but I hear it has good truffles.

The bushes are well kept, as well as dainty little flowers that grow in the window sills. Though, sad to say, the Creep has its tendrils in everything. It is here where the true battle can be witnessed, when every morning the city scrubbers spray and buff the mold away. The lower portions of the buildings are kept clean, sometimes visited twice, if not three times a day. I'm sure it costs the business owners a large sum, but it's all one can do to have an availing store front. The more difficult to reach areas are always overrun.

Originally, when I heard of Hermes Square's restoration, I was excited. But, as all things tend, a part of me withers every time I take notice of it. Oddly, all I can picture when I pass the flawless white marble statue of that profound Greek god, are phantoms dancing. I leave it all with a pain in my chest.

Further along, I step over the same spot where Emily had first spotted the Lockes.

PART III - THE SORCERER

"Look Samuel, mannequins."

I stop sharply and whip my head around, unsure of whether I had heard it or if it came from my mind; her voice, such an ethereal thing. She isn't there. No—why would she be? Nobody is. I shake my head, running my fingers over my face to whisk away the memory like a cobweb. *Mannequin,* it has different meaning now. A lot of things do.

I catch a couple of them displayed in a permanent pose starring out blankly with their flawless faces and pale physique from behind one of the store windows. A shudder tingles down to my tailbone, and I hurry my step as to avoid the misgivings that sneak up on me every time I pass them. I cannot help but imagine them moving, reaching out at me, then escaping their translucent confines and stalking me down the street. I cast a few paranoid glances behind me to better my nerves.

On the right street, just a birds-eye view from the cathedral, I turn towards the place I once swore to avoid; now, ironically, one of the most frequent places I visit. The fear that I once held for the place has long since transformed into a morbid sense of serene inevitability.

Once beneath the gates of the CitySpire's cemetery, I tap my chirper quietly in my left shoulder holster, just to reaffirm its presence beneath the fabric of my coat. It isn't the ominous shadows cast by the hanging lanterns or the foreboding nature that headstones acquire late at night that makes me edgy, but the slimy thought of some screw-job seeking refuge amidst the ambiguous tombs and distorted yew trees. You can never be too careful this time of night, especially now when the tide is at its peak. The tide has a way of messing with people, like moon madness.

I march wearily across the sidewalk, along the stretch of listless suicide victims, to Farley's creed and those who've since found comfort in a dramatic fall and the kiss of pavement. Then there are those whose spirits still haunt the Rue de Bourreau, those left behind by the massacre, a row of twelve who perished in the fires of desperation. The sorry lot. How I envy them. Scraping them off the pavement was the true horror of it all. It's one of those things that stick with you no matter how much time goes by.

My journey ends at a remote alley with three tombs, the very place many years before where I buried Richard Farley in a place of honor; one of black granite, one of limestone and the other of glass. Though, sadly enough, it isn't Mr. Farley that I planed on visiting. It is the last resting place of Miss Emily Golden Waters, her coffin still present and beyond the glass walls of the sepulcher.

The construct is marvelous, as well designed as the day I interred her. The glass is flawless and minus any smudges that tend to accrue after being bombarded by the winds. Thankfully, the Creep has yet to defile this place. I see the golden trim in elaborate vine-like design around the top and bottom portions of each wall, and a pair of glittering columns of translucent crystal that bear entrance into the place. The doors are locked by an articulate mechanical thing requiring a musical combination, safe from whatever fate befalls corpses.

Her coffin is smooth, polished and still retains the luster I gave it the first day I set foot inside the place. I picture myself on the opposite side. I envision stretching my hands across the wood, lying my head down and wishing to lie down and wait for death to inevitably take me. I could if I really wanted to, just a few feet away before I'd reach the lock, enter the correct combination, and then pass beyond the threshold of the living and into that of the dead. If I entered, I wouldn't come back out. I touch the place in my coat where my gun rests, as I remember how I've been tempted many times in the past to join my beloved in eternal rest.

I remember how she looked the day I found her lying on a bed of glass on her back on Nereid Street. Her hair was loose, like a fresh bottle of honey left to pour out across the street. Pale. Cold. So cold. It was like watching a part of me rot away to bone and then whisk away like ash. My knees, how they gave away, and I cried. They weren't just tears of sorrow—it was every ounce of me given onto the street. What was left behind was a painful echo of what once was and forever will be the remnant host of Samuel Bell.

"Emily…one day, I'll be with you again." I promise as I move my hand to my heart to stop it from quivering into entropy. I inhale a breath. I stare long into the night, doing nothing more than reliving those nights long ago.

21

The door creeks behind me as I transgress beyond the stairwell and into the unlit hallway of the old apartment building on Nereid Street. Tiny domed fixtures along the walls flicker an instance before glowing in illumination. They are motion sensitive, a positive feature about these places, as you can always tell if there's people here that shouldn't be. It is one of those sections of the city that is far outside Govennet patrols. Although, it's not like anything needs to be protected. No one has been here for years.

The hallway is decorated with wainscoting panels, plaster and then an antiquated paper border along the top. The plaster is a dark grey, spackled, possibly Venetian. The wood is a deep cherry with tiny blocked edgings. The lights flicker again, a defect in the florescent bulbs, and for a short moment I can see the grainy specters of my mind replay a scene that occurred three years prior to this day, when I spirited down the hallway, stopped at apartment twenty-three and jimmied the lock—and once barred—I kicked it in. I've since repaired it to keep the riffraff out.

It takes awhile to regain oneself after the mind turns inward. I tried keeping her body in my apartment. Hoping. Wishing. Until of course, I was visited by both Marty and Natalie. They helped me entomb her. I was no good after that. I wouldn't come out of my apartment, just sat there and stared for days. If it wasn't for Natalie's care, I don't know if I ever would have emerged from that dark grave I had dug for myself. When I got better, she left. She never told me why. Never seen her since.

I arrive at the apartment door, number twenty-three, a black painted thing with gold lettering nailed in the top center. Yellow tape stretches across the framework, one diagonally and one across, reading: "Govennet Investigation Pending, Do Not Cross." It is my way of keeping the curious out, a deterrent that implies officers frequent this place. Someone who was overly observant would notice dust gathering since it hasn't been moved in quite some time.

The Govennet was something Marty and I started. After the city council formed and members were elected, there was a unanimous understanding that any position of power makes one vulnerable to corruption. *Take nothing less than fairness and nothing beyond deserving;* a rule that, despite its origin, was ingrained in us and was to be upheld in all things. When those who govern place their own interests above those they serve, then it's the Govennet's role to step in. When corruption is low, it's the Govennet's job to keep the peace alongside the city police department. That's how things were decided. I slip the key into the lock, turn it, and dodge beneath the yellow ribbon to step into her apartment.

Shutting the door behind me, I take a deep breath. Three years and I can still smell her. It is as if her scent ingrained itself in the wooden floor, or perhaps seeped into the air circulation—hiding in the ducts—it reminded me of lilacs; a smell that had long ago dwindled away. Being here lessens the toll upon my heart. I'm able to breathe better and the slight chance of finding something new in regards to her mysterious demise lends me strength for the next night. Occasionally, I dream of her. It's what I live for.

Her configuration is very different than most other apartments. For this section of the city, it's a treasure that goes untapped as the beauty of the old style is abandoned for the security of modern fortresses built of concrete. To the right is an archway that marks the beginning of a small kitchenette surrounded by walls, no bar to open it up any. To my left is a door into the bathroom with a second door inside to the west leading into a ten-by-fifteen-foot bedroom that also accesses the living room via a door facing north.

The living room is small but comfortable, with a worn chocolate leather sofa and rickety sofa table behind it about mid-center of the room facing westward. There a half circle of windows looks out across Nereid Street and its adjoining boulevards. It is against the far eastern wall where the player piano rests, serving host to numerous piano rolls, portfolios of dusty sheet music, and a plethora of blank music sheets. Nearby is an inkwell and pen to strike down any fanciful ideas. Obviously, none have come for some time.

I select a sleeve of music out of the map case that I've been carrying, purposefully seeking Handel's Sarabande in D minor. I walk the short hallway before entering the living room and load the aging roll into the piano, engage the electric pump beneath the keys, and flip the switch. I shut the doors to the mechanisms, listening as the gears rattle within, and sit comfortably nearby on a wooden chair to hear the first notes. I sit and think about all the other artists I have planned for this evening, Johannes Brahms and Sergei Rachmaninoff, a couple of artists I've been neglecting of late.

My attention draws towards the darkest section of the living room, being which the notorious window that claimed Emily's life, now boarded shut, with tiny beams of light struggling through the cracks. I had it sealed in case it would conjure additional nightmares of her "accidental" plummet eight stories down. *Accidental* can't even describe it. I found a stool at the base of the window, overturned and kicked a few feet from. There was sheet music everywhere. I'm uncertain if the sheet music was a natural part of the conditions here, a mess Emily herself had left, or if it had been sprawled out by someone else.

I shift through one of the sheet piles, letting the music of the player piano wash over me in my contemplations—varying artists, all different sorts: Haydn, Schubert, Dussek; penned on a thin piece of parchment. Each page has tiny segments of notes circled in bright red, indicating some unknown significance. Whatever importance they held was lost upon her death. Unlike Farley, she never kept a journal. I've been through them multiple times. There isn't so much as a single pattern to it, nor had there been when it was sprawled out on the floor. I constantly reassure myself that these were left behind by Emily, that she was sporadic in everything she did, so why not in the rest of her research—that is, if she was actually researching anything at all. For all I know, she may have been circling the parts she liked the best.

Being here in her apartment allows me to think outside my usual depressions. I'm able to gaze at the knickknacks and baubles she kept. The most intriguing of them all are the child-sized tools and materials scattered across her sofa table, such as a couple push rods, tweezers, calipers, hammers, pins, musical movements, gears, glue, and other related assortments. Originally, I didn't know what they were for. It wasn't until having retraced her steps back to the silversmith's shop, the one tucked away next to B. Rick's hardware store, that I found similar items. They are all used to create watches and music boxes. Apparently, she was crafting something, because there are traces of wood shavings next to the sofa table, miniscule ones that seemed to have been missed during cleanup. The brushes that rest inside a recycled can tell of its color—red. I wonder, the gift that she had promised me that same day, if it was a red music box. Maybe a replacement for the one I already have. Whatever it was, it isn't here.

It all doesn't sit well with me. Marty, Brigit, Mr. Keasley… all of them agreed unanimously that Emily's death was an "accidental suicide". The window sits just shy of three feet off the ground, so she couldn't have accidentally crashed through the window by a misstep in balance. She lived at my apartment for some time, and the windows I have near to the floor, were it not for the wooden trim. Never did I witness anything then that would have opted for the fate everyone else had spun for her.

The stool that had been knocked over could have easily made her at window level; twenty-four inches or so tall. Did she stand on it? Did she lose her balance, perhaps a fainting spell, and plummet backwards into the pane? Or was the stool already overturned, much like her sheet music, just disheveled.

I ease out of my sophisticated stoop next to the piano and move closer to examine the stool that is set off to the side next to the sofa. I've seen it many times before, all from different angles and different perspectives. It is oak, with a light finish and slightly worn. The bottom legs are fitted with metal dowels and tightly snug screws. Pushing on it, it doesn't move. I drag it in front of the window, thinking that perhaps the floor is uneven or maybe the wood warps a particular way around this time of year. Nothing. It sits in perfect alignment. Heavy. Solid.

Once I contemplated that she might have been murdered. Perhaps someone had pushed her out the window? But nothing had been out of place and Emily's head didn't show any signs of physical trauma outside of meeting the concrete. The food was still stocked and tidy, not to mention the nineteen boxes of pancake mix that hid in a cabinet above the refrigerator. Nothing was tossed or out of place. The door was locked from the inside. There was no motive. No reason for anyone to kill her. The Count? But by his own admission he was fond of all of us. Even so, he's gone now—buried beneath a partial of ruined brick and stone when Marty and I confronted him in the cathedral a year ago. No matter which way I slice it, murder was out of the question. Logically, if it wasn't murder, then it was suicide or an accident. However, I refuse to accept either of them. Something had happened. *Something…*

I drop down into the sofa, my hand on my brow like an arched spider. I listen as the song ends and the clack of the player piano issues its final churn and falls into silence. I wipe my face, hoping to abolish the frustration from my features like sweat onto a rag. My head drops into the arm of the sofa, falling into a niche that I had carved into it long ago. I stare vacantly at the cracked ceiling, barely able to see where one ends and another begins. The light from the window is insignificant at best. I prefer the dark. A reason for why I keep the motion lighting disabled, it makes things easier to imagine and allows my mind to escape.

I run my fingers down the back cushions of the sofa. Focused, I take in the smooth feel of its texture and concentrate on hearing the swoosh of friction between my fingers. Its cold, but it won't be for much longer. For the first time tonight I realize how sore I am. I relax my gaze, allowing the shadows to play against me, as they shift in strange and alien patterns caused by the dim. I relax my breathing and feel the prodding of tiny needles as my inner pain dances across my chest. It's as if someone is pushing down on my forehead with but a finger, shushing me into slumber. I close my eyes. I dream.

I'm sitting in front of my piano back at my apartment, it is day, the sun brings in a radiant shine to the walls—everything is glowing. I run my fingers over the ivory keys, feeling their texture, the soft smooth lacquer that covers it. I can smell lilacs.

A pair of cream-colored arms slides down off my shoulders and beyond my neck; they fold around the mid-section of my chest. I can feel her breath against my neck, her bright platinum curls spill off my shoulder—brushing against me lightly—as she leans in and kisses my cheek.

I start in on the first measure of Bach's Cantata No. 140 and she brings her lips down to my ear.

"What are you doing, Samuel?" Her voice is serene and melodious.

I continue to stare at the keys, feeling the pleasures with which the song fills me with. "I'm playing your song. Don't you like it?"

"Oh, Sam." She sighs bringing her arms to wrap around my waist. She sits behind me on the bench and lends her head to my back. "You've forgotten then."

"Forgotten what?" I ask, still in perfect performance, feeling the warmth of her body squeezed next to mine.

"What you promised."

"And what was that, dearest?"

She lifts her head. "You promised that you'd finish it."

I stop playing, my fingers curling inward; slowly dying. "I can't." The words flow through me like a wounded serpent.

"Why not?" She asks.

"Because," I look down at my hands, my eyes well with tears, and I roll them from window to wall in hopes of escaping them. "Because Emily—you're dead."

I wake to the sound of my own voice echoing her words, *"But you promised me."*

I can feel the dampness of my cheeks, tiny streams of tears that have somehow escaped my dream. I wipe them away in the quiet of the room. It feels around five. Dawn is on approach. It is something I tend to avoid.

With little strength I can muster, easing into my soreness, I stagger off towards the adjoining bedroom—shedding my coat on the way, releasing my suspenders and easing off the holster—I collapse on the bed. Instead of inching beneath the covers, I just pull a quilt from the base of the bed over me. As my head drops into the pillow, I am reacquainted with my earlier paranoia and reach for my gun, check the safety, and ease it beneath my pillow. With her scent wafting in my nostrils, the rest caters to obscurity.

PART III - THE SORCERER

I sleep through the day, allowing the sun to trickle its way through the clouds without a pinch of objection and then set far in the west, once again bringing back those ideal conditions for my continued survival. I swear by the night shift, the very time when the CitySpire is at its peak for a Govennet officer. There are those who prefer to do morning to mid-afternoons, but they are mostly rookies or the occasional volunteer wanting to make up some hours. The real stuff happens at night. That's where you make the most difference. But that wouldn't be me today, at least, not officially.

I ready myself around ten, preferring to keep in awhile before slipping out into the night air. I prefer to avoid the crowds. Everyday they go to and from their respective places of employment to make just enough credits to pay rent and put food in their bellies. Then there are always the night clubs, the theatre or brimming restaurant to ease the weary-eyed soul looking for means to stave off the boredom. Unfortunately, for me it isn't boredom that I'm warring with, it's just those dreadful feelings that come when those terrible memories resurface. There is only one thing that is going to get me through this night and it waits for me at the west side pier.

The walk is brisk as I pass through the desolate streets. I stray from the main roads, keeping to the narrow alleyways and hidden passages that most people either refuse to venture or don't know at all. Between buildings I spy a few individuals, a partial crowd, all moving in different directions, each trying to get from one portion of the CitySpire to the other without being harassed.

My only company is the steam that vents up from the sewer system, which springs like geysers at times from the drains and manhole coverings. There is the soft pattering of rain against metal, remnant pools that are still draining off the skyscrapers and trickling through the storm pipes. It's really all I need, and sometimes all that I require. Too many times have I been stopped on the street by some pedestrian interested in learning about the "good old days", curious as to how everything began, others asking of the Count's demise. It's simply not a story that I enjoy telling.

That's what the Registration Office is for, to get better acquainted with the CitySpire and her limited, though violent history. That's how they know me. There's a tree of faces, a lineage of who has been here the longest. That's what established the pecking order; about who gets what, where one lives, and who is up for council election. Apparently the Registration Office isn't enough. Funny how they always come to me.

After a few hours or so, the skyscrapers morph into office buildings and the brick warehouses that, despite their constant monitoring, are always unearthing additional supplies—some missed by earlier surveyors, and others appearing out of thin air. But that isn't unusual here. There is always something new, a street that no one has heard of, a room that hadn't been there before, or an additional level to a building—the strangest of them yet. It is like the city is being renovated right before our eyes and we're unable to see it happen. It scares some people, but the worst that can be expected is a minor case of disorientation. I notice that most reports are filed right after the fogs drift through; the rest I believe, are just not noticed right away. I outright laugh when a new face asks for a map.

My hair rustles by the shore winds with the fresh air pungent with the scent of salt and fish. I step out from the tiny alley and onto Rhine where but a few feet are left before it is consumed by the wharf. I inhale, letting the fresh breeze open my lungs. It is here where one can escape the terrible taste of the Creep, a longing desire of every inhabitant of the CitySpire.

During the day, the wharf explodes in activity, people bustling between labors, aiding in the fish markets and readying the few scallop boats for the next morning. There are always high demands in resource transfers from the warehouses to deeper inside the city where they can be processed or later refined into fancy trinkets. Then there is the long line of shops built along the promenade, a straight tour of individual businesses: hemp makers, cobblers, ceramics, bakery, distilleries and so forth. They all close before dark, giving their employees enough time to return to the center of the city before the night descends upon them. That's when the patrols start.

"Can't say I blame her, a nice looking filly like that just doesn't deserve to be treated that way." Come voices from the pier.

"Well, from what I heard she packed everything up and fled outside the patrol zones. Poor Murphy has been out there looking for her for weeks, says he's been everywhere, but we all know that it's not that hard to disappear."

I spy on them from above. Caleb Grik and Bryan Sallis, first-year Govennet recruits. They are both in uniform, standing by a covered lantern atop a mooring and dealing a hand of cards while using a pile of pebbles between them to represent their ante.

"You think she's been picked up by one of the plasties? Hate to see a pretty thing like that go to waste." Sallis discards a card from the left side of his hand, and draws another from the deck at the base of the lantern.

"Who knows? It serves her right if she did. Anyone that heads out that far beyond Govennet reach is just asking for something bad to happen to them."

"Now that's not fair. She was just trying to get away from Murphy, that drunken fool. I knew that he was hittin' the bottle really hard of late, but I didn't take him for a rough handler. A couple bruises would send any respective lady out into the cold."

Officer Grik tilts his cards closer to his chest and leans his neck in. "Aye, but a black eye isn't excuse for plain stupidity. If she wants to get away from Murphy then all she need to do is file a complaint, or if she doesn't like shells or billies, then she should hide out at a friend's place. Runnin' off all teary-eyed into the lower wards is just going to get her killed or worse, if you know what I mean." He tosses a pebble into the center.

Sallis tosses one of his own in as well. "If I had half a mind, I'd go look for her myself."

"And look where? Plan on going door-to-door hoping to see if one of those deathtraps is harboring her? The only thing you'll find out there is a knife in your back. If I didn't know you better, I'd think that you have a thing for that little gal."

I decide to pay the two a visit. I'm careful to keep my footfalls quiet, as I ease down the set of stairs and onto the pier, but as soon as my boots touch off the last step it moans.

Caleb grabs the lantern and holds it high above his head, alerting his partner to potential danger. "Come out and identify yourself!"

I walk calmly into the light. "Chief Inspector Samuel Bell. Stand down, gentlemen."

Officer Sallis stoops over while grabbing at his heart, just a few inches from where his gun hangs inside his coat. "You've gone and almost made me piss myself." He heaves a couple breaths.

"It's just the chief, no need to change underwear yet. Come to scare us to death, eh?" Grik accuses.

"I thought of dropping in." I muse on their card game. "I see the two of you are hard at work."

"Just taking a breather, sir. Walkin' to and fro tend to throw spades and diamonds in your head. We figured it best to release them before they loosened our senses."

"Now we wouldn't want that to happen, now would we?" I smirk. "Any luck?"

Henry returns the lantern to the mooring. "With spades? Naw—not yet, we were just figuring ante."

"I meant with the patrols."

"Sorry sir, not a single one. It's usually quiet around this time of night. Target practice is a sorry thing lately."

"I see. Well, you might want to check those targets before shooting them. I'd hate for one of you two to accidentally plug a skinny dipper just looking for her clothes."

Caleb winks. "You can rest assured that Sallis and I would try and get all the details outta that one. You know, the usual: height, weight, age, name…address."

"I bet you would."

Officer Sallis eases back into standing. "Bout lost my skin on that one, sir. Thank you so much for that." He heaves one last hard breath. "So you've come for your usual nightcap?"

I nod. "As a matter of fact, I have."

Bryan raises an eyebrow. "Little early for that, isn't it?"

"I took the night off."

Caleb bursts out laughing. "So the clouds do part in the CitySpire. Whatever possessed you to do that?"

"Personal business."

"Ah – personal business, is it?" He and Sallis exchange glances. "It wouldn't happen to be for a lovely lady, eh? Did you find a young officer interested in the promotional fast track?"

"No, nothing like that. Besides, she'd have to be *very* good to weasel a promotion out of me."

"Hard assed, huh? I can respect that. Gives me some hope that I won't be bypassed for a girl with a beautiful smile and a nice bosom."

"I don't believe you're in any danger of that happening. But, I'll leave you two to your patrol. It looks like it is going to be a long night for all of us."

They wish me a good night and I them in return. And as I wave to them from behind, as I start back up the stairs to the promenade, I cannot help but wonder how long those two have been on this shift. I remember pulling a few months' worth of patrol duty on the beaches. It was long, boring, and nerve wracking. The thought of mannequins emerging from the depths, interested in stalking the streets with blood on their minds, doesn't sit well—especially in the dark. It tends to make one paranoid. To me, Sallis seems like he's had more than his fair share of spooks.

Normally, if I caught an officer playing cards on the job, I would have him suspended so quickly he would have thought he was waking up for the first time. But patrolling the wharf late at night is taxing on your sanity. Sometimes, it's the only thing to keep your mind sharp, to take off some of the edge, so you don't jump at every sound. I can remember drawing my weapon every time a fish jumped. Your worst enemies out here are your nerves.

I take one glance out toward the longest pier, listening to the waves lap up against the wood. Most mannequins come in with the tide, swimming up to the shores leafless and disoriented. That's where we stop the majority of them, before they steal off into the city. We can't patrol every beach, however. Some always manage to get by us. Once we dismantle them, we wait till the turning of the tide and give them back to the sea.

I walk down the lit promenade and pass the dried exterior of the shops, stopping only when I reach the sign with a lighthouse painted on it, Hopkins & Hopkins Distillery. It has a small entrance, nothing more in its lobby than a few shelves and a counter for daily transactions. I like them because they are open throughout the night. Two brothers own it. Tiny little guys, shy of five foot. They are quiet, reserved, and don't talk much. They know exactly what I want, and have it waiting for me, even when I've been infrequent with my visits. It takes but a few minutes, in and out, to acquire a familiar friend—a bottle of straight bourbon. It's what will get me through tonight.

With bottle in hand, I stroll to the ledge of the promenade and lean against the wooden railing that separates me from an eight foot drop and then the pier. I stare out across the sea, watching the inky waves roll in. I make a game out of trying to find the horizon which can be difficult at night. All I see is the black nothingness one sees behind eyelids before dreaming. I ponder about things that exist outside the CitySpire.

A sudden spark alerts my peripheral and my hand instantly draws the pistol from my coat; spinning round to face the source. And it is there, nestled in a dark niche is an aged face, grizzled by a white beard and shadowed by the wrinkles in his brow. All is set aglow by the light of a match which he wields close to his face to ignite a wood carved pipe, as he puffs on it to greater induce the flame.

"Govennet – identify yourself!" Normally the demand inspires an awkward response, a nervous tripping over of words, before the spouting of their name. But he's slow to respond, more intent on blowing smoke into the air and extinguishing the match than acknowledging the possibility of a threat. I tighten my grip. Mannequins tend to be this defiant.

I keep my chirper trained; steady in my aim to ensure that if he reaches for anything, I'll unload a sabot directly into his skull. I ask a second time.

"Again, who goes there?"

"'Tis naught but Old Waldgrave." He replies, his voice as deep as the ocean.

Caution, Samuel. Caution. "Waldgrave, is it? And what are you doing out here, Mr. Waldgrave?"

"Tending my duties, sir. You look upon the harbormaster."

I angle my pistol skyward. I note the five counting lights, each blinking in a row, to alert me of its charge. He's either touched or made of plastic.

"Harbormaster? I was not aware that there was such a position."

"Aye, as old as time, they say." He puffs again on his pipe, bringing the glow of embers to his face. He keeps calm despite the gun.

"And by 'they' you mean…?" The true question to riddle out a loon.

"Folks… everyday folks, just like you and me, Mr. Bell."

I'm caught off guard. "You know me?"

"There isn't a soul on this island who doesn't know who you are."

"I can't say that I can claim the same."

"Mind if I approach?"

His request strikes me strangely, but it isn't unreasonable. "Not at all." I bring the pistol down closer to my waist, the weapon now following his movements. "Slowly."

"'Tis the only speed I know."

He casually limps in from the dark, allowing the light from an overhanging lamp to wash over his features. He's old, late sixties or early seventies, and by all physical appearance, he's the oldest of all those who dwell here. Though he may appear ancient, he by no account has any residency over me. Not everything in the CitySpire is as it seems. His hair is long and wispy, but kept under control by a black nautical cap. His clothes are brown and dingy, with a thick grey sweater and duffle coat. His boots are wide and round, made of shiny leather that he must polish despite the wear of his socks.

"Do you frequent the pier often, Mr. Waldgrave?"

"Aye, for many years now." He looks out over the railing and toward the horizon. "'Tis a good night to be out."

"Yes, a very good night." I let him puff a few more times on his pipe before laying my suspicions out before him. "You know, I used to patrol these docks for years as well. Never once did I see or hear of a harbormaster."

He turns from the railing to address me. His wrinkled cheeks puff up in a smile as he takes his pipe from his lips just momentarily. "You don't say? We must have missed each other all that time. Destiny is a strange lass, she is."

"How long has it been since your last eye exam, Mr. Waldgrave?" I pull a small handheld device from my pocket: it has a metal grip, six inches in length, with a circular diopter lens affixed to the end of it. It's a Dr. Dreval Special, the so-called red-eye that allows us to determine man from machine. Those who've been around the block, if they're faking human, start running about now.

"Don't believe I've been subjected to one of those yet." He takes a puff off his pipe and clouds the air around him with his exhale. He holds out his hand. "Do you mind…?

"Knock yourself out." I hand him the device but then quickly add. "Careful, it's expensive."

It's an easy device to manage, just hold it up to one of your eyes and then hit the button that's mid-center of the handgrip. It's idiot proof. I guess the good doctor figured that when lives were on the line, it's best to make it as fool proof as possible.

The old man takes the device and uses it accordingly. He pushes and holds the button as he looks directly through the lens and a green light professes his humanity. My finger eases off the trigger.

He blinks to help dilate his eyes before handing the item back to me.

"I guess that means that I don't need spectacles. Been spotting ships the majority of my life. People called me 'Eagle Eyes'. Can spot things from miles away."

The poor man must have woken with dementia, as if life in the CitySpire wasn't hard enough.

"I hate to tell you this, Mr. Waldgrave." I say as I pocket the red-eye. "But the only ships that dock at the pier are fishing boats. Not too many of them can get out past the buoys due to the waves, not to mention the lack of fuel. I've seen people try it and it's not a very comforting sight."

"Oh there are ships alright. Just not too many folks around when they show up. Those warehouses don't fill up by themselves you know. They don't give much warning, but when they show they are quite the sight."

"Uh-huh." I replace my gun in its holster and decide to humor the poor man. "Just what exactly do these ships look like?"

"Well, they look like just any other ship that comes out of here. They're all windjammers, four-masted barques that are as tall as they are beautiful. They arrive around sunrise and leave at sunset. During which time they're ashore, they unload their cargo, catch up on news, and take aboard enough supplies for their voyage out."

"And these windjammers, do they ever take anyone or drop anyone off?"

"You mean do they ferry anyone across the sea? Sometimes, though no part of the crew has ever opted to stay."

"Where do these ships go?"

He empties out his pipe over the railing of the promenade and stuffs it into his pocket. "Don't rightly know. Never really asked them. Just one of life's mysteries." He looks out across the sea, listening to the lapping of water and the surf of the waves rolling in from somewhere beyond the buoys. "You'll find out one of these days. I guarantee it."

He is a crazy old coot, that's for certain. But you never know if there is some truth to his ramblings. There is a calm to him, a patience that age only brings. I give him the benefit of the doubt. Besides, there is no profit in calling him crazy. If there are ships that come to port, then perhaps they would have some answers in regards to the city.

"Mr. Waldgrave, will you do me the distinct service of letting me know when one of these ships of yours pulls into port? I have some questions for the captain."

"I'd be honored, sir. But I'm certain you'll know when the time is right."

"Why do you say that?"

"Just a feeling."

I let it be, else he'd probably take up my entire night. "You know how to get a hold of me?"

"I reckon through those officers of yours or up in that tower on Gnosh and Rhine. Is that correct?"

"That's right." I nod my head to him.

"Well then, Mr. Bell. I don't want to be taking up any more of your time. I'm sure you have more important things to do than talk to Ol' Waldgrave here. Twas a pleasure meeting you. I'm sure we'll see each other again."

"Good to meet you as well." I say as I make my way backwards. I find it difficult removing my eyes from him, still worried that he'd do something unexpected such as turn invisible or disappear in a cloud of smoke. Instead he continues to look out across the sea, ever vigilant in his watch for ships that'll never come. So, with his back turned, I silently turn my own and renew my way back up Rhine Street where I can enjoy my bourbon in peace.

22

The light, a bright beam of clouded sunlight, presses its nose against the window pane while looking in. It's been awhile since I've seen it fully. When I work, I usually sleep in my bedroom where I have the shades drawn and not a speck of light moves in. But when I drink, I sleep where ever it is most convenient. I sit here in my chair with my head leaned back and the rest of me slouched into position, my one foot stretched up on the coffee table. My neck hurts as much as my head. The bottle of bourbon is not far away, three-fourths of it are gone, 525 milliliters of momentary bliss and with it the night.

I cannot tell what time it is so I have to cheat and look at the wall clock—9:34 in the morning—too early for my tastes, especially when my shift starts at seven. I could have slept longer but the sun has decided otherwise. I don't remember when I fell asleep, but it wasn't all that long ago. It was late. I know that for sure. I start to ease myself from my chair towards the bedroom but a knock at the door pounds me back into my previous seat just when I was making progress.

"Come in!" I holler to the door knowing full well who it is.

The door knob rattles, turns and opens. I don't even have to turn around.

I pinch my sinuses to cure a minor blur. "What do you want, Marty?"

He strolls in, careful to shut the door behind him. He wears an open grey trench coat, black tie, a white shirt and black pants. The hat in his hands is meant to match his coat, a grey fedora. He pauses momentarily to examine the state of the apartment.

"I see you weren't expecting company." Marty refers to the several bottles of empty bourbon, the occasional glass, case files stacked atop one of another in tiny bundles throughout the room, clothes, dishes and dust.

"Still aren't." I reply disdainfully, although my resentment centers more on the time of day than due to his comment. I run my hand over my face to dispel drowsiness and realize the morning bristles. "What can I do for you Marty?"

"Well, I'd like to say that it is because I was curious how your day off was, but you know me better than that."

"So spill it, you're keeping me up."

"Hate to do this to you chief, but Govennet calls."

Still in my clothes from yesterday, Marty takes me to the graveyard. Better to walk so I can clear my head. Luckily, I was able to steal another drink before I left to calm the dehydration dancing in my brain. Outside the black gates, the morning officers keep outside scribbling down witness testimonies. Most likely they were passerbys who heard something, but don't claim to have seen anything. No one ever does. It makes their lives easier that way. It's well known to stay out of there at night.

"It happened around two o'clock this morning. That's what we gathered from bystanders and then judging from the time it took them." Marty recites from earlier that day. "Police officers got here around six this morning, they roused me about an hour later. Apparently, the billies are under the impression it falls under our jurisdiction. I think they just didn't want to deal with it."

"So why do you need me again?" I ask while picking out a group of men who shoulder shovels up the hill a ways. I nod in their direction. "Gravediggers?"

"Yea, they've been waiting since eight to fill the holes back in."

"Holes, what holes?"

"That's one of the reasons that I came to you. A group of misfits came into the place and started digging up the graves."

My eyes open a little wider, previously beaten down by the glow of the clouds, and I raise an eyebrow at him.

Marty notices my surprise. "Oh, it gets better. They were looking for something but didn't know where exactly to look for it. There are holes dug everywhere, even over on the south side where there wasn't anything buried. All the coffins were opened and mostly nothing was taken."

"Mostly?"

"So here's the real kicker. Remember all those poor saps we buried, the jumpers who wore white?" Marty waits for my nod before continuing. "They're gone."

"What the hell do you mean gone? As in they were taken?"

"Yup, the whole lot of them. They took the entire coffin, body and all. There were a few other holes dug here and there, but those bodies were left behind. And I hate to say this as well, considering you had a brief relationship with the guy, but Farley was taken too."

My heart sharply falls in trepidation and I lurch, grabbing hold of Marty by the collar. "What about my Emily?! Did they break into her tomb? Did they take her?!"

He grabs my hand and places his other on my shoulder. "Easy there, chief. She's fine. Not a scratch on it. You can see the coffin from the inside. Nobody's touched it."

I breathe a sigh of relief and let go of him.

"I shouldn't have done that."

He shrugs. "Don't worry about it. I knew you'd get all sensitive." He winks at me hinting at something genuine of his character. He gives me a good swat on the shoulder just in case I failed to catch it.

"So what do you think they wanted with the corpses?" I ask.

"Dating material? Sure beats the living heck out of me, boss. I can't imagine why anyone would want deadbeats like them." Marty smiles to himself. "All they do is lie around all day."

"Marty." I put in my demand for the jokes to end.

He holds his hands out in front of him. "What?" A mischievous grin marks him as guilty.

I get back to the matter at hand. "Does anyone know which direction they went?"

"No, nobody seems to know. Don't believe that anyone stuck around to find out. We were lucky, people stopped during the investigation to let us know what they heard."

"Always seems to be the case."

"Mysteries wouldn't be as fun if people gave us all the answers. Besides, it gives us something to do other than chasing plastic-heads all night."

"What have we learned so far?"

He sighs. "That there were about seven of them, some had big feet and some had little feet. They used shovels and picks to pry open the earth and a crowbar to break into Farley's tomb. That's about it."

"They must have taken them out one at a time." I ponder. "The only thing valuable would have been their ID cards that were buried with them. But why take the rest?"

One of the gravediggers, a burly man with brown mutton chops in a denim jacket busts into our conversation. "Elssekr eciffor? Onw evargs htei in nillifg ratst we anc or, ady lal rehei uot natsd to us nawt oyua do? Evohsl htei nou ridt erehts itnul iapd ont rewei."

I turn to Marty. "What did he just say?"

"He wants to know if they can start filling in the graves."

I just nod to him, knowing that I'm not going to add much more to this investigation. I do not understand why people insist on using that horrid language.

"Aehad go. Oitceridn ihts awy oury kamei nad tuosh htei rawotd enos htei on ratst. Ehtn by nodci be luohsd we." Marty replies.

The gravedigger offers more of his dock speech. "Eidobs htei uobat do to us nawt oyu do ahwt? Us vagei oyu sefinamt htei in etsild nerat ehty."

"Bodies?" Marty bellows. "What do you mean bodies?"

"Silt htei on niat ehty, disei tuosh htei on up udg rewei ahtt eidobs htei." He pulls out a tri-fold booklet, the same one we made for the city when Marty and I turned over the burial list when the council formed. Pointing to a spot on the paper, he says irritated and finally in speech I can understand, "See – they ain't on the list."

Marty grabs the tri-fold and scans over it slowly. "I wasn't told there were bodies dug up on the south side. Samuel, do you know anything about south side burials?"

"What?" My mind is gripped in a net and I struggle against previous experiences. "There shouldn't be any bodies there. The graveyard was empty before we started burying people. Is it possible that someone else happened to bury someone here?"

"No, sir. We keep detailed records here and even walk the grounds every morning. No one has buried anyone here without our knowing of it." The man with the large sideburns just crosses his arms. "Maybe someone dropped them off."

I'm taken back to when Michael brought me out to the graveyard to test his theory of creationism. The soil had easily come up, despite the growing cold. The coffin produced no body, much like the rest of the place. But it is possible that only so much of the graveyard was empty and the rest held bodies. Is it possible that Michael had dug up the grave prior to my knowledge and then led me into his machination? But why, to convince me of his sound theory of the divine, that all things were created by a single hand in a single instance? No matter what Michael had done, we made a generalization. The graveyard may not have been completely empty as we had thought.

Beneath my thoughts I return my gaze, insistent on leaving these questions for another time. "Catalogue it as today's burial. But don't bury them until our boys get a good look at them. As long as there are no signs of foul play, we have no idea where these bodies came from. Afterwards, I need you to check every grave to see if it contains a body or not. If there is anything more than an empty coffin, I want to see a report on my desk. I'll send the orders through the proper channels."

There isn't any way we can tell if the corpses were deposited by grave robbers or not. No matter how hard I try, I can't help but feel as if I was made the fool by a Mr. Michael Rawling Locke.

The gravedigger just shakes his head, throws his hands up and then moves off to relay the news to his coworkers.

"Well ain't he a gem." Marty mentions once the man's out of earshot. "He must be part of those churchers up the street. There is nothing like wasting your afternoon listening to magicians spouting on about nonsense."

"I believe they call them priests now, Marty." I wave him toward the gates before he starts in on yet another of his religious tangents.

"Priests now? So the showmen get a fancy new title? That doesn't make them any different than what they were before. You can call a turd a road apple but it doesn't change what it is. You and I both saw how this hullabaloo started, men and women in rags pointing their fingers and making folks feel guilty that they weren't good enough to be taken with the original inhabitants. Bloody rapture they called it! Follow some dope by the name of Ehcimel. They believe him to be some prophet. More like a lunatic if you ask me. One day some fool gave one of them some spare change and then they went off and bought some robes and founded a church. Doesn't that bother you at all?" He always gets steamed up whenever conversation turns in this direction.

"People should be allowed to believe what they want. Be it a fools path or not, then they'll learn it in the end."

"Now that's just turning a blind eye. You see a widow walking alone on the street and a gang of thugs comes up and bullies her into handing over her purse, you'd want to help her right?"

"Obviously."

"Well, it's the same thing with those con men in robes."

"No, that's not the same thing."

"Yes it is, boss! You have downtrodden, emotionally vulnerable individuals just trying to make it through the day. They're confused, they're upset, and to top it all off, they have to be harassed by people who claim they want to save your soul. It all comes down to this, the church says they have all the answers that the CitySpire officials don't but they're not answers, they are just false theories that if you don't believe in them, they'll curse you with eternal damnation until you do."

We pass by a few officers standing guard at the gates. I nod to them and they do in return.

"I understand your concern, Marty. But you're the prime example that proves that people are capable of thinking for themselves."

"Rational people can think for themselves. I'm done being over city-struck. I came to terms with my predicament years ago, but most people aren't rational."

"How so?"

"When people are drunk, are they rational?"

"No."

"When you're angry, are you always rational?"

"Not always."

"And when your sad, are you—" He stops upon the realization of where his sentence is leading.

"You are what, Marty?" I ask in an attempt to goad him into finishing his sentence. Already the discussion managed a poor note and Marty is now trying to salvage it.

"Look, Sam. People react differently when they get hung up on things. I'm not saying that it's unnatural, it's just the way people are. You stop entertaining guests, you turn down your best buddy's invitations, and you do nothing for yourself. It's a cruel word, but the proper term is that it isn't rational. And that's what those vultures are doing right now. They're preying upon those who are having a hard time of it. People need to be protected."

"But see that's the thing, Marty. What's the difference between you wanting to protect people from the priests, and the priests wanting to protect people from a life of supposed damnation?"

"The difference is, chief, that I don't accost people in the street by appealing to their sense of inner guilt. I don't create a church where you have to go to believe in something, or 'suggest' a tithe after emotionally bombarding people at the pulpit. You're right, boss, people should have the ability to believe in whatever they want. But religion should be left for polite conversation, not spouted to the masses who can't refute them for fear of being impolite or being chastised by their neighbors."

"I understand what you are getting at, Marty. It's just that people don't have to go to church. They don't have to believe in anything. People are the masters of their own destinies. They choose to do the things that they do. You just have to have faith that people will ultimately choose what is best for them."

"The thing is that people don't."

"Then they'll just have to live with the consequences of their mistakes. Just be happy with the select few who take the time to weight their decisions."

"I wish I could Sam." He shakes his head to clear the disappointment from his voice. "I really wish I could."

The two of us proceed back onto Rhine and slowly make our way towards our home on the corner of Gnosh. We really don't say much to one another. I sometimes catch a moment when he's looking off into the distance and watch his face as it churns over different thoughts and ideas. I can see frustration welling in his cheeks, but then smoothed over by a touch of guilt or sympathy. I cannot tell which, but whatever is gnawing at his insides, I know it's about me.

He thinks that I don't notice, but when he gets to thinking this hard about something he gets distant and fails to catch the occasional glance that I steal to better read him. It's an unfortunate side effect of my condition. I place people in an awkward situation where they are stuck between moments of silence in contemplation of whether or not they should say something. Most people fill in the gaps with: "How have you been?", "What have you been up to?", or "Any plans for tomorrow?", but with me everyone knows the answers to those. They know I haven't been doing well, that I haven't been doing much of anything save my job, and what plans I have usually hurt those that hear them. It's a human thing.

I keep my eyes affixed to the ground. I look for pebbles, bits of sand or paper that people have trudged up from the docks. In doing so, I remember a time when they were flawless, not even the gutters were touched by debris. But now there are pieces everywhere, the city obtaining its lived-in look. It all bothers me, but I keep it to myself.

In my search, I catch my image in a pool after accidentally stepping in it—too late on the warning. I watch as the ripples relax, and in it is an auburn tint over my left shoulder. I squint to perceive what's forming and as I start to see it, I notice her lips and eyes emerge from the waters. She smiles. Emily!

Quickly I turn, but there is naught—just an empty street filled with lost hopes. A cooing attracts my sinking attentions atop a lamp post and with my noticing the pigeon gives off one additional call before taking wing. I look back at the pool and see now the head of a lantern where the creature had been, cast in the reflective illusion of light and shadow. Marty calls for me and I desolate, follow.

When we reach the front doors of our apartment building Marty finally comes out with what he's been composing in his head the entire walk back.

"Listen, boss. I'm sorry for bringing up what ails you. I can't imagine how difficult things have been for you in the past three years. I know you don't really want to talk about it, and I respect that." His eyes are downcast, as if preferring to see me out of the reflection of the lobby windows than face to face. "I just see you hurtin' and it's difficult for me to just stand here and not be able to do anything about it. It's like those people up the street going for morning mass. I want to be able to help them live a stronger life and not have to be kicked down every day by people who say they're sinners. You know what I'm saying?"

He jerks away, retreats a few steps and puts his hand over his mouth. I can see that he's fighting against things he doesn't want to escape. I have to admire his courage, especially in front of me. I know how important it is to him on how I see him.

Marty drops his hand back to his waist and retraces a step forward against his own inner conflict. "That was the hardest thing in the world for me, to see my good friend locked away somewhere in his own head because something inside of him died. It's like you weren't there anymore. Don't hate me because of this boss, but when I learned this happened to you because some broad—you obviously had a thing for—threw herself out her apartment window. I was just infuriated! I wanted to take her body and just cast it out into the sea, I was so angry."

His fists are now clenched and his eyes are beginning to turn red from holding back his emotions. He forces his composure at the cost of red eyes and a paler complexion.

"But I respected your wishes, chief. I helped you entomb her and gave you your space. Now on the outside, you look like you've gotten better. But it's not that you've been able to put this behind you, but more that you've relearned how to walk and talk, to look normal in front of other people despite the pain that you carry inside you. You're almost like those mannequins—going night after night hoping that no one discovers exactly what's hidden behind the flesh." He points at me. "But I can see it, chief. Every time I look at you. I can see your pain as clearly as the clouds above me. I can see it eating away at you little by little, slowly devouring you from the inside out. And it makes me angry because there is nothing in this world I can do to help you stop from hurting."

His words touch me. They scar my insides as if scratched by the paw of some callous beast and I bleed for him. I try to speak beneath a clot of something in my throat and I have to struggle to force my voice around it.

"Marty I—"

He cuts me off with his hand. "I'm not trying to push the dagger in any further. And the last thing I want to do is add to your burden. I just wanted you to know that you're not alone in this…" he pauses and then signals to his chest. "Because these past three years… I've been hurtin' too."

"Oh, Marty. How the soul truly selects his own society. I've put you out all these years and yet you've been so vigilant at keeping my friendship. I thank you. I swear I'll make it all up to you."

"Then, how about tonight? There's this little place I've found that I just know you'll like. It'll be just the two of us and we can get a private booth. No worries about being accosted by street urchins wanting to know where they're at, or how long things have been. What do you say?"

My inner gut trembles with anxiety as I'd rather return to Nereid Street and listen to a few more rolls that I had picked out the night before. But I'm finally backed against the door, I cannot let this invite pass me by. For his devotion and friendship, he deserves my company. And so, I relent.

"Alright, Marty. I think its fair time I let you cash in one of those rain checks."

He puts his hands up in prayer against his nose to hide his smile. He sniffs and his eyes moisten. Marty starts in on a few steps backward and points at me while shaking his finger. "You sir, you're not going to regret this. I promise you. We'll get off early, call it in around 11:30 or so. It'll be great."

Marty backs up into a turn around before racing up Rhine Street. He runs as if he hopes to catch up to time itself.

He spins round to look back and calls, "You'll love it! Trust me! Don't worry about a thing!"

Before long he disappears down a side street and I am left with the horrid guilt of what I've put him through all these years, and the overwhelming sensation of breaking a promise of mourning.

The night is written with quiet solitude. Not even the most experienced officer can claim he's had such a lack of encounter. Usually something is churning in the CitySpire, the malevolent mists and abhorrent rains see to that. Foul weather always brings out the worst in people. So it is at exactly 11:30 p.m. that Marty and I decide to take off work and dress for a formal affair.

Marty meets me back at my apartment around midnight, dressed in a black and white tuxedo, fit with white gloves and shined shoes; whereas I, grudgingly pull out the old number that Emily and I had found together—a black tux fit with coat tails. After tying the white bow against my neck, I cannot repress a jet of pain in my lower breast when Marty reaches around my shoulders and jokingly says how becoming we look.

We hit the street. I find the air to be most pleasant as if a strong breeze had whisked away the scent of the Creep. Marty insists that we walk, claiming that its all part of the process—the processional—in order to see how many heads we turn on the way to our destination which, by the way, he has yet to disclose.

I keep an eye on the street names, remembering the buildings that we pass in order to catalogue our location. Our stroll takes us closer towards the wharfs, but then veers northward after passing Lexington, we then take Dollimere and Ashworth Lane. The longer we walk, the thinner the population becomes. We then cross over the invisible line that takes us beyond the patrols and into—what some may call—wild territory, marked by the disappearance of pavement and its antiquated replacement by cobblestone.

The streets are unfamiliar and the buildings take to a menacing quality. We are flanked by two to three story constructions built of a red brick that's barely noticeable beneath the black stain of the Creep. Jutting out from the higher levels are walled-in terraces and outstretched balconies that hang over alleyways and some over the sidewalks. The streets here are narrower as if only designed to allow for one way traffic.

Just as all this newness causes the hairs on my arms to raise in caution and as I'm about to part my lips to ask Marty if he remembers exactly where he's going, I hear the faint sound of music jiving between one of the neighboring alleys.

Marty hurries his step, all the while encouraging me to follow with that boyish grin of his. Together we pass between one of the many dark synapses between the moldy structures. He leads me underneath one of the overhangs that drench all beneath in an impenetrable darkness that I swear when Marty steps within, swallows him whole.

I stop at the edge of the veil, preferring to wait it out until my eyes are able to discern shapes in the ebb. Within, I hear the crinkling of paper and the slide of it through human hands. Marty speaks.

"Hiya, Job. We're here to see Ruby. She's on tonight, isn't she?"

I get the silence that muscles make, a fitting shrug, a nodding of the head; either way, I'm unable to know exactly what transpires between Marty and the night. But a thunderous rap on a metal door gives me the response that I've been yearning for. A bolt slides in its frame and a rectangular peephole opens, flooding the obscurity with a beam of music and light.

I'm able to see this Job fellow. He's a muscular man, large arms, hands and head, with half his face scarred from burn marks—a victim of the convenience store bombing, no doubt. I don't remember seeing him before, but it was a long time ago. He wears a thick black leather coat that keeps the bite of the late night chills at bay; white shirt and tie. A fedora rests on his head, positioned to keep the majority of his features blanketed from observers. Leaning up against the building next to the door, he gives me the once over. If he recognizes me, he certainly doesn't show it.

The face through the peephole gives Marty a glare before shutting the rectangular window, unlatching a series of locks and then opens the door.

The musical score of a big band latches onto me like a hook set on a line; it burrows deep in my flesh and draws me in with the wave of the doorman's hand. He wears a sleek tux, silvery cufflinks, and a red sash at his waist. He keeps his shoulders pressed down, giving him an elegant posture that I had thought long since unpracticed.

"This way, Mr. Kessler. Your table is waiting." He announces with a soft gentile voice that surprisingly is audible over the most stringent of conversations and melody.

Marty jets from the door and swoops in behind me. With a sharp intake of breath, I find myself pushed inside, into the bright shine of sparkling chandeliers, curtains of red velvet and bubbling champagne. I'm blindsided by gleams of silver: pitcher vases and fine cutlery. They rest on white tablecloths, strewn across circular tables that shrink the closer one gets to the forward dance floor and raised stage, just ankle height off the ground. The fan-shaped room is terraced, with an inclined ramp that runs down the center, connecting the multi-floors which are otherwise inaccessible due to waist high walls, forged steel and brass railings. The ten-foot ceiling rises as an upside down stairway, supported by marble ionic columns that increase an additional twenty feet the farther away from the door, giving room for both private and public balconies.

The people, all the people, well dressed gentry and their ladies-in-waiting, dazzle the already high-class establishment with the latest fabrics of silk, fur and satin. Fifty in total, maybe more, sit with their wine and champagne close at hand, while they wait eagerly for delightful dishes custom prepared just for them. I can smell a bountiful collection of spices, meats, and sauces, all flirting with the intoxicating aroma of expensive cigars.

A light breeze follows the powerful notes of a small orchestra. Gleaming trumpets, saxophones, trombones, guitars, bass, drums and a slew of varying strings are all at the beckon call of a black haired maestro whose directing baton is instead an ebony clarinet. They play various jazz tunes to inspire couples to the dance floor. A lone grand piano catches my eye, resting off to the side untouched and unsupervised, which glitters from the twinkling of light reflecting off crystal glasses.

Many couples dance, the ladies' gowns swish as they pivot to the sound of a cymbal brush. They display themselves like peacocks, yet their posture embodies them as swans. Their upper bodies are held upright and elegant and their lower limbs are kept in plié, ready for that next turn when the leg jets outward and the pairs sweep across the floor.

Marty breaks the epitome of what I once believed to be a lost society by capturing the back of my neck with the pit of his elbow. He hangs on like a drunkard or better still, a man who's doubled his fortune.

"What did I tell you, chief? The first time I laid eyes on it, I knew that this was the place for you. I've been trying to get you to come here for months, but it's like trying to get Briget to stay in one place with you."

My face droops a little and when I'm about to apologize again for my foul moods, he releases me and gives me a fair slap on the back.

"Don't worry about it, boss. What's important is that you're here now to enjoy it. Come on, we can't keep the doorman waiting." He issues me forward with an invitational wave of his hand and I nod in compliance.

We are taken to the second to last row of tables, the final terrace before a small line of table-for-twos and then the dance floor. We are seated at a table that is built to accommodate four. Apparently, Marty is expecting some company. As soon as we're settled in, the doorman snaps his fingers at a distant footman to take our drink orders. Marty asks for a martini extra dry and I decide to start the night with some gin.

Marty leans in. "Starting early on the hard stuff, huh?" He chuckles.

I shake my head. "Catching up, actually."

He cocks a crooked smile, one that if his face would allow, would reach his earlobes. He nods to the band.

"See that gent with the clarinet, that's Mr. Johnny Weber. He owns the joint. He's a nice enough guy, but I did some digging on him not long ago. Found out that he used to run with Genero's crew back when you and I were digging graves. They had some form of falling out, I'm not sure over what, and he seemingly disappeared for awhile."

"Where did he go?" I ask while straining my neck to see if I could get an estimate of how long the drinks would take. Secretly, my hands have been shaking due to a developing social anxiety. I need something to at least keep my calm.

"Occasionally, I see our old good pal coming in here to ask Mr. Weber for a favor or two. They're on speaking terms from what I gather, but I'm unsure of whether it's friendly or not." He points to the higher balconies. "They frequent up there, preferring not to mingle with us *common* folk."

I turn back around when my muscles start to pain me. "So, why are you so interested? Councilman Genero and his cronies have been clean for over a year now."

"You know as well as I do that you can't trust Genero. I don't understand why we ever agreed to let a snake like him into the city council in the first place. You bore witness to what he was responsible for."

I lean back in my chair, not wanting to embark on this same conversation again. "Politics isn't a game for ethical people, Marty. You know that. You can't corrupt the corrupt, but at least he's honorable. Besides, he was also elected because he represents a large demographic of people. Plus, it's easier to keep tabs on him now that he's in the limelight." My back arches as I spot the waiter with our order, and toss a finger up to signal him to our table as well as to dismiss the topic as I have done for years.

"Well, you can feign ignorance all you want." He falls back in his chair defeated. "I like to keep tabs on him, know who he deals with, his friends and allies. Call it a hobby of mine."

"Just be careful this hobby of yours doesn't get you into trouble." The drinks come and I thank our server before gulping down a third of the rock glass's nectar.

Amongst the plots and conspiracy theories he has churning inside his head, Marty manages to smile at the ironic. "You worried about me now? That's certainly different."

I raise my eyebrow to spur something witty that I could combat him with, but the band finishes their song, the dancers stop, and the club courteously applauds.

A couple stagehands pull out a stainless steel microphone, an antiquated piece that lends its retro style as a novelty, and deposit it center stage in front of the finely trimmed Mr. Weber. After a bow, he addresses his guests; his voice amplified over a set of hidden speakers.

"Thank you ladies and gentlemen and once again welcome to the Stardust. The orchestra is going to take a little break, but we'll be back up before you know it. These gents play so well that I constantly have to give them an eye exam to make sure they're human. Can't be too careful now a'days." A couple chuckles escape the crowd. "But seriously folks, you still have many wonderful treats awaiting you in the next few minutes. So stick around. You won't be disappointed."

The stage lights dim, showering the band members in a veil of invisibility as I watch their darkened silhouettes filter out of their high-rise seats. The loss of music is replaced by an ambiance of voices all wrapped amidst the words of their neighbors making it far too cryptic to discern what others are saying. I must confess that I miss the former and ingest another finger of my drink to compensate.

I close my eyes trying to keep the voices at bay. It's been too long since I've been around so many people at once. My stomach grows into a creeping vine and starts reaching outwards for other organs to perch atop. My heart is prevalent, beating its rhythm in my ears, whereas before I thought it was the drums. I can feel heat radiating from my face, sweat glands gasping for air. The noise all reminds me of past mobs. I finish the rest of my drink in a single backwards tilt of my head. The alcohol burns like fire.

I jolt in my seat when my eyes open again and there's Mr. Weber and a member of his waiting staff off my left shoulder.

"Mr. Kessler, how wonderful it is to see you again." He keeps his hands out where I can see them and limp at his sides. He wears a white tuxedo with a black bow-tie and a red handkerchief in his left breast pocket. He keeps a friendly demeanor in shoulders, stance and face, everything is relaxed and without an air of authority. How he came to be behind me, I haven't a clue. Perhaps he's a magician of sorts or someone with extremely soft soled shoes.

He angles his head and connects me in the eyes—hazel. They are such a startling color that I question whether they are aided by contacts or if they are natural.

"And you must be Samuel Bell." He floats to one knee and extends his hand out to me in handshake, all the while never severing his gaze. "At last I meet the legend in person. I'm absolutely delighted, I assure you. My pleasure."

I return his hospitality, not wanting to leave a poor impression on our host, despite the uncomfortable comment of being a "legend". The gesture seems to please him and he directs with his other hand towards the chair between Marty and I.

"Care if I join you?" His pencil thin eyebrows are sincere enough.

"I'm not opposed to it. You have a wonderful place here… Mr. Weber, is it?" I ask to be polite.

"My apologizes, Mr. Bell. I'm afraid I've become lazy by relying too much on reputation to take the place of introduction. Yes, I am John Weber, but most people call me Johnny. It depends on how formal you wish to be. I'm always eager to meet you either way." He eases himself in the chair and blows a breath of eased muscles. "Thank you for the seat. I believe the floor has it in for me."

"Not at all. This is your club."

"Be that as it may, Mr. Bell, there are still many places I dare not go without invitation." He looks down at my empty glass and I notice a slight twitch at the edge of his lips. He beckons to his standby attendee and points at the source of his disparity.

"Mathew, another round for these gentlemen." He returns in smile. "On the house, of course."

"Make mine a bourbon." I say before the young waiter disappears from us again.

Mr. Weber nods in acknowledgment. "A bourbon, then."

"Is this some sort of bribe?" Marty thumbs the olive into his mouth, having pillaged his martini.

"If a drink is all it takes to bribe you Mr. Kessler, then I weep for our safety. I assure you that my intentions are most sincere."

He chews slyly and narrows his eyes to see past Weber's charms. "I been here plenty of times before and this is the first time you've ever given my company a drink."

"Ah – but, Mr. Kessler, this is the first time you weren't escorting a lovely lady. I would have sent some over then, but police officers are always the suspicious sorts. And if you ask me, suspicion and women never mix. I didn't wish you to think me a cad."

Marty nods his head slowly. "Touché, Johnny boy. You're a gentleman, after all."

Our host parts his lips momentarily, but I cut him off for clarification.

"We're not police officers, Mr. Weber. We're Govennet officials. So unless you have a couple screw-jobs working for you, there isn't anything to fear from us."

"I do apologize if either of you took offense. I was merely pointing out your occupational talents and am afraid I made too broad of a generalization. Forgive me. I wasn't aware there was such a large distinction between the two."

"There's a huge difference." Marty announces as his pointer finger presses against the tabletop and he taps it to emphasize each point. "You don't see police officers chasing reds across the rooftops at four in the morning. Billies have it easy: theft, assault, domestic squabbles, or maybe even the occasional suicide to keep them occupied. Someone breaks into your place, you call the police. Think your girlfriend is a psychopathic-killer with internal wiring, then that's our jurisdiction. Then there's the occasional corruption with government officials, but that's another story."

Johnny's warmth never wanes. "Thank you for educating me, sir. I'd hate to be caught in the same conversation with less understanding individuals."

"Think nothing of it." I tilt my head in hopes of silencing Marty from any further embarrassments for our host. I can tell that he's enjoying himself way too much.

"Well, gentlemen." He gracefully draws himself out of his chair. "I need to rally backstage into their next number."

I stand with him, ready for that departing handshake that comes from polite society and when our hands grip, he pats the top of our hands with his free one. He keeps in eye contact.

"Thank you, Mr. Bell. I do apologize to cut and run, but that's show business. I do confess that I am a great admirer of yours and do hope that your visits here will be frequent." He shakes Marty's as well, with a comforting nod. "Mr. Kessler, until next time?"

"You can count on it, Johnny." Says the smug, still-seated, friend of mine.

His upper body bows slightly in reverence to our meeting and rushes off toward the darkened stage. A pity, it seems. Marty may make this gentleman a hobby of his. Sure he may have had ties to Genero at one point in his life, but Mr. Weber appeared as nothing more than a fine gentleman and gracious host. What is unfortunate is that I didn't get more time to chat with him about his club. An admirer of mine? I wonder what he meant by that.

"Seems someone holds you in high regard, Mr. Bell." Marty jokes with his usual sarcasm. His finger circles the lip of his glass.

I return to seating before honoring him with a response. A gasp of air escapes my lips in a sigh, as my muscles relax. "I think standing has it in for me."

He laughs long and deep, slapping his hand against the table to better steady himself. The sound reminds me of something years ago.

"That's the funniest thing I heard coming out of you yet. And here I thought you'd be irritated with me."

"You can't change the direction of a wave, Marty. It goes where it goes."

A hush soothes the club as if every individual's voice is stolen for a moment of silence. The lights slowly dim. I can hear the sound of violins, joined by soft drums, guitar, upright bass, and then the piano opening with a marvelous blend of jazz. A spotlight descends on the microphone, the same one previously used by Mr. Weber, and my eyes are stunned by glittering red sequins. She wears a mermaid dress, no sleeves, and long black gloves that she uses to caress the steel mic in front of her. Her hair is done in finger waves, shoulder length and dark as the shadowy band behind her. The dame's skin is flawless, pale and absorbing the light like a diamond.

PART III - THE SORCERER

As her lips kiss into the opening of a song, my mouth drops as I recognize her. The hairs on my arms extend, my heart skips and quivers, for as I live and breathe—it's *Natalie.*

23

Her voice ripples over me like a breeze of sea air, both refreshing and titillating to the senses. Natalie's alto resonates through the club, a voice that whispers into the retro-grade microphone as she begins her first number.

"Gentlemen callers and lady lovers, kiss the thought of me. Live in my fantasy as we dine on stardust and rubies."

There is an explosion of instrumentals, a sway of strings and a flirtation of brass. The drums continue their rhythm in partnership with the strum of the upright bass. Her voice swoons through the speakers like a dramatic serenade.

"Here we are dear sweethearts,

Beneath the parasol of Nyx.

Where are the stars? — come close.

Lend me the light of your eyes.

Her body bends to the music behind her. Each movement is a slow yet tantalizing motion which captures the fixed gazes of her audience. Her fingers run up the length of the stand and then cup the base of the capsule.

"We shall do as poets do

And make love to Selene.

Together we'll massage the muse,

A seduction to stay her wane.

Sweet darlings,

Embrace this reverie.

Sway to my ecstasy,

PART III - THE SORCERER

As we dance on stardust and rubies.

Natalie's hands stretch outwards to cradle the patrons in her arms. She pauses and brings them inward, and finally rests her satin gloves on her heart.

To you my sweethearts — hold me close.

A thousand breaths it seems.

Hand to cheek, lips to ear,

Whisper me your melody.

Her eyes drop and then close as her neck leans back, drawing a glove down her cheek. She gasps and then returns her eyes to the world to take in their intoxication.

And we shall lie here,

Our legs between the sheets.

Struggling beneath a swoon

For that last break of twilight.

The band repeats an earlier verse signaling the near end. Natalie holds onto the pole without shake or quiver. Her alto voice grows quiet with the lullaby-like chorus.

Sacred lovers,

Snuggle up close to me.

Breathe in my slumbering

As we dream on stardust and rubies."

As the song slowly melts away into silence, the sequined singer falls back into her whisper as if putting the crowd to bed.

363

Her finger rises to her lips and she shushes the world. *"Make love, on stardust and rubies."*

There is a pause, a moment of contemplation by the group's consciousness. I take their inaction as the chance—the first—to applaud her and by that second clap, I am followed by the thundering of palms.

After Natalie's set and in brief passing, we are able to acquire Mr. Weber's permission to go backstage. Despite the finery of the club, the hidden portions remain so for a reason. The walls are tarnished with a few open holes exposing the wooden frames and drywall. There are wires hanging too low, a few frayed at certain points, that descend into the tiny hallway behind the stage and deeper into the club. Had I not seen the face of it all, I would have rendered an unfair verdict of condemnation. Oddly, Mr. Weber didn't even mention the unfortunate disarray of things which makes me wonder whether he is even bothered by it.

Marty and I dodge a pair of trumpet players rushing out of, what appears to be, an employee's lounge, emptying their spit valves on the floor as they make their way towards the stage. They pay us no mind and go so far as to not even acknowledge our presence. Perhaps, due to how hastened everyone is, they too don't pay it any mind.

We find what Mr. Weber had described with great detail, a wooden door with a yellow star painted on the top. It has a wooden plaque fixed to it, set in a metal glide, showing that perhaps this won't always belong to their greatest star. The name reads, "Ruby Silver". Much like everything else, the star is missing some of its paint.

I take a deep breath in, a tad nervous from not having seen her in years. I remember back when I first met her and Michael. I'm hoping that it is still as fresh in her mind as it is in mine and with that, a sliver of hope that she hasn't changed her opinion of me due to my breakdown. All I can think about is how she left once I was on my feet again, didn't even say a word. I don't know why she left and thinking about it churns the hard liquor I had earlier into an unforgiving place. I knock on the door.

"It's open." Comes the muffled singer's voice from within.

I release the air that's been pent up inside and I turn the handle and push inward.

The room is as decrepit and narrow as the rest. Drywall has crumbled in some places, the ceiling is cracked, and the hardwood floors are a dull marred grey. There are changing screens, three by my count, scattered half-hazardly about the room, with varying garments, fops, boas, and the like hanging from the tops. Racks of costumes and dresses align themselves on metal roll-away carts, and off to one side is a toilet and sink left exposed and without enclosure.

At the far end is a white vanity with a mirror outlined in round florescent bulbs. Natalie herself sits on a small back bench. She delicately rolls a line of hose down her leg. No longer does she wear the red sequin dress, but is stripped down to her undergarments comprised of a black lace bra, panties and garter belt. Still concentrating on her legs, she has yet to look up at her company.

"We're going to have to get the dress loosened a little, or you're inevitably going to pick me off the floor from faint." She says to her hosiery.

"Excuse me?" I ask as Marty and I step into the room.

She looks up, startled by a familiar voice. White teeth and powdered cheeks, her excitement lifts her off her bench, giving Marty and I a full view. I can see a change in her eyes as she realizes her predicament, and joy washes away to mixture of things—one of which being embarrassment. Her hand snatches an article off a set of boxes, turns, then covers herself in a black robe of silk.

Tying at the waist, Natalie glances over her shoulder. "I'm sorry, I thought you were Johnny." Her voice is filled with a touch of awkwardness and smiles.

I want to ask if parading around in her underwear was a usual thing with Johnny, but that's none of my business. I stay silent, not knowing quite what to say.

"Hello, Marty." She tosses to the end of the room with friendly acknowledgment.

"Natalie." He blinks his eyes rapidly as if trying to capture a previous picture. He thumbs to the hallway. "I'm going to wait out here where there is a little more air, alright?—Alright." He leaves without waiting for a response and shuts the door behind him.

She turns back around. Her arms are crossed at her chest more to secure the robe, than anything else. "Well, he's off fairly quick" Natalie mentions while nodding to the door.

"Oh, him? He just figured the show was over." I sneak a grin.

"He smiles now, that's certainly a change." She flirts with her eyes; lashes much longer than those nightly affairs of piano play and ghost stories. "Are you going to keep me blushing or are you going to give me a hug?"

Thankful that there aren't spoiled feelings, I close the gap and bring her close to me, my hands rounding her back and waist.

"You were magnificent." I manage beneath a squeeze.

She cranes her neck back, staring me down like a lioness. "Do you really think so?" Her mood is poised to root out lies.

"Absolutely - one of the best performances I've ever seen."

I'm unsure of whether I pass her test as she frees herself from me and strides back to her vanity. She sits, preferring to talk to the Samuel Bell residing in her mirror than the real thing and applies a cloth to remove her lipstick.

"It's been a long time, Sam." I may have missed something, as her mood seems less cheerful.

"Yes, it has been a long time."

"How have you been holding up?" She purses her lips and then applies a shade of brown lipstick she snatched from one of the tiny shelves.

Knowing Natalie, she's trying to distract herself, but from what?

"As well as can be expected, thanks to you. Although, I must confess I never had the chance to properly thank you."

The lipstick closes slowly and then replaced on its shelf. Her hands now fidget, wringing themselves in her lap. She tries to hide it, but the mirror is positioned for my advantage.

"I'm sorry, I had to leave. I…" there's a pause. "—needed to find out what happened to Michael. After that night, I lost track of him. Something inside me said I needed to try. Though, I knew I wouldn't find him."

It seems like an empty reason, as if I just tasted the rim of the bottle. "What exactly happened between you and Michael? It wasn't because…" I trail my sentence to allow her to fill in the blank.

An ironic smirk tiptoes up her cheek. "Nothing happened. Nothing to do with you, anyways. It's what *didn't* happen with Michael."

I continue standing there, looking at her expressions through a mirror, wishing she'd turn around so I could speak with her directly.

"I'm sorry, Natalie." Adding, "For what it is worth."

She shakes her head. "Don't be." She takes a few pins out of her hair, letting the curls fall where they may. "I questioned the legitimacy of our relationship many times. It's reasonable to say that so did he. I'm led to believe that he only played his part to keep face with you and Emily. After she left he…" Her cheeks slightly swell, her eyes dart, and she bites her lip. She turns around to look at me in the eyes. "Oh, Samuel – I should have told you when Emily left, but she made me promise."

I shake my head, eyes downcast in fear she'd been carrying this for some time. I breathe in and brush my attention back into those brown eyes of hers. "I don't blame you, Natalie. I never have." I concentrate not to chip my teeth. "I blame Boenger." Such ire for that man. I try to relax. "I still retain my share."

Soft hands clasp the top of her seat's backing. "Sam." She stutters to get the next sentence out. "There's something you need to know about, Henry Boenger."

I raise my eyebrow before I'm able to ask the question. Once the words form on my tongue they are quickly kicked back in my throat by a knock and an opening of the door behind me. It's Marty.

"Ah – chief? We got to go."

Standing beside him is the rapscallion Sergeant Blake wearing his double-breasted uniform and badge.

"Llacs tudy." Mr. Blake spits out, before pivoting in the hallway and returning towards the front of the club.

Marty shrugs and says, "I guess this'll be a rain check after all." before he follows after.

I readdress her apologetically. "I'm sorry, Natalie but I have to go. Are you always here?"

She nods solemnly. "Every night."

"I'll see you tomorrow, then."

Her face brightens as if the bulbs surrounding the mirror just obtained a new level of luminescence.

Without smile she echoes, "Tomorrow then."

The aerodynes hum above the cityscape, tailing a gig registered to a Ms. Claudine Valentine. For someone with a last name associated with love, she certainly has a tough time showing it. Reportedly, she's murdered one Govennet officer and wounded another. The sergeant planned on enlisting us for a ground search, but then she took to the sky.

We've been following her for ten blocks now. She doesn't have a destination, just randomly selecting different avenues and boulevards to turn onto. She's made three left turns already at a constant speed of forty-three miles per hour. Her driving is calm and precise. That bothers me. Blue and red lights streak the exterior of buildings off our lamps, warning all of the danger.

Sergeant Blake is driving, Marty is in the back and I'm in the passenger front. I read the continual flow of police reports, Govennet profiles, and the current chatter between other department-owned gigs which display in green glowing text on the windshield. Raindrops briefly create an illusion of smeared text, and despite the situation, I find it entertaining when the wiper blades whisk off the water, failing to erase the characters. I'm sure the weather doesn't help the sergeant's driving.

We're tuned into unit six, a pair of recent officers by the name of Roy Bettle and Jack Murphy. I haven't met them yet, just a couple of boys who trained under the Sergeant. Then there is unit two containing Brigit Box and Harvey Parson.

Brigit's voice crackles over the radio. "Just —ay the word, -ammy-boy, and I'll gut th— gig with a load of electrified steel." The CitySpire is filled with interference, can't say from where, but I'm told it has something to do with the buildings. The onboard computer helps with filling in the holes.

"That's a negative. You open fire and you lose your badge. Got it?" I respond wearily. "Can't risk harming civilians." She knows this better than I do, but it doesn't stop her from trying to get a rise out of me.

"Roger —at, that's an open —ire and harm civil-ns."

I scream into my headset, "No – that's a negative! Read you're text, damn you."

Laughter blips in and out of the speakers. "Sam, you're —ays good for a – la—."

Marty leans in from the back. "What did she say?"

"That I'm always good for a laugh." I reply.

"Oh, just checking on that." He leans back with his arms behind his head smiling to himself. "So how do you plan to do this?"

I shake my head. "I don't know. All gigs are equipped with a personalized retinal scan, yet somehow she got this one going."

"You could always wait until it runs outta juice then nab her as she falls from the sky."

"Marty, I don't know if you've noticed, but its one of the newer models and it runs off electricity, the very same electricity that powers our guns. She's tapped into the city grid and won't be coming down until the ships arrive—you can thank Boenger for that. Last I checked, there's an unlimited supply and to further rub salt in the wound, I don't think mannequins need to sleep."

"—ems, like we're go—a have to force it –wn. Give her a good sq—ze and pop, sh— out –or the count." Interjects Brigit with her two credits worth.

I read off her meaning on the screen, a bit hazy on the in-and-out translation. Force her down or at least get her out far enough from the center of the city so as to reduce the possibility of casualties. Yes, it seems like a plan.

"All right folks, listen up. I know there isn't much in the Govennet training manual on this, so we're going to have to improvise. Unit six, you'll take up its passenger side flank; Brigit, take the driver's. We'll take topside and try to force the screw-job towards the street. Once it reaches a manageable altitude and there's little population, we'll open up on it. But keep close, don't allow Ms. Valentine any space for maneuvering and, above all else, watch our descent and speed. If we keep on her, she won't be able to outrun us."

"Roger --at." Replies the baritone of unit six.

I check our altitude: eighty-three feet. Mostly only apartments rise this high. We would need to get her down to at least thirty, twenty ideally. Businesses and front lobbies are tonight's safety nets. I can imagine the front page in the CitySpire Gazette already.

"So your plan's to make our friend claustrophobic and then ease her down for some soft petting?" Marty muses from the backseat. He laughs. "I can see this going swimmingly."

I reintroduce him to the prospect of danger. "You might want to put a parachute on just in case, Marty."

"Oh, yes — a parachute." He says with a hint of sarcasm as he starts to fumble with the buckles beneath the seat. "Who knows, maybe I'll be sprung into an adjacent window and into the arms of a beautiful dame. Talk about your legs between the sheets, if you catch my drift."

If it were a laughing matter, I may have chuckled out loud. On the other hand, it seems that Sergeant Blake is soaking up all the hilarity in the compartment with his straight face and unflinching responses. His stare is what bothers me the most, a vacant non-blinking stare that hasn't moved since we got in the car. The man needs to learn how to blink once and awhile.

"Units six and two are coming up on the rendezvous point. Moving into position." The Sergeant mentions as if he's narrated one-too-many of his actions tonight.

He presses down on the accelerator, boosting the aerodynes into a high-pitched whirl. Drawing back on a lever nearest the steering wheel, he leaps us up and over Ms. Valentine's gig just as Brigit and Unit-6 swing in from adjacent streets alongside the renegade gig to pin her in.

Brigit's voice crackles above the interference. "Hello, little lamb."

Reactively, Ms. Valentine veers her car to the right. Her passenger side lifts, sending her front aerodyne and left wing to skitter across the bottom of our cruiser. The feeling is utterly dreadful as the impact is mixed with the clash of metal, tearing of wires, and shattering of circuits. I can see sparks from beneath us in the reflection of Brigit's side windows—all followed by the grinding of my teeth as we're pushed upwards by the force of the impact.

"Oh, Shi—" is the last I hear as Ms. Valentine's gig thrusts into Brigit's as she accelerates.

The two collide, a shattering of the windshield, followed by a moan of steel and a screech of fan blades exploding outwards and sawing into whatever it's thrown into. Brigit's gig lurches to one side and then into a neighboring building where chunks of rock, glass and confetti-like bits of steel explode in sparks and fire.

Brigit's gig ricochets off the building like a skipping stone and spirals uncontrollably in a ball of flame towards the street below.

Valentine's gig, minus the front passenger aerodyne and a dented driver's side, wavers back towards the center; spinning like a bowl after it's been dropped on the floor. Blake drops us back, still above her whirling gig.

Unit-6—now a good car's distance ahead—cuts across Ms. Valentine's trajectory and shaves off the top compartment like a butter knife. It all comes off like a screeching and unwanted wood chip, tumbling behind it like a leaf. Remnant pieces of metal and glass are belched against our windshield in a barrage of shrapnel. Then the inconceivable.

A shadowed orb of a head pokes out of the ruined craft. The dark form slithers from its driver seat and into the back passenger before speedily pulling itself onto the trunk. It takes a running start, only a few steps, as the human-like entity rushes to the back end of the aircar and leaps towards us. Its feet push off the gig, sending it plummeting to the ground below.

A jostle and quick bang shakes our hood, as Ms. Valentine's gig strikes our front bumper. And instead of watching her vehicle hit the pavement while folding in on itself, my attention is stolen beyond our windshield and its green lettering. It is there! from the grill, drawing itself up like a deranged spider, is the battered silhouette of a woman. Her flesh is marred, revealing hard plastic, metallic inner structure and wiring. A mangled mop of black hair flaps behind her violently like a set of tentacles from an angry squid. One eye has popped and reveals a glowing red pinpoint of light that burns with the fervor of madness.

Marty throws himself between the synapse of the two front seats, grabbing onto the headrests and demands with utter disbelief, "What in the crazy bats—" his voice cuts out like a poor radio transmission.

The creature smiles wickedly from a featureless exterior, a paradox that corrects itself in pattern of thought that etches itself deeply into our souls. One of its hands punches into the hood and then its shoulder leers forward. I fumble with the pistol in my coat pocket while frantically attempting to bypass the seatbelt.

A second, a third, the automaton slams it's hand through the one inch steel hood, dragging itself closer. It's fast, despite its injuries. I can see the blood oozing off its synthetic gum and metal jaw line.

I can only scream two words as the horror reaches the border of the windshield. "Shake it!"

Blake sharply turns down an adjacent street, the aerodynes roars as he pushes harder on the accelerator. The dastardly Ms. Valentine slips, and her shoulders beat into her head, slamming it into the hood with a loud crack. I continue struggling against the confines of my tux, undoing buttons and reaching the holster which has slipped and now hides at my waist.

She grabs hold of hood's lip and then rears back with her fist and slams it into the windshield. It cracks, a wide fan of devil's fingers jets across the glass and a small hole breaches, shredding fragments into the compartment. The last thing I'm able to read on the screen before the lettering shorts out is, "*gone haywire!*"

She rears back again, even while Blake swishes the car back and forth. I finally break my gun loose and throw it into the open. My finger reflexively unlocks the safety and my ears are assailed by the high-pitched surge of electricity building in the coils and then releasing in a belch of ozone. The hit enters her torso, the back of her mouth flashes with the expulsion of a light, and then exits behind her. Fake blood, bits of melted plastic and oils expel onto the car right before I empty another shot into her shoulder.

Another shot impales directly into her head, sending her body flying off the car and into the void of the cityscape like a piece of unwanted trash.

The flames have long since burnt themselves out by the time we're able to touch down; the wreckage is unsalvageable. I sent Unit-6 to pick up Ms. Valentine's body off the street so as not to disturb some pedestrian out for a morning jog. There is always somebody who feels sympathy for a mannequin with one-inch holes burnt into it.

It's easy to feel sorry for something when you're not the one who its trying to kill. Yes, there are individuals—radicals—that believe these creatures are human, at least, human-like. But just because it thinks and breathes, doesn't make it have a soul. Once you look them in the eye and see the emptiness, the quiet mechanizations of their mind, coupled with the knowledge that they'll kill you without reason or remorse, it makes it pretty hard to feel sorry for them. At least, that's what I keep telling myself. The truth of the matter is, that once you stop caring, once you disassociate the emotions from the deed, you lose a part of yourself and become more like them. There's nothing feel-good about it, save that you may have just saved someone's life. Marty explained it once as killing nothing and getting nothing. At least it keeps me sober.

Brigit speed walks up to us underneath a light sprinkle of rain. The streetlamps reveal her face smudged with soot; beneath that, scrapes and bruises. Somehow, she survived the crash. A pity for Brigit's uniform, there's a tear in her right sleeve. Despite how much I loath him, Boenger spared no expense on safety features. A shame for Ms. Valentine, hers was a softer alloy.

"Fucking bitch!" She throws her right fist into the air taking her feet slightly off the ground in protest. "You get her? Tell me you fucking got her! I didn't get smashed into a damn building and get smeared all over Trunket Boulevard for nothing."

"Yea…" I look over her shoulder towards the flickering. They hit a lamp post. "…we got her."

Hopeless. Pieces of paneling are strewn about the street like a lover having shed her clothes. I see the leftover remains of an aerodyne laid out like the evolution of its construction. Amidst the smoldering chassis and teardrop compartment is Harvey Parson, now scavenging through the remains for anything we wouldn't want the locals to get their hands on. I'm sure the black box is worth its weight in credits. I can only imagine a very long and shocking string of profanities.

Marty wraps his arm around my shoulder. "Good ol' Sammy-boy plugged her three times right off the hood." His fingers form a gun into my kidneys. "Pow-pow-pow!"

Brigit raises both eyebrow and hip. "You're shitting me?" She looks at me. "What the hell where you doing on the hood?"

I shake my head and put out my hand as if to stop her line of thinking. "No – it wasn't—"

It seems I only spurred another as Marty cuts me off, freeing himself from his own grip in the process. "The screw-job was the one on the hood. Leapt from her vehicle when Unit-6 sliced off the upper cabbie. She punched three holes in the hood and then one in the windshield." He laughs excitedly. "You should have seen the look on Blake's face. A few more milliseconds and she would have forced him into early retirement."

Blake stands there simply, back straight, shoulders pressed. He eases his eyes towards the higher floors of the surrounding apartments and says, "Cneiduaei an uohtiwt ont."

Above the lowly street-side apartments, three maybe four windows are lit with a pallid glow. Standing in them are the tiny forms of people, pressed against the panes, looking down at us from their heights. All awakened due to the clamor, no doubt.

"So what does that bring you up to for the month?" Brigit asks while recovering from the neck strain above. "Ten?"

"Nine. The one at the Samson building was Marty's kill." I reply, while still watching the figures above. It's disturbing. They're all so still, like display models out of a fashion boutique window. That familiar shudder breathes against my neck.

"I'd be willing to share that glory, chief. I feel like being generous for you setting me up so nicely." He tosses me a wink like an unwanted coin.

"I appreciate it, Marty." I return my eyes to Brigit to ensure her of my commitment. "But this isn't a competition."

"Easy for you to say, mister chief inspector. I still have three more to catch up to Blake over there, and then three more on top of that. I only got a week left to meet the quota or I'm going to lose my streak."

"There's a quota now?" I ask with grim expectations.

"You better believe it." Marty breathes as he holds out his hands along with seven fingers. "Seven mannequins." He drops four. "Three months. That'll get you into Ace status. Once you're in, we all take bets on how long you can hold it." He points at me and cocks a sly grin. "I've got 150 credits running on you up through February. So no slacking until then, alright?"

I'm sure it was only a matter of time before something like this started. Let it inspire them to do a better job. "Just be sure that you don't get itching to meet your *quotas* and fry a human." It hasn't happened yet, but one day it might.

A whooping sound, then a short burst of a siren blares overhead, as a white and black painted gig hums in descent. Their lights flash a combination of red and blues that add strength to ours. The combination makes me queasy. A spotlight drops from higher still as another gig floats down from beneath the shadow of the high rise complexes.

Brigit's mouth drops, then she rolls her eyes as she draws out her next word in disgust. "Shit."

"Looks like the billies finally found us." Marty jests. "Probably got a call from a noise complaint. Now we get to spend the rest of the night being harassed by these assholes."

"The police are public servants too, Marty. We got to keep them in the loop or we'll start having disputes. Ignore them too much and they'll lobby the council for gun permits."

Blake speaks for the first time outside his usual gutter-talk. "They're already lobbying for them, Mr. Bell. Just not openly."

"So let's not give them any strength in their arguments." I counter.

As much as I would like to believe that the majority of the CitySpire's problems stem from or at least can be blamed on mannequins, the police are necessary to keep the peace amidst our local population. I fear that if they are able to gain weapon permits, then they may start to assert a higher form of authority over those they swore to protect. My arguments then were that there was no need to arm the police to protect an unarmed population. I still stand by it to this day. The majority of the council agreed with me. Though I will have to admit, every time their gigs drop in, they make it seem like we're encroaching on *their* territory. It's the police who answer to us, not the other way around.

One such vehicle touches down and a man dressed in a long brown coat, black tie, shinned shoes, and a collapsible baton strapped to his belt exits the passenger cab. He holds up a black wallet with his silver credentials showing in front of his angular face and hooked nose.

"Inspector Gits, CitySpire Police Department. I hope you gentlemen are willing to answer some questions."

PART III - THE SORCERER

Marty is right about one thing though, we're definitely going to be here awhile.

24

Nearly dawn and already the sun is on approach as it slowly dissipates the miasma of night off the eastern horizon. I was off hours ago, and yet here I am standing in a tuxedo in the old five-story limestone building just nine blocks northwest of Hermes Square. I was surprised that something like this existed, and swear that it hadn't until two years prior. It is an interesting find, tucked delicately amongst a nest of high-rise buildings and tiny streets.

Some call it the copper-dome for obvious reasons—resting on the corner of Govenor and Net Street—one can easily note it from the oxidized green color of its dome sticking out above the creep stained exterior. Oddly enough, copper happens to be one of the few materials that the creep keeps its tendrils out of, including glass, steels, plastics and most synthetic materials. When asked, I inform folks that I selected this building due to its rooftop observation decks which easily converted into ample gig parking, but the true reason is for the Edwardian-Baroque style of architecture. It is one of few buildings that I knew I wouldn't mind going to everyday.

Though smaller than most of its neighbors, the copper-dome now has more room than officers. The central floor is an unusual mix of desks, file cabinets, and bookshelves that once belonged to distant basements. From here, you can look all the way to the fifth-floor ceiling, which is vaulted and garners support for the massive dome. Inside its frame are detailed oil frescos depicting scenes of Greek myths and gods. Everything is lit, sporadic—if not few—florescent bulbs and shades hang from wooden beams that were erected upon our move into the building. Then there are the twin staircases towards the northern section of the lobby, just opposite the front doors, that extend to the higher levels and balconies.

Occasionally, and always between the shifts, I've seen seventeen men and women proudly bearing their uniforms and catching up with the latest reports. Last census was that we were getting close to having forty members, with the police department already doubling us in number. But then again, with a population of 18,000 and growing, it still isn't enough to cater to the nightly threats of screw-jobs, acts of terrorism enacted by sympathizers, or government corruption. All this empty space just reaffirms how short-staffed we are. Besides ourselves and a couple clerical employees, I count only three other officers reviewing reports and one working on dispatch.

Marty falls into one of the office chairs, squeaking the rusty springs, as he leans back and drops his feet on the desk like a set of unwanted luggage. The dim lighting births shadows across his features, making him appear sinister.

"If Gits was going to ask us any more questions about that damn plastic-tart Valentine, I would have snapped." He grabs a pencil off the tabletop and points the eraser at me. "Just who does he think he is, keeping us so late? Isn't he aware that we all have more important things to do than to indulge his curiosity?"

As much as I want to agree with him, someone needs to take the higher road. "He's just doing his job, Marty. All he wanted was the details."

"He can read, can't he? We send those son-of-a-bitches reports, don't we? Instead of wasting our time in field, we could have had all the paperwork finished and sent over to them in time for morning coffee. If you ask me, this Billie is just being a prick."

"It is a little strange of him keeping us so long, but perhaps he had reason to. Maybe he's stumped on how a mannequin managed to get her hands on a gig."

Brigit jumps in, her arms crossed over her chest as she rolls a cigarette in her mouth in anticipation of lighting it. "I can tell ya how – someone at Boenger Motors needed some quick cash so they took a shortcut. That's how."

"For once, I'm in agreement with you Brigit." I say while massaging my chin. "This isn't like a fake registration card, the city requires Mr. Boenger to perform an extensive background check: two years of residency, proper ID, references. You don't just walk into his store and pick up a gig. Somebody had to have screwed up." And since good old Henry insists on handling all the books, I'm positive on who it had to have been.

She thumbs to her silent partner. "You want me and Harvey to pay this Boenger guy a visit? I bet ya I'll get his confession in less than an hour." She palms a punch just to clarify her meaning.

Marty laughs and throws his arms behind his head. "Are you kiddin' me? The chief has been waiting for Mr. Boenger to mess up for years. You'd take up all his fun."

A subconscious smile works its way across my face well before I realize. "I was thinking about handling this personally, for old time's sake. But if I want to get ahead of our good pal Inspector Gits, I'll need to leave here immediately." I look down at my clothes. "Right after I change, that is."

"Chief Inspector Bell?" Shouts and echoes the voice of Sergeant Blake, coming down the stairs from the high offices. A white suited figure in a wide brimmed gambler hat descends slowly behind him with cane in hand.

It's not until he clears the flight of stairs and maneuvers through the hedge maze of desks that I'm able to identify him. His cheeks are sunken, whereas his eyes are plagued by dark circles and marred by crow's feet. His hair is long, grey and wispy, kept mostly in a comb over hidden beneath his hat. He has no eyebrows, nor does he even bother penciling them in. Despite his withered appearance, the man is renowned for his intellect – Doctor Victor Cornelius Dreval.

His voice has a touch of the nasal passages when he speaks and it's always slow. I believe he enjoys pronouncing every syllable as if he was a licking a piece of candy.

"Chief Inspector Bell, Inspector Kessler, Inspector Box," he nods his head to each of us respectively before continuing on. "It's a pleasure to see you all again. I do hope that our hard-wired friends aren't causing you too much discourtesy."

"I don't believe courtesy is in their vocabulary." Marty jests. "Or if it is, they may have redefined it with another definition, murder perhaps?"

"Yes," the good doctor breathes. "They do have quite the temperament. The ones we had subdued in the lab weren't very cooperative, to say the least."

"Cooperative?" Brigit's voice bounces out of her throat. "Everyone I've met has been extremely cooperative." She reaches into her pocket and pulls out Dreval's Optical Red-Eye and dangles it in front of him. "It's either this, or this." She opens her coat to reveal her pistol. "Lucky for me, they pick the latter."

"Speaking of such, how is the DOR-52 working for you? Having any problems? Any questions?"

"Naw – it's pretty much aim and shoot, doc." Marty exclaims, after falling forward in his chair. "But I do have one question, why do you call it the DOR-52? People round her just call it the red-eye."

"The eyes are the windows to the soul, Mr. Kessler. I simply made a door. And fifty-two, because it took me fifty-two tries to get it right."

"Ah – I see." Marty digests, while trying to feign some scientific contemplation, thumbing his chin and looking rather serious.

I shake my head to erase the scene. "Dr. Deval, just what do we owe your visit?"

"Haven't you heard?" His face sinks and his hand stretches over the head of his cane – a brass winged serpent. His fingers crack. "The city council, in acceptance of my plea for increased city-wide health, has requested that I personally see that each official and civil servant receives a thorough physical, including members of the Govennet. I believe you're all due for your quarterly exam."

"Quarterly exam!" Brigit scoffs. "Are you insane? Don't you have better things to do than telling people to turn their heads and cough, and sticking your fingers in places they don't belong?"

The respectable Dr. Dreval's brow wrinkles as his eyes narrow in agitation. "Sergeant Box, I assure you that these physicals serve your own, and the rest of the city's, best interests as far as public health is concerned. If you are uncomfortable with my fingers, as you stated, I have female nurses on my staff that would more than happily give you a physical in my stead."

"It's nothin' personal, doc. I haven't gotten sick since waking on this dismal island and I'm not about to be fondled by you or anyone else for that matter. If the sink ain't clogged, don't be dumpin' chemicals down the drain."

"I don't think you understand, Miss Box, this is a mandatory examination instructed to me by the city council."

The room just increased in temperature as Brigit thrusts her shoulders forward and jets a finger at his chest. "No, I don't think *you* understand. I don't work for the city council, I work for Samuel Bell! And if you ask me, I swear the council were oversteppin' its boundaries by mandating shit down to us. So let me mandate something to you, if you or any of your bloodthirsty bitches get near me, I'll plug em right in the fucking head."

She kicks the base of the desk next to her, sending chills to reverberate between the disks of our spine. In a hasty about face, Brigit growls. "Com'on, Harvey – we've got shit to do." And she simmers off into another shadowy portion of the building. Both clerk and officer alike are aghast in wide eyes and gaping mouth.

Dr. Victor Dreval clears his throat. "I didn't realize my services would incite such an uproar." He blinks more than his usual count, possibly attempting to clear away the incident.

I sigh. "I'll see about speaking with her, sir. We here at Govennet highly respect you for all your efforts."

"Do I then take it that you're first, Mr. Bell?" He asks with a slight tilt to his head.

I allow a frown to slip, revealing the whites of my teeth. "As much as I would love to set a good example, there is a pressing matter with a case that's extremely time sensitive."

"If not you then who, Mr. Bell?" He asks as he snails his left eye shut while enlarging the other.

I look over to Marty who immediately leans back in his chair to avoid any finger pointing. I take the hint and redirect my attention to Sergeant Blake.

"Mr. Blake, would you be willing—" I'm interrupted before I have a chance to finish.

"The Sergeant has already had his. If I may be so bold, I request that I start with the senior members of your department so as to encourage those beneath you. I assure you, it won't take but ten minutes of their time."

Marty exhales and rocks forward in his seat, causing the springs to squeak yet again. "Alright fine, I was thinking about calling it a night anyways. But I've gotta warn ya – I've been up since seven this morning, so if you try and put me on a specialized diet on the account of fatigue, I'll be grumpy."

His sigh becomes my own as I don't want Dr. Dreval's visit to be in vain. "Thank you, Marty."

As he stands, he waves me off. "Yea, yea – you owe me on this one, pal. I'll expect you to pay for the next two rounds at the Stardust."

"It's a deal then." I utter in gratitude.

I shake the good doctor's hand and bid him farewell. Hastily, I part company. With the relief of having escaped a grim future of cold hands, I barely hear Dr. Dreval's instructions for Marty before concentrating on my encounter with Henry Boenger.

"There's a room prepared, Mr. Kessler." He says in small victory. "Right this way."

I take a gig to the Boenger Building, a forty-four floor skyscraper, a modernistic blend of concrete and glass – a nearly seven-hundred foot eyesore on the southeastern horizon. The construct is terraced with converted gig parking on the lower levels so as not to disturb the higher penthouses belonging to Beonger and his most trusted staff.

Security meets me at the door. It only takes a single flash of my badge to bring their halting hands to a rest and few encouraging words to buzz me up into the elevator towards Henry Boenger's suite. Eccentric as he has become over the years, Mr. Boenger lives on the entire top floor.

The elevator is made out of glass and fastened half-exposed to the exterior with a full view of the cityscape on the ride up. Though I've scaled the outside of buildings before, it has always been the adrenaline that's kept me calm and concentrated. Here, with nothing more than past memories of heated rivalry and lingering blame for Emily's death seething inside my head, I find my nerves teetering on the edge, dreading the possibility of a freefall. As paranoid as he's become over the years, I'm sure he has a button for it somewhere.

When the carriage slows at the forty-fourth floor the metallic doors slide open, unveiling a large reception hall. Within are finely sculpted Romanesque pillars with rococo style furniture pieces: a fainting couch here and an oak desk there. He mixes the pieces with wide variety of sculptures, a few busts of ancient kings and queens, cherubs and greek heroes. There are some concept sketches of gigs hanging on the wall for future projects, I'm sure. In the center of the room, basking on the white fluffy circular rug is a glass drawing table cluttered with blueprints and statistics. The place looks more eclectic than aiming for any given style.

Boenger catches me at the threshold, the same blonde haired cretin I knew many years ago. He wears sweat pants, a white t-shirt and a blue bathrobe; his feet in slippers. He leans on an east-end window frame. The sun is muffled by the clouds at his back, casting him in a dreary backdrop.

"Security informed me that you didn't *appear* drunk, so I'm guessing your not here to throttle me." He expels over the steam issuing from his coffee mug. "So what do you want?" He takes a sip.

Exactly the type of reception I expected, but I'm not about to let him feel like he has the upper hand in this matter. Not this time.

"Nice to see you too." I give the room another glance over. "Who does your decorating?"

"It's in transition." He says sharply. "Do you have some pressing business you'd prefer to speak to me about or are you just looking for décor ideas? If that's the case, I can have security escort you out."

He's on the defensive – good. That means I intimidate him. I decide to waste a little more of his time by walking to the center of the room to get a closer look at his blueprints.

"That's private." He announces, his eyes following the crane of my neck towards his precious portfolios.

I abandon them. I'd hate for him to accuse me of spying.

"We had to force a silver Model-E7 to the ground last night." I offer casually to my random stroll about his place.

"My contracts clearly state that neither me nor my company is responsible for damages caused by the owner." He takes another sip out of his mug. "Look it up."

"It belonged to a Miss Claudine Valentine. Does that name sound familiar?"

He retreats from his lean and stands up to gain those previously lost inches of height. "If you mean by familiar, that she's the owner, then yes – she sounds familiar."

I stop my wandering and address him fully to see the reaction in his eyes. "Is your paperwork in order, Mr. Boenger?"

His face reflects the sternness of his voice. "What's this about, Mr. Bell? I haven't time to play games."

"Miss Valentine destroyed a Govennet cruiser and damaged two, among other lists of crimes including killing a Govennet officer and wounding another."

"My condolences and sympathies for your fellow officers. Again, I'm not responsible for any damages caused by the vehicle or the—"

"She was hard-wired."

"Impossible!" He yells. He looks about his place – searching for somewhere to hide, no doubt.

Henry turns his back on me and makes his egress towards the back portion of the suite. "I've overseen 147 transactions, counting the one I *gave* you four years ago." He expels with a returned condemnation.

I follow him into a back office with rows of chest high filing cabinets, each labeled with a letter of the alphabet. He stops, sets his mug on top, and then opens 'V'.

He thumbs through the pregnant file folders. "Ever since the city demanded that I conduct an extensive background check before every purchase, I've seen to each one. Just so that people like you don't try to shut me down due to an oversight. I saw what this city did to Whistler after he was caught selling a gun to a synthetic. The man couldn't shit without some official's hand in the process."

"Gives a new meaning to, 'Whistleblower' doesn't it? I have no sympathies for that man, as that same gun killed seven of our officers. It was the worst killing spree of the city's history. He got what he deserved."

"Oh, yes. Of course he did. What better punishment than to strip his name from his very own invention so that people wouldn't be reminded of the tragedy. I'm sure his later suicide was fitting as well?"

"No one forced him out that window, Mr. Boenger."

"No – they didn't have to. Whistler wasn't even given the decency to turn his own inventions on himself. They wouldn't let him near them. Give or take a few generations and no one will remember Roderick Whistler."

He pulls out a folder, a thin thing, which wrinkles his brow in confusion. He opens it and despite its apparent emptiness, he turns it over front and back. He tosses it atop the other files, points and then shakes his finger as desperation clings at his cheeks.

"This, this here was full. Someone's been in my files." He shoves his fingers back into the drawer. "Maybe it got misplaced – no, it couldn't have. Where did it go?" He rubs his hand over his face. "Who took it?"

Just the thing that I've been waiting for. A sly smile creeps across my face. I finally got the bastard.

"Having some troubles with your filing system, Mr. Boenger? Are you sure it was even there to begin with?"

He throws out his hand to stall me. "No – it's got to be in here somewhere." Fear scurries the blood from his cheeks, leaving him pale and shaking. "It's supposed to be here!" He screams. "Right here! And it's gone! Someone's been in my files. Son-of-a-bitch!"

I decide to help him out. It's not everyday you get caught selling to plasties. "Maybe you misplaced it. There are twenty-six other cabinets here."

"I did not misplace it, Mr. Bell. It was right here. It's all alphabetical. 'A' is in 'A', 'B' is in 'B' and 'V' is in fucking 'V'!" He grabs his cup violently, sending a wave of coffee onto the file cabinet. Henry shows little care as he storms back into the reception area. I follow after.

"Look, Henry. You know as well as I do that you don't have any files on Miss Valentine, otherwise you would have known that she was a screw-job. If you come clean now, it'll save you and me a headache in the long run."

He stops in mid-stride, creating a divot in his rug, before turning around. "I know what this is all about. You're trying to come down on me because of Emily. You still blame me for your little breakup."

I was calm before. But now, if there is a fire that burns in the human soul, those words ignite it within me. I feel my eyes swell with rage and my face flashes with heat.

"You think this is about Emily?" I shove a finger at his chest. "This is because you messed up and now you're trying to cover it up."

He returns in kind. "Don't give me that bullshit, you've had it in for me since day one. It bothered you that some lowly street-born gent could come waltzing into her life and try to borrow her smile. But if you weren't so damn blind you would have realized that Emily wanted nothing to do with me."

"Please!" I spit.

"You see, there it is! Emily would have given anything to share her life with you, but as I do recall it was you who threw her away when people started showing up. You weren't complaining then."

I clench my fists and grit my teeth. Everything inside me wants to kill him, wants to destroy that face that walked in my apartment door all jeering and mocking with his arm around *my* Emily. But I won't give him an easy way out, not this time. This time I'll watch as everything is stripped from him – his name, his fortune and his work.

"I hope you have some powerful contacts, Mr. Boenger. I believe you'll need to call in all of your favors to get out of this one." I start to leave.

"Oh, no you don't! I've been waiting too long to say this to you and you're going to stand here and listen to it. The truth demands it! That day she found me in the park, when I first woke, she offered to fill me in on the CitySpire if I would help her with a tiny favor. I was to pretend to be her 'new cavalier' as she put it, to make you jealous."

I continue towards the door, pretending not to hear.

"Yes – jealous, Mr. Bell! She claimed she wanted to get back at you for rejecting her; a means to find out how you really felt. She used me to get to you, as I used her to get information. I wasn't interested in your *little society*. I wanted nothing to do with it. I'm my own man, Mr. Bell. I go my own way."

I reach for the bell to summon the carriage, but something stops my hand. Something lurking in past memories as my brain trips on a curb of doubt. Henry persists, seeing my stall.

"What happened on that rooftop, Mr. Bell? While I posed for Emily, I could see the fight in your eyes. I knew your hatred of me and believed it was only a matter of time before you'd act – allowing Emily to shirk off the charade and the two of you'd live happily ever after. But something overcame you, and you gave her up! Back on the roof, you ripped her heart out."

His words sting me and for the first time since the day she died, my heart quivers with overpowering passion, an outpour of pain, anger and loss. It wounds me like devil's fingers on a pain of glass. She falls through the window in my mind and contacts with the pavement. My eyes well, and my throat gorges with bile and acid. I spin around – forgetting all decency.

"You were supposed to watch over her!" My voice powerful; commanding. He jumps a foot back startled and drops his cup. It shatters into pieces on the floor, bleeding brown. Henry grabs at his chest. "You fucking promised – you said, 'I will!' and I took you for your word. Your fucking word! And now she's dead – she's dead, Mr. Boenger! – she's dead because you failed to hold up your promise. You failed!" I swing out my arms wide to encompass his petrified form in damnation. "And you expect me to believe your lies about some pact? You're wrong! Emily was pure, she was the only happiness in my life and you took that away from me." I slowly bring my arms to my side and with it, raise my spine to its farthest extent. "As far as I'm concerned there isn't a punishment more suitable than to have everything taken away from you, much like you did with my Emily. And I will do everything in my power to bring you to ruin."

Henry Boenger, the once proud gentry, now drops to his knees. His strong offensive eyes have reduced to a swollen red. And though a few years ago I may have trusted him, may have forgiven him, and absolved him for blame – I am much older now and my resolve is unfaltering. I have seen death and I've come out cold.

He cuddles his hands close to his chest, partially begging, partially praying. He speaks while struggling with his conscience, "She wasn't the same after we left. No more than a week and then she was gone. I looked everywhere for her. Believe me, Samuel, I looked! The city is large and there are so many places she could hide. I eventually gave up. None of this is my fault, please believe me. Don't let them take my business away! It's all that I am. I won't be able to bear it!"

A noise, a slapping of feet on tile, approaching from a west-end room. Then a presence invades my left peripheral.

A feminine voice, but not from the gender I would expect. "Henry, what's going on?"

Hair is shaved to the bristle, with long womanish features: a slim body, curves and hips. A burgundy silk robe is tied at the waist, but open at the chest revealing skin and flat chest – a man. The walls crumble in my head, burying the bricks and mortar in my gut. The poison returns, the bottle uncorked.

The kneeling gent's eyes look to his housemate, to me, and then back again before biting his lip and easing himself to standing. A few moments and nothing is said, his eyes wander to the ground in search of something he had dropped. He shows his palm to his boyfriend to reassure him that all is okay and quickly returns it to his side.

He speaks slowly and humbled. "Now you know."

The truth is like a suit of needles against my skin. My tongue is choked and my heart sinks into my abdomen. The room is spinning.

I catch the wall and my straying fingers accidentally trigger the elevator doors to open.

Boenger swallows. "Please, Sam. I'm begging you. Don't let them do to me what they did to Whistler. I'll find you the files. Just give me some time."

My hand is covering my lips and I have to concentrate to force it down. I step backward into the elevator.

It takes all my strength to muster an apology.

"I'll see what I can do."

They watch me as the doors close. The two of them have the other's arm around their waist. I feel sick. Not from Boenger's affair with another man, but by the display of it. It reminds me of something I once had, a connection that I unknowingly threw away. A time when things were simpler. Before I blamed Boenger… and now? It was me. It was *all* my fault. Like the coffee, all color has spilled from my parlor and onto the floor.

The turtledoves disappear between the cracks of two sliding metal doors, and the last thing I see, before the haunting clink of the elevator's mechanisms, are the pieces of a once sterling ceramic mug. And after, I can't bare my own reflection.

I stumble through the halls of the apartment building on Nereid Street. My hand brushes against the spackled drywall and worn wallpaper. Images of Emily's pale body spirals down into oblivion like a spinning drain. I haunted by her white fabric.

I tear past the Govennet ribbons long since attached to the frame of her door and then push my way inside. The room is cold, as a breeze slinks in from the cracks between the boards that guard the ominous window. The grey of the morning dances through in miniature beams of filtered light, dispelling only fragments of the darkness of Emily's prior residence. The feeling is comparable.

Inside I'm bruised and the disparity only dilutes my memories of her. That last meeting when she played Bach's Cantata No. 140, her face was cheerful and availing. Was there malice hinged on the other side? No – I simply don't believe it. And all this time she had feelings for me, and here I believed—at one point—she had shared them with Boenger. I made the sacrifice so she wouldn't have the pain of choosing herself. What a fool I was. It all began when I rejected her the night she offered a kiss. Had I not been so fixated on a woman that doesn't exist, I could have been happy and Emily would still be alive.

The light…that damn window! It is this frame that served as the instrument in her death. It was here that she stood, high atop the stool looking out into the world. Why did she leap? Why did she fall? Why was I condemned for things that I knew not? How the window mocks me, all these years, blames me for her death. Damn it all. Damn… it… all…!

I pull out my pistol and unlock the safety. A high-pitched hum radiates from the inner coils as they charge the lights from red to green. The city's power grid, wireless electricity, pours into the weapon and the handle grows hotter. It takes a matter of seconds, a short pause, before the Ex-Whistler is fully charged with five terrifying shots. I tighten my grip. I aim and then pull the trigger!

A hole explodes through layers of boards sending splinters and planks both outward and in. I fire another, content on unloading the whole chamber of lightning against Emily's ill-fated window. The room is charged with static electricity as the hairs on my arms rise from the power of the bolt. Two more holes cut through the barrier, shaving wood like glass, and filling the room with the awful scent of the gun. Light dances in the room, filling it with empyreal beams. I empty the last two shots, before tossing the gun off onto the floor, as I charge the last remnants of the broken barrier I erected three years ago.

I rip at the remains, pulling out both board and tack, scratching at the wood while forcing splinters beneath my nails. I draw blood, but it only enrages me further. I throw them out the window, saying my farewells as I savagely clear the sill.

A powerful gust of wind dashes into the room and swirls beneath some sheet music and sends them flying to the floor. I position the once overturned stool back right-side up where it had been. I take a breath of conviction and as the last puff of air dissipates into the room, I climb atop it, now ankle-level with the window frame.

The wind combs through my hair planting frigid kisses against my cheeks and pinching my ears as it passes to stir more of the room. I can see down Nereid Street and all the apartments buildings that line it. I understand why she lived here as the breezes treat the road as a highway, constantly fluttering through at varying paces.

The buildings are fashioned in the Baroque style with detailed masonry between the floors that inspire something for the imagination. The trim is also pleasing, a light colored granite that intermingles with brick and limestone. Why have I not seen this before? Most have bay windows that are divided into nine panels by muntins. It is desolate here and away from worldly matters. As exhaustion from the past twenty-nine hours causes my legs to tremble, my eyes naturally drift to the concrete below. My mind is tantalized by envisioning what it is like to freefall over a hundred feet down.

My body is blasted by another chilling puff of wind and then my eyes are assaulted by an unusual phenomenon. Bright, warming and still very painful, the clouds part from that last push of heavenly breath and expose sun, reflecting in every pane of glass. I shield my eyes, surprised by its intensity. The glowing orb hovers in every sill, blazing in its short-lived victory over the cumulus blanket above. I am weightless as my eyes fight habitual dilation. The sting is only momentary.

As my eyes adjust, I am able to behold the solar splendor as I did that day when the four of us: Michael, Natalie, Emily and I stared at the stratus via rooftop in wonderment. And then, everything is as it had been before with the wind, the sun, its warmth, and the light tittering of friends. I step off – falling backwards to the floor.

The shock and pain are inconsequential in comparison to losing the rest of that feeling as it wafts from off my body and exits back into the city. I move and hear a light crinkle. I'm careful, knowing full well its sound to be that of music folios beneath me. I bring them with me to standing. And I don't know what it is that makes me curious, but I wonder which artist I had the misfortune of landing on. When I look my heart escapes with my prior feelings, both set adrift now like fallen leaves, and in an instant recaptured again! I can see them! There - between the pages! Circled in vibrant red are the first four notes of that once evasive song, that same callous melody that rendered frustration after frustration – night after night! She hid them: a couple one page, a few another. Only I could have made any sense of them when viewed beneath one another, where the light reveals their order. When they were so scattered it held no meaning – but now?

Another gust rolls through the room, circles and rounds again, pulling at the folios and flutters them to the ground. I take a step back, but cautiously guard the window in case any of them make a break for it. Yet they settle, scattered across the wood floor like footprints in the sand – her footprints! In that I start to smell her, start to know that sense of presence again.

"I feel you Emily." I say outloud to the dying wind.

As the clouds draw themselves over the sun, after staring at the find with awe and renewed belief in hope, I realize what it is that I must do. I gather up the folios and spread them across the sofa table. The sheer amount of them; there are too many. I'm going to need more room. Then, there is that damn window…

25

I work throughout the rest of the day. I spread everything across the floor, needing the extra space in order to work efficiently while remaining detailed and accurate. I even had to reinstate the lights. The couch is now upright and blocking the window. Best to keep the winds calm and the chill outside. It's a temporary fix.

The hardest part of the puzzle is remembering the notes, finding what pair comes next in the sequence. Even when I believe I've finished a measure, I realize the other circled notes don't align correctly and I have to start over. It's straining, especially with little sleep. All this forces me to think in multiple measures, focusing on what could come later on, before ever finding what is next. Then, a pattern! It comes from working from the corners and moving inward, circular, like a spiral towards the center.

As dusk is on approach, I am working several pages in, breaking only occasionally to lick my fingers and grab a nibble to eat—as it so happens the only thing is pancakes—when a flutter of something intrudes on my concentration from the window. I stop hesitantly, fearful that removing my eyes could lose my place and look up to see what it is that has alerted me. From out of the cold and into the fleeting heat, a pigeon has squeezed its paunchy self from around the sofa barricade and now roosts on one of the wooden legs. It cocks its head in a queer fashion and coos at me. From behind it, I notice the silent descent of snow collecting on the sofa and sill.

Already it starts, the winter months are always the worst for me. I'm reminded of nightingales and snowmen. And whenever I pass one on the street, it pains my chest and I regress – thinking of that time I held her frigid body in my hands, the light underneath my door as I lay in wake in my bedroom with Natalie in the other room. Everything closing in.

But now my feelings are replaced with an odd sense of familiarity, like this has all happened before. And in looking back at the collection of music, those ever spinning notes, I'm drawn more into it. For an instance, I'm allowed a moment of clarity and I begin to feel where everything is going. It is another run in with déjà vous, something inward that's telling me I'm on the right track.

I watch it a little longer, the pigeon, as it shakes the snow off is feathers and cleans itself with its beak. I'm mesmerized by its movements and in drifting through the corridors of memory, I am hit with inspiration. It is then that I'm able to find a couple other pieces of the puzzle and I jot it down to add with the rest of the discovered notes.

I finish shortly before seven, the folio is nigh complete and the song is written down on multiple pages. There are a few measures, missing pieces of a repeating segment, a link in the great chain. I had thought I lost a few pages, but no – they are all here. All accounted for. There must be another hint or perhaps another clue. Then again, maybe she couldn't finish it. Even now it continues to play in my head. Just to think, it's been under my nose all this time. However, as much as I would like to marvel at it longer, play it over and over again until the walls themselves have absorbed the tune, I am driven by other responsibilities.

My gig touches down a half-hour late, a first for me since Govennet's inception. I've always been one for punctuality and a good role model. Now, I can just imagine Marty's reaction when I come walking out of the elevator: *Look what the cat dragged in*, or *Get enough sleep, princess?* The entire time I'm weighted down to the first floor lobby, I'm thinking of means to combat his jives. He always tends to get one over me, but I've been known to hold my own if promptly prepared. I'm sure he's been working on something since seven.

The doors open into the lobby, a few remnant officers are at their desks finishing up on the prior mornings reports. I'm sure last night's fiasco with Ms. Valentine has been keeping a good majority of them busy, not to mention anything else that may have occurred. I'm sure Marty is interested to hear what occurred with Boenger – some of the details I may just keep to myself.

I see him leaning on the edge of a row of filing cabinets – old screw-job case files, whispering to Reginald Blake. From the look on their faces, it's something serious, although it's not much of a change for the Sergeant. I see Brigit with Harvey Parson, the duo filing some paperwork while keeping a wide birth from the other two. The funny thing is, their desks are nearest one another. They may have had another spat, Brigit and Marty that is. Once upon a time they were considered a couple, but for some reason or another it didn't work out. They're still friends, but every so often they'll get into it.

I'm more than ten feet from the elevator, where I'm caught by both Officer Grik and Sallis who are enjoying themselves by the foldout table of coffee and donuts.

"Chief Inspector!" Caleb raises his chin to me. "Fancy seeing you here, instead of the docks."

It's one of those greetings that eludes into a longer conversation. I know it's inevitable, but the two officers have grown on me.

"Indeed it is. Are you two on your way out?"

Sallis holds up a powdered pastry. "Just grabbing some breakfast before spending a night with the fishies."

The two of them raise their coffee mugs in toast. They know I paid for them. It's always the little things that make people happy. It's the least I can do.

"Well enjoy it as much as possible, boys. Seems the good Doc is on a crusade for city-wide health and has decided to start with us. Best be careful, that table may turn to celery and carrots one day." Now that I see Caleb in the light, he can afford to lose a few pounds.

Caleb looks as if he just fell off the pier. "But sir, this is Bryan's and my lifeblood. Ya can't go and take that away from us. Ol' Bryan will waste away to nothing. Can't you see he's all skin and bones?"

Officer Sallis plays into it, giving a pouting face.

"Well — I think you can afford to give Officer Sallis a bit off your tummy there? Looks to me that you're doing enough eating for the both of you."

Sallis chokes on some powdered sugar, after just inches away from a bite, and then laughs.

Grik looks offended. "Sir, I'll have you know that I've offered Officer Sallis a fair share off my belly, but he refuses to take it." He points to his partner with his head. "He's a dear friend, that one. Always, thinking of others."

"That settles it then. Officer Sallis? To break this matter of selflessness, you are to take whatever Officer Grik offers you in share of his belly. That's an order."

Still chuckling, and having cleared his throat with a swig of coffee, Bryan Sallis gives me a weak salute. "Aye – sir." It isn't much after that his face flattens.

I hear Marty's familiar voice over my shoulder.

"Don't you two have somewhere to be?" His voice is at edge of reprimand.

Both Grik and Sallis hastily grab a second pastry from off the table.

"Gotta run, boss. Good luck with that thing of yours and all that." Caleb whispers to his partner as they make for the door. "Trouble with the misses." He points at his nose, signaling something secret between them before disappearing out into the night.

I turn around after watching them go. Marty is paler than usual. Dark circles cringe beneath his eyes, as if he hasn't slept.

"You look awful." I give with my usual bout of concern. "Did the Doc give you a flu shot?"

His features are unmoving, his eyes a bastion of contempt. "You're late."

The briefness of his statement shocks me. "A half-hour and that's all you came up with? Are you feeling alright?"

Marty's eyes dodge to the side as if thinking and then back again. "I'm fine."

Definitely hiding one thing or another. "Are you and Brigit fighting about something?"

"Not that she's eluded to." An awkward pause. "Doctor Dreval has been waiting for you since seven. It's your turn, boss."

"Oh – is that what this is about?" I shake my head. "Sorry that you kind of got thrown under the bus with the Doc. Let me make it up to you. How about we go see Natalie after work. We'll get some drinks, meet some people, what do you say?"

He cocks his head and raises an eyebrow. "The Stardust?"

"Yea – why not. I'll buy."

"I'm busy."

Something's wrong. I don't know if he's angry with me, if there was a fight between him and Brigit, or if the Doc gave him some bad news. Maybe that's it. Maybe the Doc informed him of something grave.

"Listen, Marty. If there is anything wrong, anything at all, you can talk to me. I know I got my share of troubles, but I'd like to be there for you. I owe you a lot."

His brow just scowls. "I said I was fine." He motions with his head towards the stairs. "Come on, let's not keep the doctor waiting."

I shake my head. "I'm sorry, Marty, I don't have time. I have to meet Mr. Cagney over at the Registration Bureau. Our assumptions were right, it turns out Mr. Boenger doesn't have any of the paperwork on our Valentine case. He claims he must have misplaced it and swears he followed proper procedure. I hate saying this, but despite our history, I'm inclined to believe him."

He grabs me lightly by the arm. "The good doctor is a very busy man. I think you owe him a few minutes of your time."

Marty's eyes have narrowed, his cheek bones more pronounced, his words are sharp and hostile. There is something wrong here, something very wrong. Why is he so insistent? Where is the good humor? This isn't the Marty Kessler I knew from yesterday.

I decide to play the diplomat. "Just apologize for me and remind the doctor that our job takes priority over his medical examinations. If he's still willing, have him return tomorrow at seven. I'll see him then."

His hand tightens on my arm. I look to confirm that my nerves aren't lying to me and that his hand is truly constricting. His eyes are filled with haunting conviction, hollowed without remnant of good nature. It's almost as if he—

"Sam!" Brigit disrupts our standoff. I can feel the tension on my arm slacking. "I need your help on something."

She isn't far, just a few paces to the side with her strong-arm partner behind her. Harvey keeps his arms crossed in his extra large version of our Govennet uniform. With his imposing stature nearby, all arguments are off.

I readdress Mr. Kessler. "I've got to go."

Brigit's foot starts to tap. "Come on, I don't have time for you two love birds to say your goodbyes."

He looks me in the eye with a sneer. "Tomorrow then." And he releases me fully before heading towards the stairs.

Brigit watches him go. "Now that you two are finished, perhaps we can get some real work done, huh?" Her boots click against the ground as she strolls up to me, grabs me by the wrist and pulls me in close to her.

"Sumtin ain't right, Sam." She whispers. "Marty's been an asshole all night. Ever since I got here, both he and the Sergeant have been staring at me weird. I know they ain't been laid in a while, but that's not it." She looks over her shoulder and then back again. "I yelled at em about it, but they just ignored me and pretended to do sumtin else. Then, not a few minutes later, they're doing it again. There's a lot of hostility here and no one's tellin' me why."

Harvey Parson just nods to reaffirm her story.

"I used to just be able to kick it out of Marty, but that doesn't fly anymore. I once had a strong leash on em, but now…" she trails. "I don't know. For a moment, I thought it was just me. Maybe they're thinking me a threat to their running tallies and formed an alliance. But Marty thinks the world was born outta yer ass, and after witnessing what I just saw I know that I'm not imaginin' things."

I notice the Sergeant looking over at us from the case files, he has a file in his hand, but I doubt he even knows which one it is. His eyes are affixed, as if tattooing our conversation to the walls of his mind. Our eyes meet and for less than a minute, it is as if he's to stare me into submission, but then without warning his eyes casually descend to what's sitting in his hands – business as usual.

"I think you're right – then again, it could be nothing. Keep an ear out, let me know if you hear anything."

"Is this an official investigation?"

"No, keep this off the books. Like I said, it could be nothing. But again this office was built on paranoia. We can't be too careful." She nods her head. "In the meantime I've got to head to the Registration Office. You know how to reach me."

Brigit eases herself from off my hip and punches me on the arm. "You can count on me, boss! I'll make sure those screw-jobs get what's coming to them." She winks before returning to her desk with Harvey in tow.

Things are starting to get complicated. I used to know who the enemy was. Life was simple: I would give them a eye test, they'd run, I'd track them down and then kill them. At night I would return to either my apartment or Nereid Street, listen to some classical music and then drown my memories in a bottle of bourbon. Things started to go awry when Marty had me take that day off. First, there was Farley and his group of street kissers stolen from the graveyard; then, a night at the Stardust where I was introduced to Johnny Weber and later reunited with Natalie; Miss Valentine; Dr. Dreval; Henry Boenger; and Emily's portfolio – all less than seventy hours of one another. Why did all of this have to happen at once? And my night is far from over. I'm exhausted. The hours have finally caught up to me.

Shy of nine minutes in the air, I touch down in front of the Registration Office. It's a square building with lots of windows and concrete. There's a slight modernist appeal to the style, but frankly all glitz and glamour is swallowed by the creep now darkening its exterior. So dark in fact, a couple portable lights had been brought out to help illuminate the stairs so people don't trip. Its four stories high, with the stairs leading up to the second-floor doors flanked by a row of square columns.

PART III - THE SORCERER

The roof was deemed structurally unsound for gig parking when they first moved in. The city figured that since those who are registering wouldn't have a car, and since its relative close proximity to most apartment complexes, people could walk. It was a perfect match.

At the beginning, the number of people waking in the city were astronomical. The first two years the Registration Office had lines that could stretch an entire block. Then suddenly and without reason, the floodgates were shutdown and only a trickle of people were registering each month. No explanation for the phenomenon, just employee cutbacks. No use paying for people to sit on their duffs and do nothing.

All one needs to register is that little white card with gold trim, a place of consciousness, and then an eye exam. They trade your name for a registration number and a cred-card, a means for the city to recognize you as an official citizen of the CitySpire. Without it, you can't trade and you certainly can't get an honest job.

Registration was deemed necessary by all members of the council: in order to build a public record, create a census, slim down our chances for mannequin infiltration, and jump start the economy. The last was a nightmare of its own. If Farley and his band of followers caught a glimpse of the establishing of the CitySpire's laws of economy and private ownership, I wouldn't have questioned their choice in suicide. That's perhaps a story best left for another time.

I am late to meet the only employee of the Registration Office. I vid-phoned ahead and was able to convince the gentleman to wait for me at the front lobby. If the office clerk hadn't been a friend of mine, I may have been stiffed. Considering I got him the job in the first place, I figure he owes me. The man is Thomas Cagney. I can see his nose poking out of a fogged window, watching for when I would arrive. When I reach the last remaining steps to the second-floor entrance, he opens them and follows the swing outside to hold them open.

He's quick to usher me into the vestibule.

"S-sure is great t-t-to see you again, M-m-mister Bell. Your f-f-phone call is the last, th-thing I was expecting today." He cycles a couple frozen breaths into the air, pausing only momentarily to watch the slow accumulation of snow and then follows in after locking the door behind him.

"I really appreciate you staying open a little later. I hope it's not an inconvenience for you, Thomas."

The round man gives the doors a good pull before nervously watching behind his rounded glasses the key as he deposits it in his pocket.

"No, n-n-not at all. I don't have gues-s-sts all that often. I-I-I have asked the ca-ca-ouncil if-if I could stay op-open twenty-four hours. B-b-but they said it wu-woo-would cost them t-t-t-too much. I'd-d-d certainly open the doors for sum-sa-someone who needs to regist-t-ter. So, wh-why not you?" He inhales quickly as if he had accidentally left his breath outside.

"For twenty-four hours? Aren't you tapping into your sleep schedule with that request?"

He pushes his glasses closer up the bridge of his nose. "Tha-that's what the-they said. And even a-a-after I told them that I dun-do-don't sleep much, beca-ca-caus of my insomni-i-ia, they s-still said 'no' even when I offered to wor-wer-k for free. Said it-it was a liabil-ility and would mess-s-s up my in-income bracket. So-o-o-so I just don't tell them."

"If you are here twenty-four hours, where do you sleep?"

"I-I-I," he pauses to collect himself. "I sleep here, Mr. Bell. I've set-t-tled in on a hy-higher floor. It c-c-can get drafty b-b-but, there's no rent, and n-n-nobody bothers me."

After we pass through the vestibule and into the main lobby, I am perplexed by the rusted iron cages that have been erected around the front counter once used to process new arrivals. It seems the entire place has a few added features that I hadn't been aware of: rail turrets situated in the ceiling, gates with exposed wiring and black tubing that interconnect with a stationary red-eye machine, and even the occasional padlock.

"Things have changed since the last time I was here." As the place once was simply a front counter, plants, velvet rope and brass railing.

"Ye-y-yes they ser-sir-certainly have. Peh-p-people were worried that a robot would w-waltz through here trying ta-to reg-g-g-ister."

"Robot?" I ask.

"Th-that's what they are, aren't they? R-r-r-obots? J-j-just skin and mechanics?"

"Something like that."

"I-I-never have met a robot, Mr. Bell. N-n-not once. I find it st-st-strange that we had l-l-lots of people, then someone in-in-invents a w-w-way to detect r-robots, and th-then we suddenly have r-robots, an-an-and no people."

"What exactly do you mean?"

"Well, th-th-thats just s-s-strange is-isn't it? The city suddenly d-d-decides to make robots, and not people?"

"We're still trying to get down to the bottom of it. But, it's not like we're hurting on population at the moment."

"N-n-no, we are not. We aren't g-g-gaining on p-p-people, either." He blinks a couple times before realizing something. "I'm sor-sorry, Mr. Bell. I'm ta-taking up too-o m-m-uch of your time. What w-wa-ss it-t that you were lo-ooking for?"

He takes me down to the basement through a metallic stairwell. The whole place is locked up, red-eye check points, and multiple gates with padlocks. The mess is just an added security measure to prevent intruders from getting their hands on private citizen information as well as both registration and cred-card numbers.

The area he takes me to is at the far back of the basement, shielded by three feet of concrete in a vault-like enclosure. The room itself is long and cursed with a low ceiling, no more than eight-feet tall, with long fluorescent lights dangling from hooks and wires stapled into the concrete ceiling that run along each row and then down the walls. For Thomas, it is perfect, but for me, I constantly feel like I'm going to hit my head on one of the lamps – despite plenty of clearance. There is a maze of bookshelves filled with papers, books, and boxes, with many steel filing cabinets with extensive locks.

Despite the many rows of overhead lamps, only a few of them have bulbs in them. Perhaps this is the council's way of reducing costs. I'm sure it makes things difficult to find, but for some reason, Mr. Cagney is making his way just fine.

"I remem-b-b-ber a Ms. Valent-t-ine, purchasing a vehicle f-f-from Mr. Boenger man-n-ny months ago. I remem-b-er because I didn't know wh-what day Val-val-alentine's day was on."

He stops in front of a long set of file drawers. He pulls out his key ring and thumbs through the lot of them until ending on a circular shaped one. How he manages to keep them all organized is beyond me.

Unlocking the cabinet, he flips open the lid and draws out a numerical assortment of file folders, he stops at one and hands it to me, with C.14.9.20.14.5.12.1.22.5.9 labeled at the top. I look inside and it belongs to Claudine Valentine.

"How is it that you were able to remember this particular file, if it's labeled numerically?" I ask as I start fingering through the pages.

"Oh, I n-n-never stu-s-stutter on numbers, Mr. Bell. It m-makes it easier to remember. It's also m-m-my pers-s-onal system; it makes it-it hard for others to ge-get the information r-r-right away."

I hold a couple of the pages up to the light, careful not to lose its place in case it has any particular order. The last thing I want to do was upset Mr. Cagney, especially after all the trouble he's gone through.

Yes – it's here, it's all here: registration number, her white card reading, "You are Claudine Valentine", and all her papers concerning her recent purchase of her whirly-gig, red-eye test, a personal photograph, and more. There's even a notation here that no one observed her waking. I always feel bad when that happens to people.

"This is impossible." I say aloud, my voice ringing through the file drawer. "Thomas, could any of this be a mistake? Miss

Valentine is a confirmed mannequin, she's in the hands of Rockword and Slovene, being taken apart. I saw the wires myself."

"N-n-no mistake, Mr. Bell. It's all le-leg—," he inhales. "Accurate. Unless th-the stationary DORs don't w-work right and sh-sh-she slipped through. Bu-but I think that high—"

I shush my companion as the sound of footsteps catch my attention above, a couple pair of boots, and a familiar click. I seal my lips with my pointer finger, and whisper to him, "Are you expecting anyone?"

He shakes his head, his hands now trembling with anxiety.

Once their boots touch the metal of the stairway, I nab her white card and then return the file to Mr. Cagney, motioning for its return. He files it and closes the cabinet quickly, all the while my hand directing him silently—and quite vigorously—to return to my side and then behind a set of bookshelves. It isn't but a few moments until I see the emerging form of Sergeant Reginald Blake from off the stairs. What's he doing here?

I spy on him between the cracks of a shelf as he reaches the iron gate, pushing the door with his gloved finger.

"Hello?" He stops and he listens to the whine of the door's metal hinges. "Mr. Cagney?"

My trembling companion bites his lip. His eyes bounce from me to the gate with a pantomimed question as to whether he should remain or reveal himself. I pat the air to reinforce his stay. It only serves to fuel his nerves.

He may have overheard me speaking with Marty or caught wind of it somehow that I planned on heading here. Seeing my gig out front, he may have come looking for me – but for what reason? I ponder revealing myself to see what the Sergeant is up to, but then I am stalled by the next sight.

Two men follow behind him. They wear long blue coats, buttoned up to keep out the chill, and a gold badge that details a falcon and shield. Police. Yet on their belts I see black holsters and the familiar grip of a gun instead of the collapsible batons they are so widely renowned for. This isn't right. It's illegal for the police to carry a gun. They must be rogue or are at least well-supplied. You'd think they were expecting trouble. I wonder if those pistols are meant for me?

Reginald peers around a few local shelves before giving up his inquiry for Thomas and then walks back towards the cabinet where we once had been. His goons follow his every step, keeping a weary eye out for anything out of the ordinary, the ill-light working in our favor.

There are moments in which I lose sight of him. Instead, I must follow the heart-thumping click of his boots as he nears our location. But then, as he finally reaches the cabinet, I catch sight of him between a group of books. I watch as he draws out a set of keys much like the ones Thomas has and then unlocks the case.

It's only but a short leap of the imagination that I know which file he is after – Ms. Claudine Valentine. I don't even beat an eyelash as I observe him drawing it out of its holdings. He's quick, as if in some sort of hurry, looks in it briefly, nods to his associates, and then closes up the theft. He locks the cabinet back up, then proceeds back through the gate and up the stairs. The police officers escort him to where footfalls grow distant.

"Th-th-they know m-m-my system. Th-his is not good, Mm-Mr. Bell. This is not good a-at all." He says after they're gone completely.

"They have your keys, they know your system? Is there anything you're not telling me, Thomas?"

He fiddles with his hands and looks down at his feet. "I-I-I hate t-to tell you th-this, Mr. Bell. B-b-but, I recognize one of th-them. Th-th-that's Reggie Blake. H-h-he used to work here before the city l-l-let him go due to lack o-of work. H-h-he must have ma-m-made copies of the k-k-keys before leaving." He looks up at me with fear trembling in his cheeks. "He wasn't v-v-very happy w-when they told him th-the news."

"But why would he need a copy of the keys? He wouldn't make a copy unless he knew he would need them later."

He shakes his head. "I don't k-k-know, Mr. Bell. All I-I-I do know is th-that my life is-is always in dan-g-ger whenever I-I-I'm around you. I-I'm just a-a-an office clerk. N-n-not a Govennet off-f-f-icer."

I leave Thomas Cagney, thanking him again for his time and I apologize for putting him in this situation. Inside my gig, I turn her card over in my hand, reading it over and over again, "You are Claudine Valentine"

As far as I know her card is legitimate. There had been, at one time, a Claudine Valentine. Is it possible that on her way to the Registration Office she was *replaced* by a mannequin who then somehow managed to pass through the red-eye exam without being revealed? But then she had been operating in the city for months and no one had noticed. Who then tampered with the machine? Was it the Sergeant? But what motivation would he have for letting murderers into the city? Why did Ms. Valentine suddenly decide to attack Govennet officers? What was she doing prior to being found out?

Questions, so many questions, and all I have is speculation. Perhaps the machines just failed that day, but I doubt it. Jumping into her gig was the worst thing she could have done. She easily could have vanished outside the patrolled areas and hid there. It's almost as if she wanted to be found. At least I have the proof necessary to acquit Henry of failing to meet city polices. Of course, there is the matter of someone tampering with his files.

Now the bigger questions: What was Sergeant Blake doing with those police officers? Why were they carrying chirpers? And above all else, what did they want with Valentine's file, especially since he knew I was working on the case? None of this makes any sense, and with my partner down and out it makes everything more difficult. Whatever reason, this is beginning to look like it involves more than a single misplaced file or a malfunctioning piece of equipment.

There really isn't anything else I can do. Maybe Brigit will turn up something. At this point, she's the only one I can trust. I need some time to think. What better place than the Stardust?

I initialize the startup sequence of the gig. As soon as the aerodynes are warm enough, I whirl off into the city towards home to change.

As with the previous night, the place is jumping to Johnny Weber's orchestra. I see men and women dressed in their finest garments and pearls, while the wait staff – in their velvety red vests and sashes – bus tables with expensive hors d'oeuvres and champaign. It's a place untouched by the world around them, a celebration of the hour as each pretend to be famous kings and queens. Emily would have liked it here.

They all address me by name: *"Good evening to you, Mr. Bell. Tis' a pleasure to see you, Mr. Bell."* and *"Welcome back, Mr. Bell."* It is as if someone informed them to pay extra attention to my return. It's all spelled out to me when I'm shown a reserved seat dead front of the stage, and a rock glass of bourbon mere moments after sitting. It had to have been prepared the moment I entered the room. And though I appreciate all the special attention Mr. Weber's staff is affording me, I can only think about the price of favors.

I listen intently to the music exploding before me and I'm briefly yanked into the same state of euphoria as the rest of the patrons. The golden brilliance of the overhead lights remind me of those very same rays I saw peeking behind the clouds at Nereid Street. Occasionally, I can hear a set of notes that remind me of a passage in Emily's folios and I sigh as if some tiny pin was plucked from my heart. I can taste my neighbor's cigars and stranger still, I can only think of rich syrup and brilliantly baked batter.

My gaze relaxes, and though musicians play their blood-hoppers, I am lax. I begin to see the motion of light radiating from off their sleeves, leaping into position before their arm even gets there. I watch Mr. Weber as he directs his band mates with a swaying hand and flute, and I can see where they'll go shortly before they reach it themselves. It is as if I am seeing ghostly strings, as if the director is being directed. I wonder if it's my drink, but then my head pains me and all I am is tired. I close my eyes and all I can see is Emily's face.

"Doing alright, Mr. Bell?" Comes Mr. Weber's voice through the fog of neighboring conversations.

The music has stopped and the orchestra is on break. I don't know when this happened. Perhaps I fell asleep, but I'm still sitting in my chair with my hand resting on my forehead. My drink is full again.

I raise my vision to address the Stardust's host. He's in the same suit as he was the night before – a white tuxedo with a black bow tie and a red handkerchief fluffed from his left breast pocket. His blue eyes sparkle from the lights overhead.

"Just a headache, thank you." I pinch my sinuses but there isn't much relief in it.

He motions toward the seat beside me. "May, I?"

I run my hand once over my mouth, noting the bristles starting to form on my chin. "Please."

"You hadn't moved in a while, so naturally I was concerned."

My headache has radiated towards the back of my skull. "Don't worry about me, Mr. Weber. I'm sure it's due to not sleeping."

The edge of his right eyebrow twitches. "You haven't been to sleep since last we spoke? No wonder you're feeling a bit under the weather." He raises his hand to a member of his wait staff, touches his neck and returns with two fingers. The gent nods in acknowledgment and dashes off to the bar. "We must have left a good impression for you to grace us twice in one week."

"I won't lie to you, Mr. Weber, I find your establishment enthralling. I was a bit hesitant at first, especially as far outside the patrols, but I was – am certainly surprised." I nudge the bourbon with a finger, the drink not as appealing as it was the night prior. "Your staff has been extremely accommodating tonight."

"Please, call me Johnny. It's what I prefer in your company. As for your attentions, I assure you it's only to entice you for future visits. Eventually, I'll have to charge you." He smiles a set of flawless white teeth to reassure me of his friendliness. "Besides, as I mentioned before, I am much a fan of everything you've contributed to this city. From what I hear, if it wasn't for you we would have all starved to death or murdered one another."

He's sincere. I don't get the idea that he's after me for a leg up in personal contacts or destitute to find some meaning on this island. He's established. He probably has more contacts and inside information than I'll ever acquire. His fascination with me, thankfully, isn't bothersome.

"If not me, I'm sure someone else would have fallen into the role."

He shakes his head. "Don't be so modest, Mr. Bell. You've done a lot. And instead of taking a position on the council, you decided to take up guardianship. I don't think you get you're fair share of thanks. It takes a lot to step away from power when it's offered to you and to put public safety in front of your own."

"I've never wanted to rule over anyone, Mr. Weber. We all have our dreams, but politics was never one of them."

Our drinks arrive, ones that Johnny must have ordered, a red drink with two olives and a dill pickle spear.

"A Bloody Mary?"

"It always helps me when I'm feeling out of sorts," he toasts me. "Drink up, and in no time you'll feel as right as rain."

I join him in toast, following his raised glass from the air between us to lips. It's good, perhaps better than I would have ever guessed.

"The secret," he mentions. "Is using the right amount of horseradish."

"Well, thank you." I nod. "I appreciate all this."

"It's all my pleasure, sir. Personally, I feel everyone owes you a drink." He watches me as I bite into my pickle. "So where is that friend of yours Mr. Kessler? This is the first time in months he hasn't paid us a visit."

"Marty? He's—" How do I say that I don't know without sounding ignorant? "—busy working on a case, and couldn't make it." A lie, and not a very good one, but it seems to do the trick.

"Ah – always the dedicated Govennet official. When Mr. Kessler first came into my establishment, I was troubled that perhaps we were under investigation. Though the longer he was here, the more I began questioning his motives. It later occured to me that he was only *looking* for something to be out of place. But I can see that you're different, Mr. Bell. To me, you're here for the very reason everyone else is here."

"And what reason is that?"

"To forget and remember at the same time. People enjoy themselves here. It's my way of offering momentary bliss from our day to day struggles. You and I both know the burden this city places on us."

"Life here can be cruel, yes."

"I wish only to continue pampering my guests, to give them that special escape from the world. I ask you, Mr. Bell, as a man rather than your host – do I have anything to worry about from the Govennet?"

Marty must have him spooked. He never does know when to be tactful in these particular situations. "You're not under investigation, Mr. Weber. I assure you that you have nothing to fear from me or Marty, for that matter. Whatever difficulties you may have experienced with him in the past are certainly from his own curiosity."

He relaxes in his chair and lets out a month's worth of old air. "You don't know how relieved I am to hear that. I trust that you'll be upfront with me and let me know if I, or any of my staff, are in any conflict with Govennet regulations. I respect you, Mr. Bell. I certainly hope you'll pay me the same honor."

"Do not worry, Johnny. I've found you very hospitable. If something arises, I'll bring it to your attention immediately. But I can't give you preferable treatment if something warrants an investigation. What I *can* promise you is that I'll be as gentlemanly as possible and do my best not to compromise your guests' integrity."

He nods his head slowly. Johnny Weber is either in agreement or had expected that sort of answer, either way, he doesn't act too disappointed.

"That's all I can ask for, Mr. Bell." He gets up and smooths out his tux. "I do apologize for having to leave you so soon, but my staff will be in need of my attentions." He steps away from the table but then snaps his fingers. "You know, I almost forgot to tell you. Ruby wanted me to inform you that she apologizes but is not feeling well. However, she asks that you call on her tomorrow night. What should I relay to her?"

I shake my head in accordance. "Tell her that I'll be here."

He bows at the waist, his eyes never leaving my gaze. "Until tomorrow, then. Good night, Mr. Bell."

"Good night." I reply as he hoists himself back to standing.

I watch him as he leaves with a noticeable haste to his step. He weaves in and out of wait-staff and guests, never once begging their pardon or ever having the need to. He's dexterous. He's charming. He's also protective and rightfully paranoid, as there are always men of envy out there waiting in the shadows to steal what is lawfully yours. They are the worst enemies of them all, the ones you never see coming. I knew he was primping me for something but it appears that Mr. Weber was only unsure of Marty's role. He trusts me, for whatever reason. I wonder how long it's been since his last eye exam.

26

The past two days have been too much for me. It's now fair time to reacquaint myself with an old friend – sleep. I decide on Nereid Street as I am eager to look over the music folio once more before I break from this world. Beyond the hallway, I reach the door. The torn ribbons remind me of my emotional state at that time. I'm about to muse further when my thoughts are noosed and hung at the knob – the door slightly ajar.

Instincts arrest my hand as it calls forth my pistol from my shoulder holster. A quick press of a button rears the initial hum as the coils charge. I think: did I leave the door open? In my egress to headquarters, did I fail to close the door completely? Or now that the seal has been broken, has some lowly denizen decided to make this its new habitation? Perhaps something more terrible still – a screw-job seeking revenge. The pistol close to my chest, I push my shoulder into the door to bring about its swing.

Darkness haunts the room, the motion sensors taking their time in igniting the lights. Quiet. It's so silent I can hear my own breath flowing into the room. I hear the touch of my boots against the wooden floor, a delicate whisper of wind tip-toeing through the window, and a light rustling of movement toward the living room.

I peek the chirper into the kitchen, then around the bathroom door, but nothing passes my eye. The lights are returning now, painting the apartment in sepia. I can make out shapes, identifying the sofa table, couch and edge of the piano. I see the window as a little light trickles in from the streetlamps, the beams seeking shelter from the ice and snow. I can feel an intruder. My goose bumps rise as if having eyes of their own, all on the lookout for something lurking in the ebb. I smell something disrupting Emily's scent; something close.

There's motion by the window, something huddled there behind the other side of the leather sofa. I approach slowly, my heart beating in my fingers and the taste of ozone already creeping into my mouth. I step closer, my left hand now joining my right in holding the weapon. The lights increase, revealing detail: a cushion… and a handful of pigeons.

I lower my weapon and cast a glance behind me. The lights now brighter, I'm able to see the player piano completely and then a side panel removed, exposing inner gears at its hallway side – a secret compartment! Someone *is* here!

A boot scuffs in the direction of the bathroom and I catch sight of a head poking out of the framework. She spots me, pale and short black hair sprints to the open door and ducks round the hallway. Shit!

"Govennet!" I shout. "Stop where you are!"

Her boots continue to distance themselves. I give pursuit.

I push through the apartment, past the front door and slide into the hallway. I see her zigzag the latter half and then dive towards the staircase. I think about firing, but I haven't identified her yet. As far as I know, she's simply a thief. She has a brown hip satchel, canvas maybe; a short black jacket; denim shorts, and her legs are small with ankle high boots with a tiny heel.

"Halt!" I cry out and then decide to save my breath.

I rush into the stairwell and connect with the guardrail as I give a quick peek down through the floors to discern her location – down two. I speed after, trying hard to concentrate on where my feet land so not to stumble or fall. I leap the last three steps of every case to save time.

My blood rages with the heat of the chase, my breaths coming heavy and irregular. I count the steps all the while listening as she takes hers. She's leaping them as well. Short legs, I tell myself. I may have the advantage. Another round of stairs zip by. The floor rattles me to the bone after each jump, a short shock, four steps and then another jump before turning and finishing the last half of the floor. She still has the lead. Then the bang of the outside door and it slamming into stone.

I expel myself from inside the apartment building and scour the street – to the right, left. I see her no more than twenty-meters down the street heading due south on Nereid, her feet kicking up snow behind her. I throw myself forward, pushing my legs for longer and quicker strides, trying to use every trick to close the distance between us.

The snowfall is continual, the chill is arduous and the frigid air is painful to the lungs. I try and ignore it, dedicated to running the creature down. The glass panes of the local buildings pass without so much of a stayed reflection. Doubt leaps into my mind as pain rakes at my lungs. She's built for this: ninety pounds maybe less, very little clothes to impede her and with no signs of stopping. But I'm keeping the distance, the only thing I'm banking on is that she's not a mannequin. If she is, I've lost to her already.

Another few blocks and I dip into a bank of encouragement, I'm gaining on her. The confidence boosts me forward, forcing me harder into a full tilt, and I repeat a chant over in my head: *She's running out of breath. You can catch her.* It's as if she hears my thoughts for she looks over her shoulder with a snapshot of desperation imprinted on her face. She dodges down an alleyway.

This can be bad. I have no idea if anyone is waiting for her in the darkness of the narrow passage. The CitySpire holds many places for people to hide, and ambush is at the foremost of my mind. I'm dicing on the fact that she hid in the apartment because she didn't expect anyone. Cautious, I turn the corner and onto the lane with my gun tucked close. Nothing – just a steam, ventilation ducts and empty brick. Then the sound of boots on textured steel and a clump of snow from above. She's climbing the fire escape. Why do they always go on the roof?

I holster my gun, run for the ladder hanging just shy of the wall, and start pulling myself up to get a hold on one of the rungs. I manage to acquire traction on a couple uneven bricks off the sidewall, enough to give me enough room to maneuver and inevitably pull myself up onto the first landing. I spot her, can't really say how far up. Far enough.

I give diplomacy another try. "I just want to talk to you!" I yell up the metal escape.

She looks down, her hair dangling in her face, before jetting back, curious if I made it onto the stairs and still following her. No time to catch my breath. The chase continues.

Twelve stories, about average height for this section of the city. I climb a short ladder from the final landing and overtop a three-foot guard wall. The roof is comprised of black tar covered in snow, with the equipment for vents, air conditioning units and an elevator. I see her tugging at the lock preventing her access into the building through a trapdoor, with one foot on the portal.

"End of the line, sweetheart. I think it's time you—" the crazy dame takes off.

She sprints towards the opposite side of the building and she does the unthinkable. In my mind I scream, yelling at her to stop, but the short athlete steps up on a piece of ventilation, a foot touches the concrete wall and she kicks off. She hangs in the air for a few seconds, pausing in a semi-glide before descending completely.

I rush over, fearful of seeing yet another body splattered against the concrete, but she made it to the roof of an adjoining building; ten feet down, six feet across. Already she's picked herself up and is now bounding off seeking another form of escape. I shake my head as I walk back to the entrance hatch to the lower floors. I can't believe the night I'm having. Why do they always make it so difficult?

Exhale. I stretch my legs and arms quickly, and pop my neck with a stretch to the right. I try to outrun the thought of impacting the second roof, to stop my muscles from tensing before making the leap. I run – I build speed, feeling winter's spite in my throat. *Faster!* I step up on the piece of ventilation, and then land a foot on the guard-wall. I leap.

There is a brief moment when I feel as if I'm flying. It's at the pinnacle of the jump where that feeling of weightlessness grabs hold like some invisible hand lifting from beneath you and through the air. The ground comes quicker than I expect.

My shoulder takes the impact then my arms, hips and legs. It's as if the rooftop slammed into me on all sides, wrapping itself around me like a tortuous cocoon which then spits me back out and across the blacktop. The snow only adds insult to the pain.

I hold my chest and gasp for air – the wind is knocked out of me! and for the life of me I can't open my eyes. I try to get my feet beneath me but the lack of oxygen makes the ground spiral out of control. I fall a couple times, having thought my left was under my right. Though as soon as I'm able to gulp air, my throat is grabbed and my feet drag across the tarred surface.

I force open my eyes just as my knees knock into and then dangle over the wall, my legs now free floating over the side of the building. His body is all in bandages, wrapped delicately and plentiful, yet what flesh that does show is as black as coal. I can smell burnt flesh flaring in my nostrils and his eyes bare down into me like blazing embers. It's none other than, Count Champ de Croix. He's alive! All this time. His voice is truly as dark as any pit.

"We are all subject to a tyrant, Mr. Bell, a sorcerer, that by his cunning hath cheated you of this island."

I cough beneath the pressure of his tight fingers, gasping like a drowning fish. My hands try and hoist myself up on his single outstretched arm. I try to kick—to climb, to reach anything!—but he has me dangling waist deep above the abyss with no intention of giving slack.

"You're alive?" I rasp.

"You're letting it all slide out of your fingers." He smiles a wicked gleam from sharp pointed teeth. "I've stood by watching you cry in the dark, and I've pondered, why haven't I put you out of your misery?"

He squeezes even harder and up until now I thought it was his best. But as I feel his grip closing in, crushing my windpipe, I know his power is without end. My air is squeezed out in a, 'yulp', now gone forever. I can't breathe, I can't breathe!

"It's out of no adoration that I spare you the pitiful fate that you've always longed for. But do so out of the consideration of *my* city—"

I realize the death I wield closest my heart. I tear away at the inside of my coat and pull out my gun. If I die, then I'll take the city's greatest villain with me a second time. Yet, in one single motion of his free arm, he swats it away to the darkness below.

"Heed this, Bell!" His eyes exhume a fire, the likes of hellish brimstone. He draws me within tongues length of his marred and excruciatingly foul face. "You must put an end to this usurper!" He demands. "The staff must be broken! The cycle must end!"

He hoists me back up over atop the roof; me skidding my knees, my hands and face now planted in the snow. I spin around like a crab and back up, desperately searching, seeking for a weapon to aid me against this horror. But when I look back to the spot he once inhabited, the fell creature is gone; disappeared into the fluttering snow and the pacifying silence of the city.

I sit there staring at the emptiness of his prior spot, both awestruck and terrified. My heart is pounding hard in my chest, my lungs feel bruised and battered, and my throat feels as though it nearly collapsed. I touch it, the pain to remind me that I'm still alive and I was assaulted by the demon from the Rue du Bourreau and not by some figment of my imagination. I see the footprints of where he once stood, like too impish eyes glaring out into the dark. He let me go?

This wasn't a chance encounter, otherwise he'd probably have assigned me an unmarked grave somewhere in the city's sewer or even stuffed down a coal-baked chimney. He said he had been watching me, but for how long? Why, and of what use does he see in me? First with the writing on the glass, the picture of Rachel, then back on Terrace Hill. What is it that he wants? Why does he continue to stalk me? He spoke nothing but nonsense! The Count is nothing but a madman!

I drop my head into my hands. So tired. I can't go on like this anymore. It's fine time I dropped and let the world pass into listless dreams. Its odd how everything makes sense when you're dreaming, no matter the bizarre, and then not when you're awake. The girl! I look, but I know well that she's gone and taken whatever that was hidden in the secret compartment of the player piano with her. How did I happen to miss it? It could have been the gift Emily had said she had for me. It could have been the last segment of the song, the very last few measures that would complete it all. Gone to who knows where?

PART III - THE SORCERER

Picking myself up, the pain radiates from joints to spine and then settles into my feet, making the stiff walk burdensome. I think I'll take the roof access to the bottom floor and then home again. The folios aren't safe on Nereid Street any longer. I fully hope the intruder saw them as nothing more than worthless notes. I'll spirit it away with me to my home apartment, and it'll be there that I collapse and say farewell to the past few days in slumber. Now, where is my gun?

It rests safely on my glass coffee table protected by a diligent guard of empty bourbon bottles and other case reports – the song that I labored so long on. I remember the day she finally came to, fumbling into the living room and lulling me with her, "I heard music." It's the very thing that brought her out of her illness, the melody she hummed on the street to Open, and the same she had me promise to never play it for anyone until it was finished.

How is it that she was able to come up with the rest when the melody began in my mind? Did it inspire her to muse out the rest, like some fancy turned obsession? Or is it more than that? Undoubtedly, I recognized the notes immediately once I read them, like being reunited with that long lost lullaby sung to you by an absent parent. Did it come from a time before? Is it proof that we had been some place, at some previous time, and that the two of us are trying to remember? That or perhaps a bond formed between us, a subconscious exchange of information. Maybe I hummed it in my sleep and she would sit and listen to it at night. Too many possibilities for this exhausted investigator.

I am sure to lock the door to my apartment. In my bedroom, I shed my clothing with malicious protest shouting from every pain receptor in my body. I squint, I squirm, but in the end I am free. I haven't even the time to store my reclaimed chirper beneath my pillow—unharmed from the fall—before my head reaches the cotton sheets and all is drowned by a field of white.

I wake near to my shift, still banged up and bruised, but with little time to spare if I am able to make it on time. My neck displays the worst of last night's ordeal as I have a perfect imprint of the Count's right hand; nothing but black and blue. I'm eager to return to headquarters and let Marty know of every detail. Then again, I'm unsure whether his moods have improved in the last twenty-four hours.

I know as soon as I step off the elevator. He's waiting there, leaning up against the wall but a few feet from the doors. Marty's eyes look worse, as if he spent yet another sleepless night here beneath the copper dome.

"Chief." Is his only form of greeting, hollow and worrisome. His head lulls to the right as if his neck can no longer support its weight and nods to my own. "Run into some trouble?"

"Naw—" something about the way he looks at me puts me on edge. I feel as if I've just walked into a wolf's cage. "I was chasing a suspect, then Count got the drop on me."

"I see." Is his monotone response.

No follow up – no question as to my well being, the situation regarding the suspect, or how the Count is still alive. Nothing. I nod an uncomfortable nod, and with a cobweb of nervousness descending on us in silence, I start towards my desk in search of recent reports. He tails quietly behind.

I scan the lobby, desks and then the hidden sections of the Govennet center. I see a total of seven officers, many of whom I trained myself, once cheery and well-conversed individuals, who now watch movements with hungry eyes and shut mouths. The click of my boots climb far above our heads, unimpeded by the silence that's enforced by the figures in the Greek frescos above. Brigit is no where to be found.

I find a stack of papers on my desk in a neat pile and I slowly shuffle through them to catch up on any leads on Ms. Valentine. I hope to look busy so that he'll leave me alone.

Marty closes in. "I took care of it all for you."

I drop the papers and spin cautiously around, seeing that he had been peering over my shoulder in a queer fashion.

His eyes are vacant, hopeless, yet his eyebrows lurk in the halls of aggression.

"Everyone has been properly assigned." He continues from a slight lapse in clarification.

"I see." I try to read him, try to peer beyond his skin and know what it is that's possessed him so unkindly, but see only daggers in that dull face of his.

"Dr. Dreval is here to see you. First thing, as you promised."

There's a hint to his voice, a squirming thing that burrows from the back of my brain to warn of danger. I pause, and hide a cheek.

"I don't know, Marty. I –"

The officers drop their busy work, papers on desk, feet on the floor, and they all slink towards us, as if rallied by my hesitation. A few desks away, their hands are disturbingly at their sides, but ready at a moment's notice. Their eyes have the same qualities as Marty's: vacant, yet domineering. I see it on their faces, a strange change that's infected them like some callous disease tearing away at their souls. They're lifeless, emotionless suits of flesh that now surround both Marty and I, he the ever-unblinking husk that he is. It frightens me.

He doesn't say a word. He doesn't need to. I nod in compliance, petrified of what might occur if I refuse.

"Alright, Marty. I'll see Dr. Dreval."

The white suited physician chuckles as he shifts through his leather carpet bag for random medical implements. "It took some coaxing, but I see your associates finally got you here."

Dr. Dreval is snug inside a canvas lab coat, with industrial-sized buttons that run all the way to his knees. He wears shined leather shoes. His hat, coat and cane are in the corner, leaving his balding head exposed to mirror the overhead fluorescents. With the warm escort I received from the front lobby, I'm surprised no one came in to watch the door to ensure I wouldn't struggle.

I expect him to pull out a syringe, but instead he yields a stethoscope and rests it round his neck.

"I'm assuming you've seen to all the officers who brought me here." I ask with no intention of hiding my apprehension.

"Yes, Mr. Bell. I was able to see each of them in due process. A grand majority of them in perfect health, so there isn't much worry for you there."

I was lead by the arm into one of the unused offices on the first-floor. It is small, barely enough room for files or cabinets. Previously, it was used for storage. Now there are only a few empty desks occupying the opposite walls; one for his mysterious carpet bag and the other for the patient. They took my coat and hat. They were even so kind as to relieve me of my gun.

"Can you unbutton your shirt, please? You can leave your undershirt on if you'd like."

I do so out of respect for the man, but after watching the display outside I'm convinced that he must have medicated them. Refusing would only put him on the defensive and I don't need to be rough-handled by my own men.

He checks my heart rhythm, has me inhale-exhale and then returns back over towards his bag to scribble on an adjacent clipboard.

"What did you give them, doctor?" I finally ask, careful to watch his pen for any interruption.

He continues writing without a hint of hesitation. After setting it done, he replaces his stethoscope in the bag and digs for something else. Victor's expression are unchanging.

"Give to whom, Mr. Bell?" He's playing coy.

"Well, Marty for starts, then the rest of my officers."

He blinks, trying to paint himself innocent. "Nothing, why?"

"My people don't act like this, especially Marty. I've never seen him with such ire. He's been obsessed with having me undergo your physical since he underwent your care. I'm an investigator, Dr. Dreval. I know when things are out of place."

"Oh, I see." He pulls out a tiny flashlight and rolls it with both hands like a cigarette. "You think their behavior is due to something

I've done. Mr. Bell, may I ask you a personal question?" My silent suspicion gives him his answer. "When was the last time you had a drink?"

I'm confused by his question, puzzling over it as if it may have hidden meaning. "Just last night, why?"

"Hmm." He puts the end of the flashlight close to his mouth and then points at the emptiness in front of him as if highlighting his words. "And how about yesterday and the day before? How much did you drink then?"

"I don't see how this is important, doctor."

"Humor me, how much?"

He stands there like an overbearing parent demanding a confession. Already ill at ease, I start to feel uncomfortable – like he's trying to get more from me than just a physical.

"Last night I had a drink at the Stardust, the night before that I had another –same place. Then the night before that, I nearly finished out a bottle."

"I see." He makes a quick notation. "Mr. Bell, to answer your previous paranoia, a lot of your fellow officers—including your dear friend, Mr. Kessler—have expressed their concern for your overall health. Not just for your physical health mind you, but your emotional health as well."

I dance between his eyes, searching for treachery, looking for some matter of deceit.

He sighs from a heavy heart. "I was informed that you had undergone a mental breakdown in the past and since then you've done nothing but work. You've shrugged off the help of your friends' and colleagues' invitations, and have locked yourself up in that apartment of yours – if I'm not mistaken. How long ago was it?"

My eyes sting and I feel desolate. Could it be that my own friends, my fellow officers, have been so worried? Is that why they've been so aggressive? No, this isn't right. I feel it in my—

"Four years." I blurt out. "Five days." An automated response.

The venomous snake shakes his head. "I do apologize to you, Mr. Bell, for I encouraged them to be a little stern with you. I felt you were avoiding me and thought it my duty as a citizen of the CitySpire—and who we all owe you a grand debt—to help you through your time of pain." He puts his hand on my knee and speaks with such gentility. "You're wounded, Samuel. Not of body, but in your heart. It's a terrible poison you've concocted. All these years tormenting yourself. It's time to let that go. Time to let this city take care of you, like you've done for us."

The memories, her face, it all floods to the front. I see her lying there on the street, still in her white silky dress, cold and broken. The pain, now, the guilt. It's all there, welling in my eyes and I try to bite it all back. I shake my head to drive him away.

He leans in. "It must have been awful for you – having to carry the one you love through the city with no one there to lend you a hand. Desolate, alone, afraid. You must have felt powerless to save her. The guilt of not being there when it happened. I'm so sorry, Mr. Bell. It's absolutely heart wrenching."

My heart is cleft in twain, my muscles weakening, my eyes betray me in a single tear.

"That's what I was looking for." He says with a cold inhuman voice.

He quickly shines the light into my eyes as my emotions drop. Nothing but white…

The white luminescence descends above me, basking the room with its effluence. I see white ceilings, glowing walls; everything is warm.

I'm lying on a table of sorts, metal by the feel of it. I have no clothes. So warm. There's a parallel table not but an arm's distance away, stainless steel and shimmering. Another leafless form rests atop it, catching her in my peripheral, a woman with long platinum-blonde hair. I roll my head to see her.

Beautiful. Her skin catches the light magnificently, both pallid and pure. She's milky white, flawless. Her breasts are round and perky, her hips are curved and shapely, her eyes as blue as a cloudless sky. She rotates her neck towards me in reaction to my movement. Luscious lips, delicate curls, she smiles at me.

I return one filled with utter longing. "Is this a dream?"

Rachel blinks slowly. "No…" her cheeks hide dimples. "Not a dream."

"How did I get here?"

She laughs, like the sound of tiny bells kissing my soul. "You've always been here." She says.

I shake my head. "I don't understand." I pause, listening to a distant electronic humming. "What are we doing here?"

"Hmm." She purrs. "Being born."

The tension in my cheeks fade as confusion sets in. She looks back toward the ceiling, just as a silvery object hovers up her opposing side. It's spherical, no larger than a basketball, with a center blue lens that opens and closes like the shutter on a camera. Its hands are long metallic instruments comprised of polished steel, plastic tubing and a variety of unknown tools; some jagged, others not. It holds a human arm in one of its industrial appendages, her arm! and joins it to her side with a light buzz and heavy sparks.

I try and escape, but my limbs aren't responding. When I look, I see myself in halves. My bottom portion is lain out as a metallic skeleton, with panels of flesh resting alongside tiny screws, microchips and tubes. I can feel my heart pulsing mechanically in my chest, racing as I panic. It can't be! It isn't possible!

Another sphere floats along my flank, *blinking* quizzically at my sudden rise in heart rate. One of its arms ascends towards my face, a pencil-sized flashlight that buries the light of the room into my corneas. Drowsiness forces me to succumb to unconsciousness, an empty horrid place – stillness.

There, it's cold and unforgiving. I hear voices, both familiar and unfamiliar, echo around me.

Emily's voice sweeps in with the distant sound of waves, *"What did I dream about?"*

My own follows after. *"Do you know where you are?"*

"Do you?" A pause. *"You're so polite to me."*

From the shadows of nothingness emerges seven spinning rings levitating in a row, the last on each end are more obscured than the others. Each one spins at a different speed and direction.

Marty's voice chimes from their rotations.

"Well boss, whad'ya think? Should we choose door number one, door number two, or door number three?" and then, *"Rational people can think for themselves. I'm over being city-struck."*

I hear myself again, an echo of what once was.

"I wondered whether you and Mr. Locke had any recollection about the past. I see now that we all suffer the same."

"Michael pretends that nothing is wrong, that everything is the way it should be. I wish I could adopt his beliefs, but no matter how hard I try, I cannot deny this feeling. Call me crazy, but there is something wrong with this city." And Natalie.

Michaels interrupts, casting himself overtop the others. *"You'll both have to excuse me. I've picked up a copy of Shakespeare's 'Tempest'. I can't get the character Caliban out of my head. He's quite the villain, you know."*

The haunting tones of the Count, crackles in my ears above the sound of a roaring flame. *"You are the face. I am the hand."*

Then someone I don't know, a woman's voice. *"You're just lucky you are who you are. If you were anyone else, we would have killed you."*

"Why, you have a thing against killing govennet officers?" I echo.

She then sharply replies, *"Something like that."*

The rings continue to twirl, relaying mysterious messages and unknown feelings. I am captivated by their wonder, and the longer I stare at them, the more I realize the meaning of purpose and all who are caught within it. Yes, everything is so clear.

Then I hear that familiar song once more followed by the scent of lilacs. I can hear Emily once more. *"Three times and then declines forever. It's not safe. Go! Go now!"*

The rings fade with the voices, the dark erased by the night formation of walls and furniture, now taking form in my bedroom. The feeling is gone, the whole thought of purpose, meaning and why. I had it, I believe I had it all! The future was only a hand's grasp away. But it all washed away like sand on a shore, drifting back into the crevasse from wince it crawled.

I gather myself and look about the room, everything in its place. Why am I here? What happened with Dr. Dreval? I remember the light in my eyes, his sudden change in disposition, and then? Everything is blank from then on. I don't feel any different, no change or unexplainable urges. Yet I know, deep down, that something did happen, but what?

I'm still in my clothes. *Not safe.* I check my surroundings: nothing in the corners, the closet open but empty of danger. A crustacean of paranoia scuttles across my backbone and I shudder to chase it away. Emily said, "Not safe," and with that, the chords of the song form in my mind. The folio! I have to hide the folio. I don't know why, just an urging, just the feeling of something impending on the horizon. A foul breeze, a crinkling of dried parchment? Call it what you will. A lot of things don't make sense right now, but I intend to get to the bottom of it.

I rush out of bed and head straight for the living room.

My gig is gone, most likely back at the station where I originally left it, which means someone else dropped me off. Someone didn't want me to have it. They knew that I'd have to return to the station to acquire it. But I can't go back. It isn't safe. I don't know who I can trust anymore. Dr. Dreval has turned Marty and the rest of the officers against me, that's for certain. What plagues me most is whatever he did to the others, why didn't it work on me?

Dr. Dreval, that son-of-a-bitch! I was already suspicious he had something to do with how everyone's been acting, yet I was still lured by his lies to think it was all my fault—it's as if he needed me emotional. *"That's what I was looking for,"* is what he said. But why? Why did he do it? To torment me? Did he do it simply to flaunt some demented need to bring up painful memories? What was it that Marty said, something about rational people? All my effects were left waiting for me in the usual spaces, my gun on the table.

I exit the lobby doors to my apartment building and walk out onto the street. It's still night time and the snow has ceased its fall. An unusual desolation grips this portion of the CitySpire. It's all foreign where it should feel familiar. There are the same lampposts, the building across the street, the recent fallen powder and tracks from those who ventured atop it earlier. Everything is as it should be, but I can't shake the feeling of sinister things.

The concrete walls appear taller, stretched high into the canopy of gloom that shields the unlit floors above. Light, if it can so be described, is twisted to diabolic purpose, only revealing so far to solicit a false belief in sanctuary. It conspires cunningly with whatever devils lie beyond its reach. I watch the darkness, much as I had the day I confronted the dastardly Edgar. The very same recognizable sensation I had walking down those dreadful steps lingers with me now.

Then my throat leaps into my brain, as I swear I see him, there between the shadows of the buildings, a form of a man snug in his coat and fedora, watching me from the dark. A spy? A pursuant? An executioner? If I'm being watched, then there must be reason for it – to determine if whatever Dr. Dreval did, actually took affect. I can't stay here.

I start off towards the west side pier, walking slowly in the snow while keeping my ear to the wind. I don't hear anyone following me, no extra crunch in the snow or swish of fabric. But the feeling refuses to abate, still lingering in the black windows and empty streets. Those precious feelings of security, confidence and power in my associates has dissipated, replaced by those of anxiety, of feeling small in a giant and overbearing world – feelings that the whole city is clawing to get me.

Every time I stare down a deserted alleyway I can count a few odd shapes that I can't quite place and so my mind envisions them with animation. Are they mannequins or are they men with black bags intent on indoctrinating me into empty servitude? Lost. Everything is so lost. I turn northward after passing Lexington to later take Dollimere and Ashworth Lane towards the Stardust. My only hope is to enlist Natalie's help. She could stash me somewhere, just long enough until I can get to Drevel or find some other means to right whatever it is that's gone wrong. How could I have been so blind to it?

Who do I trust? Who else can be in on it? My head keeps spinning with conspiracy and treachery. The true horror emerges from the shackles of my mind when I ask myself, what does Dr. Dreval have in store for the men and women of the Govennet? I look over my shoulder after hearing an unfamiliar noise. What follows me in the dark? I brush my fingers against the gun handle stowed away beneath my coat. Only time will tell.

27

I arrive during the change of the orchestra. The doorman saw that I wasn't dressed properly and at first was unwilling to admit me inside, but when I explained to him that it was a Govennet emergency the deadbolts release without a moment's hesitation. I find Mr. Weber backstage in a state of worry, directing hurried stagehands and half-dressed performers into their next act. He doesn't even realize the state of my appearance when I approach him.

"Johnny, I need to talk to you!"

"Not right now, Mr. Bell." He points to a shorter lad with red hair and freckles. "Jimmy!" Fingers beckon him to his side. "Jimmy." He tries calmly with limited success. "Go find Sal. He was supposed to be here an hour ago, all right? Now go!"

Jimmy backs away but almost collides with a band member. He then spins back around after an epiphany widens his eyes.

"What if he don't wanna come, sir?"

"Listen Jimmy—" he says a little flushed. "I don't care how you do it," Johnny bares the whites of his teeth and barks, "but get him here!"

"Yes, Mr. Weber." Spouts the stammering gentleman as he dashes off down a hallway.

The white tux host pinches his sinuses.

"Mr. Weber." I announce again, this time with a little more assertiveness. "This can't wait. I have something extremely important to tell you."

Natalie emerges from a side room, setting an earring while stamping her feet into high heel shoes. She wears a black cocktail dress with sequins that have little luster in the poorly lit backstage.

"What's the hold up, Johnny?" She looks me up and down. "Hi, Sam…" a pause and concern. "What's wrong with your neck?"

I try and dismiss it for more important matters. "It comes with the job. Look, I need to talk to Mr. Weber."

The stage director releases his nose, pretending as if he didn't even hear me.

"Natalie." He manages a smile beneath his headache. "We have to stall for time." He grits his teeth. "Sal's not here yet."

"Surprise, surprise." Her hands land on her hips. "So what's the problem? All these people and you don't have a piano player?"

"Not a good one."

Her blackened eyelashes blink nonchalantly. "Use Sam. He's good."

Johnny's cheeks draw back, his emerald eyes catch a glint of light and he raises and eyebrow or two. "Mr. Bell is a pianist?"

She sails over and hooks my arm with hers. "Only the best in the CitySpire. He's the reason I learned to sing." Natalie entices me with a wink. "Think you still have it in you?"

I sigh. "Mr. Weber, I really don't have time for this."

"What are you wearing, Mr. Bell? How did you get into my club wearing *that*? This won't do at all. Here—" he unbuttons his jacket, all the while Natalie removes my coat. "Anyone who had inspired Ruby to sing deserves to be out on that stage."

"Enough!" I cry. "Both of you, just listen to me for one minute."

She puts her hand on my sternum and hushes my heart. "Please, Sam? Just this once? It'll mean an awful lot to me, and you'll really be helping us both out of a bind."

I bite back my urgency as they sweep me up in the affair. I try to garrison support from Johnny.

"I've already taken off my jacket, do you need me to beg as well?" He cocks his head like a starving pigeon.

She touches my cheek. "It's just one song, Sam. Barely anything to it. All you have to do is look pretty and you got that down already."

Damn it. I relent and unbutton my shirt to get down to the tee.

"Good show, Mr. Bell. I cannot tell you how much this means to me." He says while handing over his jacket and bowtie.

"Thanks, handsome." She drops her hand. "It's a slow count – Johnny will get you the music. You don't have a lot of time to memorize it, so just get the idea and improvise the rest if you need to." Natalie kisses me on the lips. Smooth and warm. "I'll see you out there." She whispers before walking off.

My eyes drop to the sway of her hips as she disappears into the crowd of people. Difficult as it may seem, as I can't quite shake a tickle down my spine, I'm able to readdress my host.

He shrugs his shoulders. "Don't look at me, I just run the show." He blinks. "What's wrong with your neck?"

A triad of spotlights expel their brilliance down atop the stage, with a single drawing of the circuit. I sit at a black grand piano. I was led by one of the available stagehands so I wouldn't trip amidst the darkness of the stage. I was told not to move.

I shake the ivory keys by no will of my own. The audience, I try not to look at them, but instead fixate on the startling beauty at the microphone. I can still see them in my peripheral, shadowy silhouettes, both men and women of the CitySpire transfixed on my every move. I can taste a touch of bile creeping up the back of my throat as my stomach churns with anxiety. Nervousness – no matter how many mannequins I plug, it'll always be here in wait.

I try and remember back when I played for such a large audience, back when we all celebrated our accomplishments as comrades after burying the dead that littered the streets. Then I recall how the chords infuse me, how they take away the world and leave me with simple uncomplicated emotion, but that was years ago. I also had a few drinks in me at the time. Ready or not, I get the nod and am forced to play.

The notes come as easily as they had then. The dexterity in my fingers hasn't waned from exchanging piano practice for a gun. The music is tasteful, slow, and with a steady rhythm. The alto then breathes into the microphone and her voice tantalizes the audience like fine lace.

PART III - THE SORCERER

"Waking's good and well,

But dreams are better,

Not the other way.

The starling singer raises her hand to block out the light, and then gently draws it back to her heart.

"Mirthless clouds

Cold winds and water

Block my love of day"

Natalie draws her hands beneath her head, closes her eyes singing, *"And lying here — Images slowly,"* she pops them open again, wide eyed and hands outstretched to catch a fleeting memory, *"Disappear. Darling..."*

Waking's good and well,

But dreams are better.

Not the other way."

I shift the melody, jumping into a few measures of improvisation, just a series of added notes to fill in a gap of memorization, keeping steady in the counts so not to confuse her. With a dramatic upscale, I cue her into her next measure — she catches it without fail.

"But love, my heart

Belongs to you.

In the land of Nod.

Your kiss, dear sweetheart

Is surely missed

433

When I glimpse the morn.

My chest,
Painful in flutter
When the day's begun.

My hands drive the next part back to the original melody, using a variety of soft keystrokes for a smooth transition. Meanwhile, the raven-haired beauty keeps her counts and choreography, never to stammer on any given beat. It's as if it was all prewritten, as if everything came together as it's meant to be.

"Waking's good and well,
But dreams are better.
Not the other way.

Brilliant lights
Warm breath and body
Slumbering I'd rather stay.

Natalie grabs at an imaginary blanket and draws it over herself, hugging the fabric she continues to sing, *"As sleeping here — Images slowly."* A pause, before she extends her arms as if tossing flowers. *"Reappear, Darling…"*

"Waking's good and well,
But dreams are better.
Not the other way."

The song continues, a short repeat of the prior measures including a compelling array of lyrics and notes. Natalie looks at me emphasizing, *"Darling, reappear."* She winks, and in the moment everything stands still.

"Waking's good and well,"

Her voice builds in steps, *"But—dreams—are—better."* Holding that last note as her angelic voice reaches for the ceiling, before exploding with, *"Not the other way."*

Loud and ravenous applause fiercely descends upon my ears from both patron and backstage hands alike. It's a sound more inspiring—more glorious!—than the very song we performed, as nearly a hundred people give themselves into a standing rapturous ovation.

Natalie's smile opens to swallow it all, her teeth in glow from the spotlights above. She curtseys, as best as she's able in that tight-fitting dress, and then acknowledges me with an open palm.

Overwhelmed by it all, I scoot out the bench and come to standing. I smile to them, all the hidden faces in the audience – prominent members of the CitySpire. As I take my bow – a scream!

One, perhaps the second or third, but many others dispel the happy occasion with horrifying chaos. Blackened figures swarm in from the front door, pushing past both patron and wait-staff alike. Those who resist are knocked to the ground, and a club bears down atop them from a vicious hand.

"This is the Govennet!" Shouts a voice from amidst the mob. "Everyone stay where you are!"

I look to Natalie, her face both confused and awestruck. Her eyebrows rise in accusation, but I desperately shake my head to ward off her suspicions.

"We have to get out of here!" I scream to her.

"Johnny!" She calls out. "The lights!"

Everything goes dark.

People scream and panic. I hear tables topple, glass shattering and the rushing of feet in unknown directions to escape the pandemonium. Someone grabs my wrist and draws me away from the spectacle. I fear that the entire time I'm going to run into something.

Tiny handheld lights illuminate the backstage, barely enough to recognize fleeing feet and hastened fabric. The stagehands, quick to retreat, vanish down the hallways and into curtains of oblivion.

Our host holds a prop sphere to his face that ferries us with an orange glow.

"You promised me, Mr. Bell!" He points accusingly. "You swore you'd be a gentleman! Now look what has happened!"

"This isn't my doing!" I scream back at him over the sounds of turmoil. "It's what I tried to tell you, the Govennet has gone mad!"

I can see Natalie beneath the mild illumination as she grabs my effects and a coat for herself off a local rack, already planning our escape.

Johnny tosses his anger over my shoulder and presses his teeth together. "How much danger are we in?" He returns with stern though apologetic features.

"I don't know." I shake my head. "I think it's me they're after. They've done something to my men to turn them against me. They tried to do the same to me, but something went wrong and now they're here to finish what they started."

He points behind him into the dark. "Then go! Natalie will get you to safety. I can't have them find you here or they'll shut me down. Go! I'll deal with the interlopers."

"What are you going to do?"

"Stall them. Plus I've got guests to consider, Mr. Bell." He puts his globe in my hands. "Besides, it'll look suspicious if the club owner is nowhere to be found. I have to keep face."

I nod to him. "Thank you, Johnny. I knew when I came here that I could count on you."

His hand drops on my shoulder and he looks me in the eyes. "As I see it, Mr. Bell. We all owe you one. Consider this my debt for the work you've done."

He holds out his hand and I take it up, but when I let go he catches me by the cuff.

"I'll still be needing my coat back, Mr. Bell. After all, a good suit is hard to find." I blink as my mind processes the request, but am quick to shed it into his hands without the time for rebuttal. Once it's safely back on his shoulders, he offers us a salute before retreating down the hallway. I hear a *good luck* before he's swallowed by darkness. I don't know why, maybe the suddenness, but I get the feeling that I'll never see him again.

I haven't long to muse on it before Natalie tugs at my arm. "Come on! This way. We're wasting time."

I follow her through a maze of costume racks, desks, and boxes of clutter then into one of the dressing rooms. There, she kicks a hidden latch that sets the center pane of a three paneled standing mirror ajar, no longer affixed to the wall. She pries it open and urges me forward. Pushing forward, she secures the passage behind us.

We're in a short but narrow hallway, with a rusty staircase towards a higher portal waiting at the end of it. I hold the globe above my head in order to better examine the battered drywall and exposed insulation that occurs every few feet.

"What is this place?"

She snatches the globe from my hand, replacing it with my coat and shoulder holster. Natalie briefly places her finger to her lips before whispering, "This was originally part of the building. Johnny just covered it up so as to have an escape route."

The thought strikes me funny, but not in the laughing sort of way. "Why would he need an escape route?"

"He likes to be prepared." She replies as together we start up the staircase. "He's a good man. Johnny always thinks ahead."

I find now that Marty's interest in Mr. Weber is justified. "Don't you think that this is just a little too suspect of Mr. Weber's activities?" I ask.

"Don't be so suspicious. He just doesn't trust that many people. He's taken quite the shine to you though. Not that I'm surprised."

Natalie leads the way up the rickety stairs and then stops at the door. It is here that I feel the cold from the outside seeping in from the hinges, already threatening to nip at my cheeks. She adorns a brown fur coat she took from the downstairs as well as some elbow-length gloves.

As soon as I'm ready, she opens the door onto a third-story balcony. It's a tiny overlook that looms above a narrow alleyway opposite the Stardust entrance. She snuffs the light and tosses it into a snow pile. I can barely hear the hum of idling gigs from off the street, and at times I notice the passing of a spotlight weave between the cracks of the buildings before carrying on elsewhere. Natalie searches the sky for the vehicle, waiting patiently for the surge of aerodynes to distance themselves before stepping onto the stone promenade. Her high heels click delicately, as they pass through the snow to a drift where it's all collected. She tugs at a corner of it, unveiling a piece of tarp and creep-stained wooden boards.

"Help me with this." She whispers while grabbing an end.

I rush to her aid, pull back the canvas and hoist a two-foot wide plank up the railing and across the five-foot expanse to a neighboring balcony all by her direction. She sits along side it to slip off her heels.

"I hope you're not afraid of heights, Sam." She holds out her hand. "Help me up."

I help her climb the stone rail and atop the board. It certainly looks strong enough, if its weight is of any consternation. But I cannot shake dread from stalking my nerves. I don't quite fear the total lack of balance or the danger of the board slipping off the railing, but more the sudden hit of vertigo or the passing of an ill-wind to send her tumbling over the edge. I hold my breath as she starts out across the plank. I note a missing hesitation on her part and assume she's done this before. She makes it across—one foot in front of the other—without waver. Once on the other side, she slides her shoes back on and motions for me to follow.

I look up at the sky and listen for any approaching hum or whirring that could indicate the return of the gig, but here churns only the static sound of those on the street-side.

PART III - THE SORCERER

I hoist myself onto the railing, careful not to get my feet stuck between any of the rungs of the banister when I first step onto the makeshift bridge. I test it for sturdiness and once satisfied plant both feet on the end. All I can see is the blackness of the creep from the board blending into that of the adjacent wall. I imagine a black line drawn over the white snow, but looking down would risk the feeling of being drawn in. I keep my eyes forward to avoid smacking the pavement. The pain from the night before reminds me of what such an occurrence would entail. My best solution is to picture a line, stare ahead, and place faith in my abilities to complete this hellish sobriety test. I focus on Natalie.

One foot after another, I slowly cross the chasm sending prayers to whatever arbiter presides over misfortunes. The bite of the season is upon me, but the winds have calmed enough not to leave a whisper. So with little complication from either mind or nature, I'm able to cross the synapse and end with two feet on the opposite side. Yet before I'm able diffuse my anxiety, I hear the gig returning our direction.

Natalie leans over the balcony looking skyward to see the pair of flashing bulbs and a search light painting the nearby rooftops. Pressed for time, she pushes the board back over the railing and together we break for shadows as it clanks its way to the ground below. I glance over my shoulder as a beam of light hits our previous location and then fixates on the fallen board. We quickly duck around a corner before the light swoops upward to tag us – narrowing our escape.

Slowly we make our way to other buildings, up derelict ladders, across walkways and window ledges, until we're a block away and out of view. We stop at the last building that overlooks a vacant street far from the Stardust. Here the snow is flawless, untouched by foot or hand. Together our gaze wraps around the empty buildings, the reflections of glass, and the sparkles cast by the street lamps across the fields of white.

"Makes you wish for better times, doesn't it Sam?" The finger-wave beauty pulls out a case of cigarettes, taking one for herself before handing one to me.

I shake my head in its refusal, but thank her just the same.

She snaps the compact shut, replacing it in her coat pocket. "Seems now is good time to start." Her hands shake while trying to light the cigarette, a brass lighter held firmly in both hands, but the trembling only encourages the flame to dance around its end.

I take the lighter from her before she gets too frustrated and hold it steady while she inhales at her end. She lets the smoke trail out of her mouth, like water running upwards. I can't tell if she's scared or cold, maybe a little of both, but she's always hidden things well. Her cheeks are smooth with a hint of redness and her eyes are thick with mascara.

"Are you alright?" I ask her while listening to the silence that has snuck up on us.

"I'll be fine." She looks down, avoiding me. "But it's you that I'm worried about."

"I'm always full of trouble." I say while trying to catch her gaze. "Can't seem to catch a break."

"Until it catches up to you." She nods to my neck. "I just hope I'm there to help you when it does." She looks up. "I'm frightened for you, Sam. The Govennet—this city—it's just eating you to pieces."

Most women would have dew in their eyes, but not Natalie. She's strong, always has been. Considering the circumstances, I wouldn't blame her if she had. Yet I fail to understand what she means.

"People flock to you, Sam. I can't explain why, but everyone feels it. Michael, Marty, Johnny, even Boenger thought kindly of you even after the whole affair with Emily. It's like everyone sees something in you, something they can't quite put their finger on. They all demand so much out of you, you never get a moment's rest. And where some people see salvation, others find it threatening – especially those who recognize the hold you have over people." She lets the cigarette burn between her fingers. "It's like you're important – meant for something. I've known this about you since the day I met you, both Michael and I did. It's like the city has something in store for you. It's like the day on the roof when you refused to come with us, you knew you had to stay behind. Then after Emily died, and you eventually got better, it didn't take long before you and

Marty were taking up the calling and talking about forming the Govennet. Then night after night, fighting those creatures, Sam? It's as if it's all building to something and no matter what there is nothing that can be done to stop it – and it frightens me, thinking that dreadful things will become of you."

She trembles even more and I can almost see the run of emotion that she's been holding back. I take her up in my arms, hugging her to scare the tears out. Her hand is placed on my chest and she lays her head against my sternum, sober as ever.

"Things will be all right." I whisper. "I'll figure this out. I can fix this."

"Oh – Sam." She sighs. "And what will you do then? Continually patrol the beaches, standing ever vigilant against that which goes bump in the night? Will there ever be a time when this city no longer needs you?"

I place my cold hand on the back of her head feeling the softness of her hair. She's frightened for me and I don't blame her.

I try my best to console her. "We make our own way, Natalie." I pull back, still holding her at the waist. "The Govennet, my friends, the trouble they're in is all due to greedy men, not by some hidden being. But now I have to set it right. I won't rest until I punish those responsible – not until everything is back the way it was."

Her eyes bounce between mine, a quiver in her lips. "Things will never be the way that they were." She touches my face. "But we can still make the best of how things are now."

My heart skips and I see the meaning in her eyes. Her kiss from earlier, her fears, it all points to this. They've always been that way, even before that night we spent together when Emily disappeared. Natalie and I have fancied one another since the beginning, though never quite understanding it. It's like a pull that's hard to fight. My soul jumps from her to Emily, then to Marty and all the other members of the Govennet. Why here? Why now? Why am I always stuck between a kiss or finding a means to escape it?

I remember back to Emily, her words echoing painfully through my head, *"I'm not her."* The haunting disappointment on her face burned an impression in my heart and it pains me still.

I collect her hands in front of me, causing her to drop what little of her cigarette was left in the snow. In her features I see a patient suffering, a tiny torture caused in waiting for an answer to a proposition that's not yet been spoken. I open my mouth to decline but I halt – damn it all, do I really want to throw this away? What good is left for me in this world? I owe her much, and it's not as if there isn't love. For Natalie, all I hold is love. The moment is still, she waits for me with all her heart, I can see it staring longingly beneath her makeup. Decide – seize it for what it's worth, or else never be again!

Forward, I choose. I lean in, directing my lips to encapsulate hers. The poison in my veins is given pause and I realize what it is like to be free from it all. My heart suffers guilt, but I'm convinced that it'll pass. Emily is gone and I'll never be able see her again, but does it mean I must brave the city empty and alone? Must I constantly be pained by the memory of what should have been? I was stalled once by a woman of mere imagination, and now Emily has become that same fixation. Rachel, nor any—wait!

A figure is there on the street making her way northward. She clutches tightly to a black long coat, walking with a constant look over her shoulder, keeping a weary eye for all horrors this city has to offer. I see her hair, shorter now, a dull wheat curl that glimmers as the light brushes against it.

I recognize the face by a scream in my veins—echoes from my dreams—both in vocals and spirit I shout, "Rachel!"

With a start, the pedestrian whips her head around to see who it is. I rush to the railing, plant my hands on the top of the banister and call out to her again. She doesn't recognize me, cannot see who it is that's cast so ghoulishly on the dark balcony. Her eyes squint her hand tries to cast off the overhead streetlamps to see whether it's friend or foe. It does her no good and leaving little to chance, Rachel sprints, laying tracks northward into the silence of the city.

I plea towards Natalie, then back to the street. She's alive! The woman from my dreams is alive! And I cannot let her escape. Not that I know she exists! Not now that everything doesn't seem for not! I start after. Then, I remember another.

PART III - THE SORCERER

"Natalie, I—"

Her lips are drawn back, her eyes now damp with tears, yet she holds herself up. "Go." She mutters. I pause shortly to try and explain, but she waves me off. "Go!" She commands. "There's little sense stopping it." She sniffs.

I cannot let time tick against me. I break our company – invigorated by the knowledge that all this time I wasn't dreaming of phantoms, but left with a horrid taste in my mouth.

I toss back at her. "I'll come for you." As a storm pipe caters my escape to the ground below. Natalie will be okay. I have to keep on her! Once I catch her, I'll explain things. She'll understand.

Farther up the street I run, not knowing where she'll take me, but committed to searching this city until fatigue claims me. Rachel holds the key, the answer to everything: the light under my apartment door, my dreams of her, my lack of memory, the secrets of the CitySpire – all of it! My continued existence depends upon it. I cannot let her slip through my fingers, I won't allow it.

She takes me six blocks up and then a few westbound. The streets become hazier the longer the pursuit stretches on. At one point, I think I lose track of her. Quick as I may have been, she's gone and proved the faster. But all is well when I find that she has run through a narrow alley with tiny patches where the snows have failed to accumulate. She's trying to shake me. As fate would have it, a few pieces of ice dropped off her shoe and point me in her direction.

Once she believes me gone, she returns to the street to keeps a steady pace to whatever her destination may be. I decide to take a more subtle approach, trail her at a reasonable distance so not to inspire yet another flight. I follow her shoeprints and keep out of sight. I use the shadows, hiding behind lamp posts, trees and other hideaways to keep a close eye without attracting attention. I have to be cautious as she looks over her shoulder every-so-often as if she knows that I'm there. But she never stops or indicates that she's spotted me, as after checking the road behind her, she continues on without the slightest change.

All the while I think back on dreams. Always they have been with longer hair, but her tresses match; the background was white, bleached out by some obscure source of illumination; blue dazzling eyes infused with a supernatural glow. It was a dream then and such things could easily be dismissed as embellishments. When the Count gave me a photo of her, I did not know whether it was some form of a trick or whether it was genuine. At the time, I couldn't afford to dismiss her as a figment spawned out of loneliness or desperation. After Emily's death had rendered me ill, the dreams of Rachel were replaced with those belonging to Emily – especially ones filled with self-blame, guilt, and anguish. Then there was Dr. Dreval who unintentionally triggered something in my mind to bring her up again – pleasant at first, then a nightmare.

I feel the warmth of hope flowing through my veins quicker than ever before, an irregular push in my arteries that beg me to rush over her and draw her into my arms. But no, wait – breathe and be patient. Eventually, she'll have to stop somewhere and it'll be then that I'll have my chance to introduce myself properly. That way, she won't panic. That way, I won't risk losing her in this labyrinth of empty blocks.

Still night, but I'm unsure of the time, Rachel enters a five-story brick building of sorts. We're close to the sea, I can smell the saltine fragrance push back the tinge of the creep, and I can slightly hear the rolling of waves. It's a worn warehouse, stained and antiquated. The outside windows are filthy, making it difficult to see past the grime. Those on the higher levels are cracked or even shattered.

She ascends a small set of concrete stairs with a missing rail, then atop a shoulder height loading dock and through a metal door. I give her a few minutes before I travel up the same steps and try the knob - soon entering as quietly as I'm able.

I expected fine furnishings, maybe some draperies or a four-post bed, but no – nothing of that sort. It's dark, with only a few emergency lights on the concrete support beams that hold up the twenty foot ceiling. Above, long strips of opaque plastic crinkle from the wind, flowing over standing boxes and plastic silhouettes. Department store mannequins are everywhere. Each glossy figure is posed in some expression of pantomime, both men and women bare-chested and exposed legs, appear as if reenacting some piece of drama or dance.

Creepy – enough that my neck hairs chance an escape through the door behind me but are caught by their epidermal masters. I draw my gun, careful and cautious. It may be Rachel, but it doesn't hurt to be on the safe side. I keep it low so not to mistake open hostility. There's an office window to my left, open and empty, just a devoid space where administration should be, even the door is missing. I catch a glimpse of some ominous stairs leading to a higher floor, nestled against the back wall.

A direct path takes me through the middle of the mannequins. Though harmless, they give me the heebie-jeebies. Maybe it's all about word association, or maybe it's because I don't like things staring at me from behind panes of glass. Whatever it is that causes my aversion, I force a concession as I brush past a piece of plastic as I stealthily move across the center floor.

I try not to look, but it is *they* who look at me. Ambiguous features stare blankly, mirroring my discomfort in their plastic shine whenever I get too close. My eyes play tricks as I attest to the moving of fingers, the turning of heads and the nearing of feet. My mind leaps to the convenience store massacre, seeing those figures in the windows, pounding away at the glass, detached like the specters in the windows on that fateful trek towards Nereid Street. I turn away, repeating to myself that they're only casted shapes – nothing more. Yet the feelings linger, the thought of them being alive, as if something had given them soul, and they outreach with their synthetic fingers to drag me into some dismal prison.

Sheet plastic impedes my journey at every turn, and once free, I'm but feet away from a naked figure and I flee only to be entangled again! My heart throbs in my thighs, a cold sweat builds across my brow, and I acquire a tightness in my lungs, making it hard to breathe. I try to keep my calm, try not to panic, but air comes sharper and quicker and then the room grows smaller. I run to the other end of the warehouse, uncaring of how my boots strike tellingly against the concrete floor and echo up the walls. They pass as they had the day

445

Emily died, like smoke and mirrors, all blurring together like pictures on a wall.

I make the stairs without stopping, slamming my shoulder into the adjacent wall. I lean there, gathering my nerves and forcing my lungs to expand, a hand to rub the pain out. I dare not look behind me or over my shoulder to assess the distance. I've beheld my share of demons for the night. I still have to find Rachel, and the only direction left for me to go is up.

Music hits me about mid-way, faint, but growing by the stair. Once near the top, I'm able to hear the string of notes clearer and reminiscent of that tune that follows the Count, both in the lobby and on the violin. The landing grants access into a short hallway where, from a mundane door frame, casts a twinkling of beautiful prismatic colors across the wall. They shift like tiny fey, faint and blinking from one part to another before returning to a prescribed rotation. The lights are coming from farther inside.

I peek my head into the room and am stunned. Surrounded by crates that are piled along the walls, mixed with mannequins striking positioned arabesques, is a three-dimensional image of an ethereal ballerina performing a set of motions. She wears a white leotard and fishnet skirt puffed into a tutu, showing off her form as she dances. Once through, a good fifteen seconds at least, the image wavers with static and begins anew. Tripod set projectors feed a reel of images through their convex lenses, constructing the phantom with aide from an overhead dome that drizzles a light fog.

From out behind a set of boxes dances a young belle, perhaps younger than I've yet to see. Her height is dwarfed by the ghost-like ballerina, she the size of a child, a few inches short of five feet, straight black hair with an angled bob cut. She concentrates, oblivious to me—now a shadow's length into the room—and attempts the same movements as the image. Her form is precise, her grace is transcendent, and when she twirls in incandescent pirouette, I simply marvel as if in view of a goddess. As she travels into the light, I recognize her as the thief from night before.

At ballet's end, she catches me in the dark, now frozen in surprise. I take it upon myself to dissuade any rash action, to speak my good intentions. But when I step forward, I'm thwarted by a jolt to the head from behind. The pain rolls down me like an open faucet. The room descends on me like the melting of wax and then I with it.

28

The light digs through my eyelids like a surgical scalp, forcing caution as I open my lids. The glow makes it hard for me to focus, everything fuzzy, for my head feels like it's trying to turn inside out.

I'm lying on my back atop an examination table, metallic though with a give. To the left of me is another such table, beaming tangents of light back at the ceiling from the ever-intrusive florescent above. I look up at the large ring-shaped bulb that scores the center ceiling, my arm span at least in diameter. I shield my eyes before it singes an imprint on my retinas, blinking to wash it away.

This room – circular, with paneled white walls, floors and ceiling. I know this. Yes - the very room where Rachel had lain beside me, there on the other examination table. My eyes adjusting ever still, I see windows about twelve feet to the ceiling, dark tinted things that shroud a few silhouettes peering down from an adjacent room. I cannot tell who they are. They simply observe, some with arms crossed whilst others lean on the frame. Some appear to be conversing, but I cannot hear what they are saying, nor do I understand what they want with me. Patting my left breast I realize that my chirper is missing, taken obviously by my captors. I watch as one of the figures move off my right and then towards a reinforced steel door not ten feet from my heels. I brace myself for what comes.

The monster-of-a-hatch grinds and screeches from hidden mechanisms, then a release of air with a retraction of what sounds like latches. The handle turns and the door eases open, a good six inches of steel withdrawing in its hinge. Down a pair of plastics steps, the blonde beauty, I've been chasing all these years, emerges like a star from the void of space. Her hair catches the light, reflecting in a warm halo that scintillates down her body, dispelling the drab that I first witnessed from the balcony.

She still wears her black coat which she keeps snug around her, a grey turtleneck and scarf, black pants and belt. All these things were procured long ago from the clothing stores of Hermes Square. I remember them well, pieces that were rejected by Emily for being too "plain" despite my encouragements. Then again, that was a long time ago.

I now sit up despite the wooziness that comes from being hit over the head. Together we take in every detail, count the buttons on each other's coats, identify the fabrics in our garb and study the features of one another's face. What it is that we're looking for? Deceit? A trick? But all I see is the embodiment of a dream, a glimmer of the mind made manifest before me and I cannot help but be held in awe.

Rachel's the one who trespasses on the silence, she still poised at the base of the stairs.

"Who are you? And why were you following me?"

The question catches me off guard. Not exactly the response I was anticipating. How can she *not* know who I am? Dreams aside – I thought everyone, even those who recently woke in the CitySpire have some idea of what I look like, my general office and deeds. It's the story everyone's given about why things are and how they've come to be – the first of many that the Registration Office is required to detail as part of a brief history of the city.

This must mean she isn't registered, and if she isn't registered, it must mean she has recently woke or she might be a screw-job. But if she's a plastie, why am I still alive? No. I refuse to accept that she's a mannequin, not after all I've gone through, not after all this time.

"Am I not the least bit familiar to you?"

She winds up her neck as if to indicate a 'no', but relaxes her muscles. "Not in the same sense of familiar that you're implying. My friends tell me you're Samuel Bell."

Not in the same sense? Then she *must* have dreamt of me as well.

"Yes," I nod with encouragement. "My name is Samuel Bell. I'm the chief inspector of the Govennet." I pause to savor this. "Is your name Rachel?"

Her previous winding fuels her now shaking head. "You must have me confused with someone else. My name is Felicia Rhodes."

"Felicia?" I brew it over in my head. "Felicia…Felicia…" I look down to help swallow it, then up again. "You said I look familiar?"

"I said, 'Not in the same sense of familiar' as you were thinking."

"What do you mean?"

"It means what it means." She crosses her arms. "You still haven't told me why you were following me."

I touch the back of my head—blood there—but at least the pain is subsiding.

"Would you believe that it was all because you looked familiar to me?"

"How so?" Had I been blind, I'd easily tell she holds a hint of antipathy.

How so, indeed. "Ever since I woke in this city, I've… *known* you. I've seen you in dreams, here—" I slip off the table only to stall from a moment of dizziness. Then I place my hand on the table beside me. "Lying, in this place."

She scrunches her face. "Is this some kind of joke?"

I start towards her. "No, I –"

Rachel pulls out a gun from her coat pocket, *my* gun. And the lights blinking indicate the safety is off and fully charged.

"That's far enough."

I follow her command, eager not to be shot on a simple misunderstanding.

"Rachel, let me explain."

"My name's not Rachel," the anger building in her nostrils. "It's Felicia."

"Rach—" I stop so not to provoke her. "Felicia, I'm not trying to pull anything over on you. I'm trying to be forthcoming and sincere. The day I first woke in the CitySpire, I witnessed the knob to my apartment door close itself shut, and a light from beneath the door disappear. I had no idea who I was, why I was here, but one thing that lent me belief in a past was dreams of you. Every time that I would sleep, you were there. Occasionally, I'd see you in waking – like a figment of my mind or a phantom. I know it sounds crazy, but I wouldn't make something like this up. For a long time I didn't think you existed, until the Count gave me a picture and—"

Her brow now marked with confusion, causes her hostility to wane. "You have a picture?"

"Yes –" I jump with excitement. "A picture! It's in my apartment behind one of the picture frames on the ledge behind my piano. You're wearing the same coat as you are now, standing in front of Hermes Square. Champ de Croix gave me the picture after a summons from Farley's apartment. I knew then that you were something more. Up until I saw you on the street, I had given up hope of finding you."

Her eyes recede into her sockets and her pupils dance between mine as if only one held any truth. I feel as if I am losing her, as if she's suspecting that I'm making the entire thing up.

"Please, Felicia, believe me. It may seem strange, but everything I am is because of you. There's so much of our lives unaccounted for. So many memories have been lost. Is it so difficult to think that maybe, just maybe, there is something to all this? I've never told anyone, not my fellow officers, not the Office of Registration, not even my best friend, because I knew they'd look at me as you do now. I don't claim to completely understand it. All I know is that on that street I found you familiar. And I thought—I hope, that maybe you find me familiar as well."

I've said my piece, there's nothing left. I've gone my entire life wondering if Rachel was alive and if so where she resided. I have so many questions that are unanswered, so many things I want to talk to her about. But now that I'm here, seeing that look of animosity and suspicion, it pains me in such a way so as to strike my questions mute. I've always assumed that we would share the same dreams, that she'd recognize me for who I am, and together bask in this spiritual connection. But now it seems that I'm the only one to have experienced it. I just wish that, for a moment, she could borrow my mind.

Rachel rears the chirper upwards. She calls out behind her, back to those looming shadows watching from behind the glass.

"We're taking him back with us. Once there, we'll let *him* decide what's to be done." She replaces the gun inside her coat. "No funny stuff. Try to run or attack any of us, and we'll kill you. Understand?"

I nod my head in compliance. "Whatever you say."

In the darkness emerge a few figures, some muscle bound, others slim; people dressed in frayed rags, cut jeans, slacks and coats, a ragtag collection of garments. It's as if they helped themselves to all the throwaways once belonging to street waifs. They escort me out of the room, keeping an uncomfortable proximity.

They push me forward through the large steel door and into the hallway. I'm bewildered at the transition, from a celestial shine to a rusty iron. The walls are worse, a thick metallic tube with arc welder burns and bolts the size of fists secure the pipes together. It must leak from time to time, as the area around each bolt is stained with a permanent rusty drip. The smell of salt and mildew flutters past my nose. From the look of things, I'd say we were underneath the city.

I glance briefly into the dim single bulb rooms that are adjoined to the previous chamber by the windows. They're small with just enough space for unusual electrical equipment that are both damaged and lifeless. I'm not given much leniency before I'm pushed ahead, a means to deter additional stalling. I give into their game of 'follow the leader', preferring them to see me more as a willing participant than a prisoner. It'll be easier on all of us.

I don't know where I am, but it seems irrelevant now. As long as I'm following Rachel, I'm on the right track. The Govennet will have to wait until later. It's not like I have much choice.

Our journey is wrought with a long list of turns, straightaways and stairs that drop a few levels or so. The pipes are wide enough for the entire crew of seven to pass through three-by-three, though they seem more apt to being scattered. Each one takes turns keeping an eye on me, more to ensure that I'm aware of their suspicious nature than to check if I'm still with them.

Rachel heads the party, keeping her back turned to me without the frequent over-the-shoulder paranoia that I had grown accustomed to. Beside her is a lanky man in a brown leather coat that's missing its right sleeve, short blonde hair and motorcyclist goggles. To my left is bald-headed man, average height, muscular and poorly dressed for this time of year. He wears cargo pants with more patches than pockets, heavy boots and a thin vest with a fuzzy-lined neck. On my right is a redhead, thin, with wiry exposed legs, a powder blue coat, fingerless gloves and funky yellow shoes. I doubt they started out that color. She's perhaps the most interested in me, transfixed on my every move even when I stare back at her. Most would look away; she on the other hand isn't shy about it.

Then of course there are the two gentlemen behind me: one who wears all black and enjoys the click of his boots far more than he should, and a gruff looking fat man with looks as if a brick from off Open smashed in his face. Tagging off to the side is the tiny ballerina-thief. This raven haired mote may appear sixteen but something about her, perhaps the way she carries herself with a straight back and weathered eyes, envelopes her in maturity. The CitySpire can be cruel and no one is free of its cold realities. Maybe that's why I've never seen any children.

"Can't thank you enough." Vibrates the man in black.

I continue walking, concentrating on my pace so as not to give them an excuse for another shove. "I beg your pardon?" I reply.

"Your gun, Mr. Govennet man. We're always needin' spares." He snickers through his nose. I can just imagine the smile freezing up into his cheeks. He must think himself clever.

"Stow it, Frankie." Rachel barks from the front.

"Aw – come on, Miss Rhodes. I'm just playing with the guy. I'm not meaning anything by it. Did I hurt your feelings, Govennet man? Do you miss your gunny-wunny?"

I crack a smile to myself. "If that was your intention, then no. You amuse me."

"Amuse you?" his voice riled with aggravation. "Tell me, oh great assassin of the populous, how is it that I amuse you?"

The she-wolf turns around, eyes flaring without losing step. "Shut the fuck up, before I fuse it shut!" She's cute angry.

"She sure told you." Comes the bald-headed base off my left. "You think she's angry now, just keep talking. Felicia is a terrifying woman when she needs to be. I've seen it."

"Oh yea, well maybe I'm not a flea-bitten pussy like—"

Rachel stops, pirouettes in a half-spin, draws my gun and fires. I'm given fair enough warning by the hum of the coils building charge, to duck out of the way. The sabot whizzes down the hallway, sparking against anything it passes. The shot thunders over Frankie's shoulder, momentarily lighting the rear tunnel.

"Whoa—just whoa!" He waves his arms as if ready to catch the next discharge. "What the hell are you doing?! Are you insane?!"

"Damn I missed." Rachel calmly addresses. "Keep it up, Folks. The angrier I get, the better my aim."

It's so quiet that I can hear the breath suck back into him. It appears she doesn't have patience for fools.

Rachel glances at me before taking her spot at the lead.

The red head in the blue coat locks her arm around mine, and calms me with a pat from her hand.

"Now don't you be worrying about, Frankie Folks. He may have a mouth on him, but he's a swell guy once you get to know him better. Frankie's just miffed about all those harlequins, or whatever you call them, that you put under." She leans her head onto my shoulder, the sensation of spiders running from beneath her hair informs me of her taunt. She sighs. "Those poor, poor dears."

The man with a squished face adds his notes to the choir. "Who knows, maybe they could have become prominent members of society if it weren't for gents like you with a superiority complex."

Sympathizers. It's all coming together now. I've heard reports of mannequin sympathizers hiding beyond the patrols, acting as a form of resistance against the Govennet and police forces. A regular pain in the neck, but never doing anything big or overly dramatic. Kidnapping a Govennet officer is an all new level for them.

"So easy for you all to say that, hiding down here in the tunnels while innocent men and women are slaughtered by the day by those soulless aberrations. They have no pity for you, no cares as to whether you live or die. I've seen men and women beg for their lives only to be ripped apart by the cold- blooded hands of the same 'people' you protect. Murder? I've been doing this city a favor. I rest easier knowing the good I'm doing for people like you."

The lass pulls hastily away as if I were dirt. "A favor!" she yells.

Brick-face interjects. "You need to stop doing us favors there, Sammy old boy. Aint't nothing *good* about the favors you lend."

Then the woman in blue lashes out. "You're just lucky you are who you are. If you were anyone else, we would have killed you."

"Why, you have a thing against killing govennet officers?" I ask.

She looks away. "Something like that."

Rachel stops and yells, "Everyone, just be quiet! For the love of all creation, he doesn't know!"

The pipes lose their echoes.

"What do you mean? What don't I know?"

Baldy is the first to speak up. "You'll find out soon enough."

Our journey ends at the mouth of a massive expanse. It appears to be some sort of silo, a cylindrical shaft where both ceiling and floor are shrouded in a veil of blackness. There is but a single rail serving as a buffer zone between a gruesome plummet into the abyss. The lights here are minute, making it treacherous to approach the edge without severe risk of a misstep. Had it not been for a rusty caged elevator suspended by equally dilapidated chains, I would have believed this my personal end.

As far as the ceiling is concerned, I knew that we were beneath the city, but not *that* far. Even with our long walk through the tunnels, taking possibly every staircase down farther into the underground, I figured twenty or thirty feet tops. They must have carried me farther than I thought. How long did that blow put me under?

The air here is humid, pushed up from below, making it slightly strenuous to breathe. I hear the sound of wind whistling through an opening above, a faint though recognizable sound that circles and carries down the shaft. There must be an exit of some kind, though from the look of the steel-plated walls and pie-sized rivets, it would be impossible to scale without the aid of climbing gear. With the opening above, along with the adjoining tunnels – a vent, this has to be an exhaust or steam vent. I've seen hot air travel out of sewers and storm drains before. It is possible that they are also connected to this shaft, or one of many.

Rachel unlocks the elevator door, tossing the chains that bound them together off to the side and then screeches them open. My traveling critics shuffle into the elevator, I along with them, as Frankie gives me a shove forward.

"That's not necessary." I say to him, my irritation now turned to ire, as I fix my gaze on his face.

He strokes his chin. "Aye, you're probably right about that, but it makes me feel better."

I ignore him for the moment, noting this in my brain for later.

After we're all inside, Rachel and the man with goggles close the doors shut and then pull the lever. I hear the whirring from above. From the roof of the cage I can see the workings of a motor, slow at first but then quickens as it feeds chains through a complex gear and pulley system. The elevator rattles and shakes its way down the chains as a few built-in wall lights are triggered by proximity, offering us just enough illumination to make out one another's faces.

It's a long descent, a long wait in the dark suspended in the air by a piece of antiquated equipment that's probably as old as the city itself. As predicted, the closer we are to the bottom, the more the heat rises. Sweat builds on my brow, perhaps the first ever because of the outside temperature.

I look out into the ebb, beyond the grated enclosure of the carriage. All those moments dreading the inevitable nothingness that comes after death pales in comparison to the anxiety I currently feel in this nether. The elevator invokes a sinking feeling, the dark — fear of the unknown and the heat just builds in my imagination the place we all know is reserved for the damned. The silence of these strangers offers me little comfort, even with the occasional look to Rachel. It's now I wonder just what saying a few prayers could do to increase my chances of escaping it. Here, I doubt anyone can hear me.

After what seems like fifteen minutes I finally spot a landing beneath us. With an end in sight, the visions of a torturous afterlife lift from my soul like a magician's cloth. Once the chains rattle to a halt, the swaying cage's doors are released by Rachel and her goggle wearing gent. I'm quick to exit the foul thing with only lingering fears of having to make the ride a second time.

The landing is small with just enough room to land a gig on. There's another reinforced steel door, but this one is heavier than the last and solid.

Rachel points to a wheel on the side door. "Biff, think you could do the honors?"

The man with a smashed face meanders up to the wheel and slowly and strenuously cranks it. All the while, I hear a knocking, like the popping of a corkscrew off a bottle of champaign. At the door, a panel opens as a keypad attached to a mechanized pole eases out. Rachel punches in a string of numbers, too quick for me to catch and then there is a rumbling, as gears squeal. Steam hisses out from the hinges and the door folds in like an accordion, separates and then slides into the walls.

Hidden behind the mammoth door is a brightly lit entryway with white paneled walls, ceilings and floors, a small ten-by-ten foot room with a second doorway already opened. Beyond that, as we all follow Rachel's lead, is a hallway with side doors and additional rooms. I can hear the fans coming off technical equipment, large towers that quietly buzz with computations and unknown processes. There's a familiar scent to the air, the clean smell of lilacs.

I'm taken through a collection of interconnecting hallways, varying rooms, and then down a few flights of steps before being stopped in a receiving hall.

"Wait here." Rachel says. "I need to fill him in on the situation."

She tosses my chirper to the bald gent.

"If he tries to leave, shoot him."

"Yeah!" Frankie tosses his hands behind his head and viciously pelvic thrusts the air. "That's what I'm talkin' about!"

The blonde points at him, shaking her finger. "And if he gets any more annoying, you can shoot him too."

"Patches won't shoot me, him and I are good buddies. Ain't we, Patches?"

Patches wipes the remaining sweat off his brow. "To what extent classifies more annoying, do you mean like continues to be annoying, or annoying'er than he already is?"

"What?!" He throws his hands out and tries to make himself look bigger by puffing out his chest. "Man fuck you, Patches. I don't need to take this shit." He stomps up the stairs. "I don't know why the hell we're spending so much damn time on this murderer anyway—" his voice trails, becoming inaudible once he rounds the corner.

"To answer your question," Rachel says while watching the stairs in case he comes back. "Continues to be annoying."

"Well, shoot." He snaps his fingers. "There went a perfectly good opportunity."

She smiles to his comment before turning her back and walking down a hallway.

"Patches?" I ask while smiling at the edge of my eyes. "Your name is, Patches?" I look around the room. "And I suppose his name is Goggles, right?"

"Actually." He speaks from a leaned position against the wall. "It's Spence." Not a tear of emotion bleeds from his features.

Perhaps that was said in poor taste. "My mistake." I mutter.

Patches in his fur lined coat points with the gun to a local chair. "Alright, smart guy. Take a seat. We might be here awhile."

For an hour I wait, sitting around with a bunch of misfits. The redhead cuddles close to Patches while sitting on the stairs, snuggling beneath his arm while doing her best to pretend that she's entertained. The man who introduced himself as Spence writes in a small pocket-sized journal. Meanwhile, the overly large and cosmetically challenged member of their coterie leans up against the wall next to my seat. His body aroma forces back the lilac perfume, all the while tickling my nose with the recent expulsion of sweat.

Across the room, sitting with her feet barely touching the floor, is the little thief from Nereid Street. She's been staring at me since I sat down, never once moving her eyes or diverting them when I look back. She makes me uncomfortable. There isn't malice there, nothing hidden deep inside her that wishes me harm, but her gaze is bothersome just the same. I've had just about enough of it.

"Is there something I can help you with?" I demand.

Her eyes are unfaltering.

"You're not going to get much out of that one." Patches defies from the stairs. "She won't talk."

"Why, is she mute or something?"

He eases back onto the stairs. "You know, for a big shot Govennet detective—"

"Chief Inspector."

"Right…Chief Inspector – you certainly don't listen very well. I said *won't* talk, not, *can't* talk. Only person she talks to is Felicia. Trust issues and all that."

"Don't we all?" They all stare at me as if I were the plague. I return to my earlier complaint. "So why does she keep staring at me?"

"You'll have to excuse Roz, she's just never seen one of you alive before."

"And just what does that mean?"

"A dead man." Murmurs the big guy beside me. His voice is like the grinding of stone, half-way between a cough as he says it.

"Is that supposed to be some kind of a threat?"

The redhead speaks up. "No way, Mister. It's not a threat at all. So don't worry, gov–," she gives me a wink. "You'll find out soon enough."

Everyone lifts their eyes, a signal that someone had entered the room. It's Rachel. Her eyes are downcast, shoulders slumped. She swings her arms as if they're lifeless and then points beneath her hip to the hallway behind her.

"He wants to talk to you." Her voice on the verge of a whisper.

"Bout time," Patches taps the woman in his lap to get up. "We've been waiting forever—"

"With Mr. Bell," Rachel then adds, "Alone."

Their expressions all collapse in a heap of open jaws, scrunched foreheads and prominent cheeks. But none of them say a word, just sit where they're at and dwell in the place where question marks make their nests.

I ease out of my seat expecting someone to say something, but instead only a shrewd awkwardness follows. I walk by Rachel, pausing only briefly to see her hide behind her hair. Without any word of encouragement or otherwise, I step into the hallway and proceed towards the door she had just entered through.

The door opens into a darkened space where the light from the hallway trickles into the room like a streaming brook. Here is where the smell is the strongest, the distinct aroma of lilacs. I can hear little save the soft rhythmic beating of something unknown though reminiscent of past lullabies. I must have triggered the motion sensors as the lights slowly brighten while I step inside.

At first there are only shapes, dark pieces of equipment and individual touch panels. Then I see lengths of rubber tubing torn out from behind the white wall paneling and drawn towards a bulky shape located at the back wall. The room is all walls, save for a small steel-framed door on the left-hand side. As the room takes form, I see a large circular ring-like apparatus, metallic, with ceiling wires and tubing attached to it. I see the figure of a man, or what appears to be a man, nestled partially in the construct with its arms outstretched as if hung on a rack.

With the light brightening, its silvery body reflects the glow from above: white plastic knee coverings, shins, pelvis and torso. I see the inner workings of its chest, a blue circular thing where its heart should be that pulses slowly but definitively like a drum. Then I make out its face, an almost clay and cream, human-like in its features, and eyes that radiate with an otherworldly blue.

The mannequin looks up at me from its niche in the wall. "Hello, Mr. Bell. It's been a long time." The automaton pauses as if to siphon my breath. "Allow me to introduce myself, my name is Richard Farley."

I shake my head. "That's impossible. Richard Farley is dead. I buried him myself." Just being in the same room as the obviously deranged creation puts me on edge. I take no comfort in his entombment in the apparatus and worry that my safety is in jeopardy. If I had my gun, he'd be in pieces on the floor.

"I assure you, I am one and the same."

"You can cut out the act," I say while examining his bounds from afar. "I'm not buying it, especially not from a screw-job who has his wires crossed. So whatever game you're playing, you might as well end it and get to the point of all this."

He shudders as a lax tube grows taut with the sound of liquid forcing its way inside his body. A tiny hiss of air then the tube falls limp, it isn't much after his demeanor returns to a misplaced serenity. It's possible, by some long stretch of the imagination, that whatever happened was not the least bit enjoyable.

"I do hope that the scissors didn't scar you too much, Mr. Bell." His fingers make a sad attempt to point towards my brow.

My heart jumps over beats like cracks in the sidewalk; the hiccup ripples through the rest of my body like a punch to the sternum. Dread. It clings to me like a drowning child.

"I see I've reached you. At least something good will come of this conversation." His porcelain-like face tilts, then manages a lazy smile before reverting to sobriety.

He couldn't possibly—no, it's a manipulation. I may not have been able to meet Richard Farley face-to-face, and aside from his magic tricks, I know for certain that he couldn't have been a mannequin then – because all mannequins come from the sea.

"No—" I shake my head to rid myself of his implications. "It was an old wound that just happened to open. As I recall, it was Farley with the scissors. It was just good old-fashioned happenstance."

"Happenstance is only one word for it Mr. Bell, depending on your point of view. From my perspective, I knew how to cut, but not why to cut and so I did. I watched as your arm rose and your nails dug into your forehead. Either way you look at it, it doesn't change that it happened."

"I didn't scratch my forehead." I watch him carefully for signs of treachery until I remind myself that mannequins have no emotion – as it is hard to discover a subconscious reaction to lying when there isn't a semblance of guilt. He says nothing. "For the sake of argument, let us assume that you are Richard Farley. Tell me, what was the last thing you did before you jumped?"

"I wrote in my journal."

"What did you write?"

"A note for you, Mr. Bell. It read: 'I am not dead and neither are you. It is imperative that you understand this in all things.' Need I go on, or does it satisfy your question?"

The words, though so many years ago, are deeply familiar to me. It's what he wrote, *exactly* what he wrote. The only way he can know this is – by the arbiter, he is Richard Farley, and he didn't come from the sea.

I cringe in the horror of the thought. "Then, why did you do it?"

"Throw myself to the pavement?" He doesn't miss a cue. "It was my purpose; following dreams of tomorrow and yesterday. We all follow them, whether we willfully acknowledge them or not, or maybe it is they who follow us."

"Are you saying you committed suicide because of dreams? And you believed that was your purpose?"

"Purpose is the driving force of all things, Mr. Bell. Some know to follow and why, whereas others simply do without understanding it. Gravity still weighs upon us, whether or not we acknowledge it. It's what makes us who we are, what we do, and who we become. You're led by it as well, but you know not where it takes you. It's the Great Spiral, Mr. Bell. We are forever a part of it, from start to finish and then around again, an inevitable descent into completion when all things become one. It's our end as well as our beginning. It's our dreams that tell us what we're doing right."

He's obviously been hanging there for far too long. "You almost sound like you're talking about destiny: that everything we've done, everything that has happened and will, is all predetermined."

"Not predetermined, Mr. Bell – predesigned."

"I'm sorry, I don't understand."

"It's alright, Samuel Bell. You're not supposed to, at least not yet. I was simply answering your question."

My mind is still caught in the spokes of my prior realization. If Richard Farley was a mannequin, who had appeared suddenly in the apartment across from mine, then that means *anyone* could be a mannequin. He had a card with his name on it, a previous place of residence, he had the requirements of passing an eye exam. Yet it was Dreval who invented the red-eye after all. What if—what if, the red-eye never tested for mannequins. What if…

"You look pale, Mr. Bell. Is there something the matter?" He looks at me with a hint of concern. It's harder to tell without him having any eyebrows.

"I need to sit down." My hands coming to my head to halt a spell of dizziness.

He looks over towards a section of the room where a chair has been set off to the side. I shuffle towards it and collapse.

Assassin, murderer – the very reason why Frankie and the rest weren't so receptive to me. I've chased down anyone who came up red, both men and women. They ran, they always ran, as if they knew there was something horrid waiting for them if they stuck around. What of those who were overtly violent? Sociopaths, regular cold-blooded types, whose minds would reflect nightmarish things: bodies in the streets, murder in plain daylight. In four years I've seen it all. So what of them? There's more to it than this—there has to be. I never once doubted the validity of the tests as the individual always displayed some manner of derangement, some human detachment, some—Farley waits patiently, his eyes never wavering from my seat. Occasionally, I hear the tightening of a tube and I watch it as a black substance jets into him. Some leaks from the fittings, down his flanks and onto the floor below. Every time I see him flinch, his face is stricken with an indescribable shiver. His jaw slightly drops, his eyes partly wander, and when the air releases, he falls back into himself – pretending to ignore what just occurred. His spine takes a little longer to relax in his holdings.

"What was that?" I ask.

"One can't simply die and expect not to suffer consequences. It's what I need to survive. Nothing more. Spencer Lobes has been kind in keeping me sustained. "

"It looks painful."

"Be careful, Mr. Bell. Saying things like that would imply a belief that I can feel."

I pause for a while and so does he.

"What do you know about Dr. Dreval?" I finally ask over a few moments of rubbing my palms together and erasing everything the good doctor ever told me.

"The man who's proclaimed the discoverer of synthetic machines, inventor of the DOR-52 dubbed 'red-eye' by the Govennet, who uses it to identify mechanical menaces living amidst the population? Not much, Mr. Bell. Although, I do find it interesting that he named his invention DOR."

"Why do you say that?"

"If you intended to look inside an individual, wouldn't you only need a window?"

I lean forward in my chair, gravity now working against my mind. "Do you believe that the eye exams are doing something other than identifying mannequins?"

"I would certainly hope not, Mr. Bell. However, if you were Dr. Dreval and your invention did something different—as you say—what would you do with it?"

"I don't know. I'm not Dr. Dreval. But judging by what I've witnessed, I'd say that he has been taking too many liberties with that DOR of his."

"Has Dreval been taking liberties? I'm curious as to what design."

"Maybe he's trying to seize the Govennet for himself. Maybe he's in league with the police, or maybe there is something else that he's after. I still don't quite understand his motive."

"Some people just want to be able to control things, Mr. Bell. We all do it to some degree. People fear uncertainties."

"Maybe Dr. Dreval see's the Govennet as a threat! First it started with Marty, then the rest of the officers followed with every new visitation. He tried doing it to me but something went wrong."

"Or maybe something went right."

"What was that?" I ask, confused by his answer.

"Perhaps the mistake didn't happen with you, Mr. Bell. Perhaps, the reason Dr. Dreval went after the Govennet had something to do with an earlier mistake."

"Claudine Valentine." I think aloud.

"What's that?" The mechanical man blinks.

I stand up. "I have to go."

"Has something happened?" His innocence is surely feigned.

"Dr. Dreval has turned the Govennet against me, Mr. Farley. He tried doing it to me but something went wrong, which tells me that it doesn't always work. My coworkers, friends and people I've trusted for years are now different – more hostile in ways that I've never imagined them being. It's as if they're acting as if they were—"

"The very creations you swore to destroy?"

Dread grips me by the chin. "Exactly."

Richard sighs. "Allow me to introduce a scenario to you, Mr. Bell: Take a man who wakes in a mysterious city in the middle of the sea without concept of identity or given past. What if in that very city people also wake, their arrival is as mysterious as his own and who hold no recollection of their identities or prior existence? Then, while struggling to identify themselves, the proverbial *other*—our illustrious Count Champ de Croix—is introduced and defined as undesirable. Sharing a common goal—in this case, eradication of the so-called *other*—creates a sense of stability amidst the general population. This, in itself, acts as a form of control, a means by which to subdue the conflicting psyches of multiple city factions and redirect it towards a single industrial gain. Those who swear to serve the public's interests—in the eradication of the *other*—are given special privileges of authority. In these privileges spawns an oath of submission by the public to those of authority. Essentially, those who rally against a common foe march beneath a single banner. Are you following me?"

"Yes, I follow." I say.

"Then allow me to introduce another scenario to you: What if those of authority eliminate the so-called *other*, or at least lay cause for the public to believe in its extermination. Would not then, those in authority, have to lay down their privileges by those they serve since the threat to the public has been eliminated? Would not one, in order to keep one's authority, essentially need to find another *other* to throw at the feet of the public? What if in a city filled with multiple identities, is minus a single *other* to focus on for their differences and undesirable qualities on?"

I shrug. "I couldn't tell you.

His eyes flash a stronger blue. "You make one."

I mull it over in my brain, but I find that not everything fits. "There's just one problem. With that line of logic, you're making the assumption that mannequins do not exist and you're living proof of the proverbial *other*. In that case, the threat didn't have to be made because it was already there. Unless you're trying to tell me that mannequins aren't in the least bit dangerous. Hate to say this, but I'm living proof that they are."

"No, Mr. Bell. I am not trying to argue that those you've hunted these past years weren't in the least bit dangerous. But I believe it's you who is making the assumptions."

I eye him suspiciously. "How do you figure?"

"Because, Mr. Bell, you're assuming that not everyone is human."

My mind is set adrift in a fog by his choice of words, a building pressure of vaporous confusion that can only be released by reasoning it out. "By not assuming everyone is human, Mr. Farley, you're saying that everyone must be human and I know that's not possible – that or everyone is a mannequin."

"That's the ticket, old boy. The revelation of the next proverbial *other.*"

"You're wrong!" I shout while pointing at him. "If everyone is a mannequin, then everyone I've loved, everyone I known is like you and I refuse to believe that. I refuse to believe it because I know I'm not a mannequin."

He digs into me with his gaze. "How do you know?"

"Because I would know! That's why!"

It bothers me how he keeps a placid face, not a ripple of emotion swelling in those cheeks of his. Whether it's due to the amount of pain he's in or because of some sadistic pleasure he gains in these sorts of conversations is unbeknownst to me. Either way, I despise him for it.

"You know because you know is not a suitable answer, Mr. Bell."

"I've been tested!" I hiss at him.

"With a contraption that we've both already established isn't to be trusted."

"Well, the only other way to know is to cut me open and I'm not willing to submit to either."

He rears back in a spasm of pain as the tubes fill up again, shoving more of the black material into his body. In my head I can hear screaming as his face betrays excruciating tortures, the likes he's experienced through our entire conversation. When the pressure escapes into the room and the tubes fall, his spine collapses and he hangs once more fully from the apparatus. His head is low and from his mouth as he coughs, spews a string of black fluid onto the ground, letting it drip from his mouth as if he were a water spout.

After a few sputters and a wheeze, the recovering Richard Farley manages to lift his head to meet me. "There is…" he coughs. "There is another way, Mr. Bell." His features struggle to descend again into a loss of expression.

He points with his left hand towards a small door at the other side of the room. "All will be answered through that door. All I ask is that you not let it consume you and to remember what it is that I wrote those many years ago."

I look between him and the door. "And what is that?" I ask.

"You are indeed alive." He waves me off like a fly. "Now go. It was a pleasure finally being able to meet you Samuel Bell, face-to-face."

Reluctantly, I find myself answering, "And I you."

I listen as his breathing becomes hoarse. He has been in pain the entire time, perhaps an extraordinary amount. The face he made the last time those pipes filled refuses to escape my mind but instead they taunt me with everything he just said. It reinforces everything and though I'm still struggling to resist it, I cannot help but feel pity for the man. What would possess someone, even an intellectual such as Richard Farley, to go day-after-day enduring such suffering. A dedication to purpose, he says, a strong belief in whatever it is he thinks he's accomplishing. I watch him for a few seconds longer before passing through the door and into the adjoining room.

Everything is black, a complete lack of lighting, and when I wave my hand inside the motion sensors are unresponsive. Someone must have deactivated them. My hand fumbles around the inside frame of the room, looking for that plastic plate that'll bring some life to the place. After finding the outside edge, I follow it to the center control and press it.

The lights flash on in a series of rows beginning with the one closest overhead and proceeding farther down the length of the room until they all ignite brilliantly. Under each line of florescent bulbs, are a pair of examination tables opposite one another, much similar to the ones I encountered before, no more than twelve in all. This time, instead of me laying across them, there is a single black bag containing an all too familiar shape. They aren't just any bags, they're body bags.

Already the hairs across my body struggle to see through the bag's exterior. I shudder, letting a draught of courage to spill down my spine before I'm able to step first into the room. When I do, I hear a crunching sound as my boots grind a missed collection of dirt into the textured steel flooring. I see traces of it everywhere, small bits hidden in cracks and other inaccessible recesses that a broom can't reach. Why would there be this much dirt in an area that contains bodies? Then it comes to me, if Farley is here, then these must be the corpses snatched from the graveyard.

I walk to the first table. My fingers crawl into my palm when I grab for zipper, like crumbling an invisible handkerchief. I'm hesitant to open it. I know there's a body inside, perhaps one of the original white suicides. I know what they looked like so it isn't that which stays my hand. It's the fear of what else it may be. Farley said in this room would be my answers, my head swims in a brine of horrific maybes and what ifs. But here, I'm wasting time. I swallow what little fear I have, pull the zipper across the top so as to reveal the head and with one heavy intake of breath I pull the cover down.

My palms sweat, my head screams, my eyes bulge, and my mouth hangs open to let escape my soul as there – beneath the curtain of death, is the terrifying face of *a once living Samuel Bell.*

29

I turn away from the fake – it has to be a fake! – and rush to another. I find the zipper and split open the teeth. With one harsh tug, I pull down the cover and again I am stricken by the face of Samuel Bell!

"No – this isn't possible!" I yell at the corpses. "This can't be!"

I make towards a third, my boots crunching the remnant soil with every stride, filling the room with the scent of the grave. I rip open that one like the rest and reveal yet another!

"What is this!?" I scream. I punch one of the examination tables, leaving a large dent in the top. My fist echoes the impact as I move onto the next.

I open a fourth one, then a fifth, again and again, one after another, I am besieged by Samuel Bells! Each with a different wound than the other, a scratch here, bullet wound there, a cracked skull, they were all once living, breathing Samuel Bells. Their faces are pallid, their lips are blue and though peaceful in their eternal slumber, I cannot help but imagine all sorts of demonic fates that snuffed them forever silent.

Then finally, when I open a ninth bag I find that same familiar face as before, but this one with a scar across his brow in the same spot as my own. My hands shaking from the shock of it all, I reach out and feel the groove. Cold and chilling. For a second, I'm caught up in the miasma, a cycle of thoughts that spiral into a pseudo-history of multiple Samuel Bells.

"Emily." I mouth as I touch my own scar.

I imagine it all, time and time again of different Samuel Bells meeting different Emily Waters. Each respectively living their lives, going through the pain and hardships that I myself have endured. The pain of losing Emily, how many times has Samuel Bell lived it? How many times have they had to endure it? And dreams, all those comforting dreams, have they been dreams at all? Or are they true memories, memories of past Samuel Bells living Samuel Bell lives?

And Farley, talking about purpose? There's no purpose in this! A constant cycle, a downward spiral of longing and loss?

Here in this room, I demand if any of it matters.

"Of course it matters." The voice is feminine and as soothing as those dreams basked in white. Apparently, I spoke aloud.

She leans on the door frame, still dressed in her black coat and keeping it snug around her to push back the frigidity from the dead.

"How?" I ask her in my mild hysteria. "How does any of this matter? There's nothing real about it, it's just as Farley said – synthetic."

"Synthetic or not, you still breathe and feel, don't you? You have loved ones and people who care about you, right? Of course things matter. You have to make it matter."

"You knew?" I ask her, my right hand condemning the corpses behind me as I take a few steps forward. "You all knew about this?"

Rachel crosses her arms. "We all knew. That's why we took a chance bringing you as far underground as we did, though we had to be sure you weren't all scrambled up inside."

"But –" I stare at the nearest replica. "How was there this many? I thought you only took the jumpers."

"We didn't take the window-wishers." She claims. "We just swapped them around a bit, to mislead any investigation. It was you we— it was them," she nods at the bodies. "That we were truly after."

"But why?" Rachel enters the room and begins to zip up the bags. "Why did you take them?" I ask.

She shakes her head. "I don't know. Richard told us to dig them up. He told us where to dig and what to look for, but didn't tell us why. He never explains why."

"But Farley was taken the same time these others were, how could he have told you what to look for if he was entombed at the time?"

"You have no idea how disturbing it is to be walking through the graveyard at night and suddenly hear a voice. I had nightmares for weeks after that. He was in pretty poor shape, but Spence has been working hard to keep him alive."

Keeping him alive? Richard Farley experiences excruciating pain nigh every moment of his existence and she calls it, 'being alive'?

"Don't look at me like that!" She returns a spiteful glare and then walks between the examination tables to close the rest of the bags. "It's not my doing, he insisted on being brought back. Everyone thought I was crazy when I told them how a dead guy talked to me. But he knew things about people that no one else knew."

I recall something from the past. "Here lies one whose name was writ in water."

"What?" Rachel belts out as if I just stepped on her shadow.

"Nothing," I look off to the black body bags as if expecting a response. "Just something I heard someone say." I catch her shivering in my peripheral. "Are you cold?"

"No, I'm just not comfortable being here with *them*. And you certainly don't help things much. It's uncanny."

I keep staring at the black bags, thinking about the men inside who own my face. I start to think about what Farley said, about pre-design. Am I doomed to follow the same fate as these other synthetics? How long before a different Samuel Bell will be standing in this very same spot looking down at me, wondering the same things as I?

I then hear her voice creeping up beside me. "Do-do you want to go someplace warmer?"

Her request garners my attention. Unsure of how long I've been in contemplation of dark and dreadful things, I'm eager to accept her invitation and glad for her company.

Rachel takes me through the complex, a long collection of varying rooms of use, interconnecting hallways, stairs, and elevators. The farther we journey, the warmer it becomes. Occasionally, as we pass, I ask her the purpose of several rooms though she replies without a clue of its use. She claims the majority of the computer consoles are locked out and the electrical equipment seems content to run on its own so no one touches it. I accept the answer disappointed.

We arrive in a terraced auditorium-like area with high ceilings and a steppe balcony with stairs on either side. At the front of the room is a half-circle wall outcropping, with a few monitors embedded into it and touch panels. Unexpectedly, she grabs my hand and pulls me in front of it.

"I have a surprise to show you." Rachel exclaims as she inputs a series of buttons on one of the panels.

My head shakes against my will. "I don't think I can handle any more surprises."

"It's alright." She places her other hand on top of mine and steps closer. The sensation carries all the way up my arm. "I think you'll enjoy this one." She purrs.

Rachel looks me in the eyes and, for a moment, I'm caught in the replaying of a dream. And when my heart trepidates in flutter, I swear our pupils orbit. Then without moving, perhaps a faint trickle of vertigo, I feel myself falling into her.

She shakes her head as if to cast off blurry vision, looks down at her hands, and then withdraws her own.

"Oh, um…" She leans into the wall and presses a final button. She fidgets while stepping back. The above lighting dims, the wall separates and then slides apart.

The room is bathed in a widening line of white, orange and yellow. My eyes squint against the tepid rays despite the tinted glass, which reveals a giant radiant ball of ignited gas, seething in the center of an enormous circular chamber. Spinning around it at varying speeds are enormous metallic rings, motorized by a mechanical pedestal made of dials and gears. I take a quick step back, startled by a pair of larger rings that pass mere inches from the transparent barrier.

A flare burns off the ball like a loose piece of twine, dancing like an orange string of ribbon. Inside the blazing sphere, I see colors mixing and miniature pockets exploding. Were it not for the glass, I could easily reach out and hug the buoy-size collection of plasma.

473

It's been here all along, hidden beneath the pavement and sewer drains of the city — the lifeblood of the world, the glowing ball of heated flame, our very own sun.

"It's…" I try to put it into words, what it is like to live day after day beneath the greyish brume with but a few droplets of sun to get us by. Once a year, if you're lucky, that's all one ever gets. Even then it isn't enough. Had the sun been plentiful, how things would have been different. But I would not be staring at it as I am now, breathing it in as if it were a cloud of air; not holding it in as I am now.

I'm about to form the words, to speak of the tears welling in my eyes, to not give excuse to them for the pain that comes from staring at such brilliance. Yet, I'm given fright from a sudden roar as a torrent of water drops on it like a lead house. The ceiling is open, like a large steel trap that vomits the sea from the pipes of the city, down overtop the fireball. Steam first, and when the chamber overflows with liquid, the flame continues to burn, shedding bubbles like an unwanted layer of skin. Tiny fireflies spark amidst the blue, winking like the aperture of stars — the sun never waning.

"What is this? What's going on?" I ask unable to look away from the happening.

She steps up to my side. "It happens every six hours or so, the silo we came down filters water from the ocean. The water regulates the size of the sphere — I guess so it doesn't overwhelm the machine. It'll get smaller, but give it a few hours and it'll grow again." She points to the glass. "You see those tiny lights? Spence tells us that those are the impurities in the water being burnt away. He has a way of stealing the romance of it. I find it absolutely captivating."

"It's beautiful." I say while watching a pattern of blinking embers. "But what is it and why is it here?"

"It's the sun, Samuel. We've gone and stolen the sun. It's what powers the city, and everyone in it. From you and me, to chirpers and gigs, it powers everything. I suppose that's what a lot of this equipment is for, to make sure that everything gets to where it needs to be going."

"We?"

She shakes her head. "I don't mean 'we' as in *us*. It was the architects who built the CitySpire. Be it a god, synthetic beings, humans or maybe even aliens, I really don't know. There really is no way of knowing."

I watch the bubbles as they mass around the sun, floating towards the top to boil off at some undeterminable point. By how hot the plasma needs to be in order to power the city, the steam must be able to melt the skin right off the bone.

"We're trapped here, aren't we?"

She nods. "Only for a few hours. The silo will need to cool off first. If you go out before, your boots will stick to the floor. This comes from personal experience."

Together we watch in silence as the spectacle of the sun slowly shrinks in the icy containment of sea water. It is as if together we're witnessing the birth of a galaxy or the precursor of life itself. Somehow, her hand finds mine and its presence tickles up my arm. It's seeing something like this, both fire and water existing in the same unnatural place, that does something to your mind; making the world seem small and insignificant in the whole shaping of things. Being here, watching the sea boil away, my hand in hers, I receive that moment of clarity and a glimpse of the connection of all things.

Somehow, in the course of it all, the two of us transition to the floor. We lay our coats down like blankets as the two of us cuddle in view, basking in the warmth of the fiery globe. I do not understand the mingling in which we've managed to embark upon, but I try not the question these things – especially now and who I'm with. It's rather sudden, spontaneous but without guilt or feeling of recourse.

My once captor touches my face, a means to catch the glittering sparks that reflect off my skin, smiles in her game while saying, "Tell me about this Rachel of yours."

I don't hold anything back. I tell her about waking in my apartment, about the light beneath my door, and the haunting memories of her wafting through my dreams. I tell her about how she's appeared to me, sometimes lying on examination tables, other times floating in mirrors or glass. I confide in her those hopeless feelings of longing that were born in those dreams, my belief that she was once my lost love, and by some spin of fate we were separated from one another – or abandoned. I emphasize her smile and how her eyes beamed in the return of my own affections.

She smiles at this, and from our contact, I feel her pulse racing as she nears closer; our lips soon to touch.

I try to reason it, "Felicia I—"

She seals my breath with a finger. "Call me Rachel."

We kiss.

Her hands are on my cheeks, her lips swallowing mine, together we delve into the impossible; shedding clothes with every passion, each passion a kiss or hidden touch. We bed one another, like two strong elements competing for dominance, a powerful ballet of fire and water playing across our skin – as we're warmed by the brilliance of an ever-burning sun. She moans beneath me, and I beneath her. Mating, for what truly is a past repression of love and miss. It's all surreal, watching her watching me as we both twinkle amidst a tiny sea of stars.

My mind spins in a whirlpool of sensation as my cheeks tingle with a thousand needles. She wraps her arms around my head, cradling me to her chest and I hear the vibrations of her heart. I'm reminded of Farley's heart, a cold mechanical thing with lights and rhythm. I ask myself briefly, as it pulses through my head to the motion of her hips, if hers is the same? I hear the word, *synthetic* echo through the halls of my brain as well as my question to what I had thought to be the stillness of a devoid room, *"Does any of this matter?"* But it is in her love, this union of two, that has brought some meaning to it all – if not for love… if only for love.

We enjoy one another, this moment forever captured as ours, an instance not just shared in the haunt of dreams but in the throes of the physical. Together we last beyond when time loses its sway and meaning. When finished, as the two of us collapse in the euphoria of our act, we are lulled through the veil of dreams by both exhaustion and the arduous ascent of bubbles.

PART III - THE SORCERER

My mind rests in whatever place is reserved for empty thoughts. There were no dreams, no reoccurring nightmare or undiscovered secret taunting me from my subconscious. I was simply there and nothing more; now rested.

I open my eyes, but am surprised to see the emptiness where Rachel had slept. My heart searches for her and I concerned to where she had gone. The room is in a stronger glow, now that the tinier sun has boiled away the last of the sea. Easing up, I take a glimpse at my surroundings and am given a temporary stare, as sitting like a perched gargoyle on a nearby step, not but a few feet from my bare-chested silhouette, is the young girl Roz.

How long has she been sitting there watching me sleep unclothed and vulnerable? It only adds additional warmth to my cheeks. I'm hoping that the cast of the sun hides my change in color.

"Is there something I can help you with?" Is the only thing I can think of saying in such a situation.

She remains silent next to her satchel on her stoop, staring at me with fewer blinks than one would expect with such a question. If there is to be any awkwardness, it's going to come from me.

"Right," I say more to myself. "You don't talk very much." I pull my coat closer to me, the one I had been lucky to have been using as a coverlet, as I try and sit up. "Can you at least give me some privacy so that I can get dressed?"

The petite brunette scoops a short strand of hair out of her face. "It's nothing I haven't seen."

My vocals are caught between the dilemmas of her speaking versus her seeing me naked.

"Excuse me?" Obviously the later wins out.

She motions behind her with her head. "There's more than one of you, you know."

Right – as if I'm comforted in the fact that she's gotten an eye full of past Samuel Bells. I direct her with a finger. "Then, do you mind? It's proper courtesy."

She sighs, stands and turns her back. But when she speaks, she gears her head a few degrees over her shoulder.

"It's just flesh. Synthetic at that."

I hurry to gather my clothes, as I'm a bit disturbed by her peculiar interest in me.

"I thought you didn't talk much." I say in order to change the subject.

"Only when I need to," she twists at the waist. "Are you done yet?" Noting my half-dressed state, she returns to facing the hallway. "We're objects, you and I. Beneath it all, we're both like Farley. Give or take a few parts."

"Then why the fascination?" I retort as I finish with my pants.

She shrugs her shoulders and bites on a couple fingernails. "Why not?"

As I tuck in my shirt. "You're age, for starters."

"I'm older than she is." Her hands drop and she spins with the momentum of her arms. "Relatively speaking."

"Older than whom?"

"Felise."

I pause to contemplate who she means.

Another sigh. "The woman you just slept with." She leans on one hip and crosses her arms.

"How do you figure?" I ask while finishing with the last articles of clothes.

"I'm the one who found her upon waking." She debates about which way to tilt her head to look at me with a child-like face of hidden emotions. "It's just my shape, you know? We don't age at all." She sticks out her small chest, putting her hands behind her back. "Or fill out."

"Well, you'll have to excuse me Miss Roz, but I'm not too comfortable discussing this with you. Especially considering the condition you found me in. I'm sure Miss Rhodes wouldn't be comfortable with it either."

Straight face and blinking she replies, "She wouldn't mind. She's the one who sent me down here." She looks at my waistline and then up again. "We don't keep secrets."

"I see." I respond, feeling incredibly objectified by an underage thief, which brings me to our next subject. "Back at Nereid Street you took something."

The small fry comes up to me about mid-chest. Her neck straining to look up. "Nothing that wasn't already mine to begin with."

"I highly doubt that." I hold out my hand to better separate us. "May I have it?"

"No." Is her reply and then she strolls back to her stoop as if wearing point shoes, tightening her butt and beating her thighs together.

"May I at least see it?"

Roz readdresses me over her shoulder with one shake of her head. "No."

I sigh out of frustration figuring I'll have to get it from her some other way. "What is it exactly that Felicia sent you here for?"

She drops from her tiptoes, letting her heels hit the ground as if dropping from a tremendous height. "Felise went topside. Thought she'd scout around for you, see what she could find out on your friends."

A darkness spreads amidst my insides. "What?!" I exclaim. "When?"

"About three hours ago."

I resettle my coat on my shoulders and rush past her towards the hallway.

She calls after. "Relax, she should be back already." The teenager follows me. "Come on, I'm not done talking to you."

I refuse to listen. I can't shake this terrifying feeling inside, like tiny black hands squeezing my stomach as a cloth being wrung of water. Right now the Govennet is dangerous, more so than it was to mannequins before Dr. Dreval started altering things. I bet you that if Rachel submitted to an eye exam that she'd come up red. Red, because she isn't registered. None of these people are.

That's how Dreval has been indoctrinating people, using the Registration Office as a means to categorize people as either red or green. If he wants to get rid of someone, he simply erases their file. No one had witnessed Ms. Valentine waking, I read it in her file, so she was the ideal match for whatever Dreval had planned. Was she a distraction or just another casualty to keep up his ruse? He didn't bet on her purchasing a gig that day. Just bad luck on his part, so he made a move against the Govennet.

If Rachel was caught… Before she might have been able to show enough humanity to bypass officers. Now, I'm not so sure.

I concentrate on reversing my course from when Rachel had led me down here. Navigating the complex is not much different than the carbon copy skyscrapers and look-alike alleys of the city above; it's about how many turns you make, not by landmarks.

"Would you wait one minute." Returns her voice from above the thoughts in my head.

I don't turn my head back. "I have to find her. I fear something terrible is going to happen."

Frankie is unfortunately the first to notice me enter their make-shift kitchen where the majority of them reside.

"Look everyone, it's the Govennet Man. Have a nice nap, dreaming of those murdered past?"

A step into his bubble and float mere inches from his face. "Where is she?" I say with teeth clenched. I haven't the time for his commentary. Roz grabs hold of one of my wrists and tugs, perhaps fearing I'd hit the guy. Frankie bares his whites in smile.

"She ain't back yet." Comes an ill-at-ease Patches sitting at a nearby table. Though, from the worry on his face, I doubt it has anything to do with a possible altercation with Frankie meat-sack in front of me.

His blue coat tootsie scoots atop the same table. "Felicia's probably busy running some errand for Farley. She'll be back soon."

The cosmetically challenged gent leans against the wall, staring at the floor. "She should have been back by now."

I push Frankie out of my way.

"You can all sit around here all you'd like. I'm going to go look for her." I announce, while searching for whichever hallway leads out of this place."

Patches stands up. "Now why would you want to go and do a thing like that? You looking to cause us some trouble?"

"Easy tiger," soothes the red-haired woman, "he's not going to cause us any trouble. He and Ms. Rhodes got rather friendly on each other. He's just sweet on her is all." She beams a cheery smile.

I catch an eyebrow from the lug.

"Did he now?" Patches sits back in his chair. "That's one way to go about it."

"Go about what?" I ask.

"Keeping you from spilling your guts to the wrong people, that's what. I'd hate to say, 'I told you so' to certain someones for having us bring you all the way down here just to have a chat with old tin-head in there."

"Well, you do what you want." I pick a hall and make my way in that direction.

"Why the rush, hot stuff?" Frankie jokes from his corner of the room.

Patches intercedes, "I don't know what you think you're going to accomplish. But you're better off waiting till she gets back. Who in the high hells knows where she could be right now."

I stop only briefly. "Something is wrong. I feel it. I haven't lived the past five years ignoring it. I trust my instincts when something is out of place." My palms hit the table in front of him as I lean in. "You feel it too. I recognized it on you when I first entered the room. Now, you can sit here and pretend that everything is all right, or you can get up and come with me. What's it going to be?"

His brow lowers and his lips tighten and for a few seconds he just stares into me, but then his head begins to bob and his cheeks smooth out.

"Yeah – something doesn't feel right. Damn it all – if they didn't make you chief for something. Let's go boys and girls we're not waiting around this Popsicle stand any longer."

"What?!" Cries Frankie. "You're listening to him, just like that? Govennet boy thinks he's a psychic and you're all going to—"

"Frankie!" Yells the bald-headed man. "Shut the *fuck* up." He relays his orders. "Jaime, go rally Spence and meet us up by the cage. Biff and I will grab some necessary essentials. And Roz?" The raven haired ballerina glides up next to me. "You do what you do. Just wait a few minutes, Mr. Bell, and we're with you. You got that? We're with you."

As everyone speeds off in their own different direction, I look down to my side mate and she looks up at me not speaking a word.

The ride up through the shaft is a hot one and less tolerable than before. I'm not fixated on the cruelty of the temperature, instead I'm chewing desperation. There's a physical gnawing on the insides of my lungs, a torturous crumbling of my being that warns me of something foretold in the silence of dreams. To make things worse, Roz gives witness to the entire ordeal.

Those eyes—those haunting brown eyes—staring at me as if in judgment over whether I'm worthy to exist in her world, cold and expressionless. Her glare lends the belief she's bordering on the obsessed.

The cage rattles some and my troupe widen their stance for balance. The transport has leaned towards one too many hot bathes and needs a proper inspection. It strikes fear in some of them, a minor slip that may have stolen a week off their lifespan. Yet I remain unphased in my brace, as I am committed to whatever awaits us above. It's hard to believe that it would all end here, losing to a foe of wet gears and slippery chains. Now I look to the dark bleak above, pacing in my mind for the elevator to hurry, for time itself to bend, so that I may extend my hand in the fate of things and put this horrid feeling to rest.

They lead me through the catacombs of the city sewers, a mix of waystations and unknown subsections. I can tell by every step how closer to the surface we are by the slow decline of the city's temperature. It settles into my muscles, adding a touch of fatigue that comes from frigidity. Lurking in the hidden depths of adjoining tunnels, I see hideous horned things watching us, spawned from the recesses of my subconscious, mocking with their scissor-like claws in how closer to inevitability we march. I choose to ignore my tormentors, those repressed ideologies of the ever-present spiral where all things are predetermined. For a mere instant I am frightened, but only for an instant.

We break surface through a manhole on some unrecognizable street somewhere beyond the patrols. The buildings here are black with creep, with sultry windows and brick exteriors. I help Roz out of the hole and then wait as the others follow suit, taking weapons when need be—pipes, a sledge hammer—so they can climb out quicker.

Once everyone clears the underground, we replace the lid. The street is untouched by the human foot, with perfect snow as far as the streetlamps allow us to see. The only scars on this wintry wonderland are around the storm drains and manhole covers where steam has melted it away.

"Alright everyone, tighten together." Patches orders. "We'll walk backwards about twenty feet into an alley, then follow our footprints back here before heading out. I'm not going to rely on the weather to powder them in this time." He looks at me. "Obviously, people are more venturous these days. Don't want anyone to think there's anything down there."

Everyone nods in agreement, shivering from adapting to the change in environments. I decide to put my best foot backward.

A spotlight blinds me, a second of pain as my pupils retreat in size. The sound of aerodynes whirr above us, a gig of recognizable shape – a Govennet cruiser. I reach for my chirper, but despair in the emptiness of my holster. I shield my vision with my arm and peek beneath the shade for a place to escape. But all faith in our continued survival is restored when I hear a woman's voice over the loud speaker.

"Chief! Where the fuck have you been? You're just the iodine on my wounds, it's been hell looking for you."

Brigit Box, perhaps the only person I can trust not to get caught by Dreval or any of his cronies.

"It's okay. She's with me." I spit out so those next to me don't chuck a brick at her. "Get down here, I need to talk to you!" I shout up at her.

"Talk? All of Govennet's gone to shit and you want to talk? Okay, we're game, but if don't have some sort of plan, I'm seriously going to kick your ass! And no damn speeches this time, I hate how long winded you get."

30

Brigit's gig touches down mid-center street. The snow is kicked up like a spinning whirlwind before tossed off to the side. That's one way to eliminate our impressions in the snow. Everyone stands off to the side, keeping their distance from the vehicle as if it were an unnatural thing. Something tells me that they've never been this close without fearing they'd be stopped or shot.

Brigit swings out beneath the wing as it rises from the driver's side, while Harvey has to place both feet down before easing himself out of it. They've tossed their uniforms and instead wear black suits and loose ties – like old times. They look like a pair of miss-sized gloves. Still the silent partner, Harvey just widens his stance and crosses his arms to better show his size. I'd be curious as to who'd win between him and brick-face Biff over there in a wrestling match. I catch the two of them sizing the other up.

The boyish-cut brunette slides her hand along the hood of her gig as she meanders up to me.

"I see you've made some friends, since you've been gone. Tell me you weren't tipping back cold ones and shooting pool while Harv and I've been stuck in the clouds."

"What were you doing up there?" I hesitantly ask in my sense of urgency.

"Damn Govennet's been trying to round everyone up whose not had a physical. And here I was feeling mighty bad about it when I gave the doc the shoulder, but it turns out he's got a horrible bedside manner that's been spreading around. I did some digging and saw that he's dick deep in those pansy-assed politicians you let take office. He's got friends in the police too. I also found a little on our buddy Blake, seems he used to work for the Registration Office and failed to let us in on it."

"Yes, I know about Blake. He was there when I was checking up on Ms. Valentine's file. I believe he and Dreval are good pals."

Her face tightens. "Damn it, Sam! When the hell were you going to let me in on this shit? Do you know the amount of effort I put forth in this?"

"Listen, Brigit, I'm sorry. I didn't have the time. Marty and the other officers grabbed me when I reported back in. Dreval used some sort of device on me, probably the same one he used on Marty and everyone else. It had to have failed because afterwards I woke up fine in my apartment. I think they were watching me just-in-case because I was followed to the Stardust."

I fill her in on the whole conspiracy: I tell her about Dreval using the red-eye and Registration Office to conduct his mind-altering experiments, a strange type of hypnosis, that forces people to act however he pleases; about how the whole screw-job mess is just a façade and how everyone is a mannequin; and how he used the threat to distract us from the real danger. I leave out the part about Farley and the underground, for reasons not to upset my comrades-in-arm.

"Son of a bitch!" Brigit screams. "As if I don't have enough shit riding my conscience, now I get to deal with this? A fucking screw-job, Sam? You're telling me that we're all made outta plastic and the doc's been messin' with peoples' heads to make em act all crazy-like so we can plug em? What fucking screwed up bullshit is that? If I didn't know you any better, I'd think you've gone off your rocker. Okay," she rubs her head. "So we going to waste this asshole or what? I don't like being played for a fool, Sam. This guy has it coming!"

"We will, but later. Right now we're trying to find someone: roughly your height, short blonde hair, goes by the name of Felicia Rhodes. Have you heard anything?"

"Not a Felicia Rhodes. But I did read something off the glass a half-hour ago about some dame they picked up for being a mannequin."

I grab her by the shoulders. "Where – where did they take her?!"

She punches my arm to release her. "Where the fuck do you think they took her. She was a pegged a mannequin, so they took her to the docks to be executed. Why?" she nods over to the group from below. "Friend of theirs?"

I try and push by her. "I'm taking your gig."

She throws her hands up and jabs me in the chest. "Oh, hell no! You're not taking my car. I'm not being left behind for this shit. Get in the back, I'm driving."

I take a breath of air to combat her but she's quick to shoot me down.

"You can argue with me, or you can get in the damn car. With luck, they haven't quite reached the docks."

I grit my teeth but accept the inevitable. I yell back over my shoulder as I head for the door. "They've taken her to the pier. We don't have a lot of time. Meet us there."

Patches runs up with Roz tailing behind him. He halts the close of the wing as Brigit takes to the driver's seat.

"No one here said you can go. Especially not with your Govennet friends." He says with a strong animosity.

A flash of light and a loud chirp and Brigit aims her gun at his head.

"No-no, Brigit! It's all right, stand down." She refuses to budge. "Look – Patches – they've taken her to be executed, I can't stop it in time if I don't go. You have to trust me."

His eyes dart nervously between me and the directionally blinking lights on the pistol that indicate that Brigit's slowly pulling back the trigger.

Even in the winter, I can see a point of sweat bead on his brow. He steps back. "Fine." He says. "But take Roz with you, you'll need all the help you can get. That way we'll have reassurance."

I frown at his proposal, but haven't the time to argue. I reach out with a hand to help her into the back of the cab, her small stature the perfect size to squeeze into the one-seater. As Brigit kisses the air in taunt to her new doorman, she motions with her chirper for him to shut the wing. Once Harvey is inside and the driver side door is reluctantly closed, the fiery brunette spurs the aerodynes into a roar, shifts it into high gear, and screeches out into the sky.

Both Roz and I are thrown into one another. The impact forces her to squeak, an adorable noise that doesn't fit the character, and I smile; she takes one look, squishes her face, and crosses her arms in protest.

"Careful back there." Our lady driver cautions. "This could get bumpy."

She takes us through a maze of unfamiliar streets headed toward the southwest, keeping clear of specific Govennet hotspots and checkpoints. We keep low to the ground, preferring the sharp turns and ley-lines of the city as opposed to losing time ascending and descending. The buildings also provide us with a cover, a major advantage when one is hunted by Govennet cruisers.

In mere minutes, we buzz out of the empty section of the city and onto Rhine. We follow the rest of it, passing familiar buildings and the bright neon sign of Pen. A knot grows nauseatingly in my esophagus, making it difficult to breathe as we near closer to the west-side pier.

Roz, now too jostled to keep her earlier disposition towards me, bequeaths from her satchel bag a newspaper covered affair. She unwraps it, rolling the object out like it was snug in linen. As the black hand-held device is brought out into the poorly lit cab, I realize that I'm being reunited with an old friend — a genuine Roderick Whistler special.

"How did you get this?" I ask, turning the weapon over in my hands.

But she refuses to give me answer, instead, she fixates out the front windshield with frequent looks out the side. I leave it be, not wanting to press the issue. I check the chirper over to ensure it hasn't been tampered with. As far as I can tell, it's fully charged and ready to go.

The turbines whistle as we pass a couple of Govennet gigs and their flashing lights.

"Whoa." Our driver musters. "Two guards standing at the mouth of the market. Couldn't make out who they were though." A brief pause. "We should be there any moment now. Where do you want me to touch down?"

Maneuvering around Roz, I lean forward in my seat. "Set her down just short of the promenade, we don't want to draw any —"

The gig is struck, vibrating through my teeth with the sound of crunching metals and fizzing circuits. Alarms pulse in red, bleeping to the warnings of a rear driver-side aerodyne malfunction.

"Not a-fucking-gen!" Brigit yells in tirade. "They shot at my fucking car!"

She veers the wheel, throwing Roz overtop me as I collide into the passenger side wall. The vehicle wobbles like a spinning top, before she's able to recover. I struggle to see through the windshield, hearing a surge of sabots wailing past; one puts a hole in the glass and then through the roof.

Bridget blinds them, two officers on the promenade, with her flood light. Harvey places his meaty hand on the fire control stick.

Our driver screams. "Waste em!"

I hear the hood churn and then a sharp click as the inner rail guns are pushed forward and raise out of the hood; locking into position. The aerodynes angle downwards for stabilization and I hear their humming increase as more air is forced through them. In a series of miniature sonic bombs, the weapons spray a slew of electrified rounds across the paved promenade, kicking up clouds of dust and concrete chips.

Time slows, a phenomenon that's occurred many times in the past when adrenaline charges through my veins. I watch as each round hits the ground, a slithering devastation that slinks its way up and then through the two Govennet officers. I can see puffs of blood expel outward and behind them as the projectiles cut through their skin, wires and metallic skeletons. I'm sure I had known them at some time, trained them, and occasionally worked along side them. But as their bodies fall beneath the heat of the steel, I try and imagine them as I always do those we have to kill — deranged store front mannequins.

Time returns and I watch as heat breathes off the guns and into the frigid air. Brigit retracts the weapons back inside the hood, then slows the vehicle into a descent. I ready the door.

As soon as the wheels touch the promenade, I shove open the wing and race out and then down the stairs leading down to the pier below. Brigit calls after me, demanding that I wait, but I know that time is important. Executions take place at the end of the pier, where the bodies are stolen by the tide, to return from whence they came. I run, trying not to trip as my heels pound into the wood. I leap stairs, harming my ankle in the process, but I continue regardless.

When I fall out onto the docks, I distinguish a group of sinister silhouettes against the blackness of the horizon, there at the end of the pier a good hundred yards out; barely aglow by lantern light. I push my lungs, praying to Hermes to grant me wings, to give me speed, so to reach her in time. They have her kneel, one behind, the other not far from him. Three figures standing, one off to the left. The one behind her pulls a gun – by the arbiter!

I'm not that far away, but not close enough to make a shot. I clutch the pistol firmly in my hand, stretch it out to give it that extra two feet. She's still kneeling, my heart pounding in its cage. Then, a flash of white light and a boom. Time slows once more, watching as she falls limp and lifeless. I scream in my mind, a long painful howl that echoes deep into my very being, rousing every beast of anger and setting them loose into the world. I pull the trigger.

Not once, but multiple times. Thunder echoes out into the night, all five shots released like a pack of vengeful hounds towards the men who killed my Rachel. One misses, two in the chest, while those remaining feast on his partner. Both are torn off the ground like dolls, one hits a mooring while the other is tossed into the frigid sea. The officer to the left ducks, draws his pistol from his coat pocket, spins for momentum and aims. I come to a halt, my gun extended.

I catch his face in the lamp light, the haunting visage of a friend and past ally, my one true Marty Kessler. We stare one another down the barrel, a fraction of a second. I cannot attest to what he sees in these mere moments, but in him I see the emotionless guise, that vacant painted look that's native to those inanimate figures behind the glass. Since day one, everything said and done pours into the front of my skull as a theatrical collage; all things allude to this moment. An overload of emotion and pain cries out across my soul.

I hear the chirp, my gun now recharged. A voice from within makes its demand – *Shoot!* He hesitates. I do not.

A localized boom, both ear shattering and heart wrenching, as the magnets accelerate the sabot from its nozzle and drives it deep into his shoulder. After that instant, when the blood expels in a cloud of fine mist from above the shell bit of his badge, I swear I see a sliver of Marty relax into his features. His arms and legs stretch out like an open parasail taken to wind as his body is pulled from the pier and out into the hyperborean waters. The dreaded splash and then desolation settles after.

I drop my chirper and with a few steps forward, I fall by her side. Rachel's face is lying down, the whole left side of her skull exposed, her heat trailing out it like a chimney and the vapor rising like a phantom later to disappear in the night. Wires spark from the oozing hole, expelling both blood and black ichor all over the boards. I turn her over, taking her up in my folds, pulling back the hair from her face as my eyes tear.

"Dear Rachel," I run my hand down her face. "Look what they've done to you."

I cradle her and bring her to my chest. No pulse, no warmth, just nothing more than a broken automaton. How it cleaves my heart in twain.

I shake my head. "No – no, no." Trying to deny and bite back the atrocity of it. All this for naught? Metal body, fake skin, nothing real – everything synthetic. But love, no, everything meaningful in that love. Finding meaning, she said. All is now smashed beyond repair. Her eyes are still open, and with careful caress I bring them to a close.

I whisper to her pale face. "We were one, you and I."

My chest chokes as I hear the parting of lips, a motion of speech for which I hastily take to my ear – both with happiness and despair.

She speaks in a hoarse monotone, *"Here lies one whose name was writ in water."* A dismal smile draws into my swollen cheeks, a message to damn me for all eternity. *"So, here is where you find me… At the waters edge."* Rachel—the world—falls silent.

I feel those familiar feelings, a lightheadedness that warps the distance between myself and everything around me. I remember carrying Emily through the mists, walking the streets in a momentarily devoid world. Hopelessness. It seeps into my bones, a hollowness that replaces the marrow. Then the bodies, all those Samuel Bells laying in their pallid skin and reposed conditions. I envision myself being pulled down with them into a spinning drain, caught in a whirlpool of water and black blood.

Then, a thought – she didn't scream. A scream may have alerted her captors to my approach, would have stalled her execution, may have prevented her death. She saw me coming, had to have, as her eyes were awake and trembling. Yet she was a quiet creature, accepting the fate that was woven out before her. Did she accept her death? In those last few moments of life did she realize her place in the whole scheme of things? Or was it darkness, the cruel nothingness that I once feared?

I ease her back onto the planks, her sanguine fluids clinging to my hands, desperate for a new home. I turn them over, small distant things that feel no more a part of me than the pier. A glint.

Concentrating, I focus on a little object, leaning closer to the silvery thing embedded in the wood. It's dug in fairly deep, so deep that when I pick at it with my nails I only risk a splinter. Behind me I hear the sound of feet approaching, running down the length of the hundred-yard bridge to the sea. I ignore them, as I unpin my Govennet badge and use it to pry up the item. Small and dainty, the metal piece is the very sabot that murdered my poor Rachel. I hold it up to the light, allowing it to sparkle from the iridescence of the lamp. I catch both Brigit and Roz not far away, the tiniest of them slowing in her stride and stopping just short of my stand off with Marty.

"Chief!" Brigit calls as she passes the shocked ballerina. "Holy shit, chief…" she pauses at the carnage. Her head descends on Rachel. "I'm sorry, Sam." Perhaps the most sincere I've ever heard her be.

I stand, easing slowly on the hindered ankle and board-stricken knees. Pocketing the sabot, I look out to the sea as I had done when the world was empty and I was sole.

"There's nothing I could have done." I say somberly.

She shakes her head. "Maybe if I would have gone faster or if I could have set her down quicker?"

I bite my teeth and snap at her. "It couldn't have been helped!" I exercise my jaw to ward back the tears. I can't let it get the better of me. Not this time.

"Bell – I'm so sorry." Brigit knocks a fist into her thigh. "Who done it?"

I twist my head, referencing the man at the base of the mooring.

"Rockwood. I'm assuming his partner Slovene was with him. He took a drink." I glance over the side, but see nothing but the roll of the surf. "And Brigit," my heart struggles out of my throat, and I choke it down. I cough, as some of it reaches the back of my tongue. Swallowing hard, I bring my arm up to my mouth to reinforce it shut. I breathe a few times, letting the air push back the sudden bout of nausea. As soon as I'm able to recoup my composure, I continue with the rest. "Marty too."

She steps back as if the words were a slap to her face. Pale now, the tomboy can only echo me. "Marty too?" Her brow drops, her eyes narrow and her face tightens. "And this couldn't be helped!?"

Kneeling back down, I pick up my chirper. Carefully, I release the ammo and fix the sabot with the next in the clip before shoving it back into the gun.

"No –" I viciously cock the gun, adding sound and identity to the pain in which I'm feeling. I walk up to her and give it to her straight in the eye. "It couldn't be helped."

I pass her in stride. All I have are ghosts swimming through the brime of my being, all burned into my heart like plates of hot tempered glass. Anger for the world, fury for this city and hatred for the arbiter who presides over it. My tormentor, the one who filled me with dreams of her, only to steal her away like some capacious devil in the night. This is why I rejected Emily? This is why I lost her? Just so that I could lose again? There is no rest for Samuel Bell, no fitting song of love everlasting – simply toils and servitude to my design. I refuse purpose, I refuse to be cast into an ever-continuous cycle that's set to bleed me dry. Now there is only one course of action, one path for those who seek vengeance.

I stop by Roz, who looks up at me from her mascara streaked face. Reflection, a female me scarred in her eyes, seething with inner fire for those responsible for the death of her friend. We communicate something unspoken, a mild telepathy belonging to attuned minds. All my reservations of her melt away and with it, everything that is human. Nothing is said, but everything is understood. Roz turns her head back to the sea and trudges the length to the end of the pier, perhaps in final farewell.

"What are you going to do now?" Brigit yells, still anchored to the dock.

"What do you think?" I offer back as I further my heading.

A few seconds is what it takes for the answers to evaporate out of her. She yields them up silently, listlessly, as she gives chase once more.

As I reach the gig, I grab for the door handle, but am taken by the shoulder – spun and decked in the face. The punch staggers me, turning me around to better face my aggressor, using the gig as both support and orientation. I taste a bit of nickel in my mouth, an extra flavor to the usual saliva.

Seeing the enraged Miss Box, I know what it is that's steamed her up and I can't blame her. It pains me as well, having to shoot Marty. But it came down to him or me, and though I would have easily sacrificed myself for him, he wasn't the Marty we both knew and love. In a sense, I put him out of his misery. It would have been something he wanted me to do. Yet, it still doesn't change the fact that I had to kill my best friend. And for that, I'll eternally suffer for it.

"Are you fucking deaf? You ain't taking my gig!" Brigit readies her stance for any combative opposition.

"It's as I said." I say while dabbing the corners of my mouth for blood. "It couldn't of been helped."

"To hell with that!" She barks. "I'm not talking about that. You did what you had to do. But that hit—ya had it comin'!"

"You're not going to stop me, Miss Box."

"Stop you? Did ya suddenly forget who yer speaking to? I ain't lookin' ta stop you. I fully intend on bein' part of the action. Marty was—well damn it all," she brings her hand to her forehead and slowly pushes back her bangs. "I loved em, alright? Yea – we didn't always get on, but hell he was the best thing I ever had. Now he's gone and—" she sniffs, wiping her nose with her sleeve. I can tell she's trying really hard not to show how much it hurts her. "I'm gonna fucking kill him, Sam! That bastard Dreval! That son-of-a-bitch!" She kicks the gig. "But damn you for trying to cut me outta it! Marty was my friend too!"

I turn to her partner, Harvey. Always there, standing somewhere close by in case of any need. I've always wondered, speculated whether there was something going on between him and her. He appears troubled, not fully knowing what it is that happened on the pier, but smart enough to put two and two together. He's concerned, I can tell by a new level of sternness that's built in his features. Still, he remains oppressive. Harvey makes no move to comfort her, nor indicates that I should in his stead.

A sound of boots on approach, Govennet issue, frightens us all into a dead aim towards the street from whence we had passed over the two cruisers. Our chirpers hum with the building of electricity in the coils, feeding off the city's grid—that miniature sun—and smoking from the collision of the chilly temperature.

One hits the ground belly first, his arms flail up in front of him, waving off the attack with an invisible white flag as his fellow freezes in place.

"Don't shoot! I don't want to die! Yes – we…" the fat one looks to his partner who nods voraciously. "*We* don't want to die!" The other one gets the idea, and falls to his belly as well, putting his hands up to signal his surrender. "We just heard gunshots, thought people were in trouble."

I recognize them, both from their post here at the pier: Caleb Grik and Bryan Sallis.

"Hold your fire." I tell my gun mates.

"Chief Inspector?" Sallis asks.

"Mr. Bell?" Officer Grik exclaims. "Is it you?"

"Yes – what are you two doing here?" I ask the still ground-dwelling officers.

"Well, you see, Bryan and I were just doing our rounds… you know – watching for plasties and all. I had four queens in me hand when—"

Officer Sallis interrupts. "You didn't have any queens! I had one in *my* hand. If you had four queens, then by George, I had a royal flush."

"Well, it could have been a couple aces, I'm not really sure. Anyway, so we were mindin' the usual business when out of the blue—"

"More black, really."

"Yes – when out of the black, came Inspector Kessler and those four other gents with that pretty little filly with blonde hair."

"Well not really blonde-blonde, more of a blondish-brown, strawberry blonde in a way."

"Listen, do you want me to tell the story or not?"

"I'm just trying to help you out here. Why are you being so testy."

"Cause I'm lying on my stomach getting wet from the snow and my arms hurt for keepin' so high, not to mention, you keep interrupting me."

Brigit rolls her eyes and lowers her pistol like an unwanted weight. "By the bloody maker, get the fuck up already. You've definitely proved a lack of threat."

"Is that Inspector Box you got with you?" Sallis asks. "Who else is there?"

"Harvey Parson, and a friend." I lower my weapon. "Come over here, I have some questions for you."

Caleb pokes up his head. "Very good, sir. Sallis and I can't thank you enough for sparing us from the cold." They hastily shift to their knees and then to standing, brushing the snow off their uniforms as they approach. "Can't even begin to explain to you the cruelties of a frozen tummy."

"You were saying about, Mr. Kessler."

"Right you are. Mr. Kessler brought that young girl to the pier, claimed they caught a mannequin and had to properly dispose of her. It was a right due shame too, she was an extremely pretty thing."

Officer Sallis nudges Caleb in the side. "Tell em about how things didn't feel right."

"Well you seem more predisposed towards it. I ain't going to lose rank by questioning Mr. Kessler's activities. You got us in trouble once already."

"You're not going to put us on review are you, Mr. Bell? That is, if I tell you what I thought?"

"No, it's alright. Go ahead." I say.

"See, Mr. Kessler told us to guard their gigs. The gigs can't fly without proper authorization, especially not a Govennet cruiser. We all know that. It just seemed like they didn't want us around. What also bothered me is that, well, he claimed he had a mannequin – and I'm not one to question my superior officer – but she didn't have the look of a screw-job. She was all quiet-like, didn't struggle or nothing. Just kept staring off towards the sea, like she was expecting to find something out there. I dunno," he shrugs. "It just didn't seem right to me. I started to ask questions – you know, nothing too difficult; the usual – wanted to know where they bagged her. Then suddenly I have a gun in my face and Inspector Kessler is accusing me of insubordination. I've always pegged him to be a nice fella'. I wasn't trying to be disrespectful."

He looks pretty shaken up about it. "Don't worry about it. You two are good men, and aren't in any trouble. You did what you were supposed to do."

Officer Grik glances over my shoulder and his once relieved face turns to worry.

"Is, ah – there something we need to know about, chief?" He motions to the Govennet corpses stapled to the promenade.

I nod. "Maybe you shouldn't trade that gut in of yours, it was dead on." I decide to hold a lot of it back. "There's more going on than you realize. All you need to know right now is that not all Govennet can be trusted. It is very possible that many of them have gone rogue, instituted and lead by Dr. Victor Dreval and his associates. I don't have the time to fill you in on all of it."

"Is there anything that Sal and I can do for ya?" Caleb asks with a hint of uncertainty.

"Actually, there is." I look off behind me. "I need the two of you to act as Govennet clean up. You need to confiscate their weapons and dump their bodies into the sea. Then, you'll need to get a hold of someone who can fill in these holes. If anyone asks, tell them that we plugged a few mannequins and just wanted to fix the promenade before business opened."

Sallis speaks up. "You can count on us, Mr. Bell. You've always been up front and a stand up kind of guy. But don't you think we should alert someone? Like the city council or maybe even the police?"

"In due time. The fact of the matter is, we don't know how deep this conspiracy goes. But I swear to you, I'll find out. Once we know who our allies are, I'll be more than happy to fill them in. Until then, I must ask you to try and keep things quiet. You may not realize it, but before all this, you two were in considerable danger."

"We'll try our best, Mr. Bell." Officer Grik pledges with utmost sincerity. "Come on, Sal. It looks we'll be going into overtime tonight."

I grab Caleb's sleeve before he goes anywhere. "One more thing. There's a woman down by the pier, you'll know her. She's…" I envision her exposed wiring and try to put things delicately. "…evidence. There are three tombs in the cemetery, one of granite, one of limestone and another made of glass. I need you to place her in the limestone one for safe keeping."

It was a lie, but I don't want to have to explain why I was being sentimental for a mannequin, at least not now and especially not to them.

"Yeah, sure. Whatever you need chief, we're up for the task."

He tries to move but I keep hold of his coat. "There's this little place on Nereid Street; 251 number 29, do you know it?"

"Haven't been there myself," Caleb offers. "But I'm sure Sal and I can find it."

"Good. I want you go there afterwards and stay put. It's a bit out of the patrol zones, but it's as safe as you can get. I'll meet you there before the night is out. I'll explain everything then."

They both nod, one of which seems solid in conviction, before they rush off together with the weight of the evening on their shoulders. I hate to drag them into this, but it's either this or get caught up in whatever Dr. Dreval has in store for those not quite filling out the ranks.

Brigit raises her eyebrow as soon as the officers pass, waiting for them to be out of earshot before crossing her arms in front of her chest. "Don't trust them?" She asks.

"Quite the contrary, I trust them explicitly. They've been on the post for awhile now, shooting up anything that fails the eye exam. It might be more than they can handle at the moment. Better for them to believe in a conspiracy against the Govennet and to get them off the street, than for them to be brainwashed as one of Dreval's new pets."

"Fine. I'll go with it. So what's the plan?"

"Now?" I look up the street to where I catch a hint of red and blue flashing across the buildings. "We wait for reinforcements."

"No! By the maker, you mother fuckers!" Patches slams his fists into the hood of one of the recently confiscated Govennet gigs. He spits when he curses. "This is your fault!" He points at me. "If it wasn't for your sorry ass, Felicia would still be alive!"

The rest of his posse shares a portion of his sentiment, keeping nearby to join in on the conversation.

"Can't do one fucking thing right, can ya, Govennet Man?" Frankie taunts to add salt to the wound.

I give him a nasty glare before returning to more important things. "Don't make the mistake that you're the only one who lost someone. I cared for Felicia too. Perhaps more than you'll ever give me credit for, but I lost something on top of that. I lost my best friend tonight and it was I who was behind the trigger. Yet I'm not going to sit around and place blame where it doesn't belong – there's only one man I blame for this tragedy and his name is Victor Dreval."

Biff's rumbling voice slides into the conversation like a glacier. "You thinking of going after him?"

Frankie buzzes his lips. "Oh, yeah? Nice try hot shot, and then what? Put him in jail for misbehaving? Everyone thinks he's a saint, and he's got a lot of political friends – damn politicians in his back pocket, not to mention whatever ties he may already have with the police. He'll be out before you have time to wipe your nose"

"Who says I'm going to arrest him?" I inquire beneath the gnashing of my teeth.

The blue coat wearing Jaime jumps in. "If you're not going to arrest him, what do you plan to do?"

I pause for a short moment, thinking over my line of reasoning carefully before spewing out what I've been contemplating for some time. "I'm going to kill him."

Patches rears his head back, as if the mentioning of it alone has a foul odor to it, but then starts, ever so slowly, nodding his head.

"You're going to kill him? Right!" The loudmouth counters. "You're going to walk right into the hospital, pull out your gun and waste em right there, huh? He's damn crazy!"

"But…" Patches voice raises like a ship from the bottom of the sea. "Dreval wouldn't expect anything. Not this quickly. Now would be the best time. Strike when his guard is down."

"You're both crazy!"

"No – Patches is right!" Jaime interrupts. "Felicia was a sweetheart and a good friend! It's inhuman what they did to her. I'm tired of sitting around and watching good people die. It's time we all did something to turn this messy business around."

Spence chimes in, a slow methodical individual who annunciates each of his words carefully and precisely, "If we are to assassinate this Victor Cornelius, we'll need more than simple blades and blunt implements. We'll need to make use of Roderick Whistler's legacy."

"I've got guns." Brigit claims, as she blows out the barrel of her chirper before replacing the piece back into the unit. She drops her foot from leaning on the trunk of her gig. Everyone's eyes are on her. "Harv and I got lots of guns."

I'm intrigued. An extra pistol at most is the standard for what Govennet officers carry in their gigs, a first aid kit and some flares. Brigit on the other hand, as I have found on countless occasions, is far from standard.

She punches a key code into the back trunk panel then pops the back. Everyone gathers to see what lurks inside the tiny compartment. Eyes bulge to the size of plums. Miss Box raises her jackboot up on the bumper of the vehicle.

"Feast your eyes, ladies. Bear witness to a collection not seen since the good old days of Roderick himself."

Collapsible rail assault rifles, automatic shotguns, multiple pistol clips and other assortments of ammo. I remember, she was there when the city seized his warehouse and store front. It was conceivable that many individuals, Govennet and police alike took weapons from the premises without notifying anyone. Whistler wasn't known for keeping detailed records about how many he produced. There were estimates and fears that some went missing. Now I know it was true. I bet it wasn't just Brigit who pilfered the cache.

I adopt a teasing smug. "And where did you happen to find these, Miss Brigit?"

She shrugs her shoulders. "Just fell into my lap one day. So I decided to keep em in case of an emergency. I'm not one for believing the city would keep em under lock and key forever. It's my sort of insurance policy. Guess I was right, huh?"

"You know, according to the book, you should be brought before a court hearing for this." I add just to play with her.

"This is a bad time to bring up technicalities, chiefy. Especially since you're talking about assassinating a so-called prominent member of society. Didn't you help write the damn book?" She spits on the ground. "To hell with the book."

"I'm just trying to rile you up. You came through, just like you always do." I say to try and soothe any misunderstandings.

"Damn right I did." Patches' crew grabs a few weapons, arming themselves appropriate to their size. "I expect those back when we're done so don't get too comfy with them." She mentions.

"You may want to run them through some basics before we head out, Brigit. I'd hate for one of us to get hurt."

"You got it, boss." Brigit holds up her chirper, places two fingers in her mouth and whistles. "Alright, boys and girls. This is very important, so don' touch nothin till I tell ya to. There are only five rules to using aunty Brigit's guns: number one, don't point the gun at anyone you don't intend to kill; number two, keep the safety on unless you're going to use it; number three, keep your finger off the fucking trigger unless you're going to shoot something; number four, if I see a single scratch on those babies, I'll kill you; and number five, if any of you assholes calls me aunty Brigit, I'll also kill you!"

A bit unorthodox, but I guess it'll have to do. I size up the little ragtag group of individuals. Not quite the skilled hunters belonging to the Govennet, but capable. They each check their weapons, as per Brigit's continued instruction, inserting their ammo and practicing switching off and then on the safety. It's what I have to work with. It'll have to do.

I ride in Brigit's gig along with her partner Harvey and the growing ever distant Roz. She mimics me, unintentionally of course, preferring to stare out the side window contemplating that terrible deed that's yet to come. That, among other things.

My thoughts relive the last fleeting moments of Rachel's life: the moment I rushed up the pier only to watch helplessly as they executed her right in front of me. I grit me teeth to the sound of the gunshot, shutting my eyes to the flash of light, it still playing on the lids of my eyes. Marty – dear Marty, what have I done?

PART III - THE SORCERER

I go over the events, trying to find some means in which I could have spared him. It seemed as if he hesitated momentarily, perhaps on some order to bring me in, that, or maybe he just hesitated. After I shot him there was a moment when I felt that he was the same old friend I knew prior to Dreval's handiwork. I try and put hope that it's possible for people to fight against it, to try and overcome the horrors of their actions. But after having seen the faces of many possessed mannequins, I can attest that whatever it is that made them human has far since been erased.

We may not be human, but as synthetic beings, it is what we were made to believe in. Farley talked about being alive, to accept it above all things. Rachel insisted that I find what it is that matters and then hold onto it. Even as a machine, I am a machine that thinks. I am a machine that feels. And though I am alive, I now find myself at odds with my humanity. To kill or be killed. To devolve into that same monster Dreval had me toil so long to destroy. With blood on the horizon, I cannot help but dwell amidst terrifying thoughts. Do I now act on free will, or is all this part of some sadistic game programmed into my being from an unseen arbiter? Had I truly any will to resist my feelings for a woman who would die shortly after I finally met her? Was choice ever an option for preventing Emily's death? Was everything previously orchestrated as so to reach this pivotal moment in time?

These thoughts act only to cloud my emotions, to distract me from what needs to be done. Ultimately, it is Dr. Dreval who is responsible for the mass murder of hundreds of people, including my best friend and the girl from my dreams. For this I shall make him pay and for this I shall make him suffer. I do it for the victims killed by my hands. I do it for Marty. I do it for Rachel. I do it for the people of the CitySpire. And looking over at my seatmate, the forlorn ballerina who lost her friend – I do it for her as well. For Emily… I would undo it all.

31

Our journey takes us to the CitySpire Hospital & Asylum, a place where Dreval's personal research laboratory is renown to reside. It's a number of concrete complexes, strung together by over-the-street walkways and interconnecting tunnels dug by city crews. It isn't much to look at, just as dull and riddled with the creep as the buildings next to it. Since everyone is synthetic, it explains why there aren't that many patients. It makes me wonder, just how long has the hospital known about the populous? How many members of their skeleton staff kept it secret? How many others are responsible?

I rush through the front sliding doors with little patience for the motion sensors to catch my approach. I'm flanked by Patches and Brigit, into the main lobby – our eyes assaulted by the bright florescent lights and white deco. I carry Roz in my arms, my coat slung over her body as she cringes in pain.

At the center of the room is a translucent hard plastic desk, an old lamp and a file drawer nearby. A dainty woman in a white v-neck nurse's jacket, short skirt and a quaint two-button nursing cap sits behind it all, penciling in a collection of reports stacked neatly on the top counter. The rest of the lobby is empty, save for the numerous steel folding chairs arranged in tight nine by nine rows, a couple wheelchairs and a stainless steel stretcher. A pair of muscle bound goons in white scrubs are positioned at back entrances into the structure: one at a hallway, another guarding the elevator and stairs.

The nurse looks up at our entry, sets down her pencil and folds her hands in front of her. Roz moans in pain for good measure.

"Oh – my goodness!" Cries the woman from behind the desk. "What's wrong with the poor dear?" She stands up to offer assistance.

"I don't know. She kept complaining her stomach hurts and then, about ten minutes ago she collapsed in pain. We didn't know where else to go." I reply with as much tenacity as possible.

I bundle the coat as tightly around her as possible, as I sit her up on the desk. Roz doubles over, clutching the pistols against her stomach beneath the garb to better hide our intentions.

The nurse places her hand on Roz's neck and says, "Poor little thing. Well, you've come to the right place. We have a number of doctors on standby, we'll wheel her right up." She motions to the brutes for assistance who proceed to lumber in our direction. "While they get her upstairs, I'll need one of you to fill out these forms so we can bill the city on your behalf."

She hands me a clipboard with an overwhelming number of applications, for which I pass onto Patches. The nurse then pulls a DOR-52 out of her pocket, and calibrates the optic sensor for the lighting.

"Now, how long has it been since her last eye exam?" She asks as she leans slightly over her desk and gently pulls back Roz's raven hair.

"Not since registration." I watch as her muscle grabs the stretcher and wheels it dangerously closer. I hurry else violate our masquerade before learning his whereabouts. "I was told specifically to ask for Dr. Dreval. I hear he's the best Doctor in the city. Is he in?"

The nurse stalls with the red-eye, as Roz bites her teeth and whimpers to avoid the diabolic device. "Oh, I'm sorry. He is in, but he's currently conducting strict research at the moment. The other doctors are all well endorsed by Dr. Dreval and are held in high regard by members of our community." One quick effort, the nurse leans in, holds Roz's head steady and then places the ocular up to her eye. The sensor flashes a blood red.

The nurse, so bewildered by the failed result, has little time for a reaction as Roz pulls a chirper from beneath my coat and forces it into her forehead.

"Oh, my." Is all the nurse can muster, paralyzed by the flashing fear of green. Her arms shake on the desk.

Both Brigit and Patches draw their weapons as well, halting the alerted men from coming any closer. The surprised male nurses look between one another to communicate the dire reality of their situation.

I refit my coat to my shoulders and take the remaining pistol from Roz. I nod towards the door at Patches for him to alert the rest of his crew to enter.

"I do apologize for the deception, miss. I'm sure you're a benefit to your profession and that you'd be a terrible waste if for some reason you decide not to cooperate. I'm only going to ask you this once and I want a straight answer. Where is Dr. Dreval?"

She stutters, her knuckles bleached to bone holding the red-eye ocular. "H-h-h-he's up on the twenty-first floor, room 2113. J-j-just take the elevator up, it should get you there."

The nurse is innocent in all this, a receptionist just trying to make ends meet. She has brown braided hair that's pinned back and tucked carefully beneath her cap, smooth skin and red lips.

"What's your name?" I ask to help alleviate her nervousness.

"L-loretta." The nurse manages to expel, unable to take her eyes off the chirper pressed to her brow.

"Loretta, we've all had a really bad night tonight. We don't want to run into any surprises. So in order to prevent people such as yourself from getting hurt, how many security officers are up on the twenty-first floor?"

She hesitates, having difficulties counting the seconds needed to take her life. "Two…m-m-maybe three?"

"Are they armed?"

Loretta starts to shake her head no, but then in perhaps a hiccup of thought, she nods her head yes.

I hate to put her in harms way, especially due to something that she isn't part of. But if the security guards see a familiar face, they'll be less apt to shooting first. If this is what I have to do to prevent the loss of life, to reach my objective then I'll do it.

As Jaime, Spence, Biff and Frankie file in through the front entry way, I relay my intentions.

"Well Loretta, it looks like you'll be coming with us."

I leave Harvey and Biff in the front lobby to guard the exit and keep the two male nurses in line. The rest of us take the elevator up to the twenty-first floor, labeled "laboratories" by the quick reference sheet adjacent to the buttons. Loretta twists and fidgets with her hands, wringing them, as she bites her lower lip watching the numbers climb.

Frankie sees this as a perfect opportunity to make matters worse.

"You nervous or something, pretty thing? Think something terrible might happen to ya? Well, don't you worry missy. At least you won't have to go far to get to the hospital."

"Shut up, Frankie!" I snap at him. Prefering to ride the elevator in as much silence as possible. "I won't tell you a second time."

I keep my face forward, keeping watch at the steel elevator doors, just anticipating their open as soon as the carriage slows and halts at our pre-designated floor. Frankie intakes a breath of air, a taste of some unneeded comeback, but I hear a stifling of sorts—figuring it either belong to Patches or some other member of his gang—and it all passes harmlessly somewhere between the thirteenth and fourteenth floor.

Loretta's worries are her own, and I leave her to them. There are no words by me or any here that could offer any sort of consolation. Besides, as long as she's fearful, the less likely she'll try to do something heroic. If she would, it'd be for the wrong reasons.

The elevator slows and then halts in its ascent. The chime calls out into a hallway of storage rooms filled with equipment, medicinal cabinets and research samples. I have Loretta lead the way, preferring her to be the first anyone sees patrolling the area before the rest of us.

Everything is darker, dimly lit and obscure, almost a parallel universe to the bright lobby we had just left. The windows are painted black on the inside, the white frames splotched by a rushed paint job. Occasionally, from one of the overhead bulbs, it flickers in brightness, turning on and then off again, sounding in protest like a hammer tapping at glass.

We cut down the hallway and into an adjoining one, where sit three officers behind at a tiny fold out end table. They sit at each respective end with one in the center, wearing blue and grey uniforms and a belt home to a baton, flashlight and a holstered Roderick chirper. I wonder where they got them from.

One gentleman has already stood up from his hand of cards and ante, probably from hearing us coming down the hall. He tips his brimmed hat to Loretta, and then steps forward to block our way. His hand rests on his belt holster, a couple fingers on the gun.

"Sorry, Miss Fox. No one is allowed beyond this point. Dr. Dreval's explicit orders, you know how it is."

The nurse crosses her arms in front of her for security. "George, you may want to let these people pass."

His eyebrows perk and the two other officers rise out of their seats. "Oh, is that so?" George replies condescendingly.

I initiate the draw by reaching into my coat whilst the rest of our troop brings their guns from behind him into view. The hallway echoes with the charge of coils and blinking of lights.

I counter from behind the barrel, "Yea - that's so."

George raises his arms, palms facing forward. His men do the same.

We're finally led to the double doors guarding the laboratory belonging to the nefarious Dr. Dreval. There is no hesitation, no moment of reconsideration, when I kick open the swinging doors, sending them crashing into the wall and startling the hunched over doctor. He's fiddling with some new mechanical device. A collection of hand drawn blueprints and various parts are scattered across an oak desk. A couple of examination tables, mysterious machinery and diagrams fill the room.

Seeing him with his nearly bald head, long wispy hair and labcoat infuriates me beyond anything I've yet to experience. I see the death of Rachel and Marty play over again in my mind, I imagine the deaths that my organization has caused under the name of protecting the citizenry from so-called monsters that he himself had invented. He glares at me from his sunken sockets and those miserable crow's feet that hang at the edge of his malicious eyes. All doubts, all second thoughts, vaporize beneath the fires of retribution raging inside me.

I race across the tile, one long stride after the other, keeping my poise and watching his in case of some treachery. And once I reach that wooden table, I stab across the mess of his evil designs, grab him by the throat and drag his pitiful body across it all. As his feet kick uselessly over the counter, I reverse him into the table—bruising his spine—and jam my pistol between his eyes.

My face is tight, my teeth are clenched and the pressure behind my eyes builds at every passing second as if threatening to expel my hatred for him. But the man—if he can be called a man—simply observes me, as if my actions were more than mere entertainment than anything else.

He makes no effort to fight me, just hangs onto the pain that I inflict upon both his back and throat. I ease into the trigger, causing the green lights to blink directionally towards the nozzle, and the coils to hum as they build with electricity. But it is in his calm demeanor, his lack of self-preservation, that I come to the realization that he has something to say, something he's holding back from me and will likely haunt me if I don't inquire. He's taunting me with it, like some vicious beast torturing its prey before swallowing it whole.

"What is it Doctor? No words of remorse or feelings of guilt? No words of justification to jot down for the pages of history?"

"No, Mr. Bell. None that I wish to expel. Yet it seems that you won't be content unless I offer you some sliver of rhetorical gratification. Proceed with your accusations, and I'll do my best to accommodate your feral urges to do what you feel inevitably must be done."

"You manipulated and deceived the population of the CitySpire, you misled the Govennet to kill innocent people, you corrupted good men and women, you're responsible for Marty's death and the death of one Felicia Rhodes—my Rachel!"

"I know not the name of the woman, but as for Mr. Kessler, he was alive last I saw of him unless there was something you did to change that."

"You fiend!"

"Quick to judge as I always expected, Chief Inspector. You never really took the time to appreciate all that I've tried to do for you and your friends. You'd think you'd be a little more grateful."

"Grateful!" I scream. "Grateful! The only gratitude that I hold for you is in the shape of the steel rail I pried from the docks after it had murdered *her*!"

"How very theatrical, but it is the typical reward from an obviously ignorant man. So misguided and blind to all that goes on around you, no wonder your beloved Emily committed suicide."

I strike him with the butt of my chirper.

He spits out a clot of blood. "That's the spirit! Kill me, Mr. Bell. Release your vengeance upon me so your dear friends may rest in peace! It's all so ironic that all this will happen again and you, dear Sam, will have to relive the torment of losing your loved ones over again! Oh – yes, Mr. Bell. We are all prisoners here, forced to live the same life over and over again. There will be, and has been, many Emily's committing suicide, multiple Marty Kessler's falling to some horrendous tragedy and many more Dr. Drevals you'll have to slay in his own laboratory. Because of you, all my work will be for naught, and we shall be prisoners forever. So go on, Mr. Bell, pull that trigger back and let me slide into the next life so I may begin this dance again. Perhaps next time you'll be more predisposed to listen than harsh action."

I watch the lights count five in their sequence, one after another lighting up to warn me and others the weapon is ready to fire. Currently, it is I who holds reign over whether Dr. Dreval lives or dies, and time – I have all the time in the world. Let the murderer state his case, and if I find him licentious and sans worth then I shall be minus one sabot for the trouble.

I release the trigger yet still keep my aim true and pressed against his skull. "Spill it."

A sly smile rends itself across his cheeks as if in some small victory. "Don't you get it, Mr. Bell? Of all those years you served as a govennet officer? I tried to save you. That's right! I, Doctor Victor Cornelius Dreval, tried to save you from a life of anguish and destruction. I gave you the chance at something, to shirk off your programmed responsibilities and be with those who now haunt your memories. It was your chance to escape destiny. I don't know how you did it—a pity that you threw it all away."

"Is that what you call what you did to Marty and all the others? Turning them into homicidal automatons without a soul or semblance of conscience?"

"A soul? Mr. Bell, don't be so naïve. We're objects. We're machines. We're synthetic beings with synthetic lives and synthetic beliefs. We're nothing in the grand scheme of the universe, don't you understand? Be it a tried and true friend, or a homicidal automaton—as you put it—it's all the same. Kill one it is a tragedy but destroy a machine, it's just a down right shame. Nothing more than that. Your convictions of what is right and wrong is a product of our maker and not a parade of personal choices or societal musings. What's the difference if I kill one, a thousand, or even one-hundred-thousand? I'm eradicating inventory, not the lives of living breathing people. Even still, what's it matter if I destroy one individual's existence this cycle, when they'll only return a second, third, till who knows when? I'm working to disrupt the designs of our maker, to break this forever unending. If you were an intelligent creation, you'd look past your adopted sentimentality and come to terms what is truly set before us."

"Machines or not, why do it at all? Why go to all the extra trouble to have them eliminated?"

"Population control, Mr. Bell. Of all people, you should understand that! We may have enough food to get us by, but what about space? What about access to resources? With each major spawning, generations bring with them different ideals, untold ambitions and secret agendas. What's to keep the status quo? The answer is simple: you destroy whoever threatens it, whoever is most dangerous. This city cannot handle such a large influx of population as it had in the past. It threatens the stability of all we worked for.

The DOR-52 was one solution to keep the scales balanced. It's about giving power to those who keep the city's best interests at heart. And it's easier making a dramatic change to a tapestry when there are only one-hundred threads as opposed to a million."

"Power to whom? The council? You?" I push the chirper harder against his brow. "Tell me or I'll send you into your next cycle."

"Do you honestly think I'm the mastermind behind the plot?" He giggles with the notion of absurdity. "Sad to say, I was not the one who first uncovered this whole mystery. Besides, I'm only ninth generation, Mr. Bell. I don't own a building like you do. I didn't have the time to claim my station in life. I had to work for it, by relying on the funds offered unto me by others. I'm just the one who invented the so-called 'red-eye' and am called upon to use it, from time to time, to ensure their particular… *cooperation*. No – Mr. Bell, there is another I work for. A man who acquired his fortune through the generous donations of the faithful."

"I want his name, damn you!"

Dr. Dreval pushes against the gun, leaning in as if to whisper so the room would not be able to hear. "He goes by the name of Ehcimel."

My head turns away as if Marty's own hand slaps me across the face. The head churcher himself. "Where? Where can I find him? What does he look like?"

"Oh, you'll know him when you see him. He certainly knows you. As for where he resides, I'd say check the northeast districts, well past the patrols; the tallest building with a white dome and needled point. You'll find him there."

I withdraw my gun, letting the barrel point towards the ceiling to let the coils cool off before holstering it. A round circular imprint is stamped on his forehead, and the doctor takes a moment to rub it.

"Before, you said you gave me a chance. A chance at what?" I ask.

"We all dream, Mr. Bell. It's ingrained into us. In reality we're stuck in an inevitable loop, our conscience is transferred into a new body with both our minds and world wiped anew. But with dreams, we can relive the parts we hold most dear. You had the opportunity to be with your dearest Emily again, Mr. Bell. I don't know how you woke, most don't have the strength. I don't think I would, had I the chance."

"How can something be awake and sleeping at the same time?"

Dreval smiles, revealing a row of bloodied teeth. "Think of it as sleep-walking, Mr. Bell. The conscious mind is asleep while the darker, more basic, aspects of our personality are brought to the forefront. It's always a part of us, Mr. Bell, lurking in the shadows of our psyche. The horse is difficult to control when the rider is unconscious but with proper assertion, someone else can grab the reins. As for waking them up? I guess that depends on the horse and rider. Once you give a horse an inch, it'll run for miles. Funny thing about horses though, if you let them go for too long they may run themselves to death."

Though as much hatred as I hold for his man, I shouldn't kill him. His goals aren't noble, he doesn't place any value on life and he is partial responsible for the untold deaths of hundreds of people. Would killing him be proper justice? If I gave into revenge, would I then not be any different than the very mannequins he created? Where then would be the line for distinguishing those who sleepwalk, and those who aren't? Perhaps he should be punished for his crimes, but not by me. We'll need him to undo the damage he's wrought. I believe it's a choice better left to the inhabitants of the CitySpire.

I retreat backwards and announce to the faces that eagerly wait by the door, "Dreval should be given—"

A resounding boom tosses my heart into my brain, in fright that Dr. Dreval took a shot from behind. But when I spin around, gun aimed for his deception, I only see the flattened corpse of the once standing doctor at the feet of a petite raven-haired girl. The gun still hums in her hand as she points it at his body and fires the remaining rounds into his back.

How she slipped by me, I do not know, perhaps when we spoke. Roz's legs and clothes are splattered with blood, a gruesome result for such close proximity. She rolls her head from shoulder to shoulder, tilting her nose into the air as if sniffing in the memory of it, basking in the scent of ozone mixed with a hint of copper.

The young ballerina spits on his head and gives him a swift kick. "And that," she cries, "is for Felicia!"

It seems in the CitySpire all it takes is a single vote to condemn a man to death.

Roz meets up with us, red stained hair and cheeks, the rest of us awash with crippling disbelief.

She rests the back of her chirper against her collar. "Now… it's time to find this Ehcimal and make him pay for what he has done!"

The Govennet cruisers open up the front lobby with a spray of electrically charged rails that are accompanied by a lashing of glass and splinters. A great tower is under siege, one with a tiny dome and a needle point spire. Its outside is black with the creep, with powerful walls of glass and beams of concrete.

I spy the silhouettes of the lobby guardsmen, each attempting to break for some level of protection, to avoid the finger-sized projectiles that bleed the room into a tornado of dust and debris. Most are caught in the furry of the gigs' cannons, resulting in a loss of limb or gain a body window the size of a fist. Mannequins, every one of them. They are armed with a variety of pistols and assault weaponry – such items meant to be under careful lock and key, yet somehow in the quest for dominance the shrouded Ehcimal managed to acquire them.

I wait for the drivers to get their fill, to clear the lobby of danger before the rest of us charge forth. They fire their guns, continually rotating their chain armament until it whirs with emptiness and the air is filled with steam and static. The gigs retreat, pulling out from in front of the building's entrance and then up into the sky to reload and wait until such a time if we need to escape. We're minus both Brigit and Harvey, along with the ever-so increasingly talented Spence.

Flanked by both Frankie and Roz, Patches with Jaime and Biff, we rush forward with one swipe of my hand – like those past training exercises I emphasized with Govennet recruits, to work as a team. Across the street we push, over the curb and then up twelve steps and in through the shattered walls and into the lobby. Glass crushes beneath my feet like a sound of tiny bells. The hair on my arms, neck and legs all respond to the static charge that built due to the high-velocity rails. At times I can hear it crackle as it leaps from one piece of steel to the other, especially along the railing that leads up to a second floor balcony where elevators nestle.

Something moves next to a battered overturned desk and I shoot it until it stops. Frankie rushes over to the same spot, kicks it over and fires a few into the corpse for good measure.

He smiles wickedly. "Never can be too careful… boss." His last word borders on a taunt.

A couple of gunshots fire off where Patches and his group have also located a struggling automaton attempting to resurrect itself from a pile of debris and missing components.

"I certainly hope there are more of those pricks." Frankie boasts while looting the weapon off the corpse. He slings it around his shoulder. "I think I can see why you enjoy doing this sort of thing."

"I've never enjoyed it." I bite back. "Sometimes you just have to do what you have to do because no one else is going to do it. That's life."

He shrugs his shoulders and presses on. "Whatever you say, Govennet Man."

"Are you two going to keep this up the entire night?" Jaime asks from her side of the room. She kicks over a piece of a counter, checking underneath and claiming another weapon for herself.

Patches keeps a wary eye out. "I say let them dish it out, we're always up for some prime entertainment." He sighs. "Reminds me of Felicia."

The still blood-spattered Roz, unwilling to wipe away her previous deed and instead insisting on wearing it as war paint, sneaks up besides me. "Forget about it, Sam. Focus more on important things."

"You gettin' a soft spot for Felicia's old fling?" Frankie prattles.

I ignore him the best I can while proceeding closer to the stairs to the upper balcony.

"Might want to rethink that one, little Rozie. Everyone he gets friendly with ends up dead."

I bid for his attention. "Hey Frankie?" And when he turns, I jack him in the face.

He stumbles backwards, dropping his initial pistol and grabbing at his nose. Eyes closed, he almost tumbles over but somehow miraculously reclaims his balance, unslings his weapon and points it at me. He breathes heavily and red faced.

"That's for being an asshole." I announce despite his current temperament. He could shoot me, but I'm convinced that I'd get a round off in his head before it was all over.

"Frankie!" Patches yells. "Point that somewhere else before he kills you."

Roz just stares him down. "Got to resort to a gun, huh Frankie? Can't settle your difference like a real man?"

"Big words for someone who shot the unarmed doc."

She looks back over at me to assert her message. "That's life."

The stringy man relents and eases the barrel towards the stairs. "Just joshin' ya, boss. Next time you and I'll give her a go, how's that?"

"Looking forward to it." I toss back.

We get up the stairs and to the elevators. Brass framed and elegantly engraved, the doors chime open with the push of the button. The insides are upholstered with red velvet, taught and buttoned. I look up, catching the small trapdoor that leads to its roof. In the back of my mind, I worry if this is a good idea.

"Which floor?" Jaime asks as she brushes past Biff and scrunches next to the call box.

"Ehcimel seems to be the type where he wants to be above everyone, so try the thirty-seventh floor. I'm sure he has his own private suite." I say while, examining the board.

"Alright," she shrugs. "Here goes nothing." She pushes the button and the carriage hastily ascends.

The whole ride people are quiet, perhaps due to the demoralizing cage they are so used to beneath the streets of the city. I listen to the sounds of the counter weights and the grinding of the spool of cable above, praying each floor that we arrive safely and are not cut loose by an overly paranoid maniac who's bent on terror, subjugation and murder. However, my fears are realized when the elevator halts at the thirty-fourth floor.

"What the hell is going on?" Patches asks while looking up. "Jaime hit the button again."

"I *am* pushing the button." She cries as she rapidly jabs it. "It's not doing anything."

"Try the door." He orders as he squeezes by me.

"Whose bright idea was it to take the elevator again?" Frankie puts in.

I enlist the aid from the brute next to me. "Biff, can you lift me to that trapdoor. Maybe I can get up there and take a gander."

Jaime finally snaps. "You know what, I didn't hear anyone say anything about not taking the elevator. Did you hear anyone say, 'Don't take the elevator?' Stop being a whinny little bitch and make yourself useful for once."

"Useful huh? I have half a mind to just walk out of this shit—"

I stop listening. They bicker, they press and fondle, then try prying at the doors but find difficulties getting their fingers into the cracks. Meanwhile, Biff gives me the boost that I need to pop open the trapdoor and hoist myself up to the roof.

I'm assaulted by dust and the awful scent of oil. The shaft is dark, only lit by the periodical glimmer of a little light that seeps from beneath the doors of every floor. We're stuck between levels, with, assumingly, the thirty-fifth at chest height.

"What's up there, Sam? Have you found us a way out?" Calls the young Roz from beneath.

The outside doors do not look as tight as the ones inside the elevator, especially around the bottom. I slip my fingers beneath the cracks, able to slide them under completely and grab hold from the opposite side. With as much strength as I can muster from this galling and awkward angle, I hold firm one while pushing away the other gaining only a few centimeters at first, but once there is a space in the center, I'm able to peel away the doors enough for a person to climb through.

"Hey, I think I may have found—"

A high-pitch squeal echoes down the empty shaft, as mechanisms from above start to turn. I feel the sinking feeling in my chest way before the elevator begins to move and with one quick jostle, I start for the open doors and leap. As I grab the exterior doors and kick up with my feet, the elevator drops from beneath me and descends into the darkness below. The updraft from the carriage pushes me upwards and onto the thirty-fifth floor where I unveil my weapon and nervously consider my surroundings.

I'm in a hallway surrounded by the other elevators, an empty passageway with marble flooring with that obvious Greek flair. The lighting here is poor and with no indications of it increasing due to my presence. I then place my ear to the darkness of the shaft, listening for that dooming crash or what other fate may have befallen them. For a few moments I hear nothing, just the whirring of the above motors. Then the cable stops and the engines grow silent. With it, as a breeze swims into my face, I'm relieved that spirits of the elevator took mercy on them. But with a chime, echoes a familiar scream, yelling and then gunfire.

They could be outnumbered, fighting for their very lives from the inside of the carriage. I want nothing more than to be able to help them, to climb down the cable and come to their rescue. But there isn't much I can do, not from here and by the time I make it to whatever floor below, they could be dead. No, from now on, I am on my own. I must find this Ehcimel to confront him and kill him. I'm only two floors away, but this time I'm taking the stairs.

Stealthily, I glide through the shadows of the hallway until I find the stairwell. Everything is dark with but a periodical wall-affixed plastic disc that hides the dim light bulb. A means, perhaps, to keep the public's attentions drawn away from the windows and offering just enough light for patrols. This area of the skyscraper is desolate, devoid of most furniture pieces that may have been moved to other locations, that, or it has always been this way. There isn't the slightest sound, no sliver of motion or mild hum of technology. It is the very bastion of quiet that instills the same dreadful feelings when the world was empty. Were it not for the vibrations beneath me, the echoes of gunfire emanating from the lower floors, I would surely believe all life to have extinguished the moment I leapt from the elevator.

I find my way to a heavy metal-set door that's comparable in design to other stairwells strewn throughout the city. With a bit of effort, I manage to ease the vessel slightly ajar, to listen and peek around the corner to see if there is any opposition. When I'm about to step out, I feel the foundation above shake, then a slam of something heavy, followed by the descending rumble of heavy footfalls.

I shut the door and hide on the other side, charging my chirper as best as I can without alerting those within that I'm here. I cover the lights, preferring not to be betrayed by my own weapon. My blood pounds with every leaden step as multiple individuals clamor down the stairs; throwing a noise that masks their number. Though they pass, continuing down the steps like a defiant thunder cloud off to spread its malcontent somewhere else, I still linger behind my door to better the distance. I wait till the quake is softer before trying the door again.

Once out onto the greyish concrete steps, in this darkened spiraled arena, I look out and over the silver railing towards the floor below. I can see the group of men who had emerged from above me still making their way downwards with flashlights spotting out before them. There are quiet a few—eight, possibly more. The shadows, mixed with the glare of their torches, make it difficult to tell. I hear them racing the steps as if in flight of some terrifying beast. Given the circumstances, I believe they are more apt to racing towards something—the source of the fire fight, no doubt—than away. I sincerely hope everyone is okay.

Quietly, I climb the remaining two floors, like a prowler set upon heinous deeds. I pass through the steel door of the thirty-seventh floor. I listen. I wait. And without noise or disturbance, I slowly push into another hallway. The lights are turned down as well, something of personal preference as there are no windows here, just a hallway that leads closer towards the elevators. I follow the white walls, glancing momentarily at the outcropping ionic columns that extend every so many feet along the wall. There are paintings hung between the occasional set, one of an ancient Greek trireme being tossed about during a savage storm, whilst another depicts the harrowing god, Setebos, devouring the moon. I quicken my pace in order to escape the demon's gaze.

Past the elevators, I continue down the hallway to a pair of white painted doors, whose knobs are replaced by polished brass handles. When I lay my hand on one, I can feel my heart throbbing through my thumb – it's a painful annoyance that reminds me of that growing anxiety that comes whenever I know a mannequin is right around a corner. It's a horrid feeling, a devious drag on my muscles that stiffens them, readying them for impact that may never come. I try and wish the sensation away by taking some deep breaths. I must control my fear, as it weakens my resolve and slows the reactions. I picture Rachel murdered on the docks, of Marty dropping into the sea and watching everything I've built the past few years be torn apart due to the delusions of a madman.

I'm not facing just a mannequin, some screw-job who is out on a rampage and is threatening the city. I'm soon to come face-to-face with *the* mannequin, the very one who started it all. And even though he may sound human and even though he may look human, he holds no appreciation for life or freewill, and will not stop without proper intervention.

I lean my brow against my chirper, say a prayer to my past friends both gone and lost to me and with a gathering of anger, with an infusion of hatred for all that has been done, I rear back and kick open the door.

A piece splinters into the room and slides across the wooden floor, and I not far along behind it. My jackboots resound through the chamber, a damning requiem to the blackened silhouette who stands at the other end of room. There's an old scent to the place, a strange collection of oil, leather, parchment and cigars. Spare light that shines from the streets and neighboring buildings trickles in through the cracks of the blinds. The windows are something spectacular, a long parade of glass panes that drape from the highest point of the extended ceiling to the floor. All walls are dressed with bookshelves spilling with tomes, papers and baubles. A few other furniture pieces marks this as his quarters: a four-post bed, armoire and dresser off in a shadowed section, along with a fainting couch, dining table and chairs, as well as a sofa and a few overstuffed chairs.

The man I've been looking for holds a book in one hand, reading before I intervened, nearest an ornately carved oak desk. He looks up from his selection, reflecting bits of the outside world with his rounded glasses. The darkness marks his visage.

My chirper keeps him in place. "Are you Ehcimel?" I ask as I gradually move towards him.

"Mr. Bell?" He cocks his head as if to confirm his perceptions. "Samuel Bell, is that you?"

The voice is recognizable, but like the dust in the room, it is old and difficult to ascertain. It's all from long ago, a lost memory, a forgotten dream. The closer I approach, the more gloom is dispelled from the man's features – a hooked nose, a prominent brow, a chiseled face and cleft chin. I know this man – by the arbiter it can't be!

"Michael? Michael Rawlings Locke? No – it can't be you!" I say trying to blink away the illusion, but the image stays firm.

"Samuel! It is you. And here I thought you my assassin." He takes a step forward. "I—"

I light up the chirper, allowing the greenish hue to dissuade his advance. I tighten my lip, still adrift in both shock and disbelief.

"I see." He sets his book down on the desk, removes his glasses, pinches his nose and then tosses them atop it. "Is this any way to greet an old friend?"

"Michael? You're Ehcimel?" I blunder out, my face frozen in the last pronunciation.

"If there ever were a man that went by the name of Ehcimel, I would be he."

"But?" I try to collect my thoughts, as most of them spilled from my brain like a rail to the skull. "Where—what?" I swallow a particularly foul lump in my throat that makes me want to expel the contents of my stomach.

He holds out his hand to steady me from afar. "It's alright, Mr. Bell. I assure you that everything is okay. Don't you worry. I am your friend."

"Friend?" I nod off to the side for a moment and reclaim my confidence. I squeeze the handle of my chirper and steady both my aim and resolve. "No – Everything is not, 'okay', Michael. Do you know what you have done?"

"I know very well what has transpired, Mr. Bell. It's terrible, but it is necessary."

"Necessary?" I scream. "Michael, people are dead because of you. You've killed innocent people and enslaved others. How is any of that justifiable?"

"Innocent?" He's taken aback by the mere mention of the word. "We wouldn't be here if we were innocent, Mr. Bell. Look around you, Samuel. This city is hell! It is a prison for those who lacked faith enough to transcend into the great beyond. We are all damned here. Do you not understand? There are no innocents. They proved that back at the Open convenience store massacre and then again when they burned down my house and almost killed Natalie! People don't care whether their neighbors live or die, as long as their survival is ensured. It's exactly as I predicted. It's exactly what I told you the day we left for the manors, 'Rats' down to the last."

I shake my head trying to swallow his fervor. "What happened to you, Michael? You used to be a dear friend, and now this?"

He points out the window. "*They* happened, Mr. Bell. Nothing happened to me. I was perfectly content living in your apartment building, not a care in the world, with just the four of us. Then *they* turned up, sniveling little beasts woken to the lower-class with hands out and mouths open. They're repulsive. Every last one of them."

"I recall a time when you woke into squalor, or did you so conveniently forget."

He straightens a few inches taller. "Unlike the majority of these beggars, I took myself from living in tepid conditions and bettered myself. We were a team, all of us. We held our own little society that provided for one another during difficult times. But those," he points out towards the blinds. "Those sea waifs came and ruined everything! Assassins, every last one of them! They came to my house with torches and knives, Samuel! Torches and knives! They burned down my house! They *burned* down my house."

"So you wanted to get even, is that it?"

"That's what a lesser man would do. But I saw something else in the fires that claimed my manor, I saw a sign from the arbiter himself telling me what it is I needed to do in order to reclaim this city. All this time, I had taken my intelligence and greater sensibilities for granted, believing that all men are created equal. Yet, as the flames devoured my home I realized that they lacked everything I prided myself on – logical rationality. These faithless people didn't need to be punished, they needed to be controlled."

"Through population control?"

"Population control is only a part of it. It's easier to influence a handful of people instead of an entire island's worth. Though some deaths were regrettable, it was necessary to keep things from spiraling out of control. There was another reason."

"Power over those beneath you?" I accuse.

"You still don't understand why we are here, do you? The ships have sailed, Samuel. The world left us behind to suffer in this abhorred place of woe. We are prisoners here, don't you see? We've been abandoned to live our miserable lives in this cursed city over and over again. We were left due to our faithlessness, and offense to the divine. All must repent, to seek forgiveness from the Great Maker, and perhaps he'll call the ships to port. But Samuel, those wretches are dragging us down! It's all here!" He spreads his fingers to encompass his entire collection. "We have to light the fires within ourselves before they'll be able to find us. People must be forced to accept to truth."

He's out of his mind. "What if people don't want this so-called *truth* of yours?"

"It isn't *my* truth, Samuel. It's *His* truth. Time and time again has proven to me that our lessers are ill-equipped for rational thinking. In such case, they shall have to be forced. It is our only chance to sail home."

"There are no ships, Michael." I offer in spite of his zeal. "There never were. There never will be."

"See that is where you are wrong, Mr. Bell. You're wrong because I've seen them." He points to his heart. "I've seen them here." And then he points to his temple. "I've also seen them here, in dreams. But for you, you have to believe that they are there, you have to have faith in what I'm telling you. Otherwise we are all lost."

"It seems to me that the only thing that is lost is your mind, Michael. Perhaps, you've always been this way. Ever since that night in the graveyard, I knew that there was something a bit off with you. I should have seen it then."

"Oh, yes… the graveyard." He places his fingers on his chin to recall the memory. "I knew it was only a matter of time before you would come searching in the graveyard. I knew, because that was the first place I thought to look in order to find the previous occupants of the city. I was there before. Why else would the soil come up so easily? It was there that I found your corpse."

I shake my head. "As I recall, that particular grave was empty."

"Yes – quite right, Mr. Bell. It was indeed empty the night I took you to it. Much to my surprise! I had hoped to draw some sort of a confession from you while we uncovered it for a second time, but when I found it empty I was exceedingly troubled. It took me a great deal of time to convince myself that it wasn't you playing some horrible trick on me, not to mention doubts of whether I had dreamed the entire affair. I knew then, that it was something only I was meant to see."

"Anyone could have come before you and stolen my body. Perhaps the Count had—"

"Yes, I had considered him as well. And there was a time I was content with that answer. But then I realized that he, though a creature of vast power, was no match for the omnipotence of the true arbiter. In fact, I believe he was subject to the same grand conspiracy as the rest of us."

Something tugs at the back of my mind, of a dark-haired beauty standing on a frozen rooftop overlooking a desolate street. Something personal. "What about Natalie? Why did you abandon her?"

"Natalie was…" He trails. "Natalie is a good woman. She may have been my wife, but there wasn't love there. Our relationship had been orchestrated, conveniently placed upon our waking that who would really question it? She was a distraction from my work, a constant reminder of utter stagnation. When the mob came and burned down my house, I came to the realization that the arbiter had other designs for me. I had grown complacent, grown comfortable with the idea of settling down and enjoying the luxurious life-style the mansion had afforded me. Natalie did not perish in the house, she was saved by you and your group of friends, which meant that the arbiter had other plans in mind. As he has plans for you and I, as he had plans for Emily."

My eyes narrow and my teeth clench. "What do you know about Emily?"

"That it was by no coincidence that you relented to that scoundrel Boenger up on the roof that day and he later turned out to fancy the opposite gender."

I choke. "You knew?"

"Of course I knew. We all knew the very moment we were settled into the mansion. He made it quite clear in his conversations with Emily. How she hated him. Though I believe it was mostly due to her own actions. She spirited away after that. It was unfortunate, when I heard second-hand of her demise. But, it all worked out nicely in the end, because it brought you to my doorstep."

My head feels a million miles away, reared back into some distant dimension that separates my mind with my body. I think of the day I found Emily dead on the street, the desolation that followed and the night after night of hunting mannequins in the dark, secretly wishing one of them would end it all.

"You and I are all part of the great conspiracy, Mr. Bell. Set down upon us by the arbiter to set things right in the world. Together, you and I can bring salvation to this city. We'll be able to go home."

The bang of the stairwell door, heavy feet and the bright invasion of flashlights steal into the room. There are many of them, both men and women. They wear fattening flak vests, helmets, and assault rifles as they charge in from the hallway. I keep my pistol still, preferring to keep Michael in my sights then let up and be shot for the surrender. In less than a minute, I have nine of his personal security force surrounding me by the flanks and rear. They keep me pinned beneath their barrels, just waiting for orders like a pack of well-trained dogs.

Michael smiles with the advantage. "You can't fight it, Sam. We can't rely on the depraved and destitute to make rational decisions. And frankly, I'm not willing to sacrifice my soul because of someone else's stubbornness. We all must be ready for the tide, else be doomed here forever. You can help make that happen. You and I can bring this city together."

He places his hand on his desk, keeping it arched like a spider. "The time to choose is now. So what's it going to be, Mr. Bell? What's it going to be?"

With a slight glance, I acknowledge my adversaries. It is in seeing their programmed resentment that I truly understand the predicament at hand. I then wonder, is there really an escape for any of us? Is there truly a choice? I think on his words. I think on everything.

I steady my grip and make my decision as I launch a sabot into his head, a resounding boom that rattles the foundation of the aged building.

"Choice is all we have."

A swirling of smoke and his body strikes the floor. I then fire a few additional pieces of steel into his chest just to be sure the deed is done and watch as his red fluids soak the wood.

I close my eyes as the sharp bitter scent of ozone and iron cloud the air, injecting it in through my nostrils and settling in the back of my throat. I relish in the moment, feeling the city fall from my shoulders like a pile of red bricks. I place my chirper on the desk, letting my hand slide off of it as if brushing a bushel of long grass. When I open my eyes, I swear the room has grown a bit brighter.

Turning to face my captives, I catch a ballerina in the doorway, her eyes alight by both surprise and warning.

I try to speak, try to call out to her but am silenced by a disrupting boom coming from my left. My lungs feel as if they are drawn into my mouth and I cough, expelling the contents of my stomach like a rejected glass of water. My abdomen cramps and when I look down, I am perplexed by the now gaping hole where flesh once had been. Blood, it pours from the wound like a fountain.

They fire again, as another explosion rips into my shoulder, and then another in the throat. The impact murders my balance and I fall, landing face first on the cold floor. Tired. I can't feel anything, just the frigid touch of wood. Between a collection of human legs, I can see Roz screaming. Her mouth is agape, her face red, eyes laden with tears. Not a sound emerges from it, just the distant sound of the surf that grows.

I am shaken by something, a feeling of being tacked to a wall, but I'm unsure what it is. Just motion and the slowing of time. Roz lifts a weapon to the tune of the oceans lullaby, yet everything is blurring, the room growing lighter until flooded by a luminescence so brilliant it passes through my eyelids. She opens fire.

I stop breathing. A seagull…

32

I wake beneath the sheets, finely tucked and warmed by the beams of sunlight that drift in through the window of my apartment bedroom. I haven't moved, lying mostly on my back throughout the night. The room smells like recent rain and lilacs, a refreshing scent free from the acrid malodor of the creep.

My fingers shift as I will them, both arms and legs. There isn't any pain involved. I touch my stomach, feeling the wholesome skin and smoothing it with my palm. Both neck and shoulder are also without injury. I stir, letting the covers rustle and bunch as they please. Stretching lifts the stiffness from my joints, a paralyzing after effect that comes from dreams.

Dreams… what was I dreaming?

Whatever happened between the then and now? I remember… I remember seeing Roz screaming. She didn't have time to warn me. I never expected them to let me go, especially since their strings had just been cut. They were mannequins after all. I watched her raise her gun, I saw her pull the trigger. Then the light… I dress and open the door into the next room.

The living room is vacant, just a few old friends: the pearl microfiber loveseat, the glass coffee table, and my beautiful white baby grand piano nestled against the wall nearest the window. The feel of newness is here as well, something vibrant about the walls, glowing from the day. But the buildings, by the maker, the buildings! They are all clean. Not a trace of the creep anywhere. Just as perfect and unmarred as the day I woke. The sky is still grey, but with enough holes to paint the world differently.

There's a newspaper on the coffee table. Sunday, the CitySpire Gazette. I let it lay. My picture frames are bare, without any smudges on the glass. Someone's been here. They came in while I was sleeping and wiped everything down, not a trace of what once was the life of Samuel Bell. My files are gone, the room devoid of empty bottles and partially filled rock glasses. Michael's desk is also missing from its usual corner. The folios are missing, no longer hidden in their resting place. It is as if everything is as it was, a replica of that time long ago when not a single creature stirred from the recesses of the CitySpire and I was sole.

There aren't any travelers on the street, particularly strange for this time of day. Usually there would be a few here and there transporting goods from the docks further into the city. Yet nothing but an unnatural vacancy, no peddlers, clerks or Govennet patrols, just emptiness and a peaceful quiet that permeates the view. Across the way, at the neighboring apartment complex, the windows are empty. There aren't any pieces of furniture, blinds, or inhabitants, just a large space fairly similar to mine, with flawless grey carpet and shadows.

But the main item, a fanciful bauble that rests on the edge of the piano, is a red painted music box shielded in glass, secluding the two dancers—one with tux and coat tails, whilst the other a ballerina—hold one another hand in hand. A ribbon is tied along the outside and topped with a bow. A card rests alongside it, white matte, gold lettering. "You are Samuel Bell". Everything is so uncanny.

The wall clock holds the time, "9:43 a.m."

I lean against the window frame as I stare out across rooftops and along the side streets. Everything is in its original place as if the whole world was rewound and started anew. It's impossible for any one person to fix all this: not able to scrape off the creep, empty the rooms or set mine back to how it once was.

I was shot. It's only logical to presume that I'm dead, yet I feel the same. I remember things, such as Michael and Natalie, Marty and Brigit, Dr. Dreval and the Sergeant, Rachel… and Emily – I remember her most of all.

I shift to a familiar spot and fog the window with my breath and I trace, "YAWA OG". I stare at it, keeping it close to my heart, thinking back when she had first written it in a like curse against the Lockes. Just the two of us together, that's all Emily ever really wanted. She didn't need the company of others. It was me she wanted and nothing else.

Absorbing the words, I think on them. "YAWA OG," whatever it is that possesses me, brings my finger to the glass and beneath it, in a different script I write the words, "AWAY GO" and then, "RETAWS EDLOGN LIMEY."

"I'll be damned." I mutter beneath my breath. "Emily Golden Waters."

I pick up the treasure from the piano, leaving the card right above the keys for safe keeping. The music box is flawless, a beautiful work of hand craftsmanship and detail.

A voice. *"Here lies one whose name was writ in water."* A melodious thing, that soothes my heart like a heated blanket.

She hovers there, inside the glass window pane, shining through like a radiant spirit set adrift by an unfelt breeze. Rachel smiles at me.

"So, tell me about this Rachel of yours." Her voice echoes through my mind.

Keeping hold of the box, I walk up to her and reach for the glass feeling nothing but the smooth texture and frigid outside weather.

"You're not really here are you?" I ask as I stroke the area where her cheeks are.

Her image wavers like a curtain floating in water before speaking a second time, *"You've always been here."*

She then fades into my reflection.

I look down at the music box. "Perhaps I have."

Dreams, visions, maybe all of these were simply a trick of the mind – all part of some programmable existence meant to live out a series of events. I hold up the item a little higher. Some weren't so bad.

I sit down on the loveseat and wind the shiny brass key. The dancers dance. The music plays. I watch the two of them twirl beneath the glass, each moving to the notes of the continual sixteen note melody that chimes like tiny bells. As I watch them spin, listening as the song loops in over itself a second time, I fall into a grand realization.

It fills my body with warmth, drawing from my toes and then up my legs and into my chest. It fills me with such a vehement understanding of things that it inflicts a tear from my left eye. It has something to do with everything, a cycle of motions, a cycle of feelings and songs. How could I have missed them? Sixteen notes of truth and revelation. They are the final sixteen, the remainder of that great familiar love song. By themselves, they are flighty things and seemingly without purpose. Yet when combined together with a stringent of notes, it finishes what otherwise likely would have been, without end. But that's the thing isn't it? All things must end.

I return the music box to its rightful place and then collect myself in the kitchen with a glass of ice water. After a short sip, I hear a tapping at the window and see feathers. A pigeon sits there, nestled up against the glass with its beak. The greyish bird looks at me, watches me, tries to catch my eyes and communicate something that I can't truly explain. It reminds me of Emily.

I swim with memories of her dimples, her auburn hair and grey eyes. I'm swept away in a maelstrom of sensations and emotions, of chasing her around Hermes Square, of late night piano playing, and her snuggling against me when the covers turned too cold. If ever there was true love in my life, it was for her. She was a physical being, a true creature of the sea, and she captured all that was good and well in me. She was a child and I was a child. In the end she was right. She was right about everything.

I set the glass of water on a side table nearest the piano, sit down and lift the fall. My hands delve into the ivory keys, letting all that has occurred, all that I know and love and pour it into the song – Emily's Song. I bend with the notes, flow like the rolling surf, and breathe in the music like a mist. I feel light, like the melody is lifting me up and out of my apartment, ready to be carried to some distant horizon. I allow the piece to temper my soul, to take hold of that very thing that gives me life and sacrifice all that I am to its substance.

Then, as I finish off the last few notes, having added the last sixteen, I slump forward, exhausted from the entire ordeal. I lay my head just above the keys, staring at them with heavy lids. I inhale the glory, the self-righteous accomplishment of finishing a major work.

I sigh, allowing sleep to overtake me.

I'm stirred by a brightness that stems from beneath the door. A white light that encroaches on the dark that hides behind closed eyelids and a slumbering mind. I pull myself from my seat, a bit dreary, but balanced and capable of keeping a straight walk. I glide across the carpet. The light is warm, yet not hot or scolding. It beams through the cracks like a brilliant sun, and inside I can hear it calling like the whispers of the ocean.

Placing my hand on the knob, I catch a figure behind me through my peripheral. There, still resting beneath the embossed card bearing my namesake is the still slumbering form of Samuel Bell. Though knowing deep inside that there lies my former self, I am not fearful. Odder still, I welcome whatever it is that waits on the other side.

I say my farewells, and bid the sleeping Bell sweet dreams and a kinder wake than I endured. With a sturdy turn of the knob, I let the light encompass me as I step out into the hallway – pulling the door shut and latching it softly behind.

The pigeon takes flight, out into the cold CitySpire air. The wind rustles its feathers, sending a shiver down its back as the bird turns onto an updraft. The creature soars high above the empty rooftops, now able to see the vacant streets. It refuses to make a sound, preferring instead to watch the horizon, keeping an eye for its intended destination.

The grey bird knows of the docked windjammer, the large wooden ship with masts of gold and sails of white, that periodically makes its berth at the west side pier. It knows that if he is late, the boat may sail out with the coming tide, yet there is another reason for his well-placed haste. It is there that a young woman has been waiting for a long time, waiting for him to make his way and join her on the voyage into the great beyond.

"Is he coming? Is he here?" The auburn haired nymph demands. She shifts anxiously in a coil of hemp, searching the skies with a hand to shield her eyes.

"Aye, he shouldn't be that much longer, lass. He shall be here soon enough. Old Waldgrave won't let the boat leave without em'."

She eases back into her makeshift bed releasing a long pent-up sigh. "I'm tired, Mr. Waldgrave. It seems like forever." Emily bites her lip then pulls herself back to sitting. "Do you think he brought me pancakes?"

"Pancakes, young missy? There'd be plenty of that up in that ship. You tell the Captain that Waldgrave insists he makes ya his golden pancake surprise. Best coins you've ever tasted."

She falls back into herself. "I certainly hope so. I'm so hungry I'd likely eat a pigeon."

"No – youngling, ya don't want to be doing that. You could swallow your cavalier and then what would ya do?"

"I'd cough out feathers. Enough for three pillows full. After that, I wouldn't know what to do with myself."

"Cry yerself an ocean, that's what'd happen. There'd be nothing left of the good city, cept' a soggy harbormaster. Ya don't want ta get me beard all wet, do you lass?"

Emily grows smug. Her face morphs into teeth and smiles as she points at the sky at the flapping of little wings. "There he is, Mr. Waldgrave! You won't have to wash your beard afterall! He's here! Oh, my dearest little bird! He's finally here!"

The silk sails expand to their fullest, as the wind pulls them out toward the distant horizon where lays the mysterious beyond. They embrace at the bow, holding onto one another as the crew bustles about, securing the rigging and other sailor duties. Both creatures are lost in the other, stroking both cheek and hair, until one falls into the other and they meet in kiss.

The sun has yet to set, but is high and good for sailing. The lovers, both Bell and Waters, are claimed by the parting of the clouds above and the relinquishing of sunlight that shines through the gates of mirth. Together they disappear, the windjammer bound for the great beyond, forever wrapped in each other's arms.

Yet from the docks, another creature stirs. A bloodied pistol lays at her feet, a brown satchel at her side, and an object of sorts clutched tightly in her fist. She squats just shy the edge of the promenade, looking out across the sea as if searching for the hidden thing that dwells in empty spaces.

"Pretty sight, ain't she?" The grizzled old man exclaims after taking a puff off his gnarled pipe. A sweet serenade of tobacco drifts out across the shore.

She neverminds the fossil, preferring to let him rattle on about the annoying nothings that come out of friendly conversation. The tiny Rozaline thinks on darker things, more specifically the recent tragedy.

His rough cardboard voice assaults her again. "Ya keep yer eye affixed to that horizon and you be spotting ships before you know it."

Her patience has well been worn to the marrow. "And what do you know of ships?" Roz demands.

"Quite a great deal, lass. You look upon the harbormaster. Old Waldgrave is my name." He puffs a few clouds into the air.

She forces air out her nostrils and scoffs. "Harbormaster."

The two remain in silence, she seething in hatred for those who murdered her friends—those who are rare and few—and, irritated at the unwanted attentions of the obviously deranged man behind her, and he in simple observation of the surf.

"Well, young miss. I'm not going to take up yer time. I'm sure you've got thoughts worth considering." He taps his pipe out on his boot. "If you be ever needing conversation, you can find me ere'." He tips his nautical hat to excuse himself from her company. "You have a nice afternoon, Miss Bell."

Rozaline inhales, as if it would catch his sleeve, but she holds her breath. She watches him go, as he strolls slowly down the promenade whistling some unknown shanty.

She questions how he knows her, an overheard conversation perhaps? Yes – that has to be the reason for there really isn't any other explanation. In a moment of vulnerability, she opens her hand and admires the sixteen-prong cylinder in her hand, the object entrusted to her by a woman who had taken her life. It's the only thing she has left, the only piece of a friendship that ended abruptly.

With great detest fuming in her hair, she closes her fist. Angry at the world once again for taking those she loves. Her eyes are inflamed with red, as she grits her teeth and snarls at the memory of Samuel's death.

"The fool." She mutters as she wipes her eye. She hates it when they tear up without her permission.

With a swift hand, the resentful Rozaline Bell replaces the musical cylinder in her satchel, ensuring to its security. Then, without word or return glance to the sea, the petite woman claims the chirper off the ground—her father's gun—and steals off into the city.

Epilogue

Weightless, torpid, and discarded. The hyperborean waters claim my body as its treasure, a piece of fallen antiquity to add forever to the bottom of the sea. There to drift. There to die. Floating as the world turns beneath me.

I see the waters deep. I can barely move, my limbs frozen in the dark. Am I alive? My lungs, I can feel them swelling with old air. My head… everything is light and foggy. My neck twitches, my fingers and now my arms. Concentrate Marty, you can do this.

Beneath me floats the startling silhouette of a woman, her blonde hair scintillates with the firefly glimmers that shine from the lamps above. She wears a white dress, one that flows about her like seaweed. Peaceful. Lifeless. Drowning! I push against the confines of my skull, sending those electrical impulses down into my limbs to force them into compliance. I try to reach for her, but my arms still refuse to budge, paralyzed by the numbness that's settled within my chest.

My will overpowers the frozen state of my veins and I thrash, but it only disrupts the water, tossing bubbles into the realm above and her deeper where tiny ribbons of incandescent lights twinkle like stars, a reflection from the city lights.

I try and scream for her, to wake her out of whatever spell has besieged her, but my desperation is replaced by icy waters. I kick in reaction to the invasion, then with an empowerment of fluidity, paddle down into the ebb to reach her. Dystrophy wrestles my every gain, a shedding of frost that's colored me blue, slowing my actions as I tread water.

With all my strength and force of being, I tear at the walls of my mind, demanding from whatever arbiter presides over the ill-fated to grant me mobility. My commands connect, as I reach out my hand to grab hers, as the last remnant of breath pours out in payment, escaping in a string of bubbles. I touch flesh.

Beneath, the stars grow larger, like a swirl of festival lights strung out across a carousel. They change in shape, a black blob against the murky blue, growing a hand at first, then arms and heads! People,

EPILOGUE

no – mannequins! all swimming from the dark, pulling themselves through the water, out from some abysmal crevasse that hides deep along the ocean bed. They lurch themselves like specters, physical apparitions whose hands grip the water like nefarious claws, to escape the frozen waters that dig into their naked bodies. Their mouths are all agape, as if wailing from the torturing of their devilish spirits. Hundreds of them!

They grab her!–those bastards grab her by the ankle and wrench her hand from mine, climbing her like a human ladder. They swarm over her body, to push off, to give them that extra lift toward the surface above – to sacrifice her life to the umbra in their stead. With one last expulsion of adrenaline, I make one desperate grasp for her hand, but it's too late! She's pulled beneath the water and my fate becomes hers.

One mannequin grabs my hand, his eyes alight with an unnatural glow, he pulls and I tug. I kick him off, but another seizes my foot and then up my leg. Another grabs hold my waist, then draws himself upwards, one my shoulder, then my head. Each horror sinks me deeper, with a stray blow landing in my chest, and I swallow water. My air exhausted, my vim extinguished, I can do nothing but tumble into the darkest corners of the world.

My eyes roll, my brain drifting and detached. I inhale water as if it was oxygen and I feel myself give into the blanket of unconsciousness. Before the silence overtakes me, I glimpse something of a dream, as there many feet below, glows the pink illumination of a gigantic O, lined in neon bulbs. It flickers to me a code of future dreams.

When all is dark, and the remaining luminance of the neon glow fades to nothing. I feel the sensation of being lifted quickly into the realm above. When my face breaks the surface, it is stung by the callousness of winter's breath and my mouth gasps as it inhales a painful taint of air bringing life to this frozen corpse—still alive.

Appendix

Such an eye pleaser, the several months have been worth it, tolling over those old sheets of music, playing them over and over again to appease that longing tickle that's feather-dusted my mind since the first time I heard its melody. So soothing, it clamors over my body like the rays of the sun—each competing to see who can court me best—that brilliant familiar love song that has now bloomed beneath my hand and chased away the grey above.

My fingers peruse over the top page, letting the parchment lick my thumb, counting with each sensation and speaking then after, "What a nice kiss."

The folios remain silent in their place on top of the sofa table. With imagined smile, I curtsy to the dormant stack. I note how the shadows cast against the wall and I ask with wonderment at the future rendezvous, "Won't he be surprised?"

The color red waves to my attention, shining in its pretty base, with its two prissy dancers under glass—the way it was supposed to be. It's an exact replica of the one Sam has at his apartment, except this one isn't scuffed, banged or chipped and it plays so beautifully. Snatching it up from its resting place like a doll, I bare it close to my chest, letting my dress pinwheel as I spin in play.

I tap at the glass, trying to vie some affection out of the plastic figurines within but they enamored with one another, are focused on their static dance. A couple rotations of the turnkey rallies the cylinder, the very one that took weeks to create, and the pins plink off those glorious sixteen notes. I watch in heavy heart as the two-in-arms twirl about the stage with sigh.

"Won't be long now…" I say to their promenade.

We've wasted so much time, he and I. Were I a stronger woman then, I would have stayed and not given into a fear of mannequins expelling their windows. Were I not so naïve to think him glad to be rid of me, I would have rushed into his arms and refused to clamor into that horrid whirly-gig. We could have been happy by now. Patience is the best prescription when dealing with a man of fixation. That Rachel of his…

APPENDIX

Dreams are fuzzy things that you rub and rub until they stick to the ceiling. You can talk to it and marvel at its extravagance, but once touched it loses its cling and drops to the floor. It's a passing fancy, but time proves you the better when he finally looks up and sees what still stands before him. Perseverance proves the better, and he'll later swear he hadn't a clue what he saw in it to begin with. I know now his heart, the way he looked at me in his apartment is enough for me to climb onto his chest and lie there until the city sinks beneath the sea

A sparkle! The glass captures the radiance from outside and releases it into the room like a net of butterflies. The sunlight warms the floor boards and my feet thank the sun. The clouds, I see the blue returning its vaporous lint into a hidden pocket and blinks at me with its single glowing eye. Oh, how it flirts with me. Replacing the music box, I grab a stool and drag it in front of the window. With one courageous step, the white capped Emily Golden Waters steps into the spotlight of the world.

The glass brings the breath of the empyreal, a strong heat that resides only from the arms of the sun and my bright star is coming. He's making his way from his apartment, up Rhine and soon eastward. I can feel him in every braid of sunlight that magnifies through the muntins and in the dispelling of the cold. I inhale it all, like a hot shower in my lungs and I smile.

I'm startled by the rattling of the doorknob and I feel the cold of the outside hallway spit against my back. I turn, too early for it to be my beloved bird. I gasp as the pigeons in my heart take wing.

Feathers escape my throat in the form of words. "Hello, me."